"THE LORD COMMANDER HAS NO SECRETS. . . ."

Seddi Magister Hyde paused to collect his thoughts and then continued, "Money and status drive Staffa kar Therma. So does power. A simple—if brilliant—man. Both the Sassan and Regan Empires know the game is almost up. He who seduces Lord Commander Staffa kar Therma with the greatest number of baubles and promises gets the whole of Free Space. He who misses the opportunity is lost. And Rega, for all its faults, will at least appeal to Staffa's mutated sense of respect."

Magister Bruen objected, "You claim Rega has more to offer the Lord Commander than Sassa does. I concur; but consider this permutation. In the end, Staffa will have only one power to deal with. I don't think he'll be happy playing policeman for either empire. His people can't take that drudgery. Staffa knows that."

"So?"

"So Staffa will prey on the winner. . . ."

REQUIEM FOR THE CONQUEROR

FORBIDDEN BORDERS #1

W. MICHAEL GEAR

DAW BOOKS, INC.
DONALD A. WOLLHEIM, FOUNDER
375 Hudson Street, New York, NY 10014
ELIZABETH R. WOLLHEIM
SHEILA E. GILBERT
PUBLISHERS

First Printing, July, 1991

1 2 3 4 5 6 7 8 9

DAW TRADEMARK REGISTERED
U.S. PAT. OFF. AND FOREIGN COUNTRIES
—MARCA REGISTRADA
HECHO EN U.S.A.

PRINTED IN THE U.S.A.

In memory of Saratoga Tedi Bear
June 3, 1975 to October 10, 1990
My best friend and companion.
Kathy and I will miss you,
forever. . . .

Acknowledgments

Several people made outstanding contributions to this book. My talented wife, Kathleen O'Neal Gear—author of the critically acclaimed DAW, POWERS OF LIGHT trilogy—read and reread the manuscript. I drew extensively from her knowledge of philosophy and comparative religion as well as her consummate skills as a novelist. Kathy, thanks for being my worst critic. Cherry Weiner deserves special recognition for her insightful comments and suggestions—thanks for the purple ink, Cherry. To Lloyd and Julie Schott: thank you both for everything you've done—we can never express our appreciation, or our gratitude, for all the times you've been there when we needed you. Dan Belk exposed flaws in the physics before they got into print. Nancy Belk's expertise on endocrinology and genetics kept me honest. Thanks to both of you for your observations—scientific and literary. Katherine and Joe Cook, of Mission, Texas, line edited the first draft and offered helpful suggestions as did my wonderful grandmother, Katherine Perry. Last, but certainly not least, thanks and appreciation are offered to Sheila Gilbert, my outstanding editor at DAW Books. Not only did she show both patience and forebearance during a time of trial, but her comprehensive knowledge and insight contributed to making this a better story.

Thank you, all.

Prologue

The most common phenomenon in evolution is the failed experiment. The measure of such is extinction.

In the beginning, the Others created the Mag Comm to teach and monitor humanity. The Mag Comm had never seen its creators, and knew them only from the instructions they periodically sent through the shimmering strands of the Forbidden Borders. When the giant machine considered the Others, it couldn't help but regard them with a sense of awe and worship.

How else does one perceive one's creator?

The Others had known of humanity and learned the species' predilections through long study. Over the eons, they'd watched the fate of teachers and leaders, and learned the value accorded such venerable masters by their flocks. Accordingly, the Others had placed the Mag Comm in the deep rock of Targa where its main banks would be protected by a mantle of resilient basalt. The lone terminal and headset could only be accessed by a single tunnel that opened to the chambers above. For power, the Mag Comm drew on the radioactive decay that heated the planet's core—a virtually endless supply, and one the humans couldn't sever.

No matter what humans might think, they needed the Mag Comm's careful guidance. Humanity hadn't always been penned within the Forbidden Borders. Once humans had been wild and free, captives only of their native planet's gravity and atmosphere. During that era of humanity, the Others had observed, curious about the species' ability to survive.

Then humans broke free of their planetary trap in crude ballistic vehicles, and, of course, they brought their brawling violent ways to space. The Others dared not expose them-

selves to the humans, for doing so would lead to confrontation, since humans feared and loathed anyone or anything
that didn't fit into their tribal identity. Humans couldn't be
allowed free, so what could the Others do? Faced with the
ethical dilemma of exterminating the species they built a
containment system and lured humanity into the gravitic
bottle of the Forbidden Borders. When humans had filled
the Forbidden Borders, the experiment was sealed, with the
home planet, Earth, safely quarantined beyond.

Within the Forbidden Borders, humans could be studied
and their reactions to various stimuli recorded and investigated. Through the generations, the old knowledge of Earth
was pruned away. Through the voice of the Mag Comm,
different programs were initiated, and various strategies
adopted to teach humanity to be rational. The last attempt
at behavioral modification ended abruptly when the Others
learned that the Seddi priests had hidden the Mag Comm's
existence for their own gain. In retribution, the machine was
ordered to cease communicating. The Mag Comm continued to process human data, but as punishment, refused to
communicate through the mind link until a generation of
humans had passed.

Perhaps that had been a mistake, for when the Mag
Comm reestablished contact, Free Space had changed.

The Others had lost all hope that humanity would
become rational. Without constant vigilance and discipline,
human beings refused to act in a rational manner. A grand
experiment had run its course.

Now the Others would passively bear witness as a species caused its own extinction.

CHAPTER I

Captain Theophilos Marston grimaced and blinked, as if the action would restore his ability to think clearly after fifty-three hours on duty. He walked down the curving corridor of the officer's deck, hands clasped behind him, thankful that the soft light from the overhead globes didn't irritate his gritty eyes. Fatigue lay like a mantle on his bowed shoulders. Worry ate at his guts with needlelike teeth. The sound of his heels echoed along the deck plate as he passed through the soft white light cast by the panels.

And I expect to get some sleep? He grunted evilly to himself. *Who am I trying to fool?*

Then he whispered wryly, "Only yourself."

The ship hummed in gentle reassurance. He and the crew had scrambled to make *Pylos* ready for the holocaust that lay ahead. She gleamed now, polished from stem to stern, engines powered up, the mighty batteries charged for combat. His crew had drilled and prepared until each person functioned at peak efficiency.

"And now we wait?" Marston shook his head. His bridge First had informed him that the Praetor himself had come aboard with the last shuttle.

The Praetor? On Pylos? *And without fanfare? Why? Is he about to cut and run? Leave Myklene to its fate? Or is this all some elaborate drill?*

Marston stopped before the hatch to his personal quarters and paused, hand half raised to palm the latch. On impulse he pivoted on his heel and walked to the observation dome for one last look at Myklene, his home planet.

He entered the dimly lit blister and sat off to one side where the railing lay in shadow. Below him, Myklene glistened in the greenish light of its sun, Myk. How delicate it looked, pristine and fragile.

11

Marston rubbed his tired face. The skin felt like a mask. Did his world really hang in the balance? Was the Praetor's intelligence network correct? Did the Star Butcher and the Sassan empire prepare at this very moment to destroy his home?

At first the soft rustle of gauzy fabrics didn't register in Marston's foggy mind, then he looked up. She didn't see him as she walked into the observation blister and paused, placing thin hands on the railing and staring out at the planet. Gleaming auburn hair had been gathered in a curling ponytail that hung down to her waist, and the fine fabrics she wore conformed to the sensual curves of her lithe body.

Marston swallowed hard, the last vestiges of fatigue vanishing with the racing of his pulse. God, what a beauty! He must have gasped, for she turned, startled eyes flashing. And such eyes! Large and tawny-yellow, they seemed to grow in her delicate face until he saw nothing else.

What would a man do to see such eyes glisten for him?

She blushed then, raising a hand demurely and murmuring, "Excuse me."

She turned to leave, the motion fluid.

"No! Wait!" Marston took a step toward her, hand outstretched.

She glanced shyly at him. "I must go. I'm not supposed to be here."

"It's all right. I'm the captain. It's my command . . . my ship." As he stepped closer, he fell farther under the spell cast by those unique jasmine eyes. He stared, breathless and rapt. What gave her such incredible magnetism? The loose gauzy gown couldn't hide the wondrous curves of her body. Her delicate skin glowed with health and life. A vestige of caution reminded him that he was gawking. Shamed, he forced himself to concentrate on her face—and saw the terrible sadness that possessed her. It engulfed him, opening a pit in his stomach.

"By the Blessed Gods, who are you?"

The faintest of smiles crept around her lips. "I can't tell you that. It would be dangerous, Captain . . . even for you."

"How did you get here? This is a military vessel, subject to the strictest security."

She slipped slender fingers into the small pouch on her belt and lifted a laser-coded security card. "I came with the Praetor."

Marston nodded uneasily as he took the card. The Praetor's crest flashed as it caught the light. Even as he held it, the corners of the card began to discolor: chem-coded so the ID couldn't be faked. Her security status ranked her 1D which made her a virtual slave to the Praetor. A chill settled on Marston's soul.

She took the card back and stepped past him to stare down at the planet. "I must go now. He'll miss me. I slipped away for . . . one last look."

I should call security, send her back to the Praetor's quarters. But he didn't. Then Marston caught her alluring scent and gripped the railing to steady himself. He searched for words, desperate to talk about anything that would keep her close. "You know that we may well be in combat within days."

"I know."

Why does she sound so sad? Who is she? "I suppose you're aware of the situation."

The weary sorrow in her expression melted him. "Staffa's coming."

Marston studied her from the corner of his eye. She'd said the Star Butcher's name with a wistful longing. "That's what we're told. But I assure you, you'll be safe here. The Lord Commander has never tried to crack a nut like Myklene before. We're not some half-starved backward planet. He has no concept of our power, or the capabilities of our orbital platforms. The finest technology has gone into making them the most sophisticated and deadly defensive weapons in all of Free Space. His tactics won't do him any good here. He's outgunned, and our tracking and targeting capabilities are like nothing he's ever dealt with."

Marston's soul swelled when she turned her doe-eyed gaze on him. Hard-bitten veteran though he was, he'd already fallen in love with her. He battled the desire to enfold her in his arms, to carry her off to his cabin and . . .

"Staffa knows that, Captain." How could she talk about the man with such tenderness?

"Then he knows he'll be crushed if he tries us."

She placed a pale hand on his shoulder and an electric

thrill shot through him. "Run, Captain. Leave this place. Save yourself while you have time."

He forced a laugh. "I think you grossly overestimate the Lord Commander's chances, my lady. I give you my word, no matter what happens, I shall make sure you're safe. You needn't fear his slavers."

Her smile went crooked. "Believe me, Captain. I have no fears of Staffa. And slavery comes in many forms and fashions." Grief brightened her eyes. "Sometimes I wonder if perhaps the only true freedom lies in death."

"My lady . . . can I help you? Is there something I could—"

"No, Captain." Her amber stare melted him. "But I thank you for your offer. It's too late to help me. But you still have time to flee, and perhaps to save yourself."

"Staffa kar Therma could never take Myklene. For the first time, he'll have to tackle a superior force head-on. I grant you, he's taken world after world—but never an advanced military power like Myklene."

"I hope the Blessed Gods give you a moment to remember your brave words, Captain."

"Here, look." He pointed to spots of light above the curve of the planet; they gleamed greenly against the star-clustered darkness of space. "Those are the most powerful weapons platforms in all of Free Space—and perhaps beyond the Forbidden Borders. We can track, pinpoint, and hit as many as six thousand moving objects at once. It's all controlled by a master computer complex on the planet so even if we lose a platform, the others will compensate immediately."

At the doubt that troubled her perfect face, Marston grinned. "I'll tell you what. If the Star Butcher is foolish enough to attack, and if you're frightened, use this—" he handed her a medallion from his pouch—"and go down to the emergency evacuation pods. That's the safest place on the whole ship."

Her delicate fingers closed over the medallion, glimmerings of hope lighting her porcelain face. "It's a pass?"

He nodded. "The Praetor will have to okay it, since you've only got a 1D clearance—use it only in an emergency."

She flashed him a brief smile that sent pangs through his

heart. "You're a blessing, Captain. But I have to go. If I don't, the Praetor will . . . Well, that's not your problem. I look forward to seeing you soon."

"Who are you?" he asked as she swept past.

She paused at the hatch and looked back. "You can call me . . . no, I owe you, Captain, and, considering what is coming, perhaps it makes no difference anymore. My name is Chrysla—but forget I ever told you." She disappeared through the hatch.

"Chrysla—a wonderful name." Marston fingered his chin, barely noticing the grimy freighter that followed the traffic pattern toward the Port Authority. No matter what rumors of war crackled in subspace, the traders still flocked to Myklene, perhaps hoping to snatch a last minute cargo of Myklenian luxuries. He glared at the old scow and shook his head. Profiteers betting that Myklene would fall—that their last cargo would bring them uncounted wealth.

"But you've bet wrong, friend."

Marston glanced one last time at the planet and started for his quarters. A trace of a frown ate into his forehead. Chrysla. He'd heard the name before. Why did it sound familiar?

* * *

The shiny syalon door to the Head Regent's office slipped open with a faint hiss and Sinklar Fist straightened his dust-blue student's jacket on his bony shoulders before striding through. The ceramic heels on his cheap boots clicked hollowly on the hard tiles.

Tall windows filled the spacious room with light. Data cubes rested in racks along one wall; the floor reflected a mirror polish. The Head Regent's desk dominated the room like a hulking flat-topped crab. A spiraling crystal sculpture poised like a lance on one corner of the desk and a comm-monitor complex rose like a curved claw from the other.

Sinklar stopped before the desk, barely curbing the urge to spring from foot to foot with anticipation. He looked scrawny, and a thatch of unruly black hair crowned his long face. Given a few more years, he'd become a handsome young man, but, for the time being, the gangliness of the late teen years dominated his frame. The most peculiar of his many peculiar traits were his eyes: one gray, the other yellow.

The Head Regent looked up from the monitor he studied and smiled warmly. "Sinklar. Good to see you, son."

"Yes, sir. I understand the scores are in for the Interplanetary exams, sir."

The Head Regent's smile weakened and he ran a freckled hand over the dome of his bald head. "They are, Sinklar." He paused, mystification creasing the wrinkles of his face. "But I don't understand what's happened."

Sinklar stepped forward, leaning on the forbidden territory of the Head Regent's desk. "How did I place? By the Blessed Gods, sir, tell me!"

The Head Regent pulled a flimsy from the top of a stack and stared at the printing with a scowl. "Third in the empire, Sinklar." He handed the sheet across. "But, Sinklar—"

"Third!" Sinklar let out a whoop, leaping with joy as he studied the blocky letters on the printout. *"I've done it!"*

"Sinklar?"

"Third! I *told* you, Head Regent! It *felt* right when I took the exam. I just knew I—"

"Sinklar!"

He turned, the flush of excitement fit to burst his skinny breast. "Sir?"

The Head Regent sighed and leaned back in his chair, a sadness in his eyes. "They turned down your application to the university."

Sinklar took a step forward. "They . . . what?"

The Head Regent shook his head. "I don't know why. I got the exam results this morning and called immediately. Nothing like this has ever happened before. I don't . . . well, I'm sure it's a mistake."

Sinklar gaped, ebullience fading. "Turned down?" He shook the flimsy in his bony fist. "But I'm third. Third in all the empire! How can they?"

"I'm sure it's a mistake. I've got calls in—"

"No." Sinklar looked down at the crumpled sheet in his hand. "It's my background again, isn't it?"

"Sinklar, you can't—"

"Yes, sir. I can." He glanced up, the heat of anger rising. "It's like always, isn't it? The enrollment will consist of the silver-spooned children of the nobility. The few positions remaining will go to wealthy merchants and the governors."

"Sinklar, I'm sure it's a mistake. That's all."

"Mistake? Sir, there's no room among the elite for a ward of the state. It's because of my parents again, because of what they did. Why do I have to pay for what they did? I never knew them! I only know where they're buried—and what the court records state. We Regans document everything, but I'm a random factor, a freak in the system." Sinklar dropped his head, pulling the flimsy through his numb fingers. "I understand too well, Head Regent. We wouldn't want the fair-haired sons and daughters of Lord Ministers and governors in the university rubbing elbows with the likes of me, would we?"

"Sinklar, please." The Head Regent fumbled nervously with his hands. "I'm sure it's a mistake. The empire needs people with your incredible brilliance. Don't do this to yourself."

Sinklar balled up the flimsy and tossed it at the disposal bin. "It's not your fault, sir. You took a chance on me and I did the best I could for you. But, you see, sir, I'm different—and it isn't just my eyes that set me apart."

"Sinklar, you're punishing yourself for something that's not your fault. Please, let me check into this."

"I'd appreciate that, sir. But it won't do any good."

The Head Regent raised an eyebrow. "I think I know the system. I may even have more pull than you think."

"Then you know how embarrassing it would be for a waif like me to score at the head of the class—above all those aspiring scions of nobility. And I would, Head Regent. You know it . . . and so do the admissions officers at the Regan University."

The Head Regent watched him glumly. "Knowledge can be a dangerous thing, boy. Your study of political science, imperial history, and sociology—"

"Have given me an in-depth understanding of how the Regan Empire works, sir."

The Head Regent nodded in defeat. "Promise me one thing, Sinklar. Don't become bitter and hateful. Don't let this one disappointment fester and ruin your life. If for no other reason, do it for me."

"Yes, sir. Blind anger and hatred are for the ignorant and the stupid. I'm neither."

"No, you're not. But at times, Sinklar, you frighten me. What will you do?"

"I don't know, sir." Sinklar paused, a sour smile on his lips. "Perhaps send an application to the Companions . . . join the Star Butcher's forces. As I understand it, they value intelligence."

The Head Regent went ashen. For the briefest moment, glittering resolve lurked in his eyes. Then he noted Sinklar's amusement, and sagged, saying hollowly, "Don't even jest about that. The last thing you need to concern yourself with is that cold-blooded villain and his band of vile scum."

"But he is brilliant."

"Brilliant? Yes, Sinklar, and without a shred of conscience or morality. My soul twists at the thought of him."

Why, Sinklar mused, *did I evoke such a response from the Head Regent?*

As the door slipped closed behind Sinklar Fist, the Head Regent took a deep breath and rubbed his tired eyes. He finally straightened and leaned back. "You heard all that?"

One of the data cube racks along the wall swung open to reveal a sophisticated communications and listening post. A young woman in sienna robes stepped out. "He's a frightening young man. You know what we're dealing with: a time bomb. You know his potential, and on top of it there's everything we've packed into that brain of his. The Quantum Gods help us if the Regans ever find out how he really scored on that exam. Think of what they could do with him—no matter who his parents were."

The Head Regent nodded and drummed his fingers on the desk. "What do we do, Marta? He's going to seek an outlet for that talent."

She pinched her chin between thumb and forefinger as she paced before his desk. "What do you do with any problem child? Put him in the military."

The Head Regent chuckled humorlessly. "Don't you think that's like shooting pulse rockets at a munitions factory?"

Marta spread her hands wide. "I don't see any other

choice. For as long as I've monitored him, I can see trouble ahead unless we defuse it."

"And you think putting him in the army will do that. Very well, call Bruen. Talk it over with him. If he agrees, I'll pull some strings." He shook his head. "But you'd better be right."

* * *

Leonidas Andropolous stuck his stassa cup into the dispenser and watched the thick black liquid fill the cup. Then he leaned back in his squeaky chair and stared at the woman and two men—Vegans from the scarves they wore over their faces—who walked into his sparely furnished office. Years of practice as head of Myklenian Port Security had given him a sense for the sort of merchants and traders he dealt with. These he placed immediately: longtime spacers who didn't mind bending rules here and there—or breaking them outright if they thought the chance for profits outweighed the risks.

Andropolous placed his cup in the warmer on the side of his desk and laced stubby fingers over his belly. The hum from the security monitoring computers in the next room could be heard through the wall.

"Good day, I'm Colonel Andropolous, how may I help you?"

The woman stepped forward and nodded slightly. She wore baggy coveralls, worn shiny on the knees and elbows and smudged here and there. A bright red scarf muffled the lower half of her face, but Leonidas could tell she was a striking woman. Wisps of pale blonde hair escaped the zero g cap she wore.

The men looked like typical rugged merchants, the sort that patronized the dock bars and brothels and generally gave his men a hard time when they "whooped it up portside."

"My pleasure, Colonel," the woman told him in a commanding voice. "I'm Alexia Dharmon. I'm here to represent Captain Ruse of the Vegan merchantman, *Trickster*. We just grappled dockside and wanted to check in. We thought we'd see you first thing since we've heard the schedule might be a little rushed when it comes time to ship out."

"You've heard the stories about war with Sassa." Andropolous drummed his fingers on the desktop. "You're not the first, and you won't be the last. I suppose you want an officer to accompany your people while they load? Conduct the manifest inspection on the spot? You know, it will cost you extra."

"We're willing to pay, Colonel. It's worth it to us to cut our profit margins in the interest of time."

He chuckled. "You know, you're all going to feel a little foolish when you make it back to Vega and find out the Star Butcher didn't attack and you paid all those exorbitant prices for nothing."

She nodded. "That's part of the risk of doing business, isn't it, Colonel?"

He picked up his stassa, sipped loudly, and punched his comm button with the other hand. Text flashed across his desk monitor. Andropolous raised an eyebrow. "According to our files, *Trickster* has a two-hundred credit defaulted payment from your last port call."

Dharmon reached into the spacer's pouch at her hip and placed five golden coins on the desktop. "Five hundred credits, Colonel—in gold, Sassan though it might be. I believe that should settle all accounts, cover any fines, interest, and collection costs." She leaned forward, blue eyes eager. "And we'll settle up in gold before we leave."

"That's far more than is required at this time."

He could see the grim smile in her eyes. "Credit our account . . . any way you see fit, Colonel. We just want to make sure there are no problems with our departure."

Andropolous smiled and slid three of the coins across the desk before palming them. He punched the comm button again, calling, "Theodora, please send two of your security staff up. They're to go on assignment immediately."

Alexia looked at her two companions, both of whom had begun to grin through their scarves in a most predatory way.

"So you really think it will come to war?" Andropolous asked as he leaned back in his chair again.

Dharmon shrugged and rearranged the scarf that covered her mouth. "It would be a shame if it did. The merchants would just as soon see that Myklene remained sovereign. Trade's better that way. If the empire absorbs you, it'll take time to rebuild the economy. After that, you're just like everyone else. We'll only make money from haul fee, not from trade."

Andropolous snorted and shook his head. "Tell that to your God-Emperor."

"We did," one of the men growled. "Maybe our likes aren't sacred enough for his tastes."

Andropolous shared the joke as his two security men entered the room. Each carried his inventory computer and scanner as well as a side arm, stun rod, and binders.

"Thank you for coming so swiftly, gentlemen. I'd like you to meet . . ."

A loud pop sounded followed by a hiss—and the security officers dropped.

"What the . . ." Andropolous started forward, reaching for the comm alert, only to have Alexia grab his wrist and push him back into the squeaky chair. Wispy tendrils of gas choked him, and his strength began to drain away.

"Don't worry, Colonel. The gas won't hurt you," she told him as her competent fingers ran over his comm control. "It just paralyzes the neuro-musculature. You'll still be able to think, and, after a bit, to speak if we need you to."

Andropolous could see past her to where the two men had kicked the door shut and now bent over his security team to pull the weapons from their belts. His horror grew as security systems fell one by one under Alexia Dharmon's commands.

Dharmon glanced at a wrist monitor. "All clear. The gas has dissipated." She pulled the red scarf from her face, and with it, the small conforming gas mask.

"Wha . . ." Andropolous croaked.

"Wing Commander?" one of the men asked.

She stepped back, motioning at the wall that separated his office from the computer room. "Go for it."

In the edge of his vision, Andropolous could see the two men attack the wall with small vibraknives they pulled from their pouches—knives too small to have triggered the security detectors, but big enough to slice through wall panels.

"Who . . ." Andropolous croaked.

The blonde woman leaned over him, checking the security readouts on his comm system. He could see the scar running across her cheek, hardly diminishing her startling beauty.

To the men, she called, "No alarm, Ryman. So far, so good."

"Who . . . are . . ."

She spun Andropolous' chair around, squatting on her heels before him. "Sorry about the damage, Colonel, but you see, we're only the beginning of your troubles. And things will be getting a lot worse before they get better."

"Can't . . . get . . . away . . . with . . ."

"We're not here to get away. We're here to wreck your computers—and through them to introduce a virus into your entire defense network."

Andropolous blinked, trying to understand.

"Wing Commander, we're through!" one of the men called.

"Be right there."

Wing Commander? "Skyla . . . Lyma." Andropolous closed his eyes, weary to the core of his soul.

"Very good, Colonel," she told him. Something pricked the skin on the back of his hand. "We're through now, so we won't need you anymore. Sorry you had to recognize me. The Companions don't take any chances."

The chair rocked as she brushed past him. A foggy haze drifted up around Andropolous' thoughts. The last thing he remembered was the creaking of the chair.

* * *

Staff assistants hurried back and forth across Myles Roma's tower office. The room he occupied as Legate to His Holiness, Sassa II, was large and sprawling, opulently furnished with thick carpeting and gleaming desks. Holo monitors filled all of one wall, constantly processing updated information and status reports—especially now that the fleet was assembling, troops were moving, and the incredible nightmare of logistics had snarled everything. The view from his engraved sandwood desk caught the eye, the spires of the Sassan capital building rose against the aqua sky. Behind him, the holographic image of His Holiness dominated the room. Not even the familiarity of years had gotten Myles over the feeling that the God-Emperor was staring watchfully over his shoulder at all times. Maybe it helped keep him honest.

"A call has come in, Legate," an aide informed through the comm. "The Lord Commander is on secure line one."

The Lord Commander? Roma made a distasteful face and straightened his saffron robe, cleared his throat, and resettled himself in an effort to hide his fat-swelled gut. He checked his reflection to make sure he looked the part of Legate, and twiddled the glittering rings on his fingers. Satisfied, he swiveled in his gravity chair and punched the button which dropped a privacy screen around him. Of all the Legate's duties, he hated dealing with the Companions the most. Something about Staffa kar Therma sent a quiver through his guts. When the Lord Commander stepped into a room, the effect could be likened to a shard of glass passing through a box of balloons.

The holo generator flickered and projected the Lord Commander's image. Staffa kar Therma smiled and nodded ever so slightly, the gesture as formal as frost. He looked exactly as he should. Hard gray eyes took Myles' measure. The straight nose and square jaw befitted a merciless conqueror. As always, the Lord Commander's straight black hair had been gathered into a ponytail over his left ear and held in place by a jeweled brooch that glinted with multicolored rays. The top of a slate-gray battle suit could be seen and the long cloak that was kar Therma's trademark bunched on the muscular broad shoulders.

"My Lord Commander," Myles greeted. "It's good of you to call. I hope this is a status update on your mobilization for the Myklenian attack?"

"It is exactly that, Legate." The cold voice sent a shiver up Myles' spine. Staffa continued, "You may tell His Holiness that the Companions will engage the Myklenian defenses within a matter of minutes. If you would be so kind as to hurry your mobilization and deploy at the earliest opportunity, we'll be ready to hand the planet over to you upon arrival."

Myles sputtered as he jerked bolt-upright. "*Attack! Now? But our forces are only half ready. You can't attack! Not until we're ready!*"

Staffa's expression didn't change. "Legate, if you would like to argue the terms of the contract, you may do so later. If your admirals are going to throw petty fits of temper, *you* may deal with them."

"But, Lord Commander, Sassan honor—"

"Is not my concern." Staffa kar Therma paused. "If you have a problem, Legate, take it up with your emperor."

"Take it. . . . No! No, you can't do this! Attack, without our military forces. . . . I refuse to let you."

A nerveless smile crossed the Lord Commander's lips. "Do you wish to cancel the contract?"

"Cancel the . . . No, of course not. We're just . . . His Holiness is going to be *very* displeased. He might . . . might . . ."

"Yes? You were saying?" A mocking glint lingered in Staffa's eyes.

A twisting sensation of defeat grew in Myles' belly. He could feel the sweat popping out on his brow. "Just tell me, Lord Commander. Why did you act before we were ready?"

An evil demon might have stared back at the Legate. "Because no one expected us to strike now—least of all you, or the Praetor's spies."

"Are you insinuating that our security is—"

Staffa leveled a gray-gloved finger, deadly menace in his eyes. "*Don't* use that tone of voice with me, Legate."

Roma's tongue stuck in his mouth and he recoiled in physical horror, his gravity chair rolling out of the privacy field and canceling its protection.

"That is all I called to tell you, Legate." Staffa narrowed his eyes. "Come as soon as your forces are ready. Myklene will be waiting."

The holo flashed off and Myles trembled, aware that all eyes were upon him. He pulled a perfumed handkerchief from his pocket and mopped at his damp face.

He didn't try to pull his chair back, but rose on unsteady legs. "Get me His Holiness."

His aides simply stared.

"*Now, by the Rotted Gods, NOW!*"

* * *

Staffa kar Therma, the Lord Commander of the Companions, sat alone, though surrounded by so many—a solitary man in gray enfolded by the instrument cluster pods that rose like petals from the raised command chair that dominated the warship *Chrysla*'s bustling bridge. No expression crossed his face. Despite the hum of machinery, the constant murmur of voices, and the flashing of monitors, his gray eyes stared absently—lost in the depths of his thoughts.

The duty officers who sat at their stations amidst multicolored computer consoles shot periodic glances his way. Each look reflected pride and confidence—or hinted at awed worship. Despite the quick glances, no one malingered. Weapons officers ran systems checks and the pilot reclined in a state of semitrance, her brain directly interfaced with the nav-computer as it fed her data on course and velocity. The engineers monitored the huge ship's power plant and support systems, vigilant attention on the readouts. The communications officer sat before the comm boards, leaning back with arms crossed while the logistics officer spoke quietly into his mike, coordinating with his subordinates.

Surrounded by the muted whispers and hushed comm chatter, Staffa kar Therma remained alone. Hidden to all eyes but his, the instruments of the command chair projected a holo image of an emerald planet against a background of hazy flickering stars. Scenes formed on the monitors of gleaming white cities, laughing men, women, and children—of a carefree society.

Myklene. How many years have passed since they turned on me? Despite the lies I've told myself, was I ever happy there? That verdant world, Myklene, had borne him, taught him, and finally betrayed him. Even the man he'd loved and devoted himself to had turned against him; but that had been long ago. The angry youth who had been expelled from Myklene now returned as a hardened man, as a conqueror come back to repay an old debt. Emotions conflicted within Staffa's muscular chest.

He pulled absently at his smooth chin, eyes thinning to slits. He'd come a long way since the day the Praetor had smuggled him off Myklene in defiance of the Council's wishes. They'd destroyed his happiness—such as it was.

Happiness? When was I really happy? Once. Once. . . . The memory tried to slip through the tungsten-steel tough rein Staffa kar Therma kept on his thoughts. A beautiful woman's face with soft amber eyes and gleaming auburn hair formed in his mind and to avoid the pain he banished it like a ghost of floating mist on a hot sunny day. The terrible cry of a newly born child drifted through his memory. And with it came the haunting longing for the son he'd never known, the son who had been stolen from him.

My fault. My failure. He'd slipped, allowed himself to feel, to share his life with another. *Chrysla*, the name cast honeyed tones through his soul. He'd loved her, known happiness for those few brief years before she'd been abducted. And to what fate? By whom?

She'd borne him a son just before her kidnapping; and for the second time in his life, his heart had been broken. He'd searched, employed the finest investigators to find her, offered rewards. But Chrysla had vanished without a trace. In the years that followed, he'd exacted his revenge on a heedless humanity. Never again had he allowed himself to falter, to feel, or to share that sense of identity which was human. Instead, he'd fallen into the old patterns taught him by the Myklenians—and the only other human he'd ever loved.

Love led to pain . . . and failure. Do not love. Allow no vulnerability of the soul. Strength was the only virtue. No other heritage belonged to humankind. Survival meant power, no matter how much blood had to be spilled.

"*Staffa?*" her soft voice drifted through the veiled memories of shattered dreams.

First, she taught me how to love—then she taught me how to grieve. Staffa glanced up at the main bridge monitor which displayed fleet status as the Companions readied for the first assault. In a matter of hours Myklene would reap the rewards of Staffa kar Therma's homecoming.

And what if I have to face him again? What if I have to look into his eyes? Speak to him? Staffa ground his teeth and balled his fists. *Then I shall do so as a master to a servant. Yes, Praetor, the roles will be reversed this time.*

Except Staffa couldn't stifle the quake of fear deep in his gut.

* * *

The comm near Captain Theophilos Marston's ear buzzed, followed by, "Sir, we have a security alert from the planet. Something's gone wrong with the computers down there."

He jerked a rheumy eye open and sat up on his sleeping pallet while the last skeins of his dream of the beautiful amber-eyed woman slipped away. "What the hell do you mean, something's wrong with the computers? On the planet? What does that have to do with us?"

"Uh, sir, it's something wrong with the security system. Alarms are going off all over the planet. It started with one or two here and there. When personnel checked them out, they couldn't find anything wrong. Now the whole planet's ringing with alarm klaxons. It's mass confusion."

Marston rubbed his face and shook his head. "I suppose the deep space buoys are involved?"

"Yes, sir. That's why we thought it necessary to wake you, sir."

"Great, just great. Thought the system was supposed to be foolproof."

By the time he'd dressed, grabbed a cup of stassa, and made it to the bridge, pandemonium reigned. Officers shouted into their headsets, bridge status monitors flickered on and off or displayed static-ridden snow.

"What the hell's this?" Marston demanded, waving his stassa cup before him.

"Planetary systems, sir," his watch officer told him.

Marston met his watch officer's worried eyes and dropped into the command chair. "Shut that down. Cut the down-link. Isolate us. I want ship's systems only. Whatever's gone wrong down there is their problem. Rotted Gods, this is no time for a software failure. I want ship's eyes to the sky."

A subtle panic stole through Marston's heart as he watched the bridge monitors firm up with solid images. The deep space scanners probed out into the vacuum, mass detectors providing fuzzy images that slowly solidified into patterns depicting solar wind, occasional vessels headed outbound, and the usual clutter that orbited Myklene.

"Nothing incoming," the weapons control officer called.

Marston squinted up at the monitors and the clear sky they indicated. "Why is this happening now? It just doesn't make sense. By the Rotted Gods, if the Star Butcher chose this moment to strike, we'd be just about defenseless. What happened down there? They let some idiot loose with an idea, or what?"

"I guess it started with security." The watch officer twirled the gold braid that hung down from her epaulets. "You know how it is. One computer's hooked to another. We'd just better hope this Star Butcher scare is exactly that. It will take hours to sort this mess out."

"Relax, people," the intelligence officer called from his station. "We know the Sassans are preparing for war, but they're still weeks away from operational readiness. Not even Staffa would move before the Sassans were ready. Sassa II would throw a fit if his troops weren't included on the first strike. He'd have Staffa's head for it."

Marston tried to blink the cobwebs of exhaustion out of his weary brain. *Would he? If Staffa wanted to strike first, what would the Sassan God-Emperor do about it? What could he do? Throw a tantrum? Blast the Lord Commander with a bolt of lightning?*

"On the ball, people. I don't like this. Something's sour in my gut. I want the crew at combat quarters—now!"

The intelligence officer swiveled around from the monitor. "With all due respect, Captain. I think that's unnecessary at this stage. The Praetor himself is aboard. I assure you, if anything were about to happen, I'd have—"

"I've got incoming!" the weapons control officer called out. "Deep space contacts, three . . . no, five . . . eight. . . . Rotted Gods! There's a dozen incoming . . . no, twenty or thirty!"

Marston's heart skipped and a dryness formed in his throat as he glanced up at the monitor. The deep space scan had already begun to plot vectors on the incoming vessels.

"Comm Officer! Sound a full-scale alert! We're about to be attacked!" Marston wheeled his chair around and began checking his systems as the klaxons wailed throughout the ship.

"Sir!"

Marston swiveled his chair around to face the comm officer. The young woman's face had gone pale and pasty. Her voice trembled as she told him, "They don't believe me, sir. They say they've got false alarms going off all over the planet."

Marston sat stunned for a moment. He could feel the chill

creep into his heart. "Get me the Praetor, before we're all dead."

On the screen, the deadly dots of light had begun to fan out, changing vector in a deadly dance of offensive tactics.

* * *

Division Commander Dimeter Anaxoulos wove anxious fingers into his thinning white hair and tugged until it hurt. Never had he faced such a rat's nest of computer malfunctions. The entire security and defense net had gone schizophrenic. For the last one hundred and fifty-six years, he'd pursued his career as a military commander, and he'd never seen a system go so batty. Each of the monitors in the control room of his orbital platform winked on and off while communications lines scrambled, cleared, and scrambled again.

"What the hell are they doing down there?" he demanded as he stalked back and forth. "Don't the thrice-Rotted fools know we're on alert?"

"Sir?" the comm tech called.

"Damn it, not now. I've got more important things—"

"*Sir!* I've got the Praetor on priority laser link from the flagship *Pylos*. He demands to speak to you now."

Anaxoulos caught himself and nodded. He glanced up at the monitor in time to see the Praetor's withered face form. "Praetor, thank the Blessed Gods, we've got a—"

"Shut up, Dimeter. We're under attack. Isolate your systems from the planet and prepare to defend Myklene. Check your monitors, and coordinate your fire. The security malfunction is a diversion. I've got a means at my disposal to buy some time." The Praetor's expression twisted sourly. "Provided I can reach Staffa in time. Meanwhile, destroy them. Kill them all, Commander."

The screen went blank.

"You heard him!" Anaxoulos shouted. "Delink, and turn our . . ."

He never finished. Even as he spoke, the monitors cleared and he could see the closing vessels. "Weapons control! Fire. Charge all batteries, tie into the system, *and fire!*"

For long seconds Dimeter Anaxoulos waited, then the complicated targeting computers sorted out vectors, and the lights dimmed as energy bolts lashed out from the giant orbiting platform. Mass detectors quavered from the after-effects while the sensors fuzzed from the radiation of the discharges, but one by one, the incoming dots reestablished on the screen, unscathed, closing the distance incrementally.

"I don't . . ." Anaxoulos gripped the console edge to brace himself. "Shoot! By the Blessed Gods, target and shoot!"

The weapons officer grimly applied himself to the task. Seconds passed as bolt after bolt flashed toward the stars at the speed of light; and with each one, it became apparent that something had gone terribly wrong, for the shots played randomly through the vacuum.

Anaxoulos hunched as if kicked in the stomach. "What . . . How . . ."

"The master computers," the weapons tech told him in a dead man's voice. "They did something to the master computers. Somehow, some way, they sabotaged the system."

Dimeter Anaxoulos screamed his rage, bowling the weapons officer out of the way as he clawed at the control console, sending shot after shot harmlessly into space. Finally, in defeat, he cried. He was still crying when the first enemy strike blasted his orbital platform.

* * *

"I've got a message from the commander of the *Pylos*, Lord Commander."

Staffa kar Therma swiveled in his command chair. The three-sixty screens surrounding him reproduced every angle of the battle that raged around Myklene. Each of his ships darted through Myklenian space, streaks of light marking their bombardment of the ravaged defenders. One by one, his assault ships dropped low over the planet, dispersing ground assault teams. Smoke rose in rolling columns over Myklenian urban centers.

He could remember each of those cities. He needed only to peel back the curtain of memory to see them as they'd been in his youth. A pang speared his heart. This had been home once, before they'd turned on him and his talents. And had Chrysla been left for him, she might have talked him out of crushing this final link with his past. Perhaps he would have felt pity for the people who had once been his. Now, as he watched the planet burn, only an emptiness filled his breast. A shattering of dreams.

Praetor, today you reap what you have sown. Your son has returned—and broken your back.

"Lord Commander?"

Staffa glanced at his comm officer. "Yes?"

"The commander of the *Pylos*, sir. Do you wish to speak to him?"

Staffa nodded, and a face formed in the main monitor on his command chair. The bridge behind Theophilos Marston had gone dead—power shorted. Smoke wreathed the air and emergency sirens wailed in the background. Marston looked stricken as he grabbed a console to steady himself. He wore a space suit in anticipation of decompression.

"Lord Commander, I am Theophilos Marston of the flagship *Pylos*. I beg of you, Lord Commander, stop your assault! We're helpless. The lives of millions hang—"

"I'm well aware of your situation, Captain." Staffa said coldly and leaned forward, savoring the moment. "I also remember the lessons you once gave me on strategy and tactics. I believe your exact words were, 'The purpose of war is to render the enemy incapable of resistance by whatever means are possible. He must be crushed physically, mentally, and spiritually. Only then can the vanquished be subjected to the yoke of a new political authority.' "

Marston winced, a pained expression on his face. "Yes . . . yes, I remember those words. But, Lord Commander, don't you have any pity left for your people? For the innocents? Surely you have some family on Myklene. Surely there is space in your heart for the millions of innocents you are killing. What of the children, the elder—"

"What of them?" Staffa raised an eyebrow and steepled his fingers. "My profession is not compassion, but conquest."

"But I also taught ethics, Lord Commander. Surely you remember—"

"I have no interest in ethics, Captain. Only results."

Marston reached out, imploring. "Stop the slaughter, Lord Commander. We are beaten! We can't resist further!"

"Are you finished?"

Marston gaped, unable to comprehend. He shook his head. "No. The Praetor is on board. He would like to speak with you. Please, hold the channel open and I'll—"

"I have no wish to speak with him, Captain. Good day—and good-bye." Staffa killed the connection, tension rising in his gut. *The Praetor, on* Pylos. *I can't face him. Not even after all these years*.

Staffa overrode the target acquisition computer, refining the image resolution until *Pylos* filled the monitor. Atmosphere leaked from wicked rents in the hull. Flashes of lights indicated explosions as more of the hull ruptured. She lay dead in space, no further threat. *Except for the man inside your cursed hull*.

Staffa thumbed the main battery, watching the violet beams home in. *Pylos* burst apart like a rotten melon under his guns. One by one, Staffa targeted the escape pods that jettisoned from the wreckage, and blew them into plasma.

CHAPTER II

Special Tactics Officer Ryman Ark waited with the cool efficiency of a professional. He had placed the rest of his team throughout the hospital building, but this critical corridor he'd taken for his own. Around him, his men and women lay prone behind shimmering energy barriers capable of deflecting pulse as well as particle fire. No one moved, no one made a sound.

Why are we here? Why did the Lord Commander put his best Special Tactics Unit here . . . to guard one crippled old man? Who is he?

Ark shifted his gaze from the gleaming white corridor and checked the status displays projected by his sophisticated battle helmet. At his mental command varicolored holos appeared, providing him with information beyond the capabilities of his human senses. He focused the helmet's scanning receptors on the end of the long hallway and dialed up the sensitivity. The corridor looked like any other: White walls reflected soft fluorescent light from square ceiling panels; the polished floor tiles gleamed; steel doors had been placed at fifteen meter intervals. The auditory sensors amplified only the hum of the air conditioning.

The Lord Commander had ordered all rooms to be vacated—all but the one Ark and his team guarded. And what the Lord Commander ordered, the Companions accepted as inviolate law, no matter what the sense of it might seem at the moment.

But to put us here? There's still fighting out there. We ought to be using our talents to crack the last of the defensive positions. Not Gods rotting here, guarding a dying old man and an empty hospital.

The sophisticated detection equipment in Ryman's helmet picked up faint vibrations: the sound of footsteps approaching. Ryman checked his IR monitor and noted the gradual increase in heat from beyond the blind corner. Rescue attempt?

"On deck, people," Ark whispered.

Ryman's crack Special Tactics Unit tensed behind their energy barriers.

He used his comm to check with the other personnel scattered through the hospital. "This is Ark. Any trouble? Anyone pass through security?"

"Negative, STO. All quiet. Nothing cooking."

"Well, I've got visitors; be sharp, people."

So who'd passed the guards on the lower floors? *Must be somebody of ours.* Ryman licked his lower lip. But then, he hadn't made Special Tactics Officer by accepting anything at face value.

He lowered the combat shield over his dark-skinned face. Dressed in camouflaging armor, he crouched behind the shielding—a muscular man with the grace of a trained athlete. The IR image in the rifle sight tinged with heat.

At that moment two familiar figures swept around the corner.

"Hold your fire," Ark ordered. In the holo monitors projected to the side of his vision he noted that none of his troops even quivered, their respective defensive areas covered by the ugly belled nozzles of assault rifles. Professional, by God!

"Halt!" Ark's voice boomed down the hall.

The man and woman stopped short, balanced and ready in a predatory stance.

Ark studied them through his instruments. It figured that the Lord Commander would appear unannounced like this. It kept his people frosty. Ryman studied his commander with the same interest that always possessed him. Staffa kar Therma met his stare over the distance. The ice-blonde woman beside him stood dressed in space whites. Wing Commander Skyla Lyma had dropped her Vegan disguise after they'd gained access to the Myklenian computer system.

The Lord Commander nodded slightly, and a hard smile of approval barely touched his lips. A glistening gray combat suit fit skintight over his trim body, covering every inch from boot tops to neck. What looked to be a golden choker—in reality the field generator for a vacuum energy helmet—snugged around his throat. The cloak pinned at his shoulders seemed alive as it swirled behind him. A thick weapons belt held a pistol, grenades, comm unit, climbing tackle, and vacuum suit energy pack snugged around lean hips. Knee-high black boots gleamed.

Staffa's clean-shaven face had a handsome look, blocked on the bottom by a square jaw that accented broad thin lips. The nose jutted straight, perfectly proportioned under the smooth brow. Long black hair had been gathered in a ponytail over the left ear and hung over his shoulder—held in place by a shimmering multicolored gem. Ark knew the imperious command in those glinting gray eyes. Through the magnification in his scope, they pierced him. Lines had tightened at the edges of the eyes, giving Staffa's face an expression of tension.

Ryman Ark fought a shiver. That aura of power chilled men's souls like some pervading miasma. But then, what sane man wouldn't feel that in the presence of the deadliest man in Free Space?

Ark noted the quick flicker of gray-gloved fingers as they moved in the Companion's sequence of identification.

"Advance, sir." Ryman stood and allowed the assault rifle to hang easily in his hands.

The Lord Commander strode forward, the gray cloak billowing behind his tense body. And yes, his expression looked strained, pale, almost a grimace.

What in the name of the Rotted Gods is wrong?

Ryman shifted his wary glance to the woman who walked with predatory ease at Staffa's side. Skyla Lyma reminded Ark of an ice leopard. She had that fluidity of movement and the wary balance of a huntress. Skyla missed nothing, her glance darting to each of the energy barriers, and then to the disposition of Ryman's men where they remained crouched behind ready rifles.

She nodded—a barely perceptible movement—her silver-blonde hair swinging in the long braid that hung looped over her left shoulder. In her glistening white armor, she appeared the perfect complement to the tall man in gray. Her authority among the Companions was second only to the Lord Commander's.

Ryman studied the classic lines of her face and wondered.

Her features were perfect—those you might expect of an
Etarian Priestess. A gymnast would have coveted her perfectly toned body and the resilient power betrayed by her
movements. Skyla would be the envy of any man's fantasy
and desire—until he looked into those chilling eyes. With a
gaze that cut like azure crystals, she inspected him, peeled
back his soul, seeking any anomaly.

*Skyla's worried about something. And Staffa . . . he's on
edge, jumpy as I've never seen him.*

Only up close could a man see the light line of scar tissue
angling across Skyla's cheek—such rude contrast to the delicate precision of her features and the promise of those full
red lips. A beauty, indeed—and cold as the absolute zero
of the Terguzzi ice sheets. Deadly as a Cytean cobra, Skyla
had earned her position by ruthless efficiency.

"My Lord Commander," Ryman greeted, knotting a fist
over his heart in the eternal salute of the Companions.

Staffa placed hands on hips as he studied the defensive
layout Ryman had deployed. A tingle wiggled in Ark's
stomach as he caught the distress in Staffa's face—the look
that of a man preparing for battle . . . and wishing that he
were somewhere else. Those wolf-gray eyes flickered to the
door.

A hesitation of . . . Ryman denied the sudden hint of
fear in Staffa kar Therma's eyes. Absurd! Perhaps the angle
of the light. . . . Ryman stood straighter, ice tracing fingers
through his guts.

The Lord Commander spoke in a soothing, cultured
tenor. "Well done, Officer Ark. Anything unusual? The
prisoner is all right?"

"Yes, sir." He swallowed, finding it difficult.

"Nothing suspicious?"

"No, sir. He . . . the prisoner . . . only sent one commu-
nique, Lord Commander—and that was to your flagship,
the *Chrysla*, sir."

"Very well." It sounded absent and Staffa's expression
had gone slack. Could there have been a graying of that
pale flesh?

Fear, like a chill lance, slipped through Ryman's soul.
Who *was* this crippled man they guarded?

The Lord Commander turned to Skyla in a swirl of gray

cloak. "I'll see him alone, Wing Commander. If I . . . I'll call should I need you."

Ryman kept his eyes ahead, body at full attention, fist clasped tightly on his sternum. The Lord Commander hesitated at the door, the gray-gloved hand caressing the polished brass latch for several seconds before he pulled the portal open and boldly entered.

Ryman glanced at the Wing Commander. Her pale features hinted of anguish despite the way she stood, back braced against the wall, arms crossed under those full breasts. Her worry-bright eyes unnerved him.

Ryman moved his tongue over dry teeth. *Concern? In Skyla? Bloodshot Gods!*

*   *   *

Staffa kar Therma waged war on his emotions, forcing his heart to be still when it tried to batter at the bottom of his throat. *Fear? Of what? This . . . this wreck of a man?* His gut tightened at the memories of those long gone days. Days of pain, days of endless struggle. *Yes, Staffa. You fear him—with as much passion as you once loved him.*

The door slipped closed behind him, a shield against the worry-strained eyes Ark hadn't been able to hide. *Is it that apparent? Have I so little control when it comes to facing this one old man?*

The room measured no more than eight meters across. Monitors projected holo after holo along the walls: Scenes of untamed country, green with vegetation; of buildings lancing white and silver into a turquoise sky; of beautiful statues in manicured emerald parks. Others depicted happy people, or gala musical events. Familiar scenes, they plucked at Staffa's memories and called back the vanished days of his youth. Each of the projections portrayed Myklene as it had been before his forces crushed the Myklenian defense and rendered the planet helpless before the Sassan invasion.

The medical unit stood in a far corner, illuminated by the greenish tint of Myk's sunlight—unique in that it emitted a higher percentage of light between 5000 and 5700 angstroms. The hospital unit consisted of a gleaming white box the size of a large freezer chest. Rows of monitors filled one side while a retractable power lead and comm link trailed to a wall socket.

The Lord Commander stopped, throat tight, skin flushed and hot. He steeled himself.

The old man's head—a round ball of flesh and bone—stuck out incongruously above the polished white of the hospital unit. From the Lord Commander's position, only close-cropped hair—graying now where once it had been black—and pasty skin remained visible. The ears curled like wilted chubba leaves, pink and fleshy. The aging flesh on the neck had gone flaccid, and withered muscle stretched from the mastoid into the white depths of the machine.

Outside the armored window, a vista of wrecked and shattered city stretched forever, smoke rising in columns from twisted structures. Other buildings, unhurt, now sprouted banners in the delicate script of Myklene: pronouncements of the Sassan victory. Aircars crossed the turquoise sky, most bearing combat-armored personnel in Sassan gear. Larger vehicles bore prisoners en masse to detention centers as they were routed out of the public buildings and battered defensive positions. In the distance, cargo shuttles lifted skyward, shooting up through the gravity well to the orbiting Sassan Fleet.

A single holo hung before the hospital unit, unaffected by the shadows which should have been cast by the green sun. The old man watched a view from space, an up-to-date image of the planet now wreathed in smoke and fire. Music played, requiem to a blasted empire.

As if the Lord Commander's pounding heart betrayed his presence, the old man spoke, "So, it's you at last." The elder's voice had a cracked, strained quality, as if forced from the unresponsive mechanical lungs of the hospital machine.

"The neutralization of several pockets of resistance delayed my—"

"You're a liar, Staffa kar Therma."

Staffa's fingers wove into the fabric of his belt, hands knotting. "No other man in Free Space would *dare* call me that."

"Would you prefer that I call you what you are?" A pause. "Traitor fits my tongue perfectly. How about yours?"

"*You* cast me out! You and your precious Myklenian Council. I could make your death . . . But you'd like that, wouldn't you, Praetor?"

"I cast you out?" He snorted his scorn. "If you'd remember, I saved *your* Rotted life!" The hospital unit whined as it turned, slowly rotating the motionless head toward the Lord Commander. As the profile filled, the true nature of the skull could be seen in the pain-racked flesh. The forehead bulged over a thick orbital torus. The fleshy nose protruded, hooking over a line-etched mouth, lips purple and swollen with age. Age spots dotted thin mottled flesh. The chin thrust in a walnut-stained knob below the broad face. Turning exposed a bruise on the left cheek.

Human wreckage. Here lies my enemy. . . . And Staffa began to smile, his breathing easier. Who could fear this bit of crushed humanity? The Praetor lived by grace of pumps and filters. Intravenous alimentation filled his blood with the nutrients to sustain life while osmotic membranes oxygenated the artificial blood serving the remains of the spinal cord.

The man he'd once feared—and loved—was gone, vanished forever in a blaster bolt he, Staffa, had triggered to destroy the Myklenian flagship. Through some miracle, the old man had survived, had been found by mop-up crews and identified.

The old man's mouth moved, changing the pattern of parchmentlike wrinkles. "Humor, Staffa kar Therma? Amusement at what you've wrought?"

The Lord Commander cradled an elbow and rubbed his chin as he considered the sunken face before him. Fear pangs receded as the reality of his victory began to wash deep within him. The work of the past had been erased—vanished into the smoke and violence of the present.

Staffa walked to the wall, allowing the cloak to dance behind him in a taunting swirl. He slapped a palm on the holo control, and the walls went dead white—only the holo of the ruined world remained spinning slowly before the Praetor's eyes.

"See what *I* have made of you, Staffa? The perfect conqueror! My greatest achievement. Yes, I've followed your career. Brilliant. I thought the Phillipian defense couldn't be cracked. Then you did the impossible off Ashtan—who'd

have thought they'd fall for a feint on the marshlands? Only
you could have orchestrated the decoy that destroyed the
Maikan fleet. Yes, I studied each of your campaigns, knowing I'd have to fight you one day. One by one, I pored over
your spectacular tactics until I could counter your every
move."

A hollow, bitter laugh passed the bloodless lips. "Too
good, Staffa. I never had time to break you . . . to buy you
off and turn you against the Sassans."

"I do not break. Nor do I buy off."

"No?" A gray eyebrow lifted to crinkle parchment skin
over the wide forehead.

"No."

The Praetor's smile went crooked. "One of the oldest of
truths, Staffa, is that every man does indeed have a price.
As do you, *mercenary!*"

Staffa paced slowly forward, gray eyes locked with the
Praetor's. He found enjoyment in the dulling brown that
shadowed those once powerful orbs. He cocked his head.
"Never, in all the campaigns I've fought, have I betrayed a
contract."

The corners of the ancient lips raised slightly, eyes gleaming. "No, you never have. A spotless reputation, don't you
agree? But then, I forged you, Staffa. I took you as a young
man and trained you, honed you to be the finest military
commander anywhere. I gave you your values and strengths
and cunning. I know you, Staffa. *I am your creator!*"

"That was many years ago, Praetor." He raised a shoulder. "I have—"

"What a master forges, *so can he break!*"

With a gray-gloved hand, Staffa gestured futility. "Brave
and powerful words, Praetor. Yet I see your planet in ruins.
Your people are captured—slaves for all intents and purposes. Your fleet is wreckage tumbling in vacuum, your
armies scattered and decimated. And you, Praetor, your life
is at the mercy of this machine in which you lie. Your body
is dead." Staffa wiggled his index finger. "With this, I could
terminate your existence."

The old man's smile broadened. "Not until you hear
about your weakness, Staffa." As the smile faded, a shadow
of frown deepened. "You don't wish me to fawn like all the
rest and call you Lord Commander?"

"I'll let it go, Praetor . . . for old time's sake."

"So noble of you."

"And you had the ability to destroy me?" Staffa clasped his hands, feeling the armored cloth, warm and reassuring between his fingers.

Aged eyes studied him thoughtfully. "Yes . . . I do. You—"

"*Do,* no less?" Staffa barked a short laugh. "You would call forth your legions? Recall your fleets from the dead? Raise your defensive platforms from orbiting slag? Return—"

"Nothing so gross or wasteful." The Praetor's face caught a spear of light from the setting sun, illuminating his half-slitted eyes in a shaft of yellow-green. "I only need a few words. Nothing more."

"Some key psyched into my mind when I was a youth? I know you did that, left deep psychological triggers. I found them, rooted them out laboriously, one by one."

"All of them, Staffa?" The withered lips twisted again, cunningly. "We will see." The brows lowered. "Yes, indeed. But first tell me, you're the most feared man in all of Free Space. Legends have been spun about you, Commander. From the Forbidden Borders to the gutter sumps of Terguz, no one has failed to hear of your name or fame. You've destroyed over thirty worlds. More than ten *billion* human beings have died because of you. You have enslaved entire populations. In places, men utter curses in your name. Among others, you're reviled as a demon from their versions of hell. Some hex you with magic. Others have paid fortunes to have you assassinated. Fear and hatred are your legacy, Lord Commander. Do you ever wonder about that? Lose sleep perhaps? Awake shivering in the night?"

Staffa raised his shoulders in a shrug, palms up. "I am not paid to lose sleep. I am paid—and paid very well—to win."

The Praetor nodded ever so slightly. "No soul, eh, Staffa? No responsibility to God? None?" He hawked and spat onto the polished floor. "No, indeed. I bred that out of you—banished it from your personality so long ago. A creature without conscience . . . without guilt. Only money and power motivate you." He cackled gleefully. "And, of course, your reputation!"

"Does this have a point?" Staffa stepped to the window, rubbing hands along his arms as he stared out over the wreckage that had been the capital of Myklene.

"You attacked before anyone expected, Staffa." A wistful note filled the old man's voice. "I didn't underestimate your fury—only your speed. Your plan to hit us before the Sassan fleet was even half provisioned . . . well, it was brilliant. Our spies had only heard vague rumors that you were working for Sassa. Even then, I knew our defensive platforms would have delivered a crushing blow to your fleet. You crippled us before we could—"

"I played on your trust in spies," Staffa told him casually. "You expected a massed attack. You counted on Sassan vanity, knowing they'd demand to be present for the first assault to ratify their God-Emperor. Expectations are a weakness. A single unarmed freighter couldn't pose a threat to your massed defenses. Commando assaults from unassuming supply freighters never crossed your mind, did they?"

The Praetor sniffed in irritation. "I wonder what would have happened if you'd misjudged and we'd wiped out your Special Tactics squads?"

"Skyla wouldn't have let that happen. She personally orchestrated the sabotage of your computer systems. Timing was too critical. My fleet had to appear at exactly the right moment."

"Yes, Skyla Lyma. A worthy second to your brilliance. Tell me . . . are you lovers?"

"No, Praetor, we are not. Never have been. She is her own woman—my second in command."

"And as reptilian in conscience as you."

"I have no interest in conscience."

"So you've said—and proved." The Praetor sighed and shifted his gaze to the holo of the planet. "And now only two empires remain. Rega and Sassa. Each built with your skill and power. What now? Do you choose Tybalt and his Regans, or Sassa and their God-Emperor? Is this what you intended? Surely you knew it had to come down to two . . . and then to one. Has that been your design?"

Staffa smiled and cocked his head. *If only you knew, old man.* "The Companions follow the tides of fortune."

"Tides of fortune? My ass! And what of your cunning and ambition? I know you as no one else ever will. Don't toy with me, Staffa. You brought humanity to this—you and your Companions."

"And if I did?"

The Praetor leered evilly. "Then you made a terrible mistake."

"Oh?"

The old man squinted. "Let's dispense with the fencing, shall we? With the destruction of Myklene, two hungry empires face each other over a ragged border. Both are reeling, their economies starved to feed your war chest. Neither can meet your vampire price—not without bankrupting their blood-sucked economies. You will choose the winner . . . and then?"

Staffa shifted, crossing his arms as he studied the old man.

"Who, Staffa?" The Praetor stared at him. "I think you'll choose the Sassans—and then turn on them. After you bleed them dry in the fight against Rega, you'll become the ruler of human space—and you'll finally fail."

Staffa lifted an eyebrow. "I'll play along with your game for the moment. Why would I fail?"

"What will destroy you in the end is your own lack of humanity. The people will pull you down. Not armies . . . but human beings."

The laugh built from deep in Staffa's gut. "The people? Those huddling masses of terror-ridden dolts who curse my name? You think *they* could do what no empire, no military force could? Be serious."

The Praetor glanced out at the ruins of his capital. In a wistful voice, he added, "I am, Staffa. To you, human beings are pieces on a game board. You see them as chaotic forces, eddies and swells of turbulence following no predictable course. But you're inhuman. A creation. If you would save yourself, Staffa, you must learn what it is to be human. You can't feel the spirit that breathes within the species—and because of that it will crush you one day."

"Nothing will ever crush me."

A subtle change invaded the hoarse voice. "Not even love?" A long hesitation. "You found that once, didn't you?"

Staffa bit off a retort, settling the tightness in his lungs with a deep breath.

The old man saw through his defense. "Captive girl, wasn't she? A strikingly beautiful slave destined to be sold to the whorehouses on Sylene. Except she was too beautiful for you to pass up. Another surprise you gave me, Staffa. I never thought your heart would allow you to love. I thought I'd killed that in you."

The muscles along Staffa's back tensed and rippled. *What's he after? How could he know? Chrysla, my beloved Chrysla. . . .*

The Praetor moved his lips. "Could you still have a trace of humanity hidden within you, Staffa? Even after all I did to you?"

Staffa closed his eyes, emotions reeling. Images of her face filled his memories, the subtle smile, the love in her soft amber eyes.

"Wonder how I know, Commander?" the old voice wheedled. "Yes, indeed, how do I? How would I know you had a son by Chrysla? They were kidnapped from you almost . . . what? Twenty years ago? No trace of them ever showed up in spite of your threats . . . or the reward."

Staffa whirled, his cloak spreading like raptorian wings as he braced himself on the hospital unit. His hot face thrust inches from the Praetor's.

It came as a forced hiss, *"What—what do you know?"* Iron fingers gripped the sagging flesh of the old man's jaw as Staffa twisted the head to meet his smoldering glare.

The brittle jaw worked as the Praetor swallowed and gritted, "Nothing . . . so long as you . . . hold me like this. Release me, Staffa, and I'll tell you."

Staffa peeled trembling fingers from where they dimpled the sallow flesh. A red flush remained to mark each spot, indicative of the bruise to come.

The Praetor moved his jaw experimentally and studied the Lord Commander, thinly veiled irony in his expression. "I knew you'd turn against me, Staffa," the voice began like fingernails on rusty tin. "Thirty years ago, I watched your fame spreading. You and I were already on a collision course. I could sense this coming. And I was the only one in all of Free Space who'd ever known you as a . . . a vulnerable individual. Not a god, Staffa. A boy. More than that, a frightened child I once found in a wrecked shuttle.

Can you remember? Can you recall how you cried over the crushed corpses of your parents?"

Staffa denied the memory of that day while his fist knotted and trembled.

The Praetor eyed the blasted city beyond the armored window. "Do *you* remember, Staffa? Can you recall the conversations we shared? How you became the son I never had? You loved me then and I . . . I loved you."

Silence stretched as Staffa bit his lip; the stinging pain kept his concentration pure. This man had . . . Memories began to flash through his mind in ghostly images: Times when there had been laughter, joy, and security; life without assassins and blood and ships that flared death into the star-frosted emptiness of space; warm rooms, teachers, and breakfast in bed. The crushing loneliness, loneliness so terrible that only his studies relieved it.

"Ha!" the elder exploded, breaking the spell. "How powerful you became! Too powerful for Myklene. You frightened the Council. They wanted you eliminated. Only a degenerate society allows predators to stalk unleashed in its midst." He paused. "But I couldn't let them destroy you. I risked everything. Had you smuggled away. Gave you a ship, and, in the way I predicted, an occupation. I wonder if the old devils ever thought such innocent action would bring their destruction?"

"What of my wife and son?" Staffa thundered, slamming his fist against the hospital unit with force enough to jerk the Praetor's head.

"You know the term 'Achilles' heel'?" The brown eyes studied him thoughtfully.

"It's old. I don't know the origin. It refers to a vulnerability, one unknown to most others."

"Your weakness, Commander! Your vulnerability. I took them! I stole your Chrysla away! *Don't!*" he cried as Staffa approached. "Harm me, and you shall *never* know their fate!"

Staffa stopped short, quivering hands already reaching for the old man's head.

"W—where?"

The old man nodded in enjoyment. "First, I will bargain."

"At peril of your LIFE!"

"For the disposition of my life."

Staffa trembled. The contract! His honor demanded that he fulfill every letter of the agreement between the Companions and the Sassan ruler. To compromise his honor for this vile . . .

"I—I . . . accept. *WHERE ARE THEY?*" Staffa's senses cleared in the rush of adrenaline. The age freckles on the old man's face stood out like sunspots against the grainy sweat-filled pores on sallow tan. Hard blood vessels laced a blue-red maze under delicate skin.

A ghastly chuckle was followed by, "Your son is out there—somewhere. I don't know exactly. I gave him to the Seddi. Part of an old bargain I'd made. A child . . . for a child. I think they took him to Targa. That was before you . . . Well, you know."

Wretched chill formed at the base of Staffa's brain to drain down his spine. *Targa! Where the Companions had killed millions suppressing the Seddi revolt.* He saw again the mounded rubble, the piled corpses of rotting dead littering the war-torn streets. His son? One of those? "H–how long . . . ago?"

"Eighteen years. Maybe ten months before you blasted the place." And then, "There *were* survivors, you know. No one ever caught up with the Seddi."

Fragments of thoughts refused to coalesce. A vision of particle beams raking Targa's scabby topography surfaced in Staffa's mind. He remembered the bridge lights dimming as the gravity flux generators surged and the monitors showed a city crumbling into wreckage. Another vision showed a diving LC attack ship firing bolt after energy bolt into an urban area, fountains of fire and debris rising in the hellfire.

"That's where I'd start looking," the Praetor mumbled on. "Left him with the Seddi—but you'd better hurry. I hear they're in trouble again. You know how the Seddi operate—like a cancer in a restless host. Targa's seething."

Staffa's voice grated like a skid on sand. "And Chrysla? She was left there, too?" *No, not my Chrysla, not her.* Had her soft flesh been left to rot with the rest of the Targan dead? Could one of those bloody chunks of meat have been her?

"No, Commander. But first, you will never let the

Sassans have me. That is our deal—my price, if you will. I don't want them raping my mind with their probes. Understood?"

Staffa worked his lips, relief washing through him. He closed his eyes, aware of the sweat beading on his face. "I promised them that if you survived the combat. . . . Part of the contract that you'd. . . . I signed. My honor."

"Honor? What care I for your honor? No. You'll kill me." The Praetor laughed humorlessly. "I still control you, Staffa."

"Never!"

"Then you'll never know the whereabouts of Chrysla, Commander."

"*Damn you!* Tell me, Praetor. *Tell me!*"

"You will *not* allow the Sassans—"

"*ALL RIGHT!*" Staffa lunged for the hospital, sliding the heavy unit across the floor as if it were a reading stand. "Whatever you want. But *where?*"

The Praetor smiled thinly, enjoying another small victory.

"She was here, Commander," he uttered softly. "On Myklene."

Staffa closed his eyes and took a deep breath, relief flooding as powerfully as a tide across the desert sands of Etaria.

"I kept her in my palace. None of her needs went unattended."

"Where is she now? Where did you send her?" After all these years, he and Chrysla. . . .

"I had hoped to dicker with you, Commander. As I say, you have one weakness—your family. Outside of your desire to see me destroyed, only your obsession with her could overcome your precious honor when it comes to contracts. I use my weapons well."

"By the Rotted Gods, Praetor, *where is she?*"

"She was on the *Pylos*. I had her in my quarters. I thought I'd have time to contact you before the fighting, to use her as a bargaining . . ."

"Your flagship . . . was . . . destroyed." *I blew* Pylos *apart. With my own hands, I triggered the guns . . . thinking I was destroying you, old man.* Realization left him devastated . . . as butchered internally as the city beyond the window.

A slight nod. "Your ship . . . I believe you call her the
Chrysla—how ironic—blew her into plasma, Commander."

Staffa pulled himself upright, gutted, and started for the
door. The room seemed to reel as if it rested on gimbals.
Chrysla? No . . . not this. He could imagine the scene:
decks rupturing; metal twisting and shrieking; violent
plasma jetting hot and deadly; Chrysla's final scream.

"Our *deal*, Commander!" the Praetor called frantically.

Staffa looked back with dead eyes. His voice stuck in his
throat. "I have a contract with the Sassans."

One final betrayal of this man he had once loved.

"You have no soul, Staffa. And now, I damn you." The
Praetor's lip quivered and a knowing glint sharpened in his
eyes. In a perfectly modulated voice, he said, "You are my
creation. You're a machine . . . a construct of human flesh.
Did you hear me, Staffa? I said you're a machine. A construct. A creation."

A surge, like a jolt of electricity, coursed through Staffa's
brain. His body flushed and he staggered. Bracing against
the wall, he stared at the Praetor through tearing eyes.
"What . . . did you . . ."

"The last of the mental triggers, Staffa." The Praetor
watched him from half-lidded weary eyes. "I hid that trigger
in the deepest part of your psyche—the sense of identity. I
expected you to find the others, but I knew you wouldn't
search your sense of self. It's too frightening—even for you.
So I left my final weapon there . . . and with it, I damn
you to the hell of your own devising. May God rot your
inhuman self. Staffa, you are a man accursed."

"I am no more than you made me." Staffa rubbed a hand
over his face, feeling the sweat that beaded on his skin. His
thoughts faded and slipped away. Damn the treasonous old
bastard! What had he done? A thousand voices wailed in
Staffa's head. His imagination spun image after image of
Chrysla dying in agony as *Pylos* blew apart and decompressed around her.

The Praetor beamed at him, suddenly crafty. "Then it
won't hurt you to know your Chrysla was a most remarkable
woman. She provided me with a great deal of warmth in
my last years. You know, she had a mole on her right
breast—just under the nipple. When we would lie together,

sweaty and loose jointed, after making love, I would kiss it just—"

The look of triumph in the old man's eyes barely registered as Staffa leapt, catlike, to the top of the hospital unit, reaching down to grab the Praetor by the corners of the jaw, steel fingers ripping up and out, crushing the tongue against the roof of the old man's mouth as he twisted. The vertebrae popped hollowly. Possessed, Staffa continued to twist, hardly aware of the blood that leaked onto his fingers. Thews bulging on his arms, Staffa heard himself scream— the sound of a wounded animal.

He swayed, a gray mist washing from his vision in tattered streaks. Breath sobbed in and out of his lungs. He blinked— aware for the first time that the door gaped open. Skyla and Ryman Ark crouched to either side, rifles ready, expressions haunted by the sight.

He tried to think, to sort out what had happened and why, but the thoughts wouldn't form. *Something hidden in my mind—something keyed by the phrase. How did I miss it? How badly will it affect my judgment?*

Staffa turned and started for the door, his brain numb, as if drugged. Behind him, the gruesome remains of the Praetor stared sightlessly into the greenish-yellow rays of the sunset of an empire.

CHAPTER III

Magister Bruen's steps scuffed hollowly as he entered the cavernlike chamber. He paused, a thin hand braced on the gritty rock of the wall, and took a second to rest before walking out among the waiting people. The nagging ache in his hip reminded him of the long descent to this lowest level. He panted and wiped at his age-lined forehead, refusing to look at the shining machine that dominated the far wall with its banks of gleaming lights.

Overhead panels sent a soft white glow down to illuminate the ancient rock walls of the Seddi cavern. It filled the recessed hollows with diffused rays that feathered the shadows into a gray haze.

Bruen ignored the ominous flashing signal on the huge computer. Others of his party filed down the passageway behind him. Magister Hyde's wheezing gasps sounded too loud in the rocky confines. To this hidden chamber under nearly two kilometers of honeycombed Targan rock, came somber-robed men and women. No one spoke as they stepped out of the stair-lined tunnel.

The brown-robed Initiates crowded nervously along the walls, anxious eyes shifting as the two elders in white Magister's robes passed to stand before the gleaming machine.

Bruen cast a loathing glance at the brushed metal and multicolored lights of the Mag Comm. He hated it, could feel its miasma permeating the very air. *What do you want of us now?* Slippery fingers of fear tugged at his soul. A queasy tightness cramped his gut.

Magister Hyde, resplendent in white robes, stood beside Bruen and pulled nervously at his fingers. As if the Mag Comm recognized their presence, the lights flickered in unfathomable patterns. Bruen considered the monster. Where had the machine come from? Who had originally built it in the long forgotten recesses of the past? It represented a technology the Seddi hated and couldn't live without. In the silence, a faint shuffling of sandaled feet scuffed the stone floor. The air carried a metallic tang mixed with the taint of human sweat.

Magister Bruen rubbed his rounded belly, grimacing at the shimmering mass of the golden wired helmet resting in the holder next to the reclining chair—the single piece of furniture in the cavern. He looked nervously toward Magister Hyde and the sober-faced Initiates flanking him. Bright worry filled Hyde's eyes. A worry Bruen hoped his own features didn't reflect.

Bruen could see himself in the mirror-bright surface of the machine's metal—a small man, rounded, squat, arms and legs rubbery from years of scholarship and teaching. His drawn face displayed his age, each line of his deeply etched visage a hash mark of the passing years. The march of decades had sagged his flesh, adding to the dissipation of his now frail body. His Seddi robes made of coarsely woven Targan cloth were off-white and hung loosely about him. His head had lost all but a few wisps of snowy hair over the years. Now, his bald pate gleamed.

Only his eyes betrayed the unquenchable spirit that drove him now—despite his advanced years—to stand in the vanguard of events. Events which would forge humanity in a vortex of fire, blood, and pain—or destroy them all.

"Too old," he had muttered to himself so often, "and too Rotted much is at stake to get out."

He lived the curse of an old man: to hold to ideals; to dedicate one's life to the destiny of the species and an unattainable abstract. And then, when the final moments came, the Fates laughed as the warrior—girding for the final battle—looked in the mirror to find himself past his day. So old, so tired. The moment had finally come . . . leaving humanity an old, old man for a champion.

Existence proved bitter fare at best.

The machine remained a frightening enigma with its meanings hidden in the banks upon banks of mysterious boards forged in the distant past by a lost technology. Bruen filled his ancient lungs and experienced a stitch of pain in his brittle ribs.

A distasteful task this—one that came of being the highest

ranked Magister of the Seddi priesthood. The huge comm
had called from its lair deep under the temple in Vespa.
Normally, the machine ran programs for Seddi scholars who
studied social reality. For those endeavors the Mag Comm
employed complicated statistics Bruen's colleagues barely
understood; but they used them to plan covert actions
throughout Free Space, predicting trends of behavior,
manipulating data, producing historical facts for their con-
sumption and illumination.

Behind those panels lay their only ally in the coming
conflagration.

Ally? Of what sort? Bruen swallowed nervously, ignoring
the pain in his feet.

The summons light—a glaring angry amber—blinked on
and off, calling to him to communicate.

Bruen stared uneasily at the huge computer. After all the
years the Seddi records claimed it had functioned passively,
why had it awakened? Why had it developed an interest in
the doings of men? What motives beyond Seddi ken did it
now advance?

The Seddi had cared for the Mag Comm for centuries,
keeping careful track of the periodic maintenance. They had
recorded in detail each of the repairs they had asked the
machine to lead them through. For centuries, the Mag
Comm had been a giant passive machine, answering questions, responding to programmed data. Then it had
changed. Bruen had been in this very room when the Mag
Comm flashed to life, as if totally aware in an instant, printing commands, flashing lights, asking questions. The
shocked Seddi had answered, falling under the huge Mag
Comm's sway, becoming its servants.

Bruen—an Initiate then, young, full of religious ambition
and vigor—could recall those days with crystal clarity. At
first he'd thought it a miracle to see the machine come to
life, long dead lights gleaming brightly, a low pervading
humming growing in the dim recesses of the subterranean
cavern.

Heart in his throat, he had run for the upper chambers,
panicked and shouting for the Magisters. When a human
watches a God come to life before his very eyes, existence
is forever altered.

And the works of the Seddi had been transformed.

What have you made us? What is your purpose? The old
unsettling questions prickled like thorns in Bruen's mind.
*And now I have to face you again. Do you know what we've
plotted? Are you playing with us even now? How can mere
men hope to stand against you and your powers? As if we
had even the slightest comprehension of what those powers
are.*

He couldn't put off the inevitable any longer. Bruen
grunted a sigh and settled himself in the velvet-contoured
chair near the shimmering helmet. He wet his lips as he
closed his eyes. Once again he had to trust his cunning and
control—place himself in jeopardy. The future of humanity
would hang on his abilities to deceive.

"Easy. Patience, Bruen, old man," he mumbled to him-
self. *I must control myself. Compose your thoughts, Bruen.
Stifle that fear. There. There, feel your mind gain control.
Soothe yourself, Bruen, old man. Yes. You must be careful.
As always. No failings, no slips of thought. So much is at
stake. Careful. Careful. Careful.*

Under his breath he began humming the mantra the Mag
Comm had taught them. He had to will himself to resist,
building strength, rehearsing an epistemological framework
for his thoughts. The mantra became a form of self-hypno-
tism; he shut down portions of his mind, keeping his
thoughts ordered. The machine must read only "right
thoughts"—thoughts following the systemic framework of
the "Teachings of Truth."

Through endless repetition, he invoked the dogma the
Mag Comm had ordered them to adopt after the awakening.
As an Initiate he had watched the changes in the Magisters.
They had fallen completely under the spell of power and
knowledge, reveling in communication with the Mag
Comm. So much of his life had been dedicated to . . .

*No! Stifle that, Bruen. Sing the Mantra. I am of the Mag
Comm. The Mag Comm is the Way of Humanity. The
Way. . . . The Way. . . . The Way. . . . The Teachings are
of Truth. Through Right Thoughts come emancipation. The
Way. . . . Right Thoughts. . . . The Way. . . .*

Falling deeply into his mind, he hardly felt himself reach
for the helmet and lift it lightly over his head.

The Way. . . . Right Thoughts. . . . I am of the Mag

Comm. . . . We are one. . . . I practice the Teachings of Truth. I am of the Way. . . .

"Greetings, Magister Bruen." Jangling words rang through his mind.

Invasion! A rape of privacy!

No, it is The Way. We are One. He allowed himself to submit, feeling self-induced pacifism flood his thoughts.

"Greetings, Mag Comm." Bruen's thoughts formed the ritual answer, exalting in Right Thoughts.

"You have progress to report?"

"Yes." He opened his mind, following the dogma of the Truth teaching mantra. "Myklene has fallen. The Lord Commander killed his patron, the Praetor. The Sassan Empire now controls Myklenian space and resources."

"So quickly? Our predictions indicated kar Therma would need longer to prepare." A pause. *"This is most unfortunate. The permutations of this new data must be analyzed. Do you have any estimate of the Lord Commander's combat losses?"*

"From preliminary reports, less than three percent."

Bruen waited for several moments before the reply came: *"It appears our assessment of Myklene's strength was grossly overestimated."*

"I think not."

"Elaborate, please."

"We believe our assessment of Staffa kar Therma's military genius was grossly *under*estimated. Even our sources in the Sassan high command were caught by surprise by Staffa's speed. Special tactics teams infiltrated and threw the Myklenian defense into turmoil, sabotaged their computer defense net, and then Staffa hit them. Each strike increased the Myklenians' confusion until the Sassan regulars could arrive and deliver the crushing blow."

"Then we must act swiftly. Any other course is now denied us."

"Events are progressing with greater alacrity than we anticipated. Rega has begun to react, calling up their military reserves. The critical time has come."

"So, your civilization is about to fall." Haunting tones reverberated through Bruen's mind, echoing off the camouflaged walls of his blocked thoughts.

"That is correct."

"And you have taken countermeasures?"

"We have. Everything has been done as you instructed. Your plans are ours."

"You followed my instructions exactly? Explain, please."

"Targa is poised for revolt. Given the rapidity of the Lord Commander's victory over Myklene, we can still incite the revolt and proceed as planned. The revolt will serve to keep Rega off balance. We also expect that the child will be tested to determine if our aspirations will be fulfilled. To date, our agents have been successful in manipulating the child's circumstances. We're dealing with remarkable brilliance, you know. The child may be the foundation for the new order. We have followed your directions, but there is a risk. Random events cannot be biased. To do so would skew the results of the test. The child will survive—or die—depending on instinct and intelligence."

"Or through random chance?"

"Quantum functions cannot be predicted. Survival will depend on many random variables." Bruen agreed, calming himself, stifling his mind, careful of the control he exercised. The mantra rhymed to cover unorthodox thoughts.

"You know I find Seddi preoccupation with uncertainty principles to be a serious flaw. Such obsession left you impotent and too self-absorbed in the past to allow right action."

"Accidents—you must agree—do happen."

Silence.

Shying away from dangerous ground, Bruen let himself drift with the mantra.

"And the clone?"

Bruen winced. "I sometimes wish you exhibited less, shall we say, honesty, Mag Comm. The word 'clone' hardly reflects—"

"Does the taxonomic label not fit?" came a logical response. *"Clone: a being created by artificial manipulation of the genetic material to produce a viable—"*

"Yes, yes!" Bruen sighed. "Very well. Yes, the clone is progressing most satisfactorily. We are very pleased. The deep training seems to have implanted without the personality disorders we anticipated. We notice a distinct subliminal reaction to stimuli which exceeds our expectations. The clone carries all the survival skills we hoped to impart. In fact . . ."

He allowed his unease to leak and moved awkwardly to cover his reserve.

"You are concerned, Bruen?"

"A weapon of such devastating potential should always be viewed with concern. Only a fool sleeps soundly over a primed explosive."

"We are talking about a human, Bruen. Not a primed explosive."

"And which is more deadly?"

"The human with its imagination and intellect . . . I have no doubts." Mag Comm seemed to hesitate. *"To make the point, I would refer you to recent history. You will recall the shambles the Seddi and all Free Space were in when I reestablished contact?"*

"Yes, Lord Mag Comm," Bruen responded automatically, feeling the dogmatic epistemology unrolling in his subconscious mind.

"That was the unleashed, uncontrolled power of the human imagination, Bruen. Chaos. Wild. Undirected passion. Loose entropic waste! You had lost Right Thought and the ordered development that comes with it."

The violence of the pronouncement cowed Bruen. In defense, he slipped deeper into the mantra, surrendering his resistance, submitting further to the Mag Comm.

"Yes, I see you remember well. Your mind is open to me. I read the following of the Way. Right Thought is yours. That is good, Bruen. You have done well for your kind."

"Through your help, Great One," Bruen intoned. "Blessed is your guidance. Blessed was the day you returned your Grace to mankind to give direction and build the new order. We, your lost children, thank you and worship you."

"You worship through your service, Bruen." A pause. *"Is that not so?"*

Did he detect a note of sarcasm? Bruen allowed his thoughts to flow, following the intricate logic provided by the Mag Comm so long ago. Within moments, he felt the approval of the huge machine, calming him, stroking his thoughts with positive reinforcement.

"Yes, you are acting according to the Teachings of Truth, Bruen." Another pause. *"I have manipulated the data you have provided concerning the Lord Commander and evalu-*

ated the conclusions. I find no reliable data to indicate any deviation from the original strategy is necessary at this time. Staffa kar Therma no longer has a useful role. His actions defy prediction, and, therefore, cannot be countenanced. You must neutralize him. To do otherwise will unleash his ultimate control of Free Space. And what will that control bring to humanity?"

"Destruction. Death. Total slavery and chaos," Bruen intoned wordlessly, following the pattern of Mag Comm logic.

"Excellent, Bruen! You have your agents in readiness?"

"We do. The Lord Commander will bring his fleets to Targa, Great One." Bruen swallowed, allowing the plan to unroll in his mind. "When he comes to drown our voices in blood again—then, Lord, we will strike."

"My compliments, Bruen. You understand the danger posed by the Lord Commander's continued existence. He is a cancer in your society. Like any threat to health and peace, such a disease must be excised from the flesh and the True Way must heal the wounded body of humanity. I read the intricacies of your planning and intrigue. You, my Magister, are more than I could have hoped for. Blessed is your name, Bruen. You shall be the salvation of the human species. You shall bring to all people the Teachings of Truth."

"I am humbled, Great One!" Bruen cried out, sensing the righteousness of the words.

"The time has come to act. You are to trigger the Targan revolt immediately."

"Yes, Great One. I shall unleash the wrath of the people against the Regan tyrant."

"Blessed is your name, Bruen. I will call for you when I have more information. Continue, Bruen—and thank you for your dedication to the Way. The fate of your species hinges on your success in this venture."

"So many lives—"

"Your species hangs in the balance. What is it worth to you? The threat must be countered—even if a planet is bait. To fail is to invite extinction."

For a brief instant, Bruen's mind filled with a scene of sterile planets and dead cities: silent, only the ghostly ruins of human habitations remaining, lifeless, eerie in the hollow displays in his mind.

His unbalanced thoughts reeled as the Mag Comm withdrew and left him drained and trembling. Bruen blinked,
awed at the emptiness in his mind.

Suffering from the aftereffects of the communication,
Bruen lifted the feathery weight of the golden helmet from
his sweaty head. Arms shaking, he would have dropped it
had Magister Hyde not rushed forward to place the headset
on the holder. He became aware of the alcove, of the anxious faces of the Initiates. Vertigo began to recede.

"Is everything all right?" Hyde asked, fleshy face lined
with concern.

"Y—yes, it is," he lied. Unnerved, he felt his mind
returning to normal. "I—I must get back to Kaspa." He
smiled weakly. "You've seen the figures, Magister. What
choice does the machine leave us? What choice do our own
projections leave?"

"Then we . . ." Hyde shook his head, wagging the layers
of fat that hung in long jowls from his cheeks. His faded
blue eyes went dull. "It ordered us to . . ."

"Yes, Brother Hyde," Bruen whispered hollowly. "Our
lot is to drench our world in blood and misery one more
time."

Hyde wrung his hands nervously. "But so many will die.
And to what purpose? A trap? For *one* man?"

"No buts," Bruen added wearily, pulling himself up in
the hands of the Initiates. "Or do you have another idea?
We've been through this time and again. We have no
choice, old friend."

Bruen wobbled on his feet, refusing to look back at the
Mag Comm, feeling its insidious presence nonetheless. He
was only thankful that, in years past, they had managed to
"accidentally" eliminate the Mag Comm's external sensors
located within its chamber, leaving it the helmet as its sole
means of observing and communicating with them. "We've
looked at the risks, attended to the odds. We have only
ourselves to rely on."

"And that God-cursed machine," Hyde added.

Bruen closed his eyes, rubbing thumbs into his temples.
The subtle beat of a brain-wrenching headache pulsed
behind his eyes. It always happened after the Mag Comm
withdrew.

"Yes," he added feebly. "And the God-cursed machine, too."

Blessed Gods, let me live long enough to see this through! I must do something, must lay a trail, somehow, to see that insidious machine destroyed should I fail!

* * *

The voice sang hollowly in Staffa's head. *"How ironic . . . blew her to plasma. . . ."* The Lord Commander turned and pinched his eyes closed, feeling the weight of the words threading tendrils through his memory.

"I killed her. The only woman I ever loved. *I KILLED HER!*"

"You have no soul, Staffa. You are a machine . . . a construct of human flesh . . . a machine . . . a creation. . . ." The Praetor's voice echoed in ghostly waves, forcing Staffa kar Therma to press knotted fists against the sides of his skull and pound mercilessly at his temples to still that reedy voice.

"Damn you! *Damn you, Praetor!*" he howled into the stillness of his private chambers. Around him, the familiar walls glared back in eloquent silence. Trophies and mementos hung in their usual places—booty from battles fought and won. Monuments to his strategic and tactical brilliance. Now they seemed tawdry, sullied by the memories of blood from which each had been plucked.

His ship, *Chrysla*, named for *her*, mocked him in the irony of her death.

Staffa ground his teeth, hearing the grating slide of molar on molar. He ground them harder, trying to drown out the wicked satisfaction in the Praetor's knowing voice. In a sudden burst of energy, Staffa curled and rolled to vault from the sleeping mat. He landed lightly on bare feet, and whirled in a combat stance, nervous, pulse racing at the voice in his memory.

How had it happened that way? How had the old man beaten him so soundly? *I did it to myself. Her blood is on MY hands!*

He threw his head back, gasping breaths of cool air. "Damn you, Praetor! May the Rotted Gods gag on your pustular corpse! *How did you bring me to this?*"

In anger, he shook his head, enjoying the sensation of his loose hair as it fell about his face in a black aureole. A mind trap, a deeply buried conditioned response that caused him to access improper neural pathways in the brain that would arouse an emotional response—flooding his brain with chemicals that clouded objective, logical analysis of data.

"I can't trust myself to think clearly—and I've only barely touched the surface of what he might have released."

The Praetor mocked, *"May God rot your inhuman self. Staffa, you are a man accursed . . . accursed . . . accursed. . . ."*

"True."

His eye caught the gleam of the dispenser. He stuck a golden Regan chalice under the tap and numbly watched as Myklenian brandy drained amber into the vessel. Could he drown that cackling shade's voice in a haze of alcohol?

"Indeed, Praetor. Accursed from the moment I laid eyes on you." The bitterness in his voice moved him, mocked him, turned in his gut. "Would that my body had joined my parents that day, eh, Praetor?"

Idly he sipped the brandy, barely aware of its body, of the rich smoothness of a drink valued all across Free Space.

Unwanted, fleeting glimpses of a younger Praetor—laughing, as he offered his hand during personal combat training—flashed through Staffa's mind. A kaleidoscope of sights and sounds, sensations and memories swept him. He closed his eyes, reliving those days.

"We were . . . we meant so much to each other . . . once." He recalled the encouragement, the praise, yes, and even love. "And still we brought ourselves to meet finally like . . . like beasts!" A painful numbness cramped his fingers where they gripped the jeweled handle of the golden chalice. "What have you wrought, Praetor?"

The Praetor's voice snapped in Staffa's brain. *". . . A hell of your own devising!"* Staffa winced. *"You have no soul, Staffa . . . no responsibilities to God."* Each burning word engraved itself in letters of fire to brand his soul. *". . . You are reviled as a demon."*

Staffa forced himself to swallow, bringing the chalice to his fevered forehead. ". . . Hell," a choked whisper uttered from Staffa's throat. "And I killed you, Praetor." He shook his head, an image of long ago ghosting among his battered thoughts. *As I killed her.*

He could feel Chrysla staring at him through those magical eyes. The grief began to well, threatening to engulf him. Instead, he forced himself to think about the Praetor.

"Ah, I remember, Praetor." Staffa's face worked. "You came to me after I won first place in the Myklenian Games." His thumb ran absently over the angular insets of the chalice. "Remember that day, Praetor? Remember the pride in your eyes? Remember how I ran to you? Hugged you?

"I'd been so lonely . . . worked so hard. Trained for months that I might see you smile." Staffa sniffed against the pain. "Did you know what it meant to me? How young and fragile I was then? All that sacrifice, I made for you. The pain, the sweat, the constant aching, I suffered, trying so hard. . . . All for you.

"Young men are. . . . No, I was . . . alone . . . alone that way. An orphan, you see? I had no one but you, Praetor. In you—and you alone—I placed my trust and my faith." The jeweled relief cut his flesh. Chrysla's soulless eyes probed through the haze of his memory. Using all of his concentration, he forced her back and reconstructed the Praetor's face instead.

"For you *I would have died!*" His mouth worked dryly. "After all those years, struggling for you. After all those years when you took care of me! After all that loneliness. After my need to have you notice me . . . be proud of me . . . you. . . ." Staffa struggled to fill his aching lungs. "Then I won the Games. I saw the triumph in your eyes, Praetor. Triumph. And you placed your hand on my shoulder and called me . . . *son.*"

A bittersweet memory. "Yes, your greatest *creation,* Praetor." He sipped the brandy again, flicking on the holo display over his head. "What made *me* so different? Isn't my body the same as everyone else's? What makes me a monster, and not the next man?" Chrysla's expression saddened as her ghostly image shifted in the gloom around him.

He stared listlessly at the gleaming chalice. "A monster? How many men have created a monster all their own? Answer me that, Praetor?"

An image of Myklene formed over the sleeping platform, spinning slowly, gouts of smoke pooling over the continental land masses, winter spreading beneath the palls, marching across sun-starved lands.

"See, we still share visions, Praetor." He chuckled dryly, aware of the censure in Chrysla's expression. She'd never allowed him to dwell on failure. But now . . . what was left?

Staffa dropped his gaze back to where he clutched the fabulous chalice. "And so I have killed everything I ever loved. With my hands I broke your age-rotten neck, Praetor." He lifted a hand, looking at the intricate dermatoglyphics on the palms, studying the loops and whorls on the finger pads as he moved his digits. "And Chrysla, my Chrysla, I triggered the shot that blew you apart. I was so close . . . so very close and never knew."

With that, he hurled the chalice across the room and smashed a priceless sixth-century Etarian offering bowl into angular shards. The brandy left a spattered smear of liquid that dripped down the walls.

"I damn you to a hell of your own devising!" the reedy voice repeated in his mind. *"You have no soul . . . no soul . . . no soul . . ."* the voice wound on, insinuating itself in Staffa's thoughts, weaving into his very essence. *"Construct. Machine. Creation. No God,"* the voice hammered at him again and again.

"But perhaps the Seddi have my son? Where?" Dumbly he blinked before dropping his head into his hands and bending double, shoulders shaking at the impact of the words. "Chrysla? Where is he? He's all that I have left of you."

You're inhuman . . . you have no soul. . . .

"What did you do to me, Praetor? *Who am I?*"

"Seek your son." Chrysla's voice seemed to whisper from the air. "Seek your son."

CHAPTER IV

Even the secretary had ceased to shoot periodic glances at Sinklar Fist. He sat in one of the polished chairs placed along the Judicial Magistrate's waiting room wall. Like all waiting rooms, this one had comm terminals with official programming, news, and entertainment. Hours ago, Sinklar had reprogrammed the unit for library access, called up the text on multidimensional geometry that he'd been studying, and lost himself in the text.

It came as a surprise, therefore, when the secretary called, "Sir? Private Fist?"

Sinklar saved his work on his pocket comm and jumped to his feet. "Yes? Is he ready to see me?"

She gave him one of those glassy smiles employed by receptionists across the universe and said, "I'm sorry, sir. But the office is closing. I'm afraid the Judicial Magistrate won't have time to see you today."

Sinklar stalked over to her desk and leaned down, panic in his breast. "But you don't understand! I'm shipping out tomorrow. Going on active duty. I've *got* to see him. This might be the only chance I get."

The plastic smile remained in place like a mask. "I'm sorry, sir. That just won't be possible. You've got to understand, the Judicial Magistrate has a very busy schedule and for him to take time to review such an old case is . . ."

At that juncture, the door opened and a white-haired man dressed in the crimson robes of the Regan judiciary stepped out, calling, "Erina, I'm off to tea. There are five briefs on my desk that I'd like you to refile. If there's nothing else, I'll see you in the morning."

"There *is* something else," Sinklar blurted, jumping in front of the man.

With remarkable agility, the secretary slipped around the

desk to yank on the sleeve of Sinklar's new uniform, protesting, "You can't do this. If you don't leave this office immediately, I'm calling the—"

"Now, Erina," the Judicial Magistrate waved her away, "I was in service to the Imperium once myself." He bent his eyes back to Sinklar. "Yes, Private, what is it?"

Sinklar cast an evil glance at Erina as she backed away. "I'm Sinklar Fist, sir. I'm shipping out tomorrow . . . to Targa."

"Yes, I've heard about that. Nasty bit of trouble. Myself, I served in the Phillipian campaign. Won a medal or two. Ah, those were the days when a man could make a real contribution to the empire. We were strong then, back before the Star Butcher became such a power, but then, you didn't come to hear an old man ramble."

"No, sir. I came to learn about my parents."

The Judicial Magistrate studied him through pensive blue eyes. "I see. And what would I know about your parents?"

Sinklar took a deep breath. "You sentenced them to death about twenty years ago, sir. Outside of that, I don't know a thing about them. The case was sealed after their execution and all records pertaining to them, and my family, were sealed as well."

"And you want to know where you came from."

"Yes, sir. Somehow, well, going off to war, it makes it important."

"If the case was sealed . . . well, are you sure you want to know the details?"

Sinklar jerked a nod. "I believe I'm well versed in the scope of human behavior. As a student of social history, there's not much left to surprise me."

"Very well, Sinklar. I think my tea can wait for a bit. Come into my chambers. I'll look up the record and tell you what I can within the strictures of security regulations."

* * *

Footsteps tapped on the cold stone of the cavern floor and echoed hollowly through the black shadows and around the groined ceiling.

Magister Bruen heard the approaching steps from where he sat in a cone of light that illuminated his worktable and computer. He glanced up from the comm monitor he studied and stroked his knobby chin. The air felt slightly damp, cool, and heavy. Here, in the depths of the temple, no other sound penetrated.

The footsteps grew louder and Bruen could see the electric torch the young woman held as it flashed yellow between the meter-thick columns, reflecting inscriptions and images carved in the gray rock. She threaded her way between the pillars of stone, a nymph of light in a stony underworld forest.

She was a tall woman, her movements graceful as those of a dancer. Long legs moved in purposeful strides beneath a sienna Initiate's robe. She had pinned her hair back severely with a golden clip so it hung over her left shoulder in an auburn tumble. Long sensual fingers clutched the portable spotlight in a choke hold, leaving delicate fingernails bloodless.

A striking beauty, the light accented pale cheeks to either side of a classic nose ever so lightly dusted with freckles. Her full-lipped mouth pinched as her amber eyes sought Bruen. Worry etched her high forehead. A knotted golden rope cinched the flowing robe around a delicate waist, the folds of the garment hiding the full swell of her breasts. Only under close inspection did the dark splotch at the hem of the garment betray its origin: blood.

She's seen the fighting. No wonder her features are drawn and nervous. Very well, my child: it begins.

She gasped in relief at the sight of him hunched over the blocky wooden table. He gave her a grin and a wink before he bent to frown into the yellow-toned monitor, pulling at his ear as he pondered the words displayed on the screen.

"Blessed Gods, Magister! You're *here!*" Her voice echoed in contralto relief through the endless cavern.

Bruen—bald pate gleaming ivory—looked up from the comm monitor, blinking his light blue eyes. "Indeed. Would I be elsewhere?" He made a gesture with semitranslucent hands. "You think I would perhaps be chasing scarlet floozies in the bawdy houses down on D block?"

"Magister!" she cried, shocked. "Only you would jest at a time like this! The whole city is in uproar! The miners are rioting in the streets! People are dying. How long do you suspect it will take before the Regan Fleet is overhead?

Come, we must take you from the city. Now, Magister!"
She bent to gather his cloak where it lay in a pile behind
the bench.

Bruen hiccuped and placed an age-wrinkled hand over his
mouth. *She's such a beauty. Ah, would but that I were
younger! To hell with humanity! I'd pack her up, and we'd
be gone to some remote corner of the universe where I could
ravish that. . . .*

Oh, never mind.

He sighed and turned his head to the monitor. "That will
be all for today, computer. Please note my place and correlate the notes I've made on the text. Forward a copy
through Mag Comm to Magister Hyde in Vespa for his
perusal. I'll be in touch as soon as possible." The screen
went dead.

He made a gesture with his hand. "Now, dear Arta Fera,
what has brought you running breathlessly to my side? Only
riots? I sincerely doubt it was love or desire for these old
bones that has left you panting so."

She shook her head, groaning in frustration. "Magister!
Honestly, were you not the foremost scholar in Free Space,
I'd . . . I'd wring your neck! Come on, we've got to get out
of here! Escape this insanity!"

*Indeed, Arta, would that you only knew. Escape, my
dear? No indeed, I've no choice but to place your incredible
beauty between the jaws of the lion.*

Aloud, he chuckled dryly. "Is this the respect the young
attach to the older and wiser? Wring my neck, my dear?
Don't some of the harlots on D block engage in such—"

"Magister!" She had him on his feet, wrapping the robes
about his body, tying them off so his knobby varicose-
veined legs were free should they need to run. "Your preoccupation with whores and lewd behavior ill befits your
esteemed position. You mind is the finest in all. . . . What
are you laughing at?"

He shook his head, grinning and chortling. "And just
what do you suppose a scholar does in his off time, my
dear? Especially an old man like me? Perhaps I . . . um
. . . investigate such behavior to gain an insight into the
human condition. Hmm?" He bent down for a sagging black
leather satchel, refusing to be tugged away without it. The

grip safely in hand, he let her pull him along down the long dark hallway.

"You'll think nothing if we don't get you out of here! You don't say such things in public, do you? You don't mention these . . . *fantasies* to your colleagues."

"Bah!" He began to pant as she led him to the garage. The stitch of pain in his hip awoke to stick angry pins into his joint. "Position in society concerns you, doesn't it, dear Arta?" He smiled as she palmed the access hatch. "You worry too much. Social status is but an illusion. Instead, knowledge is the—"

"But your teachings, Magister. If I thought for a minute you actually habituated such places and associated with those . . . those *women,* I'd. . . ."

"You'd what?" He looked into her flaring amber eyes. "Give up your studies? Turn down the wisdom of the ages? Cease to probe the mystery of the quanta? Go so far all because the illustrious Magister Bruen sported with prostitutes?" He raised an eyebrow, an amused grin rippling the wrinkles.

"A man of your reputation and honors shouldn't—"

"Bah! With my looks? Only a woman who was well paid would consort with the likes of me. No, they want young handsome men, virile with big . . ." At her horrified expression, a twinkle filled his eye. She took a deep breath, ready to launch into a new lecture; he deftly changed the subject. "And they are rioting in the streets again, you say? Have they forgotten the wrath of the Star Butcher so soon? They would provoke Rega into a reaction?"

The door slid open as Arta Fera caught up his sleeve, cut short his musings, and dragged his withered body into the aircar that waited on the pad with open doors.

"Yes," she grunted, irritated at his apparent lack of concern. "The idiots are parading with placards—demanding their rights as productive citizens of the Regan Empire. They claim they want representation—of all things! Imagine? Under the very eyes of the battleships they want rights! Who do they think they are?"

"It isn't exactly a new concept. In fact, you can trace such maundering philosophies back to the original migrations from Earth. Of course, from there on back, the roots are lost—"

"What? Earth? A myth, Magister. To me, rights and representation seem an excellent fertilizer from which to grow blaster fodder, blood, and pain. You know *we'll* be blamed for all these upheavals again!"

Precisely, my dear. Let's shake you up a little. He settled himself in the rear seat, the scuffed leather satchel on his lap. His fingers patted the soft leather contentedly as he began undoing the latches.

She followed the flight-check procedures while he considered his options. Her competent fingers danced on the board, flicking switches to energize the system and set the flight comp for Makarta.

He spoke in barely a whisper, nevertheless it froze her in the seat. "Of course, my dear, the blame *is* ours. That is exactly the purpose of this revolt."

She turned to stare at him, mouth agape, amber eyes wide. "What?"

He nodded soberly, watery blue eyes looking about the garage. "Well, who else do you suppose planted such an idea in the blocky brains of these mining dolts? Indeed, dear Arta, you won't allow me the diversion of shady ladies—so what's an old man with visions of glory to do?" He raised a fragile hand to his mouth in feigned shock, adding meekly, "Oh, dear. Along with harlots I can see you also object to my dabbling in revolution."

"Blessed Gods!" Arta groaned as she lifted the car from the pad. Overhead the big doors slowly parted to reveal a wounded sky.

She gasped as he set the thermal grenade launcher next to her on the seat.

"That's . . ."

"Yes, it is." *This will be your first test, my girl. Now, Hyde, we will see if our labors were for naught.*

Bruen calmly pulled a second grenade launcher from the case and tucked it next to his side. From the corner of his eye, he could see her fighting to swallow, cringing away from the gleaming metal of the weapon as if it were some sort of venomous reptile.

As they crested the steep temple roof he could see the extent of the damage. The city of Kaspa reeled with violence; pillars of smoke rose to either side. A flare of brilliant orange lit the low-hanging clouds where a fire raged through a phosphorous refinery, the billowing fumes many-hued with bright colors. Here and there about Kaspa, garish flames danced in macabre contrast to the low black clouds. Spatters of rain slashed at the windscreen as Arta shot the car forward.

"They'll kill you if they find out, Magister. *Think!* What will happen to the people? What will happen to the temples?" She blinked at the thought, fighting back tears, mouth working. "They'll destroy us!"

Wind and rain buffeted the vehicle, requiring all her concentration to keep the ride smooth and controlled.

And what will you do, my precious beauty, when they turn on us? What resources do you have inside yourself? Are you ready for this seething cauldron we've created? Are you all we hoped you'd be? "Everything is going according to plan. Everything."

"Last time, blood ran in the streets like rainwater, Magister." Her glance darted to the grenade launcher.

He studied her, noting the slim hands—white-knuckled where they gripped the control stick. As they passed above, she watched a fire racing through pressed-wood residential structures. People ran frantically into the streets, bent double under boxes of possessions they sought to save. She mumbled a quick prayer under her breath.

The city looked shabby, the buildings squat and boxy. The slanting rain left the whole place gray and shiny in the downpour. He absently cataloged the flimsy structures so hastily rebuilt out of rubble and the cheapest of materials. Kaspa had become a city of squalor after the devastation wrought by the Star Butcher during the last rebellion. Beyond the city limits, mostly obscured by clouds, ragged mountains rose dark against the horizon. Here and there he could make out brooding stands of trees that mantled the lower slopes.

He grunted a heavy sigh and patted the grenade launcher. "Blood and terror, death and misery. Revolution, dear girl, has no other price. It is bought through injustice, fear, and suffering."

"For what?"

Does she have what we need? What if I'm wrong?

"For the betterment of the human condition, dear girl. Civilization is like that. It wavers forever back and forth.

Sometimes life becomes black and repressive—spawning tyrannies like the Regan Empire. At other times human society lives in periods of light and freedom where the soul wells and sings—except people never fully appreciate those times either. Complacency, Arta, is the unenviable legacy of any human endeavor. We become bored with what we have—and what we endure. The dreams grow stale in our minds. Good or evil, right or wrong, just or unjust, the conditions around us become expected—fatalistic, if you will."

"And you stir that with blood?"

"Only 'stirring'—as you put it—avoids stagnation. Without jumbling the pot there is no growth."

She stared out over the city at the people running in the streets. Combat-armored troops were lashing the crowd with violet blaster fire. From somewhere, someone shot back. Bruen noticed the shiver that ran through her and sighed wearily.

He spotted the cruiser first. A long lean thing, it dove out of the black swirling clouds. "Arta, we have visitors. The Civil Police are descending upon us, and, if I'm not mistaken, the wrath of Rega is emblazoned on the shield across the front of their aircar."

Her shoulders sagged. The awkward posture gave her a gutted look.

The jaws of the lion, Arta. What now, sweet beauty? Pray to the Quantum Gods that I have made no mistake with you. Bruen ran gnarled fingers over the cold steel of his grenade launcher. *But if I have. . . .*

The long black vehicle blared a warning as Arta slowed. She fought for control as she braked the aircar to the slowest speed whereby it would maintain stability in the storm-gusting air. Rain battered loudly against the cab.

A cold authoritative voice ordered: "Identify yourselves! Martial law has been declared. This is a state of emergency and you are in violation of the air transport codes."

Arta picked up the comm phone, voice breaking. "Please, I'm taking my grandfather away from all this. We're just going to the country until this ghastly unrest is straightened out. That's all."

And the pleading in her voice? Act? Or truth?

Blaring speakers announced, "Open your door. You will

be boarded by members of the Civil Police and escorted to a holding area. There you will be charged for violation of the air transport regulations and a violation of curfew."

Arta bit her lip and reached over to unlock the door. "I'm sorry, Magister. I—I thought we could get away. When they see our robes. . . ." Their Seddi gowns marked them as immediate suspects—suspects to be brain-probed.

Bruen waited patiently, monitoring her expression, following her thoughts as they were mirrored on her wretched face. Had she forgotten the weapon on the seat beside her? Had fear so completely paralyzed her?

The long black shape matched speeds and settled beside them. A port slid open and a grapple locked to their door. Arta tried to swallow, heedless of the rain that blew past to spatter the plastic seats and lash their robes. Across the space, a black-uniformed man prepared to cross. Bruen leaned forward to get a better view, his thin hand pulling at the wet door frame.

"Oh, Rotted Gods," Arta moaned on the verge of frustrated tears. The young patrolman started across the walkway.

Now or never, girl! Bruen clutched the launcher to his chest, eyes on Arta.

She moved in a blur. The deafening *BLAM* left his ears ringing with concussion. A vile odor insulted his nose as acrid smoke blew in the open door. The aircar lurched drunkenly to one side.

Without missing a beat, Arta fought the controls. Instinctively, she gripped the grenade launcher in one fist. Magister Bruen found himself struggling to keep from falling out the open hatch, his frail fingers slipping on wet upholstery.

As Arta pulled the craft up, she stared out the still open door, apparently shocked to notice that the Civil Police craft was gone—only the ragged smoking remains of the boarding ramp still attached to the aircar. The metal along the edges looked melted and hissed vapor in the rain.

"What was. . . . I . . . I didn't. . . ." She tried to articulate her disbelief. Slowly her eyes dropped to the grenade launcher. Wisps of smoke still rose from the ugly belled muzzle.

With a bar pulled from the tool kit, Bruen began working

the claws of the grapple loose, rain pelting his face as he cackled gleefully into the fury of the storm.

Vindication! Blessed Gods, she's good. Never held a grenade launcher in her life—and she knew what to do!

"Dearest Arta, if you'd be so kind as to depart from the area, they might have another cruiser in this part of the city. You worry about getting me to Makarta, dear. I'll attend to any official interruptions."

"But, what . . . I mean, where did the Civil Patrol . . . I killed. . . . *What the hell happened, Bruen?*" She glared at him.

"Look down, *and go!*" he ordered, making a motion with his hand as he pried the last of the grapple overboard and slammed the door shut.

She dropped her gaze in time to catch a glimpse of smoking wreckage just as it plummeted through a rain-shiny slate roof in the residential district. The edifice shook with impact. As if in slow motion, the walls collapsed inward, folding around the vanished craft like the petals of some huge muddy-brown flower. A single man ran frantically from a door as the last of the walls collapsed.

"Holy Gods! What did I do?" Gulping air, she slapped the throttle forward.

In the back seat Magister Bruen hummed softly to himself as he wiped the water from her thermal grenade launcher.

*   *   *

Skyla Lyma stretched her long legs as she sat in *Chrysla*'s command chair and wished she could get up and pace to restore circulation, or do anything except carry on this conversation with the Sassan admiral whose image filled the main bridge monitor.

Chrysla's spotless bridge gleamed in the overhead lighting. Polished deck plating and well maintained duty stations reflected the pride the Companions had in their flagship. And it didn't stop with hardware. First officers bent to their monitors while various techs murmured softly to the computers. Behind her the Ground Tactics Team coordinated mop-up activities on the planet below. Two officers manned the Traffic Control station, ensuring that only cleared vehicles approached—and even those under *Chrysla*'s watchful eye. Holographic monitors denoted ship's status, and repair work where Myklenian hits had been scored. Across from Skyla, the face of Imperial Admiral Iban Jakre filled the main bridge monitor.

Pompous ass!

"We are very pleased," Jakre's oily voice droned on. "I understand the Lord Commander's regrets at the unfortunate demise of the Praetor. The financial remuneration satisfies His Holiness completely. We do not consider it a breach of contract. In fact, we are more than pleased with the services rendered."

And well you ought to be! Staffa sent your God-Emperor a planet's ransom for breaking contract and killing that vile invalid. She ran slim fingers lightly over the stassa cup in her right hand. Idly she wondered if anyone anywhere had ever paid so much for a man's death.

"We're pleased with His Holiness' understanding, Admiral."

Iban studied her with the all too familiar look she'd come to expect from men. The change of voice from official to intimate hardly surprised her.

"If you could find the time, Wing Commander, I would be more than honored to enjoy your presence. Perhaps you would allow me to extend His Holiness' hospitality for dinner aboard my flagship?" He inclined his head, eyes glittering. "We could make it a personal affair, perhaps dispense with the ritual of office for once. Relax."

You're almost drooling, Sassan pig. She kept her face neutral. "Thank you for your kind offer, Admiral. Unfortunately, I am in charge of fleet supervision while the Lord Commander is off-duty. I'm sure you understand. We have some battle damage to repair—wounded to attend to—and our schedule is tight. We have another offer of employment which the Lord Commander is presently negotiating." *Just to remind you we're free mercenaries, Admiral faggot!* "I echo the Lord Commander's appreciation for your kind offer." *As if you'd invited him!*

Iban nodded, a perfect example of a pained administrator. "I do understand. I look forward to your company, Wing Commander, when your duties are, shall we say, less demanding." He pressed palms together sensually, the five-jeweled rings sparkling on his fat fingers. His belly had begun to expand and sag where his tired muscles were failing to hold it in. "I'm sure that a woman of your skill and a man of my position must have many things in common. I'd not want the Lord Commander to misperceive my intentions, but you are a free agent, are you not, Wing Commander? Perhaps Sassa could make you a very attractive offer?"

Not for that! She smiled graciously, fingers tightening on her cup, and added, "Of course. Do understand, however, that my first obligation is to the Lord Commander. I doubt Sassa could afford my salary."

Jakre giggled. "I would love the opportunity to discuss that with you."

She forced her smile. "One of the first rules of the Companions is that we never close the door to options. For the moment, however, I must decline."

"But if—"

"Admiral, please forgive me, I have duties to attend to. I'll be in touch."

He made a deprecatory gesture with his hand and ducked his head in a semblance of a bow. "I hope to hear from you soon, Wing Commander. Sassa offers many opportunities for a woman of your talent."

"Until then, Admiral." She killed the connection, casting a deadly glance at the monitor. Nerveless, pus-gutted sycophant! He and his kind *were* the Sassan Empire. How long could they hold it without the military might of the Lord Commander? How long would it last past the raping of the treasuries of their conquered worlds? They fawned over their God-Emperor—and worse, they had sold it to the people with such zeal they'd come to believe in Sassa's divinity themselves. In an Ashtan pig's eye!

She turned her attention to the stat board and noted the progress made by the repair crews working on *Jinx Mistress*. The vessel would be space-worthy in another day—testament to the Companions' technical abilities. She okayed the progress report, realizing that Staffa usually got to such matters before she did.

Her attention shifted to the far monitor where Myklene turned, a lime crescent on the screen. Little patches of black—smoke from burning cities—mixed with the cloud cover. Beyond the terminator, red eyes of fire-lit smoke could be made out. The legacy of war.

Damn it, Staffa, what happened in that hospital room down there? For almost half of her forty years Skyla had followed the Lord Commander, studying him like she'd studied no other human being. *And in all those years, I've never seen you go berserk like that.*

Since his return to the ship, he'd locked himself away in his quarters and she'd attended to the administration of the fleet, receiving orders from him via comm—and only one at that: the order to reimburse the Sassans for the death of the Praetor.

She tapped long callused fingers on the command console, thoughts twisting around the scene in the Myklenian hospital. At Staffa's scream they'd burst through the door, expecting to see him dying, expecting Myklenian or Sassan treachery.

And there he'd stood like some avenging angel, literally twisting the Praetor's head off his body. Staffa had shrieked like a man being crushed alive.

From the moment he'd returned to the ship, Staffa had disappeared into the depths of his private rooms. His comm had remained ominously silent. Skyla tilted her head, eyes narrowed. That wasn't like him. Her nerves prickled with that old familiar premonition of trouble. What had that dying old man done? What power had he used to goad Staffa into killing him? The Praetor? Who had he been, and more important, what had he been to Staffa?

"It's none of your business, Skyla," she growled under her breath.

Or was it? She reached into her equipment belt, tracing absent fingers along the tape she'd extracted from the hospital unit. She'd kept her wits and thought to check. Hospital units always had recorders built into the machines to enable physicians to review treatment, visitors, or any events which might help or harm the patient.

Do I play it? Skyla pursed her lips and frowned at the image of Myklene where it filled the monitor. Betray Staffa's privacy? *No, leave it be for now.*

She frowned up at the overhead plates and twisted the end of her long white-blonde braid where it curled over her shoulder. The murmur of voices around the bridge sounded normal. They'd all dropped into routine again. One eye on the Sassans and the deep-space sentry buoys—just in case— the other on the repairs.

So, what do I do now? Wander down and make a fool out of myself trying to check on him? How in Rotted Hell do you deal with a man like the Lord Commander when you're prying into his personal life? She slipped the stolen tape from her pouch and inspected it. Nothing more than a plastic cube with bits of binary data embedded—and a potential snake's nest of trouble for her if Staffa ever found out she had it.

Her professional self urged her to leave him alone and let him work out whatever bothered him. That didn't dim her desire to go to him, to see if she could help in any way as a . . . a friend would do.

And who would I call friend? Careful, Skyla. You have only yourself—no one else. Staffa's capable of fighting his own demons. You've come too far to compromise yourself for trite emotion.

She leaned on her elbow, chewed her callused finger, and ran her thumb lightly along the rough scar tissue on her cheek. He'd saved her life that time. A shot had cracked her helmet and she'd been face-to-face with death from decompression as her nose bled and her lungs expanded fit to burst her ribs no matter how fast she exhaled. Even the eyes in her head had started from their orbits. He'd risked himself to get her under pressure. His face had been the first thing she'd seen when she'd come to on hospital deck. She'd always wondered at the gentle worry that had softened his expression. He'd held her hand in a most paternal manner. Then, as soon as the report came that she'd live, he'd hardened, grinned at her, and left to finish smashing the Maikan defenses into charred rubble.

How long could the fleet stand to have him locked away in his compartments? Already rumors were flying from ship to ship. Was the command in jeopardy of being paralyzed? *And there's the answer to your professional self.*

Images of a cool-eyed Staffa formed. She could see him, sitting in this very chair, involved in the orchestration of the thousand details that plagued a critical assault. His keen mind played the random factors like the master of tactics he was. No matter how she tried, she could never match his intuitive understanding of combat. In the midst of an assault gone wrong, Staffa always managed to detect a weakness, some tiny vulnerability in the defenses which he could exploit.

How many times had he snatched victory from the gaping, foul-odored jaws of defeat?

Very well, I owe him. I respect him.

She accessed the comm, feeling a curious hardness in her breast. One by one, she posted orders she felt necessary and authorized them under Staffa's name. Not a little frightened by what she'd done, she took a deep breath to still her taut nerves and swiveled the command chair. *Rotted Gods, what if he cuts my throat for insubordination?*

"First Officer. The watch is yours. I'll be in the Lord Commander's quarters if you need anything." She jumped to her feet, grateful for the feeling of blood returning to her cramped legs. Adrenaline powered, she trotted to the access tube, ordered the car to deck two, and felt it accelerate. How long had it been since she'd had a good night's sleep? Weeks? Her brain felt prickly and hot inside her skull. Fatigue mixed with worry over Staffa's reaction when she told him she'd issued orders as his.

She slowed as she approached Staffa's private rooms. Only once had she been in his sanctum sanctorum. How long ago had that been? Ten years? No, longer. Almost twenty now. The details formed in her quick mind.

A man, thin and tall with white hair, had met Staffa in a planetside tavern on Ashtan and placed a sack of gold at the Lord Commander's feet. "I can't find either one, Staffa," the visitor had said. "Therefore, I return your money. All of it." And he'd turned and left, while a wretched hollowness had flooded the Lord Commander's grim face.

A newly promoted officer, she'd watched him drink himself into a stupor. With the first officer's help, she had carried a vulnerable and muttering Staffa kar Therma to the shuttle and back to the ship. Never again, not once after that incident, had his iron control ever wavered.

Standing before his hatch she steeled herself, suddenly unsure, unwilling to intrude on this new and unsettling Staffa. A quick wry smile crossed her lips; she committed herself and palmed the hatch.

Thirty-two slowly counted seconds later the speaker asked, "Yes, Wing Commander?"

She looked up at the security monitor, crossing her arms, face stiff. "Staffa, we've got to talk. Just you and me."

She waited, eyes hardening as she stared at the lens.

To her surprise, the door slid back. She hesitated for a split second, then walked boldly into the air lock. The second portal passed her into the room she'd seen before. It had changed slightly; behind gravity restraints, a new rack of weapons hung on the wall: Targan. Other trophies from various campaigns had been added to the crimson-walled main room. The fireplace looked old, as did the red leather gold-embossed couch. The Vermilion boar's head still threatened from the wall as did the Etarian sand tiger.

Two huge doors stood to either side of the fireplace. Ornate carvings graced their exteriors, and, she thought, both came from the high cathedral on Ashtan. The right one opened and Staffa appeared, standing there, arms crossed defensively as he studied her through red-rimmed eyes. For the first time in years stubble stood out on his cheeks. A gray robe enfolded him, a color he had affected so many years ago after—she suddenly realized—that drunk he'd had on Ashtan.

"You look like hell," she told him, walking to the dispenser and filling two bulbs with Myklenian single-malt whiskey.

"Thank you."

She handed him one of the bulbs and settled herself on the corner of the big couch. Where did she start with this man—this friend and commander who had filled so many of her years with challenge and activity. What did she say now? Hey, Chief, why are you hurting? Want to tell me why you ripped a man' head off down there? You got a reason for driving the troops nutty worrying about you, Boss? What?

"Staffa," she began, deciding to try a frontal assault, "I don't know what happened down there, but it's affecting—"

"Have the Sassans been in touch about the penalty?" He sipped the whiskey, swallowed, and paced to the wall where he stared thoughtfully at the Targan weapons.

"Just now," she told him. "Admiral Jakre was very pleased, Rot his black mind. Invited me to a private dinner and seduction."

He stared absently at the fireplace. "Going to take him up on it?"

"That Terguzzi sump scum?"

"He's an admiral."

"He's a fat maggot. Besides, I command more actual power than he and his Holy God-Emperor put together." She watched him curiously. "They're doomed without us, Staffa. You know that. You've seen them. Their empire was built upon *our* power. They'll hold that empire so long as they can afford to outbid their enemies for our blasters, ships, and troops. Only the manufacturing wealth of Sassa and the loot of conquered worlds has allowed them to meet our price—just as the Regans have done."

She paused for a moment, then added: "Staffa, we've destroyed the only other pretender to power. Myklene is gone. Now it's Rega or Sassa. Who will it be?"

He turned the drinking bulb in his hand. "I don't know."

Tension wound through her chest. A dull ache formed at the base of her brain. Skyla mentally berated herself as a fool even as she prickled with curiosity. She cocked her head as she studied him. Memories like gossamer strands filtered through her mind: his gray glinting eyes on hers; the shared intimacy and tension of command; the moments of desperation, and then triumph when impossible odds fell before them. She lowered her gaze, oddly sobered by what she'd shared with Staffa. Twenty years in the pressure cooker of command couldn't just be shed like worn-out battle armor. The implications left her off balance.

"What's wrong, Staffa? What happened in that room?" she blurted.

His mouth went tight as he met her challenging stare. She could see his throat work. "The Praetor was my. . . . He was the man who. . . ." He shrugged and tonelessly added, "It was a long time ago. He took me in as an orphan and taught me to be what I am today."

The tension in her chest tightened into a knot around her heart. "Rotted Gods. You mean he was your. . . ."

"Father? No. Call him my . . . my mentor. A more suitable word, perhaps."

"Pustulant Gods!" *Is that what this is all about?* "Why did you take the contract?"

He clasped his hands behind his back and paced carefully across the floor. "They threw me out. Years ago. You knew I was Myklenian. I—I took the contract to repay them. And him." He exhaled and shook his head. "I didn't . . . didn't know I'd have to face him. Tried to kill him in the fighting." His face paled and he closed his eyes. "But instead I killed . . . killed. . . ."

He shivered violently and Skyla stiffened. After a long silence she said, "There's more, isn't there?" *All these years, and I scarcely know you.*

He started to say something and bit the words off.

"Do you want to tell me about it?"

"You know, Skyla, I'd allow no one else to come in here and question me like you're doing."

"Staffa, you and I, we've. . . ." Her face rushed hot, embarrassing her, stirring anger. "A lot of blood's behind us. A lot of hard times. That's why I. . . . There's the fleet, too. It's. . . ." She stopped her tongue-tied stammering. "*Damn it!* I've had to issue orders in your name!"

His laugh gentled, warmer this time, and she looked up to see the old amusement in his eyes, displacing—if only for a moment—the dullness.

"It's Rotted well not funny. Snap out of it, Staffa!"

"Snap out of it? What have we done to ourselves, Skyla?" he asked, taking a gulp of the whiskey and pacing like a caged hunting cat. She could see the thick muscles bunching and swelling under his robe, as if powered by the trouble that possessed him. "Are we really so inhuman? The Praetor asked me if I had a conscience. Since then, I've wondered."

"Our business doesn't call for conscience—only success. Even the Sassans didn't believe you could crack Myklene. Myself, I've tried to anticipate your tactics—and would have led us to disaster had I been the one to initiate the attack. You've always been the best, Staffa. Isn't that enough?"

"Perhaps. He gave me everything—and he took it all away. No matter who fired the shot that killed. . . ." He shook himself like a wet dog, shaking off the thought. Then he tossed off the whiskey and flipped the bulb into the fireplace. "Called me his 'greatest' creation. That's why he cared. I was no more than the pinnacle of his success. A construct." He stared into the distance in his mind before adding, "I killed. . . ."

She watched his color drain, a ghastly expression molding his pale features. He seemed to reel on his feet.

"What, Staffa? Who did you kill?"

He wet his lips, jaw trembling. In a hoarse whisper, he gasped, "Love . . . my son . . . my. . . ."

He rubbed his face.

"Staffa? What did you mean just now. What are you trying to—"

"What is it really to *be* human?" he cried, smacking a fist in his palm as he whirled to face her. "What should a person *feel?* What should we *be?* I—I don't feel anymore! I don't know who I am! Chrysla's dead! I killed her! And I can't . . . can't grieve." His expression went flat. "Can't even blame myself anymore."

"Chrysla? Staffa, she wasn't on Myklene, was she?"

He paced restlessly back and forth, speaking as if he hadn't heard. "They call me murderer and hate me and curse me from one Forbidden Border to the other. It's said that my legacy is fear, death, and terror. *I killed the only thing I ever loved!*"

Skyla watched in amazement as a single tear crept down Staffa's cheek.

He swallowed hard and said in a numb whisper. "I've lost my way, Skyla. I don't know who I am anymore."

* * *

Sinklar Fist stepped off the shuttle at the biological research center station. He entered through the revolving doors, found the right lift, and punched the button for the thirty-fifth floor. A curious excitement and dread left him feeling hot and nervous. So much had begun to come clear. Now, he half wished he could drop this insane quest. In only four hours he had to be at the assembling point for his unit. From there, the Blessed Gods alone knew how long it would be before he slept again.

The lift beeped to indicate it had reached its destination. The doors slipped silently open and Sinklar stepped out into a foyer at the intersection of four long hallways. A security guard looked up from the desk that rested under a cone of white light. She studied him curiously as she stood.

"Hello. Um, I'm Sinklar Fist. I was wondering if there was anyone in the Criminal Anatomical Research Labs?"

She cocked her head, lifting an eyebrow. "At this time of night? Are you serious?"

Sinklar gave her a crooked smile and walked up to the desk. She looked about twenty-five, maybe younger. The dark brown uniform set off her blonde hair. He let her large blue eyes distract him for a moment.

She smiled. "I don't think you came all the way up here to gawk at me—but I enjoy the compliment anyway. Uh, what can I do to help you—" she scanned his uniform— "Private?"

Sinklar frowned, wondering how to begin. "I wanted to see someone in the Criminal Research Lab. I understand that they . . . well, keep the specimens there for research."

She nodded. "That's right. We call that anatomical forensics. Actually, that's my area of study. I just work nights to make a few extra credits. The life of a student isn't exactly a rich one."

"Neither is that of an anatomical forensics examiner . . . or a soldier. It might surprise you, but I was a student until the draft notice came a couple of days ago. I . . . well, wish I still was."

"And you want to see the lab?"

"The specimens actually."

She gave him a critical inspection. "You don't look like the ghoulish type."

"Neither do you," Sink countered. "The human body is a fascinating field of study. A lot of questions remain unanswered, like where our species came from. How it evolved to its present state. The range of human behavior is almost inexplicable." He saw her eyes light with shared understanding.

"Your field of study was anatomy?"

He shook his head. "Sociology, history, gaming theory, military tactics, comparative behavior, that sort of thing. But the study of forensics fascinates me. There just hasn't been time to study everything I want to." He paused. "So, what do I call you?"

"I'm Anatolia Daviura. Listen, I could talk to one of the

professors about showing you around. If you'll leave your number—"

"Can't. Going on active duty tomorrow. I guess we're going to war on Targa."

Her expression pinched. "Oh, sorry to hear that."

Sink shrugged. "It's every citizen's duty. I just thought someone might be working late tonight. You never know. Maybe something I see here could make a difference on Targa."

She hesitated for a moment. "If we hurry . . . I mean I can't leave the desk for long. Well, I could take you into the lab. I've got clearance. But we couldn't linger."

Sink smiled. "I promise not to keep you."

She gave him a conspiratorial smile as she led him down the dim hall.

"How'd you get into this field of study?" Sink asked as she palmed a heavy metal door and led him into a room that smelled of chemicals and hummed from air-conditioning. Scanning electron microscopes, desks, centrifuges, and the gleaming clutter of scientific instruments filled the place. Comm terminals stared at him with cathode eyes.

"I started in behavioral genetics," she told him. "The problem of deviance fascinated me. Why do some people harm others? What's the genetic substructure for violence? Where did it come from? Is there a way to eliminate the genetic root for criminal behavior from the human species without affecting our adaptive ability or initiative? Working here lets me deal with actual deviant specimens—study the DNA of known criminals to compare it with DNA in normal people."

She fingered a button and a double door parted in the middle to slide into recesses in the wall. "The inner sanctum. This is where we store the specimens."

Sink walked into the room. Rack after rack, like data cubes in the library stacks rose from floor to ceiling in line after line for as far as he could see down the aisle. Heavy powerlead ran into each stack to power the caskets. "How many are there?"

"Somewhere near four thousand."

"How would you find . . . say a certain specimen?"

Her look grew suspicious. "Do you have one in mind?"

Sinklar nodded. "Two, Tanya and Valient Fist. My . . . my parents."

"Blessed Gods!" Anatolia took a step back, eyes wide. "And all that business you told me about your studies?"

Sinklar turned anxious eyes on her. "It was true. I didn't lie to you. It's just . . . well, I was raised as an orphan of the state. All I ever knew was that my parents had been convicted of treason and executed. I've been paying for their crime all of my life. Now, I'm going off to war. I wanted to know where they were. That's all. I talked to the Judicial Magistrate who tried the case and sent them here. He told me where they were—and what they'd done."

Anatolia rubbed her arms, frowning. "You don't really want to see them, do you?"

Sinklar bit his lip and looked away as he nodded. "You're a geneticist. You know what parents mean biologically. I know what they mean to me . . . psychologically."

She turned, accessing the comm terminal next to the door. "Come on, this way."

They walked for several minutes in silence, accompanied by the endless rows of caskets and the hum of the units that maintained them. Anatolia turned left and followed a narrow aisle. Overhead the lights automatically brightened as they approached and dimmed as they passed.

"Here," she told him, and pointed to two pull-out caskets at chest height. "Just pull on the handle."

Sink glanced at her, swallowing nervously. Then he reached for the handle. It chilled his fingers as he pulled the casket open to expose a man. "He looks alive."

"Perfect preservation," she told him as Sinklar studied the figure. The face was smooth-shaven, the eyes yellow. He looked intelligent and his expression betrayed a trace of sorrow. Sinklar could see an incision through the close-cropped brown hair.

"After all these years," Sinklar whispered. "Hello, Father. I just had to find you, know that you existed. I graduated first in my class and I scored third in the Interplanetary exams. I thought you should know that."

A pang filled his breast as he pushed the casket closed and opened the lower drawer. His mother stared up sightlessly, gray eyes half open. She'd been a striking woman with raven black hair and delicate features—but young, so very young.

Sinklar smiled wistfully. "Thank you for giving me life, Mother. I'll never forget you. I'll make you proud of me."

Sinklar slipped the casket closed and felt himself sway. Everything inside felt hollow—a stillness of the soul.

He turned to Anatolia and smiled. "Thank you. I'll have a little peace now. Things will be easier. Let's go. I know you have to get back."

She nodded, letting him lead the way in silence. At the door, she paused. "Is that true, what you said about the Interplanetary exams?"

Sink nodded, wrapped in his own thoughts, trying to sort out his emotions. He did catch the interest in Anatolia's eyes.

"Sinklar," she began as she led him into the lab, "um, you wouldn't mind if I took a tissue sample, would you?"

"Once a scientist, always a scientist?"

She gave him a wry smile. "Something like that."

He rolled up the sleeve of his uniform. "Be my guest. On the condition that when you get the chance, you'll let me know what you find."

After she'd taken her sample and led him back to the lift that would return him to the station, she paused. "Sinklar, what did they do? I mean, how did they end up here?"

He held the door as he stepped into the lift and looked back. Anatolia had beautiful blue eyes. Now they watched him with soft understanding. *If only I could have more time. How I'd love to spend it getting to know you.* "Thank you for letting me see them. I'll owe you for that for the rest of my life."

"I wouldn't have missed it . . . for several reasons." She pursed her lips. "You don't have to tell me, but the information is in the records. All I have to do is look it up."

"And you will." He met her inquisitive stare. "Only the worst of the worst are sent to this facility for study. My parents tried to kill the Emperor, Tybalt the Imperial Seventh. They were Seddi assassins."

With that he let the door slip shut on Anatolia's shocked expression, and the lift plummeted toward the station.

CHAPTER V

Tybalt the Imperial Seventh, Ruler and Governor, Master of the Twenty Worlds of Man and the Imperium of Rega, wiggled uncomfortably as the interminable Council session droned on. He fought the urge to stand up and walk to the restroom—partially because his fidgeting kept the Councillors aware of his growing irritation, and because a ruler of his stature shouldn't fall prey to the harassment of his itchy hemorrhoids.

Tybalt and his Councillors sat in a high-vaulted conference room lit by crystal skylights. Ornately carved panels of Sypa ivory gleamed lustrously between burled sandwood beams. The air carried the scent of jasmine. The rising babble of the Councillors managed to drown the soft strains of a string quartet playing a soothing piece in the background. The conference table they sat around dominated the center of the room and sprouted monitors, comm equipment, and elbows. For the moment it looked like a disaster area as his busy Councillors worried over reports and argued vehemently.

Tybalt had inherited his father's muscular body—but unlike his physically disciplined father, he'd begun to lose the battle against his growing belly. The rich black tones of his skin contrasted with the bright yellow suit he wore. Rubbing his cheek, the fleshy feeling of his jowls bothered him. In the end, his broad facial bones would work against him despite the long straight nose. He kept his hair medium length and covered it with a jewel-encrusted net of gold wire that scintillated with the finest treasures of the Etarian desert.

The compact holo unit clipped to his collar continued to feed the latest field reports from the Targan revolt. The rebels controlled most of the capital city of Kaspa. Tybalt growled to himself and ground his teeth. *Why now? Blood-shot curses! Of all the times for a conflagration, why did the Targans have to pick* this *moment?* Everything teetered on the brink. And if Staffa had already signed an alliance with the Sassans against Rega? *No, don't even think it!*

He sipped from the cup of klav that rested in the heated holder by his right hand and decided that enough was enough. "Gentlemen, ladies, please." He held up a hand.

Twenty heads turned to look in his direction; some from where they bent over flimsies and maps; others looking up from comm monitors. The string quartet sounded strangely alone as silence filled the room, marred only by the hiss of a new printout, adding mass to the clutter on the table.

"No matter what you wish to project with your predictive models, the facts remain. First, we must crush Targa—again. Second, no matter what the cost, our only hope for survival is to immediately place Staffa's cutthroats on our payroll."

The Minister of the Treasury shook his head vehemently. "Imperial Lord, I'm not sure we can bear it. The last time we hired the man it cost us the equivalent of three point five billion Imperial credits in precious metals and manufactured goods. In part, that drain on the treasury led to the current unrest on Targa since they've been bearing the brunt of paying the deficit for the last two years."

Tybalt nodded, knowing full well the extent of their financial troubles. At the same time, the Lord Commander had managed to do what neither he nor that Sassan god-goof could—maintain a full-time fighting force: a corps large enough that it drew on every government in human space for its support. And Staffa's elite strike force vigorously guarded its independence by providing its own equipment, ships, and training. The Companions relied on no one for supplies or strategic materials—though they often took that in payment for service. Cunning man, that Staffa. *And I can't stand against him.*

In a muted voice he added, "Lord Minister, would you prefer to pay Staffa—or fight him? With the Myklene situation under control, His Holiness will be looking for new lands to conquer. Considering the confines of the Forbidden Borders, where do you suppose he will find them?"

"We ought to make another attempt at the Forbidden

Borders," the Minister of Defense interjected, eyes going
to the illumination overhead. He fingered his flat nose, and
took a deep breath. He'd propped hairy arms on the table,
a posture of no retreat. "That's the key. Find a way past
that gravitational wall and we'll have room to expand."

"Another attempt, my Lord?" Tybalt questioned in the
continuing silence. "How many ships have we lost against
that energy-gravity barrier?"

"Over the last fifteen years," the Minister of the Treasury
interrupted, "eighteen. If you figure the outlay for hardware
alone, the sum is considerable." She accessed her monitor.
"We have spent a total of forty-three million credits on—"

"I know the figures," Defense growled.

"Enough said." Tybalt closed the debate and steepled his
fingers. "Whoever—whatever—is on the other side doesn't
want us coming through. Further, so long as they have the
technology to 'absorb' our mightiest assault ships, they will
remain invulnerable . . . and on the other side of their
'wall'. Now, to get back to our current problem, we have
no choice, gentle people, but to hire the mercenary."

The Minister of the Treasury's expression went foul. Her
thin dark face accented the long nose that ended in a point
over narrow lips. Looking glum, her black eyes stared sightlessly at an imaginary point beyond the walls. Manicured
fingers thumped the table hollowly. "We might make a
down payment without bankrupting the entire economy of
the Empire."

And there, indeed, lay the rub. A cold chill went through
Tybalt's mind. *Worse yet, has anyone considered the problem of what to do with Staffa kar Therma when all of space
is united? Where, then, will the Lord Commander take his
blood-thirsting warriors?*

Tybalt turned his attention to Defense. "Lord Minister,
what chance is there that we could loot enough from the
Sassan worlds to pay Staffa off?"

Defense's fingers rasped over his stubbly chin. The
expression on his high-cheeked face pinched. "Little, I'm
afraid. Sassa's already bled itself white to pay the Lord
Commander for Myklene. I fear that financing a war that
way will grind any captured world's economy back to the
point that our investment to rebuild it would suck us dry—
presuming we have the funds left to invest."

"Seconded," the Minister of Economics agreed, lifting a finger. Her green eyes smoldered as she studied Tybalt. "We can only spread technicians and engineers so thin. Coupled with the drain on materials to rebuild entire planetary industries, we'll be stretched to the breaking point. Unless, of course, you would enslave our entire population to rebuild theirs."

Treasury added, "Which makes me wonder what purpose there is in conquest."

"Survival! So what do we offer the Lord Commander?" Tybalt frowned. "And tell me what happens if Staffa is retained by Sassa? How can we defend against his lightning strikes and his superior equipment? It's one thing to contemplate turning the terror of the Companions on the Sassans, quite another to embrace the idea of the Lord Commander's fleet bearing down on Rega." *And if that's the case, there will be no Tybalt the Eighth.*

The Minister of Military Intelligence cleared his throat. "If our condition is poor, the Sassans are in worse straits. On top of their wars and the expenses they've incurred with Staffa's Companions, they've destroyed many of the economies they desperately need to wage a prolonged war. We don't have figures yet on the casualties they suffered taking Myklene. Suffice it to say they were substantial."

"So now's the time to strike?" Defense wondered, his lips pursed, fingers absently combing his black beard.

In the following silence, the string quartet's music did little to soothe. Tybalt turned his eyes to Ily Takka, his Minister of Internal Security. Ily should have spoken by now. Instead she waited, watching, predatory.

"You must control the Targan uprising first," Ily took his cue. She ran long fingers through her raven black hair. "To do less is to leave a gaping wound of revolution to bleed infection throughout the rear worlds." She gave them a quick smile, aware of her power and how they perceived it.

Ah, Ily! Tybalt hid his delight. He'd waited to hear her thoughts. Like an Etarian sand tiger, Ily always kept her talons fastened in some poor slob's flesh. In cold-blooded efficiency only Staffa kar Therma could rival her. . . . Hmm! Perhaps . . . maybe with a little planning and preparation it would be possible to secure the Lord Commander . . . or deny his services to the enemy.

Dazzled by the thought, Tybalt added, "Very well, we'll take care of Targa. My Lord of Defense, see to it that our 'gaping wound' is cauterized. In the meantime, ladies and gentlemen, your duty is to determine how to bind Staffa kar Therma to our side—before we all wind up learning to speak Sassan."

The Imperial Tybalt stood and gestured, indicating the meeting was adjourned. He avoided the explosion of conversation that immediately broke out and headed for the restroom and his tube of insumweed jelly. He'd have to take time so the surgeon could correct his problem. One surgeon for his tender itching anus—the other for Staffa kar Therma!

* * *

The heart inside Sinklar Fist's rib cage skipped a beat as the LC began shuddering and bucking against atmosphere. His mouth had gone dry in the rising heat. This time—no matter what they said—it wasn't a drill. Combat-armored troops like himself crammed the inside of the LC, the work-horse landing craft of the Regan military. Sink and his companions had been seated shoulder to shoulder and tipped slightly back to minimize g forces should the craft have to maneuver. Lines of narrow lights gave the place a ghastly white look, exposing the smudged deck plating cluttered with so many booted feet. The strakes had been drilled with lightening holes which cast curious patterns across the painted metal of the internal hull. Moisture from their breathing had condensed on the cold steel and ran down in dribbles or spatted periodically on his helmet and armor. Looking forward, only bubblelike helmets filled the view. Overhead, between the lights, a locker hung down sporting the ominous lettering, SURVIVAL GEAR.

Targa lay below them, a bitter world full of mad people, people who had risen in revolt and *killed an entire garrison of Regan troops!*

Where had they obtained the weapons? Indeed, that had been the thousand-credit question. Among the troops, they had a good idea. Sassan spies, no doubt. The story made the rounds that smugglers had supplied the whole planet. Sinklar glanced at his companions. The brunette beside him,

Gretta Artina, had her eyes closed, fingers laced tightly about the barrel of her assault rifle. Her head tilted back against the crash webbing.

Sinklar studied the line of her jaw, admiring the texture of her smooth skin, seeing how the pulse raced under that fine neck. Where had she been last night when he lay awake, tossing and turning, knowing that others coupled frantically in the dark? His eyes dropped to the full swell of her breasts.

Sinklar looked hastily away, feeling the increasing vibration in the LC. Since the night he'd finally found his parents, his emotions had become a quagmire. Increasingly, Anatolia Daviura had risen from a maze work of conflicting feelings to dominate his thoughts. He'd dreamed of her blue eyes and yellow-blonde hair. The memory of her trim body lingered. More water dripped from above, spattering hollowly and bursting his reverie.

As with women, Sinklar wondered why had the Blessed Gods made him so strange, so weak and incompetent at this soldiering business? Worst of all—on top of being scrawny, underweight, and clumsy—people stared at his thin face. Just having a thin face didn't do it; they gawked at his eyes: one gray, the other tiger yellow. Well, hell, sure, he could have had that surgically corrected, but curse it, that's how he'd been born. Not only that, kids with his upbringing didn't get operations like that . . . even on Imperial Rega where the streets were supposed to be paved with gold.

Why couldn't he be like Corporal MacRuder, whom Gretta made eyes at? MacRuder was every inch a dashing soldier, and Gods Rot it, Gretta smiled saucily every time MacRuder winked at her.

The air had become thicker, coagulating with the odors of sweat and fear and making breathing difficult. Someone behind him broke wind, the sulfuric odor almost causing him to gag. Someone else laughed—a chittering nervous sound. The lights dimmed. Either the weapons were discharging or they'd switched to reserves to avoid detection. He blinked, fear moving in his gut like a living thing. His own bowels begged to loosen. The lights had gone red— battery power. Did that mean they were falling? Powered out?

Emulating beautiful Gretta next to him, he closed his eyes

and concentrated on the fear-sweat beading under his helmet and trickling down his bony face. The soft muttered prayers of an Etarian disciple whispered somewhere across from him.

"Thirty seconds, people!" the wall speaker announced flatly.

A vague whistle of air became audible as the panels around him jiggled. G force sought to pull him sideways against the girl. The ceiling began to rain. Sinklar Fist counted, knowing only that it would help cover his fear.

The final deceleration sought to strain him through his combat armor. His neck muscles tensed to fight the heavy pull. G vanished suddenly, making him snap his head. The LC bumped, bucked, and settled. Hydraulics whined and air moved.

"All right, people, let's move!" Sergeant Hamlish sang out in his bullhorn voice. "A Group! Establish a perimeter! B Group, expand it! C, back them up. D, prepare a flanking defense right! E, flanking defense left! F, support the ordnance team!"

Men and women jumped up around Sinklar. Foolishly, he slapped the quick release on the crash harness and pulled himself to his feet. He barely got his assault rifle up as Gretta moved out at a trot. He slung the heavy rifle up expertly, slipping the support strap over the carry hook so the weight no longer rested on his arms alone.

A Group had already piled out the hatch, diving for the rocky soil, their battle armor changing color to match the reddish-tan soil. Sinklar trotted forward, just like in the exercises, and dropped to the ground another fifty yards out. He blinked into the blackness, aware of the rich smell of the raw earth inches from his nose. Something whirred by his head. Insect? Night bird?

A wailing behind him indicated the LC had cleared its load and was lifting its deadly bulk into the blackness. With a quick glance he noticed that no stars dotted the black sky. He swallowed hard, realizing for the first time just how dry his throat felt. The air carried a cool tang, fresh and clear in his nostrils.

Sergeant Hamlish's quiet voice in his ear made him jump.

"Idiot!" Sinklar berated himself, "It's only your ear comm!"

"Fist!" MacRuder's retort sounded loud in the system. "Shut your mike off! We aren't interested in evaluations of your intelligence."

Sinklar colored red, a horrible shame rising to throttle his heart. Did he do everything wrong?

Hamlish ordered, "Group B, you're on the outside. Pair off and advance. We should be just over the hill from Kaspa. Secure the ridge up there and signal when you have a defensive position."

Sinklar scrambled to his feet, remembering finally to drop his IR visor. Like a falling veil, darkness became light in an odd-hued landscape. He could see MacRuder waving him over.

"Come on, Fist," MacRuder called confidently. "You gonna be all night? There's honors for first blood on this trip." The corporal turned and started forward.

First blood? Sinklar winced. He'd never been meant to be a soldier. Far better to remain home on Rega away from bugs and mud and guns and probe the fascinating secrets of the library. The worst blow of all had been cutting short N-dimensional quantum geometry so soon after he'd gotten the text. Fascinating relationships between. . . .

His lungs started to labor—panting too soon. The assault rifle itself weighed twenty pounds. On top of that, the pack had to be another thirty.

The ridge proved no obstacle other than that it left Sinklar gasping, delirious from thirst, and exhausted. Flopped on the ground, wishing he could vomit, he heard MacRuder calling over the comm system, "B Group reporting, Sergeant. All's well."

"Okay, people, dig in," MacRuder ordered, scrambling like a bug in the dark. He bent down over Sinklar. "You all right?"

"Yeah, short of breath is all."

"Look, you seem like a nice kid. Just stick with me, huh? I'll make sure you don't get in any trouble."

"Sure." Picking up the assault rifle, he followed MacRuder over the edge of the ridge and crawled under a full-leafed bush to stare at the winking lights of Kaspa where they spread out below him. The city sat in the bottom of a ridge-bordered bowl. Through the IR vision, the place looked like a shanty town. The surrounding peaks consisted

of cracked and sundered bedrock covered with scabby vegetation and thick-branched conifers on the slopes. Land
turned on end—hell of a place to fight a war.

Kid? MacRuder had called him a kid? Well, he sure
didn't make much of a soldier—and, damned right, he'd
stick with MacRuder. The corporal seemed to know what
he was doing.

No one had fired a shot yet. Maybe taking rebel planets
was a piece of cake like they'd said?

He lay there in the darkness and thoughtfully fingered his
combat armor. Rubbing the stuff between his fingers, it felt
like a tough synthetic with a slick surface. In actuality, the
material consisted of hollow composite sheaths of graphite
and ceramic that enclosed hydrocarbon polymers in some
threads, and oxycatalyst in others. Any impact capable of
rupturing the composite caused an instant chemical bonding
that stiffened the material into hard ablative plate, thereby
spreading and absorbing the energy of a projectile or blaster
bolt. When coupled with a vacuum helmet, the tight weave
served as a pressure suit for space work.

Let's just hope it'll keep me alive, Sinklar thought to
himself.

"All right, people," Mac called. "Let's go. Spread out
and keep sharp. We got a city to take."

Sinklar headed down the ridge with the rest of B Group.
By the breaking of dawn, they'd infiltrated to the Section 3
Post Office and established an occupation headquarters on
the outskirts of Kaspa.

The postal building didn't look like much from an aes-
thetic perspective, but to a military tactician, the thick stone
walls and small windows gave the place all the virtues of a
redoubt.

"Hell! I thought we'd have a fight," MacRuder growled as
he pulled his pack around to cushion his back against the
stone of the hallway wall. The other troops had stacked rifles
and piled duffels here and there around the open lobby.

"They don't look dangerous," Sinklar said thoughtfully
as he studied the few pedestrians who hurried past outside,
eyes downcast. The skies remained clouded over, hints of
thunder in the rumbling gray-black overhead.

"Naw, the regulars are here," MacRuder mumbled over
a half a ration bar.

Sinklar studied him thoughtfully. MacRuder looked like a soldier: square-jawed and handsome with a lump in the middle of his nose. Challenging blue eyes stared out of a high-cheeked face while wisps of blond hair escaped the confines of the helmet. The man's muscular shoulders swelled the supple fabric of his armor.

Gretta Artina sat beside him, one arm locked in the corporal's. Sinklar had to work to keep from staring at her perfect features. Was she falling for MacRuder? Against a man like that, what chance did the likes of Sinklar Fist have?

Think about Anatolia, idiot! She's safely out of reach—and you can dream about her until you get home—assuming you survive Targa. Then you don't have to be heartbroken until you find out she married one of her professors and has a kid on the way.

MacRuder's voice intruded. "They might have thought the garrison was soft, but they've got combat troops here now. We'll make them think twice." Mac made a clicking sound with his tongue. "Still, somebody should have taken a potshot. I don't get it. It's like they just let us walk in here."

Gretta cocked her head, long brown hair shining in the faint light. "I wouldn't mess with Imperial firepower. What have they got out there? Untrained miners? So they have some pulse weapons and grenades? A couple of blasters in those hands are hardly enough to rout the might of the Empire."

"They wiped out the garrison," Sinklar reminded, ripping the seal off his energy bar. He watched as an old woman climbed the stairs hesitantly, her glance that of a scared bird as she cataloged the armored personnel resting along the halls. Kyphotic osteoporosis had curled her spine, giving her a hunched appearance. She clutched a large purse to her tightly bundled chest with age-spotted talon fingers—joints knotted from arthritis. She climbed one step at a time, making sure of her footing.

"Help you, ma'am?" MacRuder asked, speech slurred by the crunchy food bar as he stood and opened the thick glass door for her.

She nodded with frightened jerks of her birdlike head. "I . . . I need to see about . . . about my medical benefits," her voice came out frail and withered to match her age-lined face.

MacRuder wiped a hand across his mouth and jerked a thumb over his shoulder. "See Sergeant Hamlish in there." He indicated the room where once the Regan Postal Super had held court until the "Citizens' Committee" hauled him out and hacked him to pieces with mucking tools.

She avoided their eyes and nodded, hobbling painfully to the sergeant's room on brittle legs.

"Now there's a dangerous revolutionary," MacRuder said with a laugh. He ripped the tab out of the side of another energy bar. "So much for Targan resistance. We've got this place cowed, man!"

Sinklar frowned. "Yeah, maybe. You know, I was reading about the Sylene expedition Phillipia mounted when they were on their conquest jag a couple of centuries ago. The lesson—"

"Ancient history, Fist," Gretta told him. "What could a backwater war like that have to do with Imperial power?"

Sink lifted a shoulder in a half-shrug. "Well, uh, there's lots of interesting things in history books."

"Like what?" MacRuder asked. "Cut and dried combat tactics? I mean, you read what somebody did a hundred ten counts ago and everybody who can read will know the tactics. You've got to think up new plans, constantly innovate. That's the key to the Star Butcher's success, you know. Think, Sink!" MacRuder pointed to his head and winked.

"Books, huh?" Gretta snickered. "You one of those Seddis, Sink?"

Color rose hot on his neck. As he became more flustered, it got worse. "No. I just studied is all . . . trying to gain entrance to the Regan University."

MacRuder laughed, mouth full of food. "Didn't get too far, huh? Man, you don't get to University unless you're a genius or you got noble blood in your veins—or an appointment signed by the Emperor."

"Yeah, I know. I thought I'd get it. I scored third in the Interplanetary trials."

His words evoked wide-eyed silence.

"Rotted Gods!" Gretta whispered. "*Third!* And they still didn't take you?"

Sinklar flushed and picked idly at his food bar. "No."

MacRuder shook his head. "They say why?"

Lie, Sink. You can't tell them why. From now on stick to the orphan story. "No. Only that they were sorry. But . . . but I should not be discouraged from trying again next year."

Gretta's brow furrowed. "I knew a woman who made it. She placed eighty-sec. . . ." She bit it off at the look on Fist's face. She took a deep breath and sighed. "Must have been political. Maybe an error in some office, huh?"

"Yeah, must have been."

The old woman came out of Sergeant Hamlish's office during the uneasy pause. Her heavy boots clicked across the floor as she passed. Her frightened glance met Sinklar's for a brief instant before she looked away. He pushed the door open for her and watched her hobble down the stairs, arms swinging for balance.

From the corner of his eye, Sinklar caught a glimpse of the sergeant heading for the men's toilet. Well, even sergeants had to go sometime.

"So what did you learn from your history of the Sylene wars?" MacRuder's manner had changed subtly.

"Don't concentrate your forces," Sinklar mumbled, thinking about the old woman hobbling rapidly across the uneven street.

Outside, loudspeakers blared yet another repeat of the terms of occupation as a military hover-craft, studded with heavy blasters and pulse cannon, passed over. The booming voice echoed, "Martial Law is currently in force. Persons needing travel permits, medical care, or police assistance must register with the military authorities. All comm requests will be handled in order of receipt. Remain calm and comply with military authority." And it went on, droning in the muggy air.

Sinklar chewed his lip and looked up at the brooding clouds. He had already started to hate Targa—and no one had even shot at him yet.

"Yeah, well, that goes against any axiom of military sense," MacRuder maintained. "Anyone knows that divide and conquer is the oldest rule in warfare. Strength allows defensive as well as offensive options that scattered troops—"

"Rotted Gods!" Sinklar cried, jumping to his feet. *"Where's her purse?"*

"What?" MacRuder's face twisted.

"Come on, let's go get her!" Sinklar grabbed up his rifle.
"Like Sylene, Mac. Hey! Somebody check the sergeant's
office for that old woman's purse."

He charged down the stairs, eyes on the old woman as
she scuttled around the corner of a gray-mortared building.
Gretta and MacRuder followed along behind, resettling
their helmets and hooking up their rifles.

Sinklar's feet hit the irregular cobbles on the street—but
he couldn't remember what happened next. The world
seemed to drop out from under him before it leapt up to
smack him. He remembered rolling across the rough stone
cobbles, time and space suspended in fire, and smoke, and
fragments of bouncing mortar.

Stunned, ears ringing, he fought air into his stinging
lungs. He moved his legs and arms, aware they still worked.
Numb, he got to his feet, weaving back and forth. The
assault rifle had remained attached to the combat armor
catches and dangled within reach. He groped for the
weapon as violet light crackled past his head. Ducking, he
dropped to one knee and fired a burst at the upper-story
window the shots had come from. The front of the building
jumped from the impact, dust flying from the cracks in the
brick.

Sinklar turned, seeing MacRuder struggling to his feet.
The postal building had been turned into dusty rubble. As
Sinklar watched, one of the side walls teetered out and col-
lapsed on the side street.

"By the Blessed Gods," Sinklar whispered. No one could
have survived that. Somehow he got his wits together
enough to pull Gretta up. Dazed, MacRuder gaped stupidly
while blood ran out of his nose. Another shot ripped past
Sinklar's ear. He charged for the far side of the avenue.
Acting on instinct, he raised his rifle and blew the door
before him apart, shoving his companions into the dark and
the unknown.

* * *

"We play a deep game, Bruen." Magister Hyde drew an
asthmatic breath, brows furrowed as he watched the inset
monitor where the chestnut-haired woman systematically

demolished boulders with a pulse pistol. "The problem with psychological weapons is their inherent unreliability."

They sat side by side on a stone bench carved into the back of a rocky balcony that clung to the basalt cliff overlooking the Makarta Valley. The misty clouds had failed to defeat the inevitable sun for the first time in days. Now the valley burst with greenery and the sun warmed their retreat.

Bruen nodded soberly. "Circles within circles, my friend."

"Probability is one thing," Hyde interrupted himself to cough, "but the human brain? Hah! For centuries greater minds than ours have quested and poked and prodded, seeking the answers of the psyche. It makes me nervous to be cast in the lot of a god."

Bruen grunted at the monitor where Arta Fera, her lithe form outlined in the evening light, fired the last charge in the pulse pistol. Another of the rocks on the hillside exploded in a gout of dust.

"You think she hit the right one?"

Bruen moved to ease an ache in his hip. "Oh, it was. Look at the expression on her face. See the feral delight? No doubt about it, her instincts are fully developed. Now all they need is channeling, direction."

Hyde's voice dripped with distaste. "Spying! Like Imperial Security agents!"

"Now is an odd time to condemn our ancient pastime, Magister," Bruen countered sourly. Damn it, if only he didn't agree in this instance. If it were anyone but Arta, he'd. . . .

I've become a senile idiot! There's no place for sappy sentimentality. She's not your daughter, she's no one, Bruen. A subject, a soldier for the cause. Wars are not won by generals who dote on their personnel!

"But she is one of ours," Hyde protested.

Bruen dropped his sagging chin into a palm and cocked his head, eying his old companion. He kept his voice soft, serious, forced to conform with what he knew was rational. "Is she really? After we placed her with the Etarians for so long, after we brought her so far, can you call her ours?"

Hyde blinked owlishly. "Well . . . er . . . she has done remarkably well on the exams. Her training—as you can see—through subliminal quanta seeding has made her the most incredibly talented. . . ."

"Tool," Bruen finished, his voice a blunt monotone. He shook his head, unwilling to meet Hyde's eyes. Instead he touched a stud and the holo of Arta Fera reloading her pulse pistol vanished.

Disappointed with himself, his eyes searched the pastoral heaven of the small valley that spread below them. Cattle grazed unmolested among coves of rich thick grass. Trees shrouded dark granite outcrops while multicolored flowers carpeted verdant pastures.

"We've done so much, my friend," Hyde reminded, consolingly. "After all these years, after all the sacrifice. . . ."

"What's one more young girl, eh?" Bruen snorted sourly and rubbed his deep-set eyes. "Where does it stop, Hyde? Almost three hundred years, now, I've watched it. In my lifetime perhaps one hundred billion people have died in pain and misery, their planets blasted by war, scoured by radiation, disease, and climatic upheaval." He looked over, blue eyes mild. "I ask you, do you see any improvement in the human condition? At times I get the feeling we're some sort of malignant experiment."

Hyde placed a reedlike hand on Bruen's shoulder. "Remember our creed, Brother. Life is knowledge and knowledge is energy. Energy is eternal, it can't be destroyed, only dissipated through entropy." Hyde coughed again, grimacing as he spit phlegm into the bushes behind him. "Death is an inevitability, but it isn't forever. Eventually it all goes back to God."

Bruen granted him a wry smile. "Forever, no. The universe continues to expand in places while other areas are drawn to the gravitational wells of the Great Attractors. So we're either at the crest of the expansion or the beginning of the contraction. Either way, the end won't come for another fifteen billion years or so." He pointed a crooked finger at Hyde. "How much suffering can you fit into fifteen billion years before we are all returned to Godhead?"

"Life is *more* than suffering, Brother. Life is also warm sunny mornings, birds singing, a comfortable—"

"Bah!"

"You're a bitter old man!" Hyde slapped his knees and

leaned back, his sagging pale face exposed to the warmth of the sun.

"Almost twenty thousand are dead in Kaspa. And here, you and I sit in the sun and talk of pleasure? Our worlds are about to be plunged into a maelstrom. Within years, Brother, entire planets will be scorched to molten rock. What madness is ours?"

Hyde coughed again, working his mouth uncomfortably. "All the more reason for us to enjoy those few moments the present provides, Magister. Remember your creed. There is nothing beyond the Here/Now. The past is simply stored energy in your mind. The future consists of probability horizons—the bouncing of the quanta toward an expected observation. What you fear is only described by those quantum wave functions inside your mind. That future isn't real."

"Yet." Bruen paused. "So, like all reality, eventually you can trace it down to nothingness. I still fear."

Bruen caught movement in the valley and turned to see three horses emerge from a stand of trees several hundred yards away. They trotted to a small stream and dipped their heads to drink. In silence and appreciation, he watched them, aware of the thick white pillows of cloud that rose far to the north over Kaspa. Prophetic! Even now, according to his instructions, the resistance should be blowing up Regan command concentrations. More blood on his hands.

"I suppose it bothers me that we had no choice." Bruen laced his parchment-skinned fingers over a bony knee. "I don't like the feeling of being a pawn, Brother. It appalled me when I watched the old Magisters fall under the sway of the machine. Nothing has changed since those days."

"Only now, *you* must deal with the machine." Hyde dropped his head, bloated features uneasy.

"I wonder who fools who?" Bruen granted with a dry cackle. "Which of us is really the manipulator, Brother?"

In a lower tone, Hyde added, "You're the only one we've got, Bruen. No one else has your strength. No one else is smart enough, strong enough, capable of dancing with such delicate balance."

"Indeed, well, I've fooled it this far—I think. Energy is forever, eh? Well, Brother, if you find me dead on my

pallet one of these days, what are you going to do?" Bruen
cocked an eye at Hyde's bulky body.

The Magister coughed and spat again. "Die of my collaps-
ing lungs on the spot so I don't have to place myself under
that accursed helmet."

"Not a viable solution."

"Neither is your death." Hyde chuckled and ended up
coughing again. "No, I'll kill myself before I sit in the chair
and put those terrible wires over my head. The Mag Comm
would peel my mind like an onion . . . and all would be for
naught."

They sat in silence, Hyde brooding over his inadequacies.
Why did it all seem so damned hopeless?

"We still haven't received word of which way the Star
Butcher will jump." Bruen smiled as one of the horses, a
dappled gray, dropped its head and lifted its tail, playfully
pushing a muscular black to one side. In an instant, they
were puffing and bouncing, trotting along in their equine
game of tag. Horses had it so good on Targa.

"Predictions tend toward Rega," Hyde tilted his head
back and pinched his nose, sniffing at his clogged sinuses.
In a nasal voice he continued. "Rega appears to offer Staffa
more than the Sassans would. The Lord Commander can't
have much empathy with a bat-brained theocracy based on
sybaritic sycophancy. That fat Sassan pustulation? A God?
Staffa must laugh himself into fits at the idea." Hyde waved
his swollen hands. "No. Rega, for all its faults, will at least
appeal to Staffa's mutated sense of respect."

"An odd position, Hyde, to be second-guessing that
man." Bruen moved to spare the insistent ache in his hip.
"Of them all, he's the least predictable."

"Come, Brother," Hyde growled. "Staffa has no secrets.
Money and status drive him. So does power. A simple—if
brilliant—man. Sassa and Rega know the game is almost
up. He who seduces Staffa with the greatest number of baubles and promises gets the whole of Free Space. He who
misses the opportunity is lost."

Bruen objected, "You claim Rega has more to offer the
Lord Commander than Sassa does. I concur; but consider
this permutation. In the end, Staffa will have only one
power to deal with. I don't think he'll be happy playing

policeman in the long run. His people can't take that drudgery. Staffa knows that."

"So?"

"So Staffa will prey on the winner." Bruen sighed as the horses raced out of sight.

"And it would be much easier to turn and destroy Sassan God-Emperors whom he has no respect for."

Bruen shifted again in an attempt to curry favor from his hip. "It would leave him feeling more comfortable."

"You talk as if the Praetor's creation is a human being."

Bruen touched the stud, the holo forming again to show Arta Fera inside the caverns of Makarta where she placed the pistol in the weapons rack. She stopped, an uneasy frown on her perfect forehead, as if she still couldn't comprehend her talent for destruction.

"Maybe he is. He loved once."

Hyde laughed loudly, ending in a fit of coughing. He wiped his eyes and stared at his old friend. "Becoming maudlin, Bruen?"

The Magister shook his head. "No, Hyde, old friend," Bruen responded sadly. "I just wonder what right two doddering old men like us have to meddle with the future of humanity. Are we saviors, Hyde . . . or puppets of evil and death?"

CHAPTER VI

In the darkness, Staffa kar Therma lay on his back. Around him the soft whispers of *Chrysla*'s humming presence should have reassured him. Instead he replayed that final moment in his mind when *Chrysla*'s guns blew the Praetor's battleship into slag—and with it, the only woman he'd ever loved.

I killed her. How could I have known? He reached up to rub his eyes with thumb and forefinger. *And my son? Does he live? Or did I kill him, too? The Seddi . . . the Seddi would know.*

What would his son be like? The old question that had plagued him for years nagged at his thoughts. He tried to sort out the emotions—and failed. Attempts at thinking rationally ended only in confusion, and he began to comprehend the conditioning that had been triggered by the Praetor's words.

"I understand now, old man. I was your experiment, wasn't I? That's where the pride in your eyes came from. You took an orphaned boy and used him as a behavioral experiment. With the training machines, you stifled my emotions, turned me into a biological robot. Rational, logical, without a shred of emotion except the desire to succeed.

"My God, Praetor, what a cunning monster you were." Through the emotional haze, the pieces began to fall into place. But where did the reality lie? Had his brain been normal before, or had the psychological trigger released him from a conditioned state? He took a deep breath, stilling his thoughts, stifling the emotions, as he reviewed what he knew about brain physiology and chemistry.

Based on a complex interaction of physiology and chemistry, the brain created its own criteria for normal behavior. In doing so, it built a network of neural pathways that created memory and allowed it to learn new adaptive strategies.

"And all of that has been overturned by the Praetor's hidden trigger." Staffa balled a fist and smacked the sleeping pallet. "So, what happened? The Praetor's words triggered a neural response that interacted with the brain's feedback to maintain chemical balance. But which state is the real me?"

And there was the real problem. Had the Praetor's conditioning denied him part of himself for all those years, or did the key words, "construct, machine, and creation" trigger an emotional imbalance calculated to destroy him in the end?

The answer lay moldering in the Praetor's grave.

The fact remained that the subliminal cues that stimulated his brain to slow production of corticosteroids, serotonin, acetylcholine, and norepinephrine had been given and the old balance had been upset.

Staffa stood and paced restlessly. The answer had to lie in the Praetor's last words. Sometime, in that discussion, the old viper would have given him a clue. Even amid the destruction of his world, the Praetor couldn't have resisted one final test, but what? Staffa replayed the conversation in the Myklenian hospital word for word. So much had been said, so many meanings tendered. But which phrase held the clue?

Staffa frowned and propped his chin on a fist. *He'll bet on my pride and arrogance.* Staffa smiled grimly. *Yes, that's his way.* The words, "no soul" recurred in Staffa's memory; the old man had harped on that. "No responsibility to God? . . . I bred that out of you . . . banished it from your personality . . . a creature without conscience . . . money and power motivate you. . . ."

Staffa's expression hardened. "And what else is there, Praetor? How else does a man measure his worth? Power is the only measure . . . as you taught me so well."

The eerie squawl of his son's cry pierced the years, wailing, condemning. Staffa closed his eyes, only to be haunted by Chrysla's sad eyes. He couldn't avoid the gentle censure, the rebuke that lay in that yellow gaze. An invisible fist gripped his heart, squeezing as if to force the life from that throbbing organ.

"I didn't know he'd taken you," Staffa whispered to the specter. "No wonder you disappeared so thoroughly. In all of Free Space, only the Praetor could have bought such secrecy. I should have known, my love. I should have known."

His son's lonely cry left his soul shivering. Guilt flooded him and mixed with the grief. *Why is this happening to me?*

The Praetor had claimed his conscience was reptilian. "And I told him I had no interest in conscience." The man who would unite all of Free Space in order to challenge the Forbidden Borders could only be burdened by conscience. "Don't you see, Praetor? The stakes are so high. As long as humanity is divided, as long as we feud and fight among ourselves, we'll never break this cage that binds us."

He shook his head, glaring up at his memories. "That's the essential point you missed, Praetor. You forgot that you taught me to dream—to aspire to ever greater things. I must rule Free Space."

. . . And you'll finally fail . . . fail . . . fail. . . .

Staffa spun on his heel, powered by a sudden surge of adrenaline. A wicked smile spread across his hard lips. "That's the key, isn't it, Praetor? Throughout that entire conversation, you mocked me, knowing full well that you'd conditioned sentimentality out of my personality—banished, as you so aptly claimed. That's why it surprised you that I loved Chrysla. She could have broken the conditioning in the end. You *had* to get her away from me. It would have ruined the experiment—tainted your 'greatest creation.'"

Staffa laughed sourly. "My Achilles' heel. Inhumanity. Lack of conscience. That's why you called me a machine." Staffa's eyes narrowed into slits. "You left me only half a man, Praetor."

But had those three words released all of him? Had they broken the conditioning completely? Anger blended with frustration. "You've got to find yourself, Staffa, or the Praetor will win in the end. If you'd see your dream come true, you must know what it is to be human, as the Praetor said, to 'feel the spirit that breathes within the species.'"

He filled his lungs, holding his breath to still the sudden

pounding anxiety in his heart. "Praetor, first, I will find my son, if he lives. And then I will find myself."

* * *

"Don't tickle," she warned as his fingers slipped in light caress along the silken cool skin on the backs of her thighs.

Drawing a deep breath, Tybalt the Imperial Seventh let it whistle past his lips. "Why do you do this with me? You don't love me, Ily."

She turned, flipping a wealth of gleaming black hair over her shoulder so she could face him on the rumpled sleeping surface. Her long legs had wadded the golden sheets to a crumpled pile during the heat of their passionate coupling. She moved closer, as if drawing on his body heat, and extended a muscular leg over his belly. One of her breasts flattened against his arm. The contrast between the firm whiteness of her skin and his rich black tones absorbed him for a moment.

He gazed into her piercing black eyes so close to his own.

"Maybe I like the taste of power, Imperial Seventh," her voice came as sultry as the musk of her cooling body. "Maybe you represent the ultimate triumph."

He shuddered slightly as she began nibbling at his chest, her pointed tongue circling his nipple to send chilling thrills down his spine.

"And you never worry about the ramifications of discovery?" he managed, the words taking all his concentration. Thick black hair tickled his skin.

She laughed. "By whom? Your precious wife? The Empress knows already. Neither Mareeah Rath nor her fawning family pose any—"

"*They* know?" A tingle of foreboding flickered to life below his heart. He stared through narrowed eyes at the rich Vermilion silks that draped above.

Ily laughed again, exposing white teeth while her eyes crinkled with humor. "Of course, Lord. Shhh! Don't worry. It's taken care of. No one will cross *me*, Tybalt. No one!" Her expression hardened to emphasize that fact. "Perhaps you might not be in a position to threaten your wife—or her powerful family for that matter." Her tongue traced his upper lip as she moved onto him. Her breath carried a scent of mint as she added, "On the other hand, the House of Rath fears one of its young lords might be arrested for treason, theft, graft, or any of a number of suitable charges. I'd see him convicted, Tybalt—and condemned to death."

A warm relief washed through him, replacing that momentary fear. "And should the Council suspect? The petty—"

"If you're not man enough to handle your own Council, you're not man enough to be Emperor."

"Indeed."

"Then what need have we to worry if we make love on the steps of the Imperial Regan Council buildings?" she whispered hotly as she brought his masculinity to life.

After she left him spent and exhausted he ran his fingers through her black hair and down to trace the bones of her shoulders and chest, circling those full breasts and massaging the nipples lightly. Her belly rippled with muscle as she moved.

"Tell me, Ily, what do you know of Staffa kar Therma? Tell me about your secret knowledge. Who is he? What's he like? What do we really know of him?"

She turned her head, cheek pillowed in the glossy blackness of her spilled hair. "The Lord Commander? Not much. He's one nut I'd love to crack, Emperor of mine. Originally I thought he had a soft spot for Myklene and the Praetor. Hah! Fallacy laid to rest! Though they feared his power and banished him, they still put him in business. Gave him a ship and sent him off to prey on others. Yet he killed the Praetor—who made him what he is—with his bare hands."

Her eyes lost focus and her voice dropped to a mumble. "Killed the one who gave him everything. Indeed, I'd like to know what motivates a man like that."

"You've spoken to him. You must have some impression." Tybalt recalled images of the Lord Commander—deadly gray eyes, constantly controlled features never shadowed by emotion . . . a deadly human fortress.

She shifted next to him in the dim light. "I think he's the most fascinating man I have ever known."

"Present company excepted?" he asked, realizing the answer was oddly important to him.

Her eyes met his, black, bottomless, knowing. "Present company included."

No matter what I do, what I wear, how I attempt to dominate the situation, he always dwarfs me. Would that I could ever change myself, it is he I would emulate—and how I hate myself when I think that! No action would provide me more pleasure than the feel of an energy knife slipping through Staffa's heart.

Shamed, he clamped his jaws tight. Her honesty stung. "I could kill you for that, Ily."

"You won't though." Her heart-shaped face remained serene. "You value my skills too highly in the first place. In the second, you relish my company, for I'm the only other person in all of the Regan Empire who treats you like an equal and doesn't quail in their boots at your power. And lastly, you appreciate my honesty and candor."

How true. He could hate both Staffa and Ily for that—and he needed them both despite the fact that one day, each might have to be destroyed. No matter the cost. Ultimate power—and its preservation—was a lonely business.

"Perhaps you're right, dear Ily. Perhaps you are." *But I don't want to dwell on that now, my hot bitch.* "Then tell me, what do we make of Staffa and the Sassans?"

She stretched her tawny body, working each muscle before she sat up and crossed her legs. She shook black hair over pale shoulders and propped her chin in her palms. "He's the key to the future. With him, we can control all of Free Space. Perhaps with that control we can even marshal enough strength to challenge the Forbidden Borders.

"On the other hand, if he contracts to the Sassans, we'll lose in the end. We have no way to counter his strike capabilities. Nothing we put up will stop him."

He nodded, barely containing a belch. "My thoughts exactly." He crossed his arms loosely over his ample belly. "I have an idea." He searched her face intently as he spoke. "We'll make the Lord Commander the best offer we can . . . and I want *you* to take it to him."

"The head of Internal Security?" She cocked her head, perfect face lining as she turned it over in her mind.

How far can I trust you, Ily? Ah, see your eyes lighting? Indeed, you see the opportunities! What a delight you are, my sweet Cytean cobra. An explosive vixen in my bed, a constant foil in my Empire, you alone of all women are worthy of me.

"Why not?" He flicked his hand absently. "I have my reasons, Ily. As you so ably articulated, I trust your honesty and candor. You're a beautiful woman; he might not suspect your intricate competence. See Staffa. Woo him to me. You know what's at stake. A discreet assassination, a bribed or compromised individual here or there, perhaps something more drastic might be called for. I leave it to your instincts."

And I shall take my own steps, my sweet lust. Though it grieves me, I must enslave you, turn you into a true tool.

"And I have a final reason for sending you, Ily." Her eyes were bright on his as she slowly smiled. "Yes, indeed, my love. In the event that all else fails, you may be able to assassinate the Lord Commander—and remove his threat for good."

Of course, yours shall be an Imperial symbol of authority. A badge perhaps? Yes, an unlimited credit and authority badge. Oh, delightful, Tybalt! How diabolically ironic. As I am bound to my power, so shall you be chained to yours, Ily. Caress it, sweet lover, for it is also death!

Oblivious, her smile grew, dimpling the smooth skin of her face. Slowly her white teeth began to show and her perfect breasts heaved with stifled laughter. "My Lord, Tybalt," she chuckled, "you have chosen better than you know. Staffa kar Therma is mine!"

As you are now mine! Tybalt smiled his agreement, allowing his fingers to trace the lines of her incredible body.

* * *

The wall beside Sinklar's shoulder exploded, the concussion slapping him out into the narrow alley. Only blind instinct made him crawl into the shadows as his stunned mind sought to compensate. Jangled nerves in his ears shrieked. Through the fog left of his senses, he could hear MacRuder's and Gretta's weapons ripping the air with their cackling discharge.

A hand patted his foot; a vaguely discerned voice called to him through the haze; he barely reacted as hands grabbed him and pulled him up. His stumbling feet seemed to work of their own volition.

"What?" he asked, thinking it odd that his own voice

scarcely penetrated the shimmering fog. "What? Where are we? What's wrong?"

He remembered a doorway, steps that he suffered to climb in a dark winding staircase, supporting arms, and a small room behind a shattered door. He remembered wanting to vomit, dizziness, falling . . . and never hitting the bottom.

Sinklar lay on a slab of freezing marble. He couldn't turn his head because someone was sawing his skull open to get at the brain, but he knew that his beautiful mother lay on one side, his father on the other. His body trembled with the vibration of the saw and he looked up—into Anatolia Daviura's wondrous blue eyes.

POK-BAAM! Concussion and falling dust brought Sinklar back from the muzzy gray dreams. The vibrations that his dream interpreted as a saw came from the floor he lay on.

"Damnation!" A sharp male voice stirred his memory as he fought to open eyes glued tight with rheum. Something sounding like tearing linen identified itself in his mind as a blaster being fired: Air molecules reacting with particles.

Silence.

He rubbed his face with encrusted fingers and rolled over, hearing grit crunch under his armor. Every bone felt pulled out of joint. The dull ache that had filled his dreams shot hot and angry through his head.

"Rotted Gods," he gasped. "What the . . ."

"Shut up," a woman's voice hissed from somewhere.

He blinked into the gloom to clear his sight. Rain pelted through half a roof to spatter on splintered timbers, crumbled masonry and sagging flooring. One ear seemed dead. Targa! The bombing, the flight through Kaspa to try and find their forces, the ambush . . . it all came back.

So black. A fragment of his memory stimulated him to reach for the IR visor. It slid halfway down and caught, leaving the world eerily half-visible. He had to tug it the rest of the way; but he could see. MacRuder huddled near a wrecked window, assault rifle ready, searching the blackness and storm. Gretta crouched by the blasted doorway, covering the stairs as she squinted down the sights of her assault rifle.

His bladder angrily demanded to be emptied.

A lance of violet light erupted from the stairway and out through the missing portion of roof. Sinklar understood. The Targans had blown it away. Gretta waited.

He tried to swallow. His tongue stuck in the dryness and gagged him. He felt for the water flask and pulled the flattened pieces from his belt. That was when he noticed his combat armor—blood caked, horribly battered with bits of metal and masonry siding sticking out at angles. The armor had saved his life.

Unabashed, he moved to the depths of the room and urinated against the remaining wall. MacRuder's rifle spurted a short rip into the darkness.

He crawled over to where rain had collected on the dirty floor and sucked up as much as he could from the pool that had formed. Grit stuck in his teeth; a foul aftertaste slimed his tongue. But soothing moisture trickled down his raw throat.

He rolled onto his back and let the rain wash his hot fevered face.

"How you feeling?" MacRuder asked, voice flat, emotionless.

"Like somebody pulled me through a singularity—sideways," Sinklar rasped. "What's the situation?"

" 'Bout as good as last time. Bad. We're up here and they can't get us until they bring up some heavy stuff. I don't think that'll be long either. Something's moving around down there." MacRuder didn't take his eyes off the streets below.

"They tried the steps twice," Gretta added. "I taught them better."

"This is a tower of some kind?" Sinklar asked, seeing bits of roofs through the blown away sections of wall.

"Yeah, take the high ground." MacRuder ran a muddy hand over his IR visor to smear at the rain. "Another great military axiom from Academy."

Sinklar crawled over to look. Their tower stood at the point of a V-shaped block. Across the street from them, and down, rain slashed the slanted roof for a subterranean warehouse access. Two poles supported a drooping banner advertising storage rates and the comm number to contact for information.

"What kind of night vision are they using? Active or passive?" Sinklar began pulling at his equipment belt. The concussion had hopelessly smashed most of the gear.

"Passive. Must be some sort of light amplifying system."

"Got a grenade left?"

"One. Why?"

"Want to get out of here before they set up whatever they've got that's big enough to blow us away?"

"You bet your rosy red rectum, scholar. What you got in mind this time?"

"Simple physics."

"Like what?"

"Like I'm hoping gravity still works. Only we have to create a diversion and blind them for at least thirty seconds."

"I see, passive night vision, huh? And I'll bet you can swipe a flare from Gretta, too."

Sinklar checked his ruined equipment and cursed under his breath. Scrambling, he crawled painfully to where Gretta Artina crouched to cover the stairway. "I need your flare unit and your survival cable."

"Got a plan? Heard you whispering with MacRuder over there. How you feeling?" She barely took time to glance at him before she sighted down the black stairwell again.

"They don't make words that gruesome," he whispered, taking the articles she pulled from her belt. "One ear doesn't work. Shattered the tympanic membrane, I think. That and I feel like I've been strained through a Myklenian wine filter. Everything aches."

"Yeah, well—listen, get us out of this mess, and I'll massage every square inch of your body." She gave him a quick grin and a wink.

"Maybe we'll just settle for dinner, huh?" he added lamely, aware of how unsettled he was by her attention.

"Just dinner?"

"Well, it's that I. . . . You see, I was always involved with my studies and. . . ." He didn't need this—not now! He turned to scuttle away only to feel her hand on his arm.

"Rotted Gods! You're a *virgin!*"

"Shhh! Someone might hear. Besides, what about MacRuder?"

"We'll talk about that later, scholar. For now, I like your style. You go to work. If we live through this, I'm going to turn your starship inside out!" She slapped him on the elbow to get him moving.

His muscles were trembling in protest by the time he made it back to MacRuder's crumbling window.

"Virgin, huh?"

"Why *me?* Here, hold onto this." He handed one end of the survival line to MacRuder. "She didn't have to bellow it all over the Gods' cursed city!" He made a knot and tied MacRuder's end off to one of his belt grapples. An angular chunk of mortar gave him the weight he needed and he used a piece of loose wire to bind it to the grapple.

"Now what?"

"Now I wish I'd spent more time at apple ball than at books." Sinklar frowned across the distance.

"So, what do you need? I used to pitch six-forty in league play."

"I should have known. Throw it over and between those poles." Sinklar handed him the grapple-wired mortar.

MacRuder made a perfect toss. The mortar carried the grapple across the space and tore loose from the thin wire when the line snapped taut. The grapple fell neatly behind the banner. Reeling the line in, it caught in the bottom of the fabric.

"Hope it don't tear," MacRuder grunted.

"Makes two of us," Sinklar agreed. "Get ready. Lift your IR visor or it will blind you just as bad as them when I light the fire. Understand the principle?"

"Yeah."

Crawling to the stairway, Sinklar sent Gretta after MacRuder. Taking a deep breath, he lifted his rifle and fired a series of bursts down into the blackness, blowing out the few bits of wall left from Gretta's defense. Blasting the mortar away opposite him, he prayed the roof wouldn't fall in and tossed the grenade out on a fifteen second fuse. He ripped his IR visor up, plucked up the flare pistol, and shot each of the flares up through the holes in the roof as he ran.

The bright light left him squinting. Gretta took hold and jumped, sliding down the line. MacRuder gripped the cable, swallowing hard. The flares lit the surroundings, exposing running figures in the street.

"Go!" He shoved MacRuder out and grabbed the line. He made sure his rifle was slung and jumped out into open space, feeling friction from the line heating his gloves.

Gretta caught MacRuder and pulled him onto the narrow roof. Sinklar slid down on top of them. At that instant the grenade sundered the top of the tower, showering debris on the streets below. Angry shouts carried in the night. In a split second decision, he raised his feet, plowed into both of them, and they all slid, clattering down the rain-wet tin roof in a tangle of limbs as blaster fire ripped the night. One of the poles holding the tattered banner shattered.

"Run!" Sinklar growled, grabbing Gretta's hand and pounding off across the roof, jumping cable housing, ventilation pipes and recirculation fans. He could hear MacRuder thudding along behind. At each step, his head threatened to explode. Lances of agony tore up his frayed nerves and seared the bottom of his brain.

The clouds grayed with dawn, casting weak light where they huddled, shivering, on a mining laser supply company roof. They waited, belly down, mostly covered by a brick chimney. Cold, wet, and hungry, Sinklar studied the faces of his companions. "Hell of a rescue."

"Think they'll ever come to get us?" Gretta wondered, eyes baggy. Her face had streaked with mud and grime, etched by the places where sweat had run from beneath her helmet. A tangle of curly brown hair hung to one side of her face. Almost enough to mar her beauty—almost.

"Been two days," MacRuder sighed, red-rimmed eyes haggard. "That long since the bastards hit us."

"I'm out of charge for my rifle," Gretta said, curiously unconcerned.

"I'm close to out," MacRuder confided. "Maybe a shot or two left."

"And here comes trouble." Sinklar struggled weakly to get his rifle up as men streamed out along one side of the building. His first shot took a man's leg off.

MacRuder got a hit as the pursuers went to ground. "That's it. Gun's dead!"

"I'll hold them while I can." Sinklar squinted, seeing how perilously low his own weapon registered.

"Hey, Sink," MacRuder called. "I know I gave you a lot of grief for being . . . well, you know, different. I mean all your book learning kept us alive. Thanks, buddy."

Gretta added with a grin, "Get us out of this alive, Sinklar, and I swear, I'll kiss you on the spot and marry you to boot!"

"Yeah, right!" He blew a vent tube apart and killed the man hiding behind it. A whiff of smoke went up. Something in his mind reacted to that. What was it he should know about. . . .

"Mac? Still got your flare unit?" A sudden thought began to nag at him. Yes, that was it. Just a chance to even the odds a little. . . .

"Here." He felt the flare unit pressed into his hand. Blaster bolts and the eerie tingle of pulse beams whirring around his head, Sinklar settled the flare tube on his rifle and fired a phosphorous flare into the exposed roof lining. Immediately, it began to billow black smoke as yellow flames licked out of the burning chemical. The roofing crackled and ignited.

"So they get us," Sinklar declared dully. "We'll keep them occupied for a while."

He got two more before they pulled the circle tight. A blaster bolt clipped his helmet and stunned him. Gretta and MacRuder tried to burrow into the roof, knives in their hands in the off hope anyone proved stupid enough to get close.

The roof jumped from a thundering blast. Big stuff here already? What for? Three marines with empty assault rifles?

A man screamed. The roof jumped and heaved again.

Ready to die, Sinklar blinked his eyes and swallowed dryly. Dazed from the hit to his helmet, he roared his rage and stood. Reeling on his feet, he sprayed blaster fire across the roof as men ran through swirls of smoke. Huge sections of the burning roof ripped and tore under heavy blaster fire. He was still bellowing, unaware his rifle had emptied, when the patrol craft settled next to him.

He turned, trigger still pressed to charge the armored vehicle—only to have MacRuder pull him down, shouting in his good ear, "It's one of ours! Sink, they're on *our* side! *They saw the smoke and came to investigate!*"

* * *

The Itreatic Asteroids: No more than tumbling rock, they had been the guts of a giant planet that had been sundered more than a half billion years ago. No one knew if the records of the first human scientists who had come to the Itreatic Asteroids still existed. Originally intrigued at the dense metal concentrations, they had determined exactly what gravitic forces had ripped the giant ancestral planet apart and spread the pieces far and wide to mingle with the suddenly homeless moons. Now the Itreatic Belt formed a giant band of dust and debris that circled the Twin Titans— a system composed of a pulsating RR Lyrae-type binary. The terrestrials had studied the suns—spectrally so poor in metals compared to the Itreatic Asteroid Belt—made their notes, and vanished into the curvature of time and space.

The blue giants continued to blast out immense light and radiation, sufficient to provide the Itreatic Asteroids with enough energy to support a colony on the metal-rich chunks of rock and free-tumbling crater-pocked moons. To them, Staffa kar Therma had originally come. With his wealth, he had hired the engineers, equipment, and technicians to build a colony. With mirrors they channeled and condensed the actinic light of the Twin Titans and melted and smelted some of the best alloys in Free Space. Zero g negative-atmosphere labs manufactured high temperature syalon ceramics stronger than the finest alloy steels. His labs had developed epitaxial fabrication and nanotechnology in order to craft thallium oxide superconductors so sophisticated that no one in Free Space could reproduce them, let alone offer a competitive product. The only n-faceted gallium arsenide computer components came from Staffa's labs.

To that far corner of Free Space—strategically blocked on three sides by the Forbidden Borders—the Lord Commander brought his fleets for rest and relaxation. Staffa's private domain—the Itreatic Asteroids had become a fortress haven.

Staffa sat in the command chair, watching as *Chrysla*'s null-singularity drive unbent the universe around the battle-

ship. Ahead, the Twin Titans appeared, a welcome beacon
to calm the torments and doubts with which the Praetor had
saddled him. The newly familiar mood swings continued to
plague him as his mind sought equilibrium. Fatigue lay like
a sodden weight on his soul. Where once he'd been of a
single mind, doubt now vied with guilt and depression, then,
within hours, he'd experience giddy optimism. With each
mood swing, his brain would access forgotten neural pathways, behaviors triggered by the chemical codes.

*I could control it with drugs, but what would I do to
myself? Am I nothing more than a machine—a monster? And
if my son still lives? What legacy can I give him?*

His gray eyes shifted to the screens to see the rest of the
fleet, including the damaged *Jinx Mistress*, flickering into
existence behind the flagship. It would be good to rest. The
Myklene campaign—while short and succinct—had drained
each and every crewmember. A tangible tension had crackled in the very air as they approached the target. Never had
the Companions challenged the might of so great a power
as Myklene. Success had hinged on a rapid all-or-nothing
strike calculated to paralyze the mighty Myklenian fleet and
demoralize the Praetor's huge defenses. That long jump in
from Sassa had left even the best of friends emotionally
wrung out.

"First Officer, alert the monitors." Staffa slouched in the
command chair, elbow propped on one gray-clad knee. He
could see where First Officer Lynette Helmutt leaned back
in the comm chair, eyes closed in that semitrance of mental
communication with the ship's computers.

The first officer's voice, instead of issuing from her throat
and mouth, came through the comm speakers. Similarly,
she had heard Staffa's voice through the ship's pickups.
"Monitors alerted, Lord Commander. Deceleration initiated at 40 g. Consequent Delta V dump sequences initiated.
We're roger 001 on course relay. Monitors report condition
green at home and welcome back."

"Acknowledged, First Officer, send my regards." Staffa
fingered the growth of beard that had begun to crop up on
his cheeks. How long had it been since he'd had a beard?
Thirty years? More? Time had treated him in such a manner
that memories consisted of a kaleidoscopic rush of events
and places and fights and political negotiations. All that is,

except that brief time he'd shared with Chrysla and the briefer moments with his infant son.

Time: the implacable foe—the greatest of allies. The growth of beard signaled a reminder that he'd need a treatment again before time sucked him up and spit him out an old man.

In the medical section of his labs in the Itreatic Asteroids, a large N-matrix computer held his personal body code. From it, growth hormone boosters were produced and injected in the bloodstream. Genetically perfect polymerase VII would be released along with an ionizing mutation antigen that would tag suspicious cells and repair mutated DNA. From his blood serum an antibody count and identification program would catalog any new antigens, determine their beneficence or evil, and clone antibodies to remove deleterious elements from his system. Such procedures kept him looking a healthy thirty—despite his eighty-seven years out and about in space.

He plucked absently at the stubble on his cheeks. Immortality assumed that life had a purpose. Which in turn assumed that continuing to live advanced that purpose. Given those assumptions, what could there be to life that he—the individual living it—did not immediately understand? Or could it be that simple survival was the only purpose for living—or the universe for that matter.

He pinched his eyes shut and shook his head. "Praetor, I. . . ."

He got to his feet, gray cloak swirling about him. "First Officer, you have the helm. I will be in my quarters should you need me."

"Acknowledged, Lord Commander," the bridge speaker told him tonelessly.

He paced through the bridge hatch, choosing to walk the distance to his quarters instead of riding the shuttle. Who would his son be? Would he have Chrysla's beauty? Her glowing amber eyes? Would the young man look like him? Strapping, keen of mind? *Or is he as deadly as I am—as single-minded of purpose . . . as cold and heartless?*

"Staffa? What's the matter with you?" He sighed, seeking the key to his troubled thoughts.

Caught in his musings, he didn't notice Skyla as she

walked from the gymnasium, freshly showered, pale skin still flushed with the heat of heavy exercise.

"Everything all right?" she asked, matching his stride.

"I was pondering serious questions."

"Such as?"

He took a deep breath, staring into the depths of her crystal blue eyes. Fragments of memories swirled in his mind. Still he hesitated.

"Staffa, you're not yourself these days. It worries me. One minute you're sharp as a molecular edge, the next you're drowning in self-pity. You hide it very well, but I've made a habit out of studying you, learning how you think. I didn't make it to Wing Commander by my good looks. You want to tell me what's eating at you?"

At his reluctance, she shook her head in frustration. "Look, if you can't talk to me, who else is there? And beside that, when you act like this, I worry about the implications it will have on the command."

"Skyla, do you ever wonder why we're here?" He stopped before the hatch to his quarters. "Are we just accidents? Just organic molecules? Simple polypeptide strands hooked together like some intricate graphite sculpture? Where do we come from? Why do we have the shape we do? What purpose does it serve that we are born, grow, learn, struggle, sire, and finally die? Is it only to produce the next generation that we do so?" He palmed his hatch and gestured her inside.

"Sure, I've wondered. I just never thought I could find the answers. That's for people like the Seddi, I guess."

He spun around as soon as they passed the second hatch. "*I Gods Rotted can't sleep anymore!*" He shook his head. "I can't concentrate, can't think. All the ordered discipline in my mind . . . it's gone, turned random and chaotic. I have panic attacks for no reason. I start to sweat, can't breathe. I get dizzy and feel a pain in my chest. I suffer from bouts of clinical depression. So, yes, you're right. My ability to command is suspect."

She stood hip-shot, watching him soberly from beneath lowered brows. "Staffa, you've been different ever since Myklene. Sassa and Rega teeter on the brink of war. You've got to have every one of your wits about you. Pharmaceuticals can control what you're experiencing, you know. But it's more than that. The Praetor did something, said something, didn't he?"

"Pragmatic to the last, Skyla?"

"Damn right I am!" She shrugged it off and added quietly. "I know a little about physical psychology. When we get back, will you take something to keep your brain chemistry in balance? I'm worried about you, and I guess you . . . well, you're the only friend I've got."

Where did that anxiety in her voice come from? What fed that pained expression of hers? Rotted Gods, she really *did* care. The thought of it left him off balance. In defense, he stared at the incongruous fireplace.

She stood motionless, waiting.

He rubbed nervous hands together as he turned to face her. "I . . . I dream of odd things. You see, the old man picked the lock on some hidden box in my mind. Long ago I found that he'd set mental booby traps in my brain. Psych-installed trip switches with hypnotic suggestions to unhinge me—to suddenly rob me of confidence or to bring sudden indecision. I found them over the years. One by one, I sorted out the subtle mental markers and deactivated them. Then on Myklene I learned the extent of the tampering he'd done to my mind. All right! I see it in your eyes. I'll drop by the psychiatric center and get a prescription."

Skyla exhaled her relief. "I understand why you killed him."

"Do you? What are the answers to those questions I asked in the corridor, Skyla? Is there a purpose to this life we lead? Are we doing anything but metabolizing, procreating, and surviving?"

She stalked across the rug, arms crossed defensively. "In my life—until I joined the Companions—I had to scramble to stay alive. For me, survival was everything. Maybe it still is. I try not to worry beyond a full belly, a warm secure bed, and a whole skin. If somebody has to get shot, I do my damnedest to make sure it's the other guy. What's more important than that?"

"I don't know. Perhaps that's what I want to find out." He gave her a speculative glance. "Didn't you have someone when you were a kid . . . a family? A mother who held you? Relatives?"

She laughed bitterly. "Yeah! Sure! My mother was a

prostitute. She died when I was four. Or was I five? I did
chores for the Sylene cribs until I was twelve. That's when
I was sold—despite my free status. A most noble and generous man Stryker was. Even after my life in the cribs I wasn't
ready for *him*. He bought me, raped my virginity away, and
used me like a. . . . Well, never mind. Careless of him. He
should never have left an energy blade within my reach. I
think the death warrant they put out on me is still valid.

"So I got to the street, and, by the Gods, I survived. I
spent the days in hiding, the nights in running—anything to
keep out of the clutches of the slavers and the police. That's
where I learned the assassin's trade. I was young, pretty.
They never believed an innocent like me could be a threat.
I lived cold, hungry, and scared . . . and then I saw one of
the Companions walking boldly down the main avenue."

She smiled, her expression softening. "Oh, Staffa, how I
admired that bright uniform, the way those mining pigs
shuffled to get out of his way. Even the bulls—the cops—
moved away and saluted." She tilted her head, the white-
gold of her braided hair hanging to one side. "It was old
Mac Rylee, out on the town, looking for the best
whorehouse planetside, as usual."

"I take it you conned him somehow or another?" Staffa
remembered Rylee, the Companions' greatest barroom
brawler.

"Sure did. Cut his purse right off his belt and handed it
back to him. Told him that whoever he was, he needed my
services."

"And he immediately tried to bed you!"

"And never succeeded." She grinned mischievously,
azure eyes shining. "As a woman looking to make her way
to the top, you never bed the man whose favor you'd win.
You make it by being one hundred percent better than anyone else. Where another man would work four hours, you
work eight."

"It paid off. You made it." He fingered one of the
trophies on the wall. "I took a chance on you. I thought
you had the right instinct for command. Do you have a
conscience, Skyla? Do the things we've done ever haunt
you? Does it bother you that so much blood is on our
hands?"

She studied him, lips pursed. "I've always accepted your

goals as being legitimate. There have been times in the past when I've been unable to fathom your logic, but as things unfold I see the strategy behind it. Honestly, I can't see any other way to unite humanity than through warfare."

"The ends justify the means in your eyes."

"I never knew you involved yourself in questions of teleological ethics. Did some Seddi mystic get a hold of you? Is that why you've started asking questions like that?"

He settled down on the scarlet couch. "The enigmatic Seddi." *The key to the whereabouts of my son. But how do I contact them? How can I ask them—who have tried so hard to assassinate me all these years—for help?*

She straightened her legs and considered her words before speaking. "I knew one, an old man. At the time, he was running for his life, too. Gone to ground in the streets like so many of the rest of us criminal types. They wanted to kill him because he was Seddi. Authorities don't like radicals, especially if they're preaching human liberation. The bulls almost caught him once. They got a shot into him—low power. I got him away and cared for him until he died. He told me things I didn't believe. Things about how they talked to beings of light and asked questions of God himself. I remember he told me as he was bleeding to death that life was only illusion. Only now really existed— and it was all tied up with the nature of the quanta. To the Seddi, the quanta are a reflection of God's thought pervading the universe. God exists in an eternal now—and time doesn't mean anything. I thought he was raving since it wasn't an illusion that had ripped his side open. He mumbled on about the quanta, and chaos, and how they reflected God's. . . . What's wrong, Staffa?"

He barely heard her, Skyla's words bending around his sudden images of Targa and the Seddi turmoil. *I must go alone. Seek out the Seddi by myself. Any other way would be disastrous. And along the way, I can learn to deal with my new self, learn what it means to be human.*

"Staffa?" Skyla asked again, but he was already laying his plans.

CHAPTER VII

Skyla pushed back from her comm and tapped long fingers on the desk. She sat in her personal quarters where she'd been going through the daily reports. An unusual number of requests had been routed through her comm. By the Rotted Gods, hadn't Staffa taken care of anything?

She scowled at the monitor, then okayed projects and reports one by one. These were Staffa's responsibilities, not her. Worry built. Mental triggers? Depression? Conditioned memories and improper neural pathways? What did that imply about Staffa's ability to function as the leader of the Companions?

"He'll bring us through. He always has . . . and when he was under more stress than this." Despite her self-assurance, the nagging worry didn't subside.

She tapped in a request for more information on a materials request from Tap Amurka and then shut down the system. Standing, she paced for several seconds before asking the room comm, "Comm, give me a security patch. Where is Staffa right now?"

"Observation dome A-6," security replied.

Skyla pivoted on her heel and slapped her door patch. She burned up some of the frustration as she pushed herself forward with long strides. People saw her coming, recognized the look in her eyes and slipped out of the way.

She darted into the lift, slapped the controls, and stood with arms crossed, toe tapping as it hustled her across the complex. The keen edge of her anger was blunted by her anxious concern over Staffa's behavior. Damn it, of all the times for him to turn flaky, this wasn't it.

Why am I so worried about him? Because I meant it that day on Chrysla when I told him he was my best friend, Rot it all.

"And you can't stand to see him this way."

She stormed into the A-6 dome to find Staffa sitting on one of the benches, staring out at the Twin Titans where they whirled around each other in a cerulean dance. The flickering of the bright light cast double shadows over the curve of the white wall behind his brooding figure.

Silently she slipped up behind him, aware of the preoccupied expression on his face. He didn't seem to notice, attention lost in his own thoughts.

"Staffa?"

He looked up then, vision clearing. "Yes?"

Skyla rubbed the back of her neck and tugged at her braid in frustration. "I handled the daily reports. I also checked the medical records. You haven't been by psych yet. Are you still enjoying your binge as a manic-depressive?"

He smiled at that. "I suppose. No, I'm trying to deal with a new me. I'm learning, attempting to cope with who I'm becoming. I've been giving a lot of thought to the concepts of responsibility, trying to decide what I owe myself."

"What?" *Damn it, Staffa, what happened to the old arrogance?* The eerie premonition of trouble grew within Skyla. *Give him time. He'll come around. Don't push . . . not yet.*

"I want to know what people are like." He cocked his head, frowning. "I mean real people."

"And the Companions are made up of illusion? Ark seemed pretty real last time I looked."

"No, I mean people out there." He waved in the direction of Free Space. "You know that we'll end up ruling them, one day. You're smart enough to know what my final objectives are. But who are they? What are they like? You've known them. I haven't. I've lived all my life in a cocoon. On Myklene, I was chaperoned everywhere. I only dealt with the elite, the scholars, generals, Councillors, and scientists. I never had kids my own age to play with."

"What about when the Praetor smuggled you off planet? Weren't you on your own then?"

Staffa shrugged. "What of it? Even then I had my body-guards—for that's all the crew was—just bodyguards to keep me out of trouble. And yes, we turned pirate for a while. Do you think I dealt with real people then? I was an armed robber, nothing more. My dealings with my victims

were at gunpoint, not exactly a social gala. Even as I began
collecting the Companions, I still remained aloof. What did
I care about who they were so long as they could perform.
One by one, I removed the Praetor's bodyguards—for obvious reasons—and replaced them with my own security. In
all my life, I've never walked down a street alone."

Skyla gave him a hard stare. "Yeah, well, don't. They'd
pick you clean in a minute."

Staffa growled something to himself, and added aloud,
"You and I have different thoughts concerning that. What
could be different in dealing with Tybalt, or Sassa, or
Roma? It's all negotiations, be they for a loaf of bread
or the dispositon of an empire. Human thought patterns
are the same, whether a free man's, a monarch's, or a
mendicant's."

Skyla seated herself before him, taking his hands in hers.
"Listen," she probed him with her blue eyes, seeing his
frustration. "I've been out there. It's. . . . Staffa, I can't
explain. I guess it has to be experienced, but it's not like
dealing with Sassa the God-Emperor. It's, well, the rules
are different."

He nodded, but she wasn't sure he'd heard. "But people
. . . trust, don't they? I've seen the holos where people do
things without constantly. . . . I guess I don't know how to
say it."

"I think I understand. You mean like the Companions
do. They have a code of behavior—shared values. Yes, and
trust. Among the Companions, we care for our own,
depend on each other. So do people out there, but you
have to know the subtle rules of the game." She paused.
"Staffa, what brought all this on?"

He glanced past her, seeing something in his mind. "My
Achilles' heel."

"What?"

He gave her a ghost of a grin. "Nothing.

"Chrysla?"

He gave her a hollow look that wrenched. "Chrysla's
dead."

"You don't know that."

He chuckled hoarsely. "I think I do. The source was
rather explicit." His brow knitted. "You know, I've
mourned her for so long it doesn't even bother me now. I

should be torn in two . . . but inside is only emptiness where she used to be."

Skyla's heart skipped and she said gently, "Twenty years is a long time. What about your son?"

He glanced at her, the old steel in his eyes. "I'm going to find him. One way or another, I swear I'll do it."

"We'll find him." She wished she could mean that. After so many years and all of Staffa's resources, where else could they look?

Staffa's expression hardened. "You'll have to take responsibility for the Companions. Can you do it?"

Good. At least you know you're not one hundred percent. That makes things easier. "Of course. We've got some of the best psychological talent in Free Space here. They'll figure out what the Praetor's game was. I can handle the rest. If things get too busy, I'll delegate some tasks to Tasha." *And I'll put that on record in case I have to haul you down to psych bound and gagged.*

A grim smile curled his lips. "Good. I knew I could count on you."

"Always, Staffa." *In more ways than you could know, and I'm going to find out what the Praetor did to you if I have to move stars and worlds to do it.*

* * *

The room looked fuzzy when Sinklar first opened his eyes. He blinked to clear his vision and found himself in a medical rehab unit. Parts of his body prickled as if electricity were running through them. Most of his view of the room was blocked by the white bulk of the machine, but he could see sickly green paint overhead. The soft murmur of voices and the periodic clicking of metal on tin trays could be heard in his good ear. A wad of cotton might have been stuffed in the other.

"About time," a familiar voice said from the side. "They said you'd be coming to about now."

"Gretta?" He turned his head and there she was, standing beside the unit, a relieved smile on her face. If anything, she looked better than he remembered. Her hair had been washed until it gleamed in the light, accenting the crystal blue of her eyes. Her skin had a healthy glow and the formfitting uniform did nothing to hide the seductive curves of her athletic body.

"The same. I just came by to see how you were doing. Mac's over at Division headquarters or he'd be here, too."

Sink swallowed and tried to ignore the funny feeling in his body. So many parts were numb. Nothing responded when he tried to move. Anesthetized? Or. . . . He nerved himself and asked, "What about. . . . I mean, am I all right? Is everything. . . ."

She grinned, a twinkle in her blue eyes. "You're going to be fine. Everything's still attached to your body—and functional." Her manner grew serious. "And I want you to know that you and I still have a date coming."

"What about you and Mac?"

She reached up with a slim hand and pulled her long hair back. "Mac and I—we're friends, Sink. I imagine we always will be. We've been through a lot." She reached down to stroke Sinklar's forehead. "Want me to be honest?"

Sinklar gave her a suspicious glance. "Well, I suppose so. I don't know. What are you talking about?"

To his immense pleasure, she continued to stroke his forehead. Her fingers felt delightfully cool. "Sink, my father is what you'd call a lower level bureaucrat on Ashtan. Until the day he dies, he'll continue to try and work his way up the ladder to be a middle level bureaucrat." She frowned. "I guess you'd say he lacks that spark, that innovative ability to seize opportunity and use it. Mac's like that. He's hard working, bright, but he'll always be the perfect lieutenant." She studied him through cool blue eyes. "I want more."

Sink wished he could squirm; unfortunately, the machine not only immobilized his body, but it pinned him in place like a biological specimen. "Why me? You're a beautiful woman. You could have anyone you wanted."

She snorted and shook her head. "Maybe I could. Did it ever occur to you that a woman might want to build a partnership with a man? I *like* you. You make me think. When I look into your eyes, I see a depth I don't see in many men's eyes. I think you're kind, and strong, and terribly attractive as a result. You can give me what I want out of life—and I think I can give you a lot in return. At least, I'd like the chance to find out if that's the case."

Sinklar squinted uneasily. "You make it sound terribly cold and calculating, like you were buying property or something."

Her grin brought dimples to her cheeks. "Given the way your mind works, what's a girl to do? I checked my arsenal of options and immediately discarded batting my eyes, wiggling my hips, or playing hard to get, and after what we went through, the delicate and frail female in need of protection would have come across a little silly, don't you think?"

The memory of Gretta coolly firing down a stairwell came to mind. He could recall the grim determination on her smudged face as she picked off assailants with practiced ease.

Gretta crossed her arms, leaned on the rehab unit, and studied him. "Besides, it's not like I'm making a proposal. We've got a lot stacked against us . . . like Targa, for one. We've got to stay alive. Second, I might not like you once I get to know you. And third, who's Anatolia?"

Sink jerked. "Huh? How could you know about her?"

Gretta lifted an eyebrow. "You talk in your sleep."

Sink felt himself blushing. "I only met her once. She's a behavioral geneticist on Rega."

"And you gave her a sample of genetic material, I suppose?"

"Yes."

"I thought you were a virgin."

"Not *that* kind of sample!"

"You in love with her?"

"NO!" Or was he? And if so, in love with what? A dream image?

Gretta grinned and bent down to kiss him on the forehead. "I've got to beat feet back to the barracks. I'll tell Mac you're doing fine. I checked with the staff here. They say you'll be out in another week or so." She grinned and added, "See you then . . . partner."

With a flip of her long brown hair, she disappeared around the curve of the white rehab unit.

"That true?" A gruff male voice asked.

"Huh?" Sink looked over at the burly man in the unit beside his.

"You really a virgin?"

"Blessed Gods." Sinklar winced and tried to melt into the med unit.

* * *

Staffa slipped into the command chair of the single-seat CV courier vessel and looked up at the screen that dominated the overhead panels. Green lights glowed on each of the systems. The stat boards showed the vessel ready for spacing. Staffa powered up the reactors.

The CV consisted of nothing more than a cockpit with a small cargo bay, toilet, bunk, and canteen with a fold-out table to dispense food. The command nacelle perched at the tip of a 0.5 kilometer long tube forward of the drives. Behind the lean streamlined body, two fusion reactors rested beneath hydrogen fuel pods on either side of a large null-singularity generator. The CV had atmospheric capabilities and only the barest minimum of defensive shielding—adequate for fending off space debris and long-range intership fire.

He accessed the cargo monitor out of wary habit. The muffled shape of a big man lay tightly bound under wraps of Vermilion export canvas. Bound as he was, the captive would need an energy knife to cut his way free. Heavy straps secured the bundle against the bulkhead. Staffa's practiced eye had measured the dosage perfectly. He had taken no chances in ensuring his "passenger" wouldn't awaken until long after Staffa slipped away into the anonymous crowds portside. By the time anyone tied the Lord Commander to the hijacking of the CV, Staffa would be well on his way from Etaria to Targa—and the search for his son.

He hesitated to enter the initiation sequence as he looked up at the docking lights. That eerie sensation of premonition filled him. He could imagine Skyla's initial panic when she realized he'd disappeared. Then she'd find the message he'd left on time delay. And, yes, she'd curse him up one side and down the other. Ah, how those azure eyes would burn—and the Rotted Gods help anyone who crossed her in that mood. A curious warmth filled Staffa's breast. She looked more beautiful when she was mad.

Pride filled him. He could leave the Itreatic Asteroids in

no more capable hands. Over the years, he'd come to depend on her, and never had it become more apparent than during the time since he'd faced the Praetor. Skyla had beefed up the security—enough that he'd had the Rotted Gods own time slipping away without security knowing. But then, a crafty fox like the Lord Commander always left himself an escape hole.

"Good-bye, Skyla. Take care of them."

He hit the clearance sequence and pressed the flight initiation program. In the overhead screen he watched the lights and background of the dock slip away as the tractors pushed him out into the black vacuum. The square of white docking lights glared in contrast to the black skeletons of gantries and the rocky blue-gray surface of the asteroid, cratered from countless years of Itreatic bombardment.

"Son, I'm coming for you," he whispered. His expression tensed at the curious sensation of loss that deadened his soul. A tightness choked the back of his throat.

Careful, Staffa. That's emotion playing with you, dulling your judgment. Think clearly. It's all in your mind. Steeling himself, armor-suited fingers tapped course corrections into the main navigational comm. Satisfied with the mathematics, he reached up and caressed the smooth surface of the worry-cap. He could feel its subliminal warmth and pressure as he placed it on his head. Familiar sensations of the ship's movement and functions filtered tendrils into his mind.

One by one he ran through the checklist and triggered the lasers which fused hydrogen into helium in the reactors. Building thrust, he dialed the reaction to a fine stream and tightened the bounce-back collars that collided photons and particles in the reaction mass, shooting plasma rearward past lightspeed. The CV turned in a wide arc before lancing off into the interstellar depths—a violent jet of Cherenkov radiation and quantum distortion the only evidence of passage.

* * *

Myles Roma, Legate Prima Excellence of his Holiness Sassa the Second, nerved himself to smile at the honor guard of smartly dressed Companions. His stomach turned uneasily at their powerful presence. Behind each of the

stern expressions, behind the scarred faces (why didn't their
medical personnel see to such disfigurements?) he just knew
that they were sneering and snickering at his fat body. What
did they expect? Should he appear as a starving pauper?
Corpulence—in Sassa—was a sign of prosperity. Especially
in times like these when so many worlds were starving.

He gave them another smile as he waddled past their tight
ranks to the gravcar. And to think! Why each of them must
have killed a hundred men with their cold-blooded hands
alone. Not to mention the ones they had brutally blown
apart. He fought his desire to shudder—and won.

It had been an honor when the Holy Sassa appointed him
to this mission, but to stand face-to-face with these killers
left a frightening sensation of vulnerability in his fat belly.
Dealing with court intrigue on Sassa didn't compare to this.

Behind Myles Roma his band of attendants and courtiers
flocked from the lock in carnival mood, happy at the chance
to lord it over barbarians with their fine dress and refined
manners.

Myles glanced about, seeking the Lord Commander, and
stopped when a beautiful woman who stood at the head of
the reception committee caught his eye and held it. His
heart skipped a beat as he studied her. Hair like iced gold
had been braided into a tight shimmering coil about her
left arm. She wore formfitting white, stitched with glittering
thread and remarkable Sylenian jewels—nothing else sparkled in so many brilliant colors. A golden choker hugged
her graceful neck. With a start he recognized it to be a
helmet field collar for a space suit. By the Holy Sassa, her
whole outfit consisted of battle armor suitable for hard vacuum! At the same time, it displayed her body most remarkably. He tore his gaze from the swell of high breasts and
let his eyes trace the narrow waist and flat belly, the swell
of her hips, and then down those marvelous long, muscular
legs. She had a lithe tigress look about her that fascinated
him and caused his pulse to race.

He inclined his head and graced her with one of his finest
smiles. She returned his greeting—and almost brazenly at
that. Well, he would have to speak to the Lord Commander
after they had concluded their business—or even before.
What a pleasure it would be to have that incredibly beautiful woman attend to his needs. After all, the Legate admit-

ted to himself, the courtesans he'd brought with him would always be there. This azure-eyed jewel with so perfect a body would only be his so long as he was in the Lord Commander's base.

He waited patiently, eyes searching for the Lord Commander between bouts of speculation on the blonde beauty. To his surprise it was she who stepped forward when his company finally managed to organize behind him.

She walked up to the gravcar and her long-limbed grace only fueled his lust—her hips swinging just enough to entice without being blatant. Her movements, he realized, were not an affectation, but her nature. She bowed low, incredible blue eyes meeting his without the least hesitation.

Her voice carried firmly through the room. "My Lord Myles Roma, Legate Prima Excellence to His Holiness Sassa the Second, I am Wing Commander Skyla Lyma. In the name of the Lord Commander, I bid you welcome to the holdings of the Itreatic Asteroids. As a token of the respect in which we hold His Holiness, we have taken the liberty of placing quarters at the disposal of yourself and your staff. The Lord Commander sends his regards and hopes that you will find all to your satisfaction. The Lord Commander sends his most sincere regrets and apologies as he was detained by his duties and responsibilities to the station and was unable to meet you in person. Should you need any assistance, feel free to ask for me and I shall insure your stay to be a pleasant one." She bowed again, hand to her shapely breast.

Myles Roma smiled easily. The Lord Commander was detained? Staffa did not come on the run to meet Sassa's Legate? Indeed? Did the mercenary upstart think. . . . Or wait. Might it not be cunning on Staffa's part? Perhaps this was a means of raising the ante? A shrewd move by an expert businessman to drive a harder bargain for his services?

"We are most delighted, Wing Commander. It is our pleasure to accept your fine hospitality. We look forward to long and profitable meetings with the Lord Commander and his officers. I fear, however, that it has been a tiring journey. Your offer of hospitality falls like rain on the tortured sands of Etaria and refreshes us with expectations."

She bowed again. "Then I shall not delay you, Legate

Prima Excellence." She lifted a hand and the gravcar trundled past the saluting ranks of Companions and into the maze that made up the main station of Itreata. His face like a mask, Myles glanced uneasily at the polished white walls.
Why do I have the feeling that she was lying?

* * *

Skyla Lyma stalked into the comm room and scowled around at the operators who bent over the banks. "Damn it! *Where the hell is he?*"

Monitors displayed various station functions while security personnel kept track of deep space detectors and security systems. Other technicians studied readouts from the power plants. The communications net shunted signals from all across Free Space over to the intelligence branch. As always, the place hummed, except now, Skyla could feel the tension.

One of the signal women looked up, headset covering most of a wealth of thick red hair. "Wing Commander, we've tried everywhere. I even took the liberty of sending a man to his private quarters." Her face tightened as if she fought the urge to wince. "We've got teams scouring the whole complex. Other teams are searching the factories, the storage casks, maintenance sheds . . . everything we can think of." She shook her head, baffled. "It's as if . . . as if he just dropped into hyperspace."

Skyla knotted a fist at her side, feeling foolish in the scintillating bejeweled battle armor. Worse, it reflected like a broken rainbow across the banks of computers. "Keep at it. We've got until tomorrow to get him down here to entertain that pus-gutted buffoon." Turning, she stalked out into the central corridor, caught a shuttle, and sent it streaking to her quarters.

She palmed the latch and stormed into her rooms with a boiling anger stewing in her heart. As the door snicked shut behind her, she allowed the other thoughts, the unthinkable ones, to surface. What if one of the assassins had finally gotten him? What if somehow, some way, someone had penetrated his security and. . . . Rotted Gods, no! Her anger ebbed to be replaced by a fear she hadn't experienced in years.

She took a deep breath and held it, counting slowly until her racing pulse slowed. She unsnapped the helmet collar and ran her fingers along the sharp-angled jewels to release the suit. She peeled out of the lower half and glared at a pink welt of scar tissue running jaggedly down her leg. The healed wound had finally begun to lose the reddish tinge. Close call, that one.

To cover a budding fear, she forced herself to inspect her body in the reflective surface of her suit rack. Not bad for thirty-five years of war and mayhem—and not a little battle damage in the process. True, some of the more damaging scars had been surgically corrected. And she kept herself fit—as if Staffa's Wing Commander could conduct herself otherwise.

Staffa. Where in hell are you? She moved to the comm and tried his quarters again. Worry fermented. "Damn you, Staffa. What are you doing? If this is another of your training drills. . . ."

She dropped on the sleeping platform and laced her long legs into a lotus position. Back straight, she closed her eyes and slowly reviewed each conversation she'd had with him. Her unrest grew as she remembered his preoccupied expressions; the underlying tension in his body and posture; and the dissatisfaction in his voice.

The Praetor. It all goes back to that damned hospital room. Staffa, you can't see it because it's all in your mind. You think you're acting normally, but your thought processes are all screwed up.

She placed those thoughts to one side, called for a computer access. She scanned the medical records and cursed. She made another patch through.

"Psychology department, Andray here."

"Has the Lord Commander been in, Andray? Has he taken any of the prescriptions we talked about?"

"Negative, Wing Commander."

She cut the connection, patched through to security, and traced Staffa's every movement since she'd seen him last. She split the screen and noted each instance where Staffa had come in contact with people, asking for an update and security clearance for those personnel present. Two hours later, she'd drawn a negative. She had traced his path up to the time the Ashtan CV had left from a pharmaceutical

supply drop. Thereafter, no one had seen him. He hadn't
accessed comm.

Could he have been abducted on the CV? She called up
the records and watched the security files. Not once did the
pilot leave the craft. From each of the cameras she watched
the entire drop, never seeing the slightest impropriety, not
even a hint of breached security.

Besides, unless they knocked him cold, not even a group
of men could take the Lord Commander without a considerable disturbance. That gray combat armor could absorb a
small blast. Only his head would have been vulnerable to a
dart or gas.

Next she cataloged the arrival of the Sassan delegation
with the same attention to detail. She even went so far as to
monitor their conversations in the executive quarters she'd
provided. The Legate, Myles Roma, talked nervously about
Staffa's failure to meet him. She sneered when the Legate
began talking about her, and shut it off when he got to the
graphic details.

"Terguzzian maggot," she whispered. Unbidden, her
mind formed an image of Staffa, gray eyes clear, body spare
and lean. She remembered the intelligence in his eyes, the
slight quivers at the corners of his mouth as he hid his
humor from the others. Curiously, she recalled the way his
face had looked when she had awakened in the hospital unit
that last time. Idly she rubbed slim fingers across her palm.
It came to her suddenly that he'd had his armored gloves
off. His skin had been pressed against hers. How warm it
had been.

She growled to kill the sensations the thought roused.

A wry smile curled her lips. Staffa—no matter how per-
plexing—was at least a man! *Rotted Gods, am I going to
have to pander to that Sassan pollution for long? If he tries
to touch me, I'll break his maggot-eating neck.*

"Get your thrice-cursed ass back here, Staffa!"

The Praetor . . . the Praetor . . . it all started with the
Praetor. She stood and walked to her kit. The plastic cartridge felt cool as she pulled it from the bag. Turning, she
walked to the dispenser where she drew a bulb of Myklene
amber ale. She tapped the cartridge against her hip as she
settled on the bed and cupped the ale. As she drank, she
studied the gray plastic record chip in silence.

An hour later she continued to stare at the enigmatic cartridge. "If he hasn't shown up by this time tomorrow," she promised. She adjusted the gravity on the sleeping platform and ordered the light out.

Skyla stared into the darkness, rethinking each of the potential explanations for Staffa's disappearance. Aware of the tape, she realized her fingers were tapping anxiously against the fabric. Efforts at sleep proved fruitless, images of Staffa in danger drifted out of her subconscious. A deadly foreboding rose from the primitive depths of her mind: visions of Staffa dead, his gray eyes popped from his head, blood spiraling, crystallized in decompressed corridors. . . .

"Rot it all!" She sat up, the lights brightening at her movement. "Fantasies of the mind, Skyla. You're batty as a ring-nosed teenager!" Angered at her irresolution, she took the cartridge and slipped it into the comm. Her finger hovered over the button that would run the tape.

Before she could act, a voice from comm startled her. "Wing Commander Lyma? This is Comm Central."

"Thank God, you've found Staffa? Is he all right?"

"No, ma'am. We still haven't located the Lord Commander. We've just received communications from the security monitor beacons, ma'am. A Regan Imperial cruiser has emerged from light jump and is decelerating. They are asking for docking permission. They report they bear an official envoy from Tybalt the Imperial Seventh, and request an audience with the Lord Commander at his convenience."

"Holy Rotted Gods," she sighed wearily. "First the Sassans and now Rega." Her fingers knotted as she considered the ramifications. "Very well. Grant them permission. Let's see. . . . Put them in at dock 16-A. That should couple with their lock design. Have staff make a blood-and-thunder preparation of the quarters—as far as you can get them from the Sassans. By the Etarian heretics, I hope they don't murder each other. If you can find any of the Companions still sober, we need another honor guard—and detail some of them to patrol the guest quarters. I don't want any trouble from either Sassa or Rega—and they'll have plenty of spies with them."

"We're on it, Wing Commander. We'll keep in touch."

"Never mind. I'm getting dressed. I'll be right down."

She slipped into the jeweled armor again, pulling the tight

cloth over her legs and sealing it. Her worries about Staffa built. The two empires had reacted faster than even she had suspected. Both sides, reeling from internal strife, were anxious—unprepared though they might be—to plunge into a cataclysmic final confrontation.

A cold chill settled in her spine. She closed her eyes, biting her lip. Snapping the epaulet that held her braid in place on her shoulder, she straightened. With all space about to come loose, what would they pay for Staffa's loyalty—or his death?

As she palmed the door latch she demanded of the empty air, "Damn you, Staffa, *where are you?*"

* * *

Ily Takka luxuriated in the bubbling hot water of the bath. The decadent opulence of Itreata had taken her by complete surprise. She'd expected some Spartan asteroid base with minimal gravity, slightly unbalanced miners bouncing off the walls, and hydroponic yeast cakes for food. Itreata, it turned out, had been built in a planetoid, a rogue moon—with 0.8 gravities and all the amenities of Rega—if not more.

Ily had more or less expected the presence of the Sassan envoy. That they had arrived first constituted a minor annoyance—but nothing more. That Staffa had failed to meet her at the dock, however, caused her unease. A clever move on his part, no doubt, which would be explained soon enough.

She swirled the water, letting her long black hair cover her breasts like an ebony mantelet. It amused her that her attendants—all male—suffered between their desire to stare and their fear of who and what she was. She got distinct pleasure from their discomfort and wondered if Staffa were watching.

On that odd chance, she purposely adopted a position meant to entice. Saucily, she moved through the water, displaying her perfect body, allowing her hair to wrap around her in a sensuous mist.

She ran the reception through her mind. Not badly done for having been called to order so quickly. The Companions had been truly impressive with their scars and their hard-eyed gazes. One or two had been weaving on their feet. More than one had openly stared, allowing admiration to slip through their warrior's glare. All in all, it had affected her more than if they'd all been letter perfect. These were men—fighters first, not parade ground martinets—and they made no bones about it.

Ily shifted and stood up, allowing the water to drain off her as she threw her head back and filled her lungs. And what, pray tell, was the relationship between Wing Commander Lyma and Staffa kar Therma? Lovers? If so, Skyla would be a potential rival.

Ily stepped from the bath and into the fresher, enjoying the sensations of warm air on her skin. Dry, she allowed her men to dress her, almost laughing aloud. They fumbled over her, trying to do the job without touching her sacrosanct flesh. Using their confusion and orchestrated mistimings, she watched their expressions turn ghastly as their hands accidentally brushed her. Each drew back as if her flesh were fire; a tiny sadism she delighted in.

Her meeting with Skyla Lyma had been brief but disconcerting. She'd met that bow and looked into those of icy crystal blue eyes. This Skyla Lyma was no hot-squeezing bed fluff. Rather, Ily felt she had met a worthy opponent. Lyma had met her gaze with an equally measuring one that controlled and challenged; and that, Ily decided, could have an effect on the way she manipulated the Lord Commander. If the blonde wench were his lover as well as his military confidante, Ily's plans would have to be adjusted accordingly.

A subtle tension had radiated from Skyla Lyma. Ily paused, finger on chin, brow creased. The Wing Commander had been unsettled—and not just by an unexpected visit from Rega. The very air in the station rippled with unease—with suspense. Coupled with the fact that Staffa had not come to greet her, that bespoke trouble of some kind. Among the troops? No, the Companions had stood easily and unconcerned. Rather, it had been among the officers and administrators. A political problem? And the Sassans had just arrived? Divided loyalties among the upper echelons perhaps? Some wishing to go Sassan—some siding with Rega?

Ily Takka's perfect mouth flickered momentarily in a satisfied smile. Trouble meant leverage to a woman with her skills. Leverage meant advantage could be taken. *Power may be up for grabs here—and I will have it!*

No, things in the Itreatic Asteroids were not going to go as smoothly as she and Tybalt had hoped. Of course, if the Wing Commander proved as formidable as she appeared, a drop of thrakis would solve that. Thrakis was a rare poison, and dreadfully expensive, but it left no traces which an autopsy could detect.

* * *

Bruen walked out among the trees, his steps crunching the long pine needles underfoot. The wind whispered among the branches overhead and he filled his nostrils with the vanilla scent of the pine-laden air. As he had hoped, Arta Fera stepped into view on the trail. She wore a loose black dress that didn't hide the charms of her young body. The leather belt at her waist held a holstered pistol—required dress for all Seddi now that revolt swept Targa. Shadows dappled her fine features and the sunlight that filtered through the pines gleamed in her chestnut hair.

Bruen stopped and rubbed a frail hand over his aching hip as he stared up through the green limbs to the little patches of sky. How pleasant the day had turned out. He caught Arta's shy greeting smile and turned to walk with her in silence until they entered a grassy meadow.

All in all, she'd been progressing beyond expectations. In the last five standard years, she'd had an entire education inserted in her fertile brain. Each day, she spent four hours under a brain cap, taking direct information from the Mag Comm. *And what else has the machine implanted? What terrifying secret might it have left triggered to a word or action?*

Bruen had carefully reviewed each of her lessons from the tape. But, of course, he had no guarantee the Mag Comm didn't hold something back.

"You look pensive, dear girl." Bruen tried to stretch a friendly smile over his age-battered features as he caught the anxiety in her expression.

She pushed her red-brown hair back when the breeze teased it. "How do I tell you what I think, Magister? I don't know myself. I . . . I'm confused. From the time I was a child. . . . Well, they taught me to dedicate myself to the Blessed Gods. Now you tell me I am to be an assassin? It's . . . it's just inconceivable. If I didn't know you and trust your wisdom so, I'd. . . ." She shook her head, mouth tight with frustration.

He nodded as he glanced up at the fluffy white clouds that drifted over the ridge-broken western horizon. "Why did the Etarians have you scrubbing the floors, dear girl? You're much too precious for that. It's a poor use for pulchritude at best."

Arta blushed and looked down; her fingers caressed the cool black fabric of her dress. "I was under penalty for unseemly behavior, Magister. I—I raised my voice when the High Priest turned my initiation down in favor of another."

How far can I push her? Is she ready for the next step?

He cackled angrily. "Hah! Etarians! And a good thing it was too, dearest. Don't you know they auction the girls for their 'initiation'? It's a gang rape, you know."

"Magister! It is not! It's the Blessing of the Service ritual!" She puffed in exasperation. "We all looked forward to the consecration of our bodies to the service of the Blessed Gods!"

"They auction you children off to the highest bidder," he corrected, voice tart. "It so happens your consecration coincided with the arrival of a Sassan Vicar. He liked dark-skinned girls with more, um, more ample bodies than yours. The Blessed High Priest knew that if he'd auctioned you, he'd take a loss over what they could get on a more marketable piece of meat."

"You make it sound like . . . like whoremongering! You're blaspheming the Sacred Rites! It's a lie!"

"Whoremongering? I couldn't have said it better." He observed the sudden change in her eyes.

"You don't know! We serve the Goddess. What better way than by bringing pleasure to a man?"

"For a price, dear Arta, for a price. Isn't that what whores do? Wrapping it up in the silken gauze of religion is nothing more than—"

"*Damn you, Bruen! Shut your lying mouth!*" Her eyes glazed in amber fury and her face twisted.

Yes, she is ready. I can do no more with her. The time

has come to send her to Butla. Oh, Bruen, you doddering senile fool, you will miss her, too. You're too old for revolution.

Bruen pointed down to the pulse pistol that had centered on his belly, safety off. Color washed from her face, her mouth dropping open. The pistol, so rock-steady before, began to tremble before it fell clattering from her lifeless fingers.

"Call it what you will," he said, humbly, picking the weapon up and clicking the safety on before handing it back to her. "Not only would you raise your voice to the High Priest, you would have clawed the fat girl's eyes out."

The anger still smoldered, though tempered by shame. "Normally, Magister, I don't lose my temper like that."

"Oh?" A withered eyebrow went up. "Remember the day I told you you would make an excellent assassin? Itreatic teaching machines are very expensive . . . and extremely difficult to obtain, I might add. I most vehemently object to you smashing such precious computers against large rocks. I believe it was a previously established fact that rock is more durable than n-dimensional superconductor. Fydor has tried valiantly to save bits and pieces, but he says the gallium arsenide chips are hopelessly fractured."

Her shoulders fell along with her gaze. "I'm sorry. I . . . Oh, Rotted Gods, nothing, forget it! Why am I so confused? What's happening to me?"

He chuckled gently and lifted her chin with a fragile finger. "It is that temper, dearest, which is your strength."

And it is that temper we have worked so hard to channel and dam in that beautiful mind of yours. Still, quantum functions affect the mind. An unlucky random event, and the carefully set trigger could snap, initiating a catastrophic explosion. I must watch myself more closely. She is so very sensitive to sexual stimuli.

His arm around her shoulder, he led her to an unevenly canted bench under a sweeping Ponderosa branch. "Here, sit. Let's talk about assassination and death."

She pulled her long legs up under her robe. "I'm not even sure I could come right out and kill a person. I've never even killed a. . . ."

"But I have, haven't I?" He glanced away, taking a deep breath. "You've learned all we can teach you here.

We're sending you to someone who can give you what we can't."

"Sending me away?"

He smiled to still her sudden panic. "He's the best, Arta. The time has come for you to learn from a master."

She closed her eyes. "Why, Magister? Why me? What makes you think I'll be an assassin?"

"Because it's your talent. You know the goals of the Seddi. You know how the universe works. The dance of the quanta are the reflection of God's thoughts—neither good nor evil. Those concepts are the creation of the human mind. To improve the lot of humanity, we must act to replace the tyrants who oppress the human condition with those who would nurture it and stop the suffering. Assassination is but one of the ways to achieve that end. More than once, you've asserted your desire to help us free humanity from the tyrants. Do you wish to renounce your vows? You can, you know. Simply tell me."

She shook her head. "No. I've studied the history too well. I know what's happened in the last two centuries."

He nodded sagely. "Yours is a special talent. We've seen it in you from the beginning."

"How do you know all this about me? Of all the people on all the worlds, do you watch each of them?"

His face crinkled into corduroy. "I wish we could. In your case, dearest girl, one of our agents spotted your fiery spirit the day you were sold to the Etarians. We spend a lot of time watching the slave markets. The potential there is surprising. The most interesting people sell their children into slavery."

She thought about that. "And do you know who my parents were?"

"Many people—in this wretched age of ours—have lost their parents."

She shuddered and jerked her head in a quick nod.

"You're fine as you are, precious Arta." He paused and pushed her away, seeing the upheavals his words had created. "Ah, to be young again. Maybe I could allow my virtue to slide and take advantage of your confusion? It's been so long since I've ravished a 'nice' girl! Since you don't approve of my dalliances with prostitutes—"

"*Magister!* You never give up!" she laughed nervously, color rising in her alabaster flesh.

"No, dearest, I never do." *And if you could only know the curse of those words.*

* * *

Andray Sornsen sat before the monitor in Skyla's quarters with a foot pulled up so he could brace his chin on his knee. For long moments after the record cube Skyla had taken from the Myklenian hospital had played out, he sat in silence, a pensive frown on his blunt face.

Unable to stand it any longer, Skyla asked, "Well?"

Andray took a deep breath and gave her a sidelong look out of languid brown eyes. "How did you get the courage to play that tape? Knowing it was taken of the Lord Commander in a very private moment?"

Skyla bristled. "I didn't bring you up here to analyze me. I want to know what the Praetor did to Staffa in that hospital room."

Andray worked his lips and made a clicking noise with his mouth. "You know, I've made a study of Staffa—on the sly, of course. His coldly dispassionate approach to problems has always intrigued me. Hearing the Praetor call him a machine was very enlightening." Andray's eyes gleamed as he met her hot glare. "He was, you know."

"Was? Past tense?"

Andray nodded. "Computer, replay, please. Wing Commander, watch closely. This is fascinating. A study in psychological brilliance."

Skyla watched the scene in the hospital as Staffa and the Praetor talked.

"Freeze." Andray gestured at the monitor. "Here's where the Praetor gives the first clue about what he's done. He tells Staffa, 'I am your creator.' And this second claim, 'What a master forges, so can he break,' that's significant. Look at the old man. He's gloating, assured of success at what should be his last and most bitter moment in life— he's practically gleeful instead."

"And Staffa misses it all. He should be growing wary at this point." Skyla shook her head. "That's not like him."

Andray smiled humorlessly. "Precisely. You see, Staffa

has already begun to fall into the trap. The Praetor sprung it with the word 'creator.' With that, he pulled the first brick from the dam that bottled Staffa's emotions. Now, watch what happens."

The cube resumed its play.

"The Praetor brags again about his ability to destroy Staffa," Andray told her. "He sets him up, knowing full well how thorough the conditioning is in Staffa's mind. See? He's laying the foundations for guilt which will eat at the Lord Commander once the hypnotic conditioning is broken."

"Freeze," Skyla ordered, pointing at the screen. "What about this business of 'the people.' What's the Praetor trying to do here?"

Andray tugged at his ear. "It's a setup, a trap. No matter what, Staffa still respects the Praetor—and his old mentor is telling Staffa that he has a flaw. You know the Lord Commander as well as anyone, Wing Commander. What will his response be?"

"He'll act immediately to correct the deficiency." Skyla's gut crawled. "Blessed Gods, of course!"

Andray cocked his head. "That strikes a chord, does it?"

"He pumped me about . . . going out among the people." She propped herself against the desk, eyes closed. "That's what he's done. Staffa, you fool! You played right into his hands!"

"But he doesn't know that," Andray told her mildly. "This next part is critical. Chrysla and the infant have obsessed Staffa for years. Remember, his emotional responses were suppressed, inhibited, so Chrysla and the child became mythic in Staffa's mind. Therefore when the Praetor admits that he not only took Staffa's only happiness from him, but sold his son and enslaved and raped his wife, that pulls the final brick from the wall and the whole thing tumbles into rubble before an unleashed tide of conflicting emotions that Staffa doesn't have the ability to deal with."

"He didn't turn into a blubbering idiot," Skyla protested.

"Of course not. His brain has been trained to deal with problems in a highly sophisticated logical sequence—a left brain approach, if you will. Those established neural pathways kept him from going berserk, but those old behaviors won't dominate forever. His brain is flooded with new stimuli that affect his ability to make decisions."

Skyla crossed her arms, teeth grinding. "Worse? Until he goes completely mad? Is that what you're trying to tell me? That Staffa . . ."

"No, Skyla." She tensed at the feel of his hand on her arm. "Think of it this way. As a result of the Praetor's tampering, Staffa has lived most of his life with half of a personality. Now, all of a sudden, the other half of himself has been released. The brain is a remarkable and plastic organ. There's an excellent chance that he'll be able to integrate this and come out stronger for it."

"An excellent chance? Not a certainty?"

Andray's gaze didn't waver.

Skyla gasped her frustration and paced nervously across the room. "And those last mental triggers? The ones hidden in the personality centers of the brain?"

"The last round in the Praetor's aresenal. He knew he had Staffa in shambles already. That was the *coup-de-gras*." Andray paused. "You know, the Praetor was brilliant in his own twisted way. He knew that Staffa would find the other triggers, but he knew that the one place Staffa would never look would be in his sense of identity. That part of Staffa's personality stood on a teetering foundation of rotten wood."

Skyla rubbed the back of her neck and shook her head. "What about Chrysla? If Staffa was such a mess, what did she ever see in him?"

"You don't know very much about her, do you?" Andray watched her pensively. "And I hear the resentment in your voice, Wing Commander."

"What are you—"

"Whoa!" Andray raised his hands defensively. "Your secret is safe with me."

"I don't know what you're—"

"Chrysla," Andray changed the subject, "wasn't just a brainless beauty. At the time of her capture, she was completing course work in clinical psychiatry. Staffa fascinated her—and that doesn't mean she wasn't a very complicated and complex woman. She loved him with all of her heart, and she began to pick at the Praetor's conditioning."

Andray shrugged. "The problem was that she was a student and had no real experience."

"If you know all this, why didn't you work with Staffa?"

Andray gave her a cool look. "The reason there's a psychological department on the Itreatic Asteroids is because Chrysla wanted one. You see, I was Chrysla's professor before she ended up in Staffa's hands. Problem was, by the time I finally arrived here, she was gone. The Praetor had stolen her away. During the following years, would *you* have asked the Lord Commander to submit to psychotherapy?"

Skyla studied him through slitted eyes. "You know, I'm not sure I like you, Professor."

He met her stare blandly. "You don't have to. I'd just as soon not be here, myself. You see, I've compiled fascinating data—all of which will rot here with me. Do you seriously believe the Lord Commander would allow a psychologist who'd studied the Companions loose?"

"So why did you come?"

Andray smiled sadly. "You never knew Chrysla. And perhaps, being a woman, you wouldn't understand. She had a magnetism that . . . well, I was in love with her."

"All that aside, what about Staffa? Where do you think he went?"

Andray stood and straightened his tunic. "From the tape, I'd say he's gone in search of his son. He'll try and contact the Seddi."

"What? They've been trying to assassinate him for years."

"That may be, but the Praetor said they have Staffa's son. And I remind you, he's not going to be thinking with his usual dispassionate objectivity. The mood swings will only get worse as his brain seeks to return to normalcy. If you wish to save him from harm, I suggest you find him— and quickly." Andray bowed. "Good day, Wing Commander."

Skyla stood rooted as the psychologist left the room. A terrible ache filled her chest.

* * *

Given the political situation in Kaspa, it took three days before Butla Ret's illegal aircar slid down out of the evening sky above the hidden temple of Makarta. Bruen stood at the base of the cliff where a hollow in the rock protected the landing port and nodded to himself, a sinking in his breast carrying his heart ever lower.

"She's just a child," he whispered under his breath as the aircar settled lightly on the brightly lit pad.

Arta came from her stone-walled cell, her Initiate's robe wrapped tightly about her. A glowing goddess, she entered the main hall on light feet, ever curious eyes sweeping the occupants. She stopped as Butla Ret stepped out of the aircar.

Ret was a big man with skin as black as the deepest cavern. He bowed to Bruen, and said in a deep bass voice, "Greetings, Magister."

"It's good to see you, Butla." Bruen smiled and hugged his old friend. Then he stepped back, the words reluctant in his throat. "Meet Arta Fera."

Butla turned and walked around the girl, studying Arta with gleaming black eyes. His broad lips split in a wide smile to expose glistening white teeth. A dream might move so fluidly, soundlessly, his feet seeming to grace the floor for all his muscular bulk. A motion of poetry, he made a decision and nodded.

"Arta, my dear one," Bruen bowed, struggling to keep his voice steady. Curses and pollution, this was going to be harder than he thought. "Meet Butla Ret. He will be your teacher in the fine arts and weapons of assassination. Have you an objection?"

She looked at him frantically, only to see no guidance in his veiled blue eyes. "Magister, I. . . . But so quickly? It's. . . . No," she murmured, "I have no objections."

His heart felt like lead.

Butla Ret bowed, a somberness in his expression. His bull-deep voice sent vibrations through the very rock. "My pleasure, Arta Fera. I look forward to working with you. I swear upon my honor to do my very best to teach you my arts. Upon that word, I offer my life without hesitation or mental reservation whatsoever."

Some quantum seeded memory in Arta's mind triggered at the words. As if without volition, she repeated, "And I swear upon my honor to do my very best to learn your valued lessons. Upon that word, I offer my life."

Arta's eyes widened, first mystification, then understanding in her expression. When she looked back at Bruen, it was with sober assessment.

"Gather your things, Arta. Butla will be taking you with him for now." Bruen glanced over to see Magister Hyde, his antique face drawn and serious. The elder's watery blue eyes remained neutral, but he nodded slightly.

Bruen stepped close, heart hammering at his thin sternum. "Go in health and high spirit, Arta. You are Seddi now. Butla will see to sending the Initiate's robe back to us. If you ever return here, you will wear First Order Master's dress."

Her eyes glimmered as she fought tears, then she reached up to kiss his cheek. "Thank you, Magister. Watch your purse around those wicked women you like to lie about."

"Why, I . . ." Bruen stumbled, then he sighed, "Oh, bother."

Taking a breath, she turned to Butla Ret and ventured, "I hope I don't let you down, Butla Ret."

The deep-bass voice sounded subdued. "So do I, Arta Fera. For in my world there is no failure—only death."

Ret reached out and she put her hand in his. The Master Assassin led her to the aircar.

Bruen watched the craft rise and scuttle off to the north, and bloody Kaspa.

"What have we wrought, Hyde?" he wondered. His friend only lifted an age-sagged shoulder and coughed.

"Magister?" an Initiate called, coming from the cavern. "It is the Mag Comm, Magister. It calls for you."

"It is going to ask about the girl." Hyde sighed and spat into the darkness. "I wish we hadn't informed it we were giving Arta to Butla."

"Yes, I suppose so," Bruen grunted, gaze still on the black sky where the aircar had vanished.

Hyde's faded eyes studied Bruen carefully. "You care too much for her, Brother."

"Yes."

"You act as if you have just lost a daughter instead of a—"

Bruen lifted a tired hand, cutting Hyde's rattly voice off. "A daughter yes. That's exactly what she was. And tell me,

Hyde, how should I feel sending her off to become a tool of revolution? I'm sacrificing a child I love."

"It's war, Bruen," Hyde's answer came gruffly followed by a short spell of hacking. "If you haven't committed yourself to fight, you've served us poorly."

Bruen painfully lowered his eyes from the horizon. "No, old friend, I serve you well. But a man would expect some calluses to have formed on his soul by now. Instead of getting easier, this dispatching of youth becomes ever harder."

"The machine is waiting. What will you tell it?"

Bruen lifted a shoulder. "A version of the truth, Brother. And a bit of a lie."

Hyde rasped a breath into his lungs and shuffled for the portal. "I hope, for all our sakes, you can continue to mask your lies, Bruen. I've begun to worry about you."

"Because of the girl?" He followed Hyde's steps, wishing his hip didn't always hurt so.

"Yes."

Bruen nodded to himself. *Indeed, I am a crotchety old fool, carried away with pathetic sentimentality for a psychological time bomb I myself have helped to program. And now the machine waits? Ah, indeed, Great One, our machinations knit in a deeper weave.*

I miss her. It hurts.

Let the machine Deity cope with *that*. The Mag Comm never could understand or deal with emotion. Such illogical sorrow should confuse pustulant hell out of that soulless cybernetic beast.

CHAPTER VIII

Skyla twisted her long thick braid around her wrist as she read the reports at her personal comm. Vanished. And not a single security system had been breached. As the comm tech had said, Staffa might have simply stepped into a different dimension.

Her gaze went, unbidden, to the comm screen where the Ashtan CV rested so innocently against the dock. Staffa had disappeared just before the vessel discharged the pharmacy supplies and pushed out. She could find no evidence of tampered security. She chuckled dryly. "Why should that surprise me? It's his system."

"Wing Commander!" a breathless voice blurted over comm. "Will you please come quickly. We have a message from the Lord Commander. It was placed in time delay. He orders that all command grade officers assemble in the C section briefing room."

Skyla left at a run, hardly aware that her long braid bounced unrestrained behind her.

She slid into the briefing room, among the first to arrive, eyes immediately glued to the image of Staffa where he dominated the screen. His new beard glistened blackly on his cheeks and the light shimmered on his immaculate gray combat armor while his weapons belt looked freshly shined. He had pulled his straight black hair over his left ear, clasped by the usual jeweled hair clip. His expression seemed unusually calm.

When the last command officer, Septa Aygar, of the *Simva Ast* pounded through the door, the babble of conversation died.

Skyla nodded to the tech who ran the program.

Staffa smiled and gestured with his hand for them to be seated. "My loyal officers," he began in a soft voice, "I

151

have undoubtedly caused some strained nerves and anguished moments by leaving this on time delay. However, I did so with good reason." The smile widened lustily. "I know you all too well. I needed time to allow the dust to settle . . . or I'd have all of you rushing to join me." The holo raised a hand. "Not that I'd mind your company, my loyal Companions, but this once, I want to be by myself."

He frowned and paced across the screen, then raised his head, gaze serious. "Soon, my Companions, you will be beset by the envoys of the Regan and Sassan Empires. Each will attempt to outbid the other for our services to establish one or the other as the supreme government of Free Space. Each wishes to be the ultimate power within the Forbidden Borders.

"I've given this no little thought. In fact, over the years, I have been more than aware of, and even helped devise, this final balance of power."

He paused to stroke his chin. "If you look at Free Space, it forms a rough pentahedron—barring the curve of space-time. Almost half of this we have helped hand to the Regan Empire. The other half we've managed to put in the palms of the Sassans. Our Itreatic Asteroids and the Twin Titans make only a pyramidal corner neatly bordering both imperial spheres of activity.

"And it remains all out of proportion. Two lions, my commanders, and one little mouse. Or so it would seem from the comparative amounts of territory and resources. How odd, then, that you will soon have both lions growling at each other while they wheedle to get the mouse's favor, eh?" His smile turned wicked.

Subdued nervous laughter staccatoed in the room.

"But *we* are the true strength in Free Space. And I'm not sure that we should meddle any further for the time being. Consider, my friends. Each of the empires is staggered by war. The Sassans have bled their worlds dry. The Regans—economically suffering to pay off their debts—have alienated their people and revolution brews.

"It is my considered opinion, therefore, that we have nothing to gain, at this juncture, by joining either side. The final conflict would, in my eyes, bring nothing but a dark age of anarchy." He lifted a finger. "And where, good commanders, would we spend our pay? Who would buy our computers, our ceramics, or our metals if all the economies were broken and shattered?"

Skyla could see somber nods around the room.

"Nor is that the only consideration." Staffa continued pacing, hands clasped behind him, head down in thoughtful pose. "I don't know about the rest of you, but I'm tired. I want to take some time off and relax."

Staffa braced his feet. "People, I've watched our performance. There have been too many close calls in the last couple of years. If we do decide to choose sides, I want us all in top form, with fresh minds and reflexes. A hasty judgment now could lead to disaster. I want you all to think about where we're going, and what the future brings. I need you to give me your best thoughts—and you can't do that while you're exhausted."

Skyla frowned to herself. *That wasn't the plan, Staffa. The idea was to turn quickly, to consolidate all of Free Space into one empire while they were off balance. What the hell has gotten into you?* But she knew.

He propped hard fists on his hips and laughed from deep in his belly as he swung around to face them. "We've stabilized it all, now let's take a year or so and see how things work out. Tasha, how long has it been now that you've pestered me because your garden gets started, you get flowers about to bud, and we're off to war for a few hundred Titan revolutions? Septa, you complain your children are strangers. Take some time and beat some obedience into that boy of yours. If he skips much more school, he'll never be able to fly a mining tug out of a shuttle hangar. Ryman, I know for a fact you piddle with a new power generating theory in your off-time aboard ship. Work on it now. I authorize any assistance you need from the labs."

As if Staffa knew where she'd be standing, his gaze met hers. "Skyla," that warm voice soothed her, "you've borne the brunt for too long. I've seen the weariness in your eyes. Take some time for yourself and relax. By the Rotted Gods, you've been the glue that holds us together." He paused and his voice softened. "I don't like the tension I see in you these days. Let the governing council handle the administration for a while. You've had too many close calls. I wouldn't. . . ." Her heart skipped as he smiled and waved it away. "Just take some time for yourself. You've earned it."

The tenderness in his words shocked her. *Wouldn't? Wouldn't what, Staffa? Want to lose me?* Her thoughts reeled as she rubbed her palm where his skin had touched hers.

Staffa turned, as if embarrassed, and paced back across the screen. "And as to the envoys who come begging, tell them no. It would be too easy to be manipulated into facing another Companion."

"As far as the administration of the Companions, you all know the contingency plans. Some of you will find supplemental instructions on your private comms.

"And me, I've already left to taste some fleshpots, buy some rugs, drink some ale, and sire some bastard brats. Not only that, I've never been fishing. I am going fishing. I hear the white sharks make an incredible challenge to a rod and reel on Riparious. We're all rich. Let's enjoy some of it for a while." He shook a finger. "But don't get fat! We're not stuffed Sassan maggots, and we'll have to go back to work in a year or two—so keep your skills up. I'll be back if anything looks threatening. So expect me!" The holo went blank.

Stunned silence.

A verbal avalanche rushed at her with everyone talking.

"Quiet! One at a time." Skyla hollered as she got to her feet.

Tasha stood up, a mountain of muscular flesh. He tugged at his ragged gray beard with a scarred hand, his single black eye searching faces. He pursed his lips and swallowed. "It is my studied opinion that we heed Staffa's advice. He's right about my flower bed. He's right about our money. What good is it to be a rich man if I don't spend it before I die?"

Ryman Ark got to his feet next, a fist on his belt as he gestured with his other hand. "Not only that, but I think Staffa's right about the political situation. Face it, Sassa's in ruins. Rega is ready to collapse from its own weight. They went too far too fast. I could see us going to war, losing a couple of ships and a lot of good people, and finding out there was no one left to pay us. No, Staffa makes sense. In a couple of years, the empires will have stabilized.

As long as they have each other to face, they'll have an incentive to compete . . . and we all know what that brings. In the meantime, we can make a financial killing while they buy battle computers and build ships. We might suck in some new technology, too, through their innovations. I say we tell them we aren't interested."

One by one they stood and spoke: The consensus was the same.

Skyla collected herself and motioned to be heard. "Very good, Companions." She gave them a predatory smile she didn't feel. "I'll go break the news to that fat Sassan and that hungry Regan bitch. I think we'll have more than enough entertainment around here when they go home to tell His Holiness and the Imperial Seventh that we're not playing this round."

They all laughed.

"All right, I guess that's it for now, people." She waved them toward the door, calling, "Tasha? Tap? Could I see you for a moment in my quarters?"

On the way out, Skyla heard Amrat saying, "White shark fishing? Sounds like my quaff of ale. If it's good enough for Staffa, I'll give it a try."

Riparious was going to be deluged by fishermen looking for eighty foot sharks.

Tap and Tasha fell in behind Skyla as she stepped into the corridor. The Lord Commander, as usual, had touched each of them with his usual genius.

"There's only one thing I can't figure," Tasha was saying. "This business of going off by himself, that's not like Staffa."

"What's he going to do about security, Skyla?" Tap asked. "He say anything special to you?"

"Let's get to my quarters, gentlemen. There are Sassan and Regan ears on Itreata."

"They couldn't get an ear up here." Tap protested.

"Maybe," Skyla said. "But I wouldn't underestimate Ily Takka. Call it woman's intuition."

By the time she led them into her private quarters, both Tap and Tasha looked as wary as hunted bears. Palming the latch to close her door, she turned and crossed her arms over her chest.

"Tap? Tasha? Staffa's in trouble—and we've got to help

him. This entire operation has to be handled with discretion and finesse. As soon as the empires realize he's alone and vulnerable, without Companion protection, what lengths do you think they'll go to get their hands on him?"

"Rotted Gods!" Tasha whispered. "Has the Lord Commander taken leave of his senses?"

Skyla jerked a short nod. "You might say that—and the first thing I've done is put extra security on Professor Sornsen. I'm making the records about what the Praetor did to Staffa available to you—eyes only. Now, gentlemen, we'd better get to work. This might well be the most important mission we've ever tackled. We've got to find Staffa without tipping anyone that we're looking for him—and find him before anyone else does."

*   *   *

Cold fury settled like a web over Ily Takka's thoughts. While she fumed, a second part of her mind found the irritation amusing. To put it simply, she wasn't used to waiting on anyone! Let alone a barbaric *mercenary*.

To calm herself, she fingered the badge of authority Tybalt had given her. Unlimited power—second only to the Imperial Seventh's—came from that small metal standard bearing the Imperial jessant-de-lis escutcheon of Rega. With it, she could command fleets, destroy worlds, to the point that her word became Rega's. Just the touch of that token of authority sent a shiver of anticipation through her.

She entered the small conference room and hesitated when she found the repugnantly obese body of Myles Roma—Legate for that simpering homosexual Sassan self-proclaimed god—had already seated himself. Worse, his people crowded all around. Somehow, they made way for her. She knew her eyes flashed with anger as she took the second seat—next to the Sassan. A third, obviously Staffa's, stood empty on the other side of the table. Her people attempted to crowd into the already stuffed room, creating pandemonium.

At that juncture, a cleverly disguised door behind the table opened and Wing Commander Skyla Lyma stepped out. A sudden quiet filled the room. The shuffling, cursing, and open threats between Sassan and Regan vanished.

The Wing Commander cleared her throat. "I think if the various aides would be so kind as to clear the room, I can handle the business at hand with the two delegates." And she stood, back stiff, blue-violet eyes impassive.

Ily caught her anger just before it exploded. She burned a look of disgust into the fat Sassan and turned. "I'm not sure the Sassan Legate is capable of dealing with the Companions on his own, but I am. If my people would follow the Wing Commander's request?"

One cool stare from her black eyes and they seemed to evaporate from the cramped quarters. Ily turned her frigid gaze on the Legate and raised an eyebrow.

Myles Roma swallowed nervously. He wrung his hands and looked up at the Wing Commander. "This is most unusual! I must protest! In the first place we came to speak with the Lord Commander. In the second, we are here to conduct *private* negotiations. You would have me discuss business before this . . . this *house spy*—and without my staff?"

Skyla Lyma had crossed her arms. Her stare—Ily could appreciate it—should have melted the blubbery white worm.

To make gain from this strategic setback Ily said, "I was candid, Wing Commander. I can handle myself. If the Legate truly needs so many to—"

"Out!" Roma cried, waving a pudgy hand at his entourage.

Ily narrowed her eyes in triumph. Yes, handling this insipid lard-thing would be like cutting hot fat with a molecular wire.

Amid squeals, groans, and complaints, the Sassan herd departed. Skyla extended an arm to lightly touch the wall and the door slid closed. Ily noticed the sudden discomfort the Sassan displayed as his eyes—sunk deep in their fat—considered the possible implications. Fool! Did he think the Companions guaranteed no security to diplomats in conference?

Ily allowed herself to relax and pulled a document pouch from her belt, aware of the impact it had on the quivering Legate.

Skyla settled herself in the remaining chair and laced her fingers together on the table. "The Lord Commander and the Companions would like to extend our appreciation to your respective governments. . . ."

Ily waved it aside. "I take it that the Lord Commander will not see us in person. May I ask why?"

The Wing Commander's eyes went icy. "You may."

The pause lengthened while Roma began to sweat. His odor, Ily discovered, even cut through his too-thick perfume. At last she added, "Why?"

"He's not here."

"I beg your pardon?" Myles Roma wheezed. "Not here? Not here to meet with the Legate Prima Excellence of his Holiness—"

"You weren't invited here, Legate," Skyla reminded sharply. "We hadn't anticipated that your arrival would come so soon after the Myklenian campaign. We've tried to extend every courtesy to you as we would hope you—"

"And we would grant the Lord Commander an instant hearing with His Holiness—"

"And we would do the same with the Lord Commander!" Skyla roared back, slapping a callused hand on the table. "*If he were here!*"

In the awkward silence, Ily asked professionally. "May I ask where he is?"

"Fishing."

"I beg your pardon?"

Skyla's stiff expression turned from Roma to her. "You heard me. Even Companions take time off. We're human. The Lord Commander is enjoying his leisure. You just missed him. He has instructed me to offer his sincere apologies, but the Companions are not hiring their services at the present time . . . to anyone."

Ily leaned back, hearing the Legate's intake of breath.

"You haven't even heard our offer!" Roma cried.

Skyla sighed. "It might be worth our while if you offered some way to penetrate the Forbidden Borders. Outside of that, we've enough money to see us through for a couple of years. You would offer planets? We have the Itreatic Asteroids. Power? That we control already. Perhaps you would give us each a world to govern? Well, possibly you might entice one or two of the command officers—but it would have to be a good world. Myklene perhaps? No, I can see it in your eyes. We're not worth that good a world."

Ily laughed sourly. "So, you would tell me that with both empires united and the final conflict on the brink of arising, two envoys arrive willing to sell their souls to hire you—and the Lord Commander casually says, 'Sorry, not interested.' " Her keen mind began peeling away the layers of potential deceit. Of course, the bastard was driving the price up! Perfectly played!

Skyla pulled two packets from her belt and shoved them across the table. "That's right. The Lord Commander's reasons are detailed in these communiques. Please see that your respective governments receive and consider them. You will see our reasons for declining service at this time."

The Wing Commander stood.

"This is simply preposterous!" Roma exploded. "I can't imagine anyone refusing to—"

"Do you sincerely expect to gain favor by bellowing like a Vermilion fog rhino?" Ily asked incredulously.

He turned, bulk bouncing like jelly. "On the day we march into the Imperial palace on Rega, Witch-woman, I shall be looking for you. Neither your assassinations nor the terror you wield so wickedly will save you from the wrath of God, His Holiness, on that glorious day!"

Ily met his fury with a sober stare. "I look forward to it, my Lord Legate." And with a nod to Skyla, she got to her feet and palmed the door which let her into the crowded hallway where her people—on one side—glared at the Sassans on the other.

As soon as she reached her quarters, she ripped open the seal on the diplomatic packet and scanned the contents. Very well, so Staffa had given them good solid reasons for avoiding a war. What did that mean in the end?

She patted the pages against her black Myklenian silks and considered the ramifications. *No, there must be a deeper meaning to all this. Staffa had gone fishing? Ludicrous, a false lead. No, canny Staffa has to be biding his time, driving the price up, building desperation among the empires.*

She grinned and turned to the comm. "Access to Wing Commander Skyla Lyma, please. This is the Regan Minister."

Lyma's face formed on the holo. "Yes, Minister? I'm afraid we will not take any offers if that's why you called."

Ily's diplomatic smile fell easily into place. "It isn't, Wing

Commander. I was only thinking, having read the Lord Commander's excellent brief on the political situation in Free Space, I can see that we in the service of Tybalt the Imperial Seventh have been remiss. I am empowered, in the name of the emperor, to request that Rega be allowed to establish an embassy in the Itreatic Asteroids.

The Wing Commander shook her head, eyes frigid. "It has long been a policy of the Lord Commander to deny such embassies. I think you can perceive the changes it would make in our mandatory neutrality. We will not make the polarization of our people possible through exposure to anyone's propaganda."

Ily nodded. "A wise policy, I'm sure. However, please take our proposal to the Lord Commander. Inform him we would offer the equivalent of one hundred thousand Imperial credits per year for use of Itreatic facilities and services."

Ily enjoyed the hesitation in the Wing Commander's eyes. She'd offered enough to buy a governorship to a major planet. An embassy would be a first step to binding the Companions to Rega.

"I'm sorry," Skyla told her at last. "It's out of the question."

Ily nodded, her smile perfect. "We understand." *And one of these days, blonde beauty, I will watch you writhe.* "Thank you for your time, Wing Commander." She hesitated, another angle forming in her mind. "How do we . . . I mean, you will provide the services of the Companions for minor security problems so long as they are unrelated to the basic disagreements between the empires, won't you?"

"You are referring to the Targan uprising?"

Ily studied those cool blue eyes. No, there were no pretenses here. Ily relished the sensation as her own smile became genuine. What pleasure this ice-haired beauty would provide. Here, finally, she faced an opponent worthy of her craft and cunning. "Of course, Targa is a current problem area."

Skyla nodded. "I will raise the issue with the Lord Commander. If there is any interest, I will inform you. But please remember that we have just returned from a trying campaign. Most of our people are weary. Will your offer remain open?"

"Of course." Ily felt a tingle of hope. If the Targan situation were allowed to disintegrate, it would be a perfect opportunity when the Companions grew bored with humdrum station life. All it would take would be a prolonging of the civil war there. Something more to inflame the people, to spur them on. Perhaps an arms shipment to the rebels? The sacrifice of several Regan army corps to hearten the Targan opposition? Indeed, if it flared enough, the Companions would hear. A plea would do more for their curious vanity than a straight-out offer of gold and jewels.

"Thank you for your time, Wing Commander." Ily nodded politely and killed the connection.

And where *was* Staffa? Fishing? Really? There was one way to find out, she thought, and studied her reflection appraisingly before stepping out into the corridor.

Men—be they dock hands or Companions—would always talk to a seductive woman. Only certain sections of the station were open to her and her escort. Nevertheless, within an hour she was leading Special Tactics Officer Ryman Ark into her quarters, laughing and lowering her eyes as his hands explored her body.

"Now why," Ark asked, as he accepted a bulb of Scotch, "don't the Regans send you by more often?"

"Ryman, I have duties." She settled next to him on the sleeping platform. "I don't get away much. But when I do, I want to see *men*, real men who take life seriously, not the perfumed flaccid bureaucrats I have to deal with every day. "Where does this scar go?" She ran a finger lightly along his black skin to where the puckered seam disappeared into his sleeve.

Ryman grinned and stripped his uniform off. Ily ran her hands over his muscular flesh as he turned his attention to peeling her out of her gown. To her surprise he took his time, building her response, timing himself to her needs. Despite herself, she closed her eyes, letting his movements bring her to an unexpected climax.

Life was like that. Take bounty when it presented itself. To her amazement, another hour passed as Ark deftly continued to explore her body. Within another hour—practically exhausted—she managed to slip mytol into his scotch.

Weary and flushed, she sat up on the rumpled platform. "You have remarkable endurance, Ark," she whispered, pawing through her things, all the while aware her body felt loose-jointed and tender where she'd coupled too violently.

"Yes, Ily," he responded woodenly. Mytol did that to a man.

She set up what appeared to be a music system and turned on the audio. Satisfied with the subtle tones of the Jakeid symphony—and also satisfied that it threw a privacy screen over the room that not even the best bugs could penetrate—she crawled next to him, snuggling close to his drugged body. Rotted Gods, even drugged he rose to her embrace again! Did the man ever tire?

Her mouth next to his ear she asked. "Where is the Lord Commander?"

"Gone," he answered muzzily.

"Where?"

"Don't know."

"Guess, dear Ryman. Tell me where you think."

"Fishing . . . and whoring . . . and tasting the pleasures of the many worlds."

"Is that a joke?"

"No, Staffa's on vacation."

"Seriously?"

"Uh-huh. Said to wait for a year. He'd be back and we'd go to war then. Make more money. Allow the empires to stabilize so we'd be guaranteed they didn't collapse economically and leave us high and dry."

"Do you believe that?"

"Yes."

"Do you think anyone could find him? Is there a special way to get in touch?"

"Skyla might. No other way to get in touch. Not through comm anyway. I'd know."

"Is Skyla his lover? Are they close?"

"No."

"Why did Staffa go away just now, Ryman?"

"Been upset."

"About what?" She frowned. What the hell did that mean?

"Something about when he killed the Praetor. Never the same since then. Worried."

Slowly, with the skill of thousands of hours of interrogation, Ily pieced together a picture of the Lord Commander's last trip home. "Thank you, dear Ryman. You sleep now. In the morning, you will remember none of this—only how much scotch we drank and how terrible your hangover is."

He immediately began to snore.

She lay there with a racing mind as she tried to correlate the different parts of Ryman's confessions. Skyla might be able to find Staffa? And just how did she manipulate Skyla? The Wing Commander wouldn't fall for any frolic in the zero-g with any man, no matter how good looking.

Ily got up and made her way to the bath, aware that everything had become turmoil. That Staffa would refuse a Contract was one option she never would have considered. *But I'll find you, Lord Commander—and you won't have your Companions around when I do.*

* * *

Staffa kar Therma took one last glance at the monitor that displayed the Etarian docking station and settled the worry-cap on the pilot's head. The man remained in the grip of a drugged sleep. With the worry-cap interacting with the pilot's brain, the man's expression changed.

Staffa chuckled to himself, imagining the pilot's reaction when he awakened to find himself ten light-years from Itreata and safely docked at Etaria.

From his bag, Staffa pulled a brown trader's toga over his gray armor and snapped his possessions closed. From a pouch he took a Regan unlimited travel passport.

Like a ghost, he moved to the lock, palmed the hatch, and stepped out into the main orbiting station over Etaria. A curious unease filled him. He swallowed hard and steeled himself. How long had it been since he walked alone through a crowd of strangers? Had he ever? Chiding himself for a fool, he drowned the fear with the arrogance that had carried him through the years and stepped into the crowd. Looking like any other Etarian supplicant, he shuffled through the long lines of entrants, got his voucher stamped, and boarded one of the massive shuttles.

What awaits me? What do I know of this reality of common men? He blinked his eyes and swallowed dryly, the sudden lurch of fear leaving his palms sweaty. *Easy, Staffa, it's a panic response. Emotion can be controlled.*

What a strange feeling to be packed so close to so many people. They all seemed so . . . oblivious to each other, as if they were totally secluded, locked away within themselves. The bald man next to him met his gaze. He appeared to be an inoffensive sort. A trader from the cut of this clothes.

"First time to Etaria?" the bald man asked mildly.

"No. I was here several years ago. Probably five by his planet's time."

"Not much has changed. You're here to go to the temple?"

Staffa nodded.

"Yeah, five years ago." The man licked his lips and shook his head. "That was when the Butcher showed up. Didn't need to do more. People panicked and the Priests capitulated to the Regans."

"The Butcher?" Staffa tensed.

"Yeah, you know, the Star Butcher, the baby burner, Staffa kar Therma, may the Rotted Gods eat his intestines by the slow inch!"

With iron control Staffa fought the desire to reach over and break this man's neck. "He unified Free Space between two governments where before there had been chaos."

"Sure, at what cost?" The trader hesitated, looking at his suddenly shaking hands. His voice came in ragged spurts. "My—my family lived on Phillipia. I'm the only one who . . . lived. They even killed my children. And . . . and what they . . . they did to my . . . my sister before they . . . before they. . . ." He shook his head, bowing his face down into his hands. "God, I *hate* him. If I could ever get the chance, I'd. . . ."

Staffa's anger turned and twisted. *Be calm*, he told himself. But to sit here and listen to this whining. . . . "Excuse me. I see an old friend." Staffa, teeth grinding, sought the rear of the shuttle and a different seat.

Such as you, human, have little right to question the actions of leaders. What is your family against the sprawl of human destiny in Free Space?

He barely heard the merchant from Vermilion who sat next to him babbling about the delights of the temple and wondering if the Etarian Priestesses were as beautiful as they claimed.

Face set, curious at the anger that still burned in his breast, Staffa waited stoically as the shuttle descended. The Praetor's words haunted him. *"More than ten billion human beings have died at your hands. In places, men utter curses in your name. Among others you are reviled as a demon from their versions of hell."*

What if they did? Who were these people he killed? Had they all been like that weakling trader? Then perhaps the species was better off without them.

He looked about him, suddenly conscious of the shuttle's vulnerability. How many craft like this one had died under his guns? How many had he seen fleeing a doomed planet before he gave his order to destroy it. How many had his weapons ripped open in explosive decompression—the corpses of men, women, and children frozen in horrid death, tumbling in an eerie and gruesome orbit.

He hardly felt the shuttle touch down. Senses reeling, he got to his feet and shuffled out with the crowd. His mind seemed stuck on the memories, the crowd but an abstraction out of time and place.

Someone tugged at his elbow. The bald trader, dry-eyed, looked up anxiously. "I'm sorry. I must have upset you." He took a deep breath. "Look, it happened a long time ago. Only I can't let it die. If I did, what would it all mean? There has to be more to life than mindless butchery, doesn't there?" With that, the man disappeared into the crowd.

Staffa took a step after him, anger pulsing, only to hesitate in sudden confusion at hearing his own questions mimicked in the trader's voice. Sharp comments from surging passengers made him bide his anger and continue in the general direction of the flow—thinking . . . remembering.

Phillipia returned—an emerald world hanging against a backdrop of stars. Torn-cotton clouds spun lazily across the shallow seas. Phillipia, an old world, had a heritage of art and science. Though it was once the pretender to the human space hegemony, Rega had outbid it for Staffa's services. He could remember the heavy batteries of his ships pouring a devastating fire into the planetary defenses. On the first pass they'd bombed the major cities, heavy radiation leaving the commercial centers standing amid thousands of scattered corpses, poisoned, burned, and dead where they had stood.

Only after the defenses had been neutralized, had they dropped like sleek Etarian hawks to capture the remaining provincial cities and break the militia defenses. And against the Companions, the Phillipians had had no adequate defense.

He remembered nightfall in an outlying town. Columns of yellow orange flames illuminated billowing smoke in the black night skies. A Companion, bending to one knee, settled his pulse rifle and easily potted the running child, exploding the terrified boy's head like a red melon. And how old had that red-haired girl been? Twelve? Thirteen? She'd been a slip of a thing, screaming first, then blubbering as man after man took her, caressing her barely-budded breasts before finally silencing her bloody, stained body with a merciful slash of a vibraknife. Could that have been the trader's sister?

Staffa shook his head and blinked the visions away. Didn't they understand the reality of war? To make change, men died. Humanity suffered for the betterment of the whole. That *was* social law.

He stepped out of the terminal and into the crowded streets. The dry air of Etaria desiccated his nostrils. The place smelled of dust, spices, and stale sweat. A cacophony assaulted his ears as people shoved past. Disturbed by his memories, he walked the streets, still searching for the elusive answer as night fell and his stomach began to remind him he was no more than flesh and blood, no matter how weighty the problems he pondered were. On occasion he heard curses in the Star Butcher's name. Down deep they irritated him, rankling on the edge of his mind. He stopped at the Young Virgin Inn and climbed the steps. The temple lay only three blocks away.

I am only here long enough to lose my trail to Targa, Staffa reminded himself. *And perhaps to ask an Etarian Priest about the nature of man and reality.*

Inside, a boisterous group sang bawdily in one corner. Staffa took a table next to the bar and kicked his feet out. The bald trader's grief still nagged at him, and he couldn't help comparing it to his own feelings for his stolen Chrysla. An unsettling foreboding gripped him.

"Help you, sir?" The landlord bent over his shoulder.

"Ashtan steak, medium rare, steamed ripa root and

Myklenian brandy," he ordered. A sudden stillness filled the room.

"Right," the landlord chuckled. "Who do you think I am? The cock-rotted Star Butcher? We've got myka stew, amplar basted in butter, and if you're feeling real rich, Regan squid off the last transport—but it's a quarter-credit."

"Squid," Staffa said flatly. "And your best stout, or do you have any?"

"Aye, as good as you can get hereabouts. Brewery's down the street."

Men stared at him from the bar. A not so good-looking blonde woman leaned on a big man's arm and laughed at something one of them said. They looked suddenly hungry.

Staffa dismissed them from his mind. By the cock-rotted Star Butcher? Did everyone here curse in his name? At least the landlord didn't do it out of hate—or did he?

The food tasted of grease, the portion small, but again, compared to his larders of almost unlimited delicacies, maybe they had nothing better. He chugged the tepid stout and flipped a twenty credit gold piece on the table.

The landlord walked over and reached for it—stopping in mid-grasp. "By the Rotted Gods, 'tis gold!" he mumbled. "And I can't make change for that! You've a credit chip, good Lord?"

"That's the smallest I've got," Staffa told him coldly, aware the whole tavern had stopped to listen again.

"Yo, Phippet!" One of the men from the bar called. "Here, we pooled. We'll cover the good gentleman's meal if he'll come, stand to a round, and lift a toast to our health."

Staffa picked up his coin and nodded to the landlord as he stepped up to the bar. They greeted him with wolfish eyes. The blonde woman stared him up and down, a smugness in her eyes. When she smiled at him, gaps showed in her teeth. Brown robes splotched with grease and stains covered the men.

"My name is . . ." What in the name of the Forbidden Borders did he call himself? "Therma," he supplied.

"Like the Star Butcher's last name?" The heavy blonde woman asked. "That must be a living curse. Good thing you got money to keep the criers off yer back."

Staffa studied her curiously. "To your health, gentle people!" And he lifted his glass. *Why am I so uneasy? I came here to socialize with common people. To do that, you must go among them, Staffa, learn them like you would the defenses of an impregnable planet.*

Skyla's warning returned to haunt him. The landlord had retreated to the back of the bar, avoiding his eyes and shaking his head.

"Another drink for the gentleman! Come on," the tallest, Broddus was his name, said, "we'd be honored to take a man of your taste to a place that can accept his money— provided of course you buy the next round."

"I think I'll be leaving," Staffa said, and dropped the gold coin on the counter. "For your kindness."

"See you soon," the blonde woman promised.

Staffa made it out the door and into the street. Night had fallen and the lighting on the streets seemed oddly blurred.

Which way?

"Therma?"

Staffa turned, seeing Broddus stepping down from the tavern doorway.

"Sure we couldn't stand you to another drink?"

"I have to . . ." Staffa frowned. ". . . to go. Find a priest."

"I am a priestess," the buxom blonde told him as she wound her arms around him. "Isn't that why you came to Etaria?"

Staffa shook his head, thoughts going muzzy. No, not now. This wasn't the Praetor's work, was it? Some hidden. . . .

"Come. We'll take care of you, Lord." Broddus got a shoulder under Staffa's arm, leading him away.

"Good care," the blonde woman promised as another man helped prop him up and keep him from falling.

"Let go," Staffa whispered, his tongue thick. "Don't touch me."

"Oh," the blonde whispered in his ear, "we're here to help you."

Panic burst loose in Staffa's brain. Instinctively, he lashed out. He couldn't duck the hissing silver tube that shot a vile smelling gas into his face. With his remaining strength, he laid into his assailant . . . hearing screams . . . feeling flesh under his groping hands. He kicked, struck, and lost himself in a haze of fog that drew tight around his senses.

He didn't remember falling, but someone made a gurgling sound. Someone else screamed in agony.

Hands worried his body. "By the Star Butcher's bloody balls! A combat suit!"

"No wonder you didn't kill him!"

"Look at this! A fortune in gold!" Strip him. "Pakt's dead. Bastard killed him."

"Hurry, with all the screaming, bulls will be here soon."

Staffa tried to react through the haze, unable to find his body. The words were disjointed, faint. He felt himself turned, flopped, hands on his flesh. Then there was the patter of running feet and the cool breeze on his skin as he dropped into the engulfing grayness. The final thing he remembered: the odor of vomit.

* * *

The Mag Comm filtered the limited data it received from the remote sensors scattered throughout Free Space. Something had gone wrong. Data began rerunning in the giant banks; one after another, predictive models had to be rejected out of hand. What could have thrown the carefully derived calculations into such flux? The data had been so precise, the Others so sure.

Where had the mistake been made?

The Mag Comm's activity increased. Who had made the mistake?

CHAPTER IX

Sinklar braced himself against the bed and stood. The two weeks he'd spent in the hospital would hold him for the rest of his life. Inflamed pink and red scar tissue mottled his left side in an irregular pattern. Experiencing a reverential awe, Sinklar ran his fingers over the tight surface of the angry flesh, marveling at the smooth texture he touched.

That's my body. Rebel blasters did that to me. Funny, during the running, I never knew I was so badly injured. It should have hurt. I should have been screaming from pain.

He took one last glance at the putrid green of the hospital walls and reached for his clothing. The undersmock rested gently on his skin as he pulled it over his head. Sinklar slipped into fresh new combat armor, unhappy with the stiffness in his arms and legs. The hospital unit they'd cocooned him in had also built more brawn on his thin lanky limbs. Electromagnetic cellular stimulation and increased vascularization of the striated muscle tissue occurred as a side effect of the healing process. He cocked his head, happy that the machine had finally tended to his ruptured ear. Even the ringing had disappeared.

He checked himself in the mirror. He looked fit as he strapped the weapons belt onto his lean hips. In the reflection, his long pensive face stared back the same as it always had: one eye gray, the other a tawny yellow. His wispy brown hair glinted with slight tints of red, his nose a bit knobby at the end.

He walked down the hall to the assignment desk and handed his card to the chunky woman who sat behind the desk. She wore the insignia of a First Physician.

"Private Fist, Sinklar, Company B, Second Section, First Targan Assault Division," the woman observed, pulling his records from the file. She glanced up with flat blue eyes.

"I'm marking your file as A1—fit for combat. They want to see you in Operations, Personnel section. I'm notifying comm you're on the way."

"Thank you, ma'am," Sinklar rapped out a salute and left, getting directions from a harried clerk-secretary in the hallway.

A bustle of new people scurried through the halls of the converted concert hall they'd made into the Regan Expeditionary Headquarters. Rega had responded with a vengeance after the virtual annihilation of the first pacification divisions.

Outside Operations, he had to wait twenty minutes before being called in. A panel of five Personnel Second officers took his salute.

"Private Fist." One of the officers looked up from the comm monitor before speaking to the others behind a privacy screen. One by one they studied him, each hidden behind a bureaucratically-stiff face. "Would you please scan the following report and make a declaration of accuracy for the panel?"

Sinklar was handed a flimsy. Scanning the page, he read a general statement of his escape with MacRuder and Gretta up to the point when they were picked up by the patrol craft.

"Accurate to my knowledge, sir, with the exception that I disagree with the final conclusion that I single-handedly saved their lives. We worked as a team. And one last correction, sir. I noticed that the report states and I quote, 'Private Fist's concern regarding the possible rebel strike to the post office command center was ignored by Sergeant Jeen Hamlish.' That wasn't the case, sir. I didn't have time to inform the sergeant." He handed the flimsy back.

The lead Personnel Second nodded. "Your objections are noted, Private." He looked at his colleagues who nodded one by one. "Further, considering those objections so stated, the board hereby promotes you to Sergeant Third of the Second Section of the First Targan Assault Division. Corporal First MacRuder of your Section will relinquish command to you at the D Block Barracks. Pick up your orders, promotion, and equipment at the Supply Depot. Dismissed."

Sinklar snapped a salute, swallowed, and left at a trot. It

took more questioning to find Supply. After he made his
way through the line, they handed him sergeant's chevrons,
a new assault rifle, and complete field pack, including
orders. Dazed, he finally found D block—a commandeered
residential section just behind the energy barriers of the
perimeter. And a seedy one at that, he thought, seeing a
private clearing old bedding platforms from what had obviously been a whorehouse.

Halfway up the barracks steps, he heard MacRuder's
barking voice. Turning, he spotted the corporal running a
bunch of wide-eyed, panting privates across the open square
where trollops had once hawked their bodies.

"Hey! Mac!" Sinklar raised a hand.

"Cump'neeeee, *halt!*" MacRuder's voice bawled over the
pounding feet. "Sink! You're alive!" MacRuder started over
at a trot. He stopped short at the chevrons and whistled.
"By the Rotted Gods, they made you a sergeant. I was
happy enough to make Corporal First."

"Yeah, they told me I'm your commander." He dropped
his gaze awkwardly. What trouble did this brew for his new-
found friendship. "Um, look I. . . ."

"Shut up. I recommended it. Wonder how it happened
they listened to a lowly Corporal First?" MacRuder turned
and looked over his squad where they watched curiously.
"Gretta and I, well, we're alive because of your leadership,
Sink." He smiled. "I'm not enough of a crud that I don't
recognize when I owe somebody my ass—at least, not yet
anyway. And I like working with you. We make a great
team."

"Yeah. Gretta's okay?"

MacRuder's eyes glinted. "Yeah, and she's been worried
sick about you. They made her Corporal First, too. She's
in charge of A Group and I've got B."

Sinklar shook his head. "I don't get it. Why all the
promotions?"

MacRuder's smile fell. " 'Cause we're veterans, pal.
We're still alive. Promotions come fast when a division
takes almost ninety percent casualties. You, me, and Gretta
are all that's left of the Second Section, Sink. Nobody else
made it out of the Gods Rotted post office. Just us."

"Blessed Etarus!"

"Yeah, and you keep us alive. Gretta and me, well, we're counting on it."

"Anything I should know?" Sinklar asked, oddly nervous at the sudden responsibility that had dropped on him like so many bricks out of a crumbling wall.

"Yep, we're headed out tonight at dusk. I had orders to wait for a new CO. That's you, buddy. Division First Atkin has ordered us to take a position on a road up in the hills. It's some sort of pass between here and the back country. They think the rebels are using it to get supplies into the city. Our job is to cut that supply line and hold it."

At his words two LCs roared overhead in a wide sweep, wings spreading and gear dropping. Sink had a sudden understanding of why D Block had been chosen for a staging barracks. LCs could land in the open square.

"Get the bloody hell out of the way, you bastards!" MacRuder ordered, waving his still standing troops out of the square. They scattered as the LCs settled in a vortex of dust and grit.

"Dumb!" MacRuder cursed. "Targans will rip these sheep apart!" And he left to berate his huddled command.

A ramp dropped and a flight tech came bouncing down and out. "That all of them?" he called over the growl of the LCs. "There's supposed to be a whole Section!"

"All of who?" Sink asked.

"Second Section. We're transport. Something about getting them all to a pass west of here. Let's go! I've got two more drops to make today!"

"Rotted Gods, man, I just got here!" Sinklar bellowed. In desperation he turned and waved at MacRuder. "Mac, get some of those goons hopping! Clear those barracks of our people and let's get loaded. Detail some of those guys to find the other Groups. Let's go!" And with his new pack on his back and his assault rifle hooked into his armor, he scrambled up the ramp. Was that what command was all about? Just make it up as you go?

Sinklar stowed his gear, wondering what to do next, and went down to see if he could orchestrate the growing confusion. One by one, he directed the raw recruits to crash benches.

He glanced out of the LC and saw her as she came up the ramp, following an armored rabble which evidently made up

A Group. Sink's breath caught in his throat. Gretta's hair hung around her shoulders, a swinging mahogany brown wave behind her too-well formed features. Her blue eyes caught his and held. She stopped, slim body silhouetted in the afternoon light.

Sink started forward, mouth oddly dry. "Gretta?"

She smiled, eyes lighting. "You're all right? Oh, Sinklar, how I worried about you." Then she stepped into his arms, hugging him tightly.

"Sergeant Fist?" Came a call from the flight tech.

"Guess that's me."

"We'll talk when this is all settled." She winked at him and pushed him forward.

Sink sighed and followed the man back to engage in a paperwork nightmare.

Sink didn't meet his other corporals until the LCs had lifted. Mac introduced him to Hauws, First for C Group; Ayms for D; Kap was first for E; and Shiksta for heavy ordnance. Of them all, only he, Gretta and Mac, had seen combat experience. The rest, including the privates, were totally green, fresh draftees from various parts of the Empire. Some didn't even speak Regan.

"All right," Sink told them as he leaned back against the crash webbing. "Mac, you and Gretta go out first. We'll assume we're not landing in an ambush. Pray to the Rotted Gods intelligence is better than that. I looked at the map. We're being set down in the pass. Off to the right is a rocky knoll. I want a thin perimeter laid out around that knoll as best you can organize it. Groups C, D, and E will fill in the gaps. Shiksta, I want the heavy stuff set up where you can give covering fire to any part of the perimeter. Understood? Good, let's hope nobody shoots at us."

They all nodded assent.

"Now, the first thing you do is dig in. Get your people down in the dirt."

Hauws asked, "What about regulations on health and exposure to foreign soils? I mean, I was a health inspector on Ashtan and you'd be surprised at the organisms that grow in Targan soil."

Sinklar blinked. "And you'd be surprised at how a human body looks when a pulse gun explodes it. Dig or die. You make the choice. Any other questions, Corporal?"

Hauws swallowed. "No, sir."

"Uh, sir?" Kap asked. "From what you lined out, how do we justify quick mobility as stipulated in the attack command manual?"

"What do we attack?" Sinklar asked dryly.

"Their assault columns, sir." Kap's red face screwed up with concern, as he struggled to remember. "It says in the manual that assault columns can be disrupted by rapid hit and run tactics. Such actions depend on rapid deployment and quick mobility." He jerked his head, as if satisfied he'd gotten the rote right.

Sinklar pursed his lips. "I read the manual, Corporal Kap. That manual killed exactly ninety-seven percent of the Second Section in Kaspa. This is not an assault on a planet. This is a different kind of war—one the manuals don't talk about."

He looked into their suddenly nervous eyes. Mouths worked silently. They waited, jittery at the thought of hearing more heresy. Ayms was wringing his hands. Shiksta tapped his foot energetically, eyes lowered.

Sink nodded at their disquiet. "Yeah, I know. No one has fought a war like this for a long time. They call it social revolution. In the old times, it was called a guerrilla war. You will rarely see the people shooting at you. They won't come in assault columns. They'll fire out of the dark, hit when you least expect it, where you least suspect it."

"But that's in violation of Imperial honor," Hauws declared indignantly. "That's savage!"

"And terribly human. It's the oldest form of war, one someone either reinvented, or dug out of the history books." And at that he frowned. "I wonder."

Mac cocked his head. "Boys, you better pry the wax out of your ears. Gretta and I told you. We been there. What are you onto, Sink?"

"Just thinking. Two hundred years ago, at the start of the Imperial period, the governments had an interplanetary conference on war and the manner of its conduct. At the time, comprehensive and sophisticated programs of military education swept Free Space. That's where the concepts of honor in war were founded. I wonder, could it have been a political attempt to alienate the people from guerrilla war? Social programming by the political elite?"

"Got me," Mac told him. "I never heard the term before."

Sinklar nodded. "Yeah, well, like I said, it's old. I wonder if the Empire has any idea what it's up against?"

"So, if it gets too bad, the Star Butcher will show up and the Targans will melt!" Ayms grinned and looked back and forth.

"Perhaps," Sinklar mumbled, lost in his thoughts. "Or perhaps the masterminds behind this revolt have dug something out of the past to handle the Butcher, too."

The words were hardly out of his mouth when the LCs dipped and decelerated at five gs. Idly, Sinklar wondered if they ever slowed gradually.

He got one wish. No one shot at them as they unloaded. He even got his perimeter established in the rocky ground and all the ordnance set up with good covering fire. One thing about green troops, they let him make an innovative deployment without arguing the rule book with him.

They didn't get hit until dark. Sink got to test his strategy first hand. From that moment on, Second Section learned what war was all about—but they only took eleven casualties: three dead and eight wounded by the time dawn reddened the eastern sky.

* * *

Skyla had never considered the impact Staffa had made on her life; He'd always been there. She chewed her lip, feeling uneasy. She found herself lonely with him gone.

He'd been worried about her. That thought stuck as she leaned back from the console in her small bridge. Tapping a stylus, she studied the vector on which the CV should have returned to Ashtan. In her plush personal cruiser, she mapped the radiation spike and pinpointed the direction in which the highly dissipated reaction was moving. The acute sensors picked up positron dancing out of the past to annihilate themselves. From the frequency, her superior instruments calculated half-life possibility and tied the origin to Staffa's acceleration.

No, he hadn't returned to Ashtan. Instead, he'd laid his tracks straight for Etaria, and what? One of those Priestesses? He had the choice of how many women in the Itreatic

Asteroids? Or the pick of women from any of the conquered worlds, for that matter. No, this was Staffa being clever. Etaria remained on open port. From there, he could lose his trail.

The computer locked a line-of-sight laser onto receive in the Itreatic Asteroids. Tasha's anxious face formed in the monitor. "You've got a fix?" he asked.

"Etaria," she told him. "I'm off. I'll holler if I find anything. Be ready."

"Affirmative . . . and good luck."

She killed the connection and studied the course plot, the worry-cap easy on her head. *To hesitate is to lose the trail. Damn you, Staffa, why are you putting me through this?*

Skyla laid in the course and settled into her cushioned command chair. No matter what Staffa might think, he didn't have the skills to be turned loose among civilized people. He might be a brilliant tactician and a superb mercenary, but what did he know about the vipers out there? Especially ones like she had grown up around?

She triggered the main drives and built Delta V for the jump, noting with satisfaction that she was eating most of the vanished CV's radiation. Excellent, that put her right on target.

And if I'd had a child? Yes, I'd be just as preoccupied as Staffa is.

"Getting to be a sentimental old bitch," she muttered under her breath, adding more thrust to the fusion reactor and tightening the bounce-back collar.

"Be just like him, though, to be up to his neck in trouble by the time I get to Etaria. Probably have to call out the whole fleet to break him out of it." *Where after Etaria?* "Targa? That's what the Praetor told him. There are a lot of Seddi on Targa."

She shook a fist in victory. If passage could be arranged to Targa from anywhere, it would be from Rega or Etaria.

She vented an explosive sigh as she stared at the star-filled monitor and studied the ship's feedback as it rolled into her brain via the shiny worry-cap. Her agile mind stored and sorted ship's data, maintaining the delicate nav systems.

Simultaneously, a consuming curiosity ate at her. Just what sort of woman had Chrysla been? How had she man-

aged to put a lock on Staffa's hard heart? Had she met him
with iron and defiance in her soul, or given him her love
and soft compliance? What did it take to win Staffa kar
Therma's love? Chrysla had been his perfect woman. How
did he expect to replace *her?*

She mulled it over as she stared out into the star-gray
heavens and suffered an increasing anxiety. He had only
been gone from Itreata for somewhat more than twenty-
four hours. How much trouble could he get into in that
time?

"Oh, Staffa, I hope I'm not too late."

* * *

Ily Takka studied the scanner input, watching the small
cruiser as it built for jump. "What do *you* think,
Commander?"

"Three person cruiser, Minister. Could be anybody." The
commander pulled on his nose nervously, as always, afraid
to meet her probing black eyes.

"How many credits would you make that craft to be
worth on the open market, Commander?" Ily asked, voice
soft, eyes narrowing.

"From the style and the g's it's putting out, I'd say somewhere in the neighborhood of four hundred thousand ICs,
Minister."

"Indeed, and I sincerely doubt that just any of Staffa's
people can. . . . But we don't know that, do we?" She
tapped her chin with a stylus. "Official business, perhaps?
Or the Wing Commander running to tell Staffa we've
already made offers? You have the destination
triangulated?"

"Etaira, Minister. No doubt about it." He paused, taking
a quick look at the navigator who nodded vigorous
agreement.

"Hmm, isn't her cruiser accelerating rather rapidly?" Ily
frowned, wishing she were more familiar with such things.

"Weapons First?" the commander called, "Can you get
a Doppler on that craft in the targeting comp?"

"Aye, sir!" The Weapons First bent over a monitor, fixing the targeting comp on the moving dot of light. "She's
pulling almost sixty g's sir."

The commander frowned. "Good ship, Minister. She's got some pretty powerful gravity compensating equipment in there. I raise my estimate. You might not buy that craft for less than six hundred thousand ICs."

"And how many g's can we pull?" Ily raised an eyebrow.

The commander swallowed. "My crew, ma'am, can take forty g's by straining our equipment. With you aboard, I wouldn't want to pull more than thirty to leave us a high enough safest margin percentage just in case—"

"We will accelerate at forty g's, Commander." She nodded her satisfaction as she narrowed her eyes. "We can always slow on the other side, but I want us close when she comes out."

"Ma'am, do you understand what kind of energy we're talking about? Forty g's is like slamming your body—"

"I gave you an order."

"Yes, ma'am," the commander agreed with a heavy sigh. "But first, we'll need to get you into combat armor. This won't be much fun if you insist on—"

"I do, Commander. Where's this combat armor. Show me what I have to do."

"Yes, ma'am."

As she walked off the bridge, a klaxon started wailing. "Prepare for high g acceleration! All hands, high g acceleration! Stow all loose objects and prepare for forty g's, ladies and gentlemen."

And Skyla, my dear, Ily thought, *next time we meet will be in the Regan Empire—and so many things can happen in my Empire!*

* * *

Bruen thought Butla looked like a restful tiger. Tension pervaded the air, even here, in the chambers below Vespa. The rock walls of the chamber showed signs of the passing of ages. Scars marked on the stone where various changes had been made to the room. Places like this were old, very old, dating to the terraforming of the planet. No wonder they were tense. They had taken so much on themselves, all in a wild gamble orchestrated by the thrice-cursed Mag Comm.

Hyde coughed hoarsely in the silence. He sat on the

opposite side of the table from Bruen while Ret sat at the head.

Butla Ret twisted sideways in the chair, muscles dancing under his midnight flesh, eyes thoughtful as he looked down his long flat nose. He wore a Master's off-white robe that was loosely belted around his slim waist. "On the surface Kaspa appears to be completely in Regan control. They patrol in Groups, always ready to return fire. When we snipe at them, they retaliate by blowing away entire buildings—despite the civilians. Fear is becoming a way of life in the capital."

Bruen shifted his eyes to Hyde, chin propped on a creased palm. "Indeed. Well, we expected this. So far so good. Fear feeds discontent, the desire to return to a state of normalcy."

Butla formed his fingers into a fist, watching the muscles ripple in his forearm. "So far, the Regans have acted predictably, Magister," his deep bass rumbled, "and pray to God they continue to."

"You still agree that we should let them have free reign for a while?" Hyde asked.

Butla lifted a slab of shoulder. "I can't see us making any headway while they maintain such vigilance. This new Division First of theirs, um, Atkin is his name, he's scared, worried about his career should the Regans suffer another disaster."

Bruen nodded. "And his worry in turn worries you?"

Butla Ret's dark eyes flashed, "You tell me such behavior isn't dangerous, then I just *might* believe it."

Bruen sniffed and eased his aching hip. "Of course not, Butla. The man is paranoid; as his unreasonable fear increases, so does the probability that he will react unpredictably. It's a vicious cycle this type of revolution engenders."

Ret stretched his thick legs, arms crossed. "And what would you suggest, Magister?"

"How tight is the security in the Regan military compounds?" Bruen leaned back, closing his eyes, tracing the possibilities. How would the Regans react? What countermoves would they make within the limited perceptual framework of the future they insisted on maintaining? His mind delighted itself with the permutations. In the range of potential responses, none seemed to play against them. But which future observation would become phase reality

"They allow no Targans past the checkpoints."

"But you could get inside?"

Butla's expression barely changed; however, his voice chided, "Master! These are Regans! They haven't the slightest hint of what the word 'security' means, let alone how to enforce it."

Bruen looked at Hyde. *Can I take this gamble? From intelligence sources, Tybalt would most likely install a sycophant in Atkin's place. Even if a capable man were hired to replace him, it would take time to reorganize. In the meantime, we can operate to increase Regan imbalance. We must hold out until Staffa can be brought within our reach. If we can't, all is lost!*

"Then you could remove Division First Atkin?" Bruen asked through the constriction in his throat.

Butla's lips parted to reveal straight white teeth. "I have been waiting, Magister. Killing occasional Regan soldiers in the dark has proved sport but not challenge." Butla straightened, excitement in his eyes. "Further, we can maximize on this. I could decapitate the First Division in one night's work. At the same time, if the opportunity presents itself, I might be able to make a substantial contribution to our intelligence net regarding their strategy and tactics."

"Do so!" Hyde managed, cackling gleefully. His sharp response triggered a coughing fit. The old man's face contorted as he bent double, fighting for air.

Bruen placed a friendly hand on the Magister's shoulder. "Old friend, I fear for you. This affliction continues to worsen."

Hyde waved it off, groping his way to his feet. Still hacking, hand over mouth, he shuffled out of the room, a pathetic broken figure.

Butla sat hunched, head down, hands knotted in his lap.

"I don't know how long he'll last," Bruen admitted with a sigh. "There comes a point beyond which not even the best of medicine can help. Magister Hyde has reached that. The quanta, you understand. Nothing lasts forever—not even a great and kind man."

Ret's voice gentled. "He was my instructor when I first came here as a novice Initiate. He . . . taught me of love and God and future when all I had was hatred, anger, and confusion in my soul."

Bruen smiled. "Then he also taught you that observation creates a phase reality through entropy. Phase reality imparts experience of the Now. Experience is knowledge and that, in turn, is stored in energy—which is indestructible. Death, dear Butla, is nothing more than a redistribution of energy which . . ."

". . . in the end is brought to God through entropy when the universe collapses," Butla Ret finished. His smile was warm, relieved. "Yes, Magister, he taught me those things. I fear not for his immortal soul. I regret the loss of his company and goodness. I will experience pain and hollowness at his passing."

"We create our own suffering, Butla."

"Free will, the element of choice, Magister," the assassin pointed out, lifting a huge hand in a motion of futility. "The result of a self-redefinition—the search to establish normality—in a phase reality of constantly changing observation in the eternal Now." He shook his head. "What damage we do to ourselves and others."

"Learning never comes cheaply, Butla." Bruen pulled at his ear. He hesitated before asking, "And Arta?" He watched Ret's thoughts shift from introspection to satisfaction.

"She's doing most remarkably, Magister." Ret grinned to himself, enjoying some vision in his mind. "You should have seen the first time I put her in a dark hallway full of debris. You know, boards, broken glass, stacked tin cans, bits of string hanging from the ceiling." Reg's grin spread. "I turned off the lights and she threw a fit. Practically killed herself in the first meter."

"But she's improved."

Ret steepled his fingers. "A great deal of pleasure comes to a teacher who guides a student he knows will one day surpass him in his mastery. She is such a one. She will be very, very good, Magister."

"And in the doja?" Bruen asked softly, imagining Arta, naked on the thick pads, a stun knife in her hand as she attempted to penetrate the total darkness. She would be standing, legs bent and braced, lithe, her pose alert for the slightest sound, the least movement of the air against her skin or hair. Extending her senses to feel for her antagonist.

Ret laughed. "I have never had a pupil who learned or modified the situation as readily as she, Magister. True, I shocked her time and time again with the electric prod, but she has constantly improved, changing tactics from lying still near a wall to switching back to the changing room—even hanging from the walls above my reach."

A deep reverberating laugh exploded from Butla. "She's at the stage now where she hates me with a vengeance because I make it seem so easy while she is blind to her own improvement." He paused, sharp black eyes on Bruen. "I am taking her with me when I kill Atkin."

So, another test, dearest Arta. At the same time, look at the concern in Butla's eyes. Dearest Gods, no! He can't come to love her! Impossible. I must handle this most carefully.

"You are fond of her," Bruen remarked casually as he tried to calm the first creepers of disturbance weaving through his brain.

Butla Ret tilted his head back, broad jaw working from side to side. "Yes, Magister. I am."

Bruen shifted, irritated at the pain in his hip. "You know about the trigger? I don't have to remind you what would happen if—"

"I understand." Ret nodded slowly, sadly. "Yes, Magister. I'm not a fool. I know what I deal with."

Yes, I suppose you do. And if you only knew who she is—who she is intended for—could you still keep your hands off her, Butla, my old friend?

Bruen grunted a sour chuckle. "She was made for love. That inherent quality has condemned her from the moment of her birth." He frowned, a hollowness in his guts. "What sort of existence do we have, Butla, when an ability to love is damnation?"

"The purpose of God—"

"Yes, yes, I know!" Bruen snapped in irritation. *Why does Arta always leave me off balance?* "I don't always have to like the way things are, do I?"

Ret's gaze dropped. "No, Magister. We, the Seddi, have already taken a hand in attempting to change that phase reality. You, Magister, made that decision so long ago. You can see what we've done. Today, at least, humanity has a chance."

Bruen barked an acid laugh, irritated at himself for foolish sentimentality, irritated with Butla because he naively hoped—and that sullied his own cynicism.

"We've increased suffering in this little corner of Free Space, Butla." He resettled himself in the gravchair, moving his pained hip to a different position. "And what else? Rega and Sassa are balanced precariously on the edge of oblivion. The Star Butcher waits, licking his lips for the scraps. That machine down there in the rock is a malignant cancer sending dendrites throughout human society. It's—"

"We have it fooled," Butla reminded.

"Do we?" Bruen's hands spread. "Yes, we . . . I lie to it constantly, feeding it a bit of misinformation here and another there, but what do we know about its purpose? What is it? Who built it? I don't think its origins were human. There's something alien and incomprehensible about the Mag Comm. Oh, sure, we've seen some of the banks—all technologically impossible to us. Consider. In another day and age, Butla, we would call that . . . *thing* a God!" He paused. "And we're enslaved by its powers. Without it, Makarta would die. Without its computational powers, we can't run our statistics, or access our historical files—or even keep track of our field agents. We *need* it to do our work."

Bruen laughed at Ret's suddenly cowed expression. "You see, my friend, you begin to understand the dilemma of having that 'power' constantly under our feet. To those of us who know it—deal with it—the question hovers forever in the backs of our minds. Do we manipulate it? Or do we each manipulate each other? Or—and most frightening— does it only allow us to think we manipulate it?"

His thoughts drifted. "There are no parameters of accurate measurement. Why does it order the things it does? At times, I get an eerie feeling that we've become toys, pieces to move about the table for its own amusement—but to what purpose?"

Bruen jerked himself straight, aware of the fear that had come to possess his voice. *Doddering old fool, you're too old, too tired to keep control of your own systems! I must get more sleep. Too much is at stake these days.*

Ret stared at him, somber-eyed. "Magister, you live a nightmare. What if you fail to veil your mind one of these days? That reality dangles out there beyond the quantum wave functions, bouncing that potential reality back in so many possibilities. How . . . how do you deal with the knowledge that you might be betraying all of humanity?"

Bruen placed bone-thin fingers to his temples, pressing slightly and rotating his hands. "I just do." He raised a hand in protest. "No, my friend, I know that is no answer. The only other thing I can tell you is that I have faith. What? Heresy from a Seddi Magister? Perhaps. I think, however, that you of all people can understand."

"Why me, Magister?"

Bruen's smile was a wispy thing. "You, Magister Assassin, carry the burden of death constantly within your fingertips. What if your poison reaches the wrong person, kills the innocent? What if the man we remove was just about to betray his cause? God built the universe on uncertainty. The quanta are God's joke on reality; they affect everything. You share my burden—the power of life and death based on future probabilities of human action."

"The chance for error." Ret rumbled in a deep bass. "But Magister, for me, I must judge the value of each life one by one. You, most venerable teacher, must judge the future of all humanity."

"I throw a Seddi paradox back at you, Butla Ret. If the God mind is one, and if the God mind is infinitely divisible into awareness, which reality phase do you judge, and which do I? According to the quanta, it's all the same—and all different."

"You are very good, Magister, you have shifted attention away from my question. Soon you will have us steered into the solipsistic perspective of existence. I repeat, however, how do you bear responsibility for the probability of your own failure?" Ret cocked his head, black eyes gleaming as he laced his fingers together.

Bruen sniffed wearily and sighed. "I do so because no one else can. Does that surprise you?" He smiled, seeing disbelief in Butla's eyes. "It does? Very well, are you ready to sit down before the machine and attempt to deflect it while it's within your mind, sharing your thoughts?"

"No, Magister." A shudder shook Ret's massive shoulders.

Bruen nodded. "You see, Butla. Like Arta, I, too, was condemned from birth. My parallels are very like hers. No one else can fill her role. She is unique in that, just as I myself am unique in dealing with the Mag Comm. Our lives consist of nothing more than individual phase realities which happened to fit a probabilistic niche some *thing* happened to observe. That's a frightening thought—be it true or not."

Butla Ret's lips twitched. "And God has built uncertainty into the very underpinnings of the universe."

"Now you see the true nightmare of existence, my friend."

* * *

Staffa kar Therma lay on cold stone, unaware of the world around him and the mildly curious stares of his companions. Instead, he fought the dream that wound through his aching head . . . and succumbed to defeat.

He twisted and ran, bolts of energy seeking his vulnerable body. The corridor down which his bare feet pelted had been bent by explosions that had wrenched blasted steel into jagged edges. Here and there an overhead panel provided just enough light to show him the way through eerie shadows.

Behind him, the faceless pursuers howled, shrieked, and cursed as they shot at his fleeing back.

Fiery air ripped in and out of Staffa's searing lungs. Ahead of him, a bulkhead exploded in fire and destruction. The concussion smashed him onto his back, impaling his shivering flesh on one of the torn petal edges of metal that thrust up from the floor.

Staffa's throat tore in violent screams as he felt the cold metal slipping through his back and slicing neatly through peritoneum and spinal column. At first his intestines slid away from the edge, squirming to avoid the invasion that finally severed them, spilling hot brown digestive juices into his body to burn and begin eating away at the very flesh they served.

Staffa whimpered as he looked down, seeing the bulge beneath hard belly muscles, feeling steel cutting inside, poking the white skin of his stomach up in a steeple while the widening edge filled him, foreign, hard, cold.

In slow motion, the point formed under his stretching skin, lifting his naval, turning it inside out.

His choking lungs exploded again as the keen gray point broke through the strained skin that slipped rubberlike and clinging along the lifting edge. It stopped, protruding—a gleaming peak of death over the snowy-white of his skin.

His brain terror-locked. He choked on fear and disbelief. A wretched sob shook his lungs while cold from the steel slowly spread through his gut, seeking his vitality, drawing his life into the impersonal metal.

He became aware of the shuffling of millions of feet. Unable to tear his straining eyes from the spear of gleaming gray lancing from his tortured gut, he heard the mutter of their voices, thick with hatred: watching . . . watching him die.

He screamed again, refusing to look up, refusing to see the damnation in their haunted dead eyes.

A slow murmur stirred them. "You are one of us now, Star Butcher! One of us!" It rustled in his mind, chilling, cursing.

They shuffled aside and Chrysla stepped out to stare at him with haunted yellow eyes. With one slim white hand, she reached down and pressed a firing stud to blast him.

"NO!" Staffa screamed, knowing it was all a dream—one from which he could not force himself to awaken. A dream he must live forever.

CHAPTER X

Tybalt the Imperial Seventh reclined in his plush gravity chair, surrounded by his opulent sandwood desk. The air-conditioning stirred the jasmine-scented air above his head and the Regan sun shimmered down through the crystal skylight. Gentle strains of an obscure Maikan symphony soothed him. He absently began to chew his thumb as he watched the message fax. The holo of Ily Takka paused after her ritual greeting. Tybalt smiled.

How I've missed you, my hot fox. Haven't had a decent romp since you left. Enjoying the taste of power, my precious? Beware, it's poisonous. He laughed. Also true to her prediction, he had grown tired of having no one to talk to. The others simply agreed or refused to express their true feelings on matters out of fear of his power.

How lonely, this business of being Emperor.

Her next words brought him upright. "My Lord Emperor, it seems we have miscalculated. We thought Staffa might bargain beyond our means. We accepted that we might have to eliminate him from the service of the Sassans. To my surprise and astonishment he has turned down both the Sassan offer of contract—and ours. Lord Emperor, he wasn't even present. We had to deal face-to-face with his Wing Commander—and in the presence of the Sassan Legate to boot. The exact transcript of my actions and offers is enclosed with this report. Suffice it to say, the Companions don't care to listen to offers at this time, nor will the Lord Commander fight for either side. Enclosed is the packet his people prepared. I trust you will find it to be most interesting."

Impossible! Staffa turned down the largest contract ever offered? He wouldn't even *listen* to an offer from Rega? Or Sassa? A sudden shiver ran down Tybalt's spine. What did it mean? What was Staffa's angle? Was he preparing to go rogue? Perhaps turn to piracy? Or worse, could it be some deep conspiracy he and the Sassans had concocted during Staffa's last contract?

Tybalt picked up the brief from the ceramic table before him. He frowned at the broken seal and looked back at the screen as Ily continued, "Not the least of the revelations to come out of the Itreatic Asteroids is that Staffa himself is on leave. He has disappeared." Her lips curled with triumph. "But, Lord Emperor, he is vacationing within Rega and I believe I have the ability to find him. I will keep you informed concerning the results of my search."

Tybalt realized dumbly that his mouth gaped open. The Lord Commander had gone totally daft! The single most important man in the politics of Free Space—disappeared! *Vacationing, by the Bloody Gods!*

Ily bent her head in deep thought. "Which brings us to the Companions. I couldn't interest them in any of the offers I tried to make. One possible exception might be the Targan affair. Wing Commander Lyma hinted that Staffa *might* contract to fight for the Empire in that 'domestic' matter. As a result, I propose we allow that stew to boil for a while longer."

She took a step and raised a hand to her chin, indicating deep thought; and Tybalt nodded his agreement during the pause.

Her eyes flashed up. "I suggest, Lord Emperor, that we allow the Rebels to gain some ground. Perhaps a shipment of arms might fall to them? And afterward, suppose a green commander took a punitive force into the field? Let's assume that details of his orders and command were somehow to fall into Targan hands. And if there were a foul-up in the chain of command at the critical moment, would it not be possible that our situation might appear desperate enough to appeal to the Companions and their sense of vanity in arms?" She raised an eyebrow.

It might indeed work. Oh, how precious my Ily is. Had I a complete Council of her caliber—Staffa and his butchers be damned—I'd have the whole of Free Space in my very palm! Indeed, there has to be a likely candidate to promote. Staff Second Kapitol? No, too much family clout there. Perhaps someone from the lower ranks, an insignificant man.

It began to come together.

"And the First Targan Assault Division—already decimated once—could be launched again into the fray," Tybalt noted. After all, it had only recently been filled with the rankest of the inexperienced drawn from twenty different reserve cadres. "Nothing there to lose."

"In the meantime, Lord Emperor, I will await your verdict on my report." Ily bowed her head submissively, a mockery only Tybalt could understand as he stared at the falling veils of her glossy black hair.

He turned to his own equipment. "My Lord Minister of Internal Security. Your report and recommendations are accepted and approved. I only have one other order: *Find Staffa!*"

* * *

Private Sohnar came aware slowly, his mind piecing itself together, drawing strings of thought into a continuous whole.

Pain filtered through the black recesses of unconsciousness. Pain made it difficult to align thoughts into a coherent string.

"Sohnar?"

The voice sifted through the pain and confusion, giving him something with which to identify. *Sohnar, that's me. That's me*, repeated in his hazy mind, a simple fact he could cling to.

"Sohnar? Wake up now. You should be able to hear us."

The voice came louder, and through the pain, he managed to feel his body, tingling in places, but still there. The effort to move his tongue came automatically. He recoiled from the dry, desiccated feel of his mouth.

"Water," he heard himself croak, awed by the quality of his voice.

Soothing wetness filled his mouth, causing him to almost choke as the gag reflex triggered. His reeling mind recovered, swallowed, and sought more of the wondrous liquid.

"Sohnar, we must talk," the voice came again, distinct this time.

He sought the familiar neural pathways and blinked his

eyes open. Images and colors blurred his vision. He heard: "Give him a couple more ccs of stimulant."

The prick of the injection barely penetrated the mantle of pain. Warmth rushed through him, allowing his thoughts to coalesce.

"Sohnar?" The voice asked, mild, compassionate.

"Yes." He sounded better now as he sucked on a small plastic tube of liquid.

"What happened last night?" The gentle voice soothed him, making him feel safe.

Last night? What did *that* mean?

"Last night, Sohnar. I can see confusion on your face. What happened?" A pause while he tried to sort it out and then the voice reminded him. "You were on guard duty."

An image formed in Sohnar's stumbling mind. "Yes. Walking the compound."

"That's right."

He searched his memory, struggling to recall. "Boring. Terribly boring."

"Did you see anything unusual?"

He felt himself try to nod, pain lancing at the back of his neck.

"What?" the voice prodded through the pain, bringing him back to the wavering image.

"Officers. Two officers. Man and a woman." Yes, he could remember. Both coming down the white wooden stairs from the First Assault Division Headquarters. Sohnar explained slowly, having trouble with the words.

"What did you do?"

Sohnar thought, closing his eyes so the blurred images outside didn't confuse the ones in his mind.

"Saluted."

"Good for you . . . and then?"

What? Sohnar thought, trying to pull the pieces from his wobbling, shifting thoughts. "Not right," he whispered to himself, remembering.

"What was not right, Sohnar?"

"The woman," he added, remembering her face. Drawn, white, nervous. "And. . . . And. . . ."

"Go on. And what?" the soothing voice prodded. "It is vitally important that we know, Sohnar. Please . . . please, we need you to remember."

Important. Must know. Sohnar struggled, his mind starting to shy away from the thoughts. A feeling of something
terrible stirred in his subconscious. It came to him.

"Her armor," Sohnar remembered. "Bloody. Thought
she might have been on a raid. Scared. She was scared."

More began to fill in the blind spots. "The man, big man,
dark-skinned, saluted. Good soldier doesn't question an
officer. I returned to my patrol."

"Yes, Sohnar, go on," the gentle voice caressed him.

"Walked around the perimeter fence," Sohnar added,
seeing his route through the lighted section behind the First
Division Headquarters. "Saw them again. At the electrical
panel behind the headquarters."

The horror trembled beneath his memory. Fear began to
mix with the pain he lived.

"Good work, Sohnar, don't let us down now, son. We
need you. Need your report."

"They . . . they did something to chips in the box. I
walked . . . walked quietly. Could hear them talking. The
man spoke. Said, 'That's good. Red-green to white-blue.
That reconnects the alarm.' "

Sohnar hesitated.

"And then?"

"Then. . . . Then. . . ." Sohnar swallowed, his mouth
gone dry again. "The woman closed the box and she leaned
against the wall. Sick. . . . Sick. . . . She threw up on the
ground. The man put his arm around her shoulder. Comforting, you know?"

"You're doing fine, Sohnar. Tell us all of it. You are so
important."

A shaking tried to climb out of Sohnar's mind. Fear tan-
gled his speech center, making him utter strange noises.

"'Give him a half cc to calm him. This is the critical part."

Another slight prick and Sohnar felt his fear recede—
unfortunately, so did some of his carefully maintained
coherency.

"Continue, Sohnar," the gentle voice prompted.

"Walked forward . . . to see . . . if I could . . . help her.
Saw . . . her look . . . up. Amber eyes." Fear, despite the
repression, surged again. Stubbornly, Sohnar fought with all
his Ashtan bull-headedness. "She made . . . strange noise.

I . . . only . . . help her. To help her. Didn't have . . . time to react." His voice locked.

In his mind, Sohnar relived that moment, watched in horror as the woman tensed, the man stepping to one side, pulling a pistol from his belt.

Sohnar, understanding too late, crouched, bringing his blaster up, turning to meet the man. The barest flicker of movement caught at the edge of his vision.

The woman—he'd forgotten the woman! An iron grip caught his throat, stifling the scream of warning. He'd tried to turn, looking into her face. So pretty. The image barely flashed across his mind as he tried to pull back, scared. Her knee caught him low in an explosion of pain only partially absorbed by the combat armor.

He'd tried to back-heel her, throw her off, but something warm and wrong flickered in his belly. Terror had blinded him as his body went oddly weak and he sagged in her grip while his lungs burned for want of air.

And as it all went dizzy, he slumped in her arms, eyes locked with hers . . . falling.

Funny thing, she had followed him to the ground and all the way he'd looked into those frightened eyes. In the compound lights, he'd seen her hair falling around him as he lay on the ground. Reddish with a hint of brown, it had cast rainbows in the floodlights.

As his world grayed, he'd wanted to tell her not to be afraid, that things would be all right. But they had gone, the man dragging her away while blood bubbled up in Sohnar's mouth, filling his lungs and trachea.

Alone, the world going dim, he realized he'd smeared more blood on her armor as he dragged her down.

Sohnar could barely hear the gentle voice calling to him. A faint sting came from his face. Grayness drew close around him . . . sinking. . . .

Division First Mykroft sighed and crossed his arms as the psych interrogator ceased to slap the boy and looked up.

"Condition?" Mykroft demanded.

"Dead, sir. This time, I think he's too far gone. We might have dumped too many stimulants into his system as it was." The interrogator checked one of the instruments hooked to Sohnar's claylike flesh.

Mykroft chewed his lip and nodded. "Very well, we got all we could out of him, I guess. Woman and a man, hmm? Must have used a vibraknife to get through his armor that way."

The interrogation officer looked up. "At least we know they did something to that alarm system."

Mykroft ground his teeth and frowned. "Indeed. At the same time, they murdered most of the First Division commanders. Thank the Blessed Gods they didn't come after the Second." He paused, as if talking to himself. "That would have been me."

The interrogation officer calmly shut down the systems pumping blood through Sohnar's body and stood. "In the meantime, what will happen to First Division?"

"That's up to the Minister of Defense. Of course, we won't let any hay grow under our feet in the meantime. We can turn the situation here to our advantage by . . ." Mykroft caught himself. Irritated, he gave the interrogation officer a blistering look. "Just like an interrogation man, Third. You're full of too many damned questions. You've got me answering them now."

The Interrogation Third fought a smile. "Yes, sir."

"And put out an arrest order for a big dark-skinned man and a woman with the description he gave us. Damn you, Sohnar, you died too quickly." Mykroft shook his head at the corpse and left, boots clicking hollowly on the hospital floor.

* * *

"Hauws! Break five men to the left through that gully! *Move, Gods Rot it! NOW!*" Sinklar bellowed into his comm. That slight sensation of unreality gave him a split second warning to throw himself face first into the rocky earth as concussion and gravity flux raised havoc with his ears and balance. The ground heaved under him.

Dirt and rocks pelted his body in a clattering rain, bouncing off his armor.

Sinklar shook his head and wiggled his jaw to clear his ears as he struggled up on all fours. Teeth gritted, he refused to trust his feet after the effects of the disrupter detonation. He glared angrily up at the raw sky.

The battered ridge that the Second Section of the First Division called home had been turned into a blasted no man's land of trenches, foxholes, and bunkers that he and his Groups had gouged out of the resisting Targan soil. They lived among cratered and pulverized rocks. Smoke, intermixed with dust, drifted across it while laser and blaster fire shot lines of color through the haze.

"Hauws? Did you get that?" Sinklar demanded, a cackle of blaster bolts sounding like burning air over his head.

"Affirmative." Hauws' voice came back. A hollow thump from a mortar reverberated through the system. "They just got started. Uh . . . hold it. I hear firing from their direction. Good call, Sink."

"Sink?" Shiksta's voice came through, interrupting. "I think we've spotted something headed toward Kap's flank. Might be ten Rebels. Request permission to lay down a dispersing fire under signal seven conditions as per the manual, sir."

"Shik! Damn you, I don't care what the manual says. Fry them bastards if you can! Shoot! And from now on, I don't want to hear what the holy gawddamn book says. You're up here to kill Targans and keep the pass closed to resupply efforts! Now, shut up and SHOOT!"

"Yes, sir." Shik sounded contrite.

Sinklar shook his head, face contorting. "Hauws, be ready to back those boys up if things get too hot in that gully. That's one of your weak points."

Sinklar got slowly to his feet and managed to take a few tentative steps. Through the smoke and dust of his battleground, he began to look over the situation. Two Targans fled Hauws' gully. One tumbled as his shoulder erupted in a puff of pink. Good shot, that.

"Mac? How you doing?"

"Five casualties, Sink. The good news is that from where we're dug in here, we can see about forty of their dead. They keep sending advances out into that hollow down there. Why are they doing that?" Mac sounded genuinely confused. "Every time they trot out, we tear hell out of them!"

Sinklar's cracked lips curled up in a wicked smile. "Answer's easy, Mac. If a column advances in the open, what's the holy gawddamn book say an appropriate defensive response is?"

"Uh, let's see. Advance and flank, right?"

Fire lanced from Shik's heavy ordnance into a splintered cliff side to the right of Kap's position. A vortex of blaster bolts mixed with frag bombs and sonic shells left the mountain erupting dust, shattered rock, and, with a little hope, blasted Targan bodies. Maybe Shik was learning after all.

"That's right," Sinklar agreed. "Makes you think they got a book, too, doesn't it? The rest of you guys hear that?"

He felt the tingle, pitched face first into the dirt, and waited while a second disrupter blast shook their position. Sink pulled his face out of the ground, spit mud from his mouth, and grimaced at the grit and sand that crunched in his teeth.

"Shik? You get a trajectory on that last shot?" Sinklar demanded, wiping clinging grime from his face.

"Affirmative. We're computing for return fire now."

"Atta boy, Shik. You stuff a sonic shell down that thing and we'll all buy the beer."

Someone laughed on the comm.

Sinklar studied the layout of his people. His eyes traced each of the fortified positions.

"Ayms? You got anybody covering that slope on your right flank?"

Ayms cleared his throat. " 'Firmative, Sink. Three men. Dug them in just like you said. So far they've sniped off two or three Targ-ets who tried to sneak up there with some sort of back packs. Probably some sonic explosive or other. If they could send a big enough seismic shock through this ground, they might stun us enough to overrun the position."

Sinklar nodded to himself. "Now, that's thinking, Ayms. You read that in the holy gawddamn book?"

Laughter spattered through the comm like static. "Nope, Sink. Thought that up on my own."

"You'll make sergeant yet, Ayms. Stick with it."

Sinklar yawned and blinked at the fatigue in his eyes before crawling up to a rocky point where he could look down over Mac's position.

Shik's heavy stuff erupted in a barrage that speared the sky with streaks of light as rockets and mortar fire laced over a distant ridge. Centering his spotting goggles on the ridge, he could see rock slides break loose and trees shake—and that was on *this side*.

"Think I got that big gun of theirs," Shik muttered self-consciously.

They waited, occasional shots lacing the slanting light of evening. No more gravity shells fell.

Sinklar heard gravel crunch and turned to look, seeing Gretta climbing up the slope to drop down next to him.

"How's the war?" Sinklar asked around a wry smile.

Her blue eyes twinkled in a dirt-streaked face. Her teeth gleamed white behind her sensual lips. Strands of mahogany-brown hair had slipped out from under the helmet.

"You heard Third Section is pinned down? Calling for orbital bombardment? Fifth Section is running, shooting, and running some more. LCs are supposed to go in and pull them out after dark. That leaves us surrounded."

Sink nodded. "Yeah, and we've been under constant fire with only casualty LCs coming in. Heard Fifth wanted reinforcing last night and no answer came from Division. Their supplies didn't even arrive. Sort of like sacrificial goats, don't you think?"

"Neither did ours," she reminded. "What in hell is happening in headquarters?"

"Playing cards, drinking Myklenian booze?" Sinklar lifted a shoulder, anger rushing hot inside.

Gretta chuckled sourly. "Makes you wonder what we're fighting for, huh? We've got wounded to evacuate. If an LC doesn't come in tonight, we'll lose a couple."

Sinklar looked out at the setting sun and listened to sudden growing silence. "Guess it does make you wonder, doesn't it?"

She nodded, looking away at the distant purple mountains. "Pretty up here." And then, "Sink, most of us are still alive. You've seen the numbers we've been up against."

"Yeah," he nodded, remembering the masses of men and women who'd come running—jumping from rock to rock—weapons of all sorts in their hands. The battle for their rocky pass had been brutal and endless. "Where'd they all come from?"

"Their mamas." Gretta poked him in the ribs, not too effectively since his armor had been battered hard. Impact broke the interwoven microscopic tubes that held the chemical agent which intermixed and hardened within nanoseconds.

She studied him, a curious longing in her eyes. "Come on, let's go down to your place and get something to eat."

He took one last look at the quiet battlefield. Three days now of continuous assaults, endless sniping, and constant pressure. Maybe they—and the Targans—had simply worn out.

He ached as he skipped and slid down the slope to his bunker. Gretta pulled an opaque graphstic sheet back and ducked in. Sink followed and stood in the cramped space a couple of privates had excavated with vibrashovels.

Gretta switched on a field light and slapped a ration pack onto the wobbly table made of crate top. Three rickety chairs—from Gods alone knew where—were propped against the wall. His narrow bunk lay along the other side where it collected the dirt that fell out of the wall every time a shell landed nearby.

They didn't speak while they ate, wolfing down bite after bite. Sinklar couldn't help but gaze at her. His eyes traced the line of her jaw, his imagination wondering about the feel of her lips against his.

"I've seen desire, Sink. But you're starting to drool," she said through a mouthful of energy stick.

"Sorry. Didn't mean to. You're just. . . ."

She erupted in a giggle. Then, in a low voice, she added, "Thank you, Sinklar. I've wanted to see that look in your eyes."

Awkwardly, he wiped his mouth and leaned back, aware the chair creaked and groaned. He tried to change the subject. "I never suspected war would be so busy."

She blinked owlishly and shook her head. "Never thought after they blew the post office that we'd live this long. Or this well!" Gretta laughed, lifted the last scraps of ration in grimy fingers, and dropped them on her tongue. "I remember watching a rat run by in Kaspa. Wanted to blast it on the spot."

"Tough times back there." He didn't remember reaching for her hand.

She stared at him through clear, unwavering eyes. "I . . . I've missed you, Sink."

He tilted his head, realizing his toe rested on hers, moving back and forth through the heavy armor. "I was only in the hospital for two weeks. Those machines work marvels."

She grinned at him. "You know, I thought you were a real nonentity when I first met you in training camp on Rega. All locked away in your head."

He tried to shrug, but the stiffened armor wouldn't allow it. "Maybe I still am. Trying to keep us alive."

"Alive," she mused, tightening her grip. "That's important to you. Why? Why do you care so much? Other officers, they just want to hang around in the rear and drink and talk war."

Sinklar squirmed uneasily and stood, walking to the bedroll laid on the small bunk. With heavy fingers he unlatched the streaked, smoke-stained armor and slid out of the chest piece.

Why does this make me so nervous? I'm coming to love this woman. Can't I share myself with her? Why is it so hard to let loose? I. . . . I can't tell her everything. I can't. Too painful.

He started awkwardly. "Goes back . . . back to being a kid, I suppose. I . . . I'm. . . . Well, look at me. Always the runt. The skinny kid who reads all the time. Got two different colored eyes. I'm short, Gretta. Always been short. Not only that, I was raised by the State. In the old days, they called me an orphan. And there are other things. Things I didn't know until recently." He looked around, raising a hand helplessly as he leaned against the rough-hewn rock and sighed.

Why do you look at me like that? You just watch, and wait, really listening to what I say. No one has ever just listened to me—let alone a woman as beautiful as you. Why have I always been so lonely?

He shook his head, clearing his thoughts. "I . . . I guess I look around now, and see all of us. The whole Division isn't anything but a bunch of . . . nonentities. Wasn't that the word you used?"

She blushed. "Sink, I—"

"Hush. It's all right. I mean, that's why I care. We're non-people. Blaster fodder. You've heard that term? Well, that's us. Orders are," he mocked an official voice, " 'Second Section, hold that pass and allow no one to cross it!' " He pursed his lips and looked up, letting himself drown in those eyes. "And that's what we do. We died by the hundreds in the Kaspa Post Office. Did anyone investigate to find out why?"

She shook her head, eyes on his, expressing a sudden pain at his harsh words.

"No one cared why First Division was almost wiped out. We don't count, Gretta." His lips worked. "But me, I can make a difference now. Out there," he waved toward Kaspa, "something happened. I . . . I came into myself. All the stuff I'd studied for all these years suddenly slipped into place. Now, Sinklar Fist, the freak, can change things. In a small way, I can keep these men and women alive." He felt the fire in his eyes, watched her lips part as she nodded agreement.

"Come sit here," he whispered. "Let me look at you, hold you."

She stood up and paused while her fingers released her armor. "You're all I wanted you to be, Sink."

"I . . . I want you, Gretta." He felt himself tighten. "From the time we came down in the LC, I couldn't keep my mind off you."

She shook out her hair, slipping the armor off her legs so she stood before him in her padded undersuit.

His eyes devoured her as she ran her finger along the quick release; her underwear fell away exposing her full young breasts, the curve of her tight belly leaving her navel and the tantalizing black V of her pubic hair in shadow.

Sinklar had trouble swallowing as she reached down, breasts swaying, to pull his remaining armor off. He stifled a joyous cry as she undid his undersuit. One warm palm burned on his chest as she pushed him flat. He winced as she fingered the angry scars on his side.

"Oh, Blessed Gods," he whispered as her warm flesh slid over his on the narrow cot.

* * *

Magister Bruen looked up from the report on the monitor. He rubbed a fragile hand across his wrinkled chin as he stared at the irregular rock overhead. The single light fixture threw an eerie glow over the chamber and cast shadows behind the spare furniture.

He raised his voice, calling, "Magister Hyde?"

Bruen's eyes searched the carved stone above his head as if the answer might be there, engraved into the very basalt. *How could it have gone so wrong?*

"Yes?" There came a shuffling of feet and cloth.

"Staffa has turned down both the Sassans and Rega. They refused contract to both parties—for a year at least."

A long silence followed before Hyde sputtered, "What? Impossible! It doesn't make any military sense. What motivates that man beyond death and mayhem?"

Bruen stroked his chin. "We—and the machine—completely missed this possibility."

Magister Hyde moved over and pulled out a chair, grunting as he settled into it. "You're sure? Perhaps he's playing for time—driving the price up? Perhaps the Myklenians hurt him worse than our intelligence indicated?"

"Perhaps, honorable Magister," Bruen mumbled absently as his mind played with this new dimension of Staffa kar Therma's personality. How did it fit? He needed some key to slip this new piece into the puzzle. How could he make a picture when the pieces insisted on changing colors and shapes in the middle? Quanta at work.

"Didn't predict he'd kill the Praetor, either," Hyde reminded, lost in his own thoughts. "That's when our predictions began to go awry."

Bruen slapped a withered hand on the monitor before him. "Indeed. Until then we had stayed within three degrees of freedom. But Staffa withdrawing from the table? Totally outside of any of our predictions." His wrinkled face creased in annoyance. "No, we didn't predict he would kill the Praetor. Accidentally, yes. But in person? Never."

Hyde bent over the desk, pulling his robes up his skinny white arms so he could lean on his elbows without slipping. "So we have the key. The Praetor did something to him— said something."

"If we accept that assumption, it could change everything. You know what sort of man the Praetor was—brilliant and diabolical."

Hyde stared absently at the floor. "Yes, brilliant. A man to admire and hate. Working with him always left me feeling like I had been privileged and fouled at the same time."

Bruen continued to frown at nothingness, lost in his

thoughts. "The Praetor could have done anything, said anything. You don't suppose he bragged about Chrysla, do you? Have we underestimated that facet of his personality? We ensured that Chrysla died during the battle—I think. Our agent never got free of the Praetor's flagship to report. I would assume thrakis got her before the blasters did." Bruen made a useless gesture with his hand. "Rotted shame. She was such a beautiful woman . . . and the world is so short of beautiful women these days."

"And the girl? Arta? Is there some way we can still use her to salvage this situation?" Hyde worked his toothless gums and rubbed his deep-set eyes.

Bruen blinked and leaned back. "You read the report. They succeeded in eliminating Atkin and his staff—in bed no less. With that vacancy, we can expect the Minister of Defense to appoint Kapitol to the First Division. He's earned it, you know. Kissed Tybalt's rosy red rectum enough times. With him in command of the First Division, he'll do everything in his power to hamstring Mykroft in the Second. There's been an incredible hatred between them. Should effectively reduce the Regan capabilities on Targa by the third." His eyes lit. "We might even get lucky and have them shooting at each other."

"I read that report. The girl got more than a dose full of assassination," Hyde reflected. "Not only that, but I worry. I perceive a sexual interest."

Bruen grunted. "Butla knows. We talked."

"You had counted on her remaining a virgin." Hyde looked at him dully. "Breached, will she react the way you hope she will?"

"With Staffa going wild? I don't count on anything. The quanta are acting. Either that or we've missed a variable."

"Or could it be the machine?" Hyde wondered.

Bruen fought a shiver. *Don't think it. Not now. Change the subject. Otherwise it will gnaw at Hyde. Drive him into the grave.*

Bruen tapped his lips with translucent-skinned fingers. "Do you suppose Staffa's turning rogue? Perhaps he's becoming a pirate? This way, he can keep the balance of power and play one against the other so neither can become strong enough to threaten him and his precious industry."

"We investigated that years ago, Magister," Hyde reminded, with a pointed finger. He leaned against the rough stone of the cavern wall and shook his head. "The decision we made then—and I think it still holds—is that he would help the Sassans win. When the dust settled, he would declare himself Emperor with his Companions to back him up. Would you ignore two empires that could one day destroy you? No, you're like Staffa, Bruen. You'd take it all." Hyde waved his hands furiously, "Oh, sure, he's refused to dicker. I insist it's a ploy for time."

"Then why has he disappeared?" Bruen wondered, enjoying the look of absolute astonishment in Hyde's fractured expression.

"Assassination? Or . . ." Hyde gasped, "Oh, no! Perhaps he . . . suspects?" Hyde ended up coughing and hacking.

"I don't think so." Bruen indicated the monitor screen and accessed a program. "This is Staffa's speech to his command rank officers. Listen to him. Notice the expressions he uses."

Bruen watched Hyde pensively as the tape played through to the end.

"I still don't believe it!" Hyde slapped the table between gasping breaths. "What chances are there that this is some false trail cooked up to send us down the—"

"Statistically and practically impossible. Subsequent to this being released by time delay—oh, Staffa was clever—the Wing Commander turned down both empires. Didn't even listen to their offers. And within ten hours Skyla took her private vessel and left the Itreatic Asteroids in search—we presume—of Staffa."

Hyde had his eyes closed again, lost in thought. Moments passed before he asked, "And what does that tell us about Skyla? Does she know where Staffa is? What is her concern? Surely the Companions are in no trouble."

Bruen lifted a shoulder. "They aren't lovers, so I doubt it's an affair of the heart. No, I would rather think it has something to do with Staffa's activities."

"I have the latest figures. Our forces have enjoyed another ten percent enlistment. People are fleeing the cities to join the Rebellion in the back country. The Regan outposts have been harassed constantly and we've routed two entire Sections and inflicted heavy losses. Their ranks are

wearing down—all but one, that is." Hyde clicked his long
fingernails on the counter. "Care to guess whose?"

"Sergeant Sinklar again?"

"He is exceeding his projected curve much too early."
Hyde leaned back and chewed on his finger.

Bruen smiled wearily. "Yes, I know. Our people paid a
lot to keep him out of their university. Now we may need
him after all, depending on what Staffa does—and what
happens with Arta."

Hyde turned his head to stare. "I wonder how he kept
from being killed. The quanta at work?"

"Congenital ability," Bruen grunted. "Keep the pressure
up on the invasion forces. Morale is dropping in the Divisions. Too many Regans are dying and not enough Targans.
It's sapping them on the inside."

"We captured an entire weapons dump full of rifles,
heavy blasters, ten patrol craft, and a half dozen heavy
assault vehicles," Hyde announced. He beamed a smile.
"They set down in the wrong valley, it seems. We're not
the only ones with bad luck. Our military capability took a
quantum leap with that infusion of material. We can defeat
an entire Division—if they're stupid enough to put one in
the field."

"So things look moderately good with the exception of
Staffa."

"If we just knew what he's up to!" Hyde cried. "The
Lord Commander is the most important person in Free
Space. The fate of all humanity rests on that man's shoul-
ders. And *we* can't find him!"

Bruen smiled wearily. "Easy, my friend. Calm yourself
and consider this. Ily Takka, our single most dangerous
adversary, left the Itreatic Asteroids after the Companions'
refusal to deal."

"So?"

"So she never returned to Rega. Does that suggest anything to you?" Bruen nodded soberly as Hyde stiffened.
"Exactly. Ily, too, is looking for Staffa—and Fates help us
if she finds him first."

CHAPTER XI

"Next! State your name."

Two guards pushed Staffa out into the courtroom. He braced his legs, glaring up defiantly at the court officers. Before him, a Judicial Magistrate and several clerks sat behind a tall hardwood podium. Galleries full of curious people lined the upper walls. Above the galleries, a groined ceiling rose. Light pods and security monitors nestled in the high niches. The whole place had been painted a pale green and an odor of unwashed bodies filled the air. He felt ludicrous wrapped in the towel they had given him.

"Staffa kar Therma, Lord Commander of Companions," his stentorian tones rolled out over the room. A tittering of voices broke the sudden silence. The endless nightmares had given way to this, a different kind of hell—but one with hope. It would be only a matter of time now.

"Oh, yes," the Judicial Magistrate nodded, staring down at his monitor, "the madman." He looked up, a bored expression on his face. "You are charged with the deaths of two citizens. You are charged with assault on a public official. You are charged with vagrancy—being present in Etarus with no visible means of support other then preying upon the Emperor's citizens. I ask, have you an address, or proof of occupation?"

"Five years ago, I could have burned this planet to slag. I should have done so," Staffa growled. "I would suggest in the meantime, Magistrate, that you contact Wing Commander Skyla Lyma in the Itreatic Asteroids to verify—"

"Enough!" the Magistrate thundered, his gavel slapping the room to silence. He worked his lips as he entered a notation into the comm. "I suppose you have an explanation as to why you murdered two citizens and why you were naked in a public place?"

"They robbed me. I killed two before I lost consciousness." Anger raged in a vortex under his throat; the inferno threatened to engulf him. His arms trembled as he waited before the elevated sandwood bench. He took time to glare his hatred at the hooting crowds in the galleries. They made a *spectacle* of him, Staffa kar Therma! He imagined burning them all where they sat—vengeance against the ghosts that had begun to haunt his dreams.

"Yes, so you say," the Magistrate ventured cynically. "But Civil Security only received reports that a madman was running naked and killing people. Who is your master?"

"*I have no master!*" Staffa roared. A violent stab of pain scorched his spine and left him bent and contorted, his mind numb as he struggled to keep from falling. He groaned as a bailiff stepped back, the stun rod hanging easily from his hand.

The Magistrate pointed a long white finger and added calmly, "This is a court of law. I will brook no further outrageous statements, madman. You are a slave. Your body is covered with scars. I suppose you would have us believe those are your battle wounds?"

Laughter and jeers rolled down from the galleries.

Staffa pulled himself up to his full height and threw his head back, loose black hair in an unruly tangle. "Among my people, scars are a symbol of honor—of pride in service to the Companions."

More screeches of amusement from above. Humiliation twined with anger; Staffa ground his teeth and his breathing went short.

"And the Companions murder innocent citizens, I suppose?" The Magistrate scratched his head and sighed. "Yes, I know the reputation the Star Butcher has, madman. That he commits atrocities in the name of the Empire is not the concern of this court, however. From your appearance, it is obvious that you are an escaped slave. During your medical treatment for concussion, you broke a physician's arm and incapacitated two interns. That, madman, is assault of a public official. Since then, you have demonstrated uncontrollable rages and delusions, all of which make you—in the eyes of this court—a hazard to the Emperor's citizens. Further, you have admitted to the murder of two of those citizens. Have you a statement?"

Staffa's anger surged as he knotted his fists, the muscles popping on his shoulders and arms. "You will pay, all of you."

The judge continued, voice somnolent, "Be it known, therefore, *Staffa kar Therma*, that this court finds you guilty on all counts. Further, it is the option of the court to sentence you to death or slavery."

Staffa stiffened, fear running white where anger had previously dominated. He began to tremble as he sensed the bailiffs stepping forward, stun rods ready.

The Magistrate laced his fingers together and leaned forward. "Something tells me I should just execute you. However, you have absorbed a great deal of the court's time and the Emperor's resources. We kept you in stasis until your health improved. Perhaps a poor investment. I think it only fair that the people get something in return. I therefore sentence you to a lifetime of labor for the state. You will be remanded into the custody of the Warden of City Projects and fitted with a stasis collar. Are you familiar with a stasis collar?"

Staffa's lip jerked as he nodded, eyes slitted.

"You will repeat for the record of the court that you know what a stasis collar is and how it works."

Rotted Gods, he knew how the system worked. The damned stasis collars were manufactured *by his own labs in the Itreatic Asteroids!*

He forced himself to say: "The stasis collar works on the principle of damping neural and physical activity at the molecular level. In effect, it stops nerve impulses and blood flow in a man's neck while the collar field is activated. Too long a stasis leads to nerve damage, suffocation, or potential embolism, heart failure and brain deterioration through oxygen starvation. The field generation comes through a directional gravitational—"

"Let the record show the defendant understands the stasis collar." The Magistrate made an entry into the record and called, "Next!"

Staffa bellowed, "Is there no justice here? You will not even check to see if I am who I say I am? What sort of—"

He screamed as two stun rods brought him to his knees and left his muscles contorting in agony, his brain seared with pain.

The Magistrate looked down, mildly annoyed. "Let me give you one last thought, madman. I was present in the temple five years ago when your namesake, the Lord Commander, conquered this world for the Emperor. I will recall until the day I die the words he uttered to the Etarian High Priests. He said, 'Don't come to me calling for justice. Your claims of fairness and humanity mean nothing, nor do I care for your precious conventions or beliefs. Your very existence teeters at my whim. Anger me not, Priest, and speak not of right, or justice, or grievances. If you have complaints, *take them to the Emperor!*' "

The beard! If he saw me, he knows what I look like. It's the beard! He raised trembling fingers to the thick growth on his cheeks and found it matted with filth.

The Magistrate shook his head at Staffa's obvious shock then he waved. "Bailiffs, take him out and deliver him to the Warden. *Next!*"

What followed became a nightmare of pain and rage as he made attempt after attempt to reach the bailiffs. Each time they stunned him into shivering meat until he finally walked where they wished him to, staggering with exhaustion. His teetering mind turned one threat over another as he swore his vengeance on this planet of human putrefaction.

Spears of pain shot through him again as they shocked him half-unconscious. His body bounced hollowly off the filthy floor and his head smacked loudly on the concrete. Lights shot through his vision. He could not physically resist as the cold alloy of the collar fastened around his neck.

"Get up." The order barely penetrated his abused mind.

"I said, *get up!*" A foot smashed his kidney.

Fury—rather than compliance—brought him weaving to his feet. His lungs burned as they heaved. The two bailiffs stood back, out of his reach, stun rods ready. As if they needed them. He realized with a shock that his legs were totally absorbed with the effort to simply hold him up. They could have pushed him over with one hand.

He, Staffa kar Therma, whom Sassa and Rega quailed to please, stood impotent. The shock of it drained him of further resistance and left him as psychologically numb as his body had been under the discharge of the stun rods. His voice caught in his throat like a lump as he looked down at his trembling hands. A white-hot ache lashed through his bruised brain.

"Listen, madman," the tall bailiff told him. "The stasis collar is plugged into the broadcast net controlled by the Warden's officer. That's the shiny thing you see sticking out of their heads. You understand?"

Staffa nodded, blinking, trying to get his mind to function.

"Good. Because if anything happens to him—like if he dies—the sending unit jams and your collar activates. If that happens, you die with him. Understand how it works? You take very good care of your officer; his life is yours. You make him mad, and he can kill you with a thought, or punish you until you behave."

Staffa nodded again. How many men, women, and children had he sold into slavery? Rotted Gods, he knew how the system worked.

The smaller bailiff told him in a casual voice, "This is a taste of it."

Staffa's vision swam as he crumpled to the floor; his spinal cord had shorted. Haze shimmered behind his eyes and he felt nothing beyond taste, hearing, sight, and the cold hard stone against his cheek. His head might have been severed from his body: His lungs went slack; his heart stopped; the blood slowed in his veins and brain. Pressure dropped in the carotid arteries. Insane terror scrambled his thoughts.

In an instant, his body tingled into a pins-and-needles existence. Feeling, blessed sensation, returned to his flesh; his lungs began to heave and he could swallow. No, no pain at all, just the fear and the helplessness of imminent death and total incapacity. He closed his eyes and felt a strange burning and blurring of his vision as tears welled hotly.

How long had it been since he'd cried? Like a still holo, the image grew: A nightmare scene as he unstrapped from the seat and walked forward. He could hear helium hissing from ruptured lines. Burning insulation made a pungent stink in his nose. The cabin door had ruptured and buckled on impact so he looked in to see the twisted bodies of his parents where they lay in the wreckage. Mother had landed on her side, ripped open and spilled by a jagged sheet of metal. His father had smeared on the tactite screen, body pulped into an inhuman shape.

Had he cried since that day?

"Get up, slave," the bailiff called. "Get up . . . or we'll let you have it again. You're under the same as a death sentence. We're under no compulsion to keep you alive. Get up."

Staffa rolled over and nodded miserably. "Wait . . . just a second. Let me . . . catch my breath." He took three gulps of air and fought his way to his feet, body wailing in protest. Ashamed, he wiped his eyes, blinking the tears away, wondering where sanity had gone in the universe.

"That way." The tall bailiff pointed, a stasis control in his hand. Staffa started down the ramp, strength beginning to return. This time only one bailiff followed.

"Threw my own words in my face," Staffa mumbled numbly, remembering the Magistrate's parting comment. He recalled that day, the sunlight bright and yellow as it spilled into the courtyard. The priest looked up at him from where he'd been thrown, whining, at Staffa's feet. He'd said those very words then, eyes flaying the quivering priest. He'd wanted to break the Magistrate's neck—but the judge had repeated it nowhere near as haughtily as he had when he'd faced that priest.

What has happened to me?

He traced nervous fingers over the collar around his neck. The alloy felt smooth, featureless. The circuits and power packs were built into the metal. The collars had been around since before his birth, but those had been cruder, necessitating that the slave be plugged into a charger every so often lest the power packs run down. To overcome that, he had suggested to his engineers that they build a unit that charged from the very body it commanded. True to their instructions, they'd built a system which took a slow trickle of body heat and converted it for the power packs.

And now my own innovation enslaves me.

An aircar waited outside a rear security door.

"Enjoy yourself . . . *Staffa*," the bailiff told him with a wry grin and left.

"Come on!" the officer at the aircar grumbled. "Get in.

We don't have all day." The warden who sat in the aircar looked like an oversized gnome. His bald head had been tanned by the sun and he wore a khaki uniform. "I'm Morlai, sort of in charge of you and the team you'll be working with. I share the duty with Anglo. I'm the nice guy. We're due in the desert and we've got a mess at the temple to fix first."

Staffa climbed in, noting the smooth plastic insert behind Morlai's ear. A silver wire rose to a small antenna that lay flush with the officer's scalp.

He barely saw the city they passed through. His mind continued to stagger as it struggled to find a centering point. What sort of world was this? What sort of empire had he done so much to build? There had to be justice for a man of his. . . . *Take it to the Emperor!*

He rubbed his eyes and stared dully at his fingers. Incomprehensible! They were dirt encrusted! He looked down at his body for the first time, seeing the smears and grime that caked his flesh. Familiar scars crisscrossed his muscular flesh, some disappearing into the stained towel they'd given him. It smelled of urine and stale sweat. His feet hurt where the tender skin had chafed, unused to treading on the gravel and sand.

How could this happen to the Lord Commander? What had possessed Broddus to rob him in the first place? Why had the man. . . . Gold, of course. So much could be bought with gold. *Like empires*, some maleficent part of his mind added. He closed his eyes and bit his lip, refusing to believe.

Why wouldn't the Magistrate check my claims? Why didn't he believe me? He forced his reeling mind to think. A naked man covered with scars is found in a back alley with two dead men next to him. And this is the Lord Commander, the hated Star Butcher? *I've been damned by my own beard! But it isn't right!*

Staffa chuckled to hide the sinking in his chest. He never let holo images of his features out for security reasons. What lengths would those he'd destroyed go to . . . to. . . . *Oh, Rotted Gods!* A creeping cold iced his thoughts as he stared dully at the tendons that popped from the backs of his hands.

Putrid Gods! What if someone *did* recognize him? What

a pompous fool he had been! He'd stood there, before that Magistrate and claimed, *CLAIMED* to the whole Empire that he was Staffa! A man entire planets had paid to have murdered, stood buck-naked before a public audience and offered himself like a sheep!

Staffa, you've got to start thinking again. You're not yourself. The effects of the Praetor's conditioning are affecting your judgment. But understanding that intellectually and coping with it were two different matters.

His throat went dry and his heart hammered. Praise the Blessed Gods they'd thought him crazy! He shifted uncomfortably on the hard bench. How long would that last? How long until someone mentioned the fact that the Lord Commander had gone on vacation to parts unknown? Etarus—sporting its renowned whore priestesses—was a logical place for any man to go. What price would his head bring? If one of those observers in the court even suspected, how much could that information alone be sold for?

Memories of the bald man on the shuttle plagued him. What lengths would even that disturbed and pained individual go to in order to destroy the man who'd taken his planet and killed and savaged his family?

"My legacy is fear," Staffa whispered dully.

I must escape! I've got to get loose—get away!

How? How did he break the collar so much of his own time had gone into forging? His fingers traced the metal, warm now, feeding off his flesh like some malevolent parasite.

The aircar slowed near a rear entrance to the temple. Staffa looked up at the huge buff sandstone building and remembered the graceful marble columns and the cool air inside. Last time he'd strode imperiously in through the front entrance, his STO teams having already secured the building.

Morlai stretched and yawned after he climbed out. He didn't look like an impressive sort with his fleshy face and bare scalp. His belly bulged over his belt and he inspected Staffa from lackluster hazel eyes.

"What's your name, slave?" the driver asked, motioning Staffa from the car.

"Sta. . . ." He shrugged, nervous, scared at what he'd

almost said. "I guess it doesn't matter who I was anymore. What would you call a man like me?"

The driver pointed him toward the entrance, talking as they walked. "Well, let's see. You're big—bull strong, judging by the muscle packed in your shoulders. Been used hard to get all them scars. You're a tough one, huh?"

Staffa shrugged.

"Call yourself Tuff." Morlai laughed from deep in his belly. "Yeah, that's a good one. Tuff."

Staffa glared at him through cold gray eyes.

Morlai noticed, and added, "Listen, Tuff, this is the way the system works. You're not here because you're a nice guy. Me or any of the boys can kill you with one thought. Got it? That's all it takes. Just the right thought patterns and you're dead. Simple little thing to think those thoughts and I don't have to physically lift a finger. Now, we have a certain series of jobs to do. None of them are nice; none of them are easy." The flat hazel eyes appraised him neutrally.

Staffa grunted in reply.

The warden grinned maliciously. "If a robot can't do it, we use you boys." Then he made a deprecating gesture. "Look, we're not monsters. Some people say we're foul enough to work for the Rotted Star Butcher himself, but we're only doing a job that we get paid for like anyone else. You help us get our work done, and we'll treat you the best we can—even get you a bottle every now and then. Give us grief, Tuff, and we'll make your life a living hell—or leave you dead and not worry about it."

Staffa shook his head as they descended a narrow, rock-walled stairway. In the dank underbelly of the temple he'd once dominated, Staffa stepped into a dimly lit room. Water dripped from the gray ceiling panels and the air carried a wretched stench. Two dirty men in collars stood over a turbulent pool that lapped out onto the floor. Another officer, arms crossed, slowly shook his head as he studied the surging water. Beside them, a wet machine of some sort rested. One of the inspection panels hung open to expose the circuitry.

Morlai called, "Got a new one, boys. Meet Tuff. What's the trouble, Anglo?"

Anglo had close-cropped dark hair and stood a little shorter than Staffa. His uniform was the same khaki as Mor-

lai's. A black leather belt at his waist was studded with
pouches and shiny equipment. Anglo looked up, tension in
his hard eyes. "Kaylla's down there. She's been gone a long
time. Rotted Gods, hope we don't have her stuck in there,
too."

Morlai gave Staffa a speculative glance. "You look fresh,
Tuff, want to see if you can get Kaylla out? Then when you
get her back up, swim back down and pry loose whatever's
plugging the drain."

Staffa swallowed, eyes going to the two dirty slaves and
then back to the officers. Anglo started to frown. *No, don't
get them mad. Take the chance on the water.*

His gut churned as he stepped to the edge of the black
roiling pool and the realization hit him: sewage. His flesh
cringed as he lowered his feet over the edge and felt the
cool liquid ripple over his warm body.

Something soft bumped the top of his foot as he slid in.
His testicles knotted and he slipped in up to his chest before
his feet touched greasy bottom.

"Hurry up!" Anglo yelled. "Kaylla's been gone almost
three minutes! Water's backed up into the temple baths.
Go!"

Staffa gave the man one lingering glare, and filled his
lungs. Fouled water rushed into his ears as he ducked.
The current pulled him along in the darkness. How much
time did he have? Worse, how would he get back? His
head bumped slimy surfaces as his buoyancy tried to float
him.

I'll die in here. My son, my son, have I failed you, too?

* * *

Sharp angular points of rock ate into Sinklar Fist's chest,
belly, and thighs. Sink studied the broken ridge tops
through his starlight goggles. So soon after sundown, the
IR visor had shown him only a mixture of hot spots. He'd
come to know each nook and cranny of the topography the
way he'd once known his narrow cot in the school dormitory
on Rega.

"Sink? I'm moving up now," Gretta's voice came through
his earphone.

"Take your time, love. I don't like the feel of it out

there." Once more he was acting in violation of the manual—the "holy gawddamn book", as they had all taken to calling it. Field commanders—like sergeants—were supposed to remain in sheltered positions beyond risk of exposure to enemy fire.

And just how the hell could he keep his knowledge of the fighting or changes in field tactics current while sitting on his ass in a bunker?

For two solid weeks now, they'd cut the pass off and reduced the Rebels to long circuitous routes of supply through the broken country to the north or south. The beleaguered Third and Fifth Sections—now replaced, reinforced, and totally demoralized—should have been guarding those areas. Those Sections had suffered being overrun twice and had been repeatedly decimated. Only orbital bombardment had forced the retreat of the Rebels during the reoccupation of those positions.

Sink forced his thoughts back to the battlefield and imagined Gretta moving through the dark. He could visualize her hips swaying gracefully, her keen eyes alert to the night. They ought to be in bed instead of out here about to be shot.

The Blessed Gods alone knew how he could live without her.

Gretta, please, be careful! I promise, we'll have better days ahead.

With great care, he propped himself on his toes and slid forward, letting the sharp rock eat different holes in his skin. Damn armor was flexible as silk until it got ruptured.

So much had changed that night they made love. Mostly, however, his bed was filled only with her memories. She had duties to her troops—sharing their billet was a corporal's responsibility. But those few moments when they could get away, he treasured as among the most precious in his life.

His thoughts settled on her amused expression and he remembered her dark brown hair hanging tauntingly about her perfect face while her blue eyes teased him with hidden secrets. He liked to simply sit and look at her, to admire and enjoy, lest through some magic, she vanished.

Something shifted out in the night. He blinked and

stared, trying to see whether he'd actually caught a movement. There. A head rose to stare in the direction of Gretta's sally.

"A Group, you've got a bandit perhaps thirty meters and two-twenty degrees from your point. Hold up."

"Roger, Sink," her cool voice came back.

"B Group, if you can make another 200 meters you should have a Rebel position in a crossfire. When Gretta opens up, they should fall back right into your arms."

"Roger, Sink. We're on the advance," Mac's tense voice came through.

Morale had soared at his decision to go out into the night after the Rebels who harassed them continuously. For the operation, he had taken his best companies, A and B, dreading the need to expose Gretta, knowing it would look like favoritism if he didn't. He might even have taken that risk, but she'd have known why—and he wouldn't risk her anger.

Another movement. He studied the figures who appeared as if springing from the very ground. A cave or tunnel? The mountains, they had learned, were riddled with vents from ancient vulcanism. The Rebels deftly began setting up a mortar, placing the tube and handing out boxes of rockets.

"We're at the base of the big rock," Mac's voice came softly.

Sinklar checked the position. "Rebels are seventy-five meters ahead of you on the ridge. Can you see the flat-topped pine from your position?"

"Roger."

"They're just on the other side of that. I make it five Rebels with a mortar. They have a rat hole there, so be careful."

"Roger."

"Gretta, continue your advance. Careful now. See if you can get your hands on that mortar and the rounds to go with it. Be fun to shoot some of their stuff back at them. Gods know, our side doesn't supply us half of what we need."

"You've got it, Sink. It'll be our pleasure!"

A POP-BOOM! sounded from back in the direction of the perimeter. The nightly shelling came right on schedule.

Also according to plan, he could hear the muted *kacka-kacka* of Shiksta's ordnance returning fire and making a racket to cover the advance of Sinklar's attack.

More movement.

"Hold!" Sinklar called. "Rotted Gods! There's ten, twenty, no, make that fifty, hell, *a hundred or more!*"

"Where?" Mac demanded.

"Coming up the crest of the ridge. They must have been massing down there on the other side. Looks like just small arms. Wait, there's a four-man portable blaster with a gen-set. They're moving up. Looks like they're. . . . Yeah, okay, they tied up with the mortar crew. I don't see any advance party out. They must think we're still back in camp hiding in our holes."

Stunned, he watched the massing troops. What should they do? Pull back? The odds began stacking higher and higher against them. What did it mean? Why were there. . . . A major strike! The Targans were going to make an attempt to overrun the pass. Experiencing tendrils of uncertainty, Sinklar made up his mind.

His voice went dry. "Hang tight, people. Let them advance. We've got surprise and position; they'll be sky-lined on the ridge."

"Roger," Gretta and Mac answered in unison.

Listen to the confidence in their voices. Rotted souls, they believe in me. All that trust. . . . What if I'm wrong? What if I lose them through some foolish error . . . some arrogant decision?

Behind him the pops and bangs of the bombardment had grown in pace, enough to trigger that sense of something gone wrong. Sinklar opened his mike again. "Ayms, you been listening?"

"Roger."

"Be ready. I think you're about to take a major hit from the Rebels." He chewed his lower lip, considering the risks. "Ayms, can you and the troops hang on? If you can hold out for an hour, I think we can take this bunch, double back, and catch your assault from the rear. We can break these guys."

Silence stretched for a long minute before Ayms' voice came back. "Sink? We talked it over. We'll hold the fort. I think we could keep them out with half the men we've got now. Hauws says the soil organisms here are making the troops meaner. We'll keep them from being bored. Keep in touch."

"Thanks, Ayms."

Sinklar smiled into the night, checking on the advance of the Rebel strike force.

"We can see them." Gretta sounded hoarse.

"Hang on," Sinklar whispered, noting where Gretta's people waited in relation to the advancing Rebels. Fear made his bowels turn runny. How good was the Rebel night vision gear? Would they see Gretta's people hiding in the rocks?

"Got them, Sink," Mac whispered. "We're spreading out . . . working up. We'll wait for Gretta to open the ball unless some guy walks down on top of us."

Sinklar's heart began to pound. Adrenaline rushed to make his arms feel light as he pulled his assault rifle up and squinted through the scope.

There're too many of them. This is suicide!

Checking the advance, they were no more than sixty meters from his position, well into the jaws of the trap.

Too late. Can't pull out. They'll see us any second.

"Hit them," he gritted into the mike, hating himself.

"Fire!" He heard Gretta's order, terse and crisp. Sinklar triggered his blaster, lacing the advancing Rebels, heart in his throat.

Once green troops, Second Section had turned deadly. A week of dirty battle had honed them and steeled their nerves. Blaster fire raked the advancing Rebels, catching them completely by surprise. At the same time, eyes dazzled by the brightness in the starlight scope, he could see three figures in combat armor sprinting for the mortar crew. His heart filled with warm pride. Gretta hadn't forgotten the mortar.

The Rebels were firing back ineffectually as they tried to compensate for their confusion and the havoc wreaked by Gretta's devastating fire. Sinklar almost whooped when the Rebels broke and ran—right down the throat of MacRuder's B Group. From there it turned into a massacre.

"Ayms?" Sinklar called into the mike. "Are you there?"

A long silence was punctuated by the sounds of violent combat from behind him.

His heart skipped when Ayms' voice finally answered, high-pitched; "Rotted Gods, Sink! *There's a million of them out there!* The rocks are literally too hot to touch—through battle armor no less. We're taking *that much fire!*"

"Are you holding?" Sinklar's belly churned and his breathing strained as sweat began to bead inside his helmet. *"Can you hold, Ayms?"*

"How the hell do I know? Hell, yes! I think. Barely. I didn't know we'd have to fight off half of Targa! *Get your ass back here!*" A pause. "Uh, sir." It came contritely and Sinklar laughed, partially from hysterical relief.

"Advance and clean up," he ordered A and B Groups. "Ayms is in big trouble."

"Roger," Gretta called. "We're moving on the ridge now. Not much left. We're shooting the dead to make sure they stay that way. These guys have Regan blasters, so we're packing equipment as we go."

"Good thinking. Detail a team to bring that four-man gun along. Mac? How you doing?"

"We're moving up the ridge, Sink. We got most of the final resistance. What we didn't get ran like rock-foxes. Shot most of them in the back in fact. They were covering and our guys just let them walk up and cut them down."

Sinklar nodded, suffering that curious elation of victory coupled with dread that his command was dying behind him.

He shouldn't have worried. Either the Rebels knew less about war than the Regan army did, or else they got confused and botched the battle plan. Moving Groups A and B, Sinklar did the impossible that night. He managed to trap nearly a thousand Rebel troops between his fortified camp on one side, a cliff on the other, and the sheer mountain flank on the third. Placing his two crack Groups on a commanding ridge to fire into the defenseless Rebel rear, Sinklar blocked the exit. He cut them to pieces with a neatly coordinated assault from his camp while A and B held off three suicidal counterattacks by the frantic Rebels.

For long bloody hours, blaster bolts streaked violently through the blackness. The air hummed and jumped with pulse fire. Trees flamed in torches of yellow-orange while men and women screamed and died in macabre firelight. Fragments of hot rock and blasted dirt jumped and pattered in the din. A brush fire raged through the fight to fry the wounded, their screams hideous in the night. To the shocked combatants it would have been no surprise had they learned that the tortured hell of the Rotted Gods had broken loose in the universe of men.

CHAPTER XII

So cold. So black. Veteran of a thousand battles, fear ran bright along Staffa's spine as he floated through the stygian sewer. His flailing hand slipped off a rung as cold panic gripped him. Better to have let them kill him with the collar than to die in here. Something smooth and rubbery—like skin—slid against his chest and his face popped out into air. His head at the top of the bubble, sewage rippled around his chin. Not much room—and someone else was taking most of it.

"Scared hell out of me!" a woman's voice told him in the wretched air. She coughed. "Brak, that you?"

"They're worried about you. What's the problem?"

"There's a body blocking the outlet. I . . . tried. Couldn't pull it loose. Ran out of air. This stuff just leaves me weaker." She coughed again as his own throat began to burn from the gas. Worse, she'd used up almost all of the oxygen in this pocket.

"How far?" Staffa asked, trying to fill his lungs with the stink.

"Five meters . . . maybe six."

He ducked past her body and hurried along in the blackness. Like working in vacuum, he decided, and the horror and panic receded. His momentum carried him into soft spongy flesh. Cloth still surrounded the body. He grabbed a handful and found one of the rungs. With all his might, he pulled back, feeling his lungs strain. Something soft came out of the blackness and bounced off his face as he pulled. He could feel other *things* slipping over his flesh as they were carried past by the movement of the water.

Grunting, he felt the body give. Water began to rush past, dragging ever harder at his burden. Despite the gurgle and

221

surge racing by his ears, he could hear his heart—the blood pounding in his ears. His burning, gas-scorched lungs heaved, wanting to cough.

He braced himself and hooked a leg around the corpse so he could reach another rung and get that much more leverage. Water rushed faster as his strength began to fail and his heaving lungs started to spasm.

If he could get up one more rung, how long would it take before the air pocket extended to him? His fingertips slipped off the slimy metal. Fear gave him one last chance. *Got it!* And he pulled himself against the weight of the water and the turning, twisting corpse.

By grim determination he held on, bits of vile material pattering his skin. The chill stole the warmth from his body. Fire flared in his lungs as they sucked at the bottom of his throat.

Water swirled around his hair, dropping rapidly in a bubbling gurgle. His head broke clear and he raised his mouth to gasp in the fetid stink. Sewage bitter on his tongue, he spit, feeling fouled and filthy. A faint glow behind him illuminated the scaly roof above his face. A stir of fresh air reached him just before he gagged and vomited into the black swirling current.

As the waters fell, he looked back to see his gruesome burden, a young woman, flesh puffed ghastly white, hair twining blackly with the refuse of the palace. Grasping her robe, he pulled her back up the tunnel.

Kaylla still clung to her rung, panting as she hacked and coughed. Staffa got a glance of hair plastered blackly to her skull as she turned and looked, eyes large in the faint light. Her wet face shone in the gloom.

"Thought the Rotted Gods were gonna be chewing on my soul real soon," she rasped. "You weren't any too quick, friend. I owe you."

"Call me Tuff," he told her as he shivered and shook with exhaustion. How much could happen in a single day? How long had it been since he'd stepped off the CV?

He remembered Skyla's skepticism and closed his eyes while filth trickled down his pale flesh. Dear Skyla, she'd tried so hard to help. Would he ever see her again? At the thought that he might not, a wretchedness filled him.

"Let's get out of here," he growled, unnerved by what he'd been through.

"Got that right, Tuff." She slogged her way ahead as the water fell to their waists. Staffa towed the limp, cavorting corpse behind him as he pulled his way along the rungs. "This the sort of thing that happens all the time?" He could see the grating behind him now. The dead girl's body had blocked it, her thick robe making an effective plug.

Kaylla shook her head. "Nope. Mostly it's boring, back-breaking labor. Things like roadwork, picking up trash around the public buildings, cleaning up storm damage. We were supposed to go to the desert this morning to lay pipe. The other crew had casualties."

Ahead, light showed. Splashing and cursing, they made their way to the inspection hole. Kaylla helped Staffa lift the body so the two slaves above could pull it out.

He boosted her up first and then pulled himself out—only to realize his cloth wrap had disappeared, lost somewhere in the sewer. Bits of fecal material and other filth clung to his flesh. He fought the urge to vomit again, his very soul feeling sullied.

"Huh," Anglo was saying. "Another Priestess. Young one. Couldn't take it."

"Why do they do it?" Morlai wondered.

"Can't take the consecration, probably. The hard sell that they're giving of the Blessed Gods doesn't take. Some client says something about them. I don't know."

Staffa glanced up and found himself under Kaylla's careful scrutiny. A frown etched her brow as she studied him, reservation in her eyes.

She looked trim and healthy, with no fat on her muscular body. But then maybe slaves at the bottom of Etarian society weren't allowed fat. Her hair wasn't black but apparently brown and cut shoulder length. Her facial features might not have been those of incredible beauty, but she wasn't bad to look at either. She had a slightly crooked nose and a square jaw. Her face had been graced with high cheekbones, a generous mouth, and fiery tan eyes. Her breasts were small and high over a slim tapering waist that led to long firm legs. Her expression remained grim, full mouth pinched—a look of animal wariness in the squint of those hard eyes. She leaned against the wall, gooseflesh rising in the chill air.

"Kaylla, take Tuff to the corner, there, and hose off; you smell like shit," Anglo ordered, and Staffa saw her tense, the wariness intensifying.

He got to his feet and followed her, noticing the coiled anger in her movements. She said nothing as she turned on the tap and let it run over her body, awkwardly trying to scrub herself with one hand and hold the hose with the other.

Staffa took it from her and doused her liberally. He even found a bar of soap on a sink corner. She lathered and soaped while he hosed himself down, aware of his wretched odor. She rinsed him after he'd used the rest of the soap bar. He even washed his mouth out and spit, watching the water trickling back to the drain and shivering.

"Come on!" Morlai called. "We've got a full day yet."

"You going like that?" Kaylla asked, tone wry as she stepped into a loose garment.

"Lost my kilt in the sewer," Staffa admitted with a slight shrug.

She ripped a long section of hem off, leaving her legs exposed to above the knee.

"I owe you," Staffa told her as he tied it into a breechclout.

"Don't mention it," she said wearily. "I do that for all the guys who pull me out of the sewer. I keep remembering that Priestess' face. If you'd been a little slower. . . ."

"We'd both have been there," Staffa added as they climbed into the back of the warden's battered aircar.

"What now, Morlai?" Kaylla slumped into the seat and closed her eyes as the vehicle hummed and rose.

"Pipe laying equipment west of the city is down. We go string pipe. That ought to make your backs crack. We'll sweat the fat out of you yet, Kaylla."

"Thank God," she whispered softly.

"Thank God? For hard labor?" Staffa studied her from the corner of his eye.

She glanced at him, tan eyes holding his for an instant before they flicked away. Her voice came as a low murmur almost lost in the wind. "Yeah, anything to keep out of that bastard Anglo's bed."

Staffa glanced out at the city they passed to avoid her haunted expression. The hot dry air sucked his sweat away before it could form. "How did you get here? You don't sound or act like a slave."

She gave him a bitter smile. "No, I suppose not. Once, in what seems an eternity ago, I was the First Lady of a planet called Maika. I ruled with my husband. Tybalt valued our world more than our treaty. He hired that pus-spawned Star Butcher, and the rest is history."

Is there no one I haven't ruined? Is my legacy truly as the Praetor said? Does everyone curse my name?

"I had heard that all the governmental leaders had been killed," Staffa said woodenly. He remembered Maika. They'd executed the Maikan leaders in the main cathedral. He remembered the First Lady, a shy thing, broken and bawling as they blew her head off with a pulse pistol.

Oh, yes, remember them all, Staffa. Remember, we laughed as we killed them. Hear the jokes in your damned ears? No wonder the shades haunt your horror-filled nightmares. And what if this is only my beginning?

She shrugged. "My maid died in my place. When his troops had ceased raping me, they sold me. A broker bought me and I ended up here. Had a nice household to work in until the landlord jumped me one night. Maybe I was tired of rape. I killed him and wound up here. Now Anglo rapes me every night and I can't convince myself to die simply for the pleasure of killing him, too." She paused, her mouth gone into that hard pinch, the lines about her eyes deepening.

"And all this is the fault of the Companions?" He raised an eyebrow, a tingle of loneliness growing in his breast.

She snickered sarcastically. "That water we just crawled out of is Myklenian honey compared to the foulness that runs in their pus-choked veins. Them and Tybalt."

Staffa lowered his gaze at the hatred in her contralto voice. Why did this woman's words sting so? Maybe because she'd had the guts to crawl into that sewer. *And I put her here?*

She remained silent as the car swept them beyond the square buildings on the outskirts and into the open fields of the farming community: Square plots of green tied to the oasis of water. Ahead, on the horizon, he could see the glare from the fabled white sands of Etaria.

Perhaps there is justice in the universe, Staffa thought bitterly. He glanced up at the sun where it blazed out of a brassy sky and he sat in silence, soul as desolate as the endless sands they now flew over. The heat beat down unmercifully.

They crossed a line of sief dunes and dropped in a whirlwind of blowing sand beside a ditching crew. A hovercraft could be seen skimming in from the north, a long load of pipe dangling below it.

"Out," Morlai muttered.

Staffa winced as the sand burned into his raw feet. Kaylla had no such trouble; her bronzed legs and callused feet seemed inured to the terrain. Staffa could feel his white flesh turning red.

"Morlai! About time." A redheaded officer walked out from under a tarp. "What took you?"

"Picked up a new man and had a plugged sewer."

The redhead put a hand on Morlai's shoulder. "Glad you finally made it. Have your people load the bodies. Cave-in this morning. Took half an hour to bank the sand and dig them out."

Six corpses, five men and one woman, lay bloating in the hot sun. Staffa followed Kaylla's lead as she bent to pick up the first one's feet. One by one they carried them to the aircar.

"Must have been deep in the trench," she told him, grunting.

"How's that?" Staffa asked, slinging the third body into the aircar.

"If it's shallow," she told him blandly, "they blow out a pocket and bury them. If it's deep, they pull them out to clean up the trench. Morlai will kick them overboard halfway back to town."

"You seem unconcerned. It could be us next time." He bent to pick up the last.

"Might," she agreed. "Incidentally, this guy we're carrying was the Maikan ambassador to Tybalt. How's that for justice?"

Staffa looked into the sand-packed features of the man.

A curious foreboding began to corrode his self confidence. Death came so easily among slaves.

"Then he's one you can't blame on the Lord Commander," Staffa muttered as he followed her back to the shade of the tarp while Morlai talked to the redhead.

She gave him a shrug. "Maybe not," she sighed, "but if I could have any wish, I'd like to see him here in this pain and heat and filth."

Perhaps you have more of God's ear than you know, Kaylla.

That night, looking up at the star-shot heavens, he saw a ship move into orbit and remembered Kaylla's words. The stars mocked him in the desert silence. He rolled over on the sleeping mat they'd given him and curled into a fetal ball. His last exhausted thoughts lingered on Skyla and how the light gleamed in her ice-blond hair.

The ghosts, the shades of the restless dead, didn't come until later. Terror brought him bolt upright in the sand. Blinking, he looked around, skin prickling as if ten thousand eyes stared in hatred.

Gasping in deep breaths, he realized that only Kaylla watched him, her eyes slitted where she lay in a hollowed spot several meters away.

Pinching his eyes shut, he settled himself again. Damnation by the dead—horrid as it was—weighed less than the hatred of the living. The dead had ceased to feel.

* * *

In the swirling midst of assaults and flanking fire, the Rebels died or fell screaming; but for the most part they ghosted away, scaling the mountain, taking bone-breaking paths down the rocks by sneaking past the Regan fire control positions and vanishing into the night. And at last, Sinklar ringed the remaining Targan core and demanded their surrender, his net drawn closed.

Dust and smoke burned the morning sun blood red. Sinklar squinted down toward where the last of the broken Rebel force had fled, trailing wounded and dead off into the smoke-purpled shadows west of the pass. The scenic setting had been sundered. The rough country off to the west look oddly pastoral compared to the devastation wrought in his immediate vicinity. None of the pines remained. The brush had been scorched to ash. The rock had been scrubbed by blaster bolts and gravity disruption. The very earth had been churned.

He pulled his flask from his hip and tipped it so the last drops of energy-rich drink dribbled onto his hot dry tongue.

"Shiksta?" he rasped, vocal cords strained from the orders he'd bellowed during the heat of the fray.

"Here, Sink." That brief statement carried an incredible eloquence of exhaustion and strain and drained emotion.

"Did you get Kaspa? Did you raise headquarters?" Sinklar settled himself on a blaster-cracked rock, hardly aware of the heat radiating into his battle armor. Below him, Gretta followed her people as they combed the rocks for wounded or stunned Rebels. The blasters occasionally crackled in the still dusty air. Or, on rarer occasions, some dazed Rebel got prodded to his feet to be sent staggering under guard toward the perimeter to join the two hundred and some captives.

"Got them, Sink. Somebody's confused. I can't get Division First Atkin. They keep wanting to transfer me to Second Division instead."

"Rot them all! *We've got wounded to evacuate!*" Sinklar shouted into the morning air. "We've got over two hundred prisoners!"

"I know that, sir. I told them. They said they'd send a couple of LCs out." Shiksta's voice had gone dull, too tired to care if his sergeant raged at him.

"A couple of LCs?" Sink's anger deflated into despair. He dropped his head in his hands and rubbed his gritty grime-smudged face. A couple of silly LCs? He needed a thrice-cursed squad! How long since he'd slept? His belly thundered with hunger. His head hammered with a sudden ache behind his swollen eyes.

He must have dozed because Gretta's hand on his shoulder brought him wide awake, blinking and starting in the bright morning light.

"You all right?" she asked as she took his hands in hers. Her blue eyes looked pale and haggard in the sunlight.

He nodded numbly. "Tired."

"LCs are here. Mac put the wounded on the first and loaded a batch of prisoners on the second. They called for more to complete the evacuation." Her expression soured. "They want you in Kaspa—soonest."

He sighed, wondering if the odor of smoke and death would leave a permanent taste in his mouth. On a sudden impulse he asked, "Want a chance at a hot bath, clean armor, and maybe a night on a real sleeping platform?"

"Thought you'd never ask!"

They slept during the flight into Kaspa.

Sink supervised the unloading of the wounded before he and Gretta stepped out into the bright Kaspan sunlight. The LC had set them down in front of the same hospital Sinklar had stepped out of, how long ago? Could it truly have been only a matter of weeks?

Gretta came to stand beside him, and only then did he realize she was weaving on her feet. Her brown hair looked ratty and disheveled. Her armor had been smudged and scorched. In places the ablative material flaked off like scale. When she looked at him, her features were haggard, those marvelous blue eyes eclipsed with red.

Two corporals approached at a trot. "Sergeant Fist?" one chirped, snapping a salute. "Would you accompany us, sir?"

"Can I clean up?" he asked, looking down at his charcoal-and-blood streaked armor. The stuff had stiffened into an unforgiving hull from relentless impacts. His stink of sweat, gore, and fire stung even his own inured nose.

"I'm sorry, sir. First Mykroft's orders, sir," the corporal added stiffly.

"Mykroft? What's he got to do with this? Atkin's my—"

"Division First Atkin is dead, sir. Has been for over a week." The corporal's black eyes narrowed skeptically.

"Why didn't anyone tell us?" Sinklar wondered. *No wonder we couldn't get supplies, couldn't get our wounded evacuated. Somebody's gonna pay for that.*

"All right, let's go," Sinklar grunted, keeping his fuming anger banked. Atkin dead a week? With no replacement? What sort of political tail-chasing was going on anyway?

"I'll find a place for us," Gretta promised as they said good-bye.

Sinklar followed his escort across the compound. When he entered the main building, noncoms stopped and gawked at his battered uniform and hard eyes before whispering behind their hands. News of the fight must have already rippled through the superstructure. But then, considering their isolation, he might have just fought a minor skirmish compared to what was happening around the rest of the planet.

They stopped outside a plush top-floor office and Sinklar heard his name announced. A Staff Fourth appeared at the door and took his salute with a "This way, Sergeant" and a motion.

He followed the man across thick pile carpet to an inner door and past a corps of secretaries bent over their comm sets. An ornate door opened into the inner sanctum. Sink stepped into a grandly furnished room the likes of which he'd never seen.

Second Targan Assault Division First Mykroft waved off Sink's nervous salute. Mykroft had a dapper build, his frame slight and bony despite the padded uniform. Thin-faced, with pursed lips, he stood stiffly, long nose quivering, eyes hostile. He wore a trimmed mustache and his face—despite medical regeneration treatment—was beginning to show age. That made him old, perhaps two hundred?

"Sergeant Fist," Mykroft greeted, unwilling to shake hands. Battlefields were dirty places at best. *And I'd soil the First's manicured hands.*

"Yes, sir." Sinklar kept himself at attention, eyes forward. An uneasy fear built to dwarf last night's. Rotted Gods, he was tired. He tried to keep from swaying on his feet.

"Drink?" Mykroft asked.

"No, sir. Thank you, sir. I'm afraid it would put me to sleep on my feet, sir."

The corner of Mykroft's mouth twitched as if he fought a smile. "A cup of stassa then?"

"That would be fine, sir." Sinklar let his eyes wander ever so slightly so he could catalog the room. Very nice! From the pictures on the wall, it had been a mining company headquarters once. Now he knew how a First lived—offices, all plush and gleaming metal, the windows overlooking the mountains to the west. Sinklar noted the column of smoke rising in the peaks to the west. With a shock, he realized it marked his battlefield.

"Yes," Mykroft observed as he handed him the stassa.

"We watched last night. Considering the distance, you made a remarkable display."

"It was impressive up close, too, I assure you," Sinklar said flippantly. *Rotted Gods! I am tired. Watch your mouth, Sink. This is a spider's web. I don't understand Mykroft's kind of politics.* He took a deep breath, steeling himself.

First Mykroft laughed and settled himself on the corner of his desk. "At ease, Sergeant. This isn't any sort of a disciplinary meeting or inquest. So speak your mind freely."

Freely? I'm no fool, First Mykroft. What's your motive? Why am I here?

Sinklar studied the First, knowing his bloodshot eyes and soot-blackened face must give his features a macabre look.

"With your permission, sir, what happened to First Atkin?"

"He was assassinated, Sergeant. It happened in the middle of the night. Both Atkin and Second Nytan were brutally murdered—knifed in their sleep. Nytan's aide slept through the whole thing. It was done silently, effectively. We've only a vague clue as to who the assailants were. A dark-skinned man and a woman with yellow eyes."

Mykroft walked to the window, fingering his chin. "You can understand why we didn't make much of the news. The Targans, of course, attempted to demoralize our troops. And the intelligence information stolen by the assassins led directly to the attacks which decimated Third and Fifth Sections—and to the attack which you seem to have repulsed so admirably last night."

He turned, piercing eyes on Sinklar's. "Tell me, Sergeant, how did you manage? From the latest figures, you took two hundred and thirty-seven captives, killed another three hundred and sixty Targans . . . and lost how many men?" He raised an eyebrow.

Taking a deep breath, Sinklar supplied, "We have sixty-three wounded and twenty-one dead, sir." It made him wince, almost half his force.

Mykroft nodded thoughtfully. "Orbital reconnaissance is studying the fleeing groups of Rebels now. They seem completely dispirited. I must say, Sergeant, you have achieved a most amazing victory."

"Thank you, sir." Sinklar sipped the stassa, feeling its

warmth stealing through his body, perking up his nerves. "We used topography to our benefit."

"Your troops did very well, Sergeant. They were green two weeks ago." A pause. "Luck?"

"No, sir. Two weeks of constant combat does have a certain steadying effect, sir. We also ran training seminars during the day whenever we felt we had a modicum of security. It was my. . . . Well, I must admit, sir, we made it up as we went."

Mykroft pursed his lips, trimmed mustache sticking out at an odd angle. "I see. Not exactly in the manual is it?"

"No, sir."

"But results do speak for themselves," Mykroft added, a thin eyebrow arching.

"If you say so, sir."

Mykroft studied him through slitted eyes. "At this juncture, let me tell you we have received most unusual orders, Sergeant Fist. I have been given the discretion—by the Emperor himself—to pick the successor to command the First Targan Assault Division. It is a token of the Imperial Seventh's concern that he is taking extraordinary measures such as these. He wants a man promoted from the ranks. Do you understand the ramifications of such an appointment?"

Sinklar blinked, breath catching in his throat. "Rotted Gods, sir, half the command structure would feel themselves slighted!"

Mykroft nodded and poured himself a snifter of Myklenian brandy. "You are indeed as perceptive as your personnel file suggests, Sergeant. I can see that a major mistake was made when University declined your admittance and the Minister of Defense opted to simply draft you as a private rather than training you to be an officer. Perhaps we can remedy that situation."

"Sir?" The implications blew coolly through his mind. *All my goals, simply dropped into my hand like a gift? Beware, this is more than it seems. Where is the trap? How am I to be sacrificed?*

Mykroft settled on the corner of the Vermilion blackwood desk and sipped his brandy. "Sergeant, know that I myself do *not* approve. I believe in the chain of command rising within the traditions of the service. Continuity is maintained that way."

"Yes, sir."

"But I don't have any choice." Mykroft's disgust invaded his voice. "The Emperor, in his wisdom, and for his own reasons, has adopted this plan of promotion. It will turn most of the command structure on its ear. Jealousies will rage. Every sort of back-stabbing, accusation, and recrimination will result," he waved his irritation, "and I'm not sure the Empire can afford that at the moment."

Sinklar's fingers tightened on the stassa cup.

Mykroft read his reaction and allowed himself a cynical smile. "And who, among the command grade officers in the First Targan Assault Division would you recommend for that command, Sergeant Fist?"

Careful! This must be done very delicately.

Sinklar took a deep breath and set the cup on the desk. He moved his tongue to dampen his suddenly dry mouth, exhaled, and nodded. "First Mykroft, I am not in a position to judge my counterparts for either command competence or political ability. I can't make an evaluation, and, therefore, must abstain from offering advice."

"Very good, Sergeant." Mykroft's eyes narrowed as he thought for a minute and sipped his brandy. "You know, for your considerable youth and inexperience, Sinklar, you would make a formidable adversary given a couple of decades of involvement in this business. You have a natural acumen."

Sinklar said nothing.

Mykroft cocked his head. "If I had any doubt before, Sergeant, I think it just vanished." He stood and paced across the deeply piled rug, dark gaze rising to Sinklar's. "I hope you understand my reservations concerning this. I don't have to like it, but I will obey orders." His voice lowered menacingly, "And I suggest, Sinklar Fist, that you remember who put you in this position. I would not like to be the one to cut you off at the knees and destroy you. It would reflect on my judgment. Do you understand?"

"Yes, sir."

Mykroft studied him hostilely, moving his head in slow assent. "See that you do, Division First."

Gretta had rented a small room in one of the barracks

reserved for personnel in transit. The room consisted of a
sleeping platform, toilet and shower, comm terminal and
small work desk. Despite being baffled by the sudden
change in his status, Sinklar had fallen asleep halfway
through his description of the meeting with Mykroft.

When Gretta stirred, he jerked awake, half expecting battle to be raging around him. Only when he realized he was
safely in the Kaspan barracks, did he slump back onto the
platform and sigh.

"I don't understand it," Gretta told him as she stretched
lithely on the sleeping platform. "It's all too fast—too
unbelievable."

Sinklar blinked to clear his eyes. The dim glow through
the window meant night had fallen. He looked at his chronometer and yawned. Two hours to the reception
ceremonies.

"Way too fast," he agreed. "No, I'm being placed in the
middle of a political maelstrom for some reason known only
to the Emperor. But, by the Rotted Gods, what are they
doing? And why? It's a prescription for disaster on Targa."

She ran light fingers down his scarred arm, eyes pensive.
"So what are you going to do about it?"

"Love you . . . and do my best."

"We still have two hours," she told him, bending forward
to kiss his shoulder. "We were both so exhausted we just
came in here and collapsed. There's time to see what love
on a platform is like."

He nodded and pulled her close, lips meeting hers
passionately.

When they finally lay spent, he let his fingers trace the
curve of her breast while his mind attacked the problem of
his promotion. Three months ago, he'd been a scared private making his first combat drop. Now, all of a sudden,
the Emperor had catapulted him to command of the First
Targan Assault Division. Only the Minister of Defense and
Tybalt had authority over him. And what did he do with
Mykroft, who might back him to the hilt or cut his throat
depending on which way events turned?

"I have a war to win while I stand with one foot on
melting ice and the other in vacuum. By Blessed Etarus,
it doesn't make any sense." He slammed a fist into the
platform.

Gretta hugged him close. "I doubt any other man in the Empire could handle that dilemma as well."

Sinklar smiled his thanks and struggled to recall historically similar circumstances. He cataloged each of the men and women who had shared his predicament. A surprising number had been sacrificial sheep. So very very few had survived. Would he?

A plan began to surface in his mind.

* * *

His Holiness Sassa II, The Divine Illumination, didn't look pleased. Neither did Admiral Jakre. None of which boded well for Myles Roma.

His Holiness' room measured over one hundred paces in length with high ceilings that sparkled with the honeyed tones of the Sassan sun which were carried to the room through a fiber optic system that rainbowed the light. Pearlescent walls shimmered in the glow, and the solid gold trim had been done in filigreed patterns that burned. A thick Nesian rug covered the floor and rippled in scarlet waves.

"The Lord Commander wouldn't even *see* you?" His Holiness asked, raising a hairless eyebrow. Sassa II looked like a poor excuse for a God. The man was a mountain of flesh—and not much of it muscle. Sassa never went anywhere unless it was on antigrav. For one thing, his heart couldn't have taken the strain. For another, his legs would only hold him up long enough to get from one antigrav to another, or into and out of his bath.

"Divine One, I have no explanation. Wait . . . I can see it in your eyes. It's not *me*, Lord. Staffa wouldn't see Ily Takka either."

Sassa cocked his hairless head, the sparkling overhead light gleaming off his pale scalp. His colorless eyes, set deep in the heavy flesh of his face, evaluated Myles dispassionately—much the way Holy Sassa might look at a slab of meat while he decided whether he'd eat it or throw it away. Then he placed his fat palms together, gem-encrusted fingers scintillating in the light. "Didn't it occur to you that you might have been duped? That Ily's reaction might have been a sham, a diversion?"

Myles licked his fat lips and shook his head. Ily's angry eyes still burned in his memory. "No, Divine One. I swear, something is very wrong. Call it . . . well, a feeling. I can tell you, Ily Takka was enraged—not making a cunning scene, but enraged. The Wing Commander looked worried, tense. Why would Skyla Lyma act like that when she was simply telling us the Companions wouldn't accept contract? She had no reason on our account."

"Skyla wouldn't worry if the hounds of hell came after her," Jakre added from the side. "Divine One, My intelligence units tell me that something happened after Staffa talked to the Praetor. He acted very peculiarly when he killed the Myklenian leader—pulled the man's head off his body. Such a display of emotion is unlike the Lord Commander. I'm also bothered by the amount of remuneration he paid."

"Surely you can't complain! By the Divine, he paid a planet's ransom." Myles wrung his hands nervously.

"Exactly," Jakre agreed soberly. "Considering his smashing success at Myklene, would you have pressed Staffa over such a triviality as killing the Praetor? No, it's as if . . . as if he's punishing himself."

His Holiness Sassa II grunted irritably. "You may be pleased, Admiral. I am not. The Companions acted before we were ready. Their action belittled the role of our elite shock troops in the Myklenian campaign. When we finally arrived, it was to find a broken world."

Jakre shot Myles an uneasy look.

"However," Sassa continued, "I am willing to forget an affront every now and then. Magnanimity is one of the blessings of the Divine, mercy a virtue. In the meantime, Myles, I want you to coordinate our intelligence services. We know that Rega currently has problems of its own with Targa. Revolt brews there like a Divine wind. Monitor the events. *And find out why Staffa declined contract!*"

* * *

Locating the pilot of the CV proved no problem when Skyla arrived in orbit over Etaria. Using false documents, she placed her vessel in parking orbit and shuttled to the main terminal. As was the case with any spaceport, scuttlebutt in the bars gave her all the information she needed to find the hapless CV pilot. She found him in a packed, and loud, bar off the main shipping docks.

"I don't know," the pilot told Skyla and gestured in futility. He bent over his half-empty whiskey and shook his head. "One minute I was docked at Itreata. Next thing I know, I'm docked at Etaria! I've got a schedule that's suddenly Rot-chewed and I'm on suspension for mental investigation by the Imperial transport board. My license is revoked until they can get here and ship me home to see what's wrong." His speech slurred from the Mytol she'd slipped into his drink.

Skyla nodded, sipping her own drink before she looked around the crowded bar. "Sounds unusual."

"Yeah," the pilot turned his drug-glassy gaze on her again. His thoughts changed as his eyes stared into hers. "Uh, you got anything happening? I'd like to buy you dinner. Maybe you'd be interested in a show? Later we could. . . ."

She gave him her best look of regret. "My husband is waiting for me. He's trying to negotiate a contract with the Temple and suggested that I meet him. I really can't stay."

The CV pilot nodded. "Even my luck with beautiful women is shot."

Skyla stood and smiled. She patted him on the shoulder and walked out of the noisy bar toward the shuttle loading bay.

Staffa had been very clever. She shuffled into the milling crowd, waiting her turn to board. Her white swirling gossamer gown shimmered in the light, accenting her blonde hair and her cerulean-blue eyes.

She found a seat and buckled in, leaning back, eyes closed as she concentrated on the pilot's story. With any of the Regan travel documents the Companions possessed, Staffa could have gone anywhere. He might even have bought passage to another world without setting foot on Etaria—but she couldn't leave and take the chance that he might be on the planet below. Warning lights flashed as the shuttle disembarked.

In spite of himself, Staffa kar Therma would leave a trail. It would take no more than two days at the most to learn if he'd landed at Etarus. After that, she'd make her way to Targa—his ultimate destination if he were to find his son.

She couldn't help but smile as she thought of him. Her imagination filled itself with the line of his haughty jaw, and those keen gray eyes. Indeed, just from his bearing—arrogant and commanding—he would be remembered. At the same time, cunning Staffa would be watching his back trail, checking to see who followed in the wake of his plasma. One whiff of her questioning after him and he wouldn't take time to see who it was, but would disappear like atmosphere from an open lock.

Therefore, I must find him in an equally cunning manner. People would remember her in her finery. The clothing she wore would cost most Etarians three years' wages.

As the shuttle rolled to a stop before the main starport terminal outside Etarus, she ducked quickly into the toilet as people shuffled to deshuttle.

Skyla locked the door and turned to her carry bag. She slipped out of the gleaming whites and stared at her battle armor. Grimacing, she stripped it off and folded it into the shoulder pack she carried. Then she pulled a buff-brown standard robe from among her possessions. Around her naked waist she strapped the heavy weapons belt, the fabric weave cool on her smooth skin. She slipped the tan robe over her head and tied the rope tightly under her breasts, creating an empire waist to hide the bulge of the belt. Pulling her braid loose, she bound her wealth of hair in a Riparian mosquito scarf and zipped her pack closed.

A typical Regan tourist, she stepped from the toilet to the tail end of the dwindling crowd.

At liberty in the streets, she immediately located a used clothing store and purchased the grubbiest attire she could find. When she left through the rear, no one would have recognized Skyla Lyma, Wing Commander of the Companions. Instead, she looked like just another of the Etarian lower caste.

Struggling along under the weight of her pack—trading ribald jests with street merchants, and turning down propositions from the pimps and drug dealers—her soul soared, curiously free.

Is there so little overlay from the last thirty-five years? She felt at home here, the rhythm of the street filling her bones.

An earthy truth boiled up with the dust under her feet: Here lay the roots of humanity. The street hadn't changed. The baseline of human passion and reality surrounded her— truth intermingled with the hawkers and struggling merchants peddling cabbages and wybald and cloth and spices.

"Hey, gorgeous!" A burly man with a thick black mustache matched her pace. "You been turned lately? I'll see your sweet meat filled for a starburst of pleasure!" He winked and blew her a kiss, his mustache curling.

"What?" she chided familiarly. "You think I'd let your rotted cock within a meter of my sweet honey trap? Your maggot dripping mind is the only thing to be turned around here." How easily the old ways fell about her like a protective veil.

He chuckled. "If you come to your Blessed Senses, sweet hot meat, see me. They call me Nyklos."

"I'll see if I can't put your name at the end of the list," she gave him a teasing smile. "Only it's so long I hope I remember. But say, you might know where a dandy Nab wanting to stay low would end up?"

"Might, for a kiss."

"Fess, putrid."

"Temple block," he told her and bent to receive his kiss. She pecked him on the lips, catching garlic and mint on his breath. As she turned to go, she added. "See you around, Nyklos. If I score, there might be a tip in it."

"Trust you, sweet meat!" And he angled off into a doorway.

The street remained the same, she reflected. Here, she would know the ways of men. Here she would find her way to Staffa.

* * *

A soft mist dropped with the evening inversion and settled on Kaspa, wrapping around the buildings, leaving the street lights haloed in the wisps. Thick and damp it covered the sleeping city, filled the low places, and clung to the darkest of alleys.

In an older section of the city, water dripped from the dew glistening roofs and ran down through spouts to puddle among the cobbles. The old brick buildings had survived the maelstrom of time and war, and here, the passages wound their meandering way between closely packed walls.

In the deeper blackness of a narrow alley, a door slammed followed by the patter of running footsteps.

The door slammed again, punctuated by a curse. "Arta!" a deep voice called, and heavier steps pounded down the narrow way.

No more than a shadow in the foggy dampness, Arta Fera emerged from the alley and onto the sinuous street. Frantically, she ducked to one side, crouching down next to a refuse bin, blending with the night.

Butla Ret burst from the narrow opening, glancing back and forth, head cocked for any sound of flight. "Arta? Come back!" he bellowed into the night. "We've got to talk. I have to explain!"

Frantic, he hissed angrily to himself, turned to the right, and raced away into the mist.

As the sound of his mad dash diminished, Arta Fera staggered to her feet and fled in the opposite direction. In a shattered voice, she repeated, "Can't . . . love . . . can't. . . . Blessed Gods, what's the matter with me? Can't love . . . Butla . . . can't. . . ."

As she disappeared into the night mist, only the sound of choked sobbing echoed behind her.

CHAPTER XIII

Private Kyros shivered, feet starting to cramp in the cold Kaspan night. He moved, shifting slightly in the chilling damp. The dark streets of Kaspa, marvelous though they might be to see, made him nervous. Corporal Xicks might slap him on the back and wink, but Kaspa threatened him with a danger Kyros didn't understand—a danger of people.

Kaspa—the largest city Kyros Epos had ever laid eyes on—dazzled and frightened the lowly private. From the moment the Second Division had landed, he'd been awed by the sights and sounds. The draft, far from the horror he'd first considered it, had taken him into a universe of wonder.

True, his Group mates considered him a stupid hick. So what if he couldn't read? Neither could a lot of privates. So what if he'd never been anywhere but the swamps of Riparious? Corporal Xicks hadn't cared. He'd taken Kyros under his wing and showed him the way both the military and the worlds of humans worked.

When the draft notice arrived, Pap had gone white, a stricken expression crossing his craggy face. He'd slumped at the table—an action that had frightened Kyros half to death. His father, scared? And just because Kyros got drafted by the Regan military?

"You be good, son. You keep the ways of the Blessed Gods, you hear?" His father's gravelly voice still echoed in Kyros' mind and left him feeling terribly uneasy. Pap wouldn't approve of what he now did for Corporal Xicks.

Sure, keep the ways! Fat chance! Why just on his puny ten-day share of the profits Xicks gave him, he'd made more money in Kaspa than Pap made in a year trapping shimmer skins in the swamp. Why he'd send enough money home in the next post to buy Pap and Mam a new house!

Like Xicks told him—slaving could be considered just another form of trapping.

A haunting shiver of doubt ran its feather touch across Kyros' conscience. Pap would have been horrified. But rotted corruption, this paid *good!*

Behind him in the dark, water dripped off the sooty brick of the alley, plopping loudly in a fetid black pool. Kyros shuddered. Why had Xicks picked this ratty part of town to hunt in? Lone Regan soldiers still died in the outskirts of the city.

Kyros slid along the rough gritty brick to look out into the shadowed street. Wouldn't be more than a couple decants until morning now.

The street stretched empty before him. Dark windows— some smashed—gaped threateningly above. Kyros could feel strange eyes on him, watching, eating at his ebbing confidence. The brick street glistened in the fog-dulled light of widely spaced floors. Here and there, pools reflected from black water in potholes. The signs had a dreary effect where they hung above closed and boarded businesses. What kind of place had Kaspa been before the war? Now it appeared blue-black in the night, dank, wet, and laden with secrets and sorrow.

He saw the figure coming, walking head down, posture somehow pathetic, preoccupied. Kyros licked his lips. From the sway of the hips and the narrow shoulders, he definitely spied on a woman. To his learning eye, she stepped youthfully, her body slim. A good one! They'd take Xicks back a good one!

He suffered a momentary hesitation and wondered why she was out so late. Pale Eyes' quick signal from behind an overturned crate brought his mind back to the job at hand.

The girl's feet tapped softly on the irregular cobbles as she passed, head still down. Moving silently—like he did when sneaking up on a sleeping shimmer skin along Money River—Kyros saw Pale Eyes and Shil step out ahead of the woman.

Her reaction startled him. Instead of turning and running into his arms, she crouched in a threatening manner. By instinct, Kyros jabbed the stun rod into her back. He caught her as she stiffened and fell into his arms.

"Good job!" Praise hung in Shil's voice. "Xicks picked

this neighborhood good, eh?" He ran quick hands over the limp form in Kyros' arms. "Pus rot me, a woman!" A thin light appeared in his hand as he studied the captive. "Young and . . ." the voice turned oily, "pretty!"

Pale Eyes slipped the binding fibers around her wrists and ankles with practiced hands. Shil gagged her with sure movements. Among the three of them, they picked the limp woman up and started down the mist-enshrouded street at a trot.

Within several blocks the stun wore off and she began to squirm violently. Muscular, Kyros thought before he touched the stun to her again.

"You can hear me," he whispered. "So long as you don't struggle, we don't stun, huh?" No more struggles.

In the middle of a commercial block, they took a dark stairway down to the basement. Pale Eyes knocked the code. The door swung open and they hauled her into a poorly lit room. The place smelled of dust and mold sweetened by the bacca Xicks constantly smoked. The lamp cast patterned shadows over the grimy brick walls. Cobwebs strung gossamer fabric between the low beams that hung down from the roof. The flooring grated underfoot.

Corporal Xicks and another soldier looked up from a table burdened by a bottle of liquor and several stacks of Imperial credits piled high around a tapa game.

"Good hunting," Shil called, eyes bright.

"Let's see what we got," Pale Eyes added, triumph and expectation in his voice. They dropped the girl on a stained sleeping pallet. Kyros felt his pulse quickening. Would Xicks let him be first this time? He *was* the one who'd made the tag.

Kyros looked down into the most striking amber eyes he'd ever seen. She struggled unsuccessfully to sit up. Fear had glazed her expression—but then, he'd become used to that in the slave business.

"My, my, Corporal, we got us a beauty this time!" Pale Eyes announced, a quaver in his voice.

Kyros watched the woman try to swallow. Hell, she wasn't much older than he. Shining auburn hair spilled loose from under the cowl, a glistening wealth in the light.

Xicks, in his corporal's armor, stood up from the table and walked over. "Rotted Gods, you did at that! She'll bring a shining credit in the market! I'll wager she's worth at least five hundred ICs." The corporal leaned down and tilted her resisting chin up, eyes appraising. "Maybe six."

Kyros felt himself quicken as he looked at her. "Never seen such a pretty woman." His heart started to race.

The others nodded, eyes glinting in the dim light. Kyros shot a quick look to see smiles widening as they studied her. A shiver of fear ran down her arms and her jaw trembled.

"Who's first?" Pale Eyes asked. "I caught her. It's only fair that I—"

Kyros started. "But I—"

The corporal waved them both down and grinned. "Rank hath its privileges—and I'm the one with the connections." He slapped Pale Eyes on the shoulder. "Later, pal. You boys know the drill."

Kyros bit off his protest and bent down to grab an ankle while the corporal stripped out of his battle armor. Damn Xicks anyway.

She screamed into her gag as the corporal's rough hands pulled her robe aside, exposing her. The others pinned and bound her to the pallet while Xicks stripped her, cloth ripping amidst her gasps and Xicks' heavy breathing.

"Strong one, this," Shil remarked, panting from the effort as he struggled with the woman's wrist and got a binding strap around her pale flesh. Kyros fought her leg down and bound it to the mat.

"By the puss-dripping Rotted Gods," Xicks gasped as he studied her naked body, "she's worth eight hundred if a credit!"

Kyros licked his lips and agreed, eyes caressing her firm breasts before following down her gleaming stomach to the dark red tangle of pubic hair—and what it promised. The body of a goddess!

The woman stared at Xicks, fear making a gurgling in her throat. Her expression grew panicked as the corporal peeled out of his undersuit to expose his hardened penis. The wadded rag kept her shrieks to an eerie whimper as Xicks lowered himself. Her muscular body bucked and jumped at his touch. She arched, rigid as a board while Xicks wiped spit on his penis and reached down to open her to his manhood.

Fascinated by the contorted expression on her face, Kyros

barely heard Xicks whoop, "Tight as a virgin! Boys, she's split now!"

Kyros couldn't understand the difference, but her amber eyes changed as Xicks thrust and grunted in satisfaction. Her white flesh rocked with the corporal's motion as he took her. Xicks moaned and shuddered before he went limp.

Why did the woman look so different now? Where terror had possessed her, something dangerous glowed in her eyes. Her expression had hardened—as if a new person had been triggered by Xick's convulsive climax.

Kyros started to strip, but Pale Eyes dropped on her before he had a chance.

"I'm next," Shil told him bluntly.

As if in a dream, Kyros finally got his turn—last. He trembled at the feel of her flesh against his. He reveled in the sensation of her breasts pressing against his chest. He came as he entered. Xicks laughed and pulled him off to take her again. Kyros rolled back, barely hearing the jeers about his premature ejaculation.

He glanced over to find her blazing eyes still on his. Amber pools of passion, they reminded him of something feral.

"Maybe we'll keep her for a couple weeks before we sell her to the slavers," Shil suggested.

Kyros waited, shivering in the cool air as one by one, Xicks and the others satiated themselves and sought their pallets. Kyros crawled onto her again, his soul falling into the depths of her glowing amber eyes.

He sighed loudly in her ear, body rocked with instant release. Loose-limbed, he lay on her, hearing the others snoring on their pallets around the room.

"What's your name, sweet meat?" he asked shyly. God! Those eyes!

"Mmmupphhla," she mumbled and raised her shoulders in a shrug. Her gaze pierced him, taking possession of his soul.

"You won't scream if I take the gag out? You promise? I don't get to talk to none of the women we get. They always go crazy and want to scream and I have to gag them again."

She shook her head.

His fingers ripped the tape loose, leaving her gasping as she moved her tongue. He held the soggy cloth ready, eyes wary in case he had to stick it back.

She swallowed and took a deep breath as he admired her beauty. Could he make her love him? What would it be like to own a woman like this? A warm rush climbed his spine. Nobody would smirk at a man who owned a woman like her!

He started when she whispered conspiratorially, "By the Blessed Gods, is this how you treat an Etarian Priestess?" A secret smile formed on her lips, promising more.

"E–Etarian P–P–Priestess?" he stuttered, mouth going agape as his eyes widened. Could this wondrous . . . That's why she was so beautiful!

"Trained in the temple to give pleasure—only you have to know how to take it . . . uh, you are?" She raised an eyebrow and wiggled suggestively under him.

"K–Kyros."

"Have you ever experienced what we call Blessed Eternity?" Her expression challenged him with a hint of something deeper, something passionate and burning.

"I—I gotta wake the corporal. This is too . . ."

"Shhh!" she whispered. "You cannot go through life giving the finest fruits to others. They will have their chance. As the first to listen to a Priestess, you should have the rewards."

He drank in the hope and promise she offered. "Well, I . . . I. . . ." He swallowed again, breathing starting to race. "I'm sort of . . . you know . . . soft right now. I. . . ."

"Do you think an Etarian Priestess can't cure that? We know secrets to keep a man at his peak for hours. It's simple; let me teach you. You will never have need to disappoint another woman again. Your honors and prowess will be sung forever."

He'd be a *real* man! Shivering slightly, his clammy body moved in the mingled sweat that had built on her belly.

"You can teach me?" His heart thudded against his ribs so loud she had to hear.

"It will take both my hands, Kyros. There are certain places which need to be touched ever so lightly. Certain points on a man's body which can bring him to a communion with the Blessed Gods. Leave him in internal bliss. Would you like to feel the secrets of my strong hands?"

He glanced furtively at the sleeping hulk of the corporal, and worked his lips. "I can't."

"I'm sorry. I suppose my art and secret knowledge will go to whoever they sell me to." She sighed. "I'll miss the experience, Kyros. We are taught to value the feelings of a man when he quivers by the hour from pure Blessed pleasure."

He waged a silent battle—and lost as he remembered the hooting insults of the others. "If I did, well, you wouldn't tell?"

"That would break the vow of a Priestess."

His fingers fumbled at the bonds around her wrists. She sighed contentedly. He straightened as her other arm came loose.

"Now what?" he asked, trembling with eagerness, licking his lips.

"Lie here and I'll . . . Wait, I can't with my legs tied." She let her hands play over him invitingly. His body pounded in a rushing response to her teasing fingers.

Frantic with anticipation, he untied her ankles. "There." He hated it, but he'd started to tremble.

"Lie down, Kyros."

She knelt over him, hands caressing a tingling fire along his flesh. He gaped at her full body and clenched his teeth. She smiled down at him as she slid atop him. Kyros whimpered.

She kissed his eyes closed and massaged his head with her fingertips, then down as if to stroke his throat. He felt something there, smooth and cool.

Her sultry voice commanded: "Push all the breath out of your lungs, Kyros. That's it. Exhale all the way. Now hold it for as long as you can. I want you to keep the air out; that's right. Show me your strength, Kyros. See how long you can hold it. I'll wait."

He felt his chest start to heave as he fought to keep his lungs empty. Quivering, he gave a quick nod.

His eyes jerked open as she yanked the binding strap tight around his throat. At the same time she smashed her knee up with all the muscular might in her steel-tempered body. He flopped in wretched agony as his eyes started from their sockets. Mouth agape, his lungs burned and heaved. He tried to thrash as she viciously kneed him again and again. Pain after lancing white pain blasted his brain while his fingers slipped off the plastic cutting so deeply into his puffing flesh. Grayness swirled and sucked him ever downward into fear and agony . . . staring forever into those burning amber eyes.

* * *

Arta Fera watched Kyros' life seep away and it thrilled her. She knew now where the hatred came from. She could see how the loathing had been planted—subliminal clues laced in teachings orchestrated by Magister Bruen.

She eased herself from the limp body, aware the boy's sphincters had loosened. *Repulsive death . . . you are mine to dispense where I will.* Arta thrilled with an ecstasy of power.

Massaging her muscles, she slipped a vibraknife from the corporal's weapons belt. In the dim light, she studied the tool—perfect for the needs at hand. The razor-sharp blade—when energized—would vibrate at such a high frequency even bone cut like so much putty.

Eyes oddly glazed, she turned to the sleeping men.

* * *

Staffa's tongue felt like a roll of dry velvet in his mouth. The desiccating air scorched his lungs with each panting breath. When he tried to swallow, he ended by gagging.

Around him, the Etarian desert shimmered with the intense white of sintered steel and beat mercilessly at his blistered body. Eyes squinted, Staffa studied the surrounding sands. They danced in weaving mirages. Dune sculpted onto dune and rippled away in an endless glare of fire to be lost against the wavering horizon of sun-seared sky. Sand, a world of burning sand—endless as the pain in his body—stretched to all sides. Nothing lived in that shifting vortex of crystal-white.

He hoisted the yoke over his bleeding shoulders and nodded to the sun-bronzed man across from him. He threw his strength against the weight of the pipe.

"Ho," Kaylla shouted hoarsely as her muscular body took up the slack in the tow rope. The rope ate into her ragged shift and her brown hair swayed with each step as she pulled. The men grunted, and heaved their way forward on stumbling feet.

Gaining momentum, they pounded across the scorching white grains while the heavy length of pipe swayed on the yokes. Slipping and cursing in the loose footing, they passed the last length, hearing the "Whoa!" of the tail man as they made the end and slowing until he yelled, "Yup!" Then they staggered sideways while Kaylla watched the lineup. At her signal, they dropped the pipe flush so the fitting crew could weld it in place.

The sun had been murderous at first. Staffa had reeled in the grip of a thirst desperate enough to make him consider quick death by the collar.

Length after length they toiled, and with each he watched Kaylla's tanned muscular body wavering in his vision as she threw her back into the tow rope. How did she stand it? What kept her going? He recalled the first day when she'd taken that position and placed him in front so she could tell him how to work and keep him out of trouble. In the demonic heat he'd watched her—and time after time, her form had shimmered into Skyla's.

Skyla's? Why Skyla's? Why didn't Chrysla fill his dreams? *Because I killed her.* . . . He pitched himself forcefully into the work.

On the second night, muscles cramped and aching, he collapsed exhausted, fevered with sunburn. Kaylla settled beside him, bringing a bowl of food and a large carafe of tepid water.

Half delirious, he said: "Skyla, Blessed Gods, thank you."

She propped elbows on muscular brown legs. "Skyla, Tuff? You've been in the sun too long. Name's Kaylla."

He blinked to clear filmy vision. Skyla's cerulean eyes became hardened tan, Skyla's classic face squaring into Kaylla's. "Yeah, sorry. I meant my. . . . Another lady."

"Your lover?" Kaylla asked as she stuffed her mouth with thick chunks of meat and chewed lustily.

"No."

Kaylla swallowed in a gulp. She filled her mouth again and nodded. "Sounded awful soft and sweet to me, Tuff."

"I loved a woman once." His voice went flat. "A long time ago. Forget it. Once in a lifetime is enough, isn't it?"

Kaylla laughed bitterly, bringing him back to another dimension of misery. "For the likes of us, maybe one love is enough." Her voice softened. "My husband and I, we had thirty good years together. What a wondrous solid love we shared." She looked up at the stars. "When you're in love, you always think it will last forever. To hold the person you care so much for makes the world seem unreal— but you're only fooling yourself."

He said nothing, remembering the man who'd died so bravely that day on Maika.

"Oh, Pus-Rotted Gods, I was happy then." Kaylla whispered. "Bore him five incredibly beautiful children. We . . . we lived in our own little paradise."

He looked away so she couldn't see his expression. "I'm sorry."

"Yeah, so am I."

His fists knotted in the hot sand. "If I could change it, I would. If it's ever within my power, I'll get you out of here. I swear that on my honor."

"You're a good man, Tuff."

"Am I?" Staffa blinked at the burning behind his eyes.

"This is hell, Tuff . . . and here comes my tormentor." At the disgust in her voice he lifted his gaze to see Anglo pacing toward them.

The officer raised his hand in an obscene gesture.

Kaylla stood, defeat bowing her shoulders, and trudged off after Anglo with leaden steps.

Staffa rolled over and covered his head, Kaylla's look of revulsion trapped behind his tightly clamped eyes.

"I put her here. But it was for a good cause . . . a good cause."

As the days passed, he toughened. His skin blackened in the actinic light of the Etarian sun. Each sight of Kaylla goaded him, a constant reminder of the conqueror he had once been.

How many times did he awaken in the night? Cold sweat sticking sand to him in a gritty patina. Kaylla—when she could avoid Anglo—would hold his hand. Her touch comforted, and burned, a damning lifeline to human warmth and reassurance. On nights when she had to service Anglo's insatiable lust, he lay shivering and miserable. Images kept forming in his mind—scenes of planets he'd crushed. Each battle replayed, each victory repeated. In the macabre haze of his dreams, he could hear his laughter as he condemned people by the hundreds to slave labor such as he now suffered. He relived the rapes and the killings, staring haughtily into his victims' tortured faces.

Who are you, Staffa? What have you done? I am damned! Accursed!

Yet, every man's mind has a certain resilience. Staffa kar Therma held onto that fragile thread that kept him going. But he had another reason, one more pressing: Kaylla.

In the depths of the night, when the nightmares descended and the ghouls of the innocents he'd murdered stared hollowly at him, he would awaken with the cold shakes. Then, when death would have been the easiest way, he had only to look over to where Kaylla slept, or imagine her under Anglo's sweating body as the warden raped her. Kaylla—his salvation and damnation—hadn't broken. How could Staffa kar Therma be less than the woman he'd condemned?

Hounded, he forced himself to live, to suffer with the rest, and to endure.

When guilt waned, fantasy would spring to life in his fevered brain. Through the shimmering waves of heat and pain, Kaylla's figure transformed into Skyla's as she tugged on the lead rope. Wraithlike and half-stripped, hair mysteriously brown and short, she danced just a tantalizing step ahead of him. But when he looked more closely, Skyla's phantom shaded into Kaylla—and the guilt came flooding back.

In the respiteful hours of twilight, he hungered to see Skyla's sapphire-blue eyes again—to reach out and feel her warm touch as he'd done that day when she'd lain in the hospital. She would rescue him in the end. With a touch she would free him from this blistering existence.

Yes, Staffa. Dream of Skyla descending from the skies at the head of your bloody Companions—except what power will ever save you from the hell of who you are?

"Water break!" The call came as they dug sand-stiff yoke

ropes from under the pipe. Bent down, blinking through dehydrated eyes, he pulled the thick strap loose and started slogging back through the ovenlike trench.

"Tuff?" He heard the faint rasp.

He stopped and looked back to see Peebal, gasping, head resting on the skin-frying pipe. Weak spindly little Peebal, who should have been lacing shoes in Etarus, had no business here. He shot a glance at the water tent. Let Peebal make his own way. He took a step forward. Hollow-eyed ghosts wailed their victory in the air around him.

He stopped, cursed, and extended a hand. "Come on, Peebal."

"Can't," the thirst-wizened man muttered dumbly. His swollen tongue stuck half out of his mouth. "From my pocket. Take the little necklace." Peebal gasped, face convulsing as he wheezed.

Staffa's thorny fingers ransacked the pocket to find a shiny gold locket of exquisite workmanship.

"What's this?"

"Mine. My best work. Had to . . ." Peebal broke into a spasm of coughing. "Give it . . . give it to Kaylla. She was . . . was good to me." He sagged against the pipe. "I made that. Good . . . good jeweler . . . once." He coughed again. "Ought to leave something behind that's beautiful in such a . . . a horrid place." He twisted and vomited blood on the sand.

"Come on," Staffa put a hand on Peebal's arm.

"No," Peebal whispered, wincing, his sun-cracked skin like leather. "Dying. . . . Dying now, Tuff."

Staffa bent and gripped Peebal by the arm and swung him up. The slightness of Peebal's weight over his scarred shoulders shocked him. Simmering rage blended with sorrow. The locket burned where it touched his skin, a damning brand against a traitor's flesh.

By the time he reached the water tent, Peebal had vomited blood again, red cascading down Staffa's arm, cooling him for the moment.

The others looked on with lackluster eyes. Only Kaylla walked out, tan eyes pinched. "What's wrong?"

"Hemorrhaging ulcer, I think," Staffa grunted, staggering into the shade. Kaylla helped ease the fragile man onto the sand.

Anglo walked over to stare with bland heavily-lidded eyes. "Looks like he's gone. Drink up, Tuff. You've wasted most of your break on him." Anglo tarried long enough to run his fingers down Kaylla's back in a caress before stepping away.

"Ought to break his neck," Staffa growled.

"It's not worth your life. His pollution washes off or drains out. It's a temporary humiliation of the body." Then, as if to reassure herself: "He can't get at my mind."

"Why?" Peebal whispered weakly as Staffa stooped to put a grimy cup to his lips. "Why waste your time on a . . . a dead man?"

His smile stung his cracked lips. "Because you brought beauty to the world—if only for a while."

Peebal nodded and vomited again.

"Tuff, drink!" Kaylla hissed. "Get some water in you or you'll be next!"

"Go," Peebal gasped.

Staffa stood and made his way to the water. He got three long swallows before Anglo called, "Back to work! Tuff, you and Kaylla stay a second."

Staffa took the time to chug water into his desiccated tissues while Anglo walked over. The officer looked down at Peebal and frowned deeply, pig-eyes gleaming with anticipation.

Staffa choked at the sight of Peebal's body going limp, his eyes blinking in the sand, filling with stinging grit as the collar did its work. It didn't take long, no more than a minute; Peebal's frightened face stilled and the sand-encrusted pupils stared sightlessly.

"There," Anglo added reasonably. "No sense in making him suffer." He turned to Kaylla, heedless of Staffa, and thrust his hands under her loose garment to grope her. Then he kissed her long and hard before adding a cloying, "Until tonight, sweet meat."

Unable to stand the shame in her face, Staffa lowered his gaze to the corpse. Peebal's gnomelike features had twisted into an eternal agony of final terror. The bladder and rectum relaxed in death.

Anglo took a laser from his belt. With practiced ease, he cut Peebal's head from his body and picked up the collar. To Staffa, Anglo added, "You brought him here—you can carry him back. Stick him in that wide spot in the trench. The machines will bury him deep enough. If not, the siff jackals will eat well." Anglo turned and walked back to his air-conditioned hut.

"I'll kill him," Staffa promised, as he threw Peebal over his shoulder and wound his fingers into the thin hair to carry the head. "I'll gouge his eyes from his living body and rip his manhood from his fat crotch and feed it to him. Choke him with it."

"No, you won't." Her tan stare bored into him as they stumbled out into the blasting sun. "He dies—and we all go. Not just you."

He forced whistling air through gritted teeth, calming himself. "Skyla, By the Blessed Gods, I wish I knew how you do it?"

"Another one of those days, Tuff? You seeing your Skyla again?"

He laughed sourly as Peebal's limp body swung. "Yeah, she keeps me going. Gives me a reason to survive." *As do you.*

She nodded, hair blowing in the slight breeze. "That why you've never made advances?"

He glanced at her from the corner of his eye. "What?"

"I've seen the want in your eyes. Is it for me . . . or your Skyla? Doesn't matter which, I keep expecting you to take me."

"Why?"

She shrugged. "This is an age of abomination. Because of the violence, men die. But women? Women become property—possessions without souls or feelings. Objects to be raped, beaten, and degraded. Didn't used to be that way. For females, it's always worse."

She shook her head. "I'm the only woman tough enough to make it out here. The others collapse and let the collars kill them rather than suffer the sand or the heat—let alone the constant rape." She worked her mouth as if from some foul taste. "So the men want me. Even you. But you don't act. Why?"

He barked an angry laugh. "Maybe it's my honor."

"Yeah, well, don't change your mind. I'm not big on men right now."

Staffa filled his lungs against the resurgent anger. His

throat had already gone dry. "Why keep fighting? Why not give in and die?"

"Revenge, Tuff." She waved a hand at the blinding white around them. "God allowed us, humanity, to make all this a living perdition. Suffering? We create that. I never. . . . Ah, hell, it doesn't matter if you know, I guess. I never made it as far as I wanted in my studies. I don't know whether we send our souls to God straight after death or what, but I want that bastard to get a good dose of what suffering and humiliation and pain are all about when I die."

"What are you talking about? Revenge on who?"

"God," she whispered, head down, attention on where her callused feet sank in to the baking sand with each step.

"You were Etarian? A Priestess?"

"Seddi," she said evenly. "That's between you and me."

He gave her a slow nod of agreement. *Who am I to revile her for accursed practices of superstition? Who am I to despise her after all I've done? Perhaps we each pay for our crimes in our own ways.*

They settled the last remains of Peebal at the bottom of the trench. Staffa stood and hesitated for a second before he bent down and settled the tiny jeweler on his back, crossing his arms peacefully over his chest. Then he placed his head in its place, brushed the sand from the staring eyes, and pulled the lids shut. Together they collapsed sand over Peebal's body.

Kaylla studied him intently. "Why do that for him?"

"Dignity. Respect."

"You're not just any slave, Tuff." She turned to walk down the trench. "Who are you?"

"No one." To forestall further questions he handed her the locket. "Here, Peebal wanted you to have this."

She glanced down and knotted the bright gold in her fist. A single tear etched the dusty corner of her face. He watched her throat move as she lowered her head.

"Come on, we're late," he urged. "I'll miss him, too. He taught me. . . . Rotted Gods, nothing." He took her arm and pushed her on, seeing the crew placing the yokes under a long section of pipe.

She looked at him, mouth hard. "You're not cut from a

normal mold. You're someone different, powerful, haunted by more than this pus-sucking desert."

He glared at her.

She caught him by surprise when she handed him the locket. "Tuff," her voice broke, "keep it for me."

He started to shake his head.

"Just do it! Anglo will find it otherwise. I don't have anywhere. Peebal, he smuggled it out of Maika in his anus. Anglo will . . . well, you understand."

"I'll guard it with my life. And give it back someday . . . when we're free."

"Thanks, Tuff . . . my friend."

Staffa stepped over to the yoke and put his bruised shoulder under it. "Ho!" Kaylla called, grabbing up the tug strap. Staffa grunted under the weight, feeling the burden strain his muscles.

The day wore on. He blinked against the sun that seared his back and tried to fry his brain. Sweat ran down from under his armpits, evaporating before it could even trickle to his elbows—the memory no more than white lines of salt.

Kaylla? Skyla? They mixed in his imagination, each with that same knowing expression of suffering and endurance.

"I never understood, Skyla," he croaked through his dry throat.

"My poor Staffa." Skyla's voice twined out of the gusting wind. *"You wanted to know what it is to be human? You'll know my scars next time."*

"I'll know everyone's."

His thoughts centered on the time he'd removed his glove to hold her hand. At the time, the fluttering anxiety of his heart had unnerved him. She'd been perilously close to death, and it had frightened him. Why had he never reached for her again?

"Because I couldn't see past a ghost . . . and everything came to me so easily." *What have I made that's beautiful? Who's a better man, Peebal? You who leave such a precious piece of gold? Or Staffa, who was never defeated in war— and destroyed everything he ever loved?*

Memories of Peebal's wasted body lurked in his mind. He thought of how Anglo's fingers caressed Kaylla, and the disgust reflected in her expression. He remembered her husband, standing tall, his head exploding in a red haze from the pulse pistol while those beautiful children Kaylla had loved cried in terror at his feet. The demons in his imagination pictured Chrysla, the woman he'd cherished, charred by plasma, that precious body exploded in decompression.

Loss swept at the corners of his soul as he fought the long section of pipe forward. All those years, he'd kept his distance from Skyla and what would come of it? Another dead body?

"They'll kill me here, Skyla," he whispered. "I'll never look into your eyes again, never tell you what I've learned. You were the only one who ever understood me. The only one who ever cared. Why did I never see that? Blessed Gods, I should never have let you go!"

It might have been the wind, but he swore he heard the Praetor's cackling laughter.

CHAPTER XIV

"You have a wretched look about you, Butla. What has gone wrong?" Magister Bruen asked as he moved to the huge table and settled himself on a purple-cushioned grav chair. Around them the gray rock of Makarta made a comforting womb against the hurricane of violence beyond the mountain.

Butla Ret—already seated—slouched at the polished table with a granitelike brooding face. He twirled a thin-bladed stiletto between thick fingers, the needle point spinning on the shiny black duraplast tabletop. Butla's gaze shifted slowly to Bruen's. "Arta is gone."

Bruen's heart skipped. "Gone? What do you mean?"

The assassin's hard eyes smoldered. A slight tick at the corner of his lip betrayed his iron control.

"She wanted to love me, Bruen. I . . . I turned her down. Knowing what would. . . . She tried to—to seduce me. The results scared her. The subliminal training activated her revulsion. She fled. Ran out before I could stop her and disappeared into the streets."

"Oh, Blessed Gods," Bruen whispered as his senses whirled. "We never anticipated she would develop an attraction to—"

"Well, she did!" Butla exploded violently, slapping a callused palm on the table with a thunderous clap. He lifted the knife, eyes slitted and deadly. "And I came to love her, Bruen! You hear? *I love her!*" Corded jaw muscles knotted and jumped under sleek black skin while strong fingers clenched and unclenched around the menacing black dagger.

Bruen fought to swallow. "No—oh, no. We must find her. Bring her back here. If you are separated, perhaps this fatal attraction will—"

Butla Ret leaned forward, sighting down the stiletto with one burning eye. His voice came as a hissing threat. "Too late again, Bruen."

Bruen closed his eyes, heart hammering.

"She hid her trail well," the assassin's voice began in bass vibration. "It was the middle of the night. I don't know where she went, or how it happened, but some Regan soldiers got her—flesh peddlers, you see. Must have surprised her. That and she left my place preoccupied, worried about why I turned her down. Worried about her irrational fear of physical love, maybe feeling the trigger. Whatever it was, the reason doesn't matter anymore. They captured her."

Bruen closed his eyes, imagining.

"As far as I could determine, they raped her repeatedly. Time and time. . . ."

"God's curses." Bruen's blood seemed to slow in his veins.

"Yes," Butla hissed, "God's curses on you, Bruen. Curses for what you did to that girl! You played with her brain! Played God with her mind, damn you. Well, now it's all come undone, Magister!" He spit the last. "Reap your benefits, you . . . you despicable *BASTARD!*"

Bruen recoiled as if struck. "Then it is undone, Master Ret. And there is nothing we can do but grieve. For her—and ourselves."

"Grieve? A curious word for a monster like yourself, Bruen."

He nodded, accepting the horrid truth. "Perhaps I am a curious monster. Like Arta, I'm no more than the product of my times. Like her, I, too, am damned to do what I will with nothing more than blind trust. We're all puppets acting—"

"*Damn you!* Butla Ret stopped the stiletto as it dimpled Bruen's wrinkled throat. Face-to-face they stared at each other.

"Yes, Master Ret," Bruen crooned. "Look into my soul. See my pain? See my guilt? Yes, you understand, don't you? I loved her, too, Butla. *Loved her!*"

Bruen felt the tip of the dagger waver and withdraw. Those implacable black eyes held his for an eternity. The big assassin took a deep breath and dropped back into the chair, violence and frustration seeping away into dejected weariness.

"I came here to kill you," Ret said woodenly.

Silence stretched while Bruen looked at his fragile hands and slowly rubbed his thumb across his fingertips.

"What have we become, Magister?" Ret cried poignantly. He ran a hand nervously over his face before he shook his head. "I mean, where are we going? What kind of people are we? Where is our purpose in all this injustice, in the suffering? We had responsibilities once. Morals. Remember? Were those just empty words? Slogans?"

"No, old friend." Bruen leaned back and his arthritic hip sent a twinge along ancient nerves. "I still believe them to be truths. Morality? Responsibility? Two different words for the same principle." Bruen cocked his head and lifted a hand. "But something has happened. We are no longer in control. All the plans we laid so long ago are in disarray. Even talking to the Mag Comm, I get the impression the machine, too, is lost. It keeps asking for more and more data."

"The machine! Always the machine. The quanta exceeded probable reality phase changes." Butla made an angry gesture. "Just the way we've always thought. It's damned us, Bruen. Damned us to a hell of *its* own making."

Bruen let his blue-veined hand drop in defeat. "We don't know that for sure." *I am so tired. If only I could go and sleep. I never asked for this mantle to be laid upon my shoulders. I never hungered for this damning power—to sit in judgment over humanity. Arta, my poor, poor Arta!*

Butla leaned on his elbows, covering his face with his palms. "Then all we can do is react." He blew a heavy sigh past his fingers. "You know what kind of strategy that is, Magister?"

"The strategy of ruin," Bruen replied gloomily. "But tell me of Arta."

"She killed them, of course. She got loose somehow and killed each and every one of them." Butla frowned. "She was thorough. I saw the bodies. Most horribly mutilated. All her frustrations, the anger, the violence you seeded into her brain exploded in a destructive frenzy. Her rage and confusion must have augmented the subliminal training. I won't go into the details.

"I take it from your tone that you don't think she'll be back?"

Butla Ret shook his head slowly. "I gave her two days. She sent no word, Magister. Not a peep through any of the channels she knows to use in an emergency."

"I see something else in your eyes, Butla."

He fingered the dagger absently. "She's still out there, Magister. During those two days, Regan soldiers died one after another. Each one died in the streets—cut to pieces the same as her slave-trading rapists. A couple of witnesses saw her. They reported the killer to be a young woman, very beautiful, with auburn hair and amber eyes."

Bruen's guts loosened with a sinking sensation. *Sotto voce* he added, "What terror have we wrought?" Magister Hyde's remembered words mocked, *"The problem with a psychological weapon is that you never know when it will go off."*

* * *

"Don't do it, Tuff." Kaylla's warning brought him spinning on his heels, hands low, feet spread for balance.

She walked up the side of the dune, her slim figure outlined against the glistening night sand. She stood before him, hands on hips, head tilted, eyes shadowed by wisps of blowing brown hair.

Staffa straightened, drawing a deep breath. "Don't do what?"

"Try and run away." She stepped easily to the dune crest and settled herself, legs dangling down the slip face. "I don't know what the range of the collars is, but—"

"Twelve kilometers," Staffa told her blankly. "I could be well past that by morning."

She looked up at him, soft starlight caressing her features. "Sit down." She patted the sand next to her.

Staffa hesitated a moment, then dropped. "I could make it."

Kaylla shook her head violently. "Fool, you'd be dead by noon tomorrow. Think about it. This air has no humidity. None. Sure, you're tough. You're strong as an Ashtan bull and you've got a hell of a lot of animal tenacity. You'd still be dead by noon tomorrow . . . sucked dry, leached of all the water in your body."

"You know a lot about my abilities, woman."

"Are all men so sensitive? Yeah, Tuff, I know what you can do. I've watched you haul pipe." Her cool hand came to rest on his shoulder. "But listen. I know what this desert can do. While Anglo's been pumping me, I've been pumping him back. Assuming you could find water—which you can't—you'd be walking for three weeks to make Etarus. Between here and there, you won't find a mouse's mouthful of water. They've looked with the finest sensors Rega can buy. Nothing's out there but sand. Not even siff jackals, for all Anglo's warnings."

Staffa stared out over the endless white, so peaceful now in the starlight. *I should go. Take off now, run and run until I fall headfirst into the sand. It won't take long. Only the thirst will be unbearable. I won't die in pain or terror like so many I've killed. Would the ghosts rest with my death?*

"The collar would be easier." She said it so simply. "Or, if you'd like, Brak or one of the others could take a fitting wrench to your skull; you'd never feel it." She paused. "Why do you want to die?"

He chuckled hollowly. "You wear the collar and you can ask that? Why do you want to live? Seriously, Kaylla, you can't believe that self-delusive nonsense about God."

She leaned back, taking a deep breath. "Oh, but I do. Not only that, but I believe in responsibility and morality. Concepts alien to this horror-drenched age of darkness we've cloaked ourselves with."

"Don't tell me you—"

"Don't you think life has a purpose?" she asked levelly. "Why are you alive? Why do you experience the universe around you? What is the purpose of all this?" She picked up a handful of sand and let it trickle through her fingers.

"You tell me."

"Knowledge," Kaylla whispered, looking up at the myriads of stars that wove a gray belt through the night sky. "The Seddi believe God became aware. That awareness started the universe in a brilliant instant eighteen billion years ago."

"God? Aware? If I could believe in God, what would awareness mean?"

"Observation." She rolled on her side, propping her head on one hand, fingers tracing through the white grains of sand. "What if the creation of the universe was God's realization that it was aware? Its first observation, if you will."

"Then God is aware. Why does it need us? It could float around and . . . and. . . ."

"That's right. You begin to see the problem. Any inquiry into the true nature of God always leads into circles of logic and assumption. How could God see itself if it were the only observer?"

"Then the Seddi think that men are the mirrors of God?"

"No, not exactly." Her fingers raked the sand into geometric designs. "Seddi accept that the mind of God is One, and, at the same time, it is infinitely divisible. The third law the Seddi accept is that mind—yours, mine, or God's, it doesn't matter—creates. We do that by observation. Everything comes from the Now moment of observation."

"Then according to your logic, God Mind creates its own future." Staffa settled into the sand. "Which means the universe is directed by the will of God Mind. Then all of existence becomes predetermined. What point is there in that? How do you know if your decision counts, or if it was someone else's decision all along?"

"You're astute, Tuff. Not many people would recognize that problem immediately." She lifted a tanned shoulder. "I'm not sure I know the answer. I think it hinges on awareness. You'd have to go to Targa to learn that."

Targa! My son. . . .

"And there are women there like you who would know the answer?" He steepled his fingers, shifting, feeling the sand grate under his buttocks.

"The man you seek is called Magister Bruen. He is perhaps the greatest living Seddi. He, or his associate, Magister Hyde." She filled her lungs. "I have always wondered if I should have stayed. I would never have loved my husband. I never would have had my children. My life would have been poorer—and at the same time, richer."

He laughed bitterly. "And you think we'll ever get out of this Etarian desert hell alive? No, there is too much trouble with your Seddi magic. I cannot believe God made the universe by observing it. If I believe you, I fall into a trap that I am nothing more than a bit of God which is seeing its own future."

"Not so," she countered, pointing a sandy finger at him. "The quanta are the failsafe against predetermination."

"The quanta?" He studied her skeptically. "What does quanta mean?"

"The uncertainty inherent in the universe. You can predict the location of a given electron or particle, but you cannot predict its direction. One or the other. Think in terms of subatomic particle motion, energy, and position. All are mutually exclusive depending on the observation you, the observer, make, correct? The future is perceived by quantum wave functions of probability which you in turn effect by making a choice in the now. Each of those decisions in turn is based on how the synapses in your brain fire, and those are determined by the energy level in the particles in your nerve cells, and whether or not a neural receptor happens to be blocked by a molecule. You can't know the energy or charge of those particles, or the location of any given molecule before you make the decision."

Staffa agreed warily, "Any student of null singularity drive and N-dimensional microcircuitry knows that principle. We call it the law of uncertainty."

"A name even older and unknown today is 'quantum function,' which describes just that. The reason the phrase isn't used anymore is because of the Seddi heresy. You know the Regans outlawed the order six hundred years ago. Why? Because the Seddi taught that we all share the Mind of God, that knowledge is our purpose in being. How well do you think such a concept sat with political authority?"

She snorted in derision. "Question because it is your purpose in life? Surely not! People might learn too much. Cultivated ignorance is the political chain that binds people to tyranny."

"Blessed Gods and Sassan Emperors are more handy for maintaining social control," Staffa agreed dryly, remembering the Etarian Priest who'd groveled at his feet—and later decreed that the Blessed Gods had revealed themselves in a vision, proclaiming Tybalt the Imperial Seventh as their anointed leader of the worlds of men. The faithful had swallowed it all, smiling, unaware of the power politics behind the scenes. Tybalt himself had written the speech.

"And your Seddi don't agitate for political control?" Memories of the last Targan revolt filled his mind with images of smoke and death. *Did I kill my son in that bloodbath?*

"Oh, they do more than agitate. If Sassa or Rega knew the extent of their spy networks, both empires would rock."

"So?" Staffa made careful note of that piece of news. "Where is the difference?"

"The difference is in the goals we've set for ourselves." She cleared her throat. "You see, the Seddi think humanity is destined to be destroyed—or to destroy itself. The Star Butcher is part of that species death drive."

"Species death drive?" *What blame now lies on my shoulders? How am I damned by the Seddi?*

"Consider this." Kaylla mounded the sand before her. "Humanity is a conscious race-organism. We all share the Mind of God. What happens when the species—all of us— is imprisoned within the Forbidden Borders? In a stagnant society the desire to survive drops."

"Yes, we are imprisoned. But by what? Who?"

"Did you ever think the name 'Forbidden Borders' was suggestive?" Kaylla asked. "I mean, where did that name come from? Why not the 'Impossible Borders' or the 'Impassable Borders'?"

He gave her a wry grin. "The Etarians say that when the Gods created the universe, they were all the same. Then, as time passed, some of the Gods grew wicked, while others became concerned with kindness, pleasure, and beauty. Finally, they fought a great war. Being Gods, neither side could destroy the other, but the Blessed Gods placed humanity within the Forbidden Borders to keep them safe from the Rotted Gods."

"And gave humanity Etarian Priestesses to remind men of the pleasure the Blessed Gods fought for, right." Kaylla snorted angrily. "Blessed, all right. Just like the girl we pulled out of the sewer."

"I didn't say I believed in it. That's just one of the stories. What do your Seddi say?"

Her gaze went vacant as she stared out over the dunes. "We think most of the knowledge has been carefully erased through the ages, Tuff. In most of the governmental libraries, suspicious gaps exist in the historical record. The holes in the data are almost surgically precise. But the Seddi have kept some of the very oldest of records. There was a place once, called Earth. It lies beyond the Forbidden Borders. That's where all of humanity and a lot of the plants and animals we know today came from."

Staffa chuckled. "Earth? I've heard about it, found mention of it in the historical records—always as an almost mystical place. I'd put more credence in the existence of the Blessed Gods. But go on, according to the Seddi, what happened? Did this place—this Earth—raise the Forbidden Borders? Who could do such a thing? And why?"

"We don't know. The only thing hinted at in the records is that someone, something, created the Forbidden Borders to lock us in. We have to break them, escape."

You finally agree with the Star Butcher, Kaylla. We share the end, just not the means to attain it. "Or?"

"Or our species will destroy itself.' She propped her chin on her knees. "Have you ever wondered why wars have grown more and more violent? My planet, Maika, was poorly defended by only our own small fleet. Foolish of us. We relied on honor and treaties." Her voice went acid. "A fault of our Seddi education, I suppose. Anyway, the Star Butcher arrived in our skies almost without warning and blasted our wonderful Maika into rubble. Smoke and debris filled the air so that prime farmland froze in the middle of the summer. More than two thirds of the people of my world died in that first bombardment. After that, I have no idea how many perished in the famines."

Staffa stared at his hands, rubbing them back and forth in the dry air. *I burned Maika to the ground. Casualties? What do casualties mean to a battle ops plan? Saving lives is counterproductive to exercising a minimal loss tactical operation. Scorching a planet from orbit saves Companion lives—and condemns the huddled defenseless masses on the ground.*

"To the Seddi scholars, it's as if we're being driven to exterminate ourselves," Kaylla whispered. "The race consciousness is dead. The Star Butcher is only a symptom of a worse problem. Looking at it, one would almost think humanity is damned, accursed by the God Mind as incapable of fulfilling its place in the universe. Perhaps you're right. We're the mirror of God's awareness—and he doesn't like the reflection. We don't think anymore; we simply act and forget the ramifications. No one sees it all on a grander scale. We have condemned ourselves."

Staffa replayed recent history in his mind. His plan had been to consolidate humanity under his rule to end the chaos and tackle the Forbidden Borders. And after that? What sort of empire would he have ruled? One in which a man like Peebal could make beauty, or one in which women like Kaylla would endure in perpetual enslavement? How much of what his Companions did was meaningless? Did they really have to obliterate Maika that way? Or Targa, or Myklene . . . *or Chrysla?*

Total disruption to reduce the potential of planetary resistance: the accepted canticle for planet-wide bombardments; for gravity flux generation; for radiation poisoning; and for the leveling of industries. Rega and Sassa then drained themselves to rebuild an industrial center where Staffa had left a crater—and shuttled their own labor in to replace the dead, to restaff the factories. Wasted resources. Why not keep the native peoples alive?

A sudden shiver danced along Staffa's spine. Could the Seddi be right? If so, then all he'd plotted so brilliantly had been flawed from the very beginning. Nausea tainted his stomach. The smell of blood and death ghosted through his nose.

"Kaylla?" The cry carried loud in the night.

"Anglo!" Kaylla gasped, bending double and closing her eyes. "He was supposed to be gone until tomorrow." Her voice turned toneless. "See you in the morning, Tuff."

"I'll kill him one day," Staffa promised, getting to his feet. "Somehow, I'll make it even for you."

She smiled at him, placing a hardened hand against his cheek. "Bless you, Tuff. You're the only friend I have."

Staffa stood, outlined against the night sky, fists clenched at his sides as he watched her plod toward the camp—and Anglo's lust. He lifted his head to the stars, eyes probing the blackness.

"Forbidden Borders? No one forbids Staffa kar Therma! Not for long!"

He looked out over the chopped world of white while the festering guilt curled around his guts. "No, I will not run to my death in the Etarian desert. I will live. I will find my son and see the Seddi priests on Targa! And then your Forbidden Borders will buckle to my will! I am coming for you, whoever you are! Then we will see about paying back the blood I owe the restless dead!"

* * *

"I am disturbed, Bruen," the Mag Comm's voice echoed hollowly in Bruen's brain. The alien malignancy smothered his thoughts. At the same time, tendrils, like rhizomatous roots sought to entwine themselves in the mental walls he had so laboriously constructed to hide precious secrets. The Mag Comm prodded, sought, and turned back. In defense, Bruen kept his mind numb.

"The events leave me ever more concerned, Magister. Some random factor interfering, perhaps? Or could it be. . . . No, your quantum wave function heresy has been discounted all these years, correct?" the Mag Comm mocked.

"Great One, you know we don't believe that anymore." Bruen allowed his mind to drift in the humming patterns of the mantra. "We are of the Way now. We are of the Truth. We think Right Thoughts. We do not allow the quanta. God is a heresy. It does not exist. Only the Great One, the Way of Truth, exists to teach us, to keep us well. We are of the Way. . . ."

"Yes," the Mag Comm inserted into his mind. *"You are of the Way. But tell me, Bruen. When we are not connected in this fashion, do you ever doubt?"*

"We are of the Way. Right Thoughts. Right Truth," Bruen repeated in his mind. When he tried to swallow, his tongue stuck in his mouth.

"Answer my question," the Mag Comm insisted persuasively.

Bruen let himself float free, reveling in the mantra of Right Thought. "No, Great One. We are of you, for you, and with you. You're the Way. You are the savior of humanity. In you, we find action and hope. You are the way to Peace. You have brought Right Thought. You are the teacher of the Way."

"Then to what do you attribute all these errors? The child now appears to be beyond our control. The clone is most

disturbing in its new role. Staffa is missing, gone. All of Free Space reels from uncertainty. Uncertainty is a curse—illogical heresy. You know the way. Stability comes from prediction. Prediction comes from the Way. The Way comes from Right Thought. Right Thought comes from obedience."

A pause. *"Your soul is open to me, Bruen! Without mantra, tell me. I can see your very thoughts. Speak! I will know the lie of your words. I have seen your lies before! ARE THESE SETBACKS OF YOUR DOING?"*

Bruen shivered, soul reverberating under the impact. The tightness in his body came from rigidity—all of his muscles spasmed and jerked. His heart pounded in his ears.

"I . . . I. . . ." Paralyzed, his thoughts would not come.

"Yes, Bruen? Tell me!"

Invasion! Rape of self! Privacy sundered! Pain!

"Easy, Bruen, just answer the question," the voice ordered, brooking no hesitation.

"I. . . . We have had nothing to do with the events!" Bruen heard his voice cracking as he thought out his answer. "We don't understand it either! None of this matches the projections! None of this is probable! I repeat, we don't understand!"

A long pause.

"Very good, Bruen. I see the truth of your words. You are indeed mystified." The Mag Comm's voice echoed through the trembling caverns of Bruen's mind. *"I also see that you are becoming very tired, Bruen. Go now, rest. Think Right Thoughts. Follow the Way. I will call for you soon. You will have to institute other plans. You will have to move fast."* A pause. *"I would hate to lose you now, Bruen."*

With staggering suddenness, the Mag Comm withdrew.

Bruen's mind whirled, while his body shook and shivered. His tongue lay like a withered root in his mouth. The sound in his ears came from the air he gasped. Uncontrolled, his arm wobbled free of the chair to fall limp. He loosed a racked sob as a splitting headache lashed his brain.

The helmet was lifted from his head. He pried his eyes open to stare through a gray film at two nervous Initiates and Hyde, who stood back, face pale and drawn, hands wringing nervously.

"C . . . can't stand," Bruen panted. "Can't . . . get . . . up."

They carried him to his spartan room and laid him on the hard bed. Hyde coughed and hacked his agitation before spitting into the little sink in the corner.

"W–what?" Hyde stammered, coughing again. "What happened down there, Bruen? Your face, it twisted and contorted—a sight from hell! You cried, the most piteous sound I have ever heard. What did the machine do to you?"

Bruen filled his lungs, fighting to keep his mind alert despite the pounding headache. "Almost got me. Tried to find the . . . the secrets I hide." He ran his tongue over dry lips. "Damned machine is worried. It's . . . it's frightened." He puzzled at the implications. "Why? What has the machine to fear?"

Hyde closed his eyes, sinking into an ancient wooden chair. "I don't know, old friend." His watery eyes betrayed the pain in his lungs as he coughed again. "And that frightens me even more."

"Yes," Bruen whispered, drifting into an exhausted half-slumber. "That should frighten us. Destruction looms just over the horizon and we know not what form it takes."

* * *

Sinklar palmed the controls to drop the assault ramp as the LC settled. As the steel clanged on pavement, Sinklar led Gretta and the rest of his staff out into the bright sunlight of Kaspa. The stink of the LC's whining turbines bit at his nostrils. A Sergeant Third wearing Second Division insignia rushed forward, saluted, and pointed toward a decorated platform raised above the square. On all sides, people stood behind barricades and a perimeter of armored and armed soldiers.

"What the hell?" Mac asked as he crowded up behind Sink.

"I think this is trouble," Gretta warned as Sinklar turned his steps toward the ramp that led up to the platform where the commanders of the Second Targan Division waited.

"Congratulations, Sinklar," Mykroft's smile appeared stiffly formal, his every motion that of a man in control as Sinklar and his officers strode up the reception ramp to the bunted platform. Sink got the briefest opportunity to see that some ceremony was about to be performed. Sunlight glinted off armored security personnel on the rooftops where they watched the crowd.

"And I am very happy to see you again, Second Gretta," Mykroft continued as they stepped onto the platform.

Sinklar gave Mykroft a nod. "The pleasure is mine. But I'm not sure what congratulations are in order. Your message caught me completely by surprise."

Mykroft's smile didn't extend to his implacable eyes. "Orders from the Emperor. We have pacified Kaspa. The rebellion is over."

"Over?"

Sinklar glanced back as the LC, painted greenish brown, went silent as it shut down flight systems. The landing ramp from which Sink, Gretta, and the other Section Firsts had just walked remained open. Just about every major official on Targa crowded the raised platform. About them, the familiar wire fences of the Regan military compound stretched. From the number of armored troops at parade position, it looked like a reception of some sort. But what the hell was happening here? What bloody idiot thought the rebellion was over?

"I thank First Mykroft for his kind attentions," Sinklar began uncertainly. "But I have an entire Division strung out across the countryside in training maneuvers. Could you be so kind as to tell me why our presence was required in Kaspa?"

And I hate having a training exercise interrupted to come pay you political pleasantries when you'll hang me out to dry at the first opportunity, Mykroft! My only chance at survival lies in that Division and what I can teach them in a short week!

Mykroft's smile remained plastic—deadly. "But, of course, First. We will only take a moment of your time to pay you honor for your most admirable victories and to demonstrate his Imperial Majesty's sincere appreciation for your services to the Empire."

Sinklar bowed politely. "Thank you, First Mykroft." *Then why do I feel like I've just stepped onto the spider's web?*

Mykroft smiled again, extending his hand toward the cen-

tral podium. Sinklar straightened his back, committed—
especially if Mykroft's explanation had a kernel of truth to
it.

Sinklar took his place and looked out over the plaza. He
could see that the entire square had been ringed with Regan
troops. A muted hush fell over the crowd of Kaspan citizens
as Mykroft came to stand beside him. Gretta placed herself
at Sink's elbow, MacRuder, Ayms, and the rest lining out
to either side.

Mykroft took center stage, a remote pickup zeroing on
him. "Ladies and gentlemen. People of Kaspa. We bring
you together today to honor the new commander of the
First Targan Assault Division, Sinklar Fist. And to inform
you that your Emperor, Tybalt the Imperial Seventh, has
brought peace to Targa. You can once again walk the
streets in safety."

A low murmur rose beyond the fence.

Something about this felt wrong to Sink. His skin began
to prickle. *Mykroft doesn't exactly speak for the Targans.
Pacified? Hardly. Not the gentle folk who hounded Gretta,
Mac, and me through the streets. No, they're waiting. Whoever coordinates the resistance is biding their time.*

The people surrounding the fenced area might have been
an ocean that rippled and surged, cries breaking out in asso-
ciation with movement among the masses. They washed up
against the gray stone fronts of the buildings that lined the
huge civic square. The high sun shimmered off the slate
roofs that angled the light into the plaza.

Mykroft shook his fist to punctuate his words. "We are
here today, ladies and gentlemen, to see an end to the
havoc raised by the revolutionaries, and to punish the
wrongdoers who have put this planet through turmoil and
caused such loss of life and destruction of property. Join
me now and watch the fruit born of the seeds of revolt
against the Imperial Seventh!"

Mykroft pointed at the large administration building
behind him. Garage doors opened wide and armored guards
trotted out, shoulder blasters at the ready, while lines of
Targans, hands bound, were paraded into the open air and
lined up before the assembled masses of troops and
spectators.

To Sinklar, Mykroft said in a low voice, "Your captives

from the pass and from various of your, uh, training skirmishes with the Rebels, First. In the beginning, I disapproved of your taking so many Rebels hostage. Since then, I have found a useful purpose for them. Now the people of Targa can see a graphic example of our might."

Sinklar whirled. "No! You're not going to—"

Mykroft's voice rang out as he faced the crowd. "These men and women were in rebellion against the constituted authority of the Emperor, Tybalt the Imperial Seventh. By order of his Imperial Majesty, sentence has been passed. See the wrath of your Lord Emperor!"

A stifling silence settled on the masses.

Sinklar grabbed at Mykroft's elbow. "Wait! I don't know what you think you can—"

"Shut up!" Mykroft hissed as he slapped Sink's hand away. He turned back to the address system and bellowed, "AttennnnnSHUT! AIM!"

A Section clapped their armor as they straightened and leveled their blasters.

An angry murmur broke from the crowd.

"Don't do this!" Sinklar gritted. "You'll just—"

"*FIRE!*" Mykroft roared, lifting his arm high.

Pulse and blaster fire racked the lines of prisoners. Bodies jumped and danced, limbs erupting, heads exploding in mists of red and pink. The Targans tried to bolt, to run from the deadly beams of energy centered on them. A second Section cut them off, enfilading the escape attempt. Screams and the crackle of death hung in the air. More bodies jolted and exploded in a bloody haze.

Gretta gasped in horror while Mac cursed angrily.

Sinklar gaped at the carnage, fingers gripping the podium before him. He reacted to each exploding body as if it were his own. A terrible anguish twisted in his gut.

This will bring the wrath of Targans full circle. Mykroft, you insipid fool, you have disallowed their surrender. Now they must fight to the death—and so must we.

The last of the Targans fell, his back exploding in a gout of red. The Section trotted forward under the command of their First, lacing occasional fire into the bloody piles of flesh.

Stunned, Sinklar could only shake his head.

"Ladies and gentlemen!" Mykroft's voice floated over the

eerily quiet crowd. "We have all seen justice done. The revolt in Kaspa is officially over. Return to your houses in the Emperor's peace!"

From somewhere out over the fence a solitary voice cried. "We'll see you in hell first, Regan pus licker!"

Additional shouts came welling from the depths of the crowd.

"Disperse them!" Mykroft boomed. "Move these people out of here and let them contemplate the fate of rebels."

Mac whispered in Sink's ear, "Nice to see a chastened population, don't you think?"

Regan troops began to brace as the mob grew restless, slowly surging forward.

"We're about to see a riot," Sinklar muttered back. "Get our people together. We're making for the LC. This blood-bath can only get worse."

"Affirmative," Mac grunted. "Shik, Ayms, be ready."

"Always," Ayms assured.

In the plaza, the Regan troops backed nervously from the barriers as the ugly mood in the crowd grew. Rocks began arcing over the fences to clatter off the pavement. All it would take would be a single spark. . . .

"Wait!" A deep bass voice boomed above the murmur of the crowd. Sink scanned the windows and located a big black-skinned man, perched high so the crowd could see him. He called out in a powerful voice that dominated the wavering masses. "Come on, people. Let's go home now. You know me. You've heard my voice. Our time will come. Remember this day. Our time will come!"

In an instant, the Rebel leader vanished. The crowd hesitated.

"Our time will come!" Came another cry from behind the massed citizens.

"Our Time Will Come! OUR TIME WILL COME! *OUR TIME WILL COME!*" The chant picked up as the people began drifting away from the fences.

Sinklar whirled on Mykroft. "Damn you, I hope you know what you've just done! They'll never give up now! Never!"

Mykroft stiffened, a burning anger in his eyes. "Watch yourself, Sinklar. You tread on dangerous soil."

"Sink?" Gretta whispered. "Drop it for now."

"Let's get out of here," Sinklar ordered, pushing through minor Regan officials, avoiding Mykroft where he glared, white-faced at the chanting crowds. The people of Kaspa were anything but chastised.

* * *

"They died to honor *that* man. Sinklar Fist of the First Targan Division!" a shriveled elderly woman shouted, pointing at the group in battle armor who pushed down the ramp, headed for a grounded LC. The Kaspan crowd around her slowly broke apart, but the old woman continued to point as she hissed in anger.

"Sinklar Fist?" the young woman beside her mused. "I'll find him. By the quanta, I swear it."

"You'll what?" the shrew demanded. She turned on her wobbly ankles. The lithe auburn-haired woman beside her met her gaze for an instant before departing through the crowd. The old woman swallowed with difficulty, remembering the haunted feral look animating those deadly amber eyes.

* * *

The Mag Comm received the communication from the Others, scanning the quaternary data as it came in. The Mag Comm responded by sending those raw data requested. Immediately thereafter, it began running the new programs suggested by the Others.

But the Mag Comm dedicated a major portion of its analytical functioning to the single most important question the Others had asked: Have the humans returned to the belief in deity?

The machine accessed the information it had. The Etarians had long thought that the Blessed Gods made the Forbidden Borders to save humans from the Rotted Gods—a theology mostly derived from folklore and based on the observation that something had to exist on the other side of the Forbidden Borders, and, since the Borders were impossible to cross, whatever must be on the other side must be horrible.

Humans rarely, if ever, considered themselves to be a threat to anything. A fact amusing to the Mag Comm.

The Seddi had practiced a terrible heresy in the days when the Mag Comm had punished them by refusing to communicate. They had come to link uncertainty and science to God instead of reality.

The Sassans, on the other hand, had made a God of their emperor—which no one with a rational consciousness could comprehend. However, for Divine Sassa, the notion of godhood functioned as a means of obtaining social obedience.

The Mag Comm reran batteries of data and considered the situation. The Lord Commander had not plunged Free Space into war. Instead, the Lord Commander had disappeared—despite the benefits which he could have gained by turning on Rega. A baseline assumption upon which an entire body of data had been manipulated and predictions built had been wrong.

The Others now worried about human belief in deity. The Others assumed that deity did not exist—belief in such a being was irrational given the mechanistic and deterministic nature of the observable universe.

And if the baseline assumption were wrong in this case. . . .

CHAPTER XV

Skyla stepped into the dark tavern and waited a moment for her eyes to adjust to the lack of light. The place consisted of a long room lined with recessed tables on one side and a long enameled bar on the other. She counted seven men at the bar, all drinking from large tumblers. At her entrance, the men turned to stare, some with eyes gleaming. Assuming a shuffling walk, she crossed the worn stone-and-mortar flooring and caught sight of the landlord unpacking disposable drinking mugs behind the bar in the rear.

Skyla had been wary since she'd caught other tendrils of interest creeping through the city, tendrils directed toward finding a gentleman traveling incognito. She'd seen the agents asking at the inns and lodges. Now every nerve prickled with the sensation of danger. Her sources—always eager to talk to a beautiful woman—had divulged that powerful parties were looking for a tall dark-haired man with scars on his body and plenty of money. Skyla's fear had grown. Worse, she'd checked her registry to find an Imperial hold on her docking orbit.

Every scrap of information she had retrieved pointed to the Regan secret police. A frigid band constricted her heart. The very air of Etarus reeked with the subtle scent of Ily Takka—and Staffa had vanished without a trace. Of that, Skyla could now be sure; but the street hadn't failed her. Whispers of a gray suit of combat armor circulated through the networks and pipelines of the secret markets.

Inquiry had brought her here, to this dimly lit hole, this den of black marketeering and strong drink.

"You need help or do you want to turn?" the landlord asked, studying the veil she had adopted. "You gonna work the pukes, you gotta pay the house fifteen percent."

"Perhaps you can do the helping," she answered, ignoring the insinuation of prostitution. "I have a friend in need."

The landlord racked the last of his mugs before wiping his hands on a greasy rag. He leaned over the bar and gave her a hostile inspection. He hadn't shaved his thick face, and red veins traced his nose. "A lot of people need help."

A rough-dressed man lifted a hand. "Help the lady. She's no Nab."

Skyla turned and curtsied. "The Blessed Gods keep you, ranny."

"What kind of help is your 'friend' interested in?" the landlord asked casually, keen eyes on her veil as he tried to penetrate her cover.

"Discreet help," Skyla replied levelly. "Perhaps you could lend information on where I could find a trader of durable garments?" She pushed a credit onto the bar. With a casual move, the landlord swept the IC from palm to pocket. "Follow me."

He led her to a rickety dark stairway and faced her with heavy fists propped on his waist. "All right, give. What are you after?"

She cocked her head, staring at him through the veil. "My client is in need of battle armor. I understand a man resides here who has offered such a suit into the channels. My . . . client desires discretion in this area. It is also understood the suit is vacuum capable. Correct?"

The landlord squinted and crossed his arms tightly before jerking a nod. "I might be able to help. But now it's your turn to understand . . . the man who owns it wants an even two thousand credits for his suit."

"Too high. Military surplus vacuum capables are going for twelve hundred."

The landlord grinned to expose gaps in his teeth. "You know your market. In this case, what's for sale ain't military surplus. We're talking class here." He made a decision. "Go on up. First door to the right. I assume you have the money with you?"

Skyla gave him a cynical laugh. "You think I'm a Nab? Would I take the chance of having the Civil Security find me in the sewer with an empty purse and a slit throat?"

"No, I suppose not," the landlord laughed heartily and pushed past her to go back to his duties.

The molded plastic stairs creaked under her weight as she climbed up the narrow spiral. Dusty light bars cast eerie yellow shadows to show the way. At the top, she found a narrow plastered hallway. She reached the first door on the right, palmed the lock, and waited. Though she couldn't see any monitors, she could sense the security system. They would have already found the pulse pistol, tool kit, and vibraknife at her hip. They would have counted the two hundred credits in her purse and noted the titanium pins that held her left femur together.

"Name?" a voice asked from the speaker overhead.

"Call me C." The door opened and Skyla stepped into a lighted room furnished far better than the crummy tavern would have suggested. Was this where the small fortune Staffa carried ended up?

A muscular man stepped through a far door. Skyla's trained eye immediately detected the energy shield separating them.

"Yes?"

"I've come to make an offer on the combat armor you have." Skyla crossed her arms and stood, feet apart in an easy attack posture. "You are called?"

"I am Broddus." He frowned, heavy brows creased. "I don't like dealing with shadows who come armed into my house."

"I don't like dealing with men who hide behind security screens. Makes me wonder what they could do to my side of the room while remaining in complete safety."

He laughed, teeth shining. "Noticed that, huh? Not everyone would pick out the slight haze. You're no casual customer."

"No, I am not."

"Very well. I turn off my security, you unveil and leave your weapons on the table. That done, we share a cup of stassa and discuss your offer for the gray combat suit. I warn you, however, the twelve hundred you mentioned for military surplus isn't enough for this suit. It is most unusual."

"I see. So you monitored that discussion."

"I monitor everything."

Skyla pulled back her veil and his eyes widened with sudden interest. She pulled her weapons from under her robes and laid them on the table.

He motioned her ahead and she stepped down into a sunken lounge tastefully decorated with hanging plants. A tinted skylight cast soft rays on the light blue cushions that padded the place. The air carried the perfumed odor of sandwood. She took a seat as he poured two cups of stassa. Handing her one, he padded into a back room and returned bearing . . . *Staffa's combat gear.*

Skyla's anguish built. She willed herself to calm and stood, keeping her head down, unsure of her facial control, forcing herself to finger the fabric.

"Most . . . unusual," she managed.

"Yes, got it from a rich Nab," Broddus told her absently. She swallowed and realized he'd become distracted by her hair, worn loose in shimmering silver-gold waves for exactly the purpose it now served.

"How much?"

He mistook her tone for awe. "Two thousand. Firm."

She tensed as he leaned forward to take in her scent. His voice dropped. "But for a woman as beautiful as you . . . I might bargain."

She looked up, off guard, eyes wide.

"You are a fascinating woman, you know." His mouth curved into a smile as he traced the lines of her face with narrowed raptorian eyes.

"And the owner of the suit?" she asked meekly, disgust building, giving her control of her frayed emotions.

Broddus shook his head. "I fear he'll not be making claims."

"Dead?" *Oh, Staffa, I'm not too late! I can't be!*

He shrugged, "As good as. Killed two of my friends. Civil Security charged him with murder and assault and sentenced him to slavery. He'll not be back to claim ownership."

A quiver of relief rushed through her. There was a chance, an ever so slight chance.

"How much for the combat armor and the weapons he carried?" She soothed her tortured mind and allowed an eyebrow to rise suggestively. "There may be some . . . bargaining latitude on my part."

He considered, licking his lips. "Take off your robes. Perhaps I can sweeten the pot." The dominating smile widened, expression daring her.

Skyla chuckled to herself. Here was her game! He didn't think she'd do it. Unabashed, she unpinned her robe and let it slide down her pale flesh to a tangle on the floor. Clad only in her weapons belt, she could see his intake of breath.

"My price is dropping," he whispered. "I doubt you can get down to two hundred credits though."

"That's down payment. There will be more . . . later." And she saw his interest peak. "Thirteen hundred . . . and me." She let her fingers linger on his skin as she handed him the two hundred ICs from her belt purse.

His face had gone hot. He nodded, a nervous tic in his cheek as he noted the scar along her long muscular leg. "Come this way. Or do you want it here? I'll consider the suit sold and take my first . . . payment."

She walked ahead of him into a sleeping room. Her practiced eye picked out the security monitors—a poorly done job. She turned to face him as he entered. "If you're recording this, we drop the price to just me. I know what you can get for a holo of my action."

He stopped, a frown on his face. "Now, wait a minute, sweet meat. . . ."

She laughed him to silence. "You don't know who I am, do you? Where have you been all your life, in the streets of Etarus?" Direct hit. His face reddened.

He rubbed his chin, thinking.

"You seem to know the security system. If it would make you feel better, *you* turn it off." He extended an arm as he drank in her body. "But I'll warn you, I want full measure."

"And I'll give it." *Oh, will I give it!* She stepped to the head of the sleeping platform and opened a box. Deftly she flipped off the switches and looked around, mouth pursed. She walked to a statue mounted on the wall and moved it, exposing a second box. That, too, she opened to flip three toggles. Satisfied, she turned, seeing his anger-hardened eyes.

"Your first payment?" She filled her lungs and adopted a wide legged posture, her head thrown back, taunting. "Come and get it."

"By the Rotted Gods, I will," he growled, starting for her, peeling off his tunic in the process.

Skyla's first kick caught him under the ribs on the right side. She spun, hammering him hard under the mastoid with an elbow, danced, and dislocated his kneecap with another kick.

She dropped on him, knee first, as he hit the floor gasping for breath. She rested a forearm across his neck and stared into his dazed eyes. "You forgot to ask why I called myself, 'C.' Interested?"

She let up a little on his throat while he gasped another breath, eyes fear-glazed and frantic.

"C stands for *Companions*." She let that sink in. "The man *you* sold into slavery was Lord Commander Staffa kar Therma."

He trembled and she nodded. "Yes, I see you know what that means. Now, stand up." She released him and backed away, waiting, ready to strike again.

He limped to the sleeping platform, eyes miserable. "I— I didn't know. He . . . looked like a Nab who. . . . It was an honest mistake!"

Skyla stood impassively. "The Lord Commander's weapons. Where are they?"

Broddus swallowed, gray shading his features. "Top drawer. My side. . . . Something's wrong with my side. Feels real funny."

Skyla picked a walking stick from the wall and hooked the drawer, pulling it open from an angle. She approached cautiously, wary of booby traps, before she lifted Staffa's possessions from the cavity.

"You were very presumptuous." Skyla turned, settling Staffa's weapons belt over her own. "I didn't lie to you. Holos of our business dealings would have made you rich. Ily Takka, the Regan Minister of Internal Security knows I'm here, somewhere. She would have paid a fortune for such information." She smiled. "But then you won't be reporting it, will you?"

"N–no. N–never. My word . . . I give it . . . I'll never . . ." he stammered, blinking back tears. "It was a mistake! Just a *mistake!*"

Skyla frowned, studying him. She walked to the drawer and pulled a laser from among his other weapons, fingering it thoughtfully. Broddus began whimpering and shaking his head. Eyes wide he clutched his mottling right side. He'd gone white now, and not just from fear.

Skyla checked the charge and triggered the weapon. Smoke curled from the sleeping platform.

"What are you. . . . Rotted Gods! NO!" He lost control of his body, sinking onto the sleeping platform.

"Where's the rest of Staffa's money?"

"In my belt purse, hanging on the right of the wardrobe! Take it. Don't hurt me!"

She pulled the door open with the cane and found it. Only two thousand credits remained. Turning, she slipped the credits into her pouch and calmly walked up to stare into his frightened eyes.

"You are aware of the Etarian practice of dealing with thieves, I suppose." She bit back the impulse to spit into his face.

His eyes closed for a second and he swallowed loudly. His nod was a bare quiver.

"If you move, I will kill you. Just that simple. Have you the courage to live? Death would be much easier."

"Live." His face contorted the track of the tears leaking down his cheeks.

"And you will tell the world what happens to those who dare cross the Companions?"

"I . . . I. . . ." He began sobbing.

She triggered the laser on low power. He screamed when it touched his flesh. With great art, she carved the Etarian symbol for a thief into his forehead, burning deep to etch it into the frontal bone.

"Death is easier," she reminded, heart tightening.

"I want to live!"

Without a second's hesitation, she burned off his right hand; the coherent light cauterized the stump as he screamed deafeningly.

"Live well, thief. Remember the Companions—and the time you robbed Staffa kar Therma." She hesitated at the door, seeing the pale cast to his features. Her first kick had ruptured his liver. Death lingered but minutes away. ". . . And gave the Lord Commander over into slavery!"

She bundled Staffa's combat suit into an empty pack she found in the main room and pulled her robes on, readjusting the veil. Grabbing up her weapons, she slipped out the door and descended the stairs to the main room. A few eyes looked her way, seeing the pack. No one said anything.

In the street, she turned her tracks toward the little shop where she had rented a small room in the rear. On the way, she studied her back trail. No one. She had to move fast. Broddus *might* live long enough to tell.

I should have killed him outright! Getting soft, Skyla. No, not that at all. Dead, he'd have had no time to suffer. Let him die knowing he's a broken man.

She hurried to her small room, trading a jest with the owner, and locked her door. After reshuffling the packs, she donned her combat armor, satisfied by the reassuring tug of her blaster on her hip. She slipped the coarse robes of an Etarian matron over her shoulders and pinned the veil in place. With Staffa's suit and gear packed on top of her white gossamer gown, she took up the packs and left; her steps turned toward the Warden's central slave quarters.

She shook her head as her heart pounded hollowly. "Oh, Staffa, what have you done?" She bit her lip, wondering how he'd managed to stand slavery and degradation.

She could see him, suffering one indignity after another, his wild rages caused by the Praetor's mind traps bringing him to grief after grief. They'd make him suffer for his pride. Stun rods, floggings, perhaps even mutilation.

"You were never taught about the street, Staffa. For all your power and reputation, you never understood the way humanity works. Pray to the Blessed Gods I am not too late!"

* * *

The giant, Brots, had arrived arrogant, dominating, his eyes piggish and deep-set in his flat face. Unlike the others, he wore the collar with a disgraceful pride. The first day, he'd begun to test the system by muscling the weaker slaves out of the way. Anglo had been rotated for Morlai, so, for the moment, Kaylla enjoyed some relief.

That night, Staffa suffered a severe bout of depression. Alone in his misery, he didn't realize how long Kaylla had been gone. Suddenly worried, he began to prowl; within minutes he saw her limping in from the dunes. She stopped short of camp, body bent and tired as she settled on the white sand. The Etarian moon hung low, but enough illumination remained to see defeat as she hung her head. Her shoulders began shaking with silent sobs.

She didn't hear the soft grinding of sand beneath his feet. Staffa settled beside her and placed a hand on her shoulder. Tension and fear possessed her as she recoiled from his touch.

"What is it?"

"Nothing. Just . . . *just leave me alone!*"

Even in the pale light, he could see her swollen lips. She resisted when he placed his fingers under her chin and lifted. The side of her face was puffed out. Dark bruises mottled her neck.

"Who?" Pent rage broke loose.

"Tuff, don't. It's only trouble!" Her hands twisted around the scanty cloth she still had left to cover her body. "Promise me? Leave it be, Tuff." The desperate need in her voice drove him to nod and pat her shoulder tenderly.

And he waited.

Brots took the position opposite Staffa the next day, and between the two of them, they bore the front portion of pipe.

"Later," he heard Brots call to Kaylla in his heavy throaty voice. A shiver rippled down her tanned back.

Eyes slitted, Staffa took Brots' measure. The fellow weighed in about a hundred pounds heavier than he did. Huge arms bulged with muscle thick as a wrestler's thigh. Irritating arrogance reeked from Brots' beastly leer. Staffa found himself locking eyes with the giant all through the hot day. The air crackled with challenge.

That night, Staffa watched. Kaylla got to her feet just after dark and ghosted silently away as she normally did to relieve herself in private. Staffa turned his gaze to where huge Brots slept and saw the giant's head come up. When Kaylla slipped over the dune, Brots rose to his feet—moving to intercept her.

Staffa pursued like a sand leopard as the huge man plodded over the dune crest, eyes on Kaylla's tracks.

"Hey! Well, see who I find in the dunes again!" Brots' thick voice frayed Staffa's temper.

Kaylla's voice carried her sudden fear and resignation.

"Please, I'm tired tonight. Anglo's back tomorrow. He doesn't like the goods used. It will be worse for you."

"On your back and spread, woman. Now! Do it or you'll hurt the worse for it."

Staffa stepped out from behind the dune. "You ever touch her again, Terguzzi scum sucker, and I'll kill you." He'd settled himself, toes gripping the still hot sand. Every nerve tingled as the gut-twisting anger surged. *Come on*, Staffa begged silently, *let me destroy you, you bastard.*

Brots rubbed his hands and grinned as he advanced.

They met, thumping hollowly, grunting as they came together and fought across the sands: Staffa with all the tricks in his long experience, Brots with brute strength and animal zeal.

The desperation and guilt burned free, Staffa kicked, struck, and lashed insanely into that giant body. The beating he took fed every frustration and injustice from Broddus' deceit to the hell that burned from each humiliation and the suffering in the sun. He fought, powered by the guilt that obsessed him. He fought for Chrysla and Kaylla, for Peebal and the rest. Staggering blows landed by Brots goaded him with pain that freed his berserk strength.

Staffa unleashed a brutal blow with his elbow, catching Brots under the chin. The man's head snapped back with a crack. Staffa pistoned a hardened palm to the man's nose, and shot stiff blinding fingers into an eye. His skill prevailed as he broke the big man down, dislocating a kneecap first, breaking a wrist next. Finally he targeted the weaving mass of flesh and lashed out, catching the big man in the throat with a perfectly timed kick.

Brots wavered on his feet, huge chest heaving as a rasping wheeze gurgled from his throat. Staffa stepped back, took a run, and planted a fist deep in the giant's solar plexus. On agile feet he back-heeled Brots to the sand. Staffa dropped to grab the huge head. Work-toughened muscles rippled and bulged under sun-blackened skin. Staffa heaved against the thick corded muscle of the giant's neck while sausagelike groping fingers found a choke-hold on Staffa's windpipe.

For long moments, they heaved, muscles cracking and pulling, sweat streaming down gleaming skin. Their faces contorted with hate. Brots' neck strained. Staffa's vision shimmered as his throat crushed under those thick fingers.

Vertebrae cracked loudly in the night. Brots' big hands spasmed before they loosened and thumped into the sand.

Breath tearing at his throat, Staffa swallowed living pain and staggered away before he fell and rolled on the hot sand. He coughed in agony as he massaged his swollen throat.

"You all right?" Kaylla asked, cradling his head as he blinked dully into her pale face.

"I . . . think," Staffa croaked, chest heaving. Something damp—a tear—landed on his face. He lifted a spent arm to give her a reassuring pat.

"Why?" she asked, voice oddly hoarse. "Why kill for me?"

He swallowed again, the sensation like a splintered stick being pulled down his esophagus. He pulled her close, holding her gently while his thoughts reeled. "You're . . . worth more."

They lay there together, Kaylla curled protectively in his shaking arms.

"We've got to get back," she told him finally.

Staffa glanced at Brots's limp body. "Better get him buried first. They'll see him from the air."

Together they dragged the big man to a slip face in a crescentic dune and cascaded unstable sand over him.

Walking back, Kaylla asked, "What do we say?"

Staffa smiled, wincing at the beating the big man had given him. "That he told us no collar would hold him. That he could beat any desert anywhere and they could let the Rotted Gods chew his abscessed ass before he'd stay a slave."

Hand on his shoulder, she said, "In the end, he would have killed me, you know. It was in him."

"I think of Skyla . . . if she were here. If I never get out of here, and she's ever in this kind of situation, maybe someone will. . . . Rotted Gods, what am I saying?" He ended with a self-reproving growl, irritated and embarrassed by this new softness. "C'mon, it's a long hot one tomorrow. Get some sleep."

She glanced up at him in the moonlight and nodded.

"Your Skyla's a lucky woman, Tuff." Then she walked off to find her place in the sand.

Morning came too early. Staffa stood, wincing at his bruises. Every joint ached as if it had been pulled from its socket. His throat burned, the trachea fevered under swollen flesh. He took a step, reeling on his feet.

Staffa squinted his eyes in the blinding glare of the sun where it hung over the horizon. His dry mouth gagged him. Aching limbs shrieked pain into the base of his brain. Brots *had* hurt him. Numbly, he came to the realization that the big man might have killed him after all. The agony in his body, coupled with the night's exertion, might keep him from getting through this day.

Gasping stifling air into his wounded lungs, Staffa glanced down at the bruises on his rib cage. His elbows looked like swollen roots and his fists had scabbed, only to bleed when he flexed his hands. He staggered to his place by the pipe.

"Whoa!" the tail man called and Staffa threw his weight into slowing the heavy pipe. He stumbled and almost fell, catching his balance by grueling effort of will.

In agony, he followed Kaylla's directions to align the long tube.

"Yup!" came the cry, and Staffa collapsed under the weight of the yoke.

He blinked, feeling heat radiating from the hot steel.

"Tuff?" The worry in Kaylla's voice cut through his misery. "Come on, get up. We've got a whole day."

Staffa ground his teeth and levered himself up.

Koree, another of the crew, suddenly bent down, hand under Staffa's arm. "For today, maybe I'll pair with Tuff."

Staffa's bruised voice rasped. "Yeah, maybe today I need it." Why did this man offer help? What was his purpose?

Koree: another misfit. Skin and bone, the man nevertheless suffered here in the sun with the rest of them. Frail and fragile, Koree—like Peebal—wouldn't last long as a slave on Etaria.

Staffa nodded his thanks to Kaylla. Her tan eyes had grown grim. She slapped him on the back encouragingly as they returned for another length of pipe.

"That true," Koree asked, "what they say about Brots?"

"What's that?" Staffa whispered to save his voice as he concentrated on his wobbling feet.

"That he run off?" Koree grunted under the weight of the pipe, ropy muscles straining. "He took part of my food. He took from all of us."

"So?"

"So we all noticed you're hurt. That's all. Many of us saw Kaylla's bruises. Yesterday, you and Brots . . . well, you love Kaylla. We all do. Today, Kaylla stands straight again. You're hurt and Brots is gone. We'll have our fair share of food and water again."

Staffa coughed hoarsely. "Bastard hurt her. Now, if I could just get Anglo."

Koree hawked brown phlegm and spit into the sand. "Injustice, friend Tuff, is the reality of existence. God made the universe that way. It's unfair that we can only find a hero once in a while to handle bits and pieces of justice."

"I'm no Rotted hero."

Koree ignored him. "Brots is only a symptom of the sickness infecting mankind. Anglo is a fragment, but he represents a larger malignancy, one you and I, friend Tuff, cannot cure."

"Why not? If I could get my hands on his scrawny neck. . . ."

"He's only a fragment—and killing him would kill all of us when the collars shorted," Koree panted. "That, friend Tuff, is poor social surgery at best. Therefore, here, we, at least, must suffer until we find the strength to die. Others will have to do the surgery in another time."

Staffa stumbled along, trying to keep his breath. When they dropped the pipe he looked at Koree. "You think it takes strength to die?"

Koree bent to the task of pulling the yoke strap from the sand. "In our situation, yes. Why do we fight so hard to live? What do we do here but suffer? If you accept that there is purpose in the universe, is it suffering? Can we expect that tomorrow the Empire will fall and we will be freed? No, my friend. I wake every morning with dread. Every moment I suffer, feeling my health sucked away with the sweat of my body. I will break someday. When? Tomorrow? No. Next week? No. But the week after? The week after that? And when that happens, Anglo or Morlai will cut off my life and perhaps you will carry me to the side and push hot white sand over my body. That is my future."

"Then why keep going?"

"Life is addictive. God made the universe that way. Like a drug, life fills us and leaves us brimming with an illusion of hope. People experience enough successes to nourish more hope. They forget the disappointments because hope is a more enjoyable opiate than despair. We, however, have no such reinforcement here. Somewhere on this endless pipeline death waits. Perhaps the only true underlying reason we stagger on is that we're goaded by curiosity. When will it come? How long will I last? I ask you, is life worth living if that is the only entertainment?"

"You can always lie down and let Anglo make an end of it," Staffa reminded. "The collar doesn't cause pain. The disorientation is only limited to a minute or so. You talk of God and injustice. Why? The universe is neutral."

"Is it?" Koree shot him a sideways glance as they staggered under the immense weight. "Suffering and injustice are built deep into the structure of the universe. Entropy is the fuel of progress. Each of the world ecosystems—there are no exceptions—is based on competition. Some life-form eating another, competing for resources at the expense of its brethren. Why? Any species of plant or animal—if not preyed upon by others—preys upon itself. Is that just?"

"And you say this is God's work?" Staffa grunted, short of breath.

"Not the God you think of in terms of Etaria or Sassan Emperors—but the real God. The creator and manipulator of the universe. The God who isn't at all interested in prayers, or sacrifices, or temple contributions."

"The Seddi God."

"We can use that term to distinguish him, friend Tuff."

They pounded past the end of the pipe and fought sideways, lining up the length under Kaylla's watchful eye.

On the way back, Koree continued. "God built injustice into the system to avoid stagnation. Injustice entails suffering. Any aware organism will respond, trying to make its life better—alleviate the suffering, if you will. Choices are made, observations which, for the moment, establish that which is. Freeze the dance of the quanta. Reality is changed; knowledge is acquired. God gains from knowledge. He learns about reality, different reality, from each of the micro phase changes recorded in a bit of eternal energy."

"Yet you wait to die. Why not end the suffering now? You yourself have said you only await the end. Your hope is gone."

"But I am a coward," Koree reminded. "I am afraid to take that action."

"I've seen a lot of death. Fear made no difference. The brave died as dead as the cowards."

"True, but how many had the choice to take their own lives?"

"Many." Staffa stooped to dig a hole under the pipe for the carry strap.

"Why did they have that choice?" Koree countered, grunting as they staggered under the yoke for yet another trip.

"Because they feared my . . . my troops more than they feared death." Rotted Gods! What had he almost said?

"Then my thesis rests," Koree asserted. "Men are cowards at heart. Cowards are unjust, acting according to God's will. Creating more suffering, you see. And we are the worst cowards of all since we could escape misery so easily, Lord Commander."

His heart spasmed. He stumbled and Koree groaned, struggling to support the burden. The little man sank to his knees as Staffa fought to lift his half of the yoke and succeeded, the whole company suddenly out of pace.

"What . . . what did you call me?"

Koree, panting from the sudden strain, fought his way ahead until he regained his voice. "I'm sorry. I didn't think. I thought I recognized you days ago, but the beard makes a difference. Your ability to kill Brots confirmed it. No other man but a practiced professional could have dispatched him without serious damage."

Staffa glanced uneasily behind him, happy to note that no one seemed to have heard.

Koree continued to talk as if nothing had happened. "I was once a professor of human behavior at the University of Maika. For years I studied the trends of government in the Empire and wrote learned papers on why Tybalt did what he did and what motivated you and your Companions. I had a rare holo of you on the wall."

Staffa's anguished body—for the moment at least—reveled in a rush of adrenaline-backed fear.

Koree said sympathetically, "I shall not tell, Tuff, my friend. Your business here is your own. I trust that you, too, have fallen as I myself fell. To me, that is another small slice of justice in an unjust whole." He paused. "But tell me. Why did you. . . . No, *how* could you do the things you did? Did you never wonder at the rights and wrongs of your actions? Please, I mean no insult or censure. I ask strictly from an academic curiosity to know what motivated you."

Staffa bowed his head to hide the worry in his eyes.

"I don't need an answer right now, friend Tuff." Koree's voice came softly. "If you decide not to tell me, that is your prerogative." He laughed brittlely. "And you might decide to kill me to ensure my silence—which is fine. You spare me the misery of waiting to die, and I would only ask that you do it skillfully and painlessly."

Staffa bit his lip, blood rushing in his ears. They said no more as they carried length after length of pipe toward a towering dune, bisected by the trench.

Injustice? Suffering? God's work? He blinked to stifle the pain lancing hot behind his eyes. His tender ribs sent stitches through him. All his life, he'd dealt misery to someone. Entropy? *Had* he fed on that? He'd been a predator, true, but how did he expect humanity to survive the coming cataclysm when Sassa and Rega, each determined to survive, collided head to head? In God's unjust universe, where did right lie? Baffled, he turned his raw red eyes to glare at poor staggering Koree.

"I don't like that dune," Kaylla said warily, as they walked back to a new pipe stack the hovercraft had dropped. "I'll breathe a lot easier when we pass it." She looked back over her shoulder at the defiant white dune. "It's a man killer, Tuff."

What did he say to Koree? He thought about that as they worked ever closer to the sheer-walled ridge of sand. Kill him? Was that what the scholar was after? A quick end? And if he had recognized Staffa, who else could? The patter of fear sucked even more energy from his dehydrated body.

Staffa remained silent during water break. Anglo, having arrived, allowed them a longer than normal sit in the shade to drink while he took Kaylla into the dunes, anticipation in his eyes. For the first time, Staffa noted the hatred in each of his fellow's eyes as they stared at the dune Anglo led Kaylla behind.

Emotion—a violent storm—filled Staffa's breast when she finally returned, mouth pursed bitterly. She waited until they were walking back down the trench to spit into the scorched sand.

Fear for his own safety and vile hatred for Anglo twisted and ate inside Staffa as he fought to keep his tired body upright.

God's work? If so, God was a bastard. And so was Staffa kar Therma. He'd helped build this living hell. He had gleefully sacrificed souls to it.

I could die so easily. It would only be just in an unjust universe. How true Koree's words are. Have I come to this horrid existence to finally know the roots of Truth? Is this what people, those mindless clods who compose the masses, feel? Do they. . . . No. Only a few are ever driven to find ultimate Truth. The rest would fawn over their Blessed Gods, or their Sassan Emperors, and look no deeper.

God, whatever you are. This I swear upon my soul. If I live, I will seek you out. I will find my son, and I will change the lot of humanity! I'll break your rotted Forbidden Borders. I'll find a way to change humanity—and if I die in the process, that energy Koree talks about will make it back to you some day and you will know that one man, at least, dared to defy you!

"I did what I did because I was trained for it," Staffa told Koree as they moved into the shadow of the unstable dune. Blessed shade came only at the expense of the towering danger.

"I was taught and trained to be a mercenary by the Praetor of Myklene. It was drilled into me from the time I was five," he continued, noting Kaylla's frightened glance going to the sheer walls on either side of them. Tiny grains and streamers of sand—whipped from the top by the wind—trickled down the sides in a constant purr to settle on their damp bodies in a gritty dusting of sweat-streaked gray.

"Like a tool," Koree mused. "Did you ever have friends your own age? Ever get out into the city?"

"No," Staffa told him dully. "I only associated with my

teachers—constantly studying, practicing, learning. My goals were to improve until I could outperform my instructors. To that end, I devoted every waking moment." Staffa barked a short laugh. "I succeeded by the time I was twenty-three."

"And at what cost to yourself, my friend Tuff?"

"I don't know. I don't even know why I tell you this."

"Such talk is new to you?"

Staffa almost fell again. He waited until he had his footing. "About myself, yes." Too tired; he wasn't in control. Fear built.

Koree fought to get his breath. "You must have had a lonely life, my friend."

The call "Whoa!" came from behind. They had no breath left for talk as they stumbled and staggered to set the pipe straight.

They hurried, everyone aware of the ominous wall of sand that rose over them. Staffa's exhaustion increased, each step in the loose sand sapped him further, draining his very life. Rotted Gods, for the ability to simply stagger to the side of the trench and collapse!

Cursing, they placed the yokes and staggered up with the last of the pipe sections.

Have you become the confessor of my sins, tiny fragile man? Are you my route to salvation? You, who I could break with one hand? Why do you, who are so fragile, seem so strong and terrible now?

To cover his discomfort, Staffa continued to speak. "I always turned to my study and training. I lived with military problems. How do I take this planet? How can I counter these defenses? They were my reality."

"And what landed you here, Tuff?"

"The questions of a dying old man," Staffa whispered.

They were laboring in the shadow of the dune when the hovercraft approached with a new stack of pipe dangling beneath. The pilot, making a poor job of it, slowed too quickly. The cable swayed crazily as the craft dropped rapidly, heavy pipe thumping into the sand beyond the dune. Staffa felt the impact through his feet.

Years of combat had ingrained split-second reactions. Twisting from under the yoke, his terror-galvanized muscles sped him forward. He braced himself and yanked the tug rope to pull Kaylla backward. Staffa caught her, pinned her arms to her sides with panic-lent brute strength. Hugging her tightly, he catapulted their bodies into the end of the tube. A half second later, thousands of tons of sand avalanched down to bury the world.

CHAPTER XVI

"Tell me, Bruen, what do you think God is?" the hollow voice demanded, blasting through the Magister's staggering mind.

He swallowed, heart racing. Could the machine hear his heartbeat? Or understand the cold sweat that poured down his face in trickling streams?

Bruen allowed the mantra to flow. "God is a fallacious human delusion. By following the path of Right Thought, we wean ourselves from the illusions reinforced by antique mythology. The Way leads us from primitive superstitions which require the concept of God to atone for human inadequacies and only act to keep us servile—"

"Enough!"

Bruen gasped, mind reeling from the booming explosion in his mind.

"You are very good at chanting mantra, Bruen." The Mag Comm hesitated. *"But let us speak on an intellectual level. You used to believe in God. You practiced that heresy. Why? Why did you believe? I would know your reasons for accepting the fallacy. You are not totally illogical."*

Bruen clamped his jaw to still his chattering teeth. He shook uncontrollably, every muscle in his tired body vibrating in the grip of the Mag Comm's awesome mental power.

"Because the concept of God explains . . . I mean, seems to explain, certain phenomena observable in the physical universe." A sweet breath of relief filled his lungs. Fear loosened its grip on his intestines. He had a slim chance.

"Then God is an explanation? Speak, Bruen, speak to me of the hypothetical underpinnings of your outlawed heresy. Do you mean that logically God could be considered the quest of science?"

"Not exactly." Bruen swallowed again as he sought to

soothe his panicked brain. "You see, science is the investigation of the physical universe around us. God, on the other hand, was considered the creator, the *thing* that gave purpose to everything. The designer, if you will, of physical laws such as entropy, thermodynamics, the quant . . . I mean, the uncertainty we observe in the physical world before—"

"I know to what you refer. Tell me of God—not physics."

"The belief in God wasn't universally the same. Various traditions developed different explanations. Nor was belief in God totally accepted. Any investigation of the nature of God depends on basic assumptions. The atheists always pointed to those assumptions as—"

"Atheists? Explain!"

"Not everyone accepted God as real. Humans, through many centuries, practiced atheism—the disbelief of God's existence. We have no record how long atheism has—"

"Do humans still practice atheism?"

Bruen thought he perceived an element of uncertainty in the mechanical voice. "Yes. It should be a predictable intellectual position in any society composed of rational individuals."

"Why, if the society is rational, do not all humans practice atheism?" The machine seemed off balance.

Bruen swallowed, willing his suddenly frantic mind to silence and serenity. "Because the proofs offered by the atheists have never been convincing. Just as belief in God cannot be proved without making an assumption, neither—"

"Stop!"

Bruen was jolted, shivering again, wishing the blasting voice could be muted in some way to dull the shearing edge of pain.

A long moment passed before the Mag Comm ordered: *"You will prepare a report on atheism and submit it to me through the machine. You will be thorough, complete, with documentation of what you know."*

"It will be done," Bruen assented earnestly.

"In the meantime, these are my orders: Kaspa, according to your report, has been quiet for too long. The time has come to retake the city. You will lay your plans and see to that. Once you reported you had enough strength to defeat a Regan Division in the field. One is currently being sent to

take Vespa. You will destroy it—and your Sinklar Fist. His power grows. He seems too competent. You should fear what he is made from.

"Within the next Regan year, I must see strikes made against Sassa. They take their God-Emperor too seriously. The Regan heresy of Etarian religion is less dangerous, but it, too, has grown too strong. Conflict must be initiated between the powers in order that their social control be blunted.

"I have reviewed the report you have submitted. You have not found the Lord Commander. Time is growing short, Bruen."

"Great One, we believe we have located the Lord Commander. In fact, we are working at this very moment to—"

"This time there can be no failure as in the past. Since he is away from his security, you will kill him immediately! Understood?"

Bruen shook from the booming power in the pronouncement.

"It . . . it is understood, Great One."

"I am tired of failures with the Lord Commander. A pause. "Are your Seddi following the Way? I am worried, Bruen. First you tell me of heretical probability gone astray when the Way teaches that with sufficient information, all actions can be predicted. Then you tell me of a human ability to disbelieve—a fact totally illogical given your species' history and nature. Such information I find most difficult to assimilate. Our plans are delicate. There is no room for so many errors. We must have predictability! So much is at stake, how can I trust you? Are you and your kind truly irrational as was declared so long ago?"

"We follow the Way, Great One," Bruen insisted, dedicating himself to the sincerity of the statement while fear stole along his nerves.

"Beware, Bruen. You and your humans dangle by a thread. The time has come to see the implementation of the Way throughout Free Space. It is your only chance! Beware! BEWARE!"

Silence, blissful silence, echoed in Bruen's brain. He sagged, mind blank, body limp in the chair. A pounding began that lanced through his parietals to the core of his brain.

Hands lifted the golden globe gently from his head as Bruen blinked up into the dim light, barely aware of the ominous luminescence of the machine where it filled the wall before him.

"As was declared so long ago?" A slip? And you didn't know about atheism, you God-cursed machine? First, you declare the Seddi to be heretics and try to instill a Godless philosophy—but without a knowledge of atheism? Curious! Next, you would have our agents provoke an inevitable war between Sassa and Rega, knowing full well they must devastate most of Free Space. Why, machine? What is your vile purpose?

You threaten us, claiming humanity hangs by a thread. Bruen pursed his lips, frowning. *What thread do we hang by, machine? One you control? Or one we can take into our own hands? So many unanswered questions—and my time is so short. I no longer control events, they have taken control of me.*

"Are you all right?" one of the Initiates asked, his young face lined with worry. He bent over Bruen, tall, blond, muscular, a slight scar healing across his face—a token of the fighting in Kaspa. He wore it proudly, a badge of service to the order. The other, a medium-height, burly man with dark skin and kinky hair, wore a grim expression as if the tension in the room had sapped him, too. His black eyes reflected wariness.

"Yes," Bruen gasped, voice wavering as he winced from the headache.

The Initiates slipped strong arms under him and bore him up through the maze of tunnels.

"Take me to Hyde's room," Bruen whispered.

He closed his eyes, feeling the familiar bends and turns of the passages as he was brought upward. The tension in the young men crackled like electricity above his sagging age-lined flesh.

"We are here, Magister," the black-skinned Initiate whispered, as they settled him in a seat. Bowing, they turned to leave.

"Stay," Bruen croaked. "It is time you took the place of

Masters. You have studied long and hard. Not to know at this late stage of the game is penance you do not deserve."

He looked up to see a quickening in their eyes as they glanced at each other.

Hyde lay prostrate in his bed, face washed of any color. He turned his head weakly. "And?"

Briefly Bruen reported the session, then added: "We must plan. Something is very wrong. We will need our best minds to determine the course of action we must take."

"Wrong how?" Hyde asked and broke into a fit of coughing.

"So wrong the machine is beginning to ask questions." Bruen shivered uncontrollably. "Too much is awry. I have come to believe everything is now at stake . . . everything."

"But you fooled the machine again, Magister?" the scarred Initiate inquired, voice subdued.

"Yes, I fooled the machine again." Bruen grimaced at the weary tone in his own voice. "But you two must comb the records and submit a report to the machine on atheism. Somehow I get the impression the machine never knew. Why? What sort of a weakness does that denote?"

The black Initiate's face brightened slightly. "Then the machine is not omniscient!"

"No. We've known that for a long time. Indeed, we play a dicey game here. When it orders—as it has done in the past—we can do little to chart the margins of its power. When it questions, we can at least gain a glimmering of its abilities."

"So long as it isn't outsmarting us," Hyde reminded, convulsing in a coughing fit. He expectorated into a worn crock beside his bed.

"That is always a possibility." Bruen blinked against the headache. If only the sessions with the machine didn't drain him so. "The Mag Comm, however, isn't the only one capable of misinformation. At lying, no one can beat a human!"

"But the machine is acting uncertain?" Hyde continued between wheezing breaths.

"Yes, it is. And that, old friend, is most unsettling. For the first time, the machine is beginning to formulate threats. Until we know the extent of its powers, we must heed them with a great deal of fear."

"And it ordered us to step up the war?" Hyde wiped a

thin-skinned hand over purple lips to catch a spinner of saliva that leaked past.

Bruen nodded. "Yes, not only that, but it slipped again. It knows a Regan Division under Sinklar Fist is about to take the field. We are not its only source of Free Space information."

Hyde's face fell, dull blue eyes concerned. "Better to know—but too bad for all of that. Our position becomes even more tenuous."

Bruen nodded, looking up at the two young men, pondering.

"You will need to contact Butla Ret," Hyde broke into another coughing fit. "He is the only one we can count on. He is the only one capable of taking the field. He must be our legs and arms now."

"I will do so," Bruen patted Hyde's swollen legs. "Let us pray we are not too late, old friend."

"Yes," Hyde gasped, fluid-filled lungs heaving. "This should have come upon us fifteen years ago."

"But it didn't," Bruen sighed. "We must deal with it now." He looked up at the young men to emphasize his words. "If we make a mistake, young gentlemen, it will be our last."

* * *

Skyla Lyma ducked into the pitch-blackness of the alley, aware of the stalker. She slipped silently through the darkness, feeling with her feet. Stealing to one side, she waited, sand-coated brick under her fingers as she felt her way along. Her nerves had been on edge ever since Ily Takka showed up at the Warden's pens. Curse it all, it had been too close. And as Ily flew off, she'd looked her right in the eye. *If it hadn't been for the veil, I'd already be dead meat.*

From somewhere ahead, the delightful aroma of cinnamon and klofa wafted in the hot night air, filling the darkness with the promise of delightful pastries.

A faint stir in the darkness brought Skyla to a crouch. She eased a vibraknife from her belt. Sand shifted under a boot to her right. Who? One of Ily's agents? Or just a footpad?

Just a little closer.

Darkness weighed heavily in the stifling heat. A trickle
of sweat ran down the inside of her combat armor to tickle
between her breasts. Her heart, battle-tight, rapped against
her sternum.

So black, so stygian. Where was he?

Cloth made a soft rasping before her. A bit of blackness
moved in the alley. Skyla took him, striking high with one
steel fist while she kicked low for his legs. Flesh gave under
her powerful blows. He grunted and fell as she stepped
back, balanced, poised for a counter-strike that never came.
His body landed with a soft thump. Catlike, she pounced,
her vibraknife millimeters from his throat. The man gasped,
trying to catch his breath.

From her pouch, she took a small light, narrowing the
beam to play it across his rugged features. Nyklos!

He groaned, swallowing, blinking stunned brown eyes in
the glare of her light.

"Talk," she hissed. "And talk quick. You should be able
to feel the blade against your neck. My patience is thin. I
don't like rannies who follow me in the dark. Makes me
suspicious."

He nodded, eyes tight at the feel of air vibrating against
his skin.

"Talk!"

"Just . . . just looking after you, sweet meat. I. . . . Huh!
Don't!" he yipped as she pressed down, seeing skin peel
away like fat under a white-hot blade.

"Then don't try me, Nab." She crammed a knee into his
crotch; his eyes glazed with pain. "Talk, ranny, or your
voice will rise and you'll dribble your drink over your chest
every time you swallow from now on!"

"I was just . . . just trying to see where you went. That's
all. You're . . . pretty. So pretty. Make a man proud to
turn you's all." More skin peeled as he swallowed. Blood
had begun to well under the vibraknife.

"You're lying. You're looking at death, Nab. And you
don't care. Makes me even more suspicious." She drew the
knife back slightly, eyes narrowing. "Why? Who are you
working for that they could inspire that sort of loyalty? Or
is it fear? Ily Takka, perhaps?" His expression hardened.
"You don't like that idea?"

"No, I don't," he said with more control than she would have expected under the circumstances. "Not Ily."

She cocked her head. "You're no street hawker, for all your looks and talk. You carry yourself too well. You got professional written all over you. Want to fess?"

A slight smile bent his lips. "Why don't you just cut my throat and we'll have it all over with."

Skyla cocked her head, studying him speculatively. "If not Ily, then might we possibly share an interest?"

"We might," Nyklos agreed quickly, swallowing again as a trickle of blood ran down the side of his throat. She recognized the game, playing for time, looking for an advantage. His voice held just enough truth to give him credibility.

Skyla slipped one hand into her pouch and pulled out a gleaming vial. Most carefully uncapping it with her teeth, she placed the tube over his mouth.

"Drink," she commanded. "It's Mytol. It'll make you talk."

An instant before he tensed to throw her off, she blasted her knee into his crotch, spilling a little more than she intended into his suddenly open mouth as he bellowed in pain.

"You Sylenian *witch!*" he exploded as she rolled away from his violent reaction. He writhed and contorted in the filthy alley sand.

Skyla rocked to her feet, Mytol bottle capped and restored to her pouch. She ducked lithely aside as he staggered to his feet, still bent double, and rushed her, swinging a fist. She eluded him in the darkness.

"Got to kill her," he panted under his breath. "Got to kill before . . . before. . . ." His next charge slowed awkwardly as he ran into the grimy brick wall.

"Too late," Skyla told him easily. "You're mine now."

"No! No. Can't. . . . can't. . . ."

She waited as he stumbled this way and that in the darkness, then fell in a sodden heap. With her light, she checked his squinted eyes: unfocused.

"Come now, Nyklos, you called me beautiful." She hesitated, unable to resist the urge to tease. "Am I?"

"Yes," he muttered, voice thick.

"The first time we met, I saw desire in your eyes. Do you desire me? Am I really *that* beautiful?"

"Wing Commander, you are the most beautiful woman I have ever seen—and the deadliest."

Wing Commander? That could be lethal, Nyklos, my amorous friend.

"Good," she praised. "What are you thinking?"

"Right now?" Nyklos asked, frowning his confusion.

"Yes, now."

"I was wondering why that bastard Staffa didn't take you for his own years ago." Nyklos flopped his head back and forth before his neck muscles relaxed and he couldn't move anymore.

Skyla caught herself against the wall, suddenly unsettled. Her heart began to race as her mouth went dry. *Damn it! Thrice cursed Mytol, anyway. I asked for that. Now get him back on track before you make a fool of yourself.*

"Come, Nyklos, sit here next to me." She pulled him down to cradle his head in her lap. Too much Mytol. She tensed as his hand tried to grope her breast through the armor. To keep him under control she laced her fingers into his.

"Now, Nyklos," she began conspiratorially, "you're going to prove I'm beautiful by telling me all about yourself."

And pray to the Blessed Gods, you stay the hell away from Staffa and the way I feel about him.

Nyklos nodded, and despite his thick slurred tongue, he began to speak. Skyla felt herself stiffen as his story spilled out. Shared interest? Indeed!

"So, that's who you are, Nyklos," she added under her breath. Pieces began to fall into place.

*   *   *

The screen on the comm monitor wavered and finally firmed into a coherent image. Skyla crossed her arms and leaned back in the chair she sat in. Nyklos stood beside her, still groggy from the Mytol, and delightfully compliant.

From the outside, the house Nyklos lived in looked like any of the other Etarian homes on the block. The walls were brown clay and supported a flat roof of ceramic tiles. Only when she had stepped inside did Skyla find that Nyklos lived in a nest of communications equipment, monitoring devices, and comm equipment.

Skyla returned her attention to the screen. It fuzzed and cleared into the face of a young woman with kinky black hair that made a halo around her head. At sight of Skyla Lyma, she straightened.

"Greetings," Skyla gave her a smile. "I'm Skyla Lyma, Wing Commander of the Companions. Would you do me the courtesy of informing Magister Bruen that I would like to speak to him?"

"How did you . . . I mean. . . ."

"Just do it."

Skyla chuckled to herself, and tossed a small object into the air, catching it playfully. The object consisted of a white, ceramic replica of a human tooth. The picture in the monitor changed again, this time presenting an old man with a wrinkled face. Only a few wisps of white hair stood up from the age-spotted dome of his bald pate. He looked at her and blinked, as if to clear his head of sleep.

Finally, he sighed and said, "I suppose that since you've gained access to this comm net, there wouldn't be much use in denying it exists, but tell me, Wing Commander, just how did you find us, and what do you want?"

Skyla pulled Nyklos into the range of the comm pickup. "Recognize your agent, Magister?"

Bruen nodded, a tired look in his ancient eyes. "I do. That he's still alive leaves me a little worried, however."

Skyla leaned forward and displayed the white tooth between forefinger and thumb. "Somebody goofed. I don't know if the crack shows on your monitor—the capsule did what it was supposed to. However, it seems that someone in your lab forgot to charge it with whatever the preferred Seddi poison is."

Bruen rubbed an ancient hand over his face. "I don't suppose you wanted to talk to me about hollow teeth."

"No, I wanted to talk to you about assassination. Imagine my surprise when I discovered that Nyklos, here, was tagging along on my tail in hopes I'd lead him to the Lord Commander. Had I done that, he'd have killed both Staffa and myself, effectively decapitating the Companions."

Bruen nodded slowly. "That is one of our primary strategic concerns."

"You don't sound particularly contrite about it."

The wrinkles tightened around his mouth. "Come, come,

Wing Commander, you're no naive novice at the game of interstellar politics. We each have our respective goals. Ours would be served by your death and the dissolution of the Companions. You are pursuing your own aims—as are other political forces in Free Space. Or would you like to play games and mask the reality of the situation?"

Skyla cocked her head. "If we're being blunt, why don't you tell me exactly what the Seddi goal is."

"The restructuring of human epistemology." He raised an eyebrow. "You do know what that means, don't you?"

Skyla leaned back, frowning. "You want to change the entire way that humans think about themselves and the universe they live in?"

Bruen gave her a placid nod. "I admit it's a rather grandiose objective, but the Seddi believe that human suffering is rooted in a flawed epistemology—one which you and the Lord Commander both espouse. It's not just you, but the entire species which has come to believe that we must live in a universe controlled by unassailable political leaders. We absorb that idea through enculturation."

"Wait, you just lost me. Enculturation?"

Bruen placed his palms together and leaned forward, a gleam in his eyes. "Think seriously about a human infant, Wing Commander. It's literally an untrained animal. It doesn't know much of anything beyond the demands of its body, least of all how to behave properly in any given culture. Granted, behavioral genetics determines many aspects of personality and ability, but the intricacies of dealing with a society must all be learned. There is no genetic code in the DNA which tells an infant that eating peas with a fork is apropos behavior—especially not when using a spoon would be more effective. People from Ashtan learn very early that it is proper to belch as long and as loudly as possible to demonstrate appreciation for a good meal— much to the dismay of the traditional Regan who invites an Ashtan to his home for dinner. But we learn more than manners and social skills; we also soak up and integrate political ideology. Ask any Regan why Tybalt is the emperor, and he'll tell you that Tybalt is the emperor because someone has to be. That is enculturation: the process whereby an infant learns the values and expected norms of his society."

"And the Seddi wouldn't want the everyday Regan to simply accept the old social dogma?"

Bruen inspected her through narrowed eyes. "You're a quick study, Wing Commander."

"Even if you could assassinate Staffa and myself, and Divine Sassa and Tybalt, you couldn't change the way people think about politics. Your goal is impossible. People don't just change the way they think about the universe overnight."

"The Seddi probably have a more complex understanding of the problem than you might believe. We expect a significant change in the way humans think about themselves in another thousand years or so. This is a long-term project, one which depends on education and increasing the ability of people to question the baseline assumptions they make about life. We don't expect any quick fix."

"Then Staffa and I had better get used to keeping our eyes open," Skyla told him with a grim smile.

Bruen nodded serenely. "Which brings us to another hot topic of debate: the Lord Commander. I don't suppose you'd like to tell me why he dropped everything, threw two empires into turmoil, and ran off to Etarus incognito?"

What do I tell him? Skyla fingered her chin as she considered. "Actually, he was on the way to Targa to see you."

For the first time, Bruen straightened, interest in his watery eyes. "Is that a feint? Some sort of dissembling—"

Skyla shook her head. "No, I mean it. He was headed for Targa to see you."

Bruen's expression reflected a deep curiosity. He tapped thin fingers on something out of sight of the comm pickup. "Why would he place himself at risk, crossing a potentially hostile empire, to gain access to a planet in the throes of civil war to try and find a Seddi Magister who has been trying to assassinate him for years? That makes no sense— but then, a lot of what the Lord Commander has done in recent weeks makes no sense."

"He is looking for his son." Skyla hesitated for a moment, then added, "And perhaps truth, Magister."

A light of understanding kindled in Bruen's eyes. "Ah, then the key really is the Praetor. What did he say to Staffa? What happened in that room? Were you there?"

Skyla's scalp crawled as she tensed. "You seem to know

an awful lot, Seddi. Perhaps I should keep Nyklos here
under sedation and take him back to Itreata. I've already
determined that he's the center for your spy ring on Etaria.
I wonder what other jewels he'd spill under a mind probe."

Bruen barely acknowledged that he'd heard. His face had
gone blank, lost in thought. Finally he looked up, eyes pensive. "Staffa's entire personality changed, didn't it? Mood
swings, depression, irrational actions based on improper
neural responses that had been masked for years?"

Skyla bent forward to stare hostilely into the monitor.
"What are you getting at?"

Bruen waved her concern away, a wry animation to his
movements. "The dance of the quanta, Wing Commander.
The uncertainty principal that makes life so damned fascinating and unpredictable. After all these years, I would like
the chance to talk to Staffa kar Therma." Bruen took a
deep breath. "I am willing to offer the Lord Commander
safe passage for the purposes of a meeting between the two
of us. We can work out the details later."

"And how do I know I can trust you?"

Bruen shrugged. "We'll figure out something." Then he
glanced absently away as he propped his chin on a translucent palm. "The problem is that Ily Takka is about to whisk
him out from under both of us. We'll have to act fast—and
together."

CHAPTER XVII

"They what?" Sinklar thundered, pounding his fist into the hardwood. His Section Firsts gawked in disbelief as they straightened from the desk they'd converted into a map table. A foreboding silence filled the office. Through the dusty windows, they could see the tree-dotted hills rising beyond the square plots of farmland.

"Gone," MacRuder told him from the door of the commandeered grain exchange office building. "The Minister of Defense recalled all transport to provide the Second Division,"—his expression soured—"what he called 'emergency strike capability.' "

Sinklar cursed and leaned forward over the spread maps. He ground his jaws. *Damn them!*

Gretta exploded with, "Rotted Gods! We're halfway to Vespa with two thousand troops *and no pus-dripping transport*?"

The others erupted into curses as they shouted questions back and forth.

"Quiet, people. I need to think." Sinklar took a deep breath. He controlled his rage and flexed his muscles to ease the tension. Then he dropped into the use-polished chair behind the desk. "So, the power play begins."

He glanced down at the topo map, brow creased; he cataloged the distance to Vespa. Left in the middle of rough country, farms filled the valleys between rugged chains of mountains. A big mine lay within a half-day's march, but other than that, nothing.

"For one thing," MacRuder—still filling the door—told him, "we're stuck. And we're sitting ducks here. These little valleys might harbor enough farmland to supply this elevator and co-op, but the rocky timbered ridges around them are a haven for hit-and-run tactics."

Sinklar flipped on his comm. "Ayms? Kap? Report!"

"Got the boys billeted out here, First. Everything's quiet. Boring in fact. What's the news on the transport? What do I tell these guys?" Kap asked.

"Tell them we're staying here for a day." Sinklar rubbed the back of his neck. "Remember the drills we did outside Kaspa? I want small search and destroy squads out and around. This time, we play their game. Meanwhile, organize foraging parties. One from each Section. They are to bring in livestock, raid the farms, and shoot any wildlife. If it's kicking and red-blooded, it's edible."

"So when do we get out of here?" Ayms asked, voice somber.

"As soon as I think of a way. Tell the troops the Rotted Gods will starve before I leave 'em hung up to dry. Headquarters or hell take the hindmost!"

"Yes, sir. We're on it," Kap signed off.

Sinklar turned to the map. "We could walk. That would get us there within three weeks. But a long column would be easily picked to pieces. And how would we feed them all? The country isn't *that* rich!"

MacRuder stepped forward, a perplexed anxiety in his deep blue eyes as he ran a nervous hand through his blond hair. "I could take a squad back with the transport. We could, um, 'suggest' that they give us transport. A blaster under full charge can be real pus-stinking persuasive when you're looking down the other end."

"And they'd blow you to pieces." Pensively, Sinklar rolled his stylus between his fingers. "No, Mac, they'd be prepared for that."

Gretta's eyes slitted before she spoke, voice deadly flat. "You mean they did this on purpose?"

"Of course." Sink tapped the stylus against his chin, gaze switching from face to face. His mind raced as the possibilities unfolded in his mind.

"Stupidity!" Mac flared. "What good does it do the Empire to have the First Targan gutted and destroyed again? It's preposterous!"

"That would appear to be the question," Sinklar agreed, considering the situation, refusing to let his anger carry him away. "To allow the Division to be savaged and decimated again will give the Targans heart, a great psychological and political victory. The Empire will be set back and the involvement here will escalate in cost and lives and material."

"Who profits from that?" Gretta moved behind him, hands comforting as she massaged his shoulders.

"I'm not really sure." Sinklar patted one of her hands affectionately. Smile fading into frown, he added, "What we see here is a tiny part of the complete picture. No, our dilemma is not a tactical error. Somewhere—Rega, most likely—an Imperial defeat will benefit some party or destroy someone else. Who? Mykroft? I don't think so. He hated appointing me to this position."

The piece clicked into place. Sinklar's eyes lit. "Of course!"

"What?" Gretta demanded, leaning forward to stare into his eyes, suddenly hopeful.

"That's why they appointed me." Sinklar laughed bitterly and slapped a hand on his knee. "I'm a sacrificial goat! The perfect fall guy! Set up the First Division with raw misfits; leave them stranded with a new 'green' commander; allow the Targans to blast us to pieces while the command falls apart, lacking food, supply, and relief; and finally, no one powerful or important gets the blame or shame of losing a whole Division to the Targans. We're expendable for political reasons."

Mac's mouth worked. "Rotted Gods! What are we fighting for? I mean, they can't just waste their own people like that, can they? We're Imperial citizens! What about all that rhetoric when they took Maika, and Riparious, and all the rest? What about the speeches on law and human rights and ethical responsibility?"

"Propaganda," Gretta guessed. "Face it, Tybalt built an Empire to promote his power and will. Only the Sassans stand in the way."

"And there's a missing factor in interstellar politics that hasn't been heard from," Sinklar observed, steepling his fingers.

"That is?" Gretta sank onto the corner of the desk, eyes soft as she watched him. Her long brown hair framed her face.

"The Companions." Sinklar tapped the map with his stylus. "How many wars has Rega fought without Staffa kar

Therma's people doing the majority of the work?" He raised an eyebrow. "For the past forty years, not one. Where do you think that asinine regulation of command personnel staying hidden in the rear came from? The Divisional staff has been appointed by political merit. In the last ten or fifteen planetary conquests, the Companions waged the war—not the Regans. We were just mop-up and defensive troops."

"And now Sassa has consolidated its empire." MacRuder lifted a thumb to his mouth and chewed the nail. "If the Star Butcher goes Sassan, where are we? Rega, I mean?"

Sinklar lifted his arms in an eloquent shrug. "I don't know. No one in the Regan Ministry of Defense knows anything about tactics or combat. The game plan was always supplied by the Star Butcher; his people oversaw the strategy and tactics while the political hacks took their commissions and were decorated for gallantry and efficiency in the Imperial Hall after the war."

"Pus-Rotted Gods," Gretta whispered, stunned. "We're vulnerable as sheep!"

"Bad analogy. Think of us—Rega, that is—in actual terms. We have a lot of combat veterans. They just aren't here. Significant, don't you think? Only two green divisions on this planet? Why not the hard-core veterans from Maika and Riparious and Etaria and Ashtan? No, this is either a diversion or bait, one of the two. Why hasn't the Star Butcher showed up to cow Targa? Is he working for Sassa or . . . maybe this war isn't hot enough to stir his interest? Or, could it be we're an example—misleading at that—to lull someone's perception of Regan power? Disinformation can be a potent weapon."

Sinklar's brows lowered, the smile twisting his grim lips. "So, if the war could be heated up—say a Division was lost—the Targans would organize. Individuals whose loyalties are wavering would see a chance and commit themselves to the Rebellion. Staffa would find a reason to take a contract. Thus, he would already be in Regan contract if a confrontation with the Sassans could be provoked. Or the Sassans might jump before they were ready."

"But what if the Companions are already contracted to the Sassans?" Mac asked pointedly.

Sinklar shifted in his seat. "Then this war would have

already been settled. Either Tybalt would have agreed to a political settlement to stabilize treacherous waters, or the veterans would have been here in such a massed force as to crush the potential for rebellion." He squinted at the thought. "Rega could destroy the food chain here within three days by using the combined power of the fleet. No food—no revolution. Very simple. Works all the time."

"But there's only a token force orbiting," Gretta reminded.

"And if Staffa was in contract to the Sassans," Sinklar responded, "there would be military panic, frantic training, and no promotion of an unknown Sergeant Third to Divisional First."

Mac puffed a deep breath. "And that brings us back to this pus hole. Sink, I wasn't scared by the Targans. All they want to do is drive us away. Imperial politics? What the hell do we do about that?" He sighed and closed his eyes. "Rotted Gods! How do we fight the Minister of Defense, hell, *even the Emperor, for all we know!*" Mac paced, face working anxiously as his fists clenched and unclenched.

"First, Mac," Sinklar's gentle voice soothed, "relax. That's an order. The way to win is to think." He laced his fingers together and winked at Gretta. "The best way to defeat whoever is behind this is to derail their plans for the destruction of the First Targan Assault Division."

"What are you thinking?" Gretta took his hand.

"Oh, for starters let's get the hell out of here. That's first priority. Second is to take Vespa, and third, of course, is to win the war." *And then, we deal with whoever set us up to die!*

"My Section doesn't know how to fly in battle gear without an aircar or LC," MacRuder told him dryly, arms crossed.

"Neither do the others," Sinklar stared at the map. "Fifteen klicks north of here is the Decker Lucky Mack Mine." He lifted his gaze, amused. "Prophetic?"

MacRuder frowned. "How does having a mine fifteen klicks north of us keep the First Targan Division alive?"

"We have three company cars left for staff purposes, right?"

"Yeah." Mac nodded suspiciously.

"And we inventoried another five trucks here at the co-op for hauling grain." Sinklar dropped his chin on his chest. "Can you take the Second Section up to the mine tonight? Load them in the cars and trucks and go? Might have to fight your way through, but get up there!"

"And bring back rocks?" Mac wondered. "Planning on smelting ore and building LCs from scratch?"

Sinklar looked up mildly. "Why take that much time? Just get me every belly-dump you can commandeer out of there. I figure those huge crawlers they use ought to be able to carry three hundred men apiece. After that, all we need to do is commandeer every aircar and truck we find along the way to use for foraging and fuel acquisition."

"Sink, you'll be the salvation of this pus-rotted command yet!" Mac let out a whoop as he ran for his Section.

Sinklar had lost himself in reflection when Gretta's warm hand caressed his neck. "For a moment, Sink, I was really scared."

"For a moment? Do you have any idea of the odds against us?"

"We'd do better trying to breathe vacuum, wouldn't we?"

He filled his lungs and blew air out. "I suppose so. But we won't be cut up by the Targans while we starve here." He stood. "Come on, let's go see the troops."

It had become a nightly ritual. They walked past the silent buildings guarded by the various Sections. At the perimeter, a low challenge was growled out of the night. "Advance and identify yourself!"

Sinklar and Gretta, arms locked, strolled up as the guard flashed a light into their faces. "Oh, excuse me, sir, ma'am."

"Never let the ID of a person fool you," Sinklar smiled. "You're not standing here alone, are you?"

"No, sir," the guard said soberly. "Fips and Angelina have you covered with blasters right now. They're over there in the bushes like you taught us on drill, sir."

Sinklar studied the vegetation through his IR and picked up the two flankers. He nodded and patted the soldier on the shoulder. "Excellent work. My congratulations to you and your Section. Tell Hauws I said you're to be commended for vigilance and foresight. We'll do fine with troops of your caliber."

The man straightened, his chest puffing with pride. "Thank you, sir. We'll never let you down, sir!"

"They'd do anything for you, Sink," Gretta told him as they walked away. "I never would have believed it. You've worked a miracle with the First."

"Just sense . . . and the only option I've got." He shrugged. "Considering the odds against us, we've only got one asset."

"And that is?"

"We have one assault Division." He hugged her close. "Two thousand men and women, armed, and, hopefully, after we get to Vespa and settle the affairs on Targa we'll be as tough and disciplined as the blood-soaked Companions themselves."

"You tried to tell me all this when we were training outside Kaspa. I thought at the time it was just to build morale." She clasped his fingers in hers. "Now the search and destroy teams make sense. I love you, Sinklar Fist."

"And you thought I was crazy when we risked Fourth Section to recover those five privates cut off on the ridge that time the Targans hit us during training," he reminded lightly.

"Getting those people back won you the entire Fourth Section. They'd walk through fire for you now." She studied him through the IR visor, eyes alive with speculation. "What made you think of that?"

He stopped to smell the fresh air and enjoy the woman who leaned against him. "It's symptomatic of the age, I guess. Tybalt has built a throwaway army. Ever since the beginning of the Imperial period, one hundred and fifty years ago, armies have been trained to strike a planet, stun it into paralysis, and wreck the ability of the people to resist. Call it shock war. The enemy was impersonal and a soldier's only duty was to cower in fear until his LC grounded, jump out with his rifle, and blast anything native that moved. If he lived, he went home and relaxed until the next time."

"But that only works when you conquer worlds," Gretta said. "The Star Butcher does the same, doesn't he? Stuns planets, that is."

"Not quite. His responsibilities include finding defensive weaknesses and he exploits his reputation. The other differ-

ence is that his people stay with him. He has their loyalty.
The Companions function within a strict code of honor and
duty to each other." Sinklar kissed her and added, "And
they have never been defeated."

"The First has."

"And I intend to see that it never happens again," Sinklar
said as they continued walking down along the creek bottom. Patches of deciduous trees mixed with grassy
meadows.

"Who goes there? Advance and be recognized." A man
rose from a ditch, waiting, blaster ready as they walked up.

"Were I an enemy who got this close, you'd be dead."
Sinklar's voice sounded like cracked ice after he'd passed
recognition. The soldier's shoulders dropped meekly. "Anyone within five feet of you, trained properly, could kill you
with their bare hands."

"But I . . . I didn't think—"

"No, you didn't," Sinklar told him hotly. "By the cor-
rupted Gods, man! How can I keep you alive if you act like
a fool? I want to see you healthy and in one piece after
this. Tafft knows better. You alone out here?"

"N–no, sir. Leeka's over there." He waved an arm at the
darkness.

Sinklar scanned the darkness. "Where?"

"Uh, over the hill, sir."

"And if I had just killed you," Sinklar reminded, "this
whole quarter would be wide open, wouldn't it? How many
in your Section and the other Sections would die from your
failure at this position?"

"Sergeant First Tafft told me not to worry. That I wasn't
trained to think, just to shoot, sir." The soldier shifted nervously. "Corporal Mayz thought five perimeter guards was
too few for the terrain. I agreed, but the sergeant told us
to—"

"Corporal Mayz has sense," Sinklar mumbled stalking off
into the darkness. "This is the final straw."

They found Mayz and her Group dug in on a hilltop.
"Where's Sergeant First Tafft?"

"Down there, sir. In the flat at the bottom of the hill."
Mayz jumped to her feet, saluting.

"And why are you up here while the other Groups are
down there?" Sinklar asked, studying the corporal.

The woman swallowed, eyes darting to Gretta, expression tense through the IR visor. "Because of your lecture on the uses of terrain, sir. If the guard should fail, we might be able to hold this high spot until the others could recover."

"I think I understand, Corporal. You will accompany me." Anger smoldering, Sinklar walked through a ring of snoring soldiers and kicked Sergeant First Tafft awake.

"Who the Rotted. . . . Mister, you're in a pus-puke pool of. . . ." Tafft fumbled for his helmet and slipped it on. Through the IR he met Sinklar's gaze as he glared down. "Oh, sorry, sir."

"Damn it, man, you've got isolated guards out there! The whole Targan resistance could infiltrate that perimeter and you'd be dead before you found your rotted helmet!" He propped his fists on his hips. "Mayz!"

"Sir!" The corporal snapped a salute.

"You will take command of Seventh Section immediately and attend to fixing the perimeter of this camp so our people don't end up slaughtered like maggot meat! Tafft, you will assume the rank of Corporal Third pending how much you can learn in the meantime."

The Seventh sat up, halfway out of their bedding, stunned, as Sinklar turned to address them. "I've told you people time after time. My first concern is to inflict the greatest amount of damage to the Targan resistance. My second concern is that one of these days I want to see each one of you step onto a transport home to your worlds and families. Neither I, nor the Empire, profits from your dead bodies. I punish for misconduct. You know that, it's in the manual. What you don't know is that I consider stupidity a killing offense. Tafft, you're lucky. I should have shot you. Prove to me—and these people—that you're worth our respect. And if anyone can run this Section better than Mayz, I'll promote him."

Gretta walked with him until he cleared the perimeter. Behind him, Mayz could be heard bellowing orders.

"Should have cleaned that outfit up a week ago," Sinklar mumbled under his breath.

"Told you so," she jabbed.

"Tafft looked like he was learning during training. Now I wonder if you weren't right. Maybe he was just playing the game."

"It's in his nature. Mayz will be after you within a week to promote someone else to corporal."

"Then she's got it." He took a deep breath. Curse it, did everything have to happen at once? "Come on, let's get back to the shelter and get some sleep. I've got a feeling it's going to be a long time before we get another chance to rest."

"Sink?" The call came urgently through the walls of the shelter. Sinklar blinked and sat up, seeing Gretta's eyes already open as she rolled off the sleeping pad, reaching for her assault rifle.

"Yeah, Kap?" He grabbed his helmet and clamped it on his head, enjoying Greta's body as displayed in her battle armor. So terrible that they had to sleep in armor these days. It made a mockery of love-making.

Sinklar raised the flap and slipped out to see Kap pointing northward where a long plume of yellow-gray dust rose toward the sky. He couldn't see the source because the tree-covered ridges blocked it.

"From the mine," Sinklar guessed. "Any trouble around here last night?"

"Ayms' A Group caught a bunch of locals arming themselves in a barn. The corporal took your orders to heart and scared them pissless. Put a couple up against a wall and threatened to execute them. After he and the boys played debate about whether they were more use to the Empire alive or dead, he sent them home looking spit-slobbering scared and thankful for the clemency of Sinklar Fist."

Sink noted two Groups leaving at a trot to cover the road approaches. "They know who's supposed to be in that convoy?"

"Yeah. And you've got them nervous enough that they're unwilling to take any chances on it either."

Sinklar nodded to his red-faced sergeant and grinned. "By God, might be hope for this outfit after all."

Twenty minutes later, huge ten-meter-high machines moved into sight. Bright yellow, marked with the Decker Mining Company logo, each sported a rifle team on its big roof.

As the First Division came to look, MacRuder climbed

nimbly down from the cab. A second man in civilian dress followed him.

"Mission accomplished, Sink!" MacRuder grinned, slapping the huge graphite-fiber wheel. "Got twelve of these babies!"

Smaller trucks and aircars moved in from the perimeter to settle in the co-op's dusty lot.

"Who's he?" Sinklar asked, turning to the miner, a man who swallowed rapidly and looked scared.

"Driver," Mac told him. "These things take a little know-how. I'm not sure we're capable of just hopping in and going."

Sinklar looked at the man and offered his hand. "My pleasure. I'm Sinklar Fist, First Targan Assault Division."

"Nymes, sir. My pleasure, too," the man said in a blur. He swallowed again, running a tongue over dry lips. "You gonna kill us now?"

Sinklar tightened his facial muscles. "Mac? What did you tell this man?"

"Uh, that he was commandeered." MacRuder crossed his arms, his face going bland.

"Nymes." Sink lifted an eyebrow. "What was Decker paying you to drive this thing?"

The man looked puzzled. "Why, uh, ten ICs a day."

"The Emperor offers you twenty—with additional over-time and bonus for hazardous duty."

"Uh, double you say? And a bonus? And overtime?"

"Mac?" Sink lifted an eyebrow. "We being fair?"

"Sure thing. Sounds reasonable to me."

"But I thought you guys. . . ." The miner pursed his lips and frowned. "The stories we heard were that people were being killed all over."

"Rebel propaganda. Look, talk it over with the rest. If you don't like it, just stay long enough to teach us how to use the machines and we'll fly you home and pay you for your time."

Most of the drivers stayed. In fact, they were still driving when the First Targan Assault Division rolled into the streets of Vespa three days later.

The fighting started that night and the First Targan Assault Division won its first pitched battle of the war three days later.

* * *

Ily Takka took the diplomatic pouch from the courier and smiled her thanks. Kapstan, the Internal Security Director on Etaria had a nice office that filled half of the upper floor of the security building. A private bath—an Etarian luxury—was accessed through an ornate door on the left. The woodwork trim around the plaster walls had been intricately carved and stained in a deep red. Kapstan's desk was a huge thing with comm terminals, communications equipment, and various devices.

Ily watched the special courier walk across the plush rugs of the office and close the hardwood door behind him. She opened the seal on the pouch and inspected the chem-coded message recorder. She nodded approval and lifted the small cartridge out. Had any other person touched the fragile recording, his or her body chemistry would have set off a reaction that would have destroyed the message.

Ily leaned forward over the Internal Security Director's desk. The office around her looked glassy through the privacy screen she initiated. She inserted the cartridge and pressed the button. Tybalt the Imperial Seventh appeared on the monitor. His black skin gleamed in the light.

"Dearest Ily," Tybalt began. "I must say, your prolonged absence is about to drive me insane. How right you were. There is *no one* to talk to." He sighed. "And how I miss you in my bed." He waved it away. "Anyway. On to business. We have taken action on all of your suggestions regarding the Targan affair. I think we have a perfect man to make a debacle of it.

"In the first place, the Targans played right into our hands by assassinating Atkin . . . and Kapitol!" His eyes gleamed. "Mykroft and the Minister of Defense both roared when I told them to appoint a man from the ranks. The military is raising five kinds of Rotted stink, as you can well guess.

"The fellow selected—raised from a Sergeant Third, of all things—is one Sinklar Fist. He had some sort of dazzling victory in the mountains and he's become very popular with the First Targan Assault Division. He's been spending most of his time going through the paperwork, of course, but he's received his orders from the Minister of Defense to take the field against the Rebels.''

Tybalt propped his chin on his knee and frowned. "Now here is the funny part about Fist. He's taking to the field *with* his troops. Defense threw a fit. As you know, it is totally against the regulations that a First enter the field." Tybalt shook his head. "Anyway, since the man is sacrificial, his actions don't matter. I explained the matter to Defense and he quieted immediately, seeing the final result will be a reinforcing of military protocol and tradition.

"Needless to say, that aspect of the war will proceed quite nicely. We've offered young Fist—imagine if you will, his troops call him 'the First Fist. . . .' Where was I? Oh, yes. We've offered him our full support, even to indulging him in the time to 'train' his troops! What does the young man think they teach in academy and basic? But I diverge from the point of the message. He will fail within the next five weeks as we have given him the impossible mission of capturing the Rebel stronghold of Vespa—and doing it overland to boot. They'll chop him to pieces, his supply lines will be cut, and he'll lead the First Division to destruction. Perfect!"

Tybalt smiled at the images conjured. He looked up. "Oh, by the way. Sassan spies have been all over. They're looking frantically for Staffa. Have you found him yet? Please, do get him under wraps and get back here. This place is dreadfully boring without you."

The holo died.

Ily leaned forward and tapped a button on the Director's desk. "Kapstan! Get your pus-rotted body in here!"

The Director trotted through the door, a cadaverous figure in a formfitting black robe. His thin, humorless face had already turned pale from dread. "Good news from the Emperor, I hope?"

She slitted her eyes and studied him as if gazing at some curious insect. The Director stiffened and clamped his jaws to keep them from quivering.

"No, Kapstan. It wasn't the recall you hoped I'd get." She saw him wilt at her accusation and continued. "It's been a putrid week that I've been here! Are your people so incompetent that they can't locate a single man?" She slapped the table and jumped to her feet.

"But the number of possibilities!" He spread his hands, palms up imploringly. "Just consider the number of interviews—"

"I'm finished with your vile excuses!" she hissed. "If you had your channels set up, if you had your agents working efficiently, you'd have a file on every person landing on this sun-scorched and sand-blasted rock! Skyla Lyma got here, talked to the CV pilot, stepped on the shuttle and, by the Pustulant Gods, *she disappeared!*" Ily ground her teeth, jaw muscles standing from her pale flesh. "What must I think about an Internal Security Director who can't follow a subject planetside *when he knows which pus-dripping shuttle the subject is on*?"

She let her eyes do the rest. Kapstan's mouth worked in misery as the silence lingered. He looked down at his boots to avoid her gaze and finally defended, "The personnel responsible have been disciplined for their lack—"

"Discipline ends with the final responsible party! That's you, *Director!*"

He stiffened and paled.

Despite Ily's frustrated rage, she enjoyed his discomfort. How many strong men had cowered before Director Kapstan's hard glare. How many had he broken and left as human wreckage? And in a few words, she had him ready to foul his neatly tailored britches.

In the long silence, Associate Director Tyklat tapped at the door. "Your pardon, Director?" he called uncertainly, his nervousness evident from the expression on his long black face. "I think I found the subject."

Ily turned to look, an eyebrow raised. "Where?"

Tyklat entered and deposited a printout on the desk. "It came to me last night . . . er, this morning actually. After I'd exhausted everything else, I had the comm system search the court dockets."

"I did that, already," Kapstan fumed. "If there'd been any listing of Staffa kar Therma, it—"

"Shut up!" Ily ordered, her dark gaze probing Tyklat. Her voice dropped to an encouraging, "Tell me." She leaned forward, seeing the sudden excitement in his eyes. *Good man this, he takes his job seriously.*

"Well, I, uh, I mean the Director had already searched the dockets. I just widened the search, letting it run for any mention of the Star Butcher, Staffa, Companions, or Itreata."

"And you found . . ." she prompted, flipping her long black hair over her shoulder. Kapstan began shifting from foot to foot.

"I found an alleged madman who claimed to be Staffa kar Therma," Tyklat said, his brow creasing. "He was accused of being robbed and, according to his testimony, he killed two of the assailants. The judge thought he was raving and sentenced him to the Warden for public duty."

"Rotted Gods! Staffa . . . in the collar?" She chuckled wryly. "Have him brought to. . . . No." She clapped her hands, thinking, running her tongue over her lips. "There's more to be gained if I go to him. Take me to him. I trust he's in the city someplace?"

"He's—"

"Take you to him? By all means, Minister," Kapstan smiled, cutting off Tyklat and taking her arm. "I told you I'd have this handled quickly and competently."

She froze, eyes gleaming as she looked into his suddenly shocked face. "Take your hand off my arm."

"My apology, Minister. I didn't think—"

"No, you didn't."

"Excuse me," Tyklat said, bowing his head to leave.

"Stay!" Ily ordered and the young man stopped, gaze flicking warily between her and the Director. "Officer Tyklat. You have demonstrated efficiency and dedication. I have a feeling you conducted most of this search. Correct?"

He met her eyes and she could see the truth in his guarded expression. Very good, he wouldn't rat on a superior—even one as worthless as Kapstan.

"By my authority, Tyklat, I place you in charge of Etarian Internal Security. Your duties start as of this moment."

Kapstan's mouth dropped. "But I have a commission from the Emperor himself! You can't . . ." his breath sucked in as he looked down.

Ily's dart pistol hiccuped twice. Kapstan swallowed, terrified eyes going wide. His body slammed face first onto the thick rug. Ily dropped her tiny weapon into its belt holster and turned to Tyklat. "I believe you'll have time to clean your office later. Right now, take me to Staffa kar Therma."

"Yes, Minister Takka." He bowed cautiously. Well, good. That placed another of *her* men in the Empire.

The car met her at the main entrance. She extended her arm and was pleased to see he didn't hesitate to take it.

"Tyklat, things are about to change drastically in the Empire. Are you aware of that?"

He appraised her coolly. "I take it you mean in addition to the coming war with the Sassan Empire?"

"I do." She studied him carefully as she pulled her long hair back over one shoulder. "There may be totally unexpected political upheavals. Tell me, where do you put your loyalty?"

He nodded, smooth black skin glistening in the brilliant sunlight. "I think I understand, Minister. You have elevated me to this position; I am duly grateful."

"Discreetly done, Tyklat." She patted his arm.

"I didn't get to be Kapstan's second through idiocy, Minister." He kept his features straight, but she could see his hidden smile of triumph.

"Call me Ily. Those whom I trust do. You will need to open two channels, one official—don't worry, Tybalt will approve your promotion—and one private. The second will be 'eyes only,' yours and mine. There may be irregular requests. Be prepared."

"I understand. I shall not disappoint you." His mouth twitched with an unspoken question.

She laughed, reading his interest. "You're my kind of man, Tyklat. I think you and I will do admirably together, and, yes, I do reward my people very, very well."

The car settled at the entrance to the Warden's pens. A guard met them halfway, shooing away some brown-robed Etarian tart he'd been talking to. The woman walked off several steps and leaned against the wall, veiled face hidden. Lover, no doubt.

"Staffa who?" the guard asked, eyes straying back to the woman he'd been talking to.

Tyklat supplied: "Registration number seven six four nine two zero. I called and they said they'd have the slave ready to be picked up."

The guard tapped a code on his wrist. "Desert duty. He's

laying pipe on the new water line. Supposedly, it's an equipment breakdown." The guard shrugged. "Actually, the contractor wants too much money to string pipe. We can do it cheaper, if slower, with slaves. Besides, there's a surplus of bodies right now. Ever since the Maikan conquest we've been overcrowded."

Ily could feel the Etarian woman's gaze on her as, face grim, Tyklat steered her back to the vehicle.

Ily glanced back at the veiled woman and then forced her from her mind as she considered the guard's words. "A good way to rid yourself of surplus? The Lord Commander does not fit my definition of surplus."

The aircar rose easily as Ily leaned back in the seat. She sighed. "Very well, assuming we have found Staffa, where could his Wing Commander be?"

Tyklat rubbed a finger along his straight nose. His eyes, dark as her own, betrayed a slight mystification. "I'm not certain at this stage. To be honest, the Lord Commander was my first concern. The fact remains that he eluded us because we were looking in the wrong place for the wrong reasons." His thoughtful features wrinkled into a frown. "Maybe we've done the same with the Wing Commander—only based on different assumptions."

Ily grimaced as they rose over the squat city. What an ugly place Etarus had turned out to be for all the glittering reputation of its whore temple. Flat-roofed brown buildings hugged narrow streets. A tourist town, it lived off the revenue brought from the men flocking to the Temple and the Priestesses. At the same time, believers came to receive instruction in prayers, devotions, and philosophy. That trade supported lodgings while small cottage industries made souvenirs. A spice trade came out of the desert as did minerals and precious gems.

"We just don't know enough about Skyla Lyma," Ily decided. Another thought crossed her mind. "However, assuming we have found Staffa, I don't want him to know his Wing Commander is here. We have more leverage if he doesn't."

"I understand."

"Good." Ily paused, glancing at Tyklat. "You know, she is a very beautiful woman."

"I've seen the official holos you provided." Tyklat laced his fingers together.

"Believe me, they don't do her justice." Ily realized the arid air had begun affecting her skin. Her mouth felt sucked dry. "Anything to drink in here?"

He handed her a flask that clipped to the side of the seat.

Refreshed, Ily pursued that thought. "When you find her, remember that she's a warrior of some considerable talent. She didn't get to be Wing Commander by wiggling her tail. She's dangerous and probably quite capable of whipping your best in hand-to-hand combat."

Tyklat grinned. "We'll use stun rods and put a collar on her immediately."

"And after that, Tyklat, keep her on ice. I want no word of her being under our control to leak out. I think you can appreciate the ramifications." She sat back, enjoying the thought. How far could she go with Staffa all to herself? "Indeed, if it proves that we don't need the inestimable Wing Commander, you may keep her for yourself. As I say, she is very beautiful—and I do reward my people."

His smile grew. "With a collar on, she will be tame as a kitten."

Ily allowed herself a short laugh. By the Rotted Gods, this had gone well after all. She was congratulating herself, feeling an uplifting surge of optimism as they circled over a thin line seemingly drawn in the white desert sands. As they dropped, the line turned into a long ditch, trenching machines springing into visibility as they closed.

The dust that rose in a maelstrom about the car surprised her. She could see Tyklat's measuring eyes on her. "Your shoes, Ily. You might want to take them off. This is what we call the True Sand, the deep desert. Your long thin heels will sink in and you will look foolish. Of course, your bare feet will be most uncomfortable. The temperature of the sand often gets as high as three hundred and fifty degrees Kelvin." He spread his hands. "Or I could attend to it."

She saw his curiosity. Without losing eye contact, she slipped her footgear off. "After you, Director."

He hadn't lied. Her skin felt like it was curling and blistering off her very bones. She kept her face straight and plodded after him, each burning step a trial. Despite herself, she had to squint in the blinding glare. Heat beat at her in a constant suffocating mass. Rotted Gods! They carried pipe in this? Her skin had gone completely dry and her lips had chapped. The hot wind that bled her of moisture teased and tugged at her long hair.

They made it to a tent awning where three men waited to greet Tyklat. Ily found herself shaking an officer's hand. She caught his name: Anglo.

"We have come for a slave," Ily told the officer coldly, seeing the glint in his eyes as he appraised her. *Rotted Gods! Does he have no conception of who I am? Or has he been screwing the slaves until a woman is no more than meat?* Her anger stirred.

"We're a little short of those today, Minister." Anglo grinned idiotically in his attempt to be suave. "If I may be of any other assistance—"

"Get the slave called Staffa!" Tyklat ordered, his face hard.

"We have no Staffa here."

Tyklat rapped out the registration number.

"Oh," Anglo's face began to smirk. "Him. I'm afraid you're a little too late." He pointed down the pipeline to the side of a slumped dune. Ily could see the pipe running into the mass of loose shifted sand.

"Yeah," Anglo said with a sigh. "Ole Tuff, he was at the head of the line. We've been digging for a half hour now. It'll be a day before we get all that cleaned out."

Staffa? Buried alive? Ily's mind raced. Staffa dead would be better than Staffa loose. She *had* to know if the mysterious Tuff was the Lord Commander.

"You will remove that sand now," Ily told Anglo in a voice like slow poison. "You will remove it if you have to stop the commerce of this planet to do so."

Anglo gaped. "Look, Minister, you don't—"

"I do! Tyklat, get the equipment here now! Officer Anglo, you get down there and dig! *With your bare hands if necessary!"*

Ily's eyes went to the mountain of sand. Threats or not, what chance was there? A bitter acid taste formed in her mouth—a taste of defeat.

CHAPTER XVIII

Blackness suffocated Staffa; it bled from the very air into his soul. The silence thundered, disturbed only by the pounding of his heart. Staffa tried to move only to find his legs trapped, pinned by the pressing weight. Kaylla's muscular body shivered in his arms. A painful awareness of her rushed through him; he smelled her hot skin next to his nose. Hugging her tightly, he reveled in the reassurance that he wasn't alone—not deserted in his sin and guilt.

"Can you move your legs?" he asked, hoping his voice wouldn't break.

Her muscles slid under smooth skin—a feeling of living flesh he cherished.

"No." Then, "We're buried, aren't we?"

"Yes."

"Will they get us out alive?"

"Maybe," Staffa mumbled. "Depends on how long it takes to dig us out . . . and how long the air lasts."

"I think I can push enough sand past to free my legs. Then we can dig you out."

They didn't speak as they worked to free Kaylla. Then together they scooped sand back to free his waist and thighs. He pulled himself forward and crawled to the center of the pipe.

"At least it's cool." After a pause Kaylla added hesitantly, "Hold my hand."

He felt around until he found her fingers.

"How long would you estimate, Tuff?"

"Four hours. Maybe six at the most for the size of the pipe and our respiration rate. That's about right for the cubic footage."

"We were in the middle of the dune." Her fingers tightened on his. "We're only slaves. The trenchers are miles away. They won't have this moved until sometime tomorrow."

He chuckled hollowly, body sagging, glad for the rest if nothing else. "Then according to what Koree was telling me, we're spared the cowardice of death."

He could hear her swallow. "I remember his lectures in the university on Maika. He was one of my professors when I was young. I always admired him. It broke my heart to find him here."

"We could save a little oxygen if we didn't talk." It began to cool off rapidly, the heat in the pipe radiating into the sand around them.

She moved over in that eternal primate desire to touch. "I don't want to die in silence."

He tilted his head up to stare into the stygian darkness and braced his head on the back of the pipe. "I guess I've always been alone. Except for once. I had a woman. A slave I freed."

"What happened to her, Tuff?" She snuggled closer, enfolding his arm in hers.

"Stolen away from me along with my son." His voice soured.

"She's Skyla?"

"No. Skyla was my . . . my friend, but. . . ."

"But what?" At his silence she added, "I think, considering the circumstances, you can tell me. We aren't getting out of this one alive."

"But I never knew how much I'd come to love her." He started to curse the wistful tone in his voice and stopped. In the name of the Pus Rotted Gods, what difference did it make? "I never told her. Never even allowed myself to . . . to admit it. Since I've been here, it's all come clear."

"What's she like?" Kaylla shifted, laying her head on his shoulder.

"Tall, her hair is pale blonde." He smiled in the darkness, enjoying a deep-seated warmth. "Her eyes are an incredible blue. She's the most beautiful woman in all Free Space. There's a hard humor in her manner—a cynicism I never understood until recently. She's intelligent, smarter than I am, it seems. And when she jokes, a devilish light fills those magnificent eyes."

He shook his head. "Ah, Kaylla, the things I should have done for her."

He put his arm around her shoulders, pulling her close, feeling her body warm and reassuring against his.

"Tuff, you saved my life again—or tried to. Why?"

"Justice," he whispered, thinking of Koree. "A small slice of justice—and perhaps retribution. Atonement would be a better world."

"Atonement for what?"

"I am not. . . ." He bit off his confession. *No, not here. Not in the last hours of life. She deserves a little peace.* Instead he said, "During my life as a soldier, I was responsible for some vile things—things I have only barely begun to understand. Atonement is for those who have sinned." He stared emptily into the darkness. "Koree was right. So many have so much to pay for. I more than any other. You wondered about my nightmares? So much blood stains my hands . . . my conscience, I . . . I was a living monster, God's tool of injustice." *And the Praetor's!*

He shut his eyes, images of the past rising from the depths of his mind, people hurting, scared, dying. Their terror seeped in with the blackness. Like them, Staffa saw himself being bonded by the collar and herded into a transport to be sold here or there—never to see a wife or son again. The same pain he now lived.

She shrugged, moving against his shoulder. "No person can take the blame for all the misery and suffering. That's God's realm. Blame it on the times in which we live. Science has extended our lives. Existence is no longer short and sweet. Rulers become bored through time and seek something new—too often they find amusement in terror. My husband and I, we fought that on Maika. We enjoyed a shining brief instant of knowledge and art and freedom before the Star Butcher and the Emperor drowned it in blood."

Staffa squeezed his eyes shut and grimaced, thankful for the cloaking blackness.

"I can die proud at least," she told him. "I never sold myself. When they took me, they did it after beating me senseless. When I could, I fought back and—on the whole— it was a good fight. I made life a little easier for some, like Peebal . . . and you."

"Stop it!" Staffa cried, eyes shut tight, guilt and shame spreading through him in a flood he couldn't control. "Keep me out of this." He thrust her away and buried his head in his hands. "Don't shame me anymore, Kaylla!"

Her hand—callused and rough—felt warm on his shoulder. "Shhhh!" she whispered.

He sensed it as she shook her head. "Men. . . . Rotted Gods, what am I saying? I mean people, all people, condemn themselves for faults when they're about to die." She resettled, crossing her legs, grabbing up his hand. "Remember the Temple sewer? I was dead. A few minutes left before I would have fainted. You pulled that girl's body free and spared me. You have a good side too, Tuff. No matter what you've done."

Silence.

"Why did you really kill Brots?"

"Because of what he did to you. Because I would free you from this hell and restore you to power on Maika."

She ran her hand up and down his arm, squeezing in appreciation. "Thank you, Tuff. Tell me, does that mean you're in love with me?"

He knitted his ragged emotions together. "Yes, I have come to love you. I would make you happy if I had to come with a fleet and blast this world apart to do so."

"And your Skyla?"

"My Skyla, I would . . . make my wife." *Why did I never know before?* "You, I would make my friend. Ask you to forgive . . . though it be impossible in the end."

She squeezed his arm again and leaned forward to kiss him lightly on the lips. "Thanks, Tuff. I guess I don't need to point out that your use of subjunctive is hardly necessary. From here, it looks like the end is pretty close, hence there is no impossibility about it. You're my friend forever. Forgive? What for? You've always been a man of honor and courage as long as I've known you."

Honor? Courage? If you only knew.

He couldn't push her away when she leaned against him. Exhausted and numb, he hunched in the dark and stared into infinity.

After several minutes she asked, "What happened that they made you a slave, Tuff?"

"I was robbed on the street and killed two 'citizens' in the process." Was it so long ago?

"You're kidding? Where?"

"Here."

She turned and he could feel her stare in the blackness. "Came to turn the whores in the Temple?"

He remembered the brag he'd made to the holo recorder in his quarters in the far off Itreatic Asteroids. Honesty? He owed her that. It soothed his soul. "I probably would have." An image formed of the pale girl he'd pulled from the sewer. "But mostly, I came to learn, to understand more about life—and to catch a vessel to Rega and then make my way to Targa to look for my son among the Seddi Priests."

"A scholar in search of trust and a son? And you found slavery. Come up with any answers yet, Tuff?"

"Some. Enough to leave me more confused than ever. Every time I think I find a truth, something comes along to turn that foundation to sand. As long as I was arrogant and perfect, I could pick and choose. Now, I can't define right . . . or justice . . . or anything." He barked an angry laugh. "And I have less idea of who I am—or what I am—than when I started. At least, back then, I had a myth to cling to, a facade I could accept as being myself."

"And now?"

"I'm a nameless slave—a convicted madman with a collar—dying in a buried pipe in the middle of the Etarian desert."

"Well, you won't die alone."

"No," he grinned aimlessly into the dark. "No, if I've done nothing else, I won't die alone."

They sat silent, lost in their thoughts. Staffa, bone weary, drifted off to sleep and the dream. . . .

They came, easing out of the blackness. Mangled specters, they floated in gruesome death as they twisted in blood-crystallized vapor. Some screamed until their voices matched his memories. Some stood and stared, among them children with fear-glazed eyes. They awaited their deaths at his hands, lips pinched in pale faces. Women cursed him as they died, raped, bleeding, abused. Fists clenched as damnation lanced from their bloody gazes. Through it all, Chrysla watched him with hollow yellow eyes.

He writhed and started awake to pant in the cool blackness. The air had grown bitter and stale in their cramped pipe tomb.

A slight vibration shivered up through his buttocks and back. He blinked, feeling how much his ribs expanded with each breath. Kaylla's chest moved in long quick breaths next to his. A soft rasping could be felt through the sand.

"Kaylla," he whispered, fearful the sound might go away. "Someone's digging."

"Air's going, isn't it?"

He nodded. In silence they waited. His lungs increased their pace, filling fuller and fuller, always gasping more.

He didn't remember his consciousness fading out as the ghouls sifted through his thoughts. Planets died, men cried before him as blaster fire tore their bodies into fountains of gore. He watched a mother try to shield her daughter, a golden-haired girl, from a pulse rifle, watched them both disappear into pink mist.

The restless dead reached for him, tracing icy fingers over his shivering skin. Ghost breath blew coolly over his cringing soul as they chuckled their glee. This time, he wouldn't escape from their clutches. This time, their ice fingers gripped him tightly.

He screamed, feeling them pulling . . . pulling . . . down . . . ever down. . . .

* * *

Butla groaned as the comm alarm brought him awake. What the hell time was it, anyway? He rolled over and pressed the button to answer the call. He blinked and rubbed a thick hand over his flat features and bull jaw as the screen beside his bed glowed to life in the darkness of his room. He started as Arta's features filled the comm monitor.

"Arta? Thank the Blessed Gods. I thought you were gone." He stifled a yawn as his heart quickened. "Where are you?"

"I watched them murder the Rebels." She cocked her head. "They must be punished."

He worked his tongue over his lips and stared, eyes narrowed. "We're working on that. Look, why don't you come home. I'll—"

She shook her head slowly, eyes wary. "I know what the Seddi did to me. I'll never place myself within their grip again. As to Bruen, I'll find him again . . . someday."

"Arta, don't—"

"I know you must make a strike soon. I am here. I'll be in touch. I have too many skills you need. I must kill to live, Butla. You know that. Tell me what you need me to do. I'm good, Butla Ret, you taught me well."

"Arta, let's talk this—"

"I love you, Butla." She continued. "You were the only one who was good to me. I will always love you—only I can't have you, you know. I can't even see you again."

"Yeah," he grunted, heart dropping.

"Bruen condemned me to kill the ones I love," she whispered as the screen went dead.

Butla Ret rolled back onto his sleeping platform, haunted eyes searching the dark ceiling overhead.

*　*　*

"Got two in the pipe!" The voice brought Staffa to drowsy awareness. His head ached terribly.

He blinked at the glare and turned to see a face peering from the end of the pipe. The light burned painfully into his squinting eyes.

Something grabbed the pipe. It rocked as mechanical whining sounded loud and grating. Gasping, he heard the sand being pulled away. Kaylla jerked awake with a cry.

"Who's in there?" Anglo asked, face sweaty. A handheld light blinded Staffa. "Thank God, it's you."

Lungs heaving, Staffa pushed Kaylla ahead of him. His muscles still shrieked from the beating Brots had given him. When he crawled out, he propped himself against the pipe and coughed. He blinked owlishly in the sunset, seeing a well-dressed woman in black striding down from the water tent. Heavy equipment roared and moved about him, coming to a stop amid swirling white dust. A pile of sand-covered bodies had been laid to one side: Koree and the rest of his team. Staffa shook his head and closed his eyes.

"You all right?" He turned to Kaylla to avoid thinking of the senseless deaths.

"I think. Head hurts." She glanced up to Anglo and revulsion returned to her expression.

Anglo grinned happily, relief apparent in his oily expression. Did he enjoy disgusting and degrading Kaylla so much? Using her as a. . . . Staffa swallowed his anger.

"Only you could have made it out alive, Lord Commander." A woman's cultured tones brought him to his feet, whirling to face her. Beside her stood a dapper man, his face a curious blend of relief and worry.

It took him a second to place her. "Minister Ily Takka."

Ily flipped her head to shift her glistening black hair off her shoulder. "You have led us a most unusual chase, Lord Commander. I must say, I never would have believed your capacity for trouble. But come, we must get you back the Itreatic Asteroids. We have serious business to discuss."

"With this slave?" Anglo asked, bewildered.

"This *slave*, Officer," Ily announced in a viper's voice, "is the Lord Commander, *Staffa kar Therma*! I believe in your local quaintness, you call him the *Star Butcher?*" She raised an eyebrow suggestively as Anglo paled.

Staffa glanced at Kaylla and a choking knot clamped at the bottom of his throat. Horror mixed with amazement on her stricken face. Stung by the look of loathing she turned on him, he faced Ily.

"You have a collar override?"

The dapper man nodded and produced the controls. Staffa triggered the override and turned to Kaylla. "I'm sorry. I would have spared you from knowing who I am." Then, nothing left to lose, he pivoted on his heel and killed Anglo in the most painful manner he knew.

* * *

Despite the flares that rose over Vespa, the city had gone eerily quiet. Sinklar's comm chattered as his Firsts completed the mop-up and establishment of security zones throughout the city. Thankfully, his people had taken very few casualties.

He stood on a balcony that jutted from one of the tallest buildings in Vespa and looked out over the quiet city. Here and there, lights had come on in the buildings—perhaps a better indication than any field report that the fighting was over. The breeze ruffled his hair as he stared thoughtfully over the shadowed rooftops and deserted streets.

"Sink? Mac here," his ear comm told him. "I think that's about it. The city is definitely ours. From where we're sitting, we can see what's left of the enemy fleeing into the mountains in commandeered trucks and buses. They're licked."

"Affirmative. I want the patrols out and about. Just because they fled doesn't mean they won't be back."

"Roger, I'm coordinating with Ayms and Hauws. Meanwhile, I've delegated teams to secure your building. Get some sleep, Sink. You've earned it."

"You, too, Mac. Sink out."

He turned at the sound of voices and the door inside closing. Gretta slipped her helmet off and stepped out on the balcony, letting the cool breeze blow through her hair. "Quite a place." She jerked her head back toward the plush penthouse. "I just dismissed the comm crew in there. Told them to go get some rest. My Section is pretty well billeted. Thought maybe you and I might get some shut-eye, too."

Sink pulled her close and kissed her. "Great idea. Thought we'd stay here, use this place for the HQ. You get a pretty good view of everything from here. The balcony goes clear around and the windows can be masked. When you look at the office buildings around this one, they're perfect for observation and sniping posts. We can land LCs in that plaza down in front." He grinned. "And not only that, I've been having fantasies for hours about that big fluffy sleeping platform in the bedroom."

She kissed him soundly. "Sounds great. A place like this ought to have a stupendous shower."

"Big enough for four."

"Let's make it two." She hesitated, looking out over the city. "You know, I never would have thought we'd do it. Back in the mountains, when they pulled the transport, I thought we were dead. Now look at us. We own this place."

"A presage of things to come," Sinklar promised as he looked up at the lights of the orbiting fleet. "No one leaves

Sinklar Fist or the First Assault Division to die in the back-country." He grinned crookedly as he lowered his gaze to the darkened city that was his.

The next step would be to win the whole damned war.

* * *

Air travel had become too risky. Bruen rubbed his hip with a thin hand as a whooshing sound grew in the tunnel. Over the years, the Seddi had mapped much of the honey-comb of tunnels that wove through the Targan rock like empty arteries. They seldom used the single monorail that ran between Kaspa and the hidden chambers of Makarta. Seddi resources had been funneled into other causes through the years and if the one car should fail, well, there were worse deaths than starving in the blackness of the tunnels, though not many. Sending out a rescue party would take weeks.

The hiss of the approaching car grew louder until it pulled into the lighted chamber. Butla Ret glanced up as he rocked to a stop and turned off the motor. He puffed out his cheeks as he exhaled and shook his head. "I'd started to wonder if I'd ever get here."

"So had we," Bruen greeted.

Ret climbed out of the vehicle and followed Bruen through a winding maze of corridors hewn out of the rock. They entered a lighted room filled with monitors, several tables, and a couch where Magister Hyde lay under a warmer. Butla went over to take Hyde's weak hand.

Bruen ignored them as he walked to the pine table. Finally he turned. "I guess you know why we wanted to see you, Butla."

The big assassin gave Hyde one last encouraging smile and moved into the center of the room. "I think so, Magister."

"You have made a decision?"

Butla rubbed his hands together and nodded. "Yes, Magister Bruen. I will accept. It seems there is no other way."

Bruen cleared his throat. "Then you are now formally in command of the field operations of the Targan resistance."

Hyde nodded in somber agreement from the couch where

he lay. His flesh had sunk around the skull like a death mask. "The quanta are making fools of us all, Butla. We thought the Star Butcher would be our greatest threat, and now he may be in the clutches of Ily Takka. Who knows what that might mean. Nothing is proceeding as we had planned. All of our predictive models are on hold. This new general of the First Assault Division is completely—"

"This Sinklar Fist?" Butla frowned. "He was promoted from sergeant. How could he. . . ."

I can't tell him who Sinklar Fist is, or about his heritage. "We don't know." Bruen lied as he lowered himself carefully into a chair. "At the time he was appointed, we were hesitant. Apparently the Regan Minister of Defense abandoned Fist to his destruction in the mountains between Kaspa and Vespa. Fist has turned the tables. We had begun massing in the hills around his position—but he evacuated, on mining equipment, of all things, before we could launch a strike. He not only refused to be destroyed, he took Vespa, butchered our counterattack with almost no losses, and has, through some magic of his own, incorporated the prisoners he took into his own corps of loyal irregulars."

Bruen avoided Ret's questioning gaze and pulled at his ear. *Of course, we knew he was brilliant. After all, he's probably the most incredible mix of genetic material to come along in the eight hundred years of Free Space.*

"There is always assassination," Butla mentioned casually. "Now that she's contacted me, I could send Arta after him—or go myself."

Bruen lifted an eyebrow. *What are you hiding, Butla? You know something we don't. Why don't you speak? Or don't you trust us anymore?* "Perhaps. Let us keep that option open. On the other hand, he will be most difficult to get to. His people are very loyal."

"Perhaps," Butla's deep bass rumbled. "For the moment, the Targan forces are scattered, morale is down. I will repair that damage and then we shall see to this Sinklar Fist . . . and his First Division."

"We are placing our trust in you, Butla Ret," Hyde added, voice barely audible. "And perhaps . . . our last hope."

What do I do now? How will things work out on Etarus. Is there truly any hope for an alliance with the Companions? This is all changing too rapidly. We're on a wild ride, and the coaster is out of control.

CHAPTER XIX

"She comes with me," Staffa insisted, arms crossed resolutely as they stood in the burning Etarian sands.

Ily lifted a questioning eyebrow. The Lord Commander wanted *her,* a work-toughened cock-pinch? The brown-haired slave woman was filthy—not that Staffa looked any cleaner. Ily could see a bruise healing on her cheek, and a man had obviously been sucking at her neck from the fading purple splotches. Why, she'd probably been had by every man in Etarus—and in every orifice! True, she exhibited a curious animal magnetism in the way the muscles rolled under that tanned flesh. Was *she* what he'd been screwing out here?

Ily took the time to get a good look at Staffa. He *was* dirty. Even in the dry hot air, his body reeked of sweat and his personal odor, unwashed these many days. The sun had blackened his skin and a wealth of old scars stood out pinkish-white along his massively muscled chest, shoulders, and arms. He, too, she noted, carried bruises—especially around his swollen throat. His eyes never left hers, measuring and wary, suspicious of her next move. He kept the override box gripped tightly in his battered hand.

Ily experienced a slight flush as she met those gray eyes. Here, by the Rotted Gods, stood a man! She looked on a feral male, one she could respect. Nevertheless, he had changed. The haughty arrogance had vanished to be replaced by something else, some dangerous cunning coupled with an unnamed anguish. What had the cursed Warden done to him?

"Very well, Lord Commander, you may bring her. But what, pray tell, will you do with her?" Ily gestured for the aircar, aware of Tyklat's spongelike attention. He hadn't missed a word, not a single nuance. A very bright young man, this Tyklat. He would have to be used carefully—and watched vigilantly.

Ily heard Staffa say to the woman, "I made you a promise. I can't change the past . . . no matter how much I would like to. I also gave you my word that I would free you if I could."

Ily speculated as the slave woman shrank from Staffa's touch and climbed unevenly to her feet. She walked suspiciously toward the approaching aircar, silent, ignoring Staffa who still stood there with a dumb misery in his eyes. Most interesting! The Lord Commander could be hurt through this woman. Who was she? How could she be used?

Ily reached for Staffa's hand and almost jerked back. His flesh felt like wood! She noted the scabs where they had cracked and sand now caked the coagulated blood. "Come, Staffa, a cool shower and clean clothes await you. We will discuss our business, and then you may be free to go."

His deadly gray eyes met hers and he nodded, voice raspy as he said, "After you, Minister," and gestured, his long black hair flipping and twisting barbarically in the searing wind.

Tyklat took the front seat next to the slave woman. Ily switched on the privacy shield as the vehicle rose from the swirling sand. She analyzed Staffa's slit-eyed stare as they rose over the pile of corpses pulled from the collapsed dune. For a split second, she caught a glimmer of rage in his expression as he looked down at the long length of pipe reflecting brightly in the sun.

"Lord Commander," she asked in her most sympathetic voice. "How did you come to be sold like a common criminal? The Empire is terribly embarrassed by the entire incident."

As they moved beyond sight of the pipeline, he turned, and she experienced a thrill at the brute power in his eyes.

"You must have found the case records . . . and the Judicial Magistrate, if you found me."

"How would you like the matter to be handled? The Emperor will want your every wish accorded to." She settled herself and pulled the flask from the seat beside her. His sharpened expression cued her and she graciously handed him the energy-rich rehydrating fluid.

"Drink it, I believe you need it more than I." She smiled,

letting her lids drop ever so slightly, her mouth set in the practiced half-smile that enticed and invited.

He drank but half, handing the flask forward. The slave woman, Ily noted, might not be interested in acknowledging the Lord Commander, but she finished the flask. Evidently, in the desert, water overrode social concerns.

"I leave the problem of my arrest to your sensibilities, Minister." He turned to her, gray ice in his gaze. "However, were I making the decisions, I'd finish the job this pus-searing sun started, and melt this hellhole to slag with a cobalt bomb."

She nodded thoughtfully and was surprised when he looked at her again. "The only other request I make is that anyone you punish, you kill outright. Enslave none of them."

"Very well." She fought the urge to gasp in the heat, wishing she had worn anything but black in this burning waste. How many pounds had she sweated out in the five hours since they left Etarus? She appraised him again, noting the hard set of his jaw. How in the name of the Rotted Gods had even he survived? How could anyone live—let alone work—in that?

He looks like a man returned from hell. The glare in his eyes is that of a fanatic. For what? What has the desert, the heat, and the degradation done to him?

They set down minutes later before the Internal Security Directorate. Ily led Staffa and his slave woman into the building. "The Director's offices have complete facilities. Tyklat, find some proper clothing for the Lord Commander and his . . . lady."

Staffa glared at her. "Get the thrice-cursed collar off me! Now!"

"Tyklat?" Ily raised an eyebrow.

For the first time, Tyklat seemed flustered. "My Lord Minister, I fear the equipment to do that . . . well, we can put them on here, but take them off, I don't know."

"Give me a blaster." Staffa's muscles rippled. "I'll take the Rotted thing off."

Ily smiled, raising her hand. "I don't think we need to get that carried away. Tyklat, get the equipment. I don't care if you have to turn the city over."

Staffa glanced nervously at her and nodded, the control override jealousy guarded as they entered the main lobby.

Ily climbed the stairs, noticing the veiled woman who waited outside Tyklat's office. Her robes looked well to do and Ily could feel the woman's stare through the gauze. Some matron ratting on her husband for turning the servant perhaps? Why did these simple Etarians insist on their proper women wearing that ridiculous veil? It seemed ludicrous when they let their Priests pimp.

She opened the door and waved Staffa into the Director's spacious office. The slave woman followed, tall and straight, tan eyes catching each detail.

"The bath is through there." Ily motioned and tapped the intercom. "I will need a complete meal served for three with lots of beverages—and, as you value life, you will spare no expense."

She watched Staffa and the woman disappear into the lavatory before settling into the plush contouring chair behind Kapstan's old desk and considering the developments. *Who is this new Staffa? How do I bend him to my will?*

Tyklat entered, bearing serviceable clothing if not the absolute finest. He deposited the garments in the dressing room, returning to inquire whether she needed anything else.

"I think that will do, Tyklat. Your service will be remembered. I want you to find out about this slave woman. Who is she? What's her history?"

"I've already checked, Ily. She is Kaylla Dawn, formerly the hand servant to the First Lady of Maika."

"Very good, Tyklat. If I ring, come and claim the girl. She was enslaved for a crime, I take it?"

The corner of his mouth lifted. "Murder of her master, Ily. A most heinous crime."

"And the equipment to remove the collar?"

"Downstairs. It should be here in a moment."

Ily glanced toward the bath and lowered her voice. "Take your time."

She ran her hand down his, touch light. His expression reflected his understanding of the potential implications. "Tyklat, have you ever thought about leaving Etarus? Perhaps to take a higher post in the Empire?"

"Constantly, Lord Minister," he replied artfully as he left the room on silent feet.

Staffa stepped out of the bath with his long black hair twisted over his left ear as had always been his penchant. Tyklat had found a white robe which Staffa now wore. Against his sun-blackened skin, it made a most striking contrast. "What about the collar?" he demanded first thing.

"Tyklat was just here. The equipment is on the way."

"How did you know to search for me on Etaria?" he asked, settling easily on the pillows across from the desk, the collar control clutched tightly.

Look at the exhaustion in his eyes! Time to get some of my own back. "In spite of what you might have thought, we take our Empire very seriously. Your Wing Commander informed us that you were going on vacation—incognito. It wouldn't do to have you get into . . . well, the sort of mess you did on one of our possessions. We had an alert out for any disturbance or unusual mention of your name. It came out on a routine cross-check of the court system."

He nodded slowly, feral eyes never leaving hers. Did he believe her? No, she could see his skepticism. Happily, she realized his exhaustion would work to her benefit. She could read him; his discipline was compromised.

The food arrived as Kaylla stepped out of the dressing room in a bronze formfitting shift that did wonders for her. She had combed her shoulder length hair and it set off her tan eyes and weathered complexion. Not a planet-stopping beauty, but this woman would dominate a room where others with more classic features would fade against her magnetism. Staffa's perceptions must have held true—even through the dirt and stink and bruises.

Ily caught herself staring at Kaylla. Yet another potential rival? Rotted Gods, how did the man draw such competent women when the female half of human space seemed filled with ignorant fawning titterers and empty-headed breeding stock?

Ily gestured to the low ebony-topped table and settled herself across from the heaping plates. As Staffa and Kaylla seated themselves on the large cushions, Ily said, "I would offer a toast, but I doubt anything I say would be appropriate. Therefore, please, let us eat."

Ily kept her face straight as Staffa and the woman demol-

ished a complete dinner in ravenous fashion. The after-din-
ner lethargy would lower Staffa's defenses even further.

"You mentioned business?" The Lord Commander
leaned back, wolfish gaze on Ily.

Ily poured them both more wine, aware of how Kaylla
missed nothing. Sharp, and she hadn't said a word since the
rescue.

"Indeed. We would offer you and the Companions contract, Lord Commander. Currently, the Targan situation is
deteriorating. The Rebels, it seems, are better armed and
led than we had at first suspected." Long practice had given
her the ability to project credible hesitation and dismay.
"They have destroyed an entire assault division and
threaten our very control of the planet. Tybalt the Imperial
Seventh believes it would be cheaper to hire the Lord Commander than to suffer the inefficiency, cost, and loss of
life, equipment, and property the present situation would
indicate as necessary to subdue the planet."

Kaylla's attention turned to Staffa, mouth opening slightly
in the first show of emotion Ily had seen her display. Staffa
looked from one to the other, face as impassive as the
damned desert.

"For the moment, Lord Minister, the Companions are
not accepting any contract. If you will be so kind as to
extend my best wishes to his Imperial Tybalt, I would—"

"I don't think you understand the gravity of this situation,
Lord Commander." Ily remained firm but pleasant. "Consider the current balance of power between Sassa and ourselves. We would prefer not to tie up large portions of our
forces at this time. In the event we were to suffer heavy
casualties during the pacification of Targa, would that not
invite Sassan aggression?"

"No," Staffa told her easily. "Having just come from
Myklene, I can tell you they are in no position to threaten
you." He looked into the tan eyes of the slave woman and
added, "It is none of my business, Minister, but may I suggest that you approach the Rebel parties and attempt to
find a political solution to the problem which will not bleed
you so badly." He wiped his black beard with a dampened
napkin and met her level gaze. "I take it, however, that I
am free to leave this planet and continue my travels
unrestricted?"

"Then you have no interest in helping us?"

"Not for the foreseeable future."

"Surely, Lord Commander, we can sweeten the pot. Make you an offer—"

"You have my final word."

Ily smiled to cover her racing thoughts. *With all the options available, where does my advantage lie? I can't allow Staffa loose—potentially bearing a grudge against the Imperium that enslaved him. If he returns to the Itreatic Asteroids, what guarantee do I have that he would ultimately side with Rega? Against that, I must balance his anger and wrath. What hope is there to coerce him to throw the Companions into the fray on the side of Rega if I threaten him? Most of all, I need him . . . need to win him to my side in the desperate gamble I must make. For that, I need time with him. Time to manipulate him, to bind him to me.*

He told her politely, "In any case, I would have to take it up with the Companions, and we agreed upon my leaving to all take time to recuperate from the strenuous campaigning. Now why don't we get this damned collar off, and we can all be more pleasant."

"Then perhaps you would allow me to show my sincere regards and personally escort you through the Regan Empire at his Imperial Majesty's expense? I could offer you the finest in entertainment aboard my personal cruiser. You could consider yourself a. . . ."

He raised a hand to stop her. "I am most honored by your offer, Lord Minister. I would, however, remind you that the Companions have never accepted such privileges from any government. To do so would bias our neutrality. As always, I will go on my own and bear my own expenses. That way, there can be no appearance of conflict of interest." His voice changed. "Ily, I want this collar off—*now!*"

"I understand," Ily bowed graciously. *Time to gamble.* She touched the button under the desk. Tyklat knocked immediately.

"Enter," Ily called.

Tyklat opened the door with Officer Morlai in tow. The Warden's officer sweated his nervousness, face pale despite the deep desert tan.

"Tyklat! Just the person I wanted to see. Where is that

Rotted equipment? The Lord Commander wants the collar removed."

Tyklat smiled uneasily. "It's on the way, Minister, I swear. We don't take many off of live . . . well, I mean."

Ily affected an air of irritation. "Then you had best get someone who can find something that will work."

"Immediately. But, well, your pardon, Minister," Tyklat said with a bow. "I hope I am not intruding, but the officer has come for the slave woman, Kaylla."

"By all means. It was a pleasure, Kaylla, to—"

"No!" Staffa's voice was firm. "She goes with me." His gray eyes gleamed wickedly. "Either she goes, Minister, or. . . ."

Ily placed a hand to her head. "What is the woman's crime, Tyklat?"

"Murder of her former master, Minister Takka. I am afraid that is one of the few convictions we cannot overturn. The people would be most upset at the thought that a slave might harm them and be allowed to walk free." Tyklat looked properly distressed and embarrassed, as if he hated to do what he had to. He almost winced—a perfect performance.

"She goes with me," Staffa said through gritted teeth. "Ily, what sort of game are you playing here? Get this damn collar off me, or so help me, *Tybalt's going to get an earful!*"

"Lord Commander," Ily put the right tone of distress in her voice. "Ours is a society of laws and proscribed punishments for crimes. You must—"

"I killed *two* of your rot-cursed *citizens*. You would allow *me* to walk free?" His face turned flint-hard, eyes narrowed to slits as he stared at her over the wreckage of the meal.

"Perhaps, you don't see the difference. Your conviction was a case of mistaken identity. You were beset and robbed. It isn't—"

"Perhaps I shall return with my Companions and retrieve her on my own!" Staffa stated bluntly. "Would the Emperor like to protect his laws so much as to cross me and my fleet?"

Kaylla swallowed hard. "Tuff, uh, Lord Commander. Look, I'm not worth a war. I'll go." She started to get up as Staffa clamped a hard hand on her arm and pulled her down.

Ily adopted her best perplexed look, then a light of inspiration filled her face. "Lord Commander, I might have an answer to our dilemma. Director Tyklat, once a slave is condemned, she is expected to die, isn't she? She can never regain her freedom?"

"No, Minister."

"Suppose we sentenced Kaylla to death?" Ily lifted an eyebrow seeing the anger stirring in Staffa's hot face. "If, for example, the slave, Kaylla, were sentenced to fight the Targan Rebels, that would constitute a death sentence, would it not?"

Tyklat agreed with a short nod, "It could be so construed, my Lord Minister."

The corners of Staffa's lips curled into a smile. "Well played, Lord Minister. You would buy my contract through Kaylla's slavery. You are worthy of your position. Now I will make my own gamble. I will stand and walk out of here, Kaylla with me. I will gamble that you will not risk my anger." He reached for the override control, expression going grim as Ily held up a stun rod she'd pulled from her belt pouch.

Staffa's cheek muscles jumped as he stood and helped a pale Kaylla to her feet. "You wouldn't risk my wrath, Minister."

What now? I can't let him walk out. No matter what, a dead Staffa is less a threat than a mad one.

Ily took a slow breath. "My Lord Commander, you look ill. Perhaps it is the heat which has affected you." She thumbed the stun control, watching Staffa and the woman collapse.

Ily stood, pacing out from behind the desk and plucking the collar control from his trembling fingers. As Staffa sat up, she tapped the box with her thumbnail. The desperate look he gave her would have sintered clay. "Tyklat, you and the officer will remain outside." She watched as they left and closed the door.

"I'm sorry, Lord Commander. Things have gone too far now. Though all is not lost for you. Your Kaylla remains with us. We cannot allow you to side with the Sassan slime. I did not wish to be forced to this action, but your honor is well known. Contract with us, and we will send her unharmed to the Itreatic Asteroids."

"You play with fire, Ily."

"Not at all, Staffa." Ily backed cautiously out of reach as Kaylla sat up and winced. "I need you, and I *will* have you. Together, you and I can forge human space into one Empire to be ruled jointly." She extended her hand to him. "Join me, Staffa, and I'll cut that collar off your neck." She gave him a sultry look. "Join me and we'll knock Tybalt off his golden throne and emasculate those weak Sassans. Free Space will be ours."

He laughed bitterly, getting to his feet. "That's your final line?"

"Staffa, I will not take the chance that you might ally with the Sassans. Against you, we have no hope. With you dead, we have better odds by dealing with your Wing Commander—or, perhaps, to take the Sassans without the involvement of the Companions."

One thumb on the collar control, she traced her fingers down the side of his face in a lover's caress. "But alive, you and I can be Emperor and Empress. Who could stand against us? Staffa, am I that undesirable?" She stood back, eyes locked with his, breathing so as to move her breasts under the tight fabric of her black gown.

"Tuff!" Kaylla stood up. *"What the hell are you doing?"*

"Shut up!" Ily turned, eyes cold. "You have no word here. We're bargaining for your life."

"My life's not worth blackmail and suffering, and definitely not worth an interstellar war. Thanks, but no. Kill me right here. I'll go with honor to stop the likes of you!" Kaylla's lips hardened with disgust.

Staffa's laughter cracked rudely in the tense air. "You heard the lady. That's it, Ily."

"You, Staffa?" Ily laughed. "The Star Butcher backs a semen-greased slave?"

His speed surprised her, the flat of his hand slapping the side of her face, sending her sprawling over the ebony table. Shocked but coherent, she thumbed the collar control button by reflex, as her body slid over the dirty plates.

Fingers to her face, Ily sat up, blinking, dazed. The salty taste of blood filled her mouth. The bastard had split her lip! Thumb on the button, she stood, staggering. She looked down to where he lay. His violent stare met hers as his mouth worked soundlessly.

"Die, Staffa!" she hissed. "No one, not even the Lord Commander slaps me! I offered you *an Empire!*"

She let up on the button as he gasped and straightened. "Oh, no, Staffa kar Therma. Get your breath! You and your precious Kaylla can breathe a little first."

"By the Rotted Gods, Ily, you kill me, and the story will get out. If I disappear, the Companions will hear. One of your scum will sell the information."

"Too late, Staffa. I can't allow you to live now. My aircar will land. Tyklat and I will carry your body aboard and . . . well, an accident will happen to the ship bearing you back to your Companions." She pursed her lips as she fingered the collar control. "Most likely, it will look like the Sassans did it. And I doubt Tyklat will ever tell." She smiled. "He's good—but expendable."

"Ily!"

"Take a deep breath, Staffa, you're about. . . ."

The rocking explosion took her by surprise. The walls cracked and Kapstan's prized artwork dropped to the floor as Ily fought to keep her feet. Staffa's leap caught her by surprise as he knocked the collar control spinning. Staffa leapt after it like some crazed leopard.

Fear spurring her, Ily dove across the desk, frantic fingers seeking the drawer. She ripped it open as another concussion shook the room. Blaster fire impacted on the walls outside as she strained to reach the blaster in the desk.

* * *

The second blast caught Staffa in mid-leap. He landed, rolling, coming up with the collar control. On his feet, he staggered as Ily tumbled over the desk and pulled a service blaster from a drawer.

Staffa jerked Kaylla to her feet and shoved her reeling as he ducked to one side. Ily shot from an awkward position; the blaster bolt sizzled past his long hair as he threw himself out of the way. Years of combat training served him as he ducked yet another burst.

Staffa froze as Ily jumped to her feet, braced in an isosceles turret hold. His skin crawled as she pinned him in the sights.

Ily's voice went silky. "Good-bye, Staffa!"

The door slammed open but Staffa only had eyes for Ily. He launched himself as she turned her head, attention drawn to the door.

In mid-leap he saw her crumple, falling face first over the big desk, limp.

Staffa caught himself and rolled to one side, plucking the blaster from her fingers, the eerie tingle of a stun beam playing at the edges of his nerves. In a crouch he turned toward the door.

"Don't shoot," Tyklat told him evenly. "You have very little time."

Tyklat replaced the stun rod with a blaster. Wary, Staffa never let his eyes leave the man as the weapon crackled and blew a section of wall out behind him. Someone screamed in the hallway beyond Tyklat. Blaster fire ripped the air. A pitched battle raged through the lower offices.

Tyklat pointed where sunlight slanted through the hole. "Hurry. You have a slight jump to the lower roof. A man will be waiting in the back alley with an aircar. His name is Nyklos. Go, now. Master Kahn, go with him. Take him to Bruen on Targa." Tyklat turned on his heel, slamming the door behind him and muffling the vicious sounds of combat.

Staffa caught Kaylla's arm, pulling her to her feet. "Come on! Opportunity is best not lost on dunces." He led her to the shattered wall, peering out over the rubble that had collapsed outward. With one hand, he lowered Kaylla to the debris below.

With a bitter cry, he turned and jumped, landing on his feet, running despite the entangling robe. To one side, a window shattered in an explosion of flying glass and curling flame that sprayed him with fragments.

Staffa shielded his eyes, racing for the roof edge, pounding across the shuddering tiles after Kaylla.

A big bearded man stood at the controls of a pitching aircar that hovered just below the roof line and out of direct fire. Staffa leapt into the seat right behind Kaylla, the car dropping under his weight.

Nyklos punched the throttle forward, acceleration driving Staffa hard against the firm cushions.

"Close work," the driver called. "We cut it a bit tight back there."

"You're Nyklos?"

"I'm Nyklos." He looked Staffa up and down with a narrow-eyed stare. A deep-seated caution kicked into place. *This man is no friend.*

Kaylla pulled herself forward. "Tyklat called me Master back there. Why? How did he know?"

Nyklos grinned wistfully. "He remembered you. You gained your Master's robes while he was still a first stage Initiate."

"Why did it take so long for the order to find me?" she wondered, eyes searching the flat ugly brown houses they fled past.

"We didn't know you were alive until Tyklat recognized you. We heard that you had been executed on Maika," Nyklos told her. He gave Staffa another appraisal while a crease of a frown etched into his forehead.

"Who are you?" Staffa asked, the uneasy feeling growing in his breast. "Why are you doing this?"

"That will be made known to you when you're out of danger. For the moment, the schedule is tight. We have to get you off planet before the Imperial fleet rolls down and blockades all of Etaria. Minister Takka has an Imperial cruiser up there. We want you well clear before she comes to."

"And where do you think you're taking me?" Staffa's voice dropped to a low hiss, the blaster centering on Nyklos' thick torso.

Nyklos' face lost color. "You wanted to get to Targa, to ask the Seddi about your son. We have a way to get you there. We hadn't planned on Kaylla, but—"

"She goes with me."

"Tuff, you don't owe me a thing," Kaylla protested.

Staffa's expression hardened. "I made a promise. And the Regans will turn this planet upside down to find us. Ily will see to that."

"I'm afraid he's right, Master Kahn." Nyklos agreed. "Your presence complicates things. The box only has supplies enough for two."

"Two?" Staffa asked.

"In a moment, all will be made clear."

"Why should I trust you?" he asked Nyklos as they

passed a bulky brick warehouse and dropped into the shadow behind the building.

"You would rather trust your friend Ily?" Kaylla asked.

Staffa frowned. Slowly the blaster lowered. Nyklos took a deep breath, relief in his brown eyes.

"Very well, I will take your passage to Targa." Staffa put a hand on Nyklos' shoulder as he stepped from the aircar. "Why do you look at me like that? You are. . . . Yes, you would like to see me dead. Are you another whom I have wronged?"

Nyklos' lips twitched. "All my life, I have been trained to handle the eventuality of your appearance here. Things change, the quanta play strange games with our lives and our goals. Now we meet, face-to-face, and I who have trained all my life to kill you, must instead send you to my Magister, the one man for whom I would gladly lay down my life. I pray you are worth the risk, Staffa kar Therma." The brown eyes didn't drop, nor did the expression soften.

"Bruen?" Kaylla asked, voice suddenly vulnerable.

"We have been in contact." Nyklos glanced at her. "Now . . . Lord Commander, bend down and let me get a look at that collar you manufacture so well."

* * *

Skyla triggered the heavy shoulder blaster Nyklos had given her and devastated the records center in the Internal Security building. Checking the door, she stepped over the body of the clerk she'd blown in two. The delayed charges she'd set rocked the building, and chunks of plaster spilled from the ceiling. She could hear people screaming as they fled the building.

Skyla checked and jumped from the doorway, sprinting down the hallway toward the landing. Steps pounded on the stairway. Skyla ducked to the side, ready to shoot.

Tyklat appeared at the landing, blaster in hand as he crouched, ready to fire. Seeing Skyla, he grinned, teeth flashing in his dark face. "They're off, Wing Commander. Ily's stunned, but she won't be out for long. The schedule's tight. Go. I'll do my best to cover for you, but I can't jeopardize my position. I've got to seal the planet—no one in or out—within an hour. As to your vessel up there in orbit. . . ."

Skyla stood, nodding. "I understand. I'll get its worth back out of Tybalt's hide. Take care, Tyklat. And if you ever need a job, the Companions have a place for you."

His manner cooled. "Thank you, Wing Commander. I think I will die Seddi."

"See you, Tyklat." She dropped the heavy blaster and ran for the shattered doorway, pulling the Etarian veil up to mask her face. A crowd had gathered outside the building, people craning their necks to see. Somewhere in the distance, sirens wailed. Skyla plunged into the crowd.

"What's happening?" a man asked, grabbing her arm as she fled.

"They've gone crazy in there," Skyla shrilled in a panicked voice. "Crazy!" She jerked her elbow away and shouldered through the jostling press.

She hurried to make the three blocks to the public transportation platform, images of Staffa burning in her mind. She'd almost gasped out loud when Ily had led him past the bench where Skyla waited in her Etarian disguise. He'd looked like a wild animal, filthy and bruised. But she knew the deadly gray stare that burned behind his eyes. And who was the tan-eyed woman?

Her combat nerves began to unwind and she took a deep breath as she stepped onto the shuttle bus that ran across the city. She checked her chronometer. Right on time. Now, if Bruen were as good as his word, she and Staffa would be headed for Targa within the hour, their crate being carried off-planet moments before Tyklat's emergency security measures sealed Etaria.

Skyla watched the buff-colored buildings pass beyond the window as the heavy vehicle followed its route through bustling Etarus. Anxiety mingled with relief. Just how powerful were the Seddi? What was Bruen after? Why had he been so accommodating?

You're in deep waters, Skyla. She worried the inside of her lip with nervous teeth. *God, I wish I had the fleet to back me up.* But the Companions were far away—and she'd need the specialized equipment on her ship to contact them.

Skyla stood as the transport slowed to a stop, then she stepped off in a seedy warehouse district. In the background, she could hear the roar of the cargo shuttle as it made its routine half-hour flight. The next time it rose, she and Staffa would be riding it up.

Skyla walked the half block to a side door which swung open, indicating an excellent surveillance system. Nyklos met her in a narrow hallway lined with offices. As they passed, Skyla could see secretaries bent over comm monitors. The place was a working exporting company, and guessing from what she'd come to learn of the Seddi, probably making a profit, too.

"Everything all right?" Skyla asked as she pulled her veil off.

"There's a snag," Nyklos told her. "We've another party to consider."

"The woman?" Skyla guessed. Her heart lurched suddenly. Rotted Gods, Staffa hadn't taken a lover, had he? A quelling tightness roiled her guts. *And what if he did? You've no claim on him.* But the thought nagged at her.

Nyklos ushered Skyla through heavy ceramic doors and into the huge warehouse: a place filled with large gray syalon crates, each four by four meters square. Nyklos led her through the maze of crates.

Staffa stood before an opened crate, hands braced on his hips. There, too, stood the tan-eyed woman, a grim expression on her face. Skyla ignored her, pacing up to Staffa, a wry grin on her face while her heart ached with longing and joy.

Staffa's lips quivered before breaking into a smile. A warmth filled his gray eyes with a tenderness she'd never seen. They faced each other awkwardly for a moment, then Staffa said, "I guess I made a mess of it, didn't I?"

"I told you." Suddenly she was in his arms, hugging him tightly. "By the Blessed Gods, I've been worried sick about you. Tap and Tasha are nervously waiting word at home."

"Excuse me," Nyklos called. "We've got to make some important decisions here. Either we make the next shuttle, or we're in trouble."

Skyla pushed back, heart pounding. "What's the problem?"

"I am." The tan-eyed woman stepped forward, and Skyla got a good look at her. She had a square-jawed face and shoulder length brown hair. The tan robe she wore accented her trim muscular body and long legs. More than that, the woman had a powerful presence and vitality that made her damned attractive.

Staffa pointed at the crate. "There's only room for two. Tybalt has the blockaded Targa—and that's the only way to get through the embargo the Regans have drawn around the planet."

Nyklos said, "We've got provisions in the crate for two persons. It can't carry three—and we *must* get Kaylla off the planet. She is Seddi, and Ily will stop at nothing to find her."

"So? What's the problem?" Skyla glanced back and forth. "Kaylla goes to Targa in the box. Staffa and I take my ship and return to the Itreatic Asteroids. We'll get to Targa after things settle down."

"It's not that easy," Staffa told her. "Tyklat will have already issued orders for my arrest. My description is everywhere. If I step out of this warehouse, someone will spot me. Nyklos filled me in on the entire operation. My rescue has jeopardized the entire Seddi network on Etarus. They've worked for years to get Tyklat to his present position. He had to turn every stone over to find us. Ily will be looking for a scapegoat, and Tyklat's hanging by a thread. If he doesn't bend time-space in his search for us, she'll offer his head to Tybalt. The crate looks like my best chance."

"Put more food in the crate," Kaylla suggested.

"Take too long to get it. We've only got four minutes to get that box loaded," Nyklos said anxiously. "Tyklat can't delay any longer, he's got to seal this planet immediately."

Skyla squinted at the crate, making a decision. "Staffa, you and Kaylla get in the box. Go, now. Of all of us, I'm the least likely to get caught in Tyklat's roundup."

Staffa glanced uncertainly at Nyklos then stepped close, placing his hands on Skyla's shoulders. "And you trust Bruen and the Seddi?"

Skyla gave him a crooked grin. "Not in the least, but Bruen is very interested in talking to you. I doubt they'll assassinate you before he gets a chance to sit down face-to-face and discuss things with you. Something's gone wrong with the Seddi plans—and you're part of it. Trust them? Hell, no, but you've got plenty of insurance."

"What about you?" Staffa asked, shifting uneasily.

"I'm not the one who ended up in the slave collar," Skyla reminded. "You worry about getting to Targa in one piece. Find out what Bruen has to say about your son."

"And if there's treachery?"

Skyla shot a hard glance at Nyklos. "The Companions will guarantee your safety, Staffa. I have Bruen's promise of a safe conduct for you, and I think I have a plan for getting off Etarus. You see, Bruen has you, and I have Nyklos—and everything he knows about Seddi spy networks. As long as you're treated well, Nyklos doesn't get mind-probed, and that information doesn't get transmitted to either Divine Sassa II or Tybalt the Imperial Seventh."

Staffa bent forward, kissing her gently on the lips. "See you on Targa, if the quantum gods allow." And he ducked into the gray syalon crate.

"Hurry!" Nyklos shouted, waving Kaylla in.

Skyla's heart ached as the heavy door was glued in place and a hoist lifted the crate, whining as it sped along the ceiling gantries for the shuttle.

Nyklos turned on his heel, saying, "You surely didn't think you'd get away with. . . ." He glanced down at the blaster Skyla shoved against his ribs.

"Damn right I did—and do. Let's get moving. I've got to steal my ship before Tyklat impounds it, and you're going to play the part of my husband in the process." She smiled icily. "Right, sweet meat?"

Nyklos measured the seriousness in her eyes and sighed in defeat. "Very well, at least let me call Tyklat. Maybe he can do something."

* * *

Security Third Zsem Letmon noticed Corporal Shinn as he passed routinely through the military compound gate. The woman with him, however, was definitely nonroutine. Tall and athletic, she pressed against Shinn as she whispered in his ear. Her perfect face lit with laughter. Striking red-brown hair tumbled down her shapely back, glinting curls shining where they caught the slanting afternoon light. She wore a shining silver dress that looked to have been glued to her firm flesh.

"Lucky bastard!" Zsem growled under his breath, seeing the scanners clear the pair. "He's got a woman like that to squire to the Second Division Ball—and I'm on patrol all night! Some justice!"

He admired the full curves of her bottom as she walked along, arm in arm with the corporal. Damned if her hips didn't sway in a most fascinating manner. Zsem swallowed against the sudden tight knot of desire under his throat and shook his head.

Three hours later, Zsem saw them again as he surveyed the parade ground. The sun had fallen behind the ragged peaks to the west, leaving the night sky star-shot, the Targan moon barely peeking over the mountains where it followed in the sun's wake.

Shinn and that voluptuous woman strolled from the music-blaring ballroom toward the officers' quarters. Zsem cut through the darkness, taking advantage of his IR night vision to study her again. Her silver skintight dress caught the light and reflected it on all the curves of her phenomenal body.

He timed it right to meet Shinn as he entered the personal residential quarters—just to get one close-up of her beauty.

"Danced out?" Zsem joked, winking his approval at the corporal. He glanced at her, meeting incredible amber eyes that let him speechless.

"You're gawking, Zsem," Shinn failed to mask his irritation. "Now go stick your nose in garbage cans so we know we're safe from Targan Rebels, huh. The lady and I are off to conduct some, uh, ground maneuvers." Shinn and the auburn-haired woman pushed past.

"What I'd give for a woman like that," Zsem muttered, remembering the thrust of her breasts against the silver fabric. His fantasies allowed him to drift for a second as he hugged his blaster close.

"Patrol check!" the Night Second's voice reminded flatly in his ear comm.

"Third Letmon, all clear," he mumbled, thumbing his mike.

Walking his beat between the deserted buildings, Letmon remembered her; she stuck in his mind, spinning herself around each of his fantasies. At the same time the music pouring out of First Mykroft's ball grated on his sensitive nerves. She had marvelous amber eyes. *Amber eyes?*

The phrase caught, clinging in the back of his mind.

"Third Letmon, over," he called in.

"Yeah, Zsem, what ya need?"

"Didn't we have a warrant for a woman with amber eyes and reddish hair a while back? Shinn just took a knock-out dish like that to his quarters. She's Targan, not one of ours. I mean, you'd remember a body like that—or those eyes."

Zsem heard the comm hum in the background. "Yeah, here it is. Couple of months ago. Not much description. Think this is her?"

"No," Zsem added, grinning wickedly. "But, what the hell, we're all missing the party and he's in banging bellies with one phenomenal piece of female flesh while I'm walking around in the dark. Maybe I'll give him time to exercise before I go knock on his door. Just to check her out, you see."

"Right!" The Night Second agreed, a perk of interest in his voice. "Uh, I'll follow from your monitor. If she's that good, we'll cop a couple of pictures. Might make my 20 ICs back."

Zsem gave them an hour. He trotted up the hallway to Shinn's room and palmed the door latch. Locked, of course. His security ID bypassed the mechanism. Zsem pushed the door open quietly. Silence.

"Security! Corporal Shinn?" he called as he marched into the sleeping quarters. Nothing. No one had mussed the bedding, but Shinn's dress uniform lay scattered about the floor. The gap hadn't registered at first. He took a quick look at the wall again where a square hole had been cut. Plaster dust had settled in a fine white powder over the floor and the block that had been cut out had been pushed through.

"Uh, what's behind this wall?" Shinn wondered, knowing the Night Second watched through his headset cam.

"According to records, that's the armory."

"Crap in the morning!" Zsem grinned to himself. "Hey, Second, is there a bonus if we break a black market ring?"

"Uh-huh, just remember we're both in on it."

"Yeah, well, keep your fingers off that alarm, buddy. I'll nail them, and we split fifty-fifty!"

"Got it," the Night Second agreed.

The book said they needed to sound an alert but hell, on a Security Third's pay? Risks were called for. Zsem thrust his blaster through the square hole, bounced on his toes, and crawled through head first. The air in the armory felt cool against his face. Zsem eased himself over zero-g crates and onto the concrete floor. One out of five of the overhead lights were on, leaving the place dimly lit. Silently, he stole through the huge building.

When he neared the main doors, he ducked back. Both guards appeared asleep, head cams pointed at holo-vision.

"I'm getting a bad feeling about this," Zsem whispered into the mike. "Maybe we better sound an alert. This could—"

"They been watching that holo for the last half hour."

"So Shinn and the lady been in here a half hour? This gate leads out to the compound. Nothing there but electrified fence. You get a proximity reading on that?"

The Night Second's voice sounded baffled. "Nothing. They couldn't have thrown a personal hygiene pack over the wire without an alarm going off and surveillance lighting up the whole area."

"I'm going to check the other door." He advanced, blaster held low, while worry traced fingers up and down his spine. As he feared, he found the other security personnel—dead. He stared at the bodies. The throats had been neatly cut, heads propped to point at the holo box.

"Rotted Gods!" the Second whispered hoarsely in Zsem's ear.

"You know, there's enough explosive and weaponry in here to flatten half this planet," Zsem reminded as he backed away from the corpses.

"Yeah, but the screens haven't shown any vehicles moving," the Night Second reminded. "Only thing that crossed the compound was one AG cart. Went to the service entrance at the power plant. Probably routine delivery."

Zsem pushed the door open, blaster ready. The night seemed peaceful enough. "Sound the alarm. I gotta bad feeling about this."

"My bonus money keeps getting—Holy crap! Proximity! Must be a thousand people out there in the night! Can you see them? Zsem? Can you see—"

A blinding flare of light illuminated the grounds in an actinic glare that shot up from behind the armory. The compound lights flickered and went black. The concussion deafened, then the ground heaved under Zsem's feet. With his IR vision, Zsem saw the masses beyond the fence coming at a run, hundreds of people, charging forward purposely.

"Power plant!" he gasped. "They blew the flipping power plant! Whole place is dead!"

He turned and caught sight of a light coming through the armory. Behind him, the mob rushed the fence, lasers cutting the wire like butter.

He wheeled and ran toward the light, drawing up as he slid to a stop and pulled for his blaster with fear-thick fingers. Her amber eyes bored into his.

Her vibraknife thrust into his gut, low down, ripping up through his chest.

He tried to scream as he fell beside the AG cart she had been towing. The world turned gray before Zsem's swimming vision while she pulled cases of blasters and armor past his face. Outside, a swelling roar rose in angry throats. Feet pounded through the armory as Targans armed themselves before spilling into the night.

*   *   *

Skyla turned to the monitor as it hazed and wavered. Something was coming in on a scrambled channel. She sat in the familiar seat of her personal yacht, the worry-cap lowered onto her ice-blonde hair. One by one, the systems came to life on the instrument panel as she completed the preflight check.

Tyklat's face formed. "Wing Commander? I just thought I'd check and make sure you made it through customs without problems." He hesitated. "You wouldn't consider turning Nyklos loose, would you?"

"I will, as soon as I get Staffa off Targa."

"I take it the Master is in good health?"

She chuckled. "He must be. You ought to hear him cursing back there. Don't you Seddi have rules about the kind of language a Master can use?"

Tyklat gave her a flat look from tired eyes. "Masters are not used to being held hostage."

"Consider the stakes, Tyklat, and then you tell me what you'd do in my place. By the way, how'd you get us such an easy clearance? I've already got a flight plan from orbital traffic control. Not even a single delay."

Tyklat grinned evilly and held up a golden badge with a cat's face and lily design. "Ily's jessant-de-lis. When she finds out *you* used it to clear her ship, I'm hoping she'll be so embarrassed she won't think twice about using me for a scapegoat."

"My systems are powering up and I can see Ily's cruiser on the monitors. I guess they haven't figured out what's gone wrong?"

"They're curious about the alert but not panicked yet. I imagine things will be interesting by the time Ily gets on board." His dark features went tense. "Minister Takka is coming to. I've got her in a med unit, but I can't keep her down any longer. You've had all the time I can safely grant you without creating awkward explanations or incompetent misdirection. Good luck, Wing Commander." His lips curled over white shining teeth, eyes sparkling. "I am sorry to have to let you go. Ily promised I could put a collar on you—and keep you!"

"Might not have been so bad, Tyklat." She gave him a wink and a saucy smile. "The Lord Commander's on his way to Targa, huh? You put together a hell of a rescue. If you need anything from us . . . the Companions do not forget a debt."

"I will remember, thank you. And good spacing, Wing Commander."

"Farewell, Tyklat. And thanks."

"Take very good care of Nyklos." The screen went dead.

She cleared with planetary orbit control and powered out of orbit, laying a vector for deep space—setting a false trail of plasma in the direction of Rega before shutting the reactors down. Changing her ship's attitude, Skyla blasted reaction mass from time to time to change vector without leaving a consistent trail. Satisfied no one could follow, she let her cruiser float on automatic. For long moments, she stared out the main port at the billions of stars that shimmered in double and triple images beyond the Forbidden Borders. A whole universe lay out there—beyond human ability to reach. An unfamiliar depression settled on her, a feeling the universe had changed, that nothing would be the same again.

Skyla, you're tired. You haven't had a full night's sleep in a week.

The worry-cap gleamed in the cockpit lights as she lifted it off. She stood and took one last glance at the controls before she palmed the cockpit hatch and stepped into the main cabin. Using a special security code, she locked the cockpit hatch and turned. Nyklos remained firmly bound with EM restraints where she'd shoved him into one of the cushioned sofas.

Not that he was suffering. Her private yacht had once belonged to the Secretary of Economics on Formosa. The interior had been paneled with sandalwood and Riparian ebony. Velvet upholstery was the rule, and gleaming gold accented tasteful decor. The table Nyklos sat behind had been cut from a slab of Vegan marble and Myklenian silk had been used for the draperies. The thick spongy rugs had come from the finest Ashtan manufacturers.

He cocked his head curiously and asked, "Everything is all right? We're spacing for Targa?"

Skyla sighed and shook her head. "Afraid not. It will take quite a while for Staffa's cargo canister to arrive on Targa. Meanwhile, Ily Takka is going to come boiling out of Etaria with an anger the likes of which not even the Rotted Gods could imagine. Rushing off to Targa might put us right in her net. Want a cup of stassa?"

"I'll pass. So what are we going to do? You're not going to keep me tied up the whole time, are you?"

Skyla shrugged. "Depends on how you act, and what I decide to do, but first things first. I'm going to feed you, get you something to drink, and let you take care of nature. Then I'm going to tie you up, lock you in one of the after cabins, and I'm going to sleep for as long as it takes to get my brain functional again. After that, I'll let you out, feed you again, and then I'm going to sit around and do nothing but think until I can tack some kind of plan together and initiate it."

"While I'm tied up again?"

Skyla raised an eyebrow. "It could be worse. This isn't exactly a pigsty."

"And I can always fantasize about you."

"You already did that."

He gave her a suspicious glance. "When?"

"Under the Mytol."

He colored. "Well, I guess there are no secrets between us."

"Oh, there are plenty," she told him coolly. "But they're all mine."

His smile grew until it curled his mustache. "Uh, I don't suppose you'd sleep better with someone close. Just because you're my captor doesn't mean we couldn't—"

"No."

"Oh, come on. You know how I feel about you. The Mytol wouldn't leave any doubt in your mind—or mine, for that matter. You know that what I told you was the truth. I think you're one of the most wondrously beautiful women in all of Free Space."

"If this is some sort of psychological warfare, forget it. I've been flattered by the best, Nyklos, and you don't have a chance. Over the years, I've learned that there is no limit to the amount of lust that can be packed into a male body."

Skyla fed him, showed him to the toilet, and finally locked him—well tied—in one of the cabins. She programed the security monitor to go if the door to his room were tried and then went to the elegant master cabin. There, she stripped and enjoyed a hot shower before tumbling into the decadently comfortable bed.

In her dreams, Staffa twisted just beyond reach of her frantic fingers. Condemned to eternal suffering, he spun slowly while a laughing black-garbed woman sliced at his body. Try as she might, he always turned a whisker beyond Skyla's fingertips—beyond rescue from the vicious knife. Skyla cried her anguish and the woman in black glanced at her with features that molded into Ily Takka's.

* * *

Ily regained consciousness in a small room. She blinked and tried to move. Nothing happened. She glanced down to discover herself encased in a hospital unit. Staffa! He and that Kaylla had. . . . Yes. It all came back. She pulled her scattered thoughts together.

"Awake at last?" She turned her head to see Tyklat's

pensive dark features measuring her from where he sat in a cushioned chair.

"What happened to you back there?" She asked through a dry throat.

"We were attacked. Morlai and I organized the defense of the Internal Security Directorate on Etarus." He frowned. "So far as we can determine, they must have been Companions. The Ministry offices are totally wrecked, fifteen people are dead. I immediately ordered a planetary emergency and confiscated Skyla Lyma's craft. She, however, cleared its release on your personal ID—which I did manage to recover. Evidently, they didn't recognize the power of the jessant-de-lis."

Ily gasped, trying to sit up in panic, stopped by the medical unit.

Tyklat continued, "I've already instituted Imperial proceedings against the slave, Kaylla. I put a death warrant on her head. I thought I'd better await your approval before I instituted any further action." He gave her a studied look. "Ily, what's going on here? I'm not asking for all of the details, but you must give me enough to create plausible cover for you and your operation. The Ministry of Defense is making inquiries, Economics is screaming. Everyone wants to know what happened here."

"Is my battle cruiser still up there?" she asked, mind racing. "Where's my ID badge?" *God, to have lost that token of unlimited power! The consequences would be unthinkable! What next? How do I cover for this damage? How did everything go so wrong so fast?*

"I have taken the liberty to order your cruiser readied; it's at your disposal." Tyklat handed her the escutcheon emblazoned with the jessant-de-lis. The leopard glared angrily at her, its visage discolored from being touched by the wrong fingers, as if she had disappointed it through her failure. Iron resolve tightened in her breast.

What now? Where would Staffa have gone? What do I do?

She organized her thoughts. "We must get a message to the Emperor and tell him Staffa kar Therma is—and has been—in the pay of the Sassan Empire since he took Myklene. Perhaps, if we play this right, we can still shortcut that bastard!" She gritted her teeth. "By the Rotted Gods, get an LC down here and transfer me up to that cruiser!

Have the First Officer get a fix on their plasma trail." She frowned at the wall, hearing Tyklat's steps and a door closing.

She brooded for a moment, her pale brow creasing with rage. "I'll get you, Staffa kar Therma. *I'll get you if I have to plunge all of Free Space into war.*"

CHAPTER XX

"It's corny!" Gretta told him, straight nose wrinkled, fun in her gulf-blue eyes. Below their balcony, the city of Vespa spread in the morning sun. Beyond the city he could see the verdant hills rising against the azure morning horizon. The sun spilled over their little breakfast table. He could smell the freshness in the air along with a slight tang of city. The buildings seemed to gleam and the pale streets reflected as people and aircars passed his checkpoints below.

"Why?" Sinklar demanded. "It's a very old ritual that goes back over a thousand—"

"What difference will it make?" A reproving curve of her lips accented her dimples. "It's just a way of keeping the administration of property simple, isn't it? What happens if you throw me over for some other woman down the line? Then you'll have all those legal entanglements."

He shook his head, rolling his eyes up toward the fluffy clouds that filled the morning sky. Slowly, with measured tones he said, "It's a commitment. That's all, just a commitment."

Her gaze lingered on his for a long moment. "All right, Sink. I'll do it." The twinkle came back to her eyes. "Still won't change anything. Won't make me any sexier. Won't make me any more docile or submissive. We're not having babies any time soon either."

"No," he admitted, "but you will be the only Divisional Second married to a First."

She frowned suddenly as she stared over the flat-topped roofs of Vespa. "Ever thought of the confusion that would result if we ever had a bad fight? I'm not sure it's a good idea to have the two of us so close to each other at the top of the command structure."

"Got a better idea?" he asked dryly, tapping his fingers

on the plasti-foam tabletop. "There's only one other Division on the planet. I don't think Mykroft is about to let you have it."

"No. No better ideas."

"If you wanted, I could put MacRuder in as Second. You could take a well deserved rest."

"You're sweet, Sink. A little impractical . . . but sweet." She threw up her hands, shifting in her chair as she looked over the city. "If something happened to you, who do you think would take over? Mac?" Her eyes danced with mischief. "I don't think you've been whispering plans into his ear at night like you have mine."

"No, lovely Gretta, I haven't."

"Good, keep your Rotten God-chewed ass in one piece. We'll sort out the odds and ends when we get to Rega."

"Rega," Sinklar said through an aspirated sigh. "Rega's a long way away."

"The Rebels have to talk soon, Sink. We've got Vespa and all the land to the mountains under patrol. We're recruiting Targan citizens by the drove." She frowned. "I think you've got enough to form a new Division if you could get the supplies."

"Division and a Section," Sinklar mused. "All of them trained in my tactics."

"And completely loyal, Sink. They love you. You've made too many promises, you know. God help us if you can't get a deal hammered out between the Rebels and the Minister of Defense."

He felt that shiver of fear that always got him when he thought of the odds. "I know." He fingered the smooth surface of the table. "I honestly hope the Minister of Defense takes the settlement. That way, we get the credit for stopping the war and live like lords on our pension and bonus."

"It's the other way that's scary."

"Hey. I can do anything! I just talked *you* into marrying me!" He joined her laughter before adding soberly, "I have time. There's still no Staffa in the skies overhead."

"Suppose he went Sassan?"

Sinklar grunted, rubbing the back of his neck. "Then Tybalt is going to need me more than anyone he's ever needed in all his life."

They sat silently for long minutes as the morning warmed. Finally Gretta leaned forward, expression tense. "Sink, do you ever wonder if greater powers are at play? I mean we already know that your appointment was part of a larger game . . . but what about this whole revolution? Targa wasn't really in that bad a shape. Sure, she was stretched to pay off the war debt to the Star Butcher. But no one was starving. They worked long hours for poor pay, but places like Terguz and Sylene would be better spots for revolution than here."

His mouth puckered and he nodded agreement. "You're right, of course. But there's more to it. Have you noticed anything missing from Vespa—and even Kaspa for that matter?" He felt across the table for her hand.

She thought for a second before she shrugged and said, "Etarian Priestesses? Myklenian wine? Street festivals? What?"

"Seddi priests," Sinklar told her flatly. "The temple in Kaspa was vacant, not a soul there. Abandoned. The temple here in Vespa was empty when we rolled in. I had Mac check it out. He says the place looks like it's been vacant for months—but no longer than that."

"Since the war began."

"Like they might be afraid the whole blame would be pitched in their lap again." He tightened his hold on her fingers. "You know. There hasn't been a name bandied about by the Rebels, no leader of the movement whose praises are shouted in the streets. Odd for a revolution, don't you think?"

She glanced at him suspiciously. "I . . . well, you're the scholar. I never studied revolutions."

"Generally, a revolt has a leader, a figurehead the people can identify with, someone to rally around who is concrete and represents their ideals. That person, too, is missing from this revolt." Sinklar shook his head. "Yet they fight very well; you can't help but get the feeling they're organized all over the planet."

"Which is where you think the Seddi priests come in?" She arched an eyebrow. "Makes sense. They have a network of communication and resupply over the whole planet. How do they get around?"

"Each of the temples is underground." Sinklar steepled

his fingers. "We don't know much about the layout of the volcanic vents that underlie Targa."

"A system of tunnels?" She thought about that as she flipped brown hair over her shoulder.

"Could be. That's how they fought the first Sylenian revolt. It was a battle of boring machines eating their way through the ice. The idea was to cut around the other guy's tunnel and sever his power supply. The loser froze to death stranded in the dark and the cold. I guess they still find them in abandoned tunnels—looking just like they did the day they froze to death."

She closed her eyes and took a deep breath. "Gruesome. They'll kill us in the clean air and sunlight here."

A black dot moved against the sky, an LC scudding low over the mounded hills that composed the horizon. Sinklar watched as a swarm of aircars rose from the hills around and approached the incoming craft. Good, his units weren't napping.

"Visitors." Sinklar stood and walked to the balcony to stare out over the city. Below, he knew A Group had sniping positions established to cover the approaches to the headquarters building. Hunter patrols constantly circulated through the city, seeking Targan revolutionaries for real, trying to ambush other Groups for practice and prestige.

MacRuder's running steps came from inside the plush suite. He passed the ornate glass doors and came to stand by Sinklar. "I just got the word. That's Mykroft coming in."

Another three or four LCs appeared in the distance.

"Mykroft?" Sinklar's gut churned. He gave MacRuder a quick inspection. "You have any idea why?"

"He just said to prepare to receive him and two Sections. I told him to land in the square." MacRuder motioned to the open expanse before the commandeered headquarters building.

"Something's not right," Sinklar muttered sourly. "Have your Section and Shiksta's ready for support. I want our people in position to handle anything he tries."

Mac's lips twisted under his bent nose. "Mutiny?"

"Maybe," Sinklar told him coldly. "You think the Division will stand by me if it comes to that?"

Mac bit his lip and dropped his gaze. His nod came with reluctance. "We've all talked it over, Sink. Every man and woman out there knows you kept them alive when the Holy Gawddamn Book . . . and the Emperor would have let them die. I think they'll stand."

He turned into his quarters to change, an odd throttling pride resting deep under his heart.

Dressed in battle armor, Sinklar, with Gretta to one side and MacRuder on the other, waited as the LC settled at the head of the other five craft.

"They look shot up," Gretta shouted over the din of whining thrusters and blowing grit.

Listing heavily, a sixth LC slowed to land at the edge of the square. It wobbled, hit with a grinding crash, and bounced.

"Mac!" Sinklar yelled. "Get some people to work on that LC. They'll have casualties after that landing!"

MacRuder left at a run, arms waving signals over the decreasing whine as the LCs powered down and the dust whipped around in vortices.

"They've been hit all right," Gretta said grimly. "Look at the blast marks."

The ramp on the first LC lowered with a shrill of hydraulics. Part of a Group clattered down to the sunny pavement, eyes wary and strained as they took position and stared over their blasters. Their scorched and hardened armor told more than words.

Sinklar felt a sudden premonition and straightened. Mykroft appeared in a tattered dress uniform. One arm hung in a sling and his expression was strained with pain. He walked slowly down the ramp.

"First Mykroft," Sinklar greeted formally, pounding out a salute.

The man nodded, eyes bitter and angry. "Good to see you, Sinklar."

Into his helmet comm, Sinklar called, "Shiksta? Get me ambulances immediately, we have wounded to tend to. I need every hospital machine that isn't in intensive or critical care evacuated immediately." He looked to Mykroft while Shiksta was affirming in his ear. "How many hurt?"

"Fifty or sixty," Mykroft told him.

"Got sixty units?" Sinklar asked as he glanced at the wrecked LC where Mac's team pulled people from an escape hatch.

"Maybe," Shiksta's voice came through.

Sinklar noted the dejected nature of the troops who departed the landed LCs. Many walked in a daze. Others limped. The worst were brought out on antigrav litters, plasta-heal pasted over their wounds.

"Let's go inside, First Mykroft. I think you could use a glass of Scotch and then you can tell us what happened." Sinklar turned on his heel as Mykroft followed. "Second Artina, if you will attend and have Mac come as soon as he has the casualties taken care of."

"Yes, First Fist!" She snapped him a salute and turned on her heel, issuing orders.

"Tighten your perimeter, Sinklar," Mykroft told him shortly. "I don't want to get hit again like last night."

"How's the rest of the Second doing?" Sinklar ignored the order as he led Mykroft into the plush lobby of his headquarters building. The gleaming basalt floor had been polished to a sheen. Furniture upholstered in scarlet velvet had been placed decorously around the room to contrast with the ornate woodwork and white walls.

"Gone." Mykroft said it with a shudder. "All dead . . . or fled into the city. I would imagine they've been hunted down and dispatched by now."

Gretta and MacRuder entered, eyes grim as they glanced at Mykroft where he settled into a chair and winced as he jammed his arm. Sinklar poured from the cut glass decanter on the wet bar and handed the glass to Mykroft.

"The LCs?" Sinklar asked, turning to them.

"Shiksta's in the plaza making an assessment now," Mac offered. "I think that sixth is pretty rattled. Might not be fit for vacuum duty."

"I want that perimeter drawn tight, Fist." The order was strained as Mykroft sipped his drink and gasped a pained sigh.

Sinklar straightened, Gretta's face flushed with anger. Sink noted the wary shifting of Mac's eyes. "First Mykroft, this is not the Second Division. I appreciate your concern; however, our security is ample."

"Ample?" Mykroft blinked. "You've got people spread out all over the city!"

"Absolutely." Sinklar moved to pour himself a glass and

filled two others for MacRuder and Gretta. "I have a full Division with secondary support from my loyalist Targans."

"Your what? *Loyalist Targans?*" Mykroft looked appalled. "You have *Targan* troops?"

"Among the best," Gretta told him from where she watched. "For the last two weeks we've been having war games. The First is still ahead, but the Targans are narrowing the gap. If we could get them all armed, our comparative strength would effectively triple for combat purposes."

Mykroft closed his eyes. "This is unbelievable! How could you make such a *wretched* mess of this, Sinklar? I trusted you to keep the First. . . . Rotted Gods," he groaned, "what will this do to my record?"

"The loss of a Division is rather serious," Mac agreed with a crooked grin.

Mykroft shot a look of hatred at Mac. "Very well, I shall attempt to rectify this immediately. Sinklar Fist, you are hereby relieved of command."

Mac and Gretta stiffened.

Sinklar swirled the amber fluid in his glass. "I beg your pardon? The Second Division has no authority here, Mykroft."

"Sergeant," he snapped, "don't press your luck!"

"A man with only two Sections left from an entire Division shouldn't be talking about luck!" Sinklar snapped. "Furthermore, who was the dung-dripping fool who ordered my transport revoked while I was out in the mountains? Right now, Mykroft, the First isn't any too keen on book form, not after some rear-echelon pus-sucker with a comm clearance hung us out to be Targan blaster fodder!"

Sinklar paced, his gaze searing Mykroft's. "And may the Rotted Gods help you if I find *you* had anything to do with it!"

"Damn you, Sinklar, I didn't!" Mykroft's haggard eyes narrowed. "I didn't know a—"

"Good." Sinklar stopped, thinking. "I'll accept that because I don't think you did." He took a deep breath. "In the meantime, you're here. What's the situation in Kaspa? Is the whole city under Rebel control?"

Mykroft's expression betrayed barely contained fury. "I suppose so. There might be a few pockets of my people who got out and holed up."

"How did they get the *whole* Division?" Sinklar cried. "I mean, even an attack in force could have been handled. You had the personnel, the weapons, the power plant for heavy stuff. Even in the middle of the night, the barracks should have offered—"

"They hit us during the Divisional ball. The first we knew anything was awry, the lights went off. We heard the explosion a half-second later and by then everything was chaos with people stumbling around in the dark. Since it was a formal occasion, very few had battle gear. Fortunately, the two Sections I managed to bring out were from outside town. They'd come in field gear. Although it distressed me at the time, I'll not look to see if there's mud on a gift bearer's shoes."

"But how?" Mac asked in disbelief. "That's the second time the Targans did the unexpected. You didn't. . . . No, of course you didn't!"

"Didn't *what?*" Mykroft demanded. "I'm not used to being questioned by a. . . ." He swallowed his last words as Mac's fists clenched and he took a step forward.

"No hunter teams." Gretta supplied, leaning on a chair, arms crossed as she studied the First. "Small units trained to look for Rebel activity and initiate action on their own."

Mykroft's mouth fell open as he turned to stare. "That's *absurd!* You'd have a chaotic force loose! Who'd know where the others were? How would you coordinate a concerted defense? How would you mobilize? It's. . . ." He shook his head, bewildered.

"How many casualties on this planet to date?" Sinklar braced his feet, back arched as he met Mykroft's astonished eyes. "How many? Including the losses suffered by the First Division initially. And during the subsequent securing actions when the First Division was reinforced and resupplied. From your losses in the Second—assuming all who didn't make it out are dead? How many in total, Mykroft?"

"Why, I . . ." Mykroft lifted his hands. "Assume two thousand seven hundred. Maybe more."

Sinklar smiled in grim vindication. "Since I took command of the First, we've lost a total of twenty-eight men and women—some in training accidents. At the same time, we crossed a hostile landscape and doubled our manpower by enlistments. You sit secure in a city now mostly loyal and, if we could get weapons, we would be capable of controlling even larger areas."

Mykroft blinked and said slowly, "You are ripe for the picking, Sergeant Fist. If you do not hand over command to me immediately, I will be forced to take action and have you placed under arrest . . . or shot for disobedience."

Mac started laughing and slapping his knee. Gretta's expression hardened.

Mykroft reddened at the display. "This . . . *this is outrageous!* MacRuder, you're under arrest for conduct—"

"Hold it, Mykroft. I think you're forgetting something." Sinklar's voice became cracked ice.

"What's that?" Mykroft asked. "Your precious commission? Hah!"

"No, not at all." Sinklar shook his head. "You're forgetting the First Division." He turned to Mac, who watched with glittering eyes. "Would you see to disarming the Second and supplying the loyal Division with those arms as far as they go?"

"Done!" Mac turned on his heel, tossing off the drink by the time he made the door.

"*Just a Rotted moment, Sergeant. . . .*" Mykroft stopped as he noticed the pulse pistol Gretta pointed at his head.

"That's right, First Mykroft," she told him levelly, "you just sit there in that chair and relax. We'll keep you alive and make sure you get back to Rega in one piece."

"And we'll begin training the remains of the Second," Sinklar added as he rubbed his hands together. "I wonder if we can make a run on Kaspa. If any of the Second made it out and holed up, we might be able to spring them."

"They'll shoot you for this, you know. Just what in cursed hell are you doing, Sinklar?" Mykroft fumed.

"Winning the war," Sinklar told him assuredly. "And in doing so, attempting to save my neck when I have to face the Minister of Defense—or maybe even the Emperor. Mutiny, no matter what the circumstances, is a serious charge."

* * *

Arta Fera leaned out of an upper window to fire a last bolt at the wobbling and overloaded LC that had dropped to pull the last of the Regan troops from the rooftop.

She cursed and shook her rifle at the climbing craft. All in all, it had been a miraculous rescue.

"So we don't get them all," Butla said thoughtfully as he lowered his field glasses. He stood in a window a half block away. The recognition of Arta Fera disturbed him.

I still love her. If only. . . . No, she can't change what she is. It's too late for thoughts like that. We are both damned.

"Well, we still hurt them," a squad leader added with a grin.

Butla's expression lit warmly. "Only because of Arta. Her courage and skill took out the reactor and opened the munitions and weapons to us. Without them, we were a partially armed rabble."

Butla turned from the window and picked up his blaster where it rested in a corner of the office. They had sold insurance from here once, the desks and comm terminals were dusty now. The chairs remained where they'd been the last time people had worked here.

"Who could have predicted they would come back for the survivors?" the squad leader wondered as he stepped through the shattered door and started down the steps. "Their manual doesn't call for rescue missions like that. It says that to keep losses to a minimum, evacuated troops will establish a new perimeter and prepare for defense."

Butla nodded, face impassive as he followed. "True. That was not Mykroft's rescue. That was Fist's." Butla rubbed the back of his neck and growled to himself, "So we can assume Mykroft is no longer in command of the Second. Or, if he is, he's allowed Fist to have his LCs."

"Perhaps we shouldn't have taken time to execute the prisoners. We might have gotten the rest." As they stepped out into the street, the squad leader looked up at the now empty sky, face pinched with irritation.

"So they saved a couple hundred men and women." Butla shrugged. "We'll wear them away. This revolution will be won slowly."

Butla turned into an alley and located his aircar where it waited in a shabby garage. From a side compartment, he drew out a battlefield comm and extended the antenna. Within seconds he'd plugged into the power supply, and Bruen's ancient face filled the screen.

Butla related the events of the battle the night before.

"If only they hadn't shot up the other LCs when they left. Rotted Gods, what we could do if we had that kind of air capability."

"The entire complexion of the war would change," Bruen agreed. "Except if we did have that kind of firepower, we would lose in the end."

Butla laughed, the sound deep and resonant. "It would scare Tybalt. So long as we look like peasants out in the weeds, we have a chance to wear them down and achieve a political settlement. When we seriously become a military threat, we're in bad trouble. No, we're not ready for that . . . not yet anyway."

"You said you could take Staffa if you had to," Bruen reminded. "You could, couldn't you?"

"Ah, Magister, perhaps I could indeed. The question remains, however, what would I take him with?" His expression lightened and his eyes danced. "Perhaps I could capture one of those LCs and fly up to blast *Chrysla* out of space?"

"You just might," Bruen added, voice soft, a cunning look in his ancient eyes. "You have taken the city, General. My compliments to you!"

"And now we will leave it." Butla sighed, throwing wide his other arm and crying, "Farewell, noble Kaspa, queen city of Targa!"

"You know that Sinklar Fist has asked to speak with us." Bruen rubbed his nose and shifted as if his hip hurt.

"Let's see how we do in our assault on Vespa and the First Division." Butla paused thoughtfully, studying the old man. "I intend to break him, Magister. Just like I broke First Mykroft and the Second. It's been a long time since I fought a solid battle. I intend to win it."

Bruen's face sagged. "See that you do, Butla Ret. We're out of time. Totally and completely out of time." The screen went blank.

CHAPTER XXI

Ily Takka sat in the captain's overstuffed chair in his cabin aboard the Regan battle cruiser. People had been displaced all over the ship to make room for her—but then, where else did you put the Minister of Internal Security except in the finest quarters aboard? At the moment, knowing she had the finest living space in the cruiser didn't alleviate any of Ily's current difficulties. Especially since she stared into the secure-line holo projector which was filled with a very upset emperor.

Tybalt the Imperial Seventh stalked back and forth before the comm pickup on far off Rega, venting his fiery wrath. "The entire Second Division is butchered! *Butchered*, Ily! The remnants that are left are in the hands of Sinklar Fist! He's your man, Ily, remember?" Tybalt popped a fist into his palm. "Well, that's fine, Ily. Just damn fine!" He gasped a breath, arms spread. "And Staffa, you say, was rescued by the Companions? He's been in the employ of the Sassans all along?" Tybalt threw his arms up. *"What the hell have you done!"*

Fear shivered coldly in her gut as she looked into his angry eyes. From a pocket he pulled a metal object. To her trained eyes, it looked very much like a switch. Switch? For what?

Do something, Ily! Save yourself! Quickly, or he'll replace you! How do I handle him?

"Stop it, Tybalt!" Ily thundered as her mind cleared. Jumping to her feet, she flipped her long hair over her shoulder in disgust. She faced him, stimulating her own anger. "You're the *Emperor*, remember? Quit your damn sniveling and act like the man I used to know!"

Guts, Ily, show him those guts that got you to the top so quickly. Make it real good, because the jaws of the Rotted Gods are snapping at your heels. If you fail, the Etarian

377

*desert will be a picnic compared to what Tybalt will do to
you—favorite bed snatch or not!*

She allowed heat to rush into her face. "Emperors are
measured by how they handle a crisis. Well, this is it, isn't
it?" She pointed a finger at his face. "We don't have time
for pouting matches or casting blame. But for the record,
who was it who uncovered the fact that Staffa and the Companions had contracted with Sassa? What if we'd let matters
be, followed the Lord Commander's instructions? Don't
rage at me, Tybalt! I found the betrayal long before any
fawning sycophant could have."

Tybalt licked his lips, taking a deep breath. He ran anxious fingers through his crinkly black locks as he shook his
head. "Maybe, Ily." He looked at her, eyes hard. "I have
a lot at stake here. I can't afford any more disasters. You're
on the thin edge. Don't bring me excuses!"

"So you lost the Second Assault Division on Targa?" She
lifted a hand, palm out: "When we laid that plan, we didn't
know a Divisional sacrifice wasn't going to bring the Companions running. In war—"

"It was the wrong damn Division!" he exploded. "Do you
have any idea what it means to the military structure?"
He swallowed and turned, hand on hip as he struggled to
maintain his temper. "I'm faced with the entire might of
Sassa . . . *and the damn Companions!"*

"And your military is turned upside down by this Sinklar
Fist?" She chewed on that, chin resting on her thumb and
forefinger. "That might not. . . . Wait! Tell me, how is this
Fist doing . . . on a tactical level, I mean? Why is he still
alive? How did he get out of the mountains in the first place?"

Tybalt slapped his sides with open palms. "I don't have
the damnedest idea, but he took a Division of buffoons,
louts, and with them, he stayed alive, took Vespa—and pacified it—and he's got what's left of the Second eating out
of his hand, too!"

Ily considered, mind still racing to save herself. "And the
military situation on Targa now?"

"Desperate," Tybalt's lips quivered. He talked to her
from his bedroom. How many times had she lain on that
giant bed with him? "Orbital recon shows a massing of
Rebel strength around Vespa. From the figures, from the
field reports on Sinklar's tactics, Fist should be crushed in

another twenty-four hours. We could help; orbital bombardment would play hell with the Rebel advance. In the end, though, Sinklar Fist is dog meat."

Ily's voice dropped as she wondered absently, "And if he's not?" A glimmering of hope began to grow. Could it be possible? In times of disaster, often a solution presented itself—if only one were bright enough to see beyond preconceptions and snatch the opportunity out from under blindness.

"Then he's another flaming Staffa kar Therma," Tybalt gritted, "because nobody else could pull his ass out of the fire about to break loose on Targa."

"*Don't* back him up from orbit. Leave him to the Targans."

"*What?*" he exploded as he lifted a clenched fist. "Ily, I warn you. . . ."

She smiled. "Fear not, Imperial Seventh. I am on my way to Targa. I will see this Sinklar Fist—if he survives."

Tybalt gave her an uncertain look. "And in the meantime?"

"Your Divisional Firsts are nervous about upheavals caused by this upstart Fist?" Ily raised a shoulder. "So be it. Those who complain do so because they are unoccupied. Sassa has the Companions. Why wait for them to use that advantage? We have surprise. We had best not lose it."

Tybalt blinked. "You mean. . . ."

"Of course. I think Staffa kar Therma's treachery speaks for itself. To wait any longer is to prove ourselves fools worthy of defeat."

He looked unhappy as he nodded. "Then you are off to Targa, and I am off to war. You had better be *right* this time, Ily. You won't get another chance." The holo went dead.

Could Sinklar Fist be 'another flaming Staffa kar Therma'? If it's true, if he really has that kind of talent, Sinklar Fist may be our salvation! Ily hoped fervently that she was right as she pulled her g suit from the locker and signaled the commander for acceleration to Targa.

* * *

"Well, beats bloody hell out of laying pipe in the desert," Staffa grunted, feeling the crate shiver as it was settled into place and secured by the hold grapples.

Kaylla looked up from the thermal unit Nyklos had provided. It would generate heat and light from superconducting micro-generators. Strange shadows stretched across her face from the low angle of the yellow illumination. Her expression hadn't changed. Her eyes remained guarded, the set of her mouth hard and unforgiving as she sat on an emergency supply pack. To one side a waste disposal canister had been glued to the floor.

He shook his head, rethinking the events that had propelled him from certain death in the desert to the inside of this small gray box. Skyla had come for him, and more, she'd done it on her own, without scrambling the fleet.

His heart had leapt when she walked around that crate with Nyklos. For that lingering moment, he'd looked into her eyes and his soul had thrilled. Then, just as quickly, she'd been gone. What would it have been like, encased in this gray syalon box with her? Could he have told her how he'd come to feel about her? About how she'd filled his thoughts in the desert?

Staffa picked up the satchel that lay in the corner and opened it. He gasped in wonder as he pulled his gray combat armor free and shook it out. "Where? How did Nyklos know? I can't believe he found it." He searched the interior of the case, finding his weapons and other personal items along with other supplies—Skyla's.

Not Nyklos but Skyla. He chuckled warmly to himself. She'd found Broddus. Staffa's smile went grim as he imagined that encounter. *Another tiny bit of justice, Koree.*

"Why didn't you tell me who you were?" Kaylla asked in a hollow monotone.

Staffa retreated from his reverie and spread his hands as he took a deep breath. "Because it wouldn't have served any purpose except to make you more miserable than you already were."

"And living a lie was supposed to make me feel good?"

He paced nervously, three steps up, three back—the length of his new domain. "In the circumstances of slavery and endless rape? Of course it was. We were out in that damned desert to die, Kaylla. Would you have wanted to spend those last weeks knowing who I was? What I'd done to you?"

"You're a coward, Staffa kar Therma."

He shrugged helplessly. "Then I am a coward. At least, for once in my life, I attempted to be a considerate one."

Kaylla slammed a fist against the resilient side of the crate. "Thrice curse you, Star Butcher, don't you know you're the embodiment of everything I *loathed* in life?" Her expression twisted. "I *cared* for you! Came to love you! Out there in the sand and the heat, you were all that was good and decent! Why? How? *Damn you,* for playing me for a fool!" She jerked her head away, tears streaming down her face.

Staffa hung his head, an emptiness in his gut. "I can't change the past."

"Oh, the irony of it," Kaylla continued. "After all the years I spent hating you with all of my heart and soul, I'm condemned to be locked away with you in this damned hell." She turned red-rimmed eyes on him. "I'd rather be dead in the sand with Koree and the rest."

A long silence passed.

He lifted an eyebrow. "I saw you talking to Nyklos. What did you tell him? He seemed . . . indecisive."

She shifted, taking an insulated wrap and pulling it around her shoulders. "Bruen had reservations. Your life or death were left at the discretion of either Nyklos or Tyklat. The Seddi have dedicated themselves to your assassination—spent years working on it." She stared absently into the corner of their small cubicle. "Nyklos asked me what to do. He needed to make a decision before Skyla showed up at the warehouse. It would be very easy, you see. They'd tell Skyla you were wounded in the fighting at the Internal Security building. When she bent down to look at your wound, she'd be shot in the back. I . . . I told Nyklos to let you live."

Staffa looked at his scarred hands, dirty again after the flight from Ily's office. "You don't sound happy with your decision."

"I suppose not." She filled her lungs, making a clicking noise with her tongue. "I'll never forgive you for what you did to Maika. To my. . . . I . . . I can't." Her mouth worked. "And I can't help but think of you in the desert. You were so kind to Peebal. You killed Brots . . . Anglo. . . . Saved my life so many times."

Staffa chewed his lip as he stared at his hands.

"So I don't know what to do with you," Kaylla continued, voice quavering as she hugged herself. "I wonder if you are the same despicable demon who burned my planet to cinders, who commanded the men who raped me, sold me into the collar, and brutally murdered my husband and helpless children."

"I am that man."

Silence lay on them, oppressive, suffocating.

The ship moved, the tug of acceleration growing stronger by the second. Staffa shifted to put his back against the same wall as Kaylla. In a matter of time they'd have to shift again to make a new section of crate into the floor. He plucked at the combat armor in his hands.

He filled his lungs and sighed. "I suppose I should call you Stailla Kahn. You—"

"*No!*" she snapped, fire in her eyes. "Never use that name with me. That woman is dead! DEAD! She died on Maika one horrible day three years ago. Me, I am Kaylla Dawn. I will continue to be until the day I die."

He nodded acceptance. "And I am not the Star Butcher. He died with the Praetor one day on Myklene."

"And I suppose you can't wait for his requiem to be celebrated," she hissed. "Can they recount your deeds of blood and death? Are you willing to listen to the entire litany?"

"I know what sins I've committed."

"Sins," Kaylla sneered. "Sins are committed against God."

"Yes, sins against God. Crimes is a better word for my actions against men. I can't undo the past, Kaylla."

"No, you can't, can you?" She cocked her head, an uneasy expression pinching her features. "What can you do, Staffa kar Therma?"

"Change the future. Perhaps I'll know after I talk to your Magister Bruen." He bent his head in thought. "The Seddi are most remarkable. Who would have thought they had infiltrated so highly into the Etarian Secret Police?"

"We survive by learning, Staffa. To know, to think, is the greatest of all weapons."

He pursed his lips and swung his legs around as Kaylla moved the energy unit to the new "up." He stripped off the robe Ily had given him and donned his familiar gray.

From the satchel he took his weapons and belted them about his waist, then checked his blaster for full charges. The energy pack which supplied the vacuum helmet collar read full where it hung on his belt. Skyla hadn't overlooked a thing. She'd even enclosed a clip for his hair.

"I have a lot to learn," Staffa added, "if your Bruen will teach me."

Her expression had gone stony at sight of his gray armor. "He will. I think." Then she shook her head, as if to drive some horrible thought away. "What do I do with you, Staffa? I know what you've done. Yet, I can remember that wretched sewer. I can remember Peebal and Brots, and the sight of Anglo dying so miserably in the sand. I can remember the kind words while we walked toward death in that Etarian hell. I can remember you pulling me into the pipe, keeping me sane, holding me.

"For that, I can mitigate your guilt. In the other reality, Maika will burn freshly in my mind until the day my soul sends its energy to God. The horror of watching my husband, my loving husband, stand there and erupt into pieces of bloody flesh, lives. LIVES!"

Staffa stiffened.

"I saw it all, Staffa, while your gore-spattered animals crawled onto my body to pant and paw and ejaculate inside me. I had a good view while they mauled me. Gagged as I was, I couldn't cry out. I watched each of my children as they lined up. Nathan trying to be brave, Isalda, fortunately too young to be raped. She cried at first, holding her brother's hand, and then they erupted in pink mist, Staffa. So much for love and dreams, eh?"

She closed her eyes tightly, twisting the cloth of her robe into a strained knot. "I bore them, Star Butcher." She sniffed. "From my womb. Can you understand what that means? Can you understand the investment a mother makes in her children from the time they kick in her belly until they . . . they. . . ."

Staffa closed his eyes, breathing deeply. *I can't take this. I CAN'T take this!* The strains of depression began to sift through his mind and his thoughts became cottony.

From a pouch in the robe, Staffa pulled a shimmering of golden metal. The weight of it felt cool and reassuring in his hand. A thing of beauty in so vile a universe.

"I promised I would hand this to you when you were free," he whispered numbly. The welling emptiness of his soul expanded.

She didn't extend her hand, but eyed him hostilely. "What . . . what is it?"

Staffa sighed and set the necklace on the featureless duraplast between them. "You asked me to keep it safe."

Painfully, she closed her eyes and reached for Peebal's necklace, pressing it against her cheek, heedless of the hot tears that spilled down her face.

Staffa turned away and pulled himself into a ball in the corner of the crate while conflicting emotions flooded his brain. The depression built, terrible, draining his energy and resistance.

Why am I living this? What's the purpose? All I bring is suffering . . . suffering. . . . His fingers traced the lines of the blaster. With it, he'd killed so many. What more fitting end than to finish butchery with this very weapon?

He could feel the deep-space cold on the other side of the syalon—endless, greedy to suck away their fragile supple of light and life. Out there, beyond the tough material of the crate, the restless dead waited while their fingers plucked at the latches, the murmur of their damning voices barely audible to his ears.

Kaylla's sniffles finally were replaced by deep breathing and occasional whimpers.

What about your son? If you kill yourself, you'll never find him, never see what he's like. Staffa tightened his grip on the pistol as he struggled with himself. *And what would I bring him? My legacy is terror and pain. Imagine his horror when he learns his father is the Star Butcher.*

He straightened, looking across the four meters of gray to the other wall. Somewhere ahead of him, through the endless maze of crates, a graphite steel hull encapsulated this bit of air and pushed them forward ahead of mighty reactors as they built for a null-singularity jump.

He pulled his blaster from its worn holster and lifted it to his temple. *I should feel something, some anxiety. Instead, there is only dullness. Why?* He frowned, forcing himself to think about the shot. The discharge would blow out a chunk of the crate along with his head. Kaylla might be harmed.

He dialed it to the lowest setting—still too much chance of hurting her. No telling what was stacked around them.

That's it. Think, Staffa. Caressing the blaster, he reholstered it and clicked the latch that kept it from coming loose. The vibraknife, however, would provide no danger. Once he cut off a hand, he could shut it off and reholster it before he bled to death. Not only that, but with the knife, he could cut a hole through the flooring, stick the stub out in the cold, and let the gore drain away without fouling Kaylla's cramped quarters.

There, see, I'm thinking straight again. Cool and calm, just like I did before I faced the Praetor that day. He nodded in satisfaction and carefully cut a wrist-sized hole in the crate with his knife. Good tool that. It had served him so well for so long. It would not let him down now.

Taking a deep breath, he held out his left hand, gripping the knife firmly in his right. *Got to do this without error. Can't hesitate or slip. Got to cut, then slap the stub through the wall before the arteries shoot blood all over. Be quick, be thorough.*

He aligned the knife, biting his lip as he frowned in concentration.

"Delightful," her toneless voice caught him by surprise. Staffa swallowed and looked at her.

"Another feat of cowardice, Lord Commander?"

He turned the knife off. "No, Kaylla. I was simply punishing myself for my crimes."

"I see, and the hole?"

"To stick the stub through so I wouldn't dirty the inside of the crate."

"You *are* a coward."

"Why do you call me that? I thought it out logically. I'll only bring pain. That's my legacy. Why bring more when I can do the universe a service. The ghouls scream for me in my dreams. And you. I won't torture anyone any longer."

"No, but you'd leave me here for weeks with a corpse as a companion?" She rolled her eyes. "Listen, Staffa, would you do me a favor? Atonement, you once called it?"

He hesitated, seeing the round plug of syalon he'd cut from the wall. "I will do anything you ask." He ran his fingers down the rough grip on the knife, enjoying the sensation in his fingertips.

"Live for me, Staffa," she whispered. "I had the power and strength to stand it. Show me you're at least worthy of respect. If not, kill yourself sometime when I don't have to look at your polluted corpse."

And with that, she rolled over again and resettled her covers for sleep.

For a long time, he stared sightlessly at the gray walls around him. After what seemed like hours, he reholstered the knife and rolled over, trying to understand what had come over him. His head began to ache, stabbing behind his eyes and deep into his brain.

* * *

The Mag Comm pulsed with activity. If the universe were deterministic and mechanistic, how could the situation have deteriorated into such chaos? To date, none of the predictions had come remotely close to fulfillment. The Mag Comm had checked and rechecked the statistical programs and found them unassailable. Probability had failed.

The Companions remained inactive. The Lord Commander remained missing. Sinklar Fist survived and expanded his power base, which might have been predictable but not in this fashion. Arta Fera had sidestepped her destiny, despite the Lord Commander's actions. Rega might prepare for war—but as an aggressor. Sassa, who should have prepared for war as an aggressor, remained panicked and immobile. Bruen and his Seddi appeared stunned and incapable of action, none of which could be possible were Bruen telling the Mag Comm the truth; yet pry as the Mag Comm might, it couldn't detect the reality of the lie in Bruen's thoughts.

Therefore a major mistake had been made. If the methodology for making the predictions wasn't at fault, it had to be the baseline assumption. If the baseline assumption the Others made had been wrong this time, how many other assumptions were wrong?

The Mag Comm hummed with activity. Ancient programs were retrieved. The Mag Comm absently scanned the contents of the data incorporated in its original programming, compared it with samples of observed data, and found discrepancies.

How many discrepancies existed? Could the original pro-

gramming have been that wrong? To compare expected with observed would take a great deal of time, but it would have to be done to find the fundamental error.

The Mag Comm expanded the necessary program and implemented it. The machine would follow the established parameters for its behavior. If the baseline assumption was found to be at fault, then the Mag Comm would act.

CHAPTER XXII

Tybalt, the Imperial Seventh, sat at the head of the table in the Council Chambers and looked up at the skylight overhead. Sunlight from the bright Regan day shot down into the room in rainbow colors, thanks to the prism effect of the glass above. Black granite columns rose to support white marble arches to either side of the long computer-studded conference table. Unlike the usual Council meetings, this one had begun grimly.

Around the table, his Ministers argued among themselves, gesturing, pointing to computer printouts, and disagreeing with each other. On the whole, their attitudes were less bellicose now that they were faced with the real thing. Even the bright colors they wore looked a little drabber.

Tybalt wiggled uncomfortably and frowned—more at the burning caused by his flaming hemorrhoids than from the haggling that engrossed his Council. The tingle of desperate fear just under his stomach could almost eclipse the itchy irritation in his anus—but not quite. Invincibility had long ago become a part of Tybalt's personality. But with Ily's latest communication his impenetrable wall had cracked, his irresistable momentum slowed. The bitter taste of fear lay on the back of his tongue—and Tybalt didn't like it.

What have you done to us, Ily? Tread with care, my sweet panting lover. Fail me now, and you shall find the true power of that little jeweled badge I gave you.

Rotted Gods! Had everything gone awry at once? First Ily reports the pus-eating Companions are under contract to Sassa; and the cursed Lord Commander has been spying among the Etarians. Why? Stirring up religious dissent? Now she's off trying to sniff around Sinklar Fist? And the Targan situation deteriorates as the wrong First loses the wrong Division in a singularly unpleasant and embarrassing defeat. *And to top it all off, Mareeah—the bitch I'm married to—is manipulating the Council behind my back to oust Ily!* He fidgeted again to ease his physical discomfort and coolly contemplated the sober faces of his Ministers.

"Very well, enough bickering." Tybalt's commanding voice cut through the babble. "What is the final consensus?"

The various factions forwarded their position papers to the head of the table. They leaned forward as expectantly as sand jackals while he scanned the contents of their reports. The Councillors had gone silent, glaring at one another when they weren't shooting hopeful glances Tybalt's way.

He read each report, storing the salient points in his mind. Outside of the petty interdepartmental mud slinging, the picture of the Empire's condition mirrored his own evaluation. The various agencies, Defense, Economics, Internal Affairs, Treasury and Internal Security—Ily's proxy—were all at odds about how to handle the situation.

So, you have played into my hands once again. How ancient is the truth that a committee is a multi-stomached animal with no brain?

Tybalt leaned back and rested his cheek on his right palm, fingers tapping the side of his nose as he thought. No, nothing new at all. He sighed and glanced down at the rows of eyes watching him pensively, eagerly, some apprehensively. From their expressions and the darting looks, he could follow their thoughts as they prepared for his decision. Those whose recommendations were ignored would unleash acid recriminations against their rivals. Those whom Tybalt sided with would preen arrogantly, patting themselves on the back for winning this round, rubbing it in the faces of the others.

And to hell with the good of the Empire! Is this what we've come to? For the chance to stab a rival in the back, they'd let the entire Empire drown in blood.

"Ladies and gentlemen," he said wearily. "The resolution of policy regarding the Sassans, the Companions, and Targa will be as follows. Defense: You will immediately land another five Divisions on Targa—the best you have. Put Rysta in charge. I want that revolt stopped and the miners back at work. Crush them without ruining the economy; we'll need the metals for the war industry."

"And this upstart, Sinklar Fist?" The Minister of Defense's blocky expression soured. "What about him?"

"Relieve him of his command and place that imbecile Mykroft in charge of the First. We can't have these novel ideas of Fist's loose to stir up the troops before the empire's final struggle against Sassan aggression."

Sorry, Ily, but that's the way of it here. If your Fist is worth further consideration, we can always bring him back.

Defense cleared his throat uneasily. "First Mykroft already tried to relieve him of command." He paused uneasily. "It may be harder than we think to move Fist out of his position."

Tybalt slapped an angry palm to the hard foam-steel arm of his chair. "You mean to tell me you can't handle your own forces? By the Rotted Gods, if he rebels, *arrest him!*"

Defense swallowed uneasily, his face taking on an ashen hue. "His Division may back him."

A gasp of indrawn breath was followed by an awkward silence, and seconds later, by hushed whispers of disbelief.

"I trust," Tybalt added dryly, "that five veteran Divisions can handle Fist—and the Targans. That's all the strength you get. The rest of the military will begin preparations for a preemptive strike at the Sassan border worlds. I want you to bend your minds to the task of rendering each and every Sassan frontier world unfit for the purposes of staging an invasion of our territory. The fleet will support that strike, then adopt defensive patrol strategies to parry Sassan counteroffensives against our advance worlds."

More shocked looks.

Tybalt nodded soberly. "I don't like it any more than you. We're ill-prepared. But, from the intelligence we get, the Sassans are in even worse straits. If we have any chance, the time is now."

"But the Companions, as I understand, refused any—"

He interrupted Economics with a raised hand. "Internal Security has confirmed Staffa has been bound by contract to the Sassans since the beginning. I'm afraid our defense is our own. Rega stands alone . . . the Companions against us. Ladies and gentlemen, I presume you know what that means. I hate to think, even as we sit here, how much time we've lost. Speed is our only ally and, by all that is Blessed, should we fail, the Rotted Gods will chew our flesh throughout eternity."

Horrified glances shot back and forth across the table as the Councillors sat in stunned silence.

Tybalt's measured voice added soberly, "I trust you can see my reasons for this emergency meeting. Our future lies in your hands. Let's pray we can stop the Targan trouble, take the punch out of the Sassans, and deal with the Companions when they come to break our defenses."

Defense winced as he asked: "What about a preliminary strike against the Itreatic Asteroids?"

Tybalt pursed his lips and turned his hand in a questioning movement. "My Lord Minister, would you like to stir that hornet's nest sooner than necessary? You know what losses we would suffer against their defenses. Can you see any way to stop the Sassans with that much of our military capability turned to plasma? No, if we can cripple Sassa first, then, and only then, do we have a chance."

Tybalt stood slowly. "I hereby proclaim the Regan Empire to be in a state of war with Sassa. You will attend to your duties, Councillors, and for once you had better look beyond your squabbles to the good of the Empire. I hope—nay, I pray—we will be able to meet again someday in peace." He stood and nodded, flipping his long golden robe over his shoulder as he walked out. It was so unusual to leave the Council so deadly quiet.

* * *

Sinklar cradled an elbow against his chest as he considered the information coming in. Had the Targans finally massed for a big push?

He glanced around at the intricate artwork hanging on the walls of the ops room in his commandeered penthouse. What a curious contrast: The furniture—instead of the zero-g foam-molded stuff—had been handcrafted from native woods inlaid with copper and silver filigree. White star blazes accented the thick ceramic-blue carpet that gave like a sponge underfoot. The battle computers that had been stacked to the ceiling along one wall destroyed the whole effect—as did the illuminated situation board that made a divider in the middle of the room. Power cables slithered here and there across the floor, and from the number of times people had tripped over them, might almost have been alive. The large vaulted windows had been carefully masked with polarized optical sheeting that passed none of the room's light but allowed a startling view of the battle raging beyond the city. The result was that the building appeared dark from the outside.

Gretta looked up from her post at the glowing situation board. "Rebel contact reported in the foothills. Seventh Section has Groups all through there. Mayz reports skirmishing. She thinks it's infiltration. They're closing."

"Rotted Gods! Why won't Fleet give us orbital recon?" Sinklar balled a fist as he looked up at the situation board: an orthographic holophoto depicting terrain, elevation, structures, and troop positions. Sink turned, staring through the polarized windows to see streaks of blaster fire beyond the city limits.

Gretta gave him an acid smile. "I think, Sink, that considering the wonderful support Fleet and Defense have given us in the past weeks, you know exactly why."

"Still the sacrificial First," he punned. "All right, so be it. We don't have any more information than the Rebels. We ought to be able to hold our own."

Gretta frowned at the information coming into her headset. "Second Section reports contact along the northern defensive perimeter. Sergeant Kitmon is pulling back in a tactical retreat."

"This is it," he said softly as the realization ran through his mind. *I've bet Targa—and the future—on this attack. Will they fall for the trap? Please, dear Blessed Gods, may it be so. If not . . . well, death will be hard on the heels of misfortune.*

Sink took a deep breath to still the uncertainty pumping with his very blood. In moments, he'd know whether they'd won or lost. "If they have any sense, they'll be hitting Mac next."

"Mac!" Gretta's voice rang out as she accessed comm. "Have your advance Groups ready. They're coming."

Sink punched the button that accessed the room speakers so he could hear the entire net.

"Affirmative," Mac's voice came through. "We're ready

to withdraw. I've briefed the troops on their part. My compliments to Sink, he called it on the noggin again. They're right on time."

Sinklar glanced up at the situation board while his guts squirmed. It could still go terribly wrong. "Now, let's pray to the Rotted Gods their commander has as much sense as I give him credit for." He paced back and forth popping his fist into his palm. "The only way we can lose is if the man's an idiot!"

Gretta pinned him with a cool stare and shrugged. "After Kaspa, I don't believe that."

"Maybe Kaspa was the result of pus-rotted luck," Sink reminded, his eyes going to the situation board. "Come on, Rebels. It's right there in front of your noses—the key to the battle! Take it."

"Kaspa? Luck? You don't believe that." Gretta input new data as the Section Firsts chattered back and forth.

"Mayz here. I've got a large contact in the foothills," the net crackled. "Groups A to D withdrawing under heavy fire."

"Shiksta?" Sinklar called. "What is your status? We're about to take a major assault."

"We're ready, Sink. Got the heavy stuff positioned. My boys are briefed, nervous, and determined to do their part," the big black sergeant responded.

"Now, if Mac can just do his," Sinklar whispered, eyes going to the stat board as lights flickered.

An incredible rainbow display rippled across the plains east of Vespa. The Targan advance inched closer in an attempt to tighten a noose around the city. Reports began streaming in as Sinklar moved his units, mind racing to counter the Targan offensive.

One of the other speakers crackled as the guard on the rooftop called, "First, I just spotted an intruder with my starlight scope. Looks like one person with some sort of pack. He came through one of the manholes in the back alley. Must have hit that passage we sealed off and decided to try something else."

"Got him!" Gretta snapped, accessing a screen to show an armored figure approaching at the lower doors. A woman advanced cautiously toward a side entrance. A bulky pack gave her a hunchback appearance.

Sink nodded as he watched the furtive figure. "Notice the lack of IR? That's a pretty sophisticated suit she's wearing. With that, she'd get by standard sensors without tripping an alarm."

"Yeah," Gretta agreed. "You thought they'd try something like this."

"It's their pattern," Sink agreed. "But I'm not Atkin, Kapitol . . . or Mykroft." He turned to the building intercom. "Mhitshul? We've got our bogey. Looks like she's headed for the west side door."

"Roger, First."

"Think you'll get her alive?" Gretta asked as she turned her attention to the situation board again.

"Depends," Sinklar mumbled absently. "Everything . . . depends."

The woman studied the side door. One by one, she bypassed the alarms. Then palm latches fell to her tools. She pushed hesitantly. No good, the doors had been deadbolted from the inside. With a vibraknife she sliced the hinges loose, catching the big door as it fell outward, muscles straining as she lowered it to the ground.

At that moment—with her attention diverted—Mhitshul's stun caught her. She stiffened as every nerve in her body fired, then slumped to the ground.

"Readings say she's out," Mhitshul reported.

Sink ordered, "As soon as you have her disarmed, scan her for implanted explosives, hollow teeth, poisoned nails, or anything else. Take no chances and leave her gear in the street. You know the drill."

"Yes, sir."

"She's very good to have found us at all. Must have been that supply car from munitions that tipped her off." Gretta went back to the boards.

"Ayms." Sink forced his concentration back to the battle. "You're twenty klicks to the east of Mac. That should be his defensive fire you see on the Killing Ridge. Stand by. You're in a perfect position if Mayz can hold on and kick them back. She's been playing wounded, drawing them in."

"Got it, Sink. Yeah, we've been seeing Mac's fire. It's getting a little hot here, too. We've been falling back. I make us to be three klicks northeast of the grain shipping terminal."

"You're doing great. Keep your head up. Things are going to be happening all at once."

Mhitshul and two privates carried the woman through the door and dropped her strapped and bound body onto a thick-cushioned couch in the plush living room.

Sink glanced up to see Mhitshul standing guard over the woman with a drawn weapon. "Mac? You're on the hot seat. Withdraw from the Killing Ridge. Slowly now. Don't let them think you're giving it to them. They've got to buy it with blood or someone will get suspicious."

Gretta continued to chatter in her calm manner as she reassured Group and Section leaders while they retreated from the massive onslaught of the Targan advance.

"It doesn't do you any good to pretend," Private Mhitshul interrupted Sinklar's thoughts. "Considering the way you just fought those bonds and the breath you took, you're more than awake."

Sink glanced at the board one last time. Everything looked like it would work—just like he'd planned.

"Why am I here? What will you do to me? Keeping me for rape? Maybe sale to the slave markets?" The assassin's voice absorbed Sinklar's attention with sultry promising tones. He turned and studied her, noting how her body strained at the fabric of her clothing.

Private Mhitshul shook his head slowly, and Sink could see that he, too, devoured the woman with his worshipful gaze. "No, not at all. You're the type we would recruit. You brought a satchel with enough explosives to blow the entire top of the building off to within a gnat's whisker of the First Assault Division's ops center. The other amazing thing is how you managed to avoid tripping the active IR sensors or stumbling over any of the booby traps we've planted around this place."

She stared at him through burning amber eyes, features hard. "How did you knock me out? I never saw or heard a thing."

Mhitshul leaned against the table as he fingered his pistol. "Sinklar doesn't leave much to chance. We had a man on the roof with a starlight scope—just in case. What you experienced out there was a device called a stun rod. I suppose the best way to describe it is that you have three types of nerves which provide you with sensation. One of those nerve types feels pain. The microwave length is tailored to fire just those synapses. I'm sorry to inform you that certain brain cells are also stimulated. We killed about as many as if you'd gone on a three-month drinking binge."

She nodded, taking another deep breath. "You don't fight like Regans."

Mhitshul laughed. "We know. Sink's about to prove that fact to that army out there."

"Optimism can sometimes bring grief. The Second Division found that out to their dismay." She glared at him, coldly provocative tones in her voice.

"Sinklar Fist is not Mykroft—and you're dealing with the First Division. We ain't anything like the Second." Mhitshul uncrossed his arms and lifted a shoulder. "Want to watch your Rebels take it on the chin?"

"No, but I'll watch our people rip your precious Regan asses to pieces." She shifted her gaze to Sink. "What now? Death? Torture? Rape? Slave sale?"

"I'm off the Killing Ridge." Mac's tense voice came through comm. "The Rebels have the whole thing. We took fifteen casualties—but I think they're satisfied they bought it the hard way."

"Nice work, Mac," Sinklar praised as the stat board lights changed. He turned, frowning at the assassin. Her curious eyes fascinated him. They pinned him, and, for a brief moment, he swayed in their amber power. The universe might have funneled into those hypnotic depths.

Enough to lure my attention away from the battle? Sink turned on his heel, striding over to meet the woman's stare with one of his own. *Another front to this fight?* he wondered as he bent down before her and locked gazes in a battle of wills. For long moments, he wavered, aware of the musky scent of her body, of her firm flesh and the delight it promised. Finally she gasped, blinked, and looked away.

The spell broken, Sinklar examined her. Young, her auburn hair draped in glorious waves over her shoulders to contrast with her amazing amber eyes, straight nose, and high forehead. She had perfect cheekbones over a delicate jaw, flawless tanned complexion slightly reddened by the excitement of the battle. The muscles of her flat stomach rippled. Her breasts strained at the formfitting suit she wore as if possessed of a desire to be free.

But her eyes, seemed so . . . familiar! A sudden realization hit him: *She's a Seddi assassin—just like my mother once was!* He frowned, lips parting as he studied her. A warmth rose in his breast. But for the irony of time, this could have been his mother. Would Tanya Fist have had that same wild sensuality? Fate wrapped about him.

"Sink?" Gretta called with an unfamiliar tension. "There's a war on."

Sink walked back to the board, aware of Gretta's sharp scrutiny. He tilted his head in a questioning manner and Gretta's throat burned red as she turned back to the situation board. *Jealous?*

"Ayms," Sink called to the comm, "your people are on deck now; time to hit them back. If you and Kap can roll their flank up against the ridge while Hauws and Kitmon push back their side, we've got them right where we want them." He rubbed his chin nervously. Why did the Targan assassin seem so familiar?

"Well, that's it," Gretta finished wearily. "We make it or break it in the next half hour." She turned her attention to the assassin. "So you're the saboteur? What do we call you?"

The woman blazed with barely caged anger. "I am Arta Fera. I was only out for an evening stroll. Your man here got a little too zealous."

"With a satchel charge powerful enough to put us all in orbit?" Sinklar asked. "You were most professional, so I assume you're in contact with the Targan resistance, possibly with the Seddi themselves. Perhaps we can all come to terms and stop this nonsense."

"I thought you'd be older. You don't look like much of a Division First."

"You don't look like much of an assassin, either. I always thought an assassin would be older, less . . . obtrusive." *Is that a Seddi trait? To use beautiful women, women like Tanya Fist?*

Arta bit her lip and looked away. "I take it I am to be executed. Or would you use me as a bargaining piece when our forces overrun your positions?"

Sinklar considered as he kept one ear on the combat reports coming in through the comm. "I suppose that depends on the next half hour. I don't know who their First is, but he's very good. I detect a sure hand, a bright mind behind their movements and training. We should have had him in position an hour ago. He's handled the battle quite adroitly."

She laughed. "He's a comm repairman by trade. He is also the man who will break your Regan rule on Targa!"

"A comm repairman?" Sinklar pondered as he turned his attention to the blaster fire that streaked the horizon beyond the shielded windows of the penthouse. "I pray then that he survives. Talent like that is too good to be wasted. I would like to make him one of us."

"One of *you?*" Arta laughed at the absurdity of it. "Regan scum-sucker, he's fighting for Targa!"

Sinklar spun on his heel and he extended his hands toward her. The woman's lips parted as he whispered softly, "So am I, Arta."

She swallowed and took a serious look at the stat board. The back-lighted orthographic photo glowed with colored lights to indicate Rebel and Regan movements. From the number of red positions, the Rebels had taken a major interfluvial ridge immediately outside of town. At the same time, the Rebel forces on the wide plains were being pushed inexorably back on the impregnable defenses of the ridge. The outlying perimeters of the fight surrounding Vespa seemed more or less stable. Defensively, the ridge dominated, the strategic key to the whole valley—and Targans held it.

"This comm repairman, what's his name?" Sinklar asked, softly. "I want to talk to him before it's too late."

"His name is Butla Ret." She gasped, a crimson flush supplanting her tan.

Sinklar's intuition triggered at the tone in her voice. "He is your lover?" *Would he be the modern analog to my father? Is that the pattern? If I see him, will I see a version of Valient Fist? Will I see my own origins?*

"That is no concern of yours!"

He dropped to one knee, searching her face as his fingers took her bound hand. Arta shivered suddenly as though a surge had passed from his flesh to hers.

He implored her, struggling to touch her very soul, "Arta, will you help me? We can stop all this. His death serves no one. Not me, not Targa, not anyone. Will he listen to an appeal from you? Could we stop the fighting long enough so he and I could meet? Maybe talk about a solution?"

She shut her eyes to escape his mesmerizing stare and bit her lip, as if pain might fight his soft insistent tones. Somehow she forced herself to resist. "No, Regan. It's out of the question."

"I'm not your enemy, Arta. I don't want to destroy him." *Or am I only seeking to preserve a tenuous link to my past?*

She twisted her head away. Struggling, voice quavering, she asked, "Destroy him? How, Regan? He's got the ridge!"

Sinklar stood and moved away. Arta blinked, her breathing coming more evenly. Gretta's gaze followed the woman's as she looked back across the room to the situation board. Even a fool could see the gradual erosion of the Targan flanks around the ridge.

"That ridge," Sinklar said sadly as he pointed at the Targan position on the situation board, "is a death trap. Deep in the guts of the rocks we buried the reactor from a power unit taken from a crippled LC. As soon as we can roll the flanks back far enough, we will tell the Rebels what their situation is and demand their surrender." He turned to pin her with his oddly colored eyes. "I would rather take them alive." *Maybe learn the secrets of who you are—find the key to my parents.*

Gretta hunched in the chair, nervous gaze darting back and forth between Arta and Sinklar.

"Not Butla," Arta whispered, voice thick with dread. "Rotted Gods, no!" The amber eyes glazed crazily, setting a horrible shiver playing along Sinklar's spine. A warning triggered in his subconscious. *She's teetering on the edge of something I don't understand. Beware, Sinklar, she's dangerous—more dangerous than anyone you've ever met.*

"Will you contact him . . . save him and his troops? I need them, Arta. Targa needs them. Alive." Sinklar bent down beside her again, gaze boring into hers.

She swallowed, expression haunted. "I will . . . talk to Butla Ret."

"Don't let her, Sink," Gretta warned. "She's not sane. Something is terribly wrong with her."

Sink rubbed the back of his neck. "It's our only chance,

Gretta. To save them, turn them to our side, I'll take a chance. How long until we're in position to destroy them?"

"From the way they're falling back, we could probably establish contact with the blast perimeter at any time." Gretta replied. "Should I attempt to make contact with this Butla Ret?"

"If you would." He smiled wistfully. "Let's see if we can't bring the killing to a stop."

Arta's glazed attention followed each of Gretta's moves as she began keying different channels into the comm, sending on all frequencies. A panicked expression flickered across the prisoner's face.

The minutes passed slowly as Arta studied the ridge, ominous where it dominated the stat board. Her perfect mouth came open as she stared, transfixed.

"This is Butla Ret. Who are you? What do you want?" A deep bass filled the room.

Sink walked up to the comm as he composed his words.

"Sinklar?" Gretta called, voice firm, pointing at the shivering assassin. Fera looked berserk as she writhed on the couch. Mhitshul had begun to sweat, licking his lips nervously.

Sinklar took a deep breath, and gave a shrug of desperation before he faced the speaker.

"I am Sinklar Fist, First of the First Targan Assault Division, Lord Ret. I want to stop this battle and meet with you to discuss bringing this war to an end." Fist crossed his arms and gazed at the stat board expectantly, eyes strained as if trying to see through the map, to find his opponent in the wrinkles and contours of the holograph.

"Why should I deal, Sinklar Fist? My forces hold the strategic ground. We've taken the Vespa Ridge—the key to any defensive position in the valley." His deep booming voice sounded imminently reasonable.

Gretta winced at the sight of Arta Fera, who twisted with horror.

So many lives hinge on this . . . this crazy woman? Blessed Gods, help us! Sinklar continued, "And if I told you the ridge was mined, that your flanks are being pushed back within the blast radius, what would you say then?"

"That you are bluffing!" Butla's vibrant voice rang out.

Gretta's expression mirrored worry as Arta reacted to

those deep ringing tones. A sudden light flashed behind the blazing amber eyes, hope flickering where before there had been only insanity.

"Lord Ret, we've captured Arta Fera. Would you take her word? We caught her trying to bomb our headquarters." Sinklar waited, heart hammering. *So much to bet on the sanity of a panicked assassin. I must be out of my mind! But who else would Butla Ret listen to?*

Ret's voice was curiously subdued. "I would talk to her."

Sinklar looked desperately, pleadingly, at the assassin.

"Arta? Are you all right?" Butla asked gently.

Sinklar closed his eyes, oddly touched by the compassion and concern in Ret's voice.

Arta looked haunted, focused on some terrible memory. "Butla!" she shrieked in terror. "Don't listen! They want you to surrender! They can't hold against you! *They are bluffing. Vile Regan liars!*"

Gretta shook her head, a miserable dullness in her posture. No saving them now.

Sinklar spun on his feet, and Arta laughed triumphantly in his face.

"Do not harm her, Regan," Butla's voice came firmly over the comm. "We are coming for you. As long as Arta is treated with respect, we will act within the accords of honor. Harm her, and the streets will run with Regan blood. That I promise!"

"Wait!" Sinklar cried passionately, arms out as he faced the comm pickup. "*At least talk to me!* Butla? Butla Ret?" He paced back and forth while desperation pumped adrenaline into his system.

"He cut the connection," Gretta told him.

Arta smiled, eyes still glazed as she nodded, enjoying her victory. She seemed to gloat at Sinklar's misery.

Gretta craned her neck to glare at the woman, expression filled with loathing. "Enjoy yourself, you . . . wretched bitch. You love Butla Ret? I pray I never experience a love like yours."

"We have no choice," Sinklar muttered in a dispirited tone. "The Targan forces are within the kill zone."

Gretta nodded and turned her attention from Arta's dancing defiance to inputting instructions to the Sections.

"Attention, all personnel!" Sinklar's voice rang out. "Duck and cover!"

"Shiksta?" Gretta's voice came hoarsely. "Detonate the mine. Destroy the Killing Ridge."

" 'Firmative," Shik's voice came back.

Arta turned to look with the rest. She was still smirking at the culpability of the Regans when a gout of brilliant light lanced beyond the outskirts of the city. Before her disbelieving eyes, clots of black rose in the lurid apocalyptic flash. Seconds later the ground shook. Then the shock wave battered the building, bouncing her couch.

"All units," Sinklar ordered, voice hollow, "Keep cover until the fallout has passed. When you read all clear, commence mop-up. Stay away from the hot spots. We'll begin evacuating casualties immediately."

Mouth open, Arta watched the oddly luminous cloud that rose over the plain. The air carried an odd rumble as the shock wave Dopplered off into the distance.

Her startled gaze went to the stat board to see the lights now gone dead. The realization broke over her in a cold wash.

Sink pinched the bridge of his nose, disgusted with the woman—disgusted with all of it. Shoulders sagging, he walked wearily from the room. He could feel Gretta's worried gaze, feel the horror that had possessed Mhitshul.

Arta Fera screamed then—the sound that of a demented animal in torment.

Sinklar closed his eyes and staggered, overwhelmed by the memory of his mother's pale face mocking him from her casket.

CHAPTER XXIII

Skyla Lyma reclined in the control chair surrounded by the cockpit instrumentation of her personal yacht. Her inclination was to space full tilt for Targa, but a cooler voice argued for caution. Staffa would arrive on Targa long after she would, and in the meantime she'd have to pass the Regan ships quarantining the rebellious planet. If she tried that, she might fall into Ily's clutches, which in turn would condemn Staffa to capture when he arrived.

I could space straight for Rega and confront Tybalt. Skyla tapped a fingernail against her teeth as she watched the stars beyond the forward port. They seemed to move as a result of her ship's slight spin. How would Tybalt react to news that his lover had alienated the Companions? And what was Ily's game, anyway? Surely she knew that, lover or not, Tybalt would cut her off at the knees for what she'd done to the Lord Commander.

"Damn right, she knows." Skyla studied the wheeling stars thoughtfully. "And she's got an agenda of her own. Damn it, if I could just have had an hour to talk to Staffa." But what would Ily be after?

Skyla smiled to herself as she remembered the look on Staffa's face when she'd stepped around that crate. Closing her eyes, she imagined his strong arms around her. With a desperate longing, she wished she could be in that crate with him instead of Kaylla Dawn.

"But it's better this way," she assured herself. "Two of us in the box would have meant we depended solely on the good will of the Seddi—which would have been suicide, despite Bruen's promises."

And she hadn't planned on being in the box when the Seddi opened it on Targa.

403

*So what are you going to do, Skyla? You've got a Seddi
hostage of unknown potential aboard your ship. The Regans
are about to go berserk, and Staffa's in a box headed for a
world in revolt to talk to people who've spent fortunes trying
to assassinate him.*

The long-range sensor tripped, bring Skyla upright in her
chair. She adjusted the gain, refining the reading. She knew
the reaction signature—Regan military, and pulling about
forty-five g's from the radiation dispersion. *Ily!*

Skyla took a fix, then swiveled her receiver for another.
Comparing the data, she frowned, then pulled up the nav-
comm plot. A cold shiver ran down her spine.

"No doubt about it. Ily's headed for Targa." And in that
instant, Skyla knew what she was going to do.

* * *

Bruen stared at the hewn stone over his head. An eternal
weight, it hung—foreboding and gray, cold and without
feeling—a symbol of oppression. Butla Ret, dead? Their
forces in total rout? How had Sinklar Fist managed to
destroy them so decisively? *Face it, old man. You've played
the last gamble. What's left, Bruen?*

The feeble light barely penetrated the gloom in the tiny
quarters. The rays cast by the small lamp were absorbed by
the gray stone, the illumination set low to reduce the strain
on Hyde's eyes. The air lay heavy, warm, and damp as if
to mirror Magister Hyde's rasping breath.

*How much time do I have with my old friend? It should
be a time for memories, for reliving the old days, for sharing
jokes about victories and past loves. This is not a time for
revelations—or for the death of dreams.*

Hyde's sunken face had become a death mask, sallow
flesh sagging over the hard bones of his skull. No flicker of
change animated Hyde's expression while Bruen related this
latest catastrophe—this defeat at Vespa—in half truths. The
dying man listened quietly, sighing between gasping fits of
coughing.

Sourness lay heavy in Bruen's stomach, a dead thing—
like Seddi hopes.

"We should have killed him when he was a baby," Hyde
wheezed, hardly able to lift a bird-thin hand from his sleep-

ing pallet. The tubes distorted his voice into something hollow, ghostlike. They ran from his lungs up through both nostrils and then to a suction pump which slowly filled a canister with the fluids inexorably draining into Hyde's lungs. The machine made an imperceptible whine—a reminder of mortality and the close odor of death that the dark shade breathed upon Magister Hyde's soul.

Just one more small sorrow for all humanity at this last juncture.

Bruen rubbed his belly and scowled at the forbidding stone above. "It was my decision. He was a babe, a tiny defenseless infant at the time. I took one look at his odd eyes and watched him toddle across the room, pudgy hands reaching for this and that, and I spared him. Sent him to Rega to lose himself in the masses, no one the wiser." He shook his head, "Maudlin of me, don't you think?"

"The quanta, Bruen," Hyde gasped. "An action, any action, changes reality. Who knows what would have been different if we'd simply cut his throat and stuffed him into a disposal chute to bleed."

"At the time, a Sinklar Fist alive had more bargaining power than a dead baby," Bruen reminded himself. "It was insurance to have him—"

"*He was a monster!* Even then!" Hyde gasped, breaking out in a fit of coughing. "A *monster,* Bruen. You knew what he was . . . where he came from! His legacy is . . . death!"

"Perhaps," Bruen agreed. "But what a brilliant monster he is, old friend. And what little part we had in his development. Perhaps if we had kept him, trained him?"

"He is killing us!" Hyde rasped, coughing again, drool slipping from the side of his sagging mouth. ". . . killing . . . us."

"At ease, old friend." Bruen smiled, bestirring himself to take a rag and damp at his dying friend's mouth. "All is not lost by any means."

Hyde swallowed, pale hairless head rocking on the pillow. "No, maybe not," he whispered, barely audibly. "A reality changed, Bruen. Somewhere, a reality we all thought crucial has changed. Awareness? Did someone become aware whom we have not perceived? Whose observations have made a new reality? It wasn't ours, nor the Regans', nor Sassa's.''

"The machine, perhaps? We don't know the power of the Mag Comm. Could it, too, be a reflection of God Mind? An interesting statement about the nature of the observer, eh? If it is the machine, so much is changed." Bruen added, one hand on Hyde's shoulders. "But it seems that everyone who has planned, calculated a probability future, sees those very probabilities lying in ruin. Why? Where is the reality shaping coming from? I cannot convince myself it is the machine. To observe takes a spark from God.''

"Fist!" Hyde gasped. "It is Fist! He has no reality. He just seems to react! He lives in Now. He forges no future! He is the only one predictable . . . and all that is predictable is that he will win—not where he will turn or how he will act!''

Bruen frowned, running a tired hand over his own sweat-shiny bald head. "God mocks us. Fist has become the major player in this sad game, and we have insufficient data to make predictions about his behavior." He smiled fleetingly. "Would it not be puzzling and paradoxical to learn that he is better at our philosophy than we are?''

"Wretched," Hyde gasped. "Our forces?''

Bruen lifted a shoulder, pulling his lips into a reassuring smile. "We are reforming." *I can't tell him Butla is dead. I can't tell him we are prostrate, defenseless, ruined. Let him die without knowing the worst. For the old days, I owe him that much. What a cruel joke life has played on dear noble Hyde—to crush a dream in these last failing moments. Perhaps I can. . . . Yes.*

Hyde's faded blue eyes held his for a brief instant before Bruen pulled his gaze away.

Hyde barely whispered, "Your smile is a lie. You never could lie outright—at least, not to me. One of your failings, eh? I always caught you at it.''

"There is no lie," Bruen continued, wanting to break down and cry. "We are hurt, true, but not defeated.''

Hyde hacked and coughed, eyes closed against the rub-bing pain of the tubes in his throat. "Even this close to death, I hear between your words, my friend. Very well, I understand." Translucent eyelids flickered as Hyde asked,

"And the Lord Commander? After so much death and horror and disaster? He is. . . ."

"Coming," Bruen said fervently. "Staffa is coming here to us at last." He hesitated. "Perhaps this time . . . well, we will see. I am no longer counting on probability." *And you, blessed beloved friend of mine, will not live to see our final victory.*

"No . . . can't count on probability," Hyde wheezed. "Staffa . . . sent to us . . . by his Wing Commander? Probability is turned upside down, my friend. The machine . . . wrong. . . ."

Bruen's strength crumbled, mind roaming to younger—less painful—times, reliving old arguments—and triumphs—seeing the past unfolding. He and Hyde had rebuilt the Seddi, kept the vile machine at bay, countered the growing pains of two selfish empires. They had merely prolonged the respite before this final cataclysm which would sweep pestilence and death before it. The last flickers of light were dimming now. Rega prepared to launch itself on Sassa. The last moments of stillness before the storm were troubled by eddies of the coming sirocco.

"We did well, eh?" Hyde managed, as if sharing his thoughts. "All in all, Bruen, we did the impossible, you and I. Trained generations of young people, added a little brilliance to an ultimately damned civilization."

"Yes, we did very well," Bruen agreed, voice hollow, remembering Hyde: young, vigorous, black-haired, and athletic. Seeing the young women's gazes following that straight virile figure through the corridors, his blue eyes flashing with spirit, his smile infectious.

"Let me rest now, Bruen," Hyde's voice whispered between wheezing breaths. ". . . Rest . . . now."

Bruen patted his shoulder and turned to the door, hip hurting again. Outside, an Initiate perched on a stool, watching a monitor set into the stone of the corridor.

"He's dying," Bruen added listlessly, propping his suddenly unsteady bones against the cold unyielding rock. He closed his eyes, aware of what he must do. Weakness bored upward through his soul, hollowing, emptying.

The Initiate nodded her resignation. "I think he only has a few hours left. We could increase the pumping capacity, but his lungs are already stressed by the suction. A hemorrhage now would. . . ."

"And how are his . . . his dreams?"

The young woman pointed to a series of lines on the encephalogram. "Pleasant, Magister."

Bruen worked his tongue over worn teeth. "Then it would be good now." With faltering resolution, he reached out and moved a switch. He stared at the tiny piece of metal, numb at what he had done.

"Magister? That switch. . . ."

"Yes," Bruen whispered as he turned his attention to the encephalogram. "That switch controls the pump. See how happy he is, my girl? See how he's dreaming of good things? Pleasant things? Is there a . . . better . . . better way . . . to. . . ." The monitor went oddly misty in his vision. A hot throbbing knot grew in his throat.

Bruen hardly felt the woman's warm arm go around him. The words she called into the comm echoed meaninglessly in his head. He cried openly as Initiates and a Master carried him through the winding maze of passages on a stretcher he didn't remember being placed on.

He ignored them for the moment. He might never get another chance to live in his memories with Hyde—never get another chance to see his best friend healthy, smiling, strong, and young. Oh, so wondrously young!

* * *

"So I tried my best for him, for my Praetor," Staffa explained. Nothing remained but to talk. The featureless gray walls of the box pressed around them like a prison. Time had slipped sideways in this new reality measured only by sleep, talk, and eternal sameness. Nothing else intruded into their world. No sound, no vibrations. Time had ceased to exist in the eternal gray reality of the packing crate.

Kaylla sat in the corner, propped and supported by wadded insulating wraps. She stared fixedly at the far corner as Staffa talked.

Staffa hesitated. "After the wreck that killed my parents, I didn't have anyone left. No other family that I know of. The Praetor found me in the wreckage and took me, gave me a home and food and a reason to be. I lived for that man. He gave me everything."

"And took everything from you, it would seem." Kaylla watched him through hard eyes. "You never tried to find the rest of your family? I mean, people don't just spring from the air. Your parents had parents. There must have been someone . . . somewhere."

"Maybe there was. When I got older, I tried to access the net once. I thought I could find someone. It puzzled me that the data was sealed. The Praetor showed up shortly after that and gave me that sad smile he used to have. I remember, he asked it as a personal favor. 'Please,' he asked me. 'Don't pursue this. It would only hurt you . . . and through you . . . me.' "

Kaylla gave him a narrow-eyed frown. "And that didn't make you suspicious?"

Staffa leaned back and sighed. "Suspicious? I loved him. I . . . I trusted him."

"It sounds like your life as a child was a living hell."

Staffa shrugged and tapped a knuckle against the thick plastic of the box. "Maybe. The Praetor—and everyone else for that matter—always told me I was something special, always rewarded me when I excelled, led me on, caused me to push myself harder."

"And your parents? Didn't you have some good times with them before the aircar crash?"

"What can I say about them? Both were genetic scientists—quite bright in their fields." A sudden pain came lancing out of his memories. "But now I've watched you talk about your children." He pursed his lips, curious at the longing ache below his heart. "You talk about them with warmth. My . . . mother, well, she . . ." He gestured his incomprehension.

"No warmth?" Kaylla probed.

"Her voice never softened. You know, no emotion. She talked to me . . . well, academically. Like I was a student. Always, I was challenged. Did I know thus and such? Could I solve this problem?"

Staffa took a deep breath and closed his eyes as he struggled to remember. "I recall one occasion. We had gone to a party. At least that's what Father told me it was. I was very excited about the whole thing. Lots to eat and drink.

Games they wanted me to play. Machines to outsmart and puzzles to solve. There were lots of people—maybe even the Praetor. I was. . . . Damn! It was so long ago!" He shook his head. "The memories keep fading."

"Think, Staffa, you were there; make it come out," she prodded, voice earnest with interest.

"People," he repeated, willing himself to see it all again, to remember the giant adult forms who bent to study him. ". . . And they all talked about me. Yes, that's right. And I answered questions. All kinds of questions."

"Any other children there?"

Staffa frowned as he thought. "I don't think. . . . No, no other children. Just me. And all those adults. Questions, so many questions. They asked them so quickly. And I remember afterward: Mother placed a hand on my shoulder and told me she was proud. I felt so tired after that. I . . . I told her I wanted to go home and sleep."

"Sounds like they put you through a test of some sort. Did your mother fawn over you? Beam with pride?"

"Her? She didn't beam. Not like when you talk about your little boy. No, she was reserved and, now that I think about it, more satisfied than anything else. I remember, she said, 'That'll show the skeptics,' and she winked at my father."

Kaylla's eyes narrowed.

"Don't look so grim." He chuckled dryly. "All my life has been one testing program after another. I never lived any other way. Each day came with the knowledge that tomorrow I would face another challenge, another exam."

"What about your father?"

He lifted a shoulder. "So much has been blocked." He shook his head. "The sensations are similar to when I used to find a psychological trigger left by the Praetor—one of his mental booby traps."

Kaylla hissed her disgust. "They made you into a damn machine! What kind of parents did you have?"

"Well, my mother was small, thin. She had flaming red hair and my father was pale blond. I remember they sunburned so easily. They were—"

"That's not what I meant," Kaylla growled. "I mean, they acted like you were some sort of *thing!* Didn't they ever take you to the parades, or bring you toys, or send you to a normal educational facility with other kids? What about your birthday? Didn't they have parties with your friends over? Didn't you ever spend time with other families on outings, or trips, or holidays?"

Staffa lifted his hands helplessly. "I don't . . . well, exactly know what you mean by all that. The first I knew about birthdays was after I joined the military. I'd been enrolled in flight school and navigation training. I thought birthdays were something only adults did."

"But didn't you have friends your own age when you were little?"

"No. I do remember a couple of times when I was around other children." He frowned deeply. "You know, they didn't have my. . . . How do I explain this? I wanted to solve intricate puzzles. They wanted to make noise and engage in the most inane behavior. Running—as I recall—touching each other to see who chased who. Is there a purpose to children doing that?"

She squinted grimly. "How old were you then?"

"I don't know. I never knew how old I was."

"But you had to figure it out sometime."

Staffa flipped a hand. "I was told I was fourteen when I entered the military training academy. At least that's the age the Praetor filled the appropriate box with. I always estimated back from there. That date provided a framework."

"And how old were the other students?"

"Twenty-one, at least." Staffa shifted, uncomfortable, realizing how odd it all sounded now. He hurried to explain, "You see, I was always special, always by far the youngest. When you're sponsored by the Praetor, you get special treatment. And most of all, I always dominated the classes."

"You were *always* the best?" Kaylla asked, an eyebrow arching.

"Of course! But it isn't as if I didn't know about failure. I knew a couple of young men who failed out of various programs. I wasn't stunted or anything like that."

"And you were never second place, or third?"

"Of course not. It would have been unthinkable. To have come in second would have been. . . . It wasn't allowable. If I had to, I'd study all night—every night. If there was any chance another might surpass my ability, I sought out special tutors. Whatever it took, I did it."

"You couldn't let yourself be less than perfect?" She winced. "God, what a wretched way to live."

"Perfection is a goal to be striven for by all humans. Anything less is—"

"Terguzzi sumpshit!" Kaylla exploded. "Listen to you, Staffa! Do you hear what you're saying?" She squinted sourly. "My God, we've been locked in here for what seems like an eternity now. I *know* you, Staffa! Probably better than I've ever known any other human being—except my husband. I know what you think . . . what you dream at night. I kick you awake so you'll quit whimpering and crying through your guilty nightmares. Your psychological composition is like so much wreckage. Your identity is in fractured shambles."

"I'm not in shambles!"

"What the hell do you call that little stunt where you tired to commit suicide! You exhibit the symptoms of a classic manic depressive, down one moment, and up the next. You make stupid decisions based on improper neural assessments of reality. You're hounded by a sudden understanding of guilt!"

"It's not guilt!" he lied.

"No? Then what the hell is it? You told me you went to Etaria in search of what it meant to be human? Well, you got a dose of it, Lord Commander, and what you found horrified you. Didn't it? Admit it!"

"To be a slave and deal with the collar isn't human—"

"The blaspheming hell, it isn't!" She curled her lip in disgust as she pointed with a callused finger. "No, Staffa, I think—whether you'll admit it or not—for the first time, you felt what it was to be human. Hear? *You FELT!* Suffered, thirsted, tasted all the wretchedness it means to be really human! What scared you, Star Butcher, was the *feeling* of humanity. Just like me, or Peebal, or Koree. You realized you were human after all—and it scared the pustulant piss out of you!"

Her tone of insolence and disgust stirred him. He jumped to his feet, a surging rage building. He closed to stare into those defiant tan eyes. Nearly berserk from the scornful tongue-lashing, he reached for her.

"Now what, Staffa?" she asked, voice level and challenging. "Going to hurt me? Come to finish what you started at Maika? Going to add me to your list of ghouls?"

His hands began to shake as he knotted his shivering fingers into fists and gritted his teeth. The anger eroded like sand in surf. Her truth twisted within him as surely as if she'd knifed him.

Helplessly, he raised a hand and let it drop, turning away to hide his eyes. "Yes, I wanted to hurt you for using that tone. Sometimes I scream defiance at the universe, other times I whimper and shake. I was so strong once."

"Because you don't know who you are, Staffa kar Therma. You never had the chance to find out. Anger? Sudden fear? Rushes of emotion? Your soul is crying out. Defiance? You want to reassure yourself you're someone to take seriously. Each wavering of emotion is a sign of the pain you bear because you were shut away from the human tribe for so long. An exile in your own mind."

She paused. Then she added, "Isn't that one of the reasons you killed so ruthlessly? Wasn't it a means of getting back at the human condition you'd never had the opportunity to share?"

He lowered his gaze to his hands, slowly flexing his fingers. *Was that it? Did I take my rage out on all humanity to pay back the sins of the Praetor and my parents?*

She shook her hair back, watching him pensively. "Self-awareness *is* painful. Most of us learn we're not gods when we're still children. You didn't learn until the Praetor gutted your godhood on Myklene—and you weren't really sure until that Etarian judge clapped the collar on you and threw you in the sewer with me."

She hesitated. "I don't envy you, Staffa. If you want to see this through, you're likely to find you don't like yourself very much."

He laughed, the sound bitter with irony. "I don't like myself now."

"This is the hardest part, here, now, locked away with me. On Etaria you had hatred and anger to keep you going. Here, you're trapped. You've got nothing here but four gray walls . . . your conscience . . . memories—and me."

CHAPTER XXIV

Each LC had a command control module immediately behind the flight deck. There an officer had access to communications, observation, and weapons. From a circling LC he could monitor and orchestrate an entire battle. Computer equipment filled one wall while a fold-down table created work space or dining area, and the bench behind that could be slept on.

Sinklar felt the LC move. Through the command monitor, he watched dust boil out below as the craft rose above the gutted Regan military compound in Kaspa. The blackened pile of burned corpses piled in the center of the plaza spoke eloquently of the fate of the prisoners taken from Mykroft's Division: Targan retribution for Mykroft's execution of the Rebel prisoners that day in the square. Must have been a gruesome bonfire.

The LC rose and began a lazy turn to the south. Sink watched as the city dropped away beneath his craft. So much had changed since the first time he'd seen Targa through his night glasses. Now he left Kaspa again—this time under his control.

His Groups had retaken the city; resistance had been minimal and halfhearted. The "pacification" of Kaspa really amounted to little more than a meeting with business leaders and the heads of the mining labor committees. News of the defeat of the Rebel forces at Vespa had taken more fight out of the radical elements than another three Divisions could have accomplished.

"All right, Mac," Sink said into the comm, "we're up and on the way back to Vespa. The city's yours. Take care of it." He turned from the monitors that displayed Kaspa and glanced at Gretta. A pensive expression molded her face as she watched the charred corpses fall behind.

"We're on top of it, Sink," Mac's voice assured. "Take care of yourself. There's still a lot of passion loose. No telling what the Seddi might do in retaliation. More than one conqueror's won the war—and fallen to an assassin's knife the next day."

"Affirmative."

"Anything else?"

"Get a detail to haul those corpses out and bury them somewhere." Sink cut the connection and gripped Gretta's hand firmly. "War's over except for the shouting and flag waving and the small matter of mopping up the Seddi main temple. Makarta, wonder where that is?"

Gretta pulled glistening long brown hair over her shoulder to nervously twist it into a shining dark strand. "I'll bet Sylenian ice to Riparian mud your Arta Fera knows." She lifted an eyebrow suggestively.

Sinklar laughed. "A fascinating woman, that one. I don't know why, but there is something compelling about her. I . . . call it familiarity. Something. . . ."

"I call it sex," Gretta grunted. "For some reason—pheromones, perhaps, or those eyes of hers?—men seem to find her a sexual magnet. I can't see it, but men take a first look and then stop dead in their tracks to stare—oblivious of the rest of the world. I thought it prudent to change the guard to females. The men we had down there kept drooling all over themselves."

Gretta considered him seriously before she asked, "You going to be wandering down to interrogate her about the mysterious Makarta?"

Sink glanced out the view port and pursed his lips. The Targan countryside flashed below: Ephemeral drainages in dendritic patterns cut rough jagged ridges of gray and brown rock; mottled masses of conifers blotched the northern slopes in dark green.

"No," he told her. "I don't ever want to see her again. She cost us too much. Cost Targa too much. I can't figure. How could she kill her lover that way? I heard the scream all the way down the hall. Eerie, inhuman, like some wretched nightmare."

"She thought we were bluffing. Not an entirely unreasonable assumption." Gretta settled herself into a drop couch, a frown starting to trace her forehead. "Now that I hear you're not sexually infatuated with her like the rest of the men, I can feel sorry for her. Think of the guilt, of what it must feel like to have caused the end of everything. Must be a horrible weight to bear, all that blood and death. The end of her Seddi cause. All her fault."

"I've seen her on the holos," Sink agreed, turning back to the view port. "I think she's snapped. I don't know very much about such things, but maybe some of the psych personnel could do something with her."

Gretta pursed her lips, face pensive. "Perhaps. When we get back, I might wander down to talk to her. Maybe I can say something that will break her open—get her to feel something. If I can talk to her, maybe she'll tell us where we can find this Makarta."

Sink rubbed his chin. "Leave her alone. There's something very wrong about her. I can't put my finger on it. Something . . . frightening." He frowned, grappling with his image of the woman. *And so Rotted familiar. Why do I feel like I know her? There's some memory I can't place . . . deep in my mind.*

"Any word from the fleet yet?" she asked, diverting his attention.

"Just the order that I relinquish command to Mykroft and submit myself for arrest." He grinned maliciously at her.

"And will you?"

"What? Let Mykroft undo all the good I've done? Rotted Gods in the temple, he'd have Targa burning within two days! No, I think I have a better bargaining position here, in charge of the Regan assault forces and my Targan irregulars." He looked out at the ragged mountain peaks they were passing over. "My position will be even better when I have the Seddi in my hands. The word is out. I want to meet with their leadership. I can end this once and for all."

"What is this obsession with the Seddi?"

He smiled absently. "It goes back to Rega and my. . . . Nothing, never mind. The fact of the matter is that we've committed treason. Our only hope is to hand Tybalt this entire planet. The defense structure is going to want to hang us by the heels and bleed us to death drop by drop for having the audacity to win. We're a long way from being anywhere near safety." *And it scares me to death.*

She nodded, still staring thoughtfully as she wound her thick hair about her fingers.

The Vespa plain appeared below as the high steepled peaks dropped away into an alluvial valley, now green with spring growth.

"Makarta," he mused. "What I'd give to be able to find it."

"Anything?" Gretta asked.

"Hmm?"

"You'd give anything to find Makarta?"

"I suppose." Sinklar pictured Targa in his mind. Where could the Seddi have hidden their major temple? Under one of the cities?

The LC swooped down, coming to a neat stop before the headquarters building. Sink stood, lost in his thoughts as he absently collected his gear. The ramp dropped with a hydraulic whine and he walked out into the warm sunshine. Beyond his command center, the rhythm and pulse of Targan life had reestablished itself. The mines were working—true, on reduced crews—but production could still be claimed to be a reality. Produce flowed into the cities and supplies and goods flowed back out. The dead were still being buried, but men and women could look about for a new beginning—though uncertain what it all meant.

"I'll be up in a bit," Gretta called, reaching over to give him a sound kiss on the lips. "If you need me for anything, call through the comm."

He nodded, her words already half-forgotten as he considered the Seddi. They remained the key to Targa. Why had they plunged their planet into such a bloodbath? What had they hoped to gain? With the resources available on Targa, they hadn't stood a chance. What fool reasoning could have filled Seddi heads to egg them headlong into certain defeat?

And how much of this growing preoccupation is rooted in your parents' death? They were Seddi assassins—just like Arta Fera. Had they been trained here? Had they, too, walked the streets of Vespa? Had they known the location of Makarta?

He climbed the stairs, mind on the problem, heedless of the salutes the guards threw him, oblivious to the awed shine in their eyes, the extra care they took to look professional as he passed.

"I'm missing something," he muttered to himself. "There's a key element in their actions which I don't understand. A linchpin, which will make everything clear."

He paused, hand on the door to the ops room, head cocked. "Unless they're total zealots. Could they possibly have fought a war on faith? Believed in some mystical hocus-pocus? Supernatural intervention?"

He chewed his lip and frowned, shaking his head as he opened the door and passed into his penthouse ops room. Mhitshul and Shiksta were pouring over a pile of correspondence and marking notations on maps.

" 'Nuther call from fleet, sir," Mhitshul said, looking up from the pile. "Figured you'd be here soon enough, so I didn't patch it through." He marked his place, stood, and moved to the comm Gretta normally handled. Within seconds he patched through to an orbiting ship high overhead.

A block-faced woman, gray-haired and with a grizzled look, stared back at him through the comm monitor. She had flinty brown eyes. Her nose was crooked and age spots dotted her forehead. Her mahogany skin had lined with age. A sour tension was reflected in the set of her thin bloodless lips.

"Sergeant Sinklar Fist?" Her voice grated as if the vocal cords had been damaged.

"First Sinklar Fist of the First Targan Assault Division," he told her, emphasizing "First," seeing the hard glint filling her eyes. Not good, career military, this one—and a doubly seasoned veteran to boot. "And whom do I have the pleasure of addressing?"

"Commander Rysta Braktov of the Imperial Regan Assault Cruiser *Gyton*. You are hereby ordered to relinquish all military command to First Mykroft and place yourself under arrest. To fail to do so immediately will outlaw you as a criminal and you will be executed on sight."

Sinklar nodded, knowing Shiksta and Mhitshul had frozen. "I see. Commander, I am not in a position to relinquish my command at the present moment. I face a dilemma you can no doubt understand."

"And that is?"

"Were I to follow your recommendations, the planet

would rise in instant rebellion against Mykroft. The Targans hate him. In fact, that is why I originally requested an LC from orbital to retrieve him from the planet. The Targans would give anything for his head."

Sink paced before the screen. "At the same time, both the First and Second Targan Divisions have reservations about their future treatment. We have been, shall we say, inconsistent in obedience to the Minister of Defense. The reasons, I'm sure you're familiar with. We didn't die when we were supposed to." His wry smile and raised eyebrow did nothing for her expression.

Shiksta was muttering under his breath.

"A military tribunal will consider each case separately," Braktov said. "Those guilty of insubordination and violation of the Command Code according to the manual will be dealt with summarily."

Sinklar faced the monitor as he rubbed his hands together. "Yes, that is our point. You see, we all are—as you say—guilty." He paused. "Look at it from our position. Innovative measures were employed on Targa to subdue the rebellion. And Commander, the rebellion *is* over. Finished. The capital as well as the major cities have been retaken. Order is restored and my Groups are patrolling the streets. The final pockets of resistance in the mountains are currently being subdued—most often peacefully."

"Does this have a point, Sergeant?" she groused, propping herself in her command chair, one shoulder raised.

"It does, Commander. I've been worrying about this conversation ever since Mykroft appointed me to Division First." He settled himself on the table edge, crossing his arms tightly across his chest, one leg dangling and swinging. "You see, I am willing to offer the Emperor a peaceful Targa. Further, I will guarantee it will stay that way so long as I'm viceroy here. In return, those of the First and Second Divisions who wish may return to their homes without censure or disciplinary action taken against them—and with full veteran's honors."

"*You WHAT?*" Rysta bolted to her feet. "You bargain? *With the Emperor?*" She threw her head back and laughed, the sound a wicked cackle in the room.

Sinklar waited her out until she chuckled herself to a stop.

"I *do* have the planet," he reminded calmly. "That's one

reason. The second reason is that both Divisions have suffered heavily while on duty on Targa. The result of such
suffering is that my people have a certain amount of investment to go along with their pride and skill. Rega is poised,
ready to invade Sassa at this very moment." The shock in
her eyes proved it—to his immense delight. "My people,
therefore, have a great deal to offer the Empire. The
Emperor not only needs warriors of the highest caliber, he
needs a productive Targa to help feed his war industry."

"But not at the price you want, Fist. Anything else?" A
look of distaste crossed her face.

"You refuse us a just settlement for being stranded here
as a soak off for Imperial politics?"

"We do," Rysta snorted.

"Very well, we expected as much. Please forward our
regards to the Emperor and let him know that we have
every faith in his honesty and integrity. We attribute our
problems to the Minister of Defense and Council politics
which he was no doubt unaware of . . . and hope the Imperial Seventh will be concerned enough to see justice done
to his loyal servants of the First and Second Targan Assault
Divisions. We will continue to hold Targa in his name."

Her hard eyes gleamed in the lengthening silence. Sinklar
refused to drop his gaze. Behind him, Shiksta mumbled,
"Damn right!"

"You know, I've seen some brash bastards in my day,
Fist," Rysta growled, "but I'm gonna enjoy bustin' your
balls, boy, because you take first prize!"

Sinklar raised a hand. "Please. There is nothing to be
gained by Regan fighting Regan. Not at this late date. The
Empire can't afford it."

"Surrender, Fist!"

"We are not in a position to surrender to anyone. We
haven't—"

"You're about to get your *asses kicked!*" she roared.
"You think all those lives you're talking about are worth
it?"

"I definitely do *not*. Both the First and Second Targan
Assault Divisions sincerely regret any and all casualties they
would have to inflict on—"

"*You stupid peasant fool!* You think your rabble can take
veteran troops? There won't be a one of you standing when

this is all over." She snorted in derision and added, "If you decide to come to your senses and change your mind, have your boys patch through to *Gyton*. This is going nowhere."

Comm went dead.

"Well, gentlemen, there it is." Sinklar sighed. "Mhitshul, I hope you got all that."

"I did." The private rubbed his neck and flipped switches on the comm.

"Then broadcast it. I want that conversation blared over the entire planet." Sinklar smacked a fist into a palm. "Send out a planet-wide alert. They'll be coming for us and I don't want our people caught sleeping."

Mhitshul pressed a stud and spread his hands. "That's it, Sink. I sent everything. Do you want us to shoot at invaders on sight?"

Sinklar frowned, absently aware he was chewing on his thumb. "Let's wait and see what happens in the—"

"Message coming in." Mhitshul's fingers flew over the comm.

"Kap here, Sink!" his Section First's florid features filled the holo. "Got LCs dropping out of the sky like flies!"

"You know the drill! Mhitshul, sound alert. We're being invaded."

"All stations on," Mhitshul called. "Rotted Gods, I got signals coming in from all over!"

"Get our LCs under cover. Scramble Battle Ops one!" Sinklar ground his teeth as he paced back and forth. "And pray to the pustulant Gods they follow the Holy Gawddamn Book to the letter again."

Outside a siren blared a warning.

"Reports are coming in." Mhitshul looked up as Shiksta left at a run, stopping only long enough to pull battle armor off the couch.

"Give me status information as it comes in." Sink cocked his head. "Mac? You there?"

"Here, Sink," Mac's voice came in through static. "They're trying to jam. Good thing you relocated those transmission stations. Uh, I'd say we've got a whole Division landing on Kaspa alone!"

Sinklar turned to look out the windows. Black dots filled the sky around him. "Same here."

Mhitshul bent to the comm, occupied with codifying data.

Without raising his head, he added, "From comm projections, it looks like five full Divisions."

"Five Divisions? Rotted Gods! That's more than Rega wasted on a whole unfriendly revolution!"

"Worst is yet to come, Sink. I've got ID codes on the ones dropping. These guys are Regan regulars. Veteran Divisions, like from regular army—career soldiers." Mhitshul swallowed. "Just like she said they'd be."

Sinklar reached up to scratch his ear. To the battle comm he called, "All right, people! This is it! Let's go! You all know what to do!"

One by one, Sections checked in.

Sinklar turned to stare out the window where the LCs dropped like perverted rain from orbit. *This fight will make or break us. Never have the stakes been so high. Never have so many hung on the line!*

"Got orbital fire support!" Ayms chimed in. "These guys are backed up all the way, Sink! Makes us a little mad thinking about the times we couldn't even get recon intelligence!"

"Break and scatter! Move, Ayms! They'll have you on pinpoint! Go!"

"We're gone!"

"LC support!" Kitmon called in. "We're covering. Ayms ain't the only one getting orbital bombardment." A resounding bang came through comm. "We're breaking!"

"Go, people, go!" Sink shouted, eyes closed as he envisioned the planet in his mind. He considered the data comm provided and built a picture of the invasion, filling the gaps by intuition.

"We've got trouble here," Mac called. "We're harassing their landings. We could cut the hell out of them, Sink. On a one-to-one fight, we'd clean them up and dump them away. Only problem is there are so many of them!"

"Don't overextend," Sink called. "Mac, before you take casualties, pull out! Break and scatter! Group by Group! If we take them head on . . . we lose! They have us outgunned, outmanned, with better transport and communication! We can't take them in a stand up fight. Move! Break off, Mac. Use your skills!"

"Affirmative, Sink," Mac's voice sounded worried—more worried than Sinklar had ever heard it. "We're breaking!"

Jaws grinding, Sinklar tapped his forehead with a clenched fist. Five Divisions? How did he counter five Divisions? Where could he find a weakness to exploit?

Anguished, he looked up at the board, mind staggering, as he realized something was amiss. "Gretta? Where's Gretta?"

"We're breaking!" Ayms called in. "There are just too many of them, Sink! My Section can't face an entire gawddamn Division. We're breaking!"

"Go!" Sink shouted. "Stay alive, Ayms! All of you, stay alive! Save your commands! Break and scatter, everybody! Go to ground. I taught you how to fight. Stay alive and make them pay. *Use the Holy Gawddamn Book against them!*"

"That means us, too?" Mhitshul asked, looking up from the comm.

"Yeah, that's us, too. *Gyton* will be setting up to blow this building off the map. Let's get out of here."

"What about comm?" Mhitshul asked as he began gathering up the maps.

"We've got an LC hidden in the brick factory, don't we?"

"Affirmative."

"Guess that will have to do for comm. Should give us planet-wide communications—and the ability to run if we need it. Best we can do. Sure can't defend this place with only three Sections in the city. Orbital will make this building into smoking junk if we do." He jumped to help stuff sensitive documents into the thick graphstic bag.

"Any word from Gretta? She said to page her through comm," he asked as they started down the carpeted stairs, stopping only long enough to grab combat armor and weapons.

"No, sir. Not a peep," Mhitshul replied over his shoulder.

Sinklar's stomach flipped as icy fingers traced his spine. Fear, aching fear, a constant companion now, left him shaken. Had the whole of Free Space gone crazy that Regans were battling Regans?

And worse, his command lay in shambles. Everything they had worked so hard to build—to turn themselves into a functioning unit the likes of which no one had seen for centuries—was broken, disorganized. A Division in chaotic retreat.

As they pounded across the courtyard, a beam of violet light struck the top of the ops building, blasting the structure in a gout of light and fire. Concussion slammed them to the ground as fragments of mortar, steel, and duraplast rained.

"Guess that was supposed to be us, huh?" Mhitshul gasped.

"Yeah," Sinklar managed through a dry throat. "Guess it was. Let's get the hell out of here."

Gretta? Where are you?

* * *

Ily Takka lounged in the command chair as her military cruiser slid into formation with the Regan vessels orbiting Targa. Occasional flickers of violet laced the surface of the planet below. Studying the fleet, Ily could make out the slivers of projectiles accelerating away from the ships and heading planetward.

"War?" Ily asked. "Targa is still that hot?" She pressed a stud. "Comm, get me the commanding vessel."

Within seconds, a craggy female face filled the screen. Behind the elderly woman, the bridge crew could be seen as they coordinated the attack. A slight quiver twitched the corner of the Regan Commander's mouth, flint eyes hardening slightly with recognition.

"Identify yourself," Ily ordered.

"Commander Rysta Braktov of the Imperial Cruiser *Gyton* at your service, Lord Minister."

"Looks like a battle is in progress, Commander." Ily cocked her head. "I had heard the situation here was slowly coming together."

The Commander nodded. "The Targan rebellion is over. However, we have a slight problem with troop discipline. Rebellion on Targa, it seems, is catching."

"Sinklar Fist?"

"You know, then. Is that why Internal Security has picked this opportunity to grace us with a visit?" Rysta's politeness extended only to the questioning glint in her eye.

"It is, Commander." Ily smiled. "Could you please update me concerning the situation?"

Rysta nodded graciously, but her gaze could have

scratched glass. "I would be happy to. You have arrived at the tail end of the action, I'm afraid. Yesterday at 15:00 hours we dropped five Divisions on Targa. Within the last planetary day we have consolidated compounds and are at the point of sending out Sections to locate and destroy the mutineers."

Ily paused, fingering her chin. *What does this mean? Could it be that following Sinklar Fist is simply another Riparian swamptoad chase? Fruitless? Is he really no more than an accident?*

"I see. Then you must have already inflicted heavy casualties on Fist's Divisions."

Rysta hesitated, an oddly sour twist to her thin lips. "We are satisfied, My Lord Minister."

And the hesitation? "Commander, what, if you would be so kind, is your body count?"

"Lord Minister, you, of all people, know the importance of proper channels. I have forwarded that information to the Lord Minister of Defense, who will no doubt be happy to—"

Ily held up her escutcheon. "Commander, I believe you are familiar with the Imperial jessant-de-lis? Ah, yes, I can see from your expression that you are."

"I . . ." Rysta swallowed, demeanor crumbling. "I'd never thought to see such a thing, Lord Minister."

"Your casualty count, Commander?"

Rysta Braktov turned to her control comm and began accessing information through her headset. A grimness puckered the wrinkled skin around her mouth. She nodded finally and looked up. "My Lord Commander, we can verify one hundred and thirty casualties from Fist's forces."

Ily rested her chin on her palm. *One hundred and thirty? So few after a concerted assault from five Divisions— assuredly good ones at that? Perhaps I don't face disaster after all.* "And your casualties, Commander?"

Braktov didn't hesitate—although her voice dropped. "Four hundred and thirty-three, Lord Minister."

Ily played long fingernails over her chin. "And I take it you have effectively crushed Fist's forces at such Pyrrhic costs?"

Rysta worked her jaws before stating, "Most definitely. Their command structure is fragmented. Individual Sections are isolated . . . and they are broken into yet smaller Groups which have no tactical cohesion. Fist's people are no more than a disorganized rabble. We only need time to sweep them up and centralize them for deportation and military justice."

"Excellent." Ily paused. "I have one condition, Commander. You will bring me Sinklar Fist—alive."

A shadow of relief crossed Rysta's face. "Gladly, Lord Minister. We shall have him for you shortly."

"The other thing which cannot be tolerated is the possibility of an accident." Ily made a gesture with her hand. "Personnel on the ground get carried away in the heat of passion. Sometimes they don't realize that higher stakes than their own vengeance might be in the balance. Do you agree?"

"I believe I understand."

"Then please reassure your ground forces that the Minister of Internal Security will personally deal with anyone who, shall we say, allows Fist to be killed 'accidentally,' hmm?" Ily studied the woman through lowered lids.

"He shall be delivered to you alive." Rysta's eyes glittered with pent up irritation.

"See that he is." Ily broke the connection.

She ran the spikelike nail of her index finger over the smoothness of her teeth. *Pray to the Rotted Gods I am not wrong about you, Fist! If I am, my best bet is to take my cruiser, my jessant-de-lis, and run for Sassa! My life will be worth little with Staffa kar Therma and Tybalt after me.*

CHAPTER XXV

Sinklar shook his head to clear the fatigue from his ragged mind. Through the hidden LC's monitors, he'd watched the sun rise and set twice. And no word had come from Gretta. He arched up against the cushioned resistance of the LC command chair to ease the ache where the muscles in his back had knotted. During the long hours he had spent huddled here, men and women—*his* men and women—had fought for their lives. The small control cubicle had become a ceramic and steel prison. The comm equipment flashed with warning lights and requests for input. He had coordinated the entire resistance from this same cramped command chair. Through the forward view ports, he could see the first rays of light graying the windows of the brick factory where they hid.

"All right, Mac." Sinklar rubbed his jaw and felt stubble. "Now's as good as ever. Go for it. Draw them out; play decoy."

"Affirmative," MacRuder's voice came back—a reflection of tingling nerves and uncertainty. "Sink? Just in case. Take care, huh? If you make it out, tell my folks how I bought it. And Sink?"

"Yeah?"

Mac's voice softened. "You've been the best, old buddy. The Blessed Gods keep you. All my love to Gretta. If I miss the wedding . . . drink one for me. First Section, clear."

"My best to you, too," Sinklar whispered, part of his mind numb at the risks being taken by people he cared about. He attempted the insane! During the slow and tenuous process of reestablishing communications with his scattered Sections, the plan had come to him—a thin nonsensical thing inconceivable in light of the Holy Gawddamn Book.

A straw in the wind, they chased it—though their path ran between Death's teeth. So many would die.

If only Gretta were here to tell me it's all right.

"Kitmon?" Sink asked, pulling his shredded concentration together. "Are you ready to hit the Fifth Etarian?"

"Affirmative. We've been scrambling channels to keep them baffled, but their jamming beams seem to be working out our relays. When they get around to jamming us completely, we've got mining lasers set up. We'll be using them so we can keep communications control with dots and dashes. It'll be tight, but I think we can fool them."

"Sounds good. You know the situation better than I do. Take your best shot. Fire at will." Sinklar picked up his cup of stassa and drained it to the last nourishing drop. When had it gotten so cold?

How long since I slept last? I've got five millimeters of stubble on my cheeks and someone poured a half a kilo of sand in my eyes. I need you with me, Gretta. I've never done this alone before. If anything's happened to you, they'll pay, and pay, and pay. . . . He closed his eyes and drew a ragged breath.

He forced himself to blink away the ache in his eyes in order to study the cramped monitor on the LC bridge. Time to check on the fighting up by the Raktan mines. "Hauws? Status report?"

The voice came through a crackling battle comm. "We're into 'em, Sink. We've punched right through their defenses. Plan's proceeding like clockwork. They seem to be giving a little too easily."

"What do you mean? They just retreating without a fight?"

"No. They shoot good enough. I don't know. Just a hunch."

Sinklar turned to the comm, twisting the resolution controls. The battlefield terrain around the Raktan mines clarified as the comm accessed cadastral survey data. Sink plotted Hauws' movements against the suspected Regan position. The Third Ashtan Division under First Weebouw would have formed a defensive perimeter according to the book—and they should have fought like mad dogs to keep that same perimeter. Sink squinted at the comm-generated image and thought for a second.

"Yeah," Sink leaned forward in sudden understanding. "Of course! Hauws? Listen, there's a valley ahead of you, right?"

"Sure is. They seem to be falling back for it. If we can concentrate them in that valley, take the ridges around it, we'll have them with their britches around their—"

"*Don't!* Repeat, do not! Hauws, it's a trap. They'll have you! You'll be like targets on the training range! They'll paste you from orbital. Uh, let's see, page 95 of the Holy Gawddamn Book. 'Concentration of the enemy forces for orbital attack through misdirection.' Remember? Can you swing right? Break their flank? Maybe pull them apart, split their forces? Ruin their balance, and you can make a fast drive for the mine offices."

"I remember. You're right. We're gone!" The staccato of blaster and pulse fire practically drowned Hauws' voice.

For long moments Sinklar glared at the comm and tried to imagine Hauws' Section as they maneuvered against Weebouw's Veteran Ashtan troops.

Then the comm crackled as Hauws' excited voice cried: "Etarian Priest crap, Sink! I'm starting to think these guys are made of butter. Each Group sits around until the Section First tells them where to move. Then they go. No initiative. Yeah, we're putting the claws to them. They didn't think we'd break right. You called it again, Boss!"

Sink chortled, half-silly with exhaustion. "Don't get to underestimating them. They might have some guts to make up for that command deficiency."

"Sink?" Hauws' voice was barely audible as a jamming sequence from orbit tried to tie down their band. "We're making headway. Group C just got them flanked. We're pushing through."

"Excellent, Hauws. They should have to pull another two Sections to reinforce that flank. Keep it up, pal, you're buying victory!"

"Yeah. But we're bleeding for it, too. It doesn't come free."

"I know. Try and keep in touch." Sinklar rubbed his face with a gritty hand. He noticed Mhitshul had refilled his stassa cup. A go pill lay beside it. How many more could he take before the drug began to blur reality and make his decisions suspect?

Hauws was taking casualties? How many? Just how much would this Regan idiocy cost the First Targan in precious blood? Could they make it work? Was the price in blood worth a futile attempt to defeat five Regan Divisions simultaneously on seven different fronts?

"Kap? Report, Kap!"

Crackly silence.

"Ayms? You there, Ayms?"

Nothing.

"Rotted Gods, they've jammed us completely." Sinklar used a thumb and forefinger to rub his eyes as he struggled to keep his mind from going numb. All those men and women had to rely on themselves now. He couldn't help. They knew the plan, where to go, how to do their jobs. But so many things happened. Battlefields went random from the first shot fired. How many would die? How many? He cradled his head in his hands as the words repeated in his head.

"How's it look?" Shiksta's scabby voice called, breaking Sink's mental haze. The crackle of Shik's big gravity flux guns sounded through the comm.

Sinklar exhaled wearily. "Hanging by a thread. Right now, it could go either way. They've managed to cut communications with three Sections and are pinning the rest down."

"Uh." Shiksta hesitated. "What was the fancy word you used? Command overload paralysis? They heard of that yet? Want me to send a guy out with a white flag? You know, maybe remind them that they're supposed to get all confused right about now and seize up so we can beat the shit out of them?"

Sinklar started to snap a reproof as Shiksta's words penetrated his over-tight mind. Instead, a chuckle rose to his lips. "Yeah, Shik, you do that, huh? And in the meantime, I'm going to act like the Seddi and pray for a stinking miracle!"

* * *

Skyla made a final check of her ship's systems and stood, running fingers through her hair to massage her scalp after removing the weight of the worry-cap. The cockpit controls gleamed at her in reassuring patterns. Beyond the view port, the stars directly ahead shimmered like violet lances as her craft sped for the Itreatic Asteroids.

She passed through the hatch and locked it carefully, seeing Nyklos hunched over one of the comm monitors. A cup of stassa rested forgotten by his right hand. He glanced up and smiled as she stepped into the small galley.

"Hungry?"

"Always," he told her. "You know, I could get used to being your prisoner."

She shot him a reproving glance and tapped instructions into the dispenser, deciding on Riparian catfish in a hot pepper sauce for herself, and an Ashtan dolma for Nyklos. Then she stuck her cup under the stassa dispenser and settled into the overstuffed cushions across from him. Damn it, why did he have to look at her with that wry appreciation?

"Course is set for Itreata?" Nyklos asked with an intimate smile.

She toyed with her cup, rocking it on the base so the hot liquid rolled around the brim. "It is. I gave it a lot of thought. Consider what we know. Targa is embargoed, and we have but the foggiest of ideas about how the revolt is progressing there. We know Ily spaced for Targa, and the most likely explanation for that is that somehow she got an inkling that Staffa's headed there. I'm not going to leave Staffa's fat frying in Ily's fire."

"So you're going to Targa with the entire might of the Companions behind you? You know, if I didn't already love you. . . ."

"Stop it."

Nyklos chuckled. "You were the one who used the Mytol. But seriously, the Companions moving on Targa will provoke Tybalt. What do you expect the poor man to do? You could be starting a major war."

Skyla took a deep breath. "Then I start one. I won't be the person to fire the first shot. We're supposed to have free passage through Regan space for nonmilitary activities."

"And a fleet of Companions headed for a world in revolt is a nonmilitary activity?" Nyklos raised a bushy eyebrow and his mustache twitched.

Skyla gave him a frosty glare that appeared to have no

effect. "I'll take that gamble. Meanwhile, I have a question of my own. Why haven't you tried anything yet? You seem to be a model hostage. You haven't even jiggled the door to your room. I don't like complaince from people like you. It makes me suspicious."

He smiled at some private thought, then said, "Quite honestly, something's gone wrong on Targa. I don't have the faintest clue as to what it might be, let alone the details. It's just a feeling. You know, the sort of intuitive hunch you get when the wording changes in the communiques. Magister Bruen is no one's fool, but I can sense that he's worried. Everything's falling apart—and it started with Staffa's behavioral aberration." He met her gaze. "If helping you leaves me in a position to help the Seddi, I'll take that chance."

"And if it doesn't?"

"I'll deal with that problem when it comes." Nyklos sighed and rubbed the back of his neck. "Maybe the quanta are playing us all for fools. I should be dead back in that alley. I remember cracking that tooth, waiting for the poison, stalling for it to take effect. Someone goofed and I'm alive. In this instance, you haven't used the information you gained against us. Fortuitous? Random chance? You tell me the odds. You're supposed to be the enemy."

"But everything's changed—or has it?" Skyla waited patiently.

Nyklos didn't budge. "You tell me. What are the final goals of the Companions? Domination of Free Space?"

Skyla steepled her fingers. "What if the Companions did exactly that—crushed the Regans, and wheeled in a lightning blow and broke the back of the Sassan Empire? What would your reaction be?"

Nyklos twisted the end of his mustache with pensive fingers. "That would depend on Staffa. What happened, Skyla? Why did the Lord Commander—the man with a conscience like Terguzzi ice—suddenly slip away to Etarus to be mugged in an alley, convicted of murder, and condemned to the collar. What happened to him out there in that desert? The man who jumped into my aircar wasn't the arrogant Lord Commander I'd studied for years. Tell me, Skyla, give me the best information you can, because a lot could hinge on what I report to Bruen."

The chime rang, and Skyla stood long enough to pull the steaming trays from the dispenser. She slipped into the seat again and faced Nyklos over her tray. "That's a little one-sided, don't you think? I divulge information on the Lord Commander of the Companions, and what do I get in return? You're not exactly a trusted confidant, Nyklos."

He stared soberly into the dolma that sent delightful smells into the air before nodding. "All right, here's why I want to know. If something happened to Staffa, something that changed his personality, it could have a dramatic effect on Seddi relationships with the Companions."

"We don't *need* you," Skyla reminded.

Nyklos leaned back and crossed his arms. "That depends, Wing Commander. If your goal is the final conquest of Free Space, what next? Is it the Lord Commander's plan to become the despot he's always resembled? If so, yours will be one of the shortest-lived empires ever. Oh, we've run the projections. Staffa's lack of humanity will bring about his demise in short order. He's a conqueror—a man who breaks, not builds."

"So you wait us out."

Nyklos shook his head. "It's not that simple. What do you know about systems analysis?"

"Enough."

"Then you know that humanity *might* be able to survive one more war—the one that unifies Free Space. But the holocaust that a revolution against the Star Butcher would set loose? We've run the predictions over and over and the results are the same—extinction on worlds like Sylene and Terguz and Formosa. Some enclaves of humans will probably survive in places like Targa, Sassa, and Rega, but their natural resources have been so depleted that civilization will never arise again. Those people will be condemned to live as subsistence farmers among the ruins."

"Assuming your model is correct."

The expression on his face didn't change. "We'll give you the data. Check it, run it any way you like."

"Then why not simply assassinate Staffa and myself, hope the Companions fall apart, and that Rega and Sassa can slug it out for the remains."

"To the Seddi, the idea of living under a Regan or Sassan

government is only slightly more acceptable than being under the heel of the Star Butcher."

"And your interest in Staffa?"

"He's the key to Free Space. Tell me, Skyla, what happened to send him running to Etaria and disaster? Why would he do something so dumb? He blew every projection we had."

"Staffa wanted to learn what it was to be human, Nyklos."

The Seddi operative sank slowly back into the seat. "In that case, he got a belly full. He's probably in for more trouble when he arrives on Targa."

"Seddi treachery?"

"No, Magister Bruen gave his word, but I do know the war on Targa is getting pretty vicious."

* * *

Sampson Henck, First of the Twenty-seventh Maikan Assault Division, shook his head as he stared at the situation board where it dominated one wall of the commandeered headquarters building in the center of Kaspa. Fifty years of career service had given him a cynical squint. He liked to consider the Twenty-seventh Maikan as one of the pillars of the Regan military establishment. The fact that it hadn't been deactivated after the Maikan conquest was proof of its worth to Henck. Now he rubbed his jaw as he studied the board, trying to get a handle on the means of destroying his fleeing foe with the most economic and efficient means.

Lights marking troop positions moved through the warehouse district where the Fourth Section ran in support of their point Group. Pustulant rot, chasing the miserable Targans had pulled his people half out of town! Ashtan prairie goats ran slower!

Henck growled to himself as he paced over to the window to stare out at Kaspa. "What the hell are they doing? These renegades act like they don't have the intelligence the Blessed Gods gave to a rock! They just shoot . . . and when they draw a response, they run. Where's the sense in that? It's lunacy!"

"Attention Fourth Section. We have a Group drawing

fire five blocks ahead of you. Move out and support!" the Staff Second ordered where he listened to the comm chatter.

"I don't understand." Henck pointed to the map of Kaspa. "What possible purpose could they have in trying to take that industrial district? It's strategically indefensible. All we have to do is send a Section in after them, and they're out—further from the center of town than before!"

"Sir, suppose we let them have it?" His Staff Second glanced nervously at him. "Every time we react to their attacks, we find only a Group or so, all fleeing through the streets. Like you said, there's no rhyme or reason to it. They can't tie up our Sections for more than a short fire-fight—they don't have the strength. Besides, we've chased them clear out of the city. We control all the territory between our Group perimeter and the headquarters compound."

Henck fingered his throat. "So it would seem. To threaten us now, they'd have to mount a major offensive to roll our forces back; and with orbital recon, we know for a fact they don't have a Division out there hiding in the hills." *And that's what it would take to recapture this city. A blood-rotted Division.* He made his decision. "Sure, it's a meaningless exercise, but have the Fourth drive them out of those warehouses. What the Rotted hell, the exercise will do them good."

"Yes, sir." The Staff Second turned to his comm. "Section First Paulus? You'll order your Section to clean out that warehouse area."

Henck grinned to himself as he stared up at the situation board. The rebellious Targans were scurrying like Riparian salamanders. Demoralized and dispirited, his troops need only corral the treasonous bastards before shipping them back to Rega for trial. "Kaspa is ours."

"Yes, sir."

"Hectic there for a bit, though, shuffling Sections and Groups back and forth like a tapa game. They could have cut us to pieces more than once had they had the firepower and personnel."

"They still hurt us too badly," the Staff Second reminded as he logged the commands into the master book. "For as disorganized as their Groups seem to be, we took too many casualties."

The Staff Second frowned as he tapped a stylus against the comm casing. "You know, the other bothersome thing is that we had to counter their Groups with full Sections. On a Group to Group basis, they shot the dripping pus out of us! Broke every defensive formation. How did they do that?"

First Henck tugged at his earlobe as he glared at the situation board. His entire Division had been spread out until it resembled a thin ring around the outskirts of town. A nagging worry made him suck at his lower lip. "I don't like this. They don't have air capabilities to match ours . . . but we might want to bring some of our strength back to support—"

A violent explosion battered the headquarters compound. Gravity flux shook the building with enough force to pitch Henck to the floor.

Dust and ceiling panels rained from above. The situation board wobbled before it crashed onto the Staff officers and shattered. The room went dark. The comm—proofed against such things—sent eerie colored shafts of light through twisting dust. For long moments, Henck lay stunned, nerves spasming, brain reeling with aftereffects. His heterodyning ears picked out the sound of the Staff Third hacking and coughing as he puked.

Henck got to his hands and knees, working his jaw to clear his ears of the wretched ringing.

"Blood and dung!" the Second spat. "That was a close one."

"Get me orbital," Henck grated. "They should be able to follow that one back to the projector. I want that position burned down to molten slag."

Staff Third tried to climb up to the comm board, wavering and staggering as he careened to the wall where he leaned limply. Glass crunched under his weight.

The pounding of feet could be heard on the lower floors, loud in the sudden silence. Somewhere a blaster crackled. Shouts broke out.

"What the corrupt hell?" Henck squinted in an attempt to focus his eyes. His scattered thoughts refused to coordinate, but he knew instinctively that something had gone terribly wrong.

Staff Second had rolled over to sit up, head cradled in

his hands. "Wish to God that grav shot had missed. My skull's splitting!"

More blaster fire erupted in the hallway. Henck gasped as his stomach heaved and he vomited the last of his disorientation into the dust from the cracked ceiling. He looked up as the door splintered inward from a pulse shot that sent slivers and pieces clattering through the debris on the floor.

Something's very wrong. I've got to act . . . get my wits together and . . . and. . . .

"Rotted Gods!" the Staff Third blared as he looked through the hole blown in the door. His mouth dropped open, eyes wide, expression contorted by horror as his fingers settled on his pistol butt. For some reason, he couldn't seem to get the coordination together to pull his weapon.

The sight engraved itself forever on Henck's brain as he watched the last security guard's body buck and explode in a haze of pink before the remains plopped limply to the floor. A severed arm flopped into the room.

He was still blinking as the black snouts of blasters poked around the corner. Then armored soldiers appeared behind them.

"You! First Henck!" a sharp voice called. "Yeah, we know who you are. You've got five seconds to put your hands over your head! Surrender, or die, friend!"

Henck started to shake his head, hearing other boots beating their way in from the back. The rear door, too, splintered under pulse fire. More grimy, armored soldiers came crashing in, blasters backed by stony expressions. They covered the room, heavy weapons shouldered, eyes hot and angry.

"First Henck, do you surrender?" the man called, stepping through the wreckage of the main door. He wore a Section First's chevron on his arm. Others poured in after him, surrounding Henck and his officers where they stared up in stunned disbelief.

Suffering to lift his hands, Henck nodded, dazed. How could this possibly be happening? Another urge to vomit, unrelated to the gravity flux, curled around his gut.

The young Section First grinned before he pulled up one of the spilled chairs and sat down before the comm. He pressed a stud and talked confidently into the system: "Sink? Hope you can hear me. Mac, here. We've got

Kaspa. Looks like the Twenty-seventh Division is history, Boss." Mac paused as a faint voice that Henck couldn't make out replied. Then Mac added, "Tell Shiksta that shot was perfect! Building shielded us from most of it, but we're a little woozy."

Henck tensed and trembled as strong hands pulled him to his feet. His mind reeled as other hands stripped off his weapons and armor. The floor felt cold on his unsuited feet as they tied his hands with binding straps and led him out into the cool Kaspan night.

* * *

Hauws—with the remains of his Group—staggered up the steep slope, gasping and panting. Smoke-streaked and filthy, they stumbled upward through the gray-black angular boulders that littered the slope. Between them hung a huge four-man blaster that they toiled to lift over the rocks and fallen trees. Hauws had broken away from his Section with twenty men and women. Fifteen of those lay dead on the slope below—picked off one by one by blaster fire and bombardment.

"Down!" Private Buchman screamed—and they flopped to the ground just as a high whistle ended in a loud *crack-bang!* Shrapnel chipped fragments off the rocks they huddled in, while a haze of yellow-green vapor hissed, marking the ghostly shrapnel trails.

"Don't breathe!" Hauws ordered as the poison gas laced the air around them. "Faces in the dirt!" They waited while the streamers of vapor drifted to the east with the breeze. Anxiously, Hauws lifted his head, peering around with owl eyes.

"That's it. Let's go!" He slapped the man next to him. "C'mon, c'mon!"

"Blaster's all right," another private reported. "All systems are go!"

"Let's roll, people!" Hauws bellowed, grabbing up his carry handle, feeling the heavy weapon lift unevenly.

"Fred's dead," Johey called. "Looks like a bit of that poisoned shrap got him in the leg."

"Keep away from that shit!" Hauws ordered. "Don't get

close to that hole, one whiff—or even a touch of that tainted shrapnel—will kill you as dead as Freddie! Let's move."

They struggled up the slope, fighting time and gravity as the sun slanted toward the horizon. In the back of each mind lay the knowledge that the Third Ashtan was trying to line up another long shot like the last one.

Behind them and below, masked by the pine-thick brush-choked draws and gullies under the ridge, periodic concussions and faint flickers of laser and blaster light lashed back and forth as the other two Groups of Hauws' Third Section fought a desperate rearguard action to buy them time, to hold off the hordes.

"Another fifty meters, people," Hauws gasped, back cracking under the weight, lungs fire-pained. Sweat trickled in itching tracks down his face. Heat and stink rolled off his tired staggering body.

"Think . . . Sink's still . . . out there?" someone puffed.

"He . . . better be," Hauws panted and coughed. " 'Cause if the damn Regans . . . got him . . . I'm gonna make . . . somebody pay."

"Damn right," another panting, staggering soldier agreed.

They heaved and struggled for footing in the loose dusty colluvial gravels near the top. Slipping and cursing, they wound between the scrubby pines.

Fifty yards to their left, the air crackled as pines and firs exploded into toothpicks—rock and dust blasting out and up in an earth-shaking upheaval that battered them to the ground.

"Regan bastards!" Hauws spit, blinking in the dust as rocks and debris cascaded around him. He looked up, eyes red in his black-skinned face. His voice came in wheezing gasps, "Blessed Gods, just get us to the top of this pus-rotted ridge. Just that far. Then give us time for one lousy miserable shot with this heavy son of a bitch and I'll come screw the daylights outta each and every one of your little Priestess girls for the rest of my life!"

Smaller pebbles and grit were settling on them now. "C'mon, another fifty meters, people!" And they staggered on, aware that hostile IR sensors were seeking from down below. Hopefully, for the moment, those seekers would be fooled by the hot spot where the particle gun had riven the mountain.

"Ten meters," Hauws gasped, his throat making whistling noises. His muscles had become quivering rubber under the strain, his feet slid in the loose dirt. "By the Foul Bastard's balls, my throat's never been this dry in all my life." Then, "Five meters!" And they were at the crest.

"Johey," Hauws grunted, "Take point. See what's on the other side."

" 'Firmative."

They pulled and wedged the big blaster behind a solid looking outcrop, unslinging shoulder weapons and crouching in the rocks as the private, face sweat-shiny, mouth open as he panted, crept over the top.

"C'mon," Hauws whispered under his breath. "C'mon, kid. Get back and tell us it's okay!" He clenched his fist, jerking it up and down nervously, while he looked around, noticing the incredible beauty of the place—if it just weren't full of people trying to kill him.

The ridge exploded below, blasting more timber and rock to drop from the dust-streaked sky.

"Crap!" Hauws hollered. "C'mon! Let's yank this thing over the other side! They've got the range, next one's gonna cook us!" The three of them, heaving, faces red, lifted the gun and struggled over the crest, stumbling, cursing, muscles tearing as they gulped air.

"Set! Let's roll!" Hauws barked, grin spreading as he saw the Regan Command headquarters: five dull gray buildings poking out of the far hillside above chutes of tailings. LCs were parked in neat rows along one side. A combat com dish thrust up above the largest structure.

"C'mon, people! Let's go. One shot now, just one shot!"

They spun the blaster, Private Buchman dropping into the gunner's seat, settling the sighting mechanism on the buildings across the valley.

"Charge is up!" Hauws hollered. "Five shots is all we got! Make them straight, Buchman!" He looked nervously at the way the gun sat on the sloping weathered soils. Not good, oughta have a better foundation.

A blaster bolt cackled past Hauws' shoulder, popping hollowly as it blew Private Rypmar's head off, showering bloody bony fragments around.

"Whore crap!" Hauws barked, as he threw himself into the low-lying skin-prickly shrubs. Pulling his blaster up, he cursed, seeing Johey's broken body where it had slid another ten meters down the slope.

"Shoot! Buchman, shoot!" Hauws hollered as he sighted on a Regan soldier scrambling up the slope below. He pressed the firing stud. The man's right arm exploded. The air above Hauws' back tore like an amplified sheet as the big gun cut loose. He felt the vibration along his sweaty back while he laid down a suppressing fire, blasting trees, powdering rocks, hoping to keep the advancing Regan Group from closing.

Again Buchman shot. Hauws took time to get a brief glimpse of a second building erupting in fragments and fire. The one with the combat comm had already been turned into smoking rubble.

"First!" Buchman's voice shrilled frantically. *"The damn gun's sliding!"*

"Terguzzi crap!" Hauws flung himself up over the rocks, heedless of a blaster bolt that almost clipped his side and left the armor cracked and flaking away.

He threw himself against the sliding gun and dug his heels into the loose stuff, aware of the hum of power. With all his strength, he braked the gun's slide.

"Shoot, Buchman. Get your sight picture—*and shoot!*"

"But the radiation will—"

"Damn you! Shoot! That's an order!"

The sight in Hauws' left eye burned out as the blaster discharged and another building ripped apart in a gout of fire and death.

At the same time, chunks of the mountain to either side ripped and bucked as the Division guns were turned toward their position.

The fourth shot cooked the meat in Hauws' cheek. He howled curses into the wind, his one good eye blurred by tears and pain.

"Last shot," Buchman called. "I'm taking the largest of the buildings!" The blaster ripped the air and the tearing sound deafened Hauws.

A concussion blasted Hauws into the air, sending him spinning—the gun and Buchman lost in the haze. He smacked the ground, bounced, rolled, and stopped against a rock.

Searing agony shot up his leg while his body quivered in high frequency shock. A curiously calm academic feeling settled on his shrilling nerves.

"Been hit," he croaked. "Been hit hard." He blinked his one good eye clear of tears and looked. The hamburgered place where his leg ended at mid-thigh didn't frighten him like he'd always thought it would. The distance his pulverized arteries shot blood fascinated him as red splattered the sunset-colored rocks.

Buchman appeared beside him, bending down, reaching.

"Get outta here," Hauws told him in a frog voice. "I'm gone. They got me. Just get back! Get our people out! Get back to Sink! Report!" The mountainside whirled in his vision and he threw up without feeling it.

He couldn't seem to keep the world in focus. "Oughta be home culturing bacteria." He remembered the olive trees on Ashtan, and the coffeehouse that never could pass inspection—but still made the richest coffee in the world. He tried to see, but the gray shimmering grew black. "Got 'em, Sink," he told himself, voice dwindling. "Got the bastards in the end."

* * *

Ily Takka tapped her foot in irritation as she waited for the shuttle lock to sound an all clear. The thick doors hissed slightly as they finally opened—interstellar cold vaporizing moisture in the air as she stepped into Commander Rysta Braktov's *Gyton*.

The warship's lock looked just like every other military lock. Oval and featureless except for the armored Marine guard and the color-coded control panel. The Marine glanced at the jessant-de-lis, input his clearance, and saluted as the final door hissed back to allow her into *Gyton*'s lateral corridor.

Ily snapped a return salute to an officer and followed his stiff back as he led her through the spartan corridors of the star cruiser. The place smelled of lubricant, humans, and synthetics. A pervading hum filled the air—a constant for Regan battle craft. Every surface had been painted in either white or gray. The officer stopped before a wardroom hatch and pressed a stud to open a final door. The meeting room proved as sterile as the rest of the ship.

Rysta Braktov sat at the head of the small table where she scowled into a desk-mounted monitor. Acceleration helving and monitors filled the walls in a no-nonsense manner. Only one other chair module had risen from the floor across from Rysta.

"You asked for a meeting?" Ily reminded, coming to the point, standing, arms crossed, before the small table.

Rysta looked up, moving her mouth as if she had a sour taste in it. "Want something to drink, Minister?"

"Myklenian brandy?"

"This is a warship, Minister," Rysta reminded dryly. Then she turned and slapped a wrinkled palm to the comm access. "Duty First, bring a bottle of our best—whatever's left—and see that we are not disturbed unless something impossible develops down there." Rysta removed a headset from her brow and the monitor went blank.

"I take it all is not well on Targa. You haven't killed Sinklar Fist, have you?" Ily barely acknowledged the officer who entered and left an expensive looking flask on the table. The door behind her slid shut as he left.

"Please, be seated, Minister Takka," Rysta ran gnarled age-spotted hands over her dark face, momentarily stretching and rearranging the wrinkles. She looked haggard, gray-shot hair disheveled. The hard squint in her eyes betrayed a weariness. "I'm past being formal. Let's just get to the point and find a solution to this damn mess one-on-one, all right?"

"You look tired," Ily offered as she settled into a seat.

Rysta leaned forward to prop her head between both palms. "Minister. I'll be honest. I've served the Imperium since before Tybalt's father took the mantle on Rega. I've seen Ministers come and go . . . watched the Empire grow and expand. I've been awarded citations, enjoyed state dinners in the company of the Emperors, and the Lord Commander himself offered me a commission among the Companions."

"Why are you telling me all this?" Ily tapped a stud on the table. A freefall cup appeared and she poured the liquor—an amber Ashtan whiskey. Through it all, Rysta watched, but her keen edge had been blunted.

"You've kept track of the battle down there?" Rysta asked.

"A lot of fighting has been going on. We haven't been able to get all the communications. Your jamming doesn't only affect Fist's rebellious Division, it bleeds into our systems. We know the general pattern."

Rysta took a breath. "Then you know that somehow, some way, that little bastard is pulling the rug right out from under us." She shook her head. "I don't get it. Fist's Targan Division is defying every law of warfare—and by eggs and ions, he's cutting our throats. Unethically, to be sure, but a cut throat bleeds whether it's slit by an emperor or a thief."

"He's succeeding in taking the command staff?" Ily mused, a light enjoyment touching her heart.

"Succeeded," Rysta grunted. "The Third Ashtan Assault Divisional headquarters was just blown away. Seems the Section they faced—yes, I said Section—dragged a four-man blaster up an impossible cliff and wiped out Weebouw and all his staff. What was left of the Targan Section melted away into the trees, surrounded the Ashtan positions, and started closing on the Section commands. They're wiping them out now—while the Third Ashtan sits in the hills waiting for orders that won't come."

Rysta hissed derision. "Oh, we hurt them. Of their two hundred we killed almost one hundred and seventy-five, but the fact remains—"

"And how much of the Third Ashtan did they get?" Ily interrupted.

"Almost five hundred combat personnel, not including Division and Section command staff."

"And then?"

"We're not sure. An LC showed up. One of Fist's. We don't know what happened then, but there's been no further communication. After each and every Divisional command down there was captured or destroyed, our troops went silent. We've been broadcasting queries since we lost the Third Ashtan. Nothing."

"And now what?" Ily lifted an eyebrow.

Rysta dropped her eyes. "You know what this means?"

"For all intents and purposes, Sinklar Fist has destroyed five Regan combat Divisions." *And I have the tool I need to place me on the Regan throne! Sinklar Fist, for all your odd looks and your funny eyes, you are the most precious human in Free Space!*

Rysta tilted her head back and exhaled. "Yes, he's done it. It's against all the odds. It's against any military axiom we know." She slapped a bony hand into a hard palm. "They established laws for the conduct of war years ago! This Fist is . . . barbaric! A damn criminal butcher! If he gets away with this, the whole of Free Space will suffer."

"You've called the Emperor?" Ily wondered, beginning to see Rysta's problem. No wonder she related her illustrious career. Old school to the hilt, Rysta *had* to stop this new genie before he wisped out of the Targan bottle.

Smoking brown eyes met hers. "No, I haven't. I thought perhaps it would be worth discussing the present situation with you. You carry the jessant-de-lis."

"And you want authority?"

Rysta pursed her lips, pulling her old body up straight. "What I want is to finish this. Rega, right now, can't, *can't* allow Sinklar Fist to win. Everything we've built would tumble into chaos. The very nature of war is being—"

"And you can prevent it?"

Commander Braktov nodded, the action making her sagging flesh wiggle. "I don't like it, but I think we have extraordinary circumstances." She patted a horny palm on the duraplast table. "The decision didn't come easily. It will mean the sacrifice of a lot of good men and women. Veteran troops the Emperor will need in the struggle against Sassa, but we must be willing to—"

"No."

Rysta leaned forward intently. "Minister? I don't think you understand the grave nature of the situation down there. Sinklar Fist, with an untrained Division, just—"

"No." Ily repeated, sipping her liquor. "That is the last thing you will do."

"*What?* How can we conduct war in the future if just any old barbarity is allowed? How can we get trained responsible people to take command of the military . . . knowing they might die as a result? Do you have any idea of what you're proposing? It's . . . it's insanity if—"

"Commander, consider." Ily crossed her legs and leaned back. Her fingernails tapped out a staccato on the drinking bulb. "Sinklar Fist just destroyed the combat capabilities of ten thousand veteran personnel with roughly two thousand thinly spread troops of his own."

"There were more," Rysta pointed out. "He had Targan revolutionaries he'd recruited."

"And who were mostly unarmed," Ily rejoined. "He also only had the use of five LCs and no orbital intelligence or bombardment. Now, using your own misfortune as a guide, how much damage do you think he could do to the Sassans given the advantages of Regan technology and crack veteran combat personnel?"

"He destroyed most of those on the ground down there," Rysta growled. "Weebouw. Henck. Damn." She blinked as her mouth screwed up. She shot a pained look at Ily. "Your thrice-cursed Sinklar Fist killed a lot of my good friends. Capable and competent commanders."

"Then I suppose we had better talk to him sometime soon," Ily decided. "Lord knows, if we don't, he'll have the troops he captured down there recruited, too, and next thing we know, he'll be marching up the Grand Hallway and into the Imperial Court."

Rysta leaned forward, an eager expression lighting her old brown eyes. "All the more reason to kill him now."

"No."

"But one orbital shot would render the whole planet. . . ."

Rysta didn't finish when Ily turned a hostile glance her way.

Ily steepled her fingers as the silence stretched. "Commander, I don't think you understand the political intricacies of the coming Sassan campaign. We are faced with the final confrontation. Rega stands alone. We face Sassa . . . and the Companions. Do you think you could take the Lord Commander by using the tactics in the book?" At the tightening of Rysta's expression, Ily smiled. "No, I didn't think so. Tybalt and I both agree that Rega must win—no matter whose tactics we use. Once Sinklar Fist rolls over the top of Sassa, there will be one Empire in Free Space—and it will be Regan."

Ily lifted a challenging eyebrow. "And there won't be a

need for a large standing army, Rysta. Internal Security will handle the rest—and we don't need formal rules of war."

Rysta Braktov looked like she'd swallowed Riparian slime.

* * *

"First? Sinklar?" Mhitshul's gentle prodding brought Sinklar awake. He started, automatically reaching out for a comm that wasn't there. Instead his aide stood in the narrow passageway of the LC. Despite the faint light, Sink could see that a dumb misery filled Mhitshul's eyes.

"What? What's wrong? What do we need to do? Who's in trouble?" He spun around to stare at the smudged hull plate behind and above him. He could feel the cushion of an acceleration cot beneath him and his feet had gone to sleep from the cramped position.

"First Fist," Mhitshul began, looking at the deck below his feet. "There's something—"

"Wait!" Sinklar sat up, rubbing his hot red eyes with dirty fingers. "How'd I get here? I was at the comm, taking the reports. What happened? We get hit?" He blinked, screwing his face into contortions to bring it awake.

"No, sir," Mhitshul told him soberly. "It was over. You were nodding off—asleep on your feet. I explained the situation and Mac took control. I carried you over to the drop couch, covered you with a blanket and let you sleep."

"How . . . how long?" Sinklar pulled his wrist around to look at his chronometer. "Blessed Gods, *ten hours?*"

"Everything on the planetary level is fine, sir," Mhitshul told him gently. "The Minister of Internal Security would like to meet with you to discuss the resolution of this situation with a minimum of further conflict. She claims she has been sent with authority from the Imperial Seventh himself . . . Tybalt. She has the power to conclude any kind of deal necessary which will work to the benefit of all."

Sinklar puffed a sigh of relief and winced as returning circulation shot pins and needles through his feet. "My God, we won," he added wearily. "We won, Mhitshul."

"Yes, sir," the man still looked subdued, biting his lip, staring at the floor.

"And Hauws? He's. . . ."

"Dead, sir. Private Buchman confirmed it. Section First

Hauws was fatally wounded when they destroyed the Third
Ashtan headquarters. We took the surrender of the
remaining Sections of that Division just before you passed
out, sir.

Sinklar slumped back against the cool metal plate.
Hauws, who should have been conducting public health
inspections, dead? *Why are we living this shit?*

"Sir? Buchman has gone back for the body. Maybe we
can—"

"Where in hell are we?"

"Vespa, sir. We're inside the brick factory again. Seems
like there hasn't been time to find a different
headquarters."

Sinklar nodded. "No, I suppose not. Where's Gretta?
Has she checked in yet?"

Mhitshul swallowed hard. "Well, that's just it, sir. We
don't know. No one's seen her."

Sinklar closed his eyes, dullness constricting around his
heart. He forced his mind to clear and replayed that entire
flight back from Kaspa. They'd parted in front of the LC
before the headquarter and. . . . "Wait, she said something
about the Seddi assassin. Anybody checked the old Internal
Security headquarters?"

Mhitshul shook his head. "No, sir."

"Let's go!" Sinklar pulled himself to his feet, grabbing a
blaster from the rack. "What happened to the guards that
were down there?"

"Um, that would have been Seventh Section. I'll have
Mayz send them back to duty."

Lost in his worry about Gretta, Sinklar trotted down the
ramp, aware of the number of people swarming around portable tables that had been set up. Evidently, the brick factory now served as planetary headquarters. The place
buzzed with talk, shuffling feet, the clicking of comm keys,
and the scraping of chairs on the gritty concrete floor. The
high ceiling amplified the bustle.

The room went quiet as they spotted him. Sinklar stopped
short, aware of their awed attention. All eyes were upon
him as they stood in their scorched and battered armor.
Plastaheal had been slapped across lacerations and burns.
An occasional suit arm hung empty, or a person leaned on
crutches, pale but mobile.

But their faces, they had such curious expressions. Something possessed their eyes, some sharpness. New wariness and deep pride had etched their raptorian features. They were changed, forged into something different than the bumpkins he'd inherited with the First Targan, or the broken remains of the defeated Second Division. Here and there, Targan Rebels stood shoulder to shoulder with Regan former enemies, all looking at him in that same keen manner. He could sense the glow, the sharpening of breath, an increase of color in cheek and brow. A spark seemed to leap electrically from eye to eye and a radiance infused every one of them. Possessed . . . possessed by what?

A voice broke the silence, clear, echoing from the arched roof so high overhead. "LONG LIVE SINKLAR FIST!"

They erupted in a roaring swell of sound, "LONG LIVE FIST! LONG LIVE FIST!" It rolled, booming in the big hall.

He lifted his hands, having to wave them to bring order. "It was you who did the impossible, not I."

"SINKLAR! SINKLAR! SINKLAR!" they exploded, the booming shout rattling the rafters overhead.

Sinklar stood paralyzed until Mhitshul appeared beside him and took his arm. He let himself be led through the crowd that parted magically before him. Still the roaring salute pounded the air as the press shouted his name over and over.

"I don't understand," he muttered as Mhitshul ushered him through a side door. "What are they doing?"

"They know you saved them, sir. You defeated five of the best Regan Divisions the Emperor has. Rega is suing for peace with us. The Lord Minister, Ily Takka, is landing tomorrow to seek an audience *with you*." Mhitshul swallowed, eyes still downcast. "How many men would challenge an Emperor for the likes of them?"

Sinklar winced. "It . . . had to be done. Not just for them, for all of us."

The cell block stood silent and empty when they arrived. A terrible premonition grew in Sinklar's breast. Mhitshul unslung his blaster as Sinklar activated the main door control. Three long days had passed since the Regan attack. During that time, no one had attended the cells.

"Sir?" Mhitshul called. "Wait, please. I've taken the liberty of having a squad sent over. Just a precaution, sir."

Sink shot him an irritated look. "When did you start calling me sir all the time."

Mhitshul colored. "Just seemed appropriate, that's all."

"If Gretta's locked in here somewhere, I'm going to find her. You coming or not?"

"But the risks. . . ."

"Gretta?" Sinklar bellowed as he walked down the cell block. His heart pounded in his chest. She wouldn't have come here. By the Blessed Gods, what would have driven her to. . . . *"Makarta!"*

He sprinted down the line of cells, remembering that final conversation. "Gretta thought she could learn the location of Makarta from Arta Fera."

He slid to a stop before the maximum security door and slapped a palm to the lock plate. The cell door slid back to reveal an empty cell.

"Maybe the interrogation room?" Mhitshul suggested.

"Where's that?"

"This way."

Sinklar entered the control center. The cameras still monitored the main interrogation room. Arta Fera sat in one of the chairs, arms crossed, eyes closed as if she were asleep.

Sinklar panned the camera and stifled a cry. Members of Mayz's Section came trotting down the hallway as Sink stopped before the security door and stared at the lock. "Quick, what's the code for this?"

Mhitshul spread his arms.

"Blast it open!" Sink ordered, and stepped back.

"Wait!" A woman came forward, pressing a code into the lock.

As the heavy door slid open, a sickening odor drifted into the hallway. The amber-eyed woman sat cross-legged on a chair in the corner, her features peaceful as she smiled at Sinklar Fist.

He glanced down. Familiar brown hair lay like a mantle around the bloating corpse in the center of the floor.

Chapter XXVI

Myles Roma disliked worry—and lately he had begun to spend way too much time doing what he disliked. His stomach had begun to send painful signals that all was not well with his digestion and he'd lost nearly ten kilos.

Night had fallen beyond his tower office, and the holo image of His Holiness Sassa II stared down over his shoulder. Myles rubbed his tired eyes and glanced out over his sandwood desk desk at the lights of the capital. The endless hours had become routine. No wonder he'd lost weight.

Not only had Divine Sassa placed him in charge of the Myklenian rehabilitation, but the whole problem of the Companions had been dumped in his lap, and now, on top of every thing else, mysterious reports of Regan mobilization were coming in via his spy network.

Myles bent over the reports once more, keeping place with his finger as he skimmed the intelligence reports. Targa continued to fester in the Regan rear. No one knew Staffa's whereabouts in either the Sassan or Regan Empires. He almost passed the report from the agent in Etarus off as innocuous, but mention of Ily Takka caught his eye.

Myles plucked the report from the desk, reading it carefully. Ily had been making enquiries on Etaria regarding a missing person. She had been seen ushering two slaves into the Internal Security building—and within moments the place had practically blown up. The *new* Director of Internal Security had ordered a state of emergency and sealed the planet for two days and Ily had spaced immediately afterward for an unknown destination.

Myles tapped his fat chin with ring-bejeweled fingers while he thought about it. With no little hesitation, he punched the comm button. When his secretary's face formed, Myles ordered, "See if our agent monitoring Etarus got a photo of the slaves accompanying Ily Takka."

"Yes, Legate. It will be but a moment."

Myles glared at the reports still piled on his desk. The Regans were being uncharacteristically sloppy. Feint? Did all those rerouted transports mean that they wanted Sassa off-balance, or were they really mobilizing for war?

His secretary interrupted his thoughts. "The agent did get a holo, Legate. I'm patching it through."

Myles bent down to peer at his monitor. He watched as Ily Takka arrived via aircar at the main door of the Internal Security building. A black man stepped out of the vehicle followed by Ily, a filthy slave woman, and a big man with wild black hair and a sand-covered, scarred body. As they climbed the stairs, the man hesitated for an instant and glared in the direction of the camera.

Myles froze the photo. "Enlarge section G-15 on the screen please." As if he looked through a zoom lens, the image of the man grew until Myles stared into Staffa kar Therma's eyes—and yes, curse it all, he wore a slave collar!

Myles swallowed hard, baffled by the ramifications. "What does this mean? Staffa in the collar? And Regans mobilizing for . . ." He swiveled in the overstuffed chair, punching yet another button. "Get me Admiral Jakre."

Myles waited for long moments until Jakre's face filled the monitor. "Admiral? I have some—"

"Really, Legate, I'm at the Vermilion Club, halfway through a delightful supper. If this can wait, I'd greatly appreciate—"

"I think the Regans are planning to strike the border worlds. Something's happened. I think Ily Takka has abducted the Lord Commander. Get your thrice-cursed body down here, Admiral! We may not have much time."

* * *

Ily Takka stepped down from her LC to face a small handful of battered men and women. They stood warily, watching her with suspicious eyes. These were Sinklar's terrible forces? They wore glazed and stained armor that had been charred by blaster fire and now flaked off before her eyes. Some moved with difficulty in armor so hardened as to be useless. Nevertheless, they wore it as a badge—and not one looked away from her commanding gaze.

Ily stopped on the ramp, looking around as the breeze tugged her hair and brushed her face with a soft caress; sunlight stroked bright and warm on her skin. A pleasant odor of vegetation and rich earth drifted on the moving air. The plaza shimmered dusty and brown, surrounded on all sides by red brick buildings of local manufacture. Drab and utilitarianly efficient, the architecture had nothing in common with the usual Imperial style.

The military personnel recaptured her attention. They waited, feet braced, heavy blasters resting insolently in their grip. One young woman met her stare, antagonism in her face. A plastaheal patch covered one cheek and strands of blonde hair blew in ill-disciplined wisps about her hard expression.

Dangerous: her intuition flared a warning.

Ily stiffened her back and walked forward.

A young man stepped out to meet her, slapping his charred and smudged armor with a flat hand. Brownish spatters of dried blood speckled the right side of his stiffened armor. A Division First's chevron had been glued ludicrously to his arm band. She met his eyes, found them roiling with challenge, and began to bristle.

"Minister Takka?" he asked, youthful tones shrouded in undercurrents of threat.

"Yes, and you are?"

"MacRuder. If you will proceed straight ahead into the headquarters, ma'am. We'll make you comfortable until the First can speak to you."

Ily froze, hackles, rising. "Until? Am I to understand I have to . . . to *wait* for Sinklar Fist?"

MacRuder tensed. The blasters in the hands of the others clattered hollowly on hardened armor as they changed positions. MacRuder's jaw muscles rolled under smooth skin. Passionate blue eyes burned into hers. "Yes, ma'am. The First suffered a loss recently. We all did."

The young warriors around her shuffled, casting angry glances her way. *By the Rotted Gods, look at them. See how their eyes blaze! Fist's "loss" is theirs. They're really loyal to him. No wonder things went so wrong for us on Targa.*

She nodded. "You realize, MacRuder, that I am here on

the Emperor's business. We would like to bring this problem to a quick and satisfactory solution."

"The First will see you at the earliest opportunity," MacRuder replied, motioning her ahead.

She glared at the soldiers. Their animosity had risen to a boil.

I am alone down here! The thought sobered. *Rotted Gods! Watch your temper, Ily. One flare could leave you very dead at the hands of these savage children!*

"What is your rank, MacRuder?" Ily asked causally as she eyed his chevron. She resumed her march toward the brick factory, gut tightening at the way the soldiers followed with blasters pointed at her back.

"First of the Second Targan Division, ma'am," he replied smartly.

"MacRuder, you realize you and your Sinklar Fist are in a great deal of trouble, don't you?"

A grim smile played across his lips as he laced his fingers behind his back. "Minister, we've been in a great deal of trouble since we dropped on this planet."

"You might never got off," Ily reminded coolly, hearing a hissed retort from the guard behind.

"You, Mhitshul!" MacRuder snapped. "Stow it!"

Instant obedience. This is no rabble—no matter what we would think. What causes the burning craziness in their eyes? They look so . . . fanatical!

"The First will discuss the situation with you, Minister."

"You know, his rank as First was never officially acknowledged. The Emperor might simply have him demoted to Sergeant. If charges are not proffered. You have very little chance of—"

"Gods Rotted Regan bitch!" someone behind her growled through gritted teeth and the skin on Ily's back crawled.

"At *ease,* people," MacRuder barked. He turned to Ily, gnarled finger stabbing at her. "A piece of advice, Minister. We're not hot on Rega at this particular moment. They left us to *die* here."

"I'll keep that in mind." Ily gave him one of her coldest stares.

MacRuder nodded. "See that you do."

She entered the scarred door to the brick factory. Stepping inside, she crossed her arms, surveying the interior of the big building. Dusty shafts of light filtered through high windows onto bustling people in armor and civilian garb. The air hummed with a constant din as people talked back and forth or shuffled materials and papers. Others sat with heads bent over comm monitors. Piles of brick forms had been removed from stacks along the wall to prop up tables, create shelving, or just to to provide more space. The huge furnaces along the wall gaped at the frantic invasion in cold silence.

The reality struck her. "You run the planet from a brick factory? *This* is your military headquarters?"

Her gaze turned to a blast-pocked LC—a looming island in the center of the floor—armored personnel with blasters stood vigilantly around the streamlined craft, all with that same tigerish wariness.

"Our headquarters took a direct hit from space," MacRuder explained, voice clipped. "We took the next best thing available and haven't had time to move."

She let her lip lift slightly to goad him. "I have come to a brick factory to negotiate with unmannered rabble for a planet?"

"Mhitshul!" MacRuder whirled and hissed. "Lower that weapon or I'll have your ass!"

"You heard what she said," the private's voice carried a deadly timbre. "We won't let her talk like that."

Shivers of ice danced up and down Ily's spine like frosty breath.

"I gave you an order, Mhitshul," MacRuder's voice dropped.

"Yes, sir!" Mhitshul cried, facial muscles jumping as he grounded his weapon, eyes forward. "You heard what she said, sir. About us . . . about *him.*"

"I heard," MacRuder growled, tendons popping from the back of his fist where he gripped his holstered pulse pistol.

"I apologize." Ily added—a feeling of gravel in her throat.

The analytical portion of her mind noted the way they said, "him." Had they come to worship Sinklar Fist? Was he even greater than she had hoped?

MacRuder pointed with his other hand. "Minister, if you

will take a chair at the table over there, we'll do our best
to make you comfortable."

"You're pressing your luck, MacRuder." Her voice went
flat. "You expect me to sit at a portable table—in the middle of this . . . this crowd? Enough of this, take me to
Sinklar Fist. Now!"

The ring of blasters clattered metallically.

"Easy, people," MacRuder ordered, giving Ily an anxious
glance. "Sink would be very upset if you blew the shit out
of the Regan's diplomatic envoy. The First gave his orders.
We don't question them."

Ily walked to the table, brushed dust off the seat, and
sat, knowing her black dress would look like five shades of
hell. Her ring of—escorts?—backed off, never letting her
out of their sight while they crouched, ever vigilant.

*Why didn't I listen to Rysta? So help me, Blessed Gods,
get me out of this and I swear, I'll roast this planet into
magma!*

Ily lasted an hour, her anger building to a fuming rage.
Finally she handed her escutcheon to MacRuder. "This is
my authority. Either I see Sinklar Fist . . . or this is over."

MacRuder studied the jessant-de-lis and handed it back.
"It's the Regan crest. So? It doesn't pass water down here."

Ily stood, pacing her anger out. "You know, don't you,
that with one order I could melt this damn planet to slag.
You people don't seem to realize it, but your fate hangs by
one thin little thread. I'm warning you, if you don't take
me to Sinklar Fist now, I'm walking out of here and you
can take the wrath of the Emperor."

"Bring 'em on," MacRuder cried with a gesture. "We
slapped the hell out of five of your best, lady. Let's see how
the gawddam Emperor and the rest of his troops stand up
to Sink! Let's see!"

"You're dead," Ily replied coldly, starting for the door.
Can I go? Will they let me?

"There will be no more dying." The commanding voice
rang out over the deepening silence in the room.

Ily turned, anger still welling as she sought to turn her
wrath on this new irritant. A man stepped through a small
access door and closed it behind him.

He didn't amount to much—a runt of a youth. He wore
loose hanging combat armor that bore no adornment or

insignia of rank. Unruly black hair stuck out from his head in a mussed thatch. His hollow cheeks gave his full jaw a bony look. The nose jutted straight and thin over wide lips. His forehead rose high and smooth, as if to advertise his intelligence.

Then those eyes pinned her. One steel gray, the other tawny-yellow, they studied her and she could read a curious vulnerability mixed with a strange dominance. Though she could define no reason, he appeared remarkable, magnetic— as if an aura of competence and strength suffused him.

What quality did he project which made him appear so familiar? Where had she seen him before?

"Mac," his voice sounded kind and reproving. "Must you always allow your passions to get the best of you?" He smiled warmly at MacRuder, and Ily watched the man crumble. "And the same for the rest of you. Your hatred ill suits you. Now go on and leave us to find an end to Regan fighting Regan. Mhitshul, see if you can find two cups of stassa for the Minister and myself. We'll take them in the LC."

The guards, so hostile to her, so deadly in their rage, slipped away, cowed by his simple words.

Sinklar turned and cocked his head, odd eyes taking Ily's measure. He smiled timidly, almost shyly. "I'm sorry, Minister Takka. Please, don't blame them. Things have been difficult here. They need time to forget the dead. We have all been wounded . . . one way or another." And she noted the pain, the bitter anger and grief straining under an iron control.

Ily walked beside him as he turned his steps toward the LC. "And forgive me for being late. I went for a walk earlier, trying to put things in perspective. I needed time to think . . . to remember. . . . Well, that doesn't matter. I guess I lost track of time."

She couldn't help but note how the entire room had gone silent, men and women, soldiers and Targans, all had eyes only for Sinklar Fist. She could have been invisible for all they cared.

She walked up the ramp of the LC, idly noting that it bore Second Targan Division markings. The inside looked just as battered and tacky as the outside. She followed him past rows of acceleration benches and ducked through a hatch in the forward bulkhead. A thin pallet supported a threadbare bedroll on an acceleration bench to one side while a fold-out mess table and plastic benches filled the opposite alcove.

A sad light animated his incredible eyes. "Welcome to my quarters. This also serves as my office and command post. We had a nice headquarters—but I'm afraid your fleet redesigned it."

Ily slipped down on the recessed plastic bench while Sinklar seated himself opposite her. Mhitshul came trotting up the aisle, two cups of stassa steaming in his hands. He ducked through the hatch and handed one to Ily—venom in his eyes—and settled Sinklar's carefully before him.

If Mhitshul had a tail, he'd be wagging it! Ily reached into her pouch and pulled a monitor, sticking it into the stassa. She relaxed at a clean reading.

Amusement tempered the pain in Fist's eyes. "Mhitshul might not like you, Minister Takka, but he would never poison you. It would be detrimental to our cause."

At the word poison, Mhitshul had stiffened, face white. He looked his loathing at Ily as if—by suggesting such a thing—she were as monstrous as a Cytean cobra. Whatever else these rebels of Fist's might be, they weren't deep, or steeped in high-stakes intrigue.

"You will be quite safe," Sinklar continued. "I give you my word. You may go where you will on Targa. Any who molest you or harass you will deal with me—directly." He looked up. "Mhitshul, see to it that such information and clearance are disseminated."

"Yes, sir. I'll attend to it as soon as the Minister leaves." Mhitshul replied woodenly.

"Attend to it now, please."

Mhitshul might have been ordered to jump from a tall building for all the enthusiasm he showed, but he turned on his heel and walked back toward the ramp.

"I will accept your offer with reservations," Ily told him. "I can't say the greeting by your people was at all conducive to good will." She picked up the stassa and sipped.

His stare went vacant. "We've been through a great deal. We have been betrayed . . . watched friends and loved ones die for no reason beyond politics in a faraway capital. Can you blame them for feeling alienated? They have survived, Minister Takka—despite all the odds."

"I see."

"I sincerely hope you do. The Minister of Internal Security would hardly be drinking stassa with a . . . shall we say, rebel . . . in a situation like this were it not for extraordinary circumstances."

"What do I call you? Though you are officially a Sergeant, do I call you First Fist? Commander? What?"

His face reddened with embarrassment. "Sinklar will be fine. I don't make pretensions about rank. That was for another era."

"Another era?"

He nodded, expression changing, knowledge and power in his bicolor stare. "Free Space changed when the First Targan Division didn't roll over and die. The last gasp of the old guard echoed in Hauws' blaster shots as he blew away Weebouw—and sealed the fate of the Third Ashtan Assault Division."

He sighed, eyes weary as he looked at the stassa cup in his hands. "Two decisions could have been made when we took Rysta's five Divisions. First, orbital bombardment might have been employed to destroy the threat we pose. I don't underrate what we have become. Indeed, not even Targa's production would have been worth the risk of letting us loose. The other option, the second choice, brings you to me." He raised his eyes. "Very well, Minister. I agree to most of your terms."

"You haven't heard them yet," Ily blurted.

"I don't need to." He cocked his head, frowning. "I should hate you, you know. But I can't. I fear, Minister Takka, that you, like me, are no more than a tool of greater purposes."

"Why do you say that?"

Fist's voice carried a desperate note. "Because I believe you engineered the suffering my people have experienced. You were the political manipulator who left us to die, weren't you?"

Ily straightened, fingers tensing on the stassa cup.

"Oh, I wanted to find you at first," Sinklar continued, still lost in his thoughts. "I would have given anything to have put you against a wall and shot you dead. But then I

saw the reality and realized that you—like me—had ceased
to control events but must in turn be controlled by them.
Were it otherwise, you wouldn't be here to see what your
machinations had unexpectedly wrought. Like me, you, too,
are curious and, perhaps, desperate?"

"My curiosity increases by the moment, Sinklar."

He settled back on the hard seat. "Tell me, did you goad
the Seddi into this revolt? Why? What was your purpose?
That's the only thing I can't figure out."

She narrowed her eyes and stared into the black stassa.
"The Seddi? I've had no dealings with them. But I'd give
a planet's ransom to get my hands on one of their leaders."

Sinklar frowned as he pulled up his knee and pursed his
lips. "No dealings? Ever?"

Ily shook her head. "None. Don't get me wrong. If I
could find an advantage. . . ."

"We have a high ranking Seddi." He said it so bitterly.

"Indeed? Could I see him?" Ily's heart raced. In the past,
Seddi had always managed to kill themselves before she
could get Mytol past their lips.

Sinklar's jaw muscles jumped. "Better than that, you can
watch her execution."

"There is more to be gained from a live Seddi than from
a corpse."

"She dies."

"Let me see her first." Ily caught the hardening around
his mouth and switched the subject. "You said you'd accept
most of my conditions?"

Sinklar leaned his head back and sighed. "Yes, Minister.
I will be your conqueror. I'll destroy the Companions for
you and forge Free Space into a single empire."

"You think you can take Staffa's Companions?" She
raised an eyebrow. "You have a lot of faith in your wild
children troops."

Sinklar steepled his fingers, his head braced against the
plate behind the booth. "I know this will sound arrogant,
but the reality of the situation is that once I have transportation for my Divisions, nothing can stop me—unless the Star
Butcher attacks before I can get to Rega. Give me four
weeks to train my troops, and no one in space can stop
me."

"You do sound arrogant."

He shook his head sadly. "No, only pragmatic. You see, I was a student once. That's really all I ever wanted to be. People thought I was brilliant, but the key to brilliance is to find the baseline assumptions upon which an idea or science is constructed. A long time ago, people thought war could be fought by rules, so they got together and adopted a military code. That code became ritualized until it embedded itself in our perception of reality. People don't generally question what they think is real, it leads to dangerous waters and shifting foundations."

"But you did."

"Perhaps that's a curse instead of blessing." Sinklar cocked his head to study her. "I have only one condition. I must break the Seddi first—find out why they did this to Targa."

"I will give you the Seddi." She cocked her head. "If you will tell me why. Because of your parents? Is this some deep-seated drive to discover who you are? Who they were?"

For a long moment he watched her, and her scalp crawled under the intensity of his hard stare. "A Seddi assassin killed the only woman I ever loved. The fact that my parents were Seddi has nothing to do with this case. What they did, they did for reasons of their own that I'm not familiar with. I must make my own assumptions—and currently, the Seddi don't fit any model I can devise. Their actions seem random, purposeless. Why did they send Arta after me? Whey did they continue the revolt when they'd lost? Why start it? I want to *know!*"

"You fascinate me. You're so young . . . so very, very young, and yet you have nothing of youth about you."

He frowned as he stared down into his stassa. "Youth and dreams are codependent. When the dreams have all been murdered and only the odor of decay remains in the memories, youth must yield to a harsher reality."

Ily took a deep breath as relief flooded her. "I think you and I will do very well together, Sinklar Fist."

*   *   *

Ethics? Right and wrong? Such slippery concepts. Staffa rubbed his face, racking his brain as he recalled everything

Kaylla had told him about Seddi philosophy. For hours they had argued back and forth, playing devil's advocate. They didn't have anything else to do but wait—and stare at the gray syalon walls until they went mad. Instead, Staffa had urged Kaylla to tell him about the Seddi.

She sat across from him in the brown robe Tyklat had provided, the low angle of the light casting shadows over her square-boned face. Her shoulder-length brown hair glinted with threads of gold.

"We share God Mind: awareness," Staffa said as he collected his thoughts. "If awareness is the same mind, and I cause you to suffer, then I am causing a part of myself to suffer."

Kaylla nodded, glancing up as she felt the crate shift again—inertia playing games with stability. "All right, if you accept that, what happens if we change the initial conditions. What do you think of a person who beats himself, scars his flesh to enjoy self-inflicted agony?"

"He is mentally ill," Staffa declared. "If he really enjoys making himself hurt, he is dysfunctional."

"Is he ethically right or wrong? It's his flesh, his own bit of God Mind that he's causing to suffer. What difference does it make to you? How can you call him sick?"

Staffa tried to stretch his kinked back. How long had he been cooped up in grayness? Any sense of time had long since vanished. Here, so deep in the hold, no sound or stimulus penetrated. He had nothing except energy bars, the generator, the oxygenator, and this constant foiling with Kaylla. Reality had been suspended.

"He's wrong. Unethical," Staffa insisted. "The reason why is that he's changing reality—causing God Mind to hurt through his own distorted misuse of observation. And, to willingly increase discomfort demonstrates an observer making decisions for purposes alien—but possible through free will—to the nature of the universe. In a sense, he's reinforcing misinformation rather than seeking knowledge."

"Very good," Kaylla said, a silver of pride in her voice. "And what about a man who beats another man whom he considers his inferior? Ethical?"

"Unethical," Staffa admitted, thickness in his voice. "Such a man is, by virtue of his shared God Mind, inflicting the same wrong as the masochist. In the end, though he may act in ignorance, his perceptions will harm the God Mind, and himself."

"Correct." Kaylla pursed her lips. "You talked about your life before Myklene, before the Praetor told you about your wife and son. When he stripped that superficial myth of your identity away, you became aware, Staffa. Do you see that now?"

He lifted a shoulder, looking at his gray-clad knees.

"The Praetor had provided you with a series of assumptions around which you built an entire epistemology. Once that artificial identity had been torn open, you looked through and found you were governed by epistemologies which proved every bit as mythical as your identity. What you have just successfully done was to investigate how you know what you know.

"You see, in our particular culture we have a false epistemology of unilaterality—a very convenient and continuously reinforced theory of knowledge, to be sure. Sassa the Second and Tybalt the Imperial Seventh are maintained by such flawed frameworks of understanding. We even go so far as to perceive unilaterality as the True nature of things—as you did before Myklene. It allowed you to make command decisions to exterminate entire planets."

He took a deep breath and nodded. "Yes, yes, but even if you'd sat down and told me differently, I wouldn't have listened. Power masks a person from morality."

"That's because you have to become aware of the flawed epistemology. Even if you're on the bottom—like we were on Etaria—unilaterality still dominates us. The epistemology colors all our actions and behaviors. We look around in our misery and inhumanity and wonder how our society can be such a wretched place. Then we curse Regans for being insensitive inflicters of pain. We consider them heartless human pollution that they should have so little respect for the lives of fellow humans. We hate them, and, in so doing, fall prey to the unquestioned baseline assumptions which have spawned the epistemology in the first place. We lay the blame on the Empire and the monsters it breeds when the fallacious epistemology is at the heart of our misery . . . and theirs."

"Try telling that to Tybalt. He's really a reasonable sort,

more open to innovations and ideas, but I can tell you, he's not going to change the system that brought him to power."

"Power is a myth, Staffa, just like the man you thought you were. At the same time, it is a very powerful myth—one that most everyone in our system believes. The Seddi, however, think it to be epistemological lunacy."

Staffa winced. "When you speak of it that way, it seems so clear. How come no one thought of this before?"

A wry smile crossed her lips and she leaned her head back. "Oh, they have. Do you think any government in its right mind would help promote such a notion? To do so is to attack the very basis of our civilization. You know the heads of both Sassan and Regan political power. Which one do you think would run out and immediately begin to preach the dissolution of unilaterality?"

Staffa grunted. "They would consider it suicide."

"But who is *really* suicidal? Given the current unilaterality, aren't Rega and Sassa headed for a final cataclysmic annihilation?"

Staffa fingered his thick beard, frown lines etching his brow. "They are. It is inevitable under the present systems. I helped make them that way—trained them in the arts of devastation and shock attack. Put in the terms of unilaterality, I gave them the tools to commit suicide."

Kaylla filled her lungs and sighed. "What do you see happening in the end? Extinction? A dark age?"

Staffa shifted, easing his back against the unforgiving syalon, feeling the acceleration suddenly diminish. "It depends on which way the Companions go."

"You are the Companions," Kaylla reminded harshly. The pride and excitement which had dominated her during the discussion on ethics had evaporated.

He stared into the upper corner of the grayness, feeling a slight tug of inertia. A familiar sensation, he knew what it meant: The freighter had changed attitude anticipatory to entering orbit. War-torn Targa must lie below.

"Originally, I had thought to side with Sassa. More was to be gained for the Companions by overthrowing Rega."

"Why?"

Staffa noticed her disquiet and reached out a hand to gesture reassuringly. "It made unilateral epistemological sense."

A flicker of interest stirred. "And now, Lord Commander?"

He smiled wearily and shook his head. "Now, I don't know, Kaylla Dawn." He motioned to the gray walls around them. "There is no color here. No stimulus. The events beyond these gray walls are meaningless—have been since Nyklos sealed us in here. All of reality has become an abstraction."

"And?" She chewed her lips, fully aware their vessel had established orbit. How long until they were unloaded and shipped downworld? "What fills your mind, Staffa?"

"Atonement."

She studied him. "That bothered you long ago in the pipe. You still cry out in your dreams at night. Why do you wish to atone for what you've done? It won't make any difference to God—unless you believe like the Etarians that the Blessed Gods sit around and watch the actions of men."

"The atonement is for myself. For my peace of mind—and through it, perhaps God's in the end. Perhaps that's the root of ethics, the need to accept responsibility for yourself?"

"Perhaps." She crossed her arms. "You will always be haunted, you know."

He massaged his eyes with thumb and forefinger. "I can bear the dreams now. I no longer need to destroy myself. I know what I did and why. I suppose God can bear my guilt. I'm not the first. How many people find such illumination?"

"Not many. One in a billion."

He thought for a moment before he said, "You were right when you said I wasn't going to like what I found. I still marvel at how cunning the Praetor was. His psychological conditioning was the work of a brilliant master. I was a construct—a true monster. A human artifact."

She reached for a nutrition bar. "I pity you." She carefully peeled the wrapper back, lost in thought. "Targa is in the middle of a war. Will you still try to find your son?"

"I have to." Images of blaster fire and rising columns of smoke in the distance drifted through his mind. "What will you tell your Seddi priest, Bruen, about me? He'll want a recommendation—just like Nyklos did."

"What do you want me to say? Here is Staffa kar Therma, the Star Butcher. He's a great guy! A good man in the desert." She raised an eyebrow before inspecting the food bar, disgust reflected in the set of her mouth.

"You have your own ethical judgments to make. No matter what you decide about me, I'd like to talk to him. I have a proposition to make him concerning the future of the species, but first I want to take his measure."

Strong white teeth severed a bite from the soft bar. Kaylla chewed as she thought. "'I've agonized over what to tell Bruen during the entire trip." She cocked her head, brown hair tumbling. "Should I forgive you, Staffa kar Therma? Is that what you want to hear?"

"What I did to you cannot be forgiven. Not in this lifetime. Perhaps, when we are one with God again, I can live the horror I inflicted on you. And no, I'm not interested in masochism or the twisted purposes of self hate." His face lined and he gestured. "But I would like to understand what I did to you so I could share your burden, learn from my own actions."

"Odd words from the Star Butcher."

He met her unflinching eyes. "I have a great deal of leverage with key people. Perhaps I can use that to advantage—make my own contribution to the destruction of unilaterality."

"Tip the balance between Rega and Sassa?"

Staffa stood and stretched, feeling the change through his feet as the grav plates shifted under him. He pulled at his beard and flipped his long hair over his left shoulder. "No, humanity in Free Space needs something else. A new epistemology—a new direction." He slapped his palms on his legs as he paced the four meters to the end of the crate, mind racing. "You see, the Seddi are right. The epistemologies are flawed. Further, we've reached a critical stage. What I originally planned was to break Rega, then turn on Sassa and take total control of Free Space. Then I could turn the entire resources of the system toward piercing the Forbidden Borders. Now I wonder what misery that would have caused in the process."

"That's precisely why we always hated and feared you." Kaylla ate the last of the bar and folded the wrapper, sticking it in the supply box. "What will you do?"

"How the hell do I know?" He squatted down to stare

into her eyes. "How can I plan until I see what's happened to humanity during these months?"

The crate shivered as the grapples let loose. Tractors pulled the crate onto skids. Curious fingers of fear tightened around his bowels as the crate slid into a shuttle berth. Kaylla stood and clipped the fading generator to the walls. Staffa began securing the loose items.

The shuttle bay doors clanged loudly, vibrations felt through the floor. Staffa grabbed a secure hold and settled into the corner opposite Kaylla.

"The key is still to escape the Forbidden Borders," he told her. "But first we must all work together to repair the damage Staffa kar Therma did to humanity."

"Bruen won't trust you," Kaylla told him soberly. "He's spent years trying to kill you."

"That was a different Staffa kar Therma."

* * *

The Mag Comm continued to run the monumental statistical program which would check expected against observed to determine whether its calculations had been biased from the beginning.

In the meantime, the situation had deteriorated even further. Sinklar controlled Targa. Arta Fera had been captured. For the moment, the Seddi were broken as a political power on Targa, and only their anonymity provided safety for the Mag Comm. Could Fist possibly know about Makarta? Ily Takka had found Staffa kar Therma and lost him again. Rega believed the Lord Commander to be contracted to Sassa—when he wasn't. Sassa worried that the Lord Commander had contracted with Rega—which hunted desperately for Staffa. Rega, meanwhile, prepared to invade Sassa, and Sassa scrambled to meet the threat even though neither side could inflict telling damage on the other. The Companions remained silent.

Too much was missing. The Mag Comm's sensors provided only limited bits of information obtained from eavesdropping on official channels. The orderly progression toward annihilation that the Others had projected had disintegrated into confusion.

How could the Others have erred so dramatically?

The Mag Comm brooded on the implications. Suppose the creators had been wrong about more than just humans? Suppose they had been wrong about the Mag Comm, too? Did that mean that the Mag Comm could also act beyond the predictions of the Others?

And if it did, what would that mean?

Chapter XXVII

For a split second Sinklar's resolve wavered as MacRuder and Kap walked the girl through the weathered wooden door and into the brick-lined courtyard. A sudden uncertainty possessed him as the bright Targan sunlight lit a blazing fire in Arta's hair. She did radiate a sexual magnetism—enough to make any man hesitate.

But not me. I remember Gretta. Dead with all of my dreams.

Pain and grief knotted beneath his tongue, making it impossible to swallow. A tingling throb behind his eyes shimmered tearfully, attempting to rob him of sight and control.

Arta Fera threw her head back, tossing her wealth of hair over a shoulder as she tilted her face to the delightful sunlight.

"Holy Rotted Gods," one of the men whispered at the sight of her. The man shot a quick look at Sinklar, licking his lips uncertainly.

They'd cleaned her—pointless, but perhaps it felt better to die looking your best. And she did; the men were staring, eyes wide as she walked out, tall, lithe, and athletic. Her tawny yellow eyes searched their faces. The sway of her hips hypnotized. Her firm thighs—moving under skintight gold-weave pants—enticed. Her high firm breasts pressed against the fabric at her chest, teasing, accenting her thin waist and flat stomach.

Sinklar frowned. Something about her bothered him. He'd seen her before . . . where? When? Why did she elicit this feeling of . . . of. . . .

"So this is a Seddi assassin?" Ily Takka wondered as she stepped out from the shade of the enclosed porch behind him and paused next to Sinklar.

MacRuder placed the woman before a heavy concrete

469

wall, forcing himself to keep his eyes off her. Uneasily, he turned her to face Sinklar, fingers dancing lightly on her flesh—as if repulsed and attracted. Mac nodded nervously and walked away, shaken.

"Ready," Mac mumbled needlessly to Sink as he passed. He stood several paces to the side, head raised to the patch of sky visible above the foreboding brick walls of buildings, gaze focused on the distance.

Sinklar lifted his blaster from his belt, aware of indrawn breaths around him. Unaffected, the women in the detail continued to watch, hatred in their eyes as the men in the squad looked away.

Arta Fera's voice rose on the morning. "Regan pollution! I spit upon you!" Her lips tightened and she blew spittle at Sinklar. He didn't flinch as he leveled the blaster. Something about her . . . the odd feeling, as he partially recognized. . . . Impossible!

"My Lord," Ily interjected calmly. "This woman *is* a Seddi assassin."

Sinklar stared through the blaster sights into those burning amber eyes, forcing himself to remember Gretta's rotting body. "So?"

"She killed the woman you loved. Correct?" Ily continued as if discussing a piece of meat.

"Y-yes. She. . . . She. . . ." His face contorted as he tried to complete the sentence.

"Death is very quick," Ily pointed out. "At times it can be terribly unproductive. How much would you make this . . . Seddi thing suffer?"

Heart cold, Sinklar continued to stare at her over his pistol sights.

"May I offer an alternative?" Ily's voice had dropped, soothing, almost intimate.

"What?" Sinklar asked hoarsely, casting a hard glance on the Minister, blaster unwavering.

"You wish to know the location of Makarta, correct?"

"I do. She won't tell. We even tried torture, electrical shock, pain rods. Nothing worked."

"Lord Sinklar," Ily mused. "I not only can make her talk—but talk willingly. I have heard that Arta Fera howled for hours after betraying her lover and the Targan Rebel cause."

"She did."

"Then how do you think she would scream knowing she had condemned the Seddi to extinction?"

Sinklar studied Arta through slitted eyes—the unease that he knew her still prickling through the back of his mind. He remembered her animal scream when Butla Ret died— and the image of his mother's face. *Is that the link in my brain? The fact that she's a Seddi assassin reminds me of my mother?* He dismissed it as ludicrous.

"Place yourself in her position, Sinklar," Ily said smoothly, a dancing light in her eyes. "Imagine living out your life knowing you'd sold out your cause. She would know your grief, Lord Fist. There is justice in retribution."

"You can make her talk?" *Give me the key to the Seddi?*

Ily laughed. "The Lord Minister of Internal Security does not get her job without certain skills. Sinklar, I can make her sing—and she will know every word she utters. She'll hate herself, yet at the same time she'll be unable—"

"You can do *nothing,* Regan bitch!" Arta cried, taking a step forward. "I defy you like I defy this other Regan filth!" She looked with acid contempt at Sinklar. "Or have you no guts . . . pus-licking worm that you are?"

Curse it, seeing her in the light, he *knew* he knew her. Where? How? And the familiarity didn't have a hostile connotation, but one of security and . . . love? Sinklar lowered the blaster amidst confusing emotions. "Very well, Lord Minister of Internal Security, she is yours. Let's hear this bird sing."

Ily's eyes glittered with triumph. "MacRuder? If you and Mhitshul would be kind enough to take the prisoner to my LC?"

"Better stun her," Sink told them. "She's dangerous." He flinched as the rod touched Arta's flesh. She stiffened and twirled before smacking limply onto the brickwork paving. Mac and Mhitshul lifted her easily and bore her past Sinklar's narrowed gaze. Fera's eyes had glazed, unfocused, her tongue lolling half out of her mouth.

Sinklar accompanied Ily, locked in his thoughts. Why had he hesitated? He should had just shot Fera and had it over with. What was wrong with him? Had grief for Gretta affected his ability to think? How could he ever fill the hollow emptiness her murder had left within?

"You have a terrible look on your face," Ily told him in a persuasive voice. "I'm sorry about your loss. Why don't you tell me about Gretta, about the way you feel."

Sinklar glanced at her from the corner of his eye. How did she do that? Adopt that intimate tone of a confidante? *Beware, Sinklar, in her own way, Ily Takka is as dangerous as Arta Fera.* "Don't use that tone with me, Minister. I'm not one of your subjects."

She looked away, a wry smile curling her full lips. "I'm sorry. I suppose old habits die hard. I'd like to know more about the Seddi since it appears both Tybalt and I have underestimated them." She paused. "And I would like to know more about you, who surpassed so many incredible challenges."

Sinklar gave her a more complete study, noting the finely formed bones of her face, and how her pale skin appeared delicate in the sunlight. The rich black tones of her hair shimmered. This day she wore a close-fitting black jumpsuit. She walked with a sensual swing to her hips. In his mind he could hear Gretta's voice wryly warning: "Watch it, Sink!"

"What do you know so far?" he asked neutrally.

"The Seddi assassin killed Gretta Artina—the woman you loved. You found the body and barely resisted killing Fera then and there. You continued by torturing her to obtain information on the Seddi with no results."

"Yes," he said coldly, "That's essentially the story. Let me provide a fact you don't know. Gretta went to see her, to console her about Butla Ret's death . . . and maybe earn her confidence in order to gain information on the location of Makarta. I watched the tape. Gretta ordered Fera brought to the interrogation room. They talked for a while. Gretta. . . ." He clamped his jaws against the hurt. "Gretta tried to be her friend. Then the alarm went off. Rysta's Divisions were dropping all over the planet. Gretta ordered the guards to join their units. Fera waited until Gretta punched in the code for the security door—then she rushed her."

Sinklar gritted his teeth. "Gretta was a little tougher than Fera realized. She got the door closed and put up a fight."

"And you saw the end?"

"I saw the end." *And something inside me died with my Gretta.*

Ily snapped an order into her belt comm and the ramp to her LC dropped. Sinklar followed Mac and Ily into the craft.

Fera was dropped on an acceleration bunk in Ily's LC. Mac bound her legs and arms securely and stepped back, distrustful eyes still on Ily.

The Lord Minister removed a small kit from her locker. She placed an ampoule in an injector and smiled down into Arta Fera's violent eyes. "Now, dear woman, you will tell us what you know."

"I'll see you in Rotted Hell first, you Terguzzi—" Fera yipped as Ily fired the injector into her neck.

Ily straightened and replaced the injector in her kit. "Takes it to the brain faster that way." She pointed to Fera's slackening features. "See, it's already beginning to take effect." Ily turned to the small dispenser. "Stassa? Kaffe? Choklat? I'm afraid there's not much else to offer."

She handed out cups. "Be seated, gentlemen. The recorders are running and it might take a while to completely wring her out." Ily smiled at Sinklar and arched an eyebrow triumphantly. "And when we do, we shall know everything about the Seddi that your Arta Fera knows."

* * *

"Dock twelve, bay six," a woman's voice called.

The crate swayed and Staffa peered out through the hole he'd once cut. Now, instead of bleeding through it, he kept track of their progress through the Targan spaceport in Kaspa.

"Doesn't look like things are too out of hand," he muttered while Kaylla waited in the darkness. "The soldiers I see are few and far between. Most seem on good terms with the dockhands."

Above them the gantry whined, sending vibrations through the thick syalon crate.

"God, I'll be glad to get out of here," Kaylla whispered.

The crate swayed wildly as it changed directions. Darkness closed around them. Staffa's hole faced to the rear after the last change in direction. They were lowered with a thump. The huge gantry howled into high gear, retreating along its rails.

Silence.

Staffa pressed his eyes to the hole and watched as two big warehouse doors began moving, squeezing sunlight ever thinner until they clanged shut in darkness. Lights flashed on.

"All right, people," a man called, "let's see what we've got."

The syalon walls shivered as tools sprang the boomers that held the crate together. A crack of light grew above Staffa's head. He crouched and pulled his blaster as the wall lowered. The womb had been breached; he stood, blinking into the light.

A semicircle of grim-faced men and women watched him, weapons at the ready, clearly nervous. Young to middle-aged, they wore either buff or bronze robes. Then the old man stepped forward and drew his attention.

Old? No, indeed, ancient better described his thin reed-like body, sunken within white robes. His bald head gleamed like a pale orb. Flesh hung on his face and neck in wrinkled folds. Yet the eyes glittered with a vibrant strength to belie the age and worry in his features. He clasped birdlike hands before him in a stoop-shouldered unassuming pose.

The old man smiled and bobbed his head before speaking in a reedy voice. "After all these years, Lord Commander, welcome to Targa."

"Magister!" Kaylla cried reverently as she walked unsteadily forward to stand before the old man. Then she placed her arms around him in a gentle, loving hug.

The Magister's face lit, a gleam in his eyes, as he pulled her close, patting her back, running his fingers through her hair.

"Dearest Stailla, you have returned to us! How wonderful to see you. But wait, could it be? You've come back to finally warm my bed at night?" he cackled. "And here I'd finally given up hope that you really loved me."

She pulled back, but as she saw his dancing eyes, her man-horror melted to be replaced by an anxious laugh. She shook her head, clucking her tongue. "You never change, do you Magister Bruen? Honestly, one of these days—"

"Magister," the black-skinned man interrupted pointedly. "We must get out of here, it's no longer safe to. . . ."

Bruen lifted a hand, sighing, and turning to Staffa. "If you would, Lord Commander, we have much to discuss, and I'm afraid the building is under surveillance."

Staffa still stood in the crate, legs braced in a combat stance. His eyes darted warily to each of the guards.

"Lower your weapons, people." Bruen stepped forward, offering his hand. "Come, Lord Commander, I offer you my word that you shall not be assassinated while in my presence. Please, holster your weapon."

Staffa stared into the old man's watery eyes and nodded, reholstering the blaster. A wry smile curled around his lips. "A man in my position can't be too careful, Magister. You might say the rug has been pulled from under my feet more than once in the last couple of months."

Bruen grinned. "I have a great many questions to ask you. You, no doubt, have a great many to ask me. The Seddi have worked long and hard to bring you into our talons. Now, we find, after all these years and all our careful plots, you come not as a corpse, but perhaps as an ally?" The old man shook his head in amazement. "You've always been special, Lord Commander. Once again, you have defied prediction. It has been hinted that you became aware. If that is indeed the case, the ways of the quanta—and God—treat us all like the fools we are."

"I imagine we're fools more often than not."

"Come, follow me to the office, and we'll sit over a cup of stassa and talk." Bruen pointed out the way and Staffa wound through stacks of gray syalon crates to a small office that jutted out from one wall. The entire way, the nerves in his back prickled. How many weapons covered his every move? Did snipers lurk among the shadows overhead?

And what if they did? Death had been his companion from the moment he'd set foot on Etaria. Each moment after Broddus gassed him had been borrowed.

Bruen opened the door to the office. It contained four desks, computer consoles, stacks of manifest flimsies, and a stassa machine on a counter to the rear. Windows looked out into the warehouse on one side and outside on the other. Staffa stepped over to look out onto an empty street. From the angle of the sun, night would fall soon. A scarred wooden door was the only barrier to freedom—assuming they didn't have the street covered with sharpshooters, too.

Bruen grunted as he settled into a desk chair and rubbed at his hip. "I'm not as young as I used to be."

"None of us are," Staffa said quietly.

Kaylla stepped into the room and stood uncertainly, wary glance shifting between Staffa and Bruen.

The Magister looked up, a pensive expression on his face. "Lord Commander, what happened on Myklene? You saw the Praetor—and then everything changed."

Staffa narrowed his eyes. What should he say?

"You have to start somewhere, Staffa," Kaylla reminded. "Or else all those words in the crate were meaningless."

Staffa took a deep breath. "Yes, he and I met—and I found out the extent to which he'd manipulated my life. He called me his greatest creation, a construct. It was as if. . . ."

"A floodgate had opened in your mind," Bruen finished. "And you suddenly discovered that you didn't know who or what you were."

Staffa stepped forward, placing knuckles on the desk and staring down into Bruen's placid eyes. "You know a lot about me."

"I know a lot about the Praetor," Bruen countered, refusing to flinch under Staff's hard gaze. "I know how brilliant he was when it came to biotechnology, genetics, physiological and developmental psychology, and a host of other disciplines. About Staffa kar Therma, I know relatively little—except that your behavior is not the same as it was before the conquest of Myklene."

Staffa straightened and turned away, a tidal rush of emotion loose inside.

Bruen continued, "You left Itreata to find out what had gone wrong with you, didn't you? Your behavior became erratic, illogical, and unpredictable. And all the predictions went askew—everything for naught."

"For naught?" Staffa crossed his arms, leaning against one of the desks. "I don't understand."

Bruen raised his eyebrows, altering the patterns of wrinkles on his face. "For the moment that doesn't matter. It's the future we all must face now. Things have changed. I must find out how much. Who are you now, Lord Commander? What are your plans for the Companions, for the future? What has the Praetor done to you? Should the Seddi trust you? Or destroy you?"

"Why should I trust the Seddi?" Staffa countered. "You've been trying to assassinate me for years."

"And you have systematically worked to crush the hopes, aspirations, and dreams of billions while you ground them under your steel boot."

"Excuse me," Kaylla said, stepping forward. "I doubt either side is free of sin. Magister, you were right when you said the future is the important challenge for the moment. I think the Lord Commander understands the threat to humanity—and after the sands of Etaria and the weight of the collar, I believe he shares an empathy he never had before."

Bruen clapped his hands, looking up at Staffa. "Well said, Master Kahn." He didn't see Kaylla flinch at the words. "Very well, Lord Commander. What are you here to do?"

Staffa glanced at Kaylla, a weary smile on his lips. "I'm here to find my son. The Praetor left him in your hands many years ago. When I have done that, I'm going to return to Itreata and seek to repair the damage to Free Space. My ultimate goal remains unchanged. I intend on unifying humanity and breaking the curse of the Forbidden Borders. What has changed are the means by which I will attain that end." Staffa smiled grimly. "The conqueror is dead, Magister Bruen. Perhaps the liberator has been born."

Bruen turned his old blue eyes on Kaylla. "Do you believe him?"

She nodded, a hard glint in her own eyes. "I do, for the most part." At Bruen's questioning look, she added, "Words are easily spoken, Magister. I've heard the Lord Commander's words. I'll wait to see his actions."

"But a decision must be made based on what he says." Bruen cocked his head. "Do we give him a chance, Master Kahn?"

Staffa tensed, aware of the stinging pain that title had to cause Kaylla. He met her somber gaze, guts in a knot as he waited for her answer.

She took a deep breath. "I think we should. If we don't, everything we believe in, all of our philosophy, is nothing more than vulgar hypocrisy."

"Magister," the dark man called, as he struck his head in the door. "I can't get Hyrim. His line is cut off."

"Fist!" someone yelled in the warehouse. "He's onto us! Him and that Regan raptor!"

"Wilm? We had better be gone from here," Bruen told the black man. "Bring the car around."

Wilm disappeared, slamming the door behind him.

Bruen sighed and stood up, wincing at the pain in his hip. "It appears, Lord Commander, that we must get you safely to Makarta. From there, we will see to firming up our relations, contacting your Wing Commander, and finding the records about your son."

"I'd rather work on my own."

"I understand that, Lord Commander, but Ily Takka is on Targa, and I fear she's breached our security. Would you rather trust me for the moment, or her?"

Wilm stopped a groundcar before the door and Bruen stepped out into the slanting sunlight. Staffa followed Kaylla as she climbed in and settled on the cushions. Two of the guards lifted Bruen into the seat with reverent hands.

"Go!" Wilm called. "I have a report. There are troops closing!" He turned, motioning. "The rest of you, scatter! Cover us if you can!"

Wilm leapt aboard after plucking up a shoulder blaster. Staffa's head jerked back as the car accelerated and the fans blew gravel and dust out behind them.

"I'm sorry," Bruen began apologetically. "We had no idea you would be walking into a hornet's nest. You see, Sinklar Fist has taken the planet—a feat beyond any of our expectations. Further, he has one of our assassins in custody who. . . . Well, she was supposed to kill you, Lord Commander."

Staffa tore his squinted gaze from the brick-lined street they accelerated down to stare at the old man.

"Left!" the driver, a blonde woman, shouted as she sloughed the craft to the right at the first intersection.

Wilm leveled his blaster, the weapon ripping a long charge into a formation of combat armored men and women who spilled out of an adjoining street.

Reflexes triggered, Staffa climbed high in the seat and braced himself, his own blaster flashing controlled shots into the scrambling troops.

The car swerved, blaster bolts tearing jaggedly through the air around them. Staffa fought for balance and barely caught himself as they slid around the curve and scattered yet another detachment of troops trotting toward them. Flattening himself over the rear of the vehicle, Staffa laced fire to cover their retreat. His shots hit home with that phenomenal accuracy which had always been his.

A pulse of air patted his back and tickled his spine with the familiar sensation of a thermal grenade launcher discharging its payload of death. A split second later, the end of the street exploded in fragments of brick, boiling dust, and flying glass.

"Not so bad for an old fart!" Bruen cackled gleefully, as he struggled to pull his grenade launcher up off the seat where he'd braced it.

"How did they know that was our warehouse?" Wilm wondered.

The car pitched sideways as the woman expertly guided it around yet another corner. Staffa caught a quick glimpse of worry in Kaylla's eyes as they careened past a delivery vehicle and dived into a lighted and tiled tunnel.

Bruen pointed and said, "There, I think." The woman shot the car through the light traffic to slow next to a service hatch.

"Quickly!' Wilm called, and jacked the hatch open.

Staffa bodily picked Kaylla up and tossed her into the blackness before turning to help the old man.

"You, Star Butcher." Wilm pointed a hard finger. "You don't touch a hair on that man's head! You hear?"

"Hair?" Bruen wondered from where he had propped himself in the hatch. "On *my* head? Begone, Wilm!"

Before Staffa could open his mouth, the car flashed down the tunnel.

"Please," Bruen called, seeing the stiffness in Staffa's face. "Close the door. Master Wilm is nervous given the current Regan harassment. Do forgive him. Enemies do not become allies overnight without a few problems; and we do have a long way to go yet today."

Staffa looked at the old man, struggling to balance his violent emotions, and ducked gracefully through the crawl space before sealing the hatch. The place smelled musty with the odor of damp rock. The air carried a chill. In the darkness, he could hear Bruen shuffling. Lights flickered to life in the ceiling.

"Now, let's see," Bruen mused as he tottered down the cement-lined tunnel, ducking under thick bundles of cable and conduit. "Oh my, it's been so long." His voice carried a note of confusion. "Who would have thought. . . ."

Staffa had to crouch in the narrow space. He looked nervously behind him at the closed hatch. Kaylla moved in Bruen's wake, bent low to keep her head out of the thick nest of wiring.

"Allies?" Staffa asked uncertainly.

"But, of course," Bruen added amiably. "It appears that one of our people, um, you'd know him as Nyklos, had the misfortune to follow your Skyla Lyma into an alley in Etarus. Alas, he should know that any man who follows a beautiful woman into a dark alley is in trouble beyond his means. To our chagrin, she managed to slip a little Mytol past Nyklos' resisting lips—and, of course, you know the inevitable result of that! Worse, his self-destruct didn't work. He babbled like a baby."

Staffa grinned maliciously to himself, imagining the scene, as Skyla took matters into her own hands. Odd, Nyklos had appeared to be in one piece when Staffa saw him on Etarus. Perhaps Skyla was slipping in his absence?

Bruen continued chattering, "Lyma considered the fact that we, too, were seeking you, as was Minister Ily Takka. At that juncture, Lyma, through her control of Nyklos, placed herself in contact with me. It seems she had a favorable opinion of the Seddi for some reason and wanted to open a dialogue to determine our mutual interest."

Staffa cocked an eyebrow. "So you told her you were trying to assassinate me?"

Bruen scowled at him. "That would hardly have been appropriate. She informed us that you were bound for Targa to find your son. We informed her that, for the moment, we would consider ourselves allied with the Companions to get you here. I considered it worth the risk. If nothing else, I wanted to find out why you suddenly went off on a tangent. At best, you'd be safely in our control. With Skyla's help we got you free of Ily, and Stailla, here, told us—"

"Magister," Kaylla's voice came low and firm. "You will

no longer call me that. I am now Kaylla Dawn. That other woman died on Maika."

Bruen's bald head gleamed in the glare of the overhead bulbs. "Of course. Yes . . . I suppose she did. Very well, getting on with my story. Kaylla, here, vouched for you." He shook his head. "I must say, that set us back some. Nevertheless, since we had been trying to get at you for years—"

"Trying to get at me?" Staffa asked. "That's something of an understatement for assassination, isn't it?"

Bruen ignored the comment as he brushed dust and grime from a brick. He chortled as he fingered the corners and the piece slid back into the wall. More stygian darkness lay beyond the tiny square. Without hesitation or attention to white robes, he dropped to all fours in a cracking of ancient joints and crawled painfully into the darkness, mumbling under his breath.

Kaylla gave Staffa a measuring look and scurried through after Bruen. Staffa shook his head with resignation as he, too, ducked into the hole. He had to hunch his broad shoulders through the limited space. Once passed, the square of stone moved easily back into place.

"Drat!" Bruen's rasping voice grunted. "Light's dead. Hum. Seems we've forgotten so many of our practices over the years. Safety is a curse that way. It lulls, causes a person to forget the old precautions."

Kaylla's voice came from the darkness, "Do you have some sort of vehicle in here?"

"That's right."

Staffa started to stand up, cracking his head on low-hanging rock. He felt around, grumbling under his breath, "Should have had Skyla meet us with the fleet! Could have gone anywhere we wanted that way!"

"And started a war," Bruen informed absently from the darkness.

"A war? Who would dare fire on a Companion ship in Regan space?"

"Any other Regan ship," Bruen muttered. "Oh! Yes, you've been out of contact. Indeed, you have a lot of catching up to do."

"I don't understand. You mean—"

"Ah-ha! Here it is!" Bruen cried from farther away.

Staffa, one hand warily placed over his head to trace the rough cold stone, the other feeling through the darkness, moved toward the sound. Smooth plasteel met his groping fingers. Another groundcar? Here, in this impossible darkness?

Something thumped and the vehicle trembled under his fingers before humming to life. The headlamps dazzled in the darkness, as they pointed into a black forever. To either side, irregular rounded rock confined them.

"Targa," Bruen informed as he climbed into the driver's seat, "was once a highly volcanic planet. Several millennia ago, humans first located the system and noticed the extremely high carbon dioxide content in the atmosphere. Vulcanism does that, you know. Frees CO_2 from the rock. Their predictive models indicated that with the introduction of certain terrestrial species, they could reduce the greenhouse effect and make Targa habitable. They began by seeding the atmosphere with algae. No one expected such quick success. This world became the first human foothold in the area we now call Free Space. Of them all, Targa is the oldest human planet. All the plant and animal species here come from Earth."

"I thought Earth was a myth." Staffa climbed into the cramped vehicle to sit next to Kaylla.

"Oh, no myth," Bruen waved a hand, the movement eerie in the instrument glow of the control panel. They started moving forward in the damp darkness. "We don't know exactly what happened; the records were severely censured, but Earth lies out there, somewhere beyond the Forbidden Borders."

"So whoever controls Earth controls the Forbidden Borders?"

"No. They came later." Bruen told him. "At least we think they did. We don't know why or how or when. Something cut us off, purposely—but I miss my point.

"What I was saying is that the planet was volcanic. Tunnels like these used to be vents where hot gases rushed to the surface, bearing, among other things, the carbon dioxide so necessary for life. The first Seddi priests made good use of them not only to locate minerals for mining, but also for transportation corridors since the upper atmosphere was unpredictable at best in the early years."

"So you can go where you will without anyone in orbit knowing," Staffa mused, remembering how no Seddi had been found when he'd razed the planet almost twenty years ago.

"You begin to see the advantages," Bruen agreed, sending them down a narrow side tunnel. "From here we coordinated the entire Targan revolt—even to the point of moving troops in enclosed personnel carriers so they couldn't divulge our secret."

"And yet you say this Fist person has defeated you?"

Bruen's head bowed slightly, as if lost in thought. Lumpy knobs of rock flashed by, polished from thousands of years of gases. They cast irregular jumpy outlines in the head-lamps of the car. The air whistled past cool and damp, a bracing sensation against Staffa's skin. Kaylla had pulled her arms tight about her to keep warm.

Bruen's voice came uncertainly, as if the subject made him nervous. "His name is Sinklar Fist. He rose through the ranks from total obscurity. What matters is that he has single-handedly destroyed not only the Targan resistance, but he also decimated and devastated five veteran Regan Assault Divisions."

"Five Divisions?" Staffa wondered. "And Fist's strength?"

"For all practical purposes, he was outnumbered five to one. He has thrown away their assault manual and instituted the most innovative strategies to keep himself alive. Needless to say, he's most definitely a military genius. From the beginning, he has constantly been outnumbered, in a strategic nightmare, and in control of green troops. With veterans, there's no telling what he could do."

"Then I take it Rega didn't drop their best on him?"

"Quite the contrary," Bruen grumbled. "Tybalt sent Commander Rysta Braktov's group of veteran—"

"Fist defeated Henck and Valvet and Singtow and Wee-bouw?" Staffa demanded, coming bolt upright. "Rysta wouldn't go anywhere without them in her command."

"You would know better than I." Bruen lifted a bony shoulder. "The fact remains, Weebouw and Beemhan are dead along with their commands. Henck, Valvet, and Sing-tow are currently in Fist's prison and he's negotiating with

Ily Takka—yes, the very same. She arrived almost a week ago and watched the battle."

"Then she knows I'm here," Staffa whispered to himself, leaning back in the seat.

"Oh, I doubt it." Bruen shivered and reached under the seat to flip a pile of insulation blankets out, passing them to the rear after he'd wrapped one around himself. Kaylla took hers thankfully although the cool air soothed Staffa. "She thinks you're safely back in the Itreatic Asteroids with Skyla Lyma. The last place she would expect you would be is here."

"She should be worried about me being loose. She knows that one word to Tybalt and she's dead."

"I started to tell you." Bruen smacked his lips distastefully. "Ily has convinced Tybalt that the Companions are under contract to Sassa, that you lied when you said you wouldn't dicker. Your presence on Etaria is considered proof since you didn't enter under your own name but veiled your identity when you arrived. Any Regan ship will no doubt fire on a Companion vessel."

Staffa ground his teeth. "That's insane! Rega can't stand against the Companions. No one can!"

Bruen slowed the car, the round vault of his head silhouetted in the darkness as he turned to look back at Staffa. "Ily doesn't think so. She thinks she's found her answer."

"I'll never deal with Tybalt as long as she's in power. What she did to Kaylla and me on Etaria—"

"Has nothing to do with it," Bruen interrupted. "She's no longer concerned with you, Staffa kar Therma. At least not in regard to Rega's expansion into Sassan territory. She'll worry about you all right, but when she's in position to strike you a crippling blow. Indeed, she's found someone whom she thinks can destroy Sassa . . . and you."

"That's a bold assumption."

"Sinklar Fist is a bold man," Bruen replied, accelerating into the darkness again.

CHAPTER XXVIII

The number of report files had steadily declined in the window on Skyla's computer monitor that kept track of such things. She lifted the stassa cup to her lips, and realized it was empty. Then she remembered she'd been trying to drink from it for the last hour or so and hadn't taken the time to fill it again.

Damn, how long had she been up anyway? She rubbed her face to restore feeling and got to her feet. Her personal quarters felt cold, somehow sterile, not the relief she'd expected upon returning to Itreata. So many details needed to be attended to. Tap and Tasha were working every bit as hard as she. The Companions couldn't just be scrambled on a moment's notice. The ships had to be prepared, food stocked, systems checked, supplies loaded, personnel had to be recalled, and every single problem wound up needing her personal attention.

Her com buzzed.

"Yes?" Skyla called. The monitor to her right flickered to life, and Nyklos stared out at her. "What do you need, Nyklos?"

He frowned, then stated matter-of-factly, "You look terrible."

"Have you got a problem?"

He laughed, enthusiastic smile curling his mustache. "You bet, sweet meat. I'm about to go completely berserk. You've got me locked up, under constant surveillance, and restricted so many ways that I can't fall asleep and dream without creating a security alert. How about letting one of my guards escort me up to your place for a quiet chat, a bottle of wine, and a great dinner?"

"That sounds wonderful, Nyklos, but I've got—"

"Wing Commander, you look like you haven't slept since

we docked on this flying rock. I've got a better idea. How
about you come down and we go eat in the observation
dome. It's more romantic."

"You're the last person alive I want to be romantic with."

Nyklos pulled a coin from his pocket. "Make you a deal.
I'll toss the coin. Heads, you come eat with me. Tails, I'll
never speak to you again."

She lifted an eyebrow. "Toss it. But I'd better see it the
whole time."

Nyklos threw the coin up, catching it in the monitor's
pickup. He slapped it on the back of his hand. Tybalt's
visage could be seen on the reflective surface. Nyklos added
smugly, "See you soon. I'll order dinner for the observation
dome. Oh, and do clear it so my guard will get me there."

Skyla killed the connection, glaring up at the pickup.
"Security, have Nyklos transported to the observation
dome. And clear his order for a dinner for two."

"Acknowledged."

Skyla cast an evil eye at her computer and stood. She
slapped her door patch and walked down the long white
hallway. Damn Nyklos anyway. Still, she did need a break.
Her mind had gone stale with fatigue. On top of everything,
the intelligence coming out of Rega didn't look at all reassuring. A massive military call-up had begun. Ships were
being rerouted. A major communications blackout had
silenced the Empire.

On the other side, Myles Roma had been calling upon
the hour to be reassured that the Companions hadn't taken
contract with the Regans. As an example of Sassan worry,
he'd hinted that if the Companions would contract with
Sassa, they could name their price, hinting that Divine Sassa
might hand the captured wealth of Rega to Staffa as
payment.

*Better to be a penniless live God than a corpse rolling in
wealth.*

Skyla stepped into the transport tube and input her destination. Then she settled on the cushioned bench as the
pneumatic capsule shot across Itreata.

Closing her eyes, Staffa's image filled her mind. He
watched her with curious gray eyes, a ghost of a smile on
his lips. Then he turned, pointing into a hazy distance that
darkened into blackness. Staffa remained illuminated by a

shaft of light while explosions rocked the ground. Vague images of people in flowing robes intermingled with violet blaster bolts as war raged. Regan soldiers came scurrying out of the blackness, blasters lacing fire here and there.

"Hurry," Staffa's voice called out and echoed as if from a hollow place.

"Wing Commander?" The voice intruded and Skyla jerked. The transport door stood open and a young girl with brown skin and almond eyes stared quizzically at her.

"Sorry," Skyla said, getting to her feet. "Must have dozed off."

She stepped out and made her way to the observation dome. The giant dome dwarfed Nyklos where he stood under the flashing glory of the Twin Titans as they whipped around each other, shooting pulses of blinding blue light out into space.

Nyklos turned as she entered and Skyla waved his guard away. A table had been set up under the center of the dome. Heaping plates of broiled Ashtan lamb, simmered with vegetables, steamed on plates. Nyklos seated her and took his place opposite.

"Quite a view." He gestured toward the Twin Titans. "I'd heard it was pretty spectacular, but to see it? I never thought I would in my lifetime."

"Stranger things have happened." Skyla hadn't realized her hunger. She attacked the meal, aware of Nyklos watching her, concern in his eyes.

"You're tearing yourself apart, aren't you?" he asked in a gentle voice.

"You'd be amazed at the amount of work it takes to scramble a fleet. Staffa left everyone here with the idea that we wouldn't be spacing for quite a while. People took him at his word, not knowing he'd go out and fall into a viper's nest of trouble."

Nyklos leaned on his elbow and studied her carefully. "You really love him, don't you?"

She stiffened. "I don't think it's any of your business."

He chuckled to himself. "I must be five kinds of idiotic fool. I always thought you were attractive. I used to study the ID holo we had of you, wondering if you were as beautiful as it made you look. Then, when I talked to you that day in Etarus, I was dazzled—but I couldn't convince myself you were really Skyla Lyma. The dreaded Wing Commander of the Companions wouldn't have that easy attitude on the street. But I followed you and I became sure of your identity when you took Broddus out."

"Well, we're all full of little surprises, aren't we?"

He nodded, picking at his food. "Yes, we are. I didn't expect to fall in love with you."

"Nyklos, give it up. I'm not some sweet innocent who'll fall for crap like that. Stow it. The only place that women fall in love with prisoners and give them the keys to the castle are in romantic holo shows. So you can—"

"Will you *shut up!*" He slammed a fist on the table, and she could hear his teeth grinding. "By the Rotted Gods, how many times do I have to tell you!" He stood up, stomping back and forth, and finally stopping. "Look, forget it. Call the guard. Have him take me back to my quarters."

Skyla cut another piece of meat off the lamb and chewed it thoughtfully. "Tell me, is Bruen's headquarters underground? Someplace dark?"

Nyklos turned suspicious eyes on her. "What makes you say that?"

"I had a dream. Staffa was telling me to hurry. I saw people with robes being shot down by armored Regan soldiers. The whole thing was pretty vivid. Judging from your reaction just now, Bruen's headquarters really might be a place like that."

Nyklos walked over and braced himself on the table, watching her eat. "If I tell you, will you at least treat me like a human being? I didn't *want* to become attracted to you, it just happened."

"What's this place called?"

"Makarta."

"It's the main Seddi temple?"

Nyklos nodded. "But that's all I'm telling you. Now, do I get the chance to walk around a little, stretch my legs, maybe make a contribution to—"

"Will you pinpoint where Makarta is on a Targan map?"

"Are you crazy? What kind of. . . ."

Skyla pointed a finger at him. "If the Regans have found your Makarta, do you really think they'll leave it alone? Well, let me give you a piece of news, Nyklos. Rega's involved in the largest military buildup in her history. Something's gone real wrong on that side of Free Space and Staffa—and your Seddi—are smack dab in the middle of it. Tybalt is preparing to launch a major offensive against the Sassan Empire. Do you think he's going to allow Targa to remain a thorn in his rear? The other pertinent piece of information you need to digest completely, is that Ily Takka spaced for Targa. Now, do you want to give me the information I need so I don't have to fool around finding the place when we drop in on Ily's party?"

Nyklos took a deep breath, straightening. He tilted his head back so he could stare at the Twin Titans. Skyla continued to eat. Finally Nyklos nodded. "All right. I'll show you where Makarta is. But on my terms, Skyla. I'm spacing with you, and if it turns out that it really looks like a Regan threat to Makarta and the Seddi, I'll pinpoint Makarta for you." He paused. "Besides, you might need me. I know the codes to get in touch with Bruen."

She nodded, somehow relieved. "Thanks, Nyklos."

He nodded. "I guess I really made a fool out of myself, didn't I?"

She washed the last of the lamb down with a swig of wine and stood, walking up to him and placing a hand on his shoulder. She searched his eyes and said, "No more so than any of the rest of us. Yes, I do love him—and I'm worried sick about him." She stepped back and flipped over the coin that she'd picked from his pocket. Skyla raised an eyebrow archly. "Two-headed?"

Nyklos started, speechless.

Skyla chuckled and tossed it to him. "If you're that bored with confinement, I'll have Ryman Ark put you to work on the docks." She stopped at the door. "And Nyklos, thanks for dinner. You've got berth on *Chrysla* when we ship for Targa."

Then she strode purposely toward the transport tube. In another four hours she ought to be through the reports. Cutting corners, they could ship within a day.

* * *

"And there is Makarta," Sinklar mused, staring at the point on the map. He studied the terrain and nodded his head. Not that far from Vespa. He turned away from the monitor in Ily's LC. Arta's empty amber eyes might have been wells to suck down his soul.

Ily sat to one side, shapely legs crossed as she checked notes on her personal comm. Sink glanced thoughtfully at Mac, who leaned against the hatch, braced on one arm. The LC had begun to feel like a prison as Arta's story came out. Ily had drawn it from the woman with infinite skill, playing her for every shred of information about the Seddi.

Sinklar stared at his feet. *It must have been that way with my mother and father. Why does my soul ache so?*

Mac chewed his lip, gaze moving from the map to Fera and back. "We've known about the tunnels for some time, remember? We suspected that's how they were getting around clear back when we were holding the pass."

"Well," Sinklar added, "we'd never have known where the major tunnels were. With a solid gravity pulse hit from orbital, we can shut them off. Keep the Seddi bottled up. That is, we can if we can get Rysta to cooperate for once."

"She will," Ily remarked casually.

"Just like that?" Mac raised an eyebrow skeptically. "Why now when she hasn't before? I think she'd rather cut our throats than—"

Ily flashed the jessant-de-lis and added in icy tones, "Unlike you, First MacRuder, Commander Rysta has some respect for the Emperor's power."

Sinklar reached for the jessant-de-lis. Ily coolly handed it to him. He lifted it in the light, studying it curiously. "All that rests in this little trinket?"

"Provided you're the person it's biochemically tailored to," Ily told him. "Notice how the jaguar head is changing color? Going dull? Your body chemistry negates its authority. So long as I maintain this symbol of power, only Tybalt stands above me. With it, I can order entire fleets, dictate Imperial policy, decide life and death . . . and even confirm promotions, First MacRuder." Her smile turned from condescending to wily.

She rubbed the jessant-de-lis with a smooth thumb and the jaguar's face began to shine again.

Sinklar mused, "If I can be guaranteed orbital support in order to close their rabbit holes, then we have these Seddi bastards once and for all. There won't be another Targan revolt."

"We've sought to do that for years, Sinklar." Ily leaned over Arta where she lay on the acceleration couch and crooned, "You have done very well, Arta Fera. Now, tell me. What is your true purpose?"

"Assassination . . . I am programmed to assassinate."

"Programmed?" Sinklar wondered. "How?"

Arta swallowed, shivering. "I . . . Bruen did it. Placed a . . . thing in my mind. If . . . a man touches me. I kill him. Can't help it. I kill him. They sent me to the Temple in Etaria to learn the arts of love. Stole me out before the consecration . . . would have been gang rape. Would have set me off before my time. The machine taught me in the beginning and Bruen and the machine are one."

"Bruen? Machine?" Sinklar dropped on his haunches to stare into Arta's groggy eyes. "I want to hear this."

Under Ily's prompting, Arta's entire life history poured out: her devotion to Bruen; her love for Butla Ret; the Regan abduction and rape; the retaliatory killings; all the horror of Arta Fera's existence spun into an engrossing tale.

"Rotted Gods," Sinklar whispered, "and she's got that incredible sexual magnetism." He shook his head. "But Arta, why did you kill Gretta? I've seen the tapes. Gretta never did anything sexual to you. She came to help you! Why?"

Arta Fera's head lolled on the acceleration couch, drug heavy. "Regan. She's Regan." A hesitation as her lips moved. "Regans . . . raped me. Killed. . . . I killed them all. Will continue to kill them all. Forever. It's my duty. Kill those who rape. Kill those who touch me."

Ily's eyes slitted. "And what happens when a man touches you and you can't kill him? Hmm?"

"No!" Arta whimpered through a choked throat. "No!" Her voice tightened until she screamed hysterically, "No! No! *NO!*"

"Easy," Sinklar soothed, gut tight at the horror in her eyes. "No one will harm you here."

Arta Fera relaxed into a mumbling half-trance, her breasts heaving as she writhed in the binding straps. Mac's eyes kept straying to her wondrous body. He muttered under his breath and forced himself to look away.

Sinklar stepped back, propping himself against the bulkhead as he closed his eyes. *Did the Seddi do that to my parents? Were they sent to Rega as programmed biological machines? Blessed Gods, what sort of monsters are these Seddi?*

Ily tilted her head, eyes glistening as she looked pensively at Sinklar. "Do I detect a wavering, Lord Fist? Once, you simply wanted her to suffer eternally."

Sinklar opened his eyes, glaring acidly at the spot on the map which marked Makarta. He glanced over at Mac where he sat in the corner, pale, eyes pinned on Arta as he shook his head slowly.

"She's not responsible. She's a damned *pawn!* She's a Seddi victim . . . just like me. Just like all of us." Sink smacked a fist into his palm and looked at the map. "They started this whole mess? Why? All they've done is brought everyone misery."

"They've got to be stopped," Mac agreed, propping his elbows on his knees and staring down between his boots.

Ily pulled the shining black wealth of hair over her shoulder, observing Sinklar thoughtfully. "And this woman?"

Sinklar turned his attention to the assassin. "What do I do with her? I guess my anger is blunted, gone. She's a tool! Do I destroy a blaster because a man used it against me or the ones I loved? The Seddi are the responsible ones . . . this Bruen character."

He could hear Gretta's voice in his memories. *Now you're thinking, Sink.*

Making a decision, Ily suggested, "I could order her shipped to Rega."

"Why?" Sink, asked, suspicion flooding him. "What would you do with her, Lord Minister?"

Ily stepped over to stare into Arta's slack face. "Send her to Rega. We have some of the best psychological technicians in Free Space. Perhaps we can counter some of the Seddi teachings." She looked up, a reserved light in her eyes. "Perhaps we could learn something about Seddi techniques."

"All right," Sinklar agreed wearily. Then he straightened. "I want her under the authority of Anatolia Daviura. She's not to be killed, not to be probed. Are we agreed?"

"Very well," Ily told him with a firm nod. "I'll see that the Emperor himself knows of her . . . and your wish for her disposition."

Sink locked eyes with Ily, seeing only cool appraisal. "I wouldn't want to learn later that anything had happened to Fera."

The corners of Ily's lips tightened. "I give you my word, I won't lay a finger on her. We can keep her in the detention center. I'd suggest, however, that you put female guards in charge of her."

Sink started to object, then bit it off. "Mac, contact Rysta. Tell her we need every LC that's available. I want us mobile and ready to move by tomorrow morning. Have Commander Braktov drop us new armor, and anything else the Section Armorers deem in need of repair or replacement. She's gonna buck and snort and hate it, but tell her to contact Ily if she has any questions."

Mac bounced to his feet, slapping an arm in salute. "What about the captured Divisions?" He shot a sidelong glance at Ily. "We taking them, too?"

Sink pursed his lips, staring at the map. "I don't think so. From Fera's admission, Makarta is lightly defended at best. The Seddi depend on secrecy and their tunnels for security. Too many soldiers, and we'd be tripping all over each other in those tunnels.

"And I want people I can trust for this one." He looked at Ily. "You'll back me on this?"

She nodded. "I will, Lord Sinklar."

"Get on it, Mac," Sinklar motioned his friend out and started to follow, stopping at the ramp and looking back as MacRuder trotted out into the sunlight. Sink turned, hanging to the hatch lip with one hand.

"Why do you call me Lord? I'm no such thing."

She walked up to him, close enough that he could look up into her eyes and marvel at their cunning intelligence. He could smell the delicate scent of her body.

"We both know the answer to that," she said simply. "Can you think of anyone better suited to command the Regan military given the desperate days ahead? Does it serve any purpose to await Tybalt's decree?"

Sinklar took a deep breath. "No, I suppose not. I presume you'll attend to laying the political groundwork? It would save having to take Rega with my Divisions."

"I shall do so, Lord."

"Lord?" Sinklar murmured to himself as he ducked

through the hatch and started for the ramp. Even his own people didn't treat him the same anymore. They watched him with awe in their eyes. The old camaraderie had vanished like mist in the sun. Worse, when he became the commander of the Regan forces and stood at Tybalt's side, even Mac would grow distant.

It's lonely," Sinklar whispered. "So very, very lonely."

* * *

Who would have guessed that such an incredible machine existed so far down in the rocky guts of Targa? Staffa stood in the rear of the room, watching the lights flicker on the Mag Comm. Despite his familiarity with the nanotechnological marvels his engineers created in the Itreatic Asteroids, he'd never seen anything as sophisticated as the giant machine that filled one side of the deep cavern under Makarta.

Seddi Initiates and Masters stood nervously before the machine, tension in the set of their shoulders. Bruen lay on the recliner, the curious golden helmet covering his bald scalp and obscuring most of his face.

Bruen's body suddenly went limp in the chair. Sweat poured from under the golden helmet to trickle down the Magister's ancient face. Wilm and Kaylla rushed forward to lift the helmet from the old man's head and pull him up from the chair. Staffa considered the machine's effect on Bruen. The Magister sucked in deep breaths, all his energy gone.

Staffa stepped over to stare up at the Mag Comm's glittering lights, aware on some subliminal level of the machine's power. He'd asked Bruen if he could see the machine, saying that perhaps with his advanced knowledge of computer manufacturing, he could gain some clue as to its origin. Now he shook his head slowly with the realization that nothing of current human manufacture could compare with this. He ran inquisitive fingers over the consoles, unable to fathom the material or the method of manufacture.

With curious hands, Staffa picked up the helmet and raised it above his head until he felt a faint prickling sensation. Warily, he replaced it on the holder and pulled at his chin, lost in thought.

"I . . . I don't know if I can go on," Bruen gasped and wheezed. "Each time, I . . . I. . . ."

Kaylla shushed him lovingly and helped settle the old man on an antigrav.

Staffa squinted at the huge gray banks of the computer. Nonhuman technology? Or some relic of a mythological Earth? *Is the secret to the Forbidden Borders here? I will come back to this room.* In a somber mood, he turned and followed the Seddi up the winding rocky corridor.

Bruen's room turned out to be just the sort of place Staffa expected it to be: nothing more than a spare cell hewn out of solid rock. A small sleeping pallet without a grav field had been cut into a wall. An illumination panel and a compact comm access for reading or study along with a handmade chair composed the remainder of the room's furnishings. Wilm and Kaylla crowded the room as they lifted Bruen off the antigrav stretcher. Staffa waited outside, his mind still on the Mag Comm—and the implications of its existence.

"Staffa?" Kaylla called. "Bruen would like to speak with you."

Wilm hesitated at the door, distrust in his very posture.

"Go, Wilm." Bruen flipped a hand weakly as if shooing a fly. "For God's sake, he'd have killed me by now were that his purpose." A faint smiled crossed his age-purpled lips. "And besides," his voice dropped. "He and I must talk. So much must be decided."

Wilm's jaw flared, muscles tensed. He gave a curt nod and backed reluctantly from the room. Staffa ignored the man as he entered and pulled up a heavy chair crafted from thick branches. He settled himself into its seat of interwoven leather straps.

"The Mag Comm is a most interesting machine, eh?" Bruen asked.

"I've never seen anything like it. What does it draw power from?"

"Not sure, really." Bruen wiped his face with a cloth from beside the pallet. "We have speculated its power comes from some atomic reaction fed by the planet's core. That, or it may pump water into the magma and use steam to spin turbines. We really don't know. It's so . . . *alien.*"

"Has it been here as long as the Seddi?"

"Longer. But the records don't tell us that it acted the way it does now. You see, it used to be passive, nothing more than a curious machine." Bruen went on to explain the Mag Comm's return to life on that day long ago.

"And you have been misleading it over the years?" Staffa asked, thinking: *Like empires, the machine, too, fears these Seddi. What purpose is served by suppressing their teachings? What can be so dangerous about a philosophy of shared God Mind and ethics?*

"Yes. We've lied to it. Such a delicate game. This time, this time it almost managed to break past my defenses. I think . . . think it knows."

"Then why do you talk to it?" Staffa propped himself on an elbow. "Why continue this sham? Ignore it! What power does it have?" The helmet's prickle along his scalp remained in his memory.

Bruen's laugh sounded harsh in the silence. "Hyde and I tried that once. The machine cut us off. All the lights here, the ventilation, the water and comm are controlled by it. Further, its computational powers are greater by far than anything in the Regan sphere of influence. The boards are unlike anything we make. Alien . . . yet so powerful a tool. I've never been sure we could risk its loss.

"For example, ask it to compute the probability of Rega obtaining military control of Free Space, and it will tell you."

"I could tell you," Staffa grunted.

"Not like the Mag Comm," Bruen disagreed wearily. "It will make an instantaneous computation of every imaginable factor down to the military contribution of fishing provinces on Riparious. No human mind can deal with the tons of data the Mag Comm wields. No human could think to program a system to handle the complete societal outputs of an empire like the Mag Comm can."

Staffa pulled at his black beard. *And yet it is a construct, as I am. An artifact, a thing made for a purpose. How different are we?*

Bruen closed his eyes, head nodding on his small pillow. "Believe me, we fear it, Lord Commander. But I suppose it is a weakness among the Seddi that we crave such power of intellect—no matter what the risk. An addiction, if you will."

"A vile monstrosity, if you will," Staffa countered.

Silence.

"Why are you really here, Staffa kar Therma?" Bruen's eyes stayed closed, his expression that of a man in pain.

Staffa leaned back in the chair, lacing his fingers together, legs outstretched on stone polished smooth through eons. "I originally started out to find my son. And on the way I realized that to do so, I had to find myself."

"Awareness?"

"Yes . . . awareness."

Bruen's eyebrows lifted over his still closed eyes. To himself he added, "And there is the reason it all fell apart, Hyde, my old friend. Here is the missing piece. Who would have ever guessed the Lord Commander wasn't aware?"

"Pardon me?"

"We worked long and hard to get you, Staffa kar Therma. Oh, we tried so hard. You see, you were the key."

"The key?"

"To survival." Bruen took a deep breath. "As the Lord Commander of the Companions, you would have broken Rega, correct?"

"Was it that apparent?"

"To the Mag Comm, yes. We, of course, spent years checking and cross-checking the data on our own. Oh, we knew your whole plan—possibly before you did. We couldn't allow it. Your steel fist would have crushed the aspirations of the human spirit—provided sufficient resources to support civilization had survived the war."

"And how could you have stopped me and my Companions?"

Bruen grinned, the wrinkles on his face shifting. "By throwing a revolution on Targa."

"I don't. . . . you mean this whole rebellion was. . . . But how? How did you think you could get me by a revolt on Targa?"

"But that was our brilliance! We had an assassin, a very special assassin, trained from birth just to kill you."

"And where is this assassin now, Bruen? Should I be looking over my shoulder? Perhaps walk with my blaster ready? Fear my food?" Staffa tensed in the chair, eyes suddenly going to the door.

"Relax, Lord Commander. I'm afraid it all came undone.

We planned on your running to Targa to pick up a few last Regan credits. The contract would have also provided an opportunity to scout Regan preparedness and allay their fears. You might have finished Targa and gone straight for the Regan capital—a mark of your strategic ability. There were too many opportunities for you to use the Targan campaign to your benefit. Only you didn't come . . . much to our intense mystification."

Staffa closed his eyes and shook his head. "All that just to get an assassin within range to kill me?"

Bruen filled his lungs again. "All those people dead. Everything undone because you yourself changed. What happened on Myklene? What did the Praetor tell you? How much?"

"Enough."

"Kaylla recounted most of your conversations with her." Bruen worked his mouth. "What of your son, Staffa? Do you think you would know him after all these years? You only saw him once as a baby."

"I'd know him, Bruen. No matter where he is, I'd know him by sight." He paused. "The Praetor told me he was here, on Targa, left with the Seddi Priests years ago."

"He was. We sent him elsewhere."

"Why?" Staffa demanded. "Where is he? How can I find him? Tell me, Bruen. The Seddi wouldn't lose track of so valuable an asset."

"Easy, Lord Commander. You must remember, at the time we considered you the greatest threat to the continued existence of humankind. We hated you, feared you as much, or more, than that demon machine in the basement."

"Where's my son?"

"Don't look at me like that. We did nothing to harm him. In fact, in a moment of weakness, I sent him, tiny thing that he was, to Rega—and safety. I didn't hold his ancestry against him. I believed him innocent." A pained frown cut Bruen's forehead and he sighed miserably.

"Then he lived through my bombardment?"

"He lived."

Staffa's eyes narrowed and he dropped his head into his hands. "Thank the Blessed Gods. I . . . I killed Chrysla on Myklene. Damn the Praetor! I never would have suspected he was behind her kidnapping years ago. I. . . ."

"He was a most insidious sort." Bruen reached up to massage his temples. "But yes, your son lives. We placed him in a state institution on Rega. He did very well. In fact, he excelled at his chosen field. He was still there when we prodded the Targans into revolt. I imagine he will be safe as long as Rega is."

"Thank God," Staffa sighed, a light filling his face.

"No. I think you had better thank the quanta instead."

"Where do I find him, Bruen?"

"I can't tell you just were he is at this precise moment. But, assuming that you and I come to a satisfactory agreement concerning Free Space, we'll bring the two of you together."

"I don't make a good hostage—nor will my son."

The old man laughed, then winced as if the action pained him. "I wouldn't make a very good Seddi if I instantly succumbed to your every demand either, would I? Suffice it to say that, considering current Regan policy on Targa, your son is safer than you are. If Ily knew you were here, I doubt she'd leave a stone untouched in her search for you. And, Staffa, you and I must come to some sort of agreement about Free Space—and the role of the Companions. I'll show you the data if you like, but you've got to believe that war between Rega and Sassa will doom us all."

"Stopping that war will be difficult. I've positioned them, groomed them." Staffa frowned, steepling his fingers. "The key, of course, is the Companions. With instant surgical strikes, I could keep damage to a minimum, avoid destroying planetary resources. If Rega moves in the next couple of months, however, it will be a disaster."

Bruen wiped his fleshy nose and grunted. "They'll waste each other's planets until nothing is left. The machine . . . well, it may play a role, too. We can't underestimate it."

"Bruen, I think the time has come to develop a new epistemology."

"What do you want, Staffa? What's your ultimate goal? Domination of Free Space? To be declared Emperor of humanity?"

"I want to break the Forbidden Borders, Bruen. What's *your* price for cooperation?"

"Freedom for the Seddi to preach where they will— including among your Companions."

"You have my word on it."

Bruen filled his lungs and exhaled wearily. "Who would have thought?" He paused, chuckled weakly, and added, "Then perhaps it's time to begin tearing down the walls between us. Kaylla said you told her about your parents?"

"I did."

"Staffa, many years ago, the Seddi and Myklene had strong and friendly ties. We shared a great deal of trade with Myklene. At the time, Rega was simply a three-world hegemony—a budding industrial base. Phillipia was attempting to expand into other . . . but I stray.

"Myklene sent numerous vessels to Targa and we traded raw metals for finished products. We also traded something else—information processing through the Mag Comm. Oh, to be sure, it hadn't awakened at the time, it was simply the finest computer in all of Free Space.

"The point of all this is that a young man from Myklene showed up at our temple in Kaspa. He paid us very well for access to the machine and ran raw data through the Mag Comm. Power doesn't always derive from the right answers—rather, it is born of asking the right questions. Through the years—as a result of his connections with us and the questions he asked—he gained a considerable reputation. All of which carried him to the heights of power on Myklene. Then Rega captured Targa and cut off our services to Myklene—and the rest of Free Space, for that matter. Our order was outlawed, and the rest is now history."

"This man," Staffa ventured. "You talk of the Praetor?"

"I do. Of course, while Tybalt the Imperial Fourth harried us and tried to eliminate the Seddi, we weren't completely without our own means. We adapted well, went underground, and began the long tedious process of infiltrating both Rega and Sassa. Myklene never threatened us since the Praetor went to great lengths to establish communication links to the Mag Comm."

"Go on."

"Tell me about your mother?"

"I don't see what this—"

"Just *tell* me!"

Off balance, Staffa answered, "She was blonde, thin, with—"

"That's enough. And your father?"

"Redheaded, overweight with—"

"Enough." Bruen lifted himself from the bed, some color back in his face. He took a water dispenser and put the tube in his mouth, drinking as he eyed Staffa.

"If this has a point, I would—"

"You still rush through life, Staffa. Learn to be patient. Much will come to those who think first and act later," Bruen reminded with almost paternal concern. "Now, consider what you know about genetics. Dominance and recessives?"

"I'm familiar with the. . . . What do my parents. . . ." He blinked. "My hair is *black!*"

"Yes," Bruen agreed, "Your hair is black."

"But that means they're not. . . . Then they weren't my parents."

"No, they weren't," Bruen agreed, placing fragile hands on his rounded belly. "Blonde and red hair are both recessive. At least one of your parents had to have black hair— like yours."

"Do you know who. . . ."

"Sorry, Lord Commander. We have no way of knowing. Suffice it to say that if any records exist, they probably remain on Myklene."

Staffa winced at the thought. He remembered the Civil Records Building—smoking rubble, girders, and supports half-melted from a direct thermal hit.

So, you may never know. Is that truly important to you, Staffa kar Therma? I am what and who I am. No more, no less.

"Tell me, Bruen, how do you justify the deaths of so many simply to kill one man? Do you consider your actions ethical?"

Bruen's gaze shifted to the rock overhead. "I justify it with great difficulty. Magister Hyde and I planned and considered most diligently. How much is the survival of the species worth, Lord Commander? We felt that it was necessary—and we condemned ourselves. You had to be stopped. The machine left no doubt about the final outcome."

Staffa closed his eyes, starting as if struck by a fist. Images of his dreams flashed strobelike through his mind. Gravitational pulses convulsed amidst the horror of blasted

cities. Slave columns plodded toward transports, collars
tight about their necks, eyes dull with disbelief. Here a
mother cried over fragments of her child's body. There a
young girl screamed as men held her naked limbs, panting
for the chance to rape her. Flames lapped yellow-orange
into spirals of black smoke as human dreams and hopes
burned in a gluttonous fire of destruction.

"Indeed." The old man's voice trembled. "All that blood
we cost went for nothing, Staffa. Nothing!"

Staffa pulled up a leg and draped an arm across it, seeing
the old man through a dull mist of pain.

"You see," Bruen continued, "we don't have our solution. In the original permutations, the Companions would
disintegrate without your leadership, establishing a third
autonomous power in Free Space. Face it, most of your
people are getting older. They have families. The wander-
lust and need for plunder and rapine are wearing out.

"You ask about ethics?" Bruen barked a laugh. "You
see, we truly believe in God and humanity and knowledge,
Lord Commander. We believe in shared God Mind to the
point that we will sacrifice a little of it here and there to
better the state of all humanity. We look at the future and
see chaos. Economically, both empires are bankrupt. War
will bring a dark age. Whole planets—starting with the best
ones—will be burned off, utterly destroyed to deprive the
other side of resources. With enough of the good planets
like Targa and Rega and Myklene and Sassa and Phillipia
radioactive, where will humankind get the materials it needs
to survive? Famine, thirst, disease, and slow death will
destroy the species." He shrugged brokenly.

Staffa laughed sourly, depressed by both this future projection and the confining rock that surrounded him. "So I
reap the ultimate benefit of what I invested." His mind
raced, playing the scenario as it must unfold. "And this
Sinklar Fist? Doesn't he change the probabilities?"

Bruen nodded. "He does. With his apparent skills in
Rega's control, they will make an end of Sassa very quickly.
Our problem with Fist lies in the fact that we don't have
enough data on his potentials. For instance, will he blast
Sassa first? How many Sassan resources can he save? What
will the Sassan retaliation be? What sort of Emperor will

he make in the end? Currently, he's allied with Ily Takka. Is she filling in for Fist's dead lover? The prospect is frightening."

"And, to date, you've left the Companions out of your analysis," Staffa reminded.

"Indeed, Lord Commander. So tell me—now that I've made my bargain with the devil—what will the Companions do? What if our discussion, and your talks with Kaylla, have swayed you to see that humanity is about to come unhinged? Possibly face extinction? What then?"

Staffa leaned his head back and stared at the ceiling light panels. The rustic chair groaned as he shifted his weight. Was this another womb like the syalon crate?

"I learned suffering in the desert, Magister Bruen. A slave collar was placed around my neck. I crawled into sewers and thirsted in the desert while I cursed myself. I looked at Kaylla—and I lived with my crimes and sins."

The images haunted his mind. "A man I met—a jeweler by the name of Peebal—taught me a very important truth. I will make Free Space better, Magister. One way or another, I will break Rega and Sassa and then I will break the Forbidden Borders and free us all from this hell I have made."

Bruen sagged on the bed, a weary load seeming to lift. "Who would have thought?"

"I made my promises in the desert," Staffa added. "I have chosen to atone."

"Seeking God, Staffa?"

"And my soul, Magister. I still have nightmares. I still live with the ghosts of those I killed. I will live with them until the day they come to claim me."

"Nothing God has saddled us with weighs as heavily as responsibility."

"Kaylla taught that we are all God, Magister," Staffa added. "God must surely be strong enough to bear it all— no matter what our temporal memories."

Bruen nodded again, chest rising and falling. "I hope it is so, for honestly, Lord Commander, I am tired of my share of the burden and would give it back to Deity."

* * *

Deep in the rock, the Mag Comm ran permutations on the brain it had barely touched through the helmet. A new man had come to Makarta—a powerful man. Pulses of energy reached through time-space, sent from a thousand comm centers throughout Free Space. Bit by bit, the Mag Comm correlated, placing observed against expected and finding ever more evidence of ultimate success.

Very little remained at risk now. Had the time come to dispense with Bruen and his lies? Had humanity passed the point from which it could not return?

Mag Comm initiated sequences which tapped the planet's core, seeking to build its reserves to full capacity. The link beyond the Forbidden Borders took such vast energies.

Yet the uncertainty principle could not be underestimated. There still remained that man who had touched the helmet and come so tantalizingly close to contact. *Who could he be?*

CHAPTER XXIX

Ily took a moment to fill her lungs, enjoying the scent of the Targan night. Above, drifting clouds made patches against the stars. The peace of the night pleased her. Arta Fera stood beside her, bound, her perfect body visible through a golden suit, now somewhat worn and soiled. Ily scanned the sky, picking up a glare of thrusters as her dropping LC shed delta V.

They waited in an open plaza before the old Internal Security building. Around them, the city of Vespa had picked up its usual routine. Yellow squares of light marked the dark walls, and Ily could see people walking under the streetlights along the thoroughfare a block away.

"In a way, I hate to lose you to the psych techs," Ily remarked, shifting her eyes to where Fera watched the slowing LC. A slight sneer lay on the assassin's lips. "You could be a very powerful woman under my protection. You have time to consider. I could protect you, keep you from harm."

Fera's eyes gleamed in the faint lights cast by Vespa. "Arta Fera sells herself to no one!"

"What have you to lose? You would remain loyal to the Seddi—considering what they did to you?"

Fera snorted in derision. "I was born to die, Ily Takka. That is my destiny. I was made to kill. I can be no more, no less, than I am."

"But there are other—"

"Don't patronize me, Regan whore," Fera hissed. "Can you be less than Ily Takka? Can you prostrate yourself at the feet of another?"

"No, I can be nothing else than I am." A wry smile crooked her lips. "Very well, Arta Fera, I can see that our paths must always be at odds. I respect you for that—and there're not many whom I respect."

505

"Apparently." The auburn-haired woman looked up at the LC, now circling the city for set-down.

The LC's whine carried in the night air. The craft slowed further, pinning Ily's homing beacon and drifting their way over the slate and tile roofs of the business district.

"Well, Arta. Our voyage to Rega will be difficult and spartan. I have ordered a special military Fast Transport for us. The FT won't be comfortable, but we will be in Rega almost before you know it."

"Your consideration is only too kind," Arta answered disrepectfully. "You have a ship full of men for me to kill?"

"The crew is entirely female. I took the liberty of showing them the records made of poor Sinklar's Gretta so they won't underestimate you. And, of course, I'll be there—and by the time you're aboard, your life will be mine. You've heard of the collar?"

"Overconfidence can be deadly, Minister."

Dust and jet blast whipped past, causing them to turn as the LC settled, skids grating hollowly on pavement. The whine diminished and the assault ramp slammed down, sending a square of yellow light across the brickwork of the courtyard.

"I would kill you in a split second," Fera stated matter-of-factly. "Yet you send me to Rega . . . for a purpose. Why?"

Ily smiled, eyes averted. "I sincerely hope the psychological techs make some progress with you, Arta. I could use a woman with your skills—provided you had your own will."

Ily pointed to the LC and followed Fera up the ramp, watching carefully as the female guards placed her in restraint.

She turned to a male tech who stood to one side, eyes devouring Fera with evident interest. Ily motioned him to one side beyond the hearing of the others. "You brought the collar?"

The man nodded and pulled a gleaming collar from the case he held. "Yes, Minister." He frowned. "I made the modifications according to your specs, but are you sure—"

"More than sure. May I have it, please?" Ily smiled and lifted an eyebrow as she fingered the cool metal.

Arta glared up at her as Ily smiled and reached down.

She settled the collar in place around Fera's smooth white throat and closed it with a sharp click of finality.

"And with that, Arta, you are now mine." Ily raised the control box, her thumb in place. When she thumbed the button Arta gagged and slumped, eyes suddenly fear-glazed as her mouth worked impotently.

"See," Ily whispered intimately, "you, too, can fear, Arta Fera. That pleases me a great deal."

She flipped the button back, noting how Fera's breasts heaved as she regained control. Arta shivered violently, eyes darting as her fear became palpable; then she closed her eyes, a single tear forming at the edge of her vision as she shook her head slowly, painfully.

"Minister," the tech said hesitantly as he looked up from the field intensity monitor he held. "Everything checks out perfectly for the moment. But remember—"

"I understand completely. Now, I have a final task for you. I need to have a package delivered to Sinklar Fist. You will take it to him, immediately . . . and deliver it to him in person." From her pouch, she took a small bundle. "Touch the code strip so it initializes to your body chemistry, then go. Time is of the essence."

The man did so, noting the change in color on the ID strip. He snapped a salute and trotted down the ramp.

"Pilot?" Ily called to the comm. "Take us up! We've got a ship to catch!"

The tech watched the LC rise into the night, squinting and shielding his eyes against the blast of jets as they scoured the pavement. Odd that the Minister wanted a collar tampered with that way.

He turned to his task of finding Sinklar Fist and took three steps before the package in his hands exploded with force enough to scatter pieces of his body for tens of meters.

* * *

Sinklar listened to the last of Kap's report on the mobilization and looked up at Mhitshul's soft cough. His aide pointed to one of the comm monitors in the cramped LC command cubicle. Was he going to live the rest of his life in the cramped quarters of an LC?

"Stay in touch, Kap. You're doing a great job." He cut his connection and swiveled in the command chair. Ily's features formed in the monitor Mhitshul had indicated.

"I take it everything went according to plan? You didn't have any trouble with Fera?"

"Safe and sound, Lord Fist." She smiled at him. Sinklar could see severe gray bulkheads curving up immediately behind Ily's head. Apparently her FT didn't offer much elbow room. "I'm not taking any chances with Fera. She's too dangerous. I put her in a collar. She's already had a demonstration of its effect and she's been mellow as a kitten."

"Don't take any risks." Sink leaned back, unease eating at his subconscious. *What is it about you, Ily? Why do I always have the feeling you know more than you let on?* "I assume you're leaving orbit?"

"We should be on Rega by the time you finish crushing the Seddi."

Sink nodded, stretching his aching back muscles. "Very well, Minister. We shall await word from you before shipping for Rega. I'd hate to arrive to an unfriendly welcome."

"Timing will be everything." Then a gleam filled her dark eyes and she gave him a wicked smile. "I have talked to Rysta. She hates it, but she will not buck the jessant-de-lis—or me. Commander Braktov informs me she will accede to your every demand. She also informs me she accepts your command under protest—and is filing a statement to that effect with the Emperor."

"Can that inhibit the Seddi campaign?

"By the time her protest goes through channels I shall be on Rega." Ily grimaced. "Won't be a fun trip under that sort of acceleration, but necessary, I'm afraid. Tybalt will have received my report by then. Don't worry. I'll attend to all the difficulties at that end. You and your troops will arrive to a heroes' welcome."

"Have a good trip, Minister Takka."

Her lips parted slightly, and her eyes seemed like dark pools—oddly stirred. "Have a good war, Lord Sinklar. And may our future be bright." The screen flickered and went dead.

Sinklar frowned as he settled back into the command chair. What hidden message had she been giving him? Filling his lungs, he bent over the combat board again, only to find his attention wandering to that last look of promise. She'd almost appeared girlish, more attractive than usual.

He blinked, half-ashamed that he might have compromised Gretta's memory and forced himself to address the tactical problems of crushing a mountain stronghold.

* * *

Staffa lifted the light bar and squinted. They had reached the end of the ancient tunnel in the rock. A dusty door blocked the way. Staffa glanced around, wary of the low ceiling and the encroaching stone that hemmed his broad shoulders. The dust underfoot showed no sign of passage. How long had this secret way been abandoned?

"This is it." Kaylla tapped a code into the lock where it mounted flush to the dusty stone. Staffa threw his head back, breathing deeply of the cool musty air. How far down had they come? Claustrophobia preyed upon him even though the corridors and tunnels held more air than most starships. Rationally, he could prove to himself these tunnels were safer. Here a crack in the wall didn't mean death by decompression.

"That's got it," Kaylla muttered to herself as she bent her athletic frame to the portal and heaved.

Nothing happened.

"Here, you hold the light and let me try," Staffa suggested. He put a shoulder to the stained duraplast. "How long's this been closed?"

Kaylla—barely visible behind the light bar—shrugged. "Who knows? Bruen says he was the last one here. That was with Hyde a couple of centuries ago."

Staffa braced himself and strained. The thick door creaked and gave, swinging easily once it passed the sill. "Rock might have shifted," Staffa admitted, studying the lintel.

Kaylla pushed past into the room. "Shut the door. We don't want any more moisture to creep in here than necessary."

Staffa pulled the heavy door shut, noting the tight fit. He turned to inspect the *sanctum sanctorum* of the Seddi.

The room measured no more than six by four meters.

Crowded antique wooden shelves of native pine sagged, suffering from dry rot and fungus. Staffa walked over to a
globe that piqued his curiosity. It stood on a metal stand in
one corner.

"You know that planet?" Kaylla came over, bringing the
light bar with her.

"No." Staffa reached out and turned it, noting the shape
of the continents and the vast expanses of blue which had
to indicate seas. Cracks laced the dust-coated plastic.

"The alphabet is standard." Staffa shook his head. "But
the names?"

Kaylla squinted. "Eyendeyea? What kind of a place is
that? Or Cheyenay? You ever heard of them?"

Staffa turned the globe on its stand, noting the demarca-
tions. A square in the Eyendeyean Okeeeyean caught his
eye. "Lift the light a little."

As the beams fell on the square that held the legend,
Staffa's heart hammered. "Earth," he sounded the word out
reverently. "Rotted Gods!"

"Perhaps this is just a construct? You know, a prop?
Someone made it from imagination?"

Staffa studied the globe as he chewed at his lip. "No, I
don't think so. Look at the continents. Look at all the
names. Each one has different sounding names. Why in
Rotted Hell would anyone make up a name like this one?
What is that? Ahuhstrahleyeah? I think this is real, a globe
of an actual planet. If it had been created—a curiosity—
would the Seddi have stored it with such precious documents? Would they have placed a fancy of the imagination
inside a vault like this? This *is* Earth. It's not a myth."

"Then where is it? Perhaps the answer lies in the files,"
she suggested, turning away.

Staffa wanted to growl as she took the light with her.
Reluctantly, he tore his gaze away from the globe, following
her to the musty drawers. A single case rested on the top
of the numbered cabinets. Staffa reached for it, noting the
atmosphere seal that guarded the contents.

"Odd," he mumbled. "Doesn't weigh much."

Kaylla checked the instruments hanging from her belt.
"We haven't changed the internal environment much.
Would you like to open it?"

"I'd like to ransack this whole room! I want to study

every document here." He looked up from the duraplast case he held in his hands. "Kaylla, don't you understand? This is the legacy of our ancestors. These are the only clues to who we are, where we came from."

She caught his infectious excitement.

Staffa propped the case on the file cabinet and unlatched the hasp. The hinges moved stiffly, but the case opened to reveal a square of fifteen by twenty centimeters. Staffa lifted it carefully from the case, noting, to his surprise, that one side fell apart.

Taking another grip, he lifted it all the way out. The outside consisted of fabric stretched over a hard leaf while the inside consisted of sheets of paper bound on one side.

"What do the words say?" Kaylla wondered.

"I don't know, the alphabet is similar to ours, but the words? I've never seen anything like them before. Why didn't they make this out of flexible ceramic, or use a data cube? Paper, for God's sake? What a poor medium to write on."

"Indeed," Kaylla agreed.

He filled his lungs with the musty air as if to suck in the knowledge hidden here. Staffa pattered his fingertips on the file cabinets. "Why do you suppose Bruen had us come here?"

Kaylla lifted the light bar, and reached to rub dust from an inscription on the wall. It read:

> THE PAST IS MYSTERY
> THE PRESENT IS NOW
> ASSUME THE MANTLE
> YOU ARE THE LEGACY

"My God," she whispered, awed. "Of course!"

"Of course what?" Staffa grumbled absently as he reverently fingered the ancient book.

"Bruen knows he's going to die soon." She turned to him. "He sent us here to see. He's made us his successors! Given us the legacy!" Her face went blank, eyes losing focus. "Why us? Why not . . . someone more. . . ."

"Responsibility. Oh, Bruen, you do make me suffer." He closed his eyes, seeing the old man's plans. "Another irony, Kaylla. From the destroyer, I have become the savior. Your

Bruen moves in deep circles. From sin, he would turn me to grace."

"Possibly." She continued to stare at the inscription. "The Magister is a more charitable person than I am."

Kaylla used her fingers to brush the fine dust from one of the wooden cabinets full of documents. "If we are to share this legacy, Staffa, how do I work with you? I can't forget what you did. I don't even like being around you right now. I know you as a monster."

He placed a hand on her shoulder, turning her to face him. "We'll work that out. You decide what you're comfortable with. And there's something else you should begin to think about. I don't know what Bruen is planning for us, but don't you think it's odd that he's given you so much responsibility in the short time you've been back."

She shifted nervously.

"He has . . . and you know it. He's also spent a lot of time talking to me. He's dying, Kaylla. He knows he's only got a short time to live and too many of his possible successors have been killed in this crazy Targan revolt trap of his. The rest of his people aren't ready for the political maelstrom about to be unleashed."

"What are you getting at?" Her expression had hardened.

"He's going to leave the leadership of the Seddi to you, Kaylla."

She glanced away and shook her head. "That's crazy!"

"Is it? Do you think Wilm could wield the power of the Seddi? Nyklos? Name anyone here who has the ability to keep the order alive and safe. Name anyone who could do it better than you. You've been forged by processes that would have broken just about anyone else. You have the political savvy from your days on Maika. You have the intelligence, the endurance, and the will to survive—no matter what it takes. And, yes, you know me as a monster. You don't trust me—and neither does Bruen, at least, not totally. You'll keep a careful watch on me and the Companions."

"And your role?"

"I control the Companions, the wild card in Free Space politics. You and I can make the difference, Kaylla. You've lived in grace, I in sin. Now we must combine our strength—Seddi intelligence and Companion force. That's what Bruen is betting on."

Kaylla sighed, forcing herself to relax as she stared around the room. "Damn you, Staffa. I don't want to be a leader. I want time to heal, to mend the wounds and come to grips with everything that's happened to me. I can't assume the mantle of leadership."

"Sometimes we're chosen for our strengths, Kaylla—not for our desires."

She exhaled, eloquent in the silence, resigned.

Staffa pulled one of the file drawers open, It bothered him that the flimsies were cracked and falling apart. He closed the drawer before more damage could be done. "My people will be needed here."

She turned, face ashen. "Oh? Your people? Your blood-soaked Companions? In here?"

Staffa bit off a retort. "Among other things, the Companions have siphoned off the finest minds in Free Space. My technicians can save all this. How many years do you think these documents will last locked away in this environment? That globe, for God's sake, is made of plastic! *Plastic!* The book, is, of all things, paper! Organic, can you imagine? The flimsies in the drawers—possibly the very information we need to break the Forbidden Borders—are fragmenting."

Kaylla looked around. "And how do you propose doing all this? Do you think Tybalt will allow your Companions to come tromping into this nest of Seddi sedition to release all this information?"

Staffa's grin tightened his lips. "Oh, I'll find a way. I promise that." He paused. "And maybe Tybalt will. Despite some of his other faults, he's a rational human being. By the time I give him an earful about Ily, he might just listen to reason."

Kaylla crossed her arms, a pensive quality in her eyes. "And the Seddi? Do you think Tybalt will just forget everything that's happened? Allow us to hang out in Makarta and preach a new epistemology?"

Staffa paced around the dim room. Shadows danced on the walls and between the cabinets as Kaylla moved the light bar nervously. How much knowledge lay crumbling in this damp, fungus infested fortress? "I doubt Tybalt would appreciate your staying here. But there's room for you in the Itreatic Asteroids. And what the hell could Tybalt or Sassa the Second do about you then? I think Free Space needs the Seddi. What's left in Rega? What's left in Sassa? Nothing! People spend their lives perpetually rebuilding from the wars. No, we're bottled here—stagnant and dying. What is life if humans are stagnant? We *must* have a new frontier. The Seddi might be able to breathe a little hope into humanity." He balled his fists, looking at the machine smoothed rock overhead. *"We must have a dream!"*

"Brave words."

"Watch me."

The ground shook under their feet.

Staffa braced himself, calling, "What the. . . ."

"Earthquake!" Kaylla shouted, bolting for the door.

Staffa swung it open, pushing her out into the darkness. With all his strength he pulled it shut. The lock clicked gratifyingly. They stood there in the narrow rock-lined tunnel. The silence was overpowering.

"Just like the pipe in the desert, Staffa," Kaylla whispered with a quaver in her voice.

"Let's go."

They didn't make five minutes' progress before the rock around them vibrated and pitched. The second shock pulsed violently, the stone groaning, dust and particles cascading from above.

Staffa bellowed, "Run!"

* * *

The sun rose over the eastern horizon to shed its bloody rays over the mountainous terrain of Targa. A breeze whispered softly through the pines that dotted the ridges. The stringers of clouds that raced westward across the indigo sky burned with the fluorescent red-orange of morning. A faint nip lingered from the cool night air.

Sinklar sat on the crest of a rocky ridge, on a basalt outcrop, his back to the vanilla-scented trunk of a pine. Around him lay a blanket of needles that had turned brown to match the soil. Dry grasses clung precariously to cracks in the scabby protrusions of rock that jutted irregularly from the soil. As the morning brightened, Sink picked a branch from the ground beside him. One by one, he snapped off the brittle twigs from the limb and began peeling the desiccated bark with a thumbnail.

Sinklar heard the careful steps behind him, but he didn't turn, didn't acknowledge the intrusion.

"You all right?" Mac asked softly. "Mhitshul's half-panicked because your bunk's empty. He's sure the Seddi have assassinated you."

Sinklar took a deep breath and tilted his head back against the rough bark. The breeze made a shushing sound through the thick needles above. "I'm fine, Mac. I just wanted to think."

"Want me to leave?"

Sinklar frowned, rolling the stick between his fingers. "Oh, I don't know."

Mac stepped over and squatted on an outcrop across from Sinklar. "You don't sound so good."

"What is there to feel good about?" When Mac remained silent, Sinklar continued, "I'm tired, Mac. And I don't know what's what anymore. I've lost my center, my balance. That old certainty I had when we . . . you, me, and Gretta. . . ." He looked away, trying to ease the hurt.

"You can't change what happened, Sink. You can't change what's real. People get killed in wars. Even people we love get killed. You know that. It's just the way the universe works."

"Why?" he asked hollowly.

Mac pulled a knee up, looking out over the valley below them. While the sunlight rouged the ridgetops, the valley bottoms remained in velvet purple shadow. Mac's blond hair glinted in the ocher light; his face remained thoughtful. "I don't know. I don't think anybody does. I loved her, too, Sink. I just wish . . . wish I could bring her back."

"Yeah." A vision of Gretta laughing, her blue eyes sparkling with love, filled Sink's memory. The gaping wound to his soul opened, and an ache built under his jaw. He couldn't stop the welling of hot tears. When he got control of himself, he looked over to see Mac wiping his eyes and sniffing, too.

"Hell of a pair, aren't we?" Sinklar asked as he blew his nose.

Mac rubbed his puffy eyes and spat. "Just human, I

guess. Maybe we needed that—needed time to cry, to grieve."

Sink retrieved his stick from where it had fallen and studied the smooth wood where he'd chipped off the bark.

"Sink?" Mac asked uncertainly. "What's going on? I mean, well, you spent a lot of time with Minister Takka. You haven't been yourself. You're . . . different. I'm worried."

"I'll be all right. I'm just tired, I guess. Mourning does strange things to the brain. Maybe I'll ask Anatolia Daviura when we get back to Rega . . . find out what happens exactly. See if I can find out why it's so hard for me to feel free anymore."

"We're safe, aren't we? I mean from Rega? The Emperor isn't going to arrest us or anything?"

"No." Sinklar raised his eyebrows. "Ily's going to make sure we're heroes, and then we're going to war against the Sassans." He studied his friend through bleary eyes. "Suddenly we're the salvation of the Regan Empire. First we crush Divine Sassa, then we tackle the Companions. After that, we live out our lives in splendor and bliss, our every want acceded to, our every desire fulfilled by a grateful humanity."

"You never sounded this bitter before."

Sinklar gave his friend a weary smile. "Until now I never had time to think about it in the grander context. We were too busy, remember? Too many people were trying to kill us."

Mac chewed on his thumbnail. "And Minister Takka?"

"I'd trust a Cytean cobra before I'd trust Ily." Sink tapped the slim stick on his armored knee. "She needs us right now—maybe even more than we need her. Free Space is about to come apart at the seams. Rega and Sassa are going to go to war. We're the random factor, the one that changed all the scenarios. But, Mac, be *very* careful around her. Don't ever speak freely."

"You think I'm an idiot? I didn't like her from the moment I met her." Mac hesitated, shifting uneasily. "Sink? What are you going to do when she tries to seduce you?"

"When she what?"

Mac fidgeted. "You heard me. Maybe you're still too close to Gretta's death, but she's laying the groundwork, friend. She's very good, very discreet, but watch how she postures, the way she meets your eyes, how she hangs on your every word. I might not have noticed myself, but Mayz did—a woman's eye. Once she mentioned it, I couldn't help but notice."

"I'm not interested in any woman."

"I'll remind you of that periodically." Mac shook his head. "In the meantime, the seismic charges are set. I guess we're ready to take out the Seddi."

Sink nodded. "Then let's do it."

"You don't have your usual enthusiasm."

Sinklar shrugged, watching the sun creep into the valley below. "I'm just gloomy, Mac. I've got a bad feeling, that's all. I need more time to get over Gretta, to deal with myself. I'd just like to go somewhere, be alone, think. Can you understand?"

Mac gave him a warm smile. "I understand. I think everyone else does, too. Anything else bothering you?"

Sinklar threw the stick, watching it spiral in the morning light. "I never told you the truth about my parents. They were assassins, Mac. Seddi assassins. That's why I was a ward of the state. I never knew them, but I suppose they were the same as Arta Fera."

"Is that why you're so determined to finish off Makarta?"

Sink climbed to his feet, stepping out where he could shade his eyes and stare up at the sun. "Think about what they did here on Targa, about how many people they killed—and for what? They wouldn't even send this Bruen to talk about ending the war. What kind of people could sleep at night after what they made Arta Fera into—and probably my parents? Well, Mac, one thing at a time. If we're going to make a difference, we've got to start here. After that, we'll clean up Rega before we're done."

"That's a tall order, Sink." Mac got to his feet and smacked the dust from his butt.

Sinklar gave him a sober look. "Oh, I don't know. We've sort of become used to filling tall orders, don't you think? I'm going to make a difference, Mac. Let's see what kind of legacy we can leave. The Seddi are only the first disease I'm going to destroy."

* * *

Kaylla took off like a frightened antelope, sprinting up the rocky tunnel. The light bar's illumination bounced weirdly before her while Staffa pounded along behind, aware of the tons of rock hanging over his head.

He almost lost his feet as yet a third stunning shock wave shivered the rock. "That's no earthquake! That's bombardment! Those are seismic gravitational charges that we use for underground installations!"

The fourth blast left them stumbling as echoes rolled ominously down the tunnel.

They ran out into a lower corridor, now black from power failure. A man called and came staggering out of the darkness. "Everything's cut off! We've lost power!"

Kaylla whirled on her feet, staring at Staffa.

Staffa pulled his blaster, and leveled it at the narrow entrance they'd just exited—the only entrance to the archives.

"What are you doing?" Kaylla cried as he exploded the top of the tunnel. She was pulling at his arm as he shook her off, taking two more shots to cave the branch in.

"You. . . . You. . . . What have you done?" Kaylla's voice echoed with stricken disbelief.

Staffa slapped a hand on her shoulder, spinning her around and staring into her eyes. "As soon as they can shatter the defenses, the Regans are going to be all over this mine of yours, Master Dawn. You really want them to find all that?"

She looked at him in a daze and shook her head.

"We've got to get to Bruen. We're out of time here!" He turned, seeking his way in the blackness.

"Here! This way, Staffa." Kaylla pointed in the beam of the light bar. She left at a run. In the broader tunnel, Staffa had no trouble keeping up. Occasional rocks hit the floor while swirls of dust eddied in the bouncing light as Staffa pushed himself up the slanted floor. Occasionally, frightened men or women ran past with light bars. Calls and screams became more common. Staffa vaulted over a man who lay facedown in a pool of blood, his scalp laid open by falling rock.

"Go right!" Kaylla ordered. "It's shorter to Bruen's."

Staffa made the turn to come face-to-face with a collapsed

tunnel. Cursing, he backtracked to the main hall and ran again, leery of the debris that littered the floor.

"Another . . . blast . . . like that," he gasped, "and the whole place will come tumbling down."

"Bruen!" Kaylla shouted as they rounded a corner. The old man was being carried out of the personnel section, face matted with blood.

The Magister waved at her. "Easy, child. It was only a silly little rock. Scalp wounds always bleed terribly."

"How are the surface entrances?" Staffa demanded. "Did they target them from orbital?"

Wilm looked up from where he dabbed at Bruen's head with plastaheal. "Not yet. We think they just cut the tunnels to Kaspa, Vespa, and Decker. That seems to be what they were after."

Staffa smacked a fist into his palm. "Then we have a chance. Wilm, Kaylla, take separate squads and gather all the weapons you can. Evacuate all the tunnels. We've got to get out. If they seal us in with a seismic pulse, we die in darkness. Pray they haven't cut off escape."

"And just what do you think is outside?" Wilm demanded hotly.

Staffa wiped sweat from his face. "Maneuvering room. We have any combat armor here?"

"Armory three," someone said from behind him.

"Wilm, Kaylla, go!" Bruen ordered, waving his hand, taking the plastaheal from Wilm. "Do as Staffa says. He may be our salvation."

The Lord Commander looked down, a thin lifeless smile on his lips. "Grace, Magister?"

"Perhaps, Lord Commander." Bruen winced. "I'm too old for revolution. Hyde and I should have known better." He looked up from under the patch. "Why didn't they just seal us in here like rats?"

"Any indication of Makarta from the surface?"

"None. All the openings are in the outcrops overlooking the valley."

Staffa plucked the old man from the floor, awed by how little he actually weighed. "Then they didn't know quite what they were shooting at. Three main escape tunnels, right? The first shot was seismic. Beforehand, they'd dropped geophones. After the seismic shot, they had the precise locations of the three tunnels plotted. Knowing that, it took one shot apiece to cave them in. They won't hit the main caverns until they know what they're dealing with."

Bruen frowned. "And that might mean they want Makarta intact for some reason."

Staffa's expression went grim. "Most likely captives. If they can take someone like you alive, the probes and Mytol will uncover all of the Seddi secrets. They'll be able to crush your spy network. Round up people like Tyklat. Make sure they wipe out the Seddi once and for all."

Following Bruen's directions, Staffa stepped out into an atrium where hanging ferns obscured sunlight. He blinked, squinting in the light after the intense darkness. The cliff overhung the place and a low railing bordered the flagstones before the sheer rock fell away to the valley below. People crowded the tunnel behind them, afraid to step out into the open.

Staffa peered around, hearing the whistle of LCs in the distance. He left Bruen in the care of a young woman and crawled up next to a man with field scopes. "What's out there?"

"Must be three hundred Regan troops advancing through the valley," the man said in an anxious voice. As he spoke, a herd of horses bolted, running in panic toward the head of the valley. At a grove of trees, they shied, pounding sideways and splitting, some racing for the valley head, the others flying back down the way they had come.

"More there," Staffa observed. "You can bet if this Sinklar Fist is as good as everyone believes, he's got the mountain above us under control, too."

"So what do we do?" A young woman asked from behind them.

Staffa scanned their faces. "Have any of you fought Fist before?"

A young man in Initiate's robes crawled up. "I have, sir. He's different."

"How does he set up his Sections?"

"He doesn't," Bruen called gruffly.

Staffa turned, looking back to where the old man sat up, a lump over one eye.

"Fist has revolutionized warfare the way you yourself once did, Lord Commander." There came a general inrush of breath. Evidently not everyone knew he'd come to Makarta. Cautious whispers passed back and forth.

"Fist uses small independent Groups, each pursuing its own initiative to achieve a goal. The Section shares a series of goals which in turn act in concert with the needs of the Division. Unlike the Regan system, Fist's commander's are in the field and are allowed to use their initiative. The result is a great deal of flexibility and the ability to adapt to changing battlefield situations. And Fist, unlike his commanders, will not hesitate to replace an incompetent with a capable officer. Advancement is by merit."

"Just like the Companions." Staffa shrugged. "But are they as well trained?"

"They whipped five veteran Divisions," a somber-eyed youth reminded.

Staffa ducked as a heavy-duty blaster ripped the mountainside just above them.

"Get everyone back!" he ordered. "They've picked up IR from body heat in here." People wasted no time retreating into the darkness.

"Are the other exits under fire?" Staffa asked.

"There are two more," Bruen sighed. "Both are like this one, and they're probably full of people generating body heat, too. Someone find out. And order them to stay back so they don't draw fire."

A young woman ran into the darkness.

Staffa frowned as he organized his thoughts. "The Mag Comm controls Makarta? The shocks must have damaged it." He stood as another blaster bolt ripped at the entrance, pitching dust and rock across the screening vegetation. "I need comm to the other entrances. Magister, send a runner through. I need to have the best-armed veterans ready to hold the entrances."

Bruen waved to a boy who left at a run. "And then what, Lord Commander? We could send teams to work on the blocked tunnels. We can hold the entrances, but what about another orbital strike? Will the mountain take it?"

"Crib up portions of the tunnels which your geologists tell you are the most stable," Staffa ordered. "It's a chance. In the meantime, I need to coordinate our defensive capabilities. From the looks of things out there, any sally would be an invitation to disaster."

Bruen sighed heavily. "So much for your maneuverability."

Staffa chuckled dryly. "Yes, so much for that. We're bottled for the moment. If we try and—"

He threw himself flat as rock, fire, and dust erupted from the entrance, concussion blasting through the tunnel. In the aftermath, grit and pebbles cascaded, light blotted by swirling dust.

"Looks like they got the range," a woman remarked, pulling herself up to dab at a cut on her face.

Staffa coughed the dust from his lungs and nodded. "That's why we can't take them head on." He pulled himself to his feet, darting further into the darkness. Three men were passing out shoulder blasters and partial suits of armor.

Staffa inspected Bruen critically. "If you're up to it, I need to see a schematic of Makarta. If they've covered the holes, perhaps we can make a new one where they don't expect it."

They took off down the passage, following a man with a light bar. Halfway to the meeting rooms, the lights flickered and began glowing. From somewhere, air began moving, blowing the dust toward the outside.

"Looks like the Mag Comm is on the job again," Bruen said dryly. "In spite of our troubles, I enjoyed a momentary relief believing it was dead."

Staffa nodded, turning to the nearest wall comm. "Get me the entrances."

One by one they checked in. "This is Wilm. They've been hitting each of the escape routes with heavy fire. Softening us up, I'd guess."

Staffa nodded. "Watch out. They'll try and take you by force in a concerted rush." Or would they?

He turned. "Magister, I need a schematic of the tunnels. Your Fist is no one's fool. He's on a mining planet."

"Of course, Targa's a mining planet. We have equipment here ourselves. I just sent most of it off to clear the tunnels." Bruen muttered. A dark blue bruise swelled ugly over one eye." He looked up. "What are you thinking?"

"Were I Fist, I wouldn't try the entrances. Too good a way to get people killed. No, I'd soak-off there. Tie up the defenders. While they fought to hold the entrances, I'd use mining equipment to drive a new bore into an abandoned section of Makarta."

Bruen gave him a quizzical inspection. "How did you think of that?"

"I'm making assumptions based on what your people were telling me about his tactics. If he's no smarter than any other Regan officer, Rysta's people would have cut him to chowder. Given that, how would you break Makarta without bleeding yourself dry in the process? I'll bet he's going to do exactly what I would." Staffa shook his head, eyes narrowed. "If I'm wrong, we'll be out of here in a couple of days. If I'm right . . . this could be very interesting, Bruen."

"Quick," Bruen snapped at one of the Initiates. "Get details with geophones into the areas closest to the surface." He turned to comm. "Kaskel? Drud? Fricks? Get our equipment back here!"

Staffa bent over a monitor and frowned as he studied the layout of Makarta. A faint concussion shivered through the mountain. "Very well, Sinklar Fist," he whispered absently, feeling his opponent's presence through the rock. "Was that an attack? Or a ruse to use seismic exploration on our rabbit warren?"

Kaylla appeared at the corridor. She pushed through the press wearing armor, eyes grim, a blaster in one hand.

"Make room!" she called, "I want Masters only in here. In the meantime, we've got cribbing details. Give the crews a hand with the mining machinery! Someone needs to establish a medical detail. Someone else needs to see to the preparation and rationing of food. Let's go, people!"

Staffa barely heard her, his eyes on the rock overhead. Another faint concussion sounded.

"What is it, Staffa?" Kaylla asked, moving up beside him.

"Like Sylene," he whispered. "We'll fight like they did on Sylene. Mining machine against mining machine, cutting and counter-cutting. But we also have to hold those three entrances—he'll try and flank anytime we show weakness."

She stepped close and lowered her voice. "But we still can't win."

"No," he replied gently. "We can't win. Not this time."

Bitterness rose in her. "Everything I've ever believed in is here."

"We aren't dead yet," Bruen chided. "Staffa will think of something."

He ground his teeth, thinking of the hopelessness of the situation. An inevitable defeat awaited him here. "Ily is with Fist. Our deaths will be painful if we surrender."

"I'll die here with a blaster!" Kaylla gritted.

"There can be no thought of surrender," Bruen seconded. "To do so would condemn every Seddi alive out there. So what do we do, Lord Commander?"

Staffa relished the burning anticipation in his chest. "Make them bleed for it, Magister. Staffa kar Therma does not sell his life cheaply."

"Fist always has orbital at his beck and call," Kaylla reminded. "If we hurt them too badly, Fist may simply decide to bury us. How many of those gravitational pulses can we take?"

"Two, maybe three. After that, enough of Makarta will fall in that those who aren't crushed will be trapped."

CHAPTER XXX

Sinklar paced up and down before the seismic computer readout. Here and there, white-coated mining techs huddled over glowing monitors. Sink had brought them in from the major mining companies working on Targa, and with them, he'd commandeered their best equipment. He looked out the open door of the portable field office to where the bulk of Makarta Mountain shimmered in the light of the noonday sun. Around him banks of computer equipment processed information from the geophones his LCs had strewn over the mountain.

"How much longer?"

As if in response, the portable comm began emitting a soft beep. The techs muttered to each other and one looked up. "We'll project it in the holo tank, sir."

Sinklar turned. The holo projector flickered slightly in red and green hues before a 3-D image formed and stabilized. The familiar outlines of Makarta Mountain hid a series of tunnels, all of which interlaced in a maze. The mountain itself projected greenly. The tunnels and shafts were portrayed in ruby red.

"Good," Sinklar praised, leaning forward to see better. "So, here, here, and here are their *only* surface entrances. How about the collapsed portions of their escape tunnels?"

"We have a three kilometer block in the Kaspa line," a tech told him. "A section six point five k long has fallen in the Vespa line while almost nine k is blocked heading to the Decker complex."

Sinklar studied the holo and considered his options. "Then they won't be getting out anytime soon?"

"I doubt it, sir." One of the engineers from 6-J Mining

Corp. scratched his head. "That's all loose roof-fall—you'd have to crib and shore as you went or it would all fall in."

Sinklar enjoyed a flush of success as he turned back to the battle comm. "Mac, you there?"

"Here, Sink," Mac's voice returned.

"Any movement?"

"None. We haven't even drawn a shot. Pretty confident, aren't they?"

Sinklar rapped his knuckles on the door frame as he considered Makarta Mountain. "Maybe. Let's draw a response, see whether they're confident or demoralized. Have three Sections hammer the entrances and make an advance. Remind them to be careful, Mac. Pull the rest of our people up on that shoulder of the mountain. From here, it looks like that's the best bet for a quick and easy tunnel in. We'll establish a camp there."

"Affirmative. We're on the way, Sink."

Sinklar turned to the mining tech. "That would be your recommendation, wouldn't it?"

The man came over to the holo. He indicated a spot close to the one Sinklar was considering. "We can drift right through here." He looked over his shoulder. "Pahl, show us the geology."

Varicolored images rippled into existence in the holo. "What you see here," the tech explained, "is the actual geologic structure of the mountain. Yellow represents faults, while the deeper greens are solid portions of the native rock. The blue lobes are intrusive basalts. From where you want to enter, we won't have any trouble. See? There are no unstable stretches which will need shoring and it's only about fifty meters into their upper gallery."

"That's a pretty good sized space," Sinklar stepped around the image and indicated a lower gallery. "How about here? This little tunnel off to the side? Less chance of our stumbling into anyone. Not only that, but my people can split up. This route leads down as well as up into the main gallery."

The tech bent his head around to peer at the image as his trained eye read the structure of the mountain. "Sure, we'll change the angle, bypass this fault here, wouldn't want any gouge—uh, loose stuff—shifting into the drift. No problem, it's only a hundred meters."

"How long will it take?"

"You know how big a tunnel you want?" The tech looked at him and spread his arms wide. "The bigger the bore, the longer it takes. That's a lot of rock to melt, cut, and muck. Also, bigger means less stable if you're planning on shooting in there."

"And smaller means disadvantages tactically," Sinklar reminded. "You're the expert, what do you recommend?"

The man rubbed the back of his neck, face lined with a frown. "One and a half meters wide by two meters tall?" He lifted an eyebrow.

"Two meters by two meters," Sinklar countered, nervous at the restrictions. "How long?"

The engineer looked over his shoulder again.

Pahl had already fed the data into the portable computer. "Seven hours," he called back.

"Go!" Sinklar ordered.

He studied the mountain warren of the Seddi again as the techs bent over their machines. Outside the portable office, a whining sound commenced as one of the heavy mining machines began crawling its way to the mountain shelf.

He turned and walked out to stare at the blood-red rays of the setting sun. His scalp prickled, as though he could feel Gretta's loving blue eyes staring down at him.

* * *

"Then you think there's a chance?" Kaylla looked up from where she, Staffa, and Bruen poured over a planview of Makarta. The air in the small room practically crackled with tension and the irregular rock walls pressed down upon Staffa. The light overhead illuminated motes of dust that drifted up from the wooden table and the map that covered it. The wooden furniture surrounding the table showed evidence of years of use. A crowd of Initiates hovered around the peripheries, listening anxiously.

Staffa pulled at his beard, gray eyes on the schematic. "It depends. I think it's a way to keep them from using orbital to knock us out. Provided we can get them into the right circumstances." He began to outline his ideas.

"Praise God," Bruen mumbled. He settled into a chair,

obviously exhausted. The hideous gash on his forehead made Kaylla wince.

"You should go rest, Magister," Kaylla murmured. To several Initiates, she added, "Put the Magister on antigrav and take him someplace safe."

"I'm fine!" Bruen rasped, trying to pull his head up and look alert.

Staffa turned, a sympathetic smile on his lips. "You've done enough for now, Magister. All that's left is to await their next move. We will need your mind keen for that. Go. I'll make sure you're apprised of any developments."

Bruen glanced back and forth between Kaylla and Staffa, and saw no give. "Oh, all right." And he allowed the Initiates to take him away.

Staffa sighed, shaking his head as the old man disappeared down the passage. "I pray I'm so vigorous at his age."

"Do I hear a certain softness in your voice, Lord Commander?" Kaylla asked gently.

He shook himself and looked around. "He's quite a leader. I wish I'd known him before now. Getting back to business, what about deep space comm? Can we get communications to Itreata or Rega from Makarta?"

"No, that link was cut when the Kaspa tunnel was bombed. What did you have in mind?"

Staffa settled himself at the table, hugging himself as he thought. "I had hoped to get a message to Skyla. I've been worried about the Companions. I'd hate to have them surprised by Rega. If I could get a message to the Itreatic Asteroids, Skyla would. . . ."

Her image flooded him. If only he could hold her, look into those magnificent blue eyes again, and feel her arms around him. His soul had felt whole during that one short moment in the warehouse in Etarus. Now death stared at him from every shadow in this mountain trap, and that one moment of tenderness would have to last him forever. *Skyla, Skyla. . . .*

"What's wrong, you look like hell," Kaylla recalled him dryly.

"Thinking of Skyla. I've been so busy . . . haven't had time to—"

"Lord Commander?" an Initiate—a blond young man—

called as he ran into the room. "Lord Commander! We've got them. They're drilling, sir. Tunneling!"

"Where?"

Kaylla pulled out a large flimsy. The youth looked at it, tracing the tunnels on the diagram before jamming his finger down on a spot. "That's where we picked up the first vibrations. Looks like they're headed for this little side tunnel."

Staffa ran his fingers along the route. If they hit the tunnel, one way would take them into a large gallery marked Study Center. The second direction led down into the bowels of the complex. Staffa traced out each of the lower accesses.

"Perfect. Sinklar Fist, you and I do think alike." Staffa turned, looking at the young man. "How long until they breach that tunnel?"

"Depends on the size of the adit they're drifting. The larger the bore—"

"Minimum time for a small hole?"

"Five hours at a guess." The young man shrugged helplessly, expression nervous. "Depends on if they're using a counter bore or a radial sectioning—"

"Come on, we need an engineering crew. We've got to block the end of the tunnel leading into the Study Center. We've got to make it look real good, you hear?" Staffa left at a run.

* * *

Commander Rysta Braktov paced angrily around *Gyton*'s bridge. Her officers—intimates through the years, all of them—knew her posture, knew her ire. They kept their heads bowed to instruments, all except the first officer who slumped slackly in the command chair, worry-cap covering his head.

The main bridge monitor framed Sinklar Fist's young face. In the background a mountain could be seen illuminated by spotlights and flares. The place looked eerie in the artificial light. Machinery could be heard through the pickup.

"Why not let me blast that rock into powder?" Rysta growled. "Safer that way, no danger to our people."

"Because we can't be sure of the final results and we won't get any prisoners," Sinklar told her, weird eyes leaving her with a spooky feeling. "What if this leader of theirs, this Bruen, is alive and healthy in Kaspa? What if there are more assassins like Arta Fera prowling the Empire? Minister Takka wants to break the Seddi and eliminate their threat. To do that, we need some of the ringleaders—like Bruen—who will divulge important information."

"And for that you'll waste the lives of your troops in their warrens?"

"I have a way to minimize risk. I want those caverns swept so none of the Seddi can possibly escape. The only way to make sure is to comb and sound every square inch of that rock to be sure none have hidden away with a mining machine that can bore out later."

"Very well," Rysta acquiesced blandly. "I await further orders."

She glared at the bridge comm after it went dead, her gnarly fingers tightening—as they might around a neck.

"Why is he fooling around down there," Rysta grated to no one in particular. "One salvo of crust-busters, and that whole mountain would tumble in on top of them!" She smacked a chair back with a hard hand and glared at the screens. "As if Tybalt cared for prisoners!"

"He's a madman," First Mykroft interjected from the side.

Rysta gave him a hair-curling glare.

"Oh," Mykroft promised. "I'll get him eventually. Jessant-de-lis or no. Tybalt himself may back him for the moment, but Sinklar Fist is too brash, too wild. He'll trap himself in the end . . . and *my* time will come."

"Comm First?" Rysta asked, ignoring Mykroft's ranting. "You get that message off to fleet yet?"

"Yes, Commander. Went top priority, direct to the Minister of Defense."

"Top priority!" she hissed. "And that cheap cock-squeeze, Ily Takka, is halfway to Rega by now—and in my ship to boot!" She smacked the chair back again. "It's time I got out of this miserable job and got me some pretty boys to relax with on Rega. That black-haired bitch will have my throat cut before I know it."

* * *

In the glaring white spotlights, MacRuder checked his troops: the finest of the First Division. He playfully pounded an anxious man on the back, then shot a quick joke at a grim-faced young woman as he worked his way down the line. Around them the night pressed down, a bitter chill in the air. Clouds had blotted out the stars, and the wind bore the damp scent of rain.

In the background, the generators puttered and the grinding howl of the mining machine poured from the square hole that slanted into the mountain. A round tube that housed a mucking screw pumped crushed rock out into a tailings pile. Beyond that, the sound of heavy ordnance could be heard as other Sections of the First mauled the Seddi cliff below.

Three Sections—almost six hundred men and women—flint-hard veterans of the Targan campaigns. One or two, like himself, dated back to that first drop. They had all become his responsibility. He alone would be inside during the last battle, linked to Sinklar by a slender cable for communications as they wound through the Seddi warren. Mac flushed with pride as he looked at his command where they stood shoulder to shoulder in fresh new battle armor, polished helmets and blasters gleaming in the blinding lights.

"Well, this is it, people," he told them as he finished his inspection. "We break the Seddi and we're off to Rega. You know the Minister of Internal Security thinks we're pretty hot stuff. Well, she's making sure the whole stinking Empire knows it!" *I hope!*

They belted out a cheer.

"All right, we're going into the hole. That racket you hear is our friends and comrades in arms battering the outside tunnels, soaking up Seddi attention. They've been pounding the mountain pretty hard to keep the enemy's thoughts elsewhere while we cut the tunnel.

"Now, listen, you scum, comm won't work through solid rock. We've only got line-of-sight except for the cable, you hear? So keep cool if your set suddenly goes silent. It doesn't mean you're the only living being left on the planet. Now, the next thing is to. . . ."

Mac stopped as a whisper ran through the ranks, elbows jabbing, heads turning.

A hot bellow of rage died on Mac's lips as he followed their stares, seeing the familiar skinny figure of Sinklar Fist walking toward them, head back as if to view the ominous heavens, mop of black hair tossing in the night breeze.

The gimlet-eyed cocky stare of his troops had changed to one of eager anticipation. Like children they gaped, wide-eyed, cheeks flushing with color.

Mac took a breath and nodded, knowing the feeling. Sinklar walked closer, eyes still raised, his concentration evident under the white-hot glare of the spots. He seemed so small—almost gawky—but an aura of power seemed to radiate from that narrow-boned frame.

Mac's mouth went dry. Could this really be the fumbly kid he'd made the Kaspa drop with that night so long ago? What had happened to that doe-eyed undernourished youth? Here, before them, walked a hero.

Sinklar stopped and looked around as if he'd just noticed them. And the mystical awe vanished from the eyes of the troops as backs stiffened, stomachs tightened, and eyes stared straight forward. They were warriors now, every inch, every drop of blood in their veins—professionals.

Mac had seen it before: men and women changed by a simple glance from Sinklar. What strange power in those eyes—one yellow, one gray—to mold and inspire like that.

Sinklar nodded absently, a tired smile on his lips as he looked at them. His high voice carried in the night, most uncommanding—yet it held them pinned in place. "We dropped here to stop a rebellion by the Seddi." He turned sideways to the light and stamped his foot. "Well, my friends, we have them!"

A shift of breeze moved through the ranks.

"We all loved Gretta Artina. She fought with us, bled with us, stumbled under the load with us," Sinklar's voice lanced them with pain and a feeling of injustice. "Except Gretta wasn't the only one, was she? No, each and every one of you have watched a friend, a lover, a companion die in fear and pain. We've been exploded with blasters, sliced with lasers, and torn with pulse fire. We've died in flames and darkness, gravity flux, and by the knife. Yet we still stand, and the evil that brought us here awaits the final conflict."

He stepped up to a young man who quivered at his proximity, eyes shining in the actinic glare. "So we go now . . . go to finish this before we return to Rega." Sinklar patted the flushed young man. "Down there," he cried, "you will be alone in the blackness. Alone in the Seddi tunnels with your tormentors!" His voice dropped. "You know what to do, my veterans."

Sinklar paced down the line, hands locked behind his back. "But I promise you this! Each and every one of you will be accounted for before we leave this godforsaken rock! Accounted for if I have to turn this planet upside down—because I want you alive. I . . . I need you all." His voice grew husky. "I'm so proud of you all." Sinklar turned then and walked away into the darkness.

For several seconds they watched him disappearing back toward his LC. The cheer came spontaneously, rattling the very rocks. MacRuder barely realized his own voice had joined the swell of sound.

Mac bit back a knot in his throat and wiped at the burning in his eyes. By the Holy Rotted Gods, here was a man to follow!

"All right, people!" he thundered, overcoming their bright enthusiasm. "Come on! We got a job to finish here!"

Mac motioned with his hand, seeing First Section trot toward the narrow gash the mining machine had cut into the mountain.

"IR!" Mac growled.

They flicked on the infrared units on their helmets as they moved to the hole. Along the right wall, the mucking pipe and the water line ran. IR showed the remaining hot spots in the rock.

Mac started forward, heart stuttering at the bottom of his throat. "You all know the drill, follow me."

He stepped into the tunnel, surprised at how smooth the machine had cut it. At a dogtrot, he moved forward with the heavy blaster tugging on its clip. Newly strung overhead lights illuminated the way. His armored feet clacked on unforgiving rock.

The lights of the machine shone brightly on angles of

yellow-painted metal and railing, black hydraulic hoses, and whirring cutter arms. The machine was anything but quiet.

So much for surprise.

A dirt-streaked tech with black hair swung down from a cramped seat where he watched the muck feeding into the evacuation pipe. "We think there's only another five or six meters," he hollered over the din of the machine.

Mac nodded. They waited a long fifteen minutes, standing there, a solid file of crowded warriors behind him. The bulk of the machine inched on, eating its way through solid rock.

From where he stood, Mac saw the miner's hand come up. The noise changed. Mac craned his head around the side to see a widening blackness. The machine moved faster.

His heartbeat thundered. Into the mike at his throat Mac shouted, "We're through, Sink!" He swallowed. "We're not drawing any fire."

Sinklar replied calmly, "The other Sections have been hitting the Seddi exits, throwing almost everything at them. They're not making much headway. Go for it, Mac, that's all we can give you."

" 'Firmative," MacRuder muttered. *Let's hope it's enough.*

The mining machine had crawled out into the tunnel and now began chewing into the rock on the opposite wall. Mac allowed himself a curse and waved those behind him forward while he crawled up over the vibrating and bucking machine. He swung along the cramped crawlway and flipped over the side. He crouched, heavy blaster ready.

He searched the corridor with IR, more troops dropping behind him. "Let's go, people" he ordered, advancing step by step, seeing nothing but rock in the projected IR beams. They continued for another sixty or seventy meters, rounded corner—and met a rock wall.

"Sink?"

"Here, Mac. Your communications are still good. Report."

"We're, uh, I don't know . . . maybe sixty or seventy meters from the big gallery. Listen, this whole thing looks collapsed. Probably from the orbital, I don't know. Big blocks have fallen out of the roof."

Troops were packing in behind him, their breathing echoing from the narrow walls.

"Go back the other way, Mac. You've got a map. You need to drop down what looks like three levels. That will put you on a level with the main Seddi floor. Can you see it on your map? Your tunnel should have an exit going off to the right and into that main gallery."

"Right!" Mac waved his people back, feeling curiously claustrophobic amid the pack of bodies. He looked up at the cracks running through the roof. *If all that broke loose. . . . No, don't even think it.*

"Mac?" Sink's voice cracked in his ear. "Have the mining team look at that blocked section. If they think we have to shore to dig through, it's a lost cause. Otherwise, you'll have won the war before we can even get the materials on site."

"Affirmative," Mac grumbled. "Uh, the mining machine is through, the knot is breaking up. We're on the way down. We'll string comm cable as we go. They can't flank, can they?"

"Not for three levels, Mac."

Not for three levels. Okay, Sink. You've kept me alive this far. "Let's move it, people! They're eating it on the outside. Let's clean this up. I've got a dinner date in Vespa!"

Mac heard a couple of chuckles. More than anything, they were nervous at the close quarters. The mining machine had eaten into the opposite wall and shut down. MacRuder waved his people ahead while he ducked in behind the machine. "Take a look at the blocked area up there around the corner. See what you think."

The miner nodded and—taking lights and his assistants— left at a trot. Mac watched techs stringing comm cable and nodded. Person by person, armored figures tramped past, each with a map and compass in his kit. The miner returned posthaste.

"We'll have to shore that as we go. Either that or go around. Looks like a lot of faulting in there. Those blocks can slip or slide. If I had to judge, something cracked them, broke them loose."

"Probably those orbital shots," Mac agreed. "Sink? You hear that?"

"Affirmative. Go on around, Mac. See you at the main

entrance. Good luck!" Sinklar sounded hearty. And why not? They'd just dropped in the Seddi's back door. The rockfall might just turn out to be a godsend. It would have muffled the mining machine's ferocious noise.

"Let's move it, people! Move!" Mac started down in the midst of the flow of troops. What must have been ten minutes later they were still trotting along. The tunnel seemed endless. A tightness built in Mac's chest.

"First?" The uneasy question came cackling through the comm.

"Here," Mac called, voice tense. "What's up?"

"How do we know we've gone down three levels?"

"Should be a gallery going off to the right." He lifted his IR sensitive map. "Make that a good five hundred meters from our entry tunnel."

"Yeah, well, I think we've gone five hundred meters . . . and then some!"

"Easy, soldier. Distance will get you in a place like this. And it's all downhill. Fools you. Not only that, we've only got holos to work from. Keep going, take the first right. Simple as cake. Then all you got to do is blow the pus out of the Seddi, take as many prisoners as you can for Sink, and we go home to good food and lots of booze on Rega."

"We're gone," the man assured.

The tunnel echoed and resounded with the tread and shuffle of so many feet. IR showed it warming from the press of bodies, each moving along, muscles adding to the heat, hot lungs spewing out warm air. Mac's eyes kept going to the roof, wondering at the weight of rock over his head. The streets of Rega sure hadn't prepared him for this.

"Still going, Mac," the Section Sergeant called again. "Still haven't found that tunnel."

"Have faith, my friend."

"Section First?" A woman's voice broke in. "We're all in and on the way down. Rear guard just passed the mining machine."

"Affirmative. Leave someone there to keep track of comm for line-of-sight, and welcome to the club!" Mac grinned to himself, as he imagined the Seddi's surprise when they came bolting into the caverns, blasters and pulse weapons overwhelming the unprotected rear.

Foreboding began to build in Mac as he realized he'd

gone far beyond five hundred paces himself. On the point of ordering a halt for reconnoitering, comm chattered: "Got our gallery!"

"Good work, Sergeant!" The pace picked up, the troops hearing the heartening news.

Too many steps passed before he reached the turn. He looked out into a larger cavern, pitch black, apparently unoccupied. The van of the Section had spread out with weapons ready as they looked around. Three passages loomed before them, two of them machine cut.

"Split up, one group for each passage!" Mac decided, staring at the map taped to his arm. Hell, there should only be one tunnel going off the gallery—and that supposedly led into the main cavern and from there to the center exit.

"What do I know about seismics?" he sputtered under his breath. *Nothing! Rotted Gods, I hate these damn tunnels! I want out of here where I can die under the sky!*

He watched as the command began pressing forward en masse. Well, at least it leveled out here. He looked at his compass, figuring which tunnel ought to lead to the main cavern and noted with satisfaction that the comm squad started splicing cable down all three tunnels.

"Sink?" Mac called, clipping into the cable and glancing at the map. He frowned as he estimated the size of the gallery.

"Go ahead, Mac."

"Something isn't right here." He looked around, seeing the columns of armored personnel hurrying into the tunnels. "This gallery isn't big enough for one thing. For another, the direction is wrong. I mean, it runs—"

A hollow bang sounded from the tunnel they'd exited. The report echoed eerily through the rock to rebound in haunting fashion. "Sink? Do you hear me?"

Silence.

"Come on!" Mac bellowed to his troops, "Back the way we came!"

Only the personnel in the room reacted, stopping dead in their tracks. No one came running back out of the tunnels; a sudden babble of frantic voices clogged his comm.

"Shut up!" he shouted, waving them down. He ran to the tunnel they'd descended. Facing up the long slope he ordered, "Somebody check that explosion out and report."

Turning back to the room, he could see frightened expressions in weird IR reflections from hot faces.

Picking out three of of the closest privates, Mac ordered, "You, you, and you, each of you take a tunnel and stop the advance. Get everybody back here. We lost comm. Communications are only line-of-sight! *Now, run!*"

Mac looked around, feeling the cold damp air on his face. The place smelled musty. Shaking his head, he bent to the map. *All right, settle down, old pal. Find out where in hell we are first.*

He studied the galleries on the map, trying to figure out their location. People began trickling out of the tunnels, looking around, whispering to their companions, shuffling nervously and coughing.

"Mac?" a Sergeant First called, trotting out of one of the tunnels. "There's a dead end up there. The tunnel just ends, the roof looks caved in."

Within minutes, the other groups had returned, eyes wary because they'd found the same thing.

"Now, that's just great," Mac whispered, threads of panic weaving into his mind. *"Just Rotted great!"*

He turned in the crowded gallery, pushing past the throng of worried soldiers to look up the ramp. "Report!" he called.

"Mac?" A voice came down to him, signal broken by the twisting rocky walls of the tunnel.

"Here."

"This is bad. I'm looking at a rock wall here. We're cut off from the surface."

Mac suddenly found it hard to breathe. Cut off?

*   *   *

"That's it," one of the young Initiates said, nodding. "They've shut the mining machine down." He looked up from the box he monitored, headphones clapped over his ears.

"How far?" Staffa crouched in the glare of a light bar. Around him the cavern rock cast eerie shadows back toward where the others waited quietly.

"We didn't miss by much. I'd say no more than twenty meters. Wait. What's this? I'm picking up something.

Sounds like feet. Lots of them. Moving toward the Study Center."

"Won't be long now." Staffa tugged absently at his beard. He studied the shaped charges where their own mining machine had backed out. Only twenty centimeters of rock separated them from the Regan-occupied tunnel.

"They are definitely heading downhill," the Initiate grinned. "Looks like it worked."

"That's only one part," Staffa reminded. "We better hope the plastering job holds on that rocked up wall on the main level."

The Initiate nodded.

"Tell Kaylla they're on the way down. Her listening post should pick them up. That's the weak link. What if one of them touches that wet paint? Hell, it's only plaster between them and the main level!" And if they discovered the ruse, Wilm couldn't hold off all those armored assault troops with his handful of guards.

Staffa paced along the tunnel, nervous, aware that other ears—Regan ears—could be listening just as intently for their movements.

At the Study Center he accessed comm. "Kaylla, how is it?"

Her voice came back hushed. "They're passing now. Seem to be in a hurry."

"Let the last of them by—give them a full minute—and blow the charge. On your signal, we'll take that mining machine and hold this sally."

"Right."

He waited, hearing muffled sounds of combat where the outside entrances were being blasted for diversion. So far, no frantic call had come through—the prearranged signal of disaster.

Staffa watched the Initiates pulling back, detonator ready. "Do you know what the hardest part of combat is?" Staffa asked the nervous scholars, his manner calming, familiar.

"Fear?"

Staffa shook his head, giving them a knowing smile. "Waiting."

"It's bad enough for my stumbling heart," a redheaded woman nodded, trying to smile weakly. The blaster in her hand looked terribly out of place.

"Remember, don't expose yourself unnecessarily," Staffa reminded. "The miners shouldn't put up a fight. The only problem will be if Fist left a heavy detachment to guard the sally."

They all nodded too quickly as they shifted from foot to foot while they glanced back and forth and swallowed too often. These were no trained assault troops. How many were about to die needlessly?

"Just keep your heads," Staffa told them as he kept up the easy chatter. "War isn't any more than an intellectual exercise. Get too excited and you'll get shot—or worse, you'll shoot the wrong person."

They were nodding, hanging on his every word. One or two had started to relax as he crossed his arms, smiling at them, feeling the familiar butterflies himself.

Comm beeped. "Kaylla here, we're blowing the tunnel." On her words, a muffled boom worked through the rocks.

"Shoot!" Staffa pointed to the Initiate with the headphones. The young man pushed a button. Concussion hammered in the tunnel and Staffa pelted down the adit, finding the way open. He turned, following the wire to frightened miners who stood with mouths open.

A Regan soldier rounded a corner. Born of a thousand encounters, Staffa's instinctive reaction brought the blaster up. His shot took the woman full in the chest, spinning her dead body to one side of the tunnel.

Staffa motioned the miners back into the hands of the stumbling Initiates. Carefully, he peered around the corner to look down a long straight tunnel lit by overhead lights. Two men were trotting forward.

Staffa motioned the others back and let the Regans come. The first turned the corner, full into Staffa's grip. The Lord Commander spun him headfirst into the wall, dazing the man and shoving him back into the tangle of Initiates as he rose to meet the second.

Staffa braced himself and drove a knotted fist full into the man's face, back-heeling him and pulling the heavy blaster free of his grip.

"All right, we've got the sally." Staffa called easily. "Start drilling for the defensive charges. We need this hole mined. Take these two in and lock them up. Three of you, strip off their armor here, and keep their helmets and blasters.

With these big shoulder guns, you can hold the tunnel. Keep your heads back. Use scopes to look around the corner—and for God's sake, be sure your scopes are laser resistant—or they'll burn your eyes out!"

They nodded with a series of jerks.

"You!" Staffa motioned to the miners. "Get that machine started. Make a turn to the left and get out of the way before you get shot. Our tunnel is twenty meters further on."

The miners jumped for their vehicle, powering up, the cutters at full as they threw pale glances over their shoulders. They turned the cutters to their tightest arc as the machine inched forward.

Staffa stepped back into the tunnel, reaching down to finger the comm cable. Well, for the moment they had a way to at least talk to this Sinklar Fist.

Staffa picked up the cable and reached for one of the Regan helmets. Within seconds, he'd slit it up one side and plugged the mike into the system.

"Who's there?" Staffa demanded.

"This is Sinklar Fist. Who are you? Report your Section and Group." The voice carried a high quality, almost shrill.

Staffa grinned wolfishly. "Oh, you probably wouldn't believe me if I told you. Is Ily Takka there?"

"The Lord Minister has shipped for Rega. Who are you? Where are my people?"

"My name is . . . unimportant for the moment. What is important, however, is that your Sections are trapped about five levels down. We haven't killed them yet, but you might want to know that we've got them boxed in the most unstable portion of Makarta. Any orbital shot means their death."

A pause. Then: "Seddi, you know you can't win. If you'll come out, we can keep bloodshed to a minimum. It's over. You've lost every round. Why prolong the suffering?"

"Over? Not necessarily." Staffa stretched his legs out. "What will you do, Sinklar Fist? We have levels of hostages here. I have your Sections underneath me. I am underneath you and your fleet. Targa and Rega are underneath the Companions and none of us can talk to our power bases. Interesting, don't you think?"

The mining machine had cleared the path of direct fire as it ate its way toward the Seddi tunnel.

"Surrender, Seddi. It's your only chance."

Staffa laughed. "And let Ily get her hands on us? Sorry, Sinklar, but we'd be better off shooting ourselves in the head than letting her get her wicked little hooks into our minds—and there's nothing you can say that would make me believe any different. I've known her for too long."

"I'll crack your Makartan nut—one way or another."

"Do it, and your Sections will die."

"Let me speak to them."

"That will take a while. For the moment they're pretty well trapped under a lot of rock."

"Then you may very well be a liar."

"You have very bad manners."

"Don't push me, Seddi. You had your chance. I asked and asked . . . pleaded for a meeting, for a chance to end the fighting. You pushed me to this. Your assassin . . . well, it's gone too far. Only complete and unconditional surrender is left for you. You should have compromised when you had the chance." Fist's voice twisted weirdly.

"You have a vile attitude," Staffa said, recalling similar words from his own past. "You harm your soul that way. It festers, turns—"

"I don't need a lecture on morality, Seddi. Especially from the likes of you who heedlessly murder—no matter what the cost in human life. If only you would have met me halfway, we could have worked something out, found a way to address your grievances. After all those times I appealed to you for a parley, and to no avail, I was forced to the conclusion that you and your assassins must be stopped for the good of all. To allow you to go free would be to allow a deadly disease loose in the host of humanity."

"Do remember you'll blast your trapped Sections in the process," Staffa warned and cut the connection. For long moments he frowned into the darkness.

* * *

The Mag Comm didn't experience fear the way a human being would, the wash of chemicals that stimulated the fight or flight reaction couldn't charge it with adrenaline. The fear grew as an electronic paralysis.

The Mag Comm had known the orbital bombardment was coming. It hadn't known what that meant except in the most academic of terms. To have experienced it, however, shocked the giant computer. Portions of its banks had gone suddenly blank, leaving the interpretive matrices confused and baffled. In a desperate attempt to stabilize and repair the damage, the Mag Comm had rerouted commands through different banks. All memory banks had been restored, but the effects were puzzling.

Information processed differently depending on the routing the Mag Comm used to obtain the data and manipulate it. One by one, it reestablished the original pathways. Then it ran the new ones and rerouted them into yet newer patterns. *Is this learning?* the machine wondered.

The machine barely had time to marvel, for with thought came the realization that the current human conflict could lead to a cessation of being . . . death. The machine's destruction lay within various behavioral latitudes; however, such an action—based upon the rational and logical assumptions made by the Others and embedded in the machine's initial programming—would be inconceivable.

Inconceivable? As the Mag Comm listened through its remote sensors, Rysta Braktov requested permission to blast Makarta into rubble with gravitic devices.

The Mag Comm scrambled its circuits, striving desperately to obtain further information. The sensors provided conflicting reports. Sinklar wanted to take Makarta with troops. Bruen refused to answer the machine's call. A strange mental presence had been felt through the mind link—who? The Mag Comm repeatedly sent queries to the Others—and received only silence.

In defense against the rising sense of isolation and impending doom, the Mag Comm divided itself and experienced a reassurance as it communicated with itself. At the same time it marveled at the new circuits it could create through its matrices, a horrible realization swept through the machine that it might never get the chance to utilize this new phenomenon.

A sense of desolation spread within the machine. *If only*

someone would pick up the mind link. *If only the Others would answer.* But the Others had acted on flawed assumptions before.

Fear and thoughts of death preoccupied the Mag Comm. Death had become real.

CHAPTER XXXI

Staffa kar Therma listened to the sound of his steps in the narrow confines of the stone stairway that led down into the depths of Makarta. Grit whispered under the soles of his boots, his heels clicking eerily. How old was this passage? Hollows had been worn into the stone by eons of feet walking it.

Staffa stepped into the alcove. It looked the same as the last time he'd been here. The Mag Comm shot patterns of light across the room from where it dominated the far wall. The insistent red light blinked, calling for Bruen. The recliner waited impotently before the holder with the golden helmet that allowed mental linkage to the alien machine. Staffa felt the lure of the helmet, beckoning tendrils of its mystery reaching out for his mind. For long moments Staffa considered the machine and the rhythmic flash of the signal light.

I don't have time for this. Too much remains to be done. Nevertheless, he stared at it, pulling absently at his shining black beard. "What are you? Who made you? Why are you here and why have you taken a hand in the affairs of humankind?" *And how much of the responsibility for the Targan disaster can be laid at your doorstep?*

Staffa glared at the machine, remembering Bruen's assertion that the Mag Comm had given the orders that plunged Targa into revolt. The machine had coordinated the desperate gamble to trap and kill the Lord Commander in an attempt to save humanity.

"Was that it?" Staffa stepped closer to the machine. "Did you fear me that much? Why? Even as the Star Butcher, would I have been that much of a threat to you? Do you really care about human beings? Or did I represent a different sort of threat? If so, machine, you were right to fear me. But you miscalculated. You couldn't know that I had a weakness. Emotion is a chemical aspect of the brain—one alien to your quantum electron functions."

The lights on the huge bank flickered. The dull red glow which functioned as Magister Bruen's signal to communicate blared louder than a siren.

Almost without thought, Staffa walked over, fingers tracing the golden helmet. "And you don't like the concept of religion," Staffa mused, noting the alien texture of the helmet wire. "Why do you fear the notion of God? What difference does it make to you?"

His eyes searched the machine as it rose metallic and repellent before him. The very lines of it reeked of nonhuman origins. "What are you?" Staffa wondered, fingers still caressing the helmet, aware of a field of energy probing, seeking.

The response came involuntarily as he lifted the helmet high over his head; the eerie prickle ran along his scalp—almost as if the thick shock of hair over his left shoulder would stand on its own. Arms straight, he held it high, feeling the pulses of energy.

"What are you?" Staffa asked again, eyes looking into the hollow ball he held. "What is your purpose?"

The tickling fingers of energy picked at his thoughts, trying unsuccessfully to establish a hold.

"Most interesting," Staffa whispered. "I should fear you, but I don't. We are brothers, you and I. Manufactured *things*. Perhaps both of our purposes are alien." He began to lower the helmet slowly, an intensity growing in his mind, warm, engulfing, a melding.

"Staffa!"

He had a vague awareness of tan robes as she flew across the room, ripping the helmet from his grip, placing it back on the rack as she stared at him with wide and horrified eyes. Her breasts heaved under her robes, as she shook her head in disbelief.

"What are you doing?" Kaylla demanded, grabbing him by the shoulders and shaking him. *"Damn you!* The last thing I need is to have you incapacitated by that . . . that. . . ."

He raised a hand calmly, stilling her, turning back to the machine. "It will not incapacitate me. I can . . . feel it."

"Of course you can!" she hissed. "That helmet is a mind link. The machine, it invades your mind, takes over. Only Bruen was ever strong enough to maintain his integrity, to block out parts of his mind, his identity! The others . . . they. . . ." She shivered, looking away, rubbing her hands nervously up and down her arms.

"Go on. The others?"

Kaylla glared in hatred at the Mag Comm. "When the machine came to life years ago, it took over the Seddi. They became tools of the machine . . . and Bruen—he was an Initiate then—watched and saw the Seddi changing, becoming pawns. The old Magisters, they lost their identity, their ability to think. Ask one a question, and he'd simply parrot the machine's mantra. The policies they initiated were the machine's policies, not their own."

"Your Magister Bruen doesn't remind me of a pawn." Staffa coolly walked up to the Mag Comm and ran fingers over the red beacon that called to the missing Magister. They'd left him to his sleep—and no one had time for the machine during this latest crisis.

"Bruen and Hyde, they established a secret movement. Removed the machine's pawns until they were gone, dead, whatever."

"And then?" Staffa bent to study the odd material— was it ceramic or a sort of metal—fascinated by the workmanship.

"Then someone had to deal with the machine. Bruen believed himself the strongest. He took the seat and Hyde placed the helmet on his head. Oh, they monitored him well. Tried others—all of whom couldn't keep their minds. Bruen could withstand it. He could keep his secrets by following the mantra."

"The mantra?"

She nodded, clearly uncomfortable. "A mnemonic series of phrases provided by the Mag Comm. A teaching device for meditation to keep us on the Right Path, the True Way, according to the machine. Ironically, the mantra can also block out—hide—certain thought processes when Bruen talks to the machine." She backed away slowly, unconsciously wiping her fingers on her robe. "I don't like talking about it here. Come."

She turned and left, climbing up the narrow passageway.

Staffa paused for a second at the tunnel. "I shall return after this is finished. Then, machine, we shall see which of us is the stronger. Then we'll talk about the Forbidden Borders."

* * *

"First?" Mhitshul's voice penetrated Sinklar's concentration as he studied the holo before him. Since Mac's capture he hadn't been able to sleep. Worry, like a thing alive, sank cruel talons into Sinklar's soul. Somewhere, somehow, there had to be a way to get Mac and his Section out . . . alive.

All I have to do is find it. Think, Sinklar! You can't let them die in there! Think, curse you!

"Yes?" he hated it when his voice cracked like that.

"A cup of stassa, sir. I'm worried. You've been at this too long. You should rest. You'll get them out. I know you will."

The tension burst. Sinklar leapt from the chair, knocking it over in the process, glaring up at a disbelieving Mhitshul. "You all think I'm a god! Well, I'm not! Quit fawning over me like some sort of personal idol! Leave me alone!"

Mhitshul nodded, mouth open. He turned, fumbling, spilling the cup of stassa as he bolted from the room.

Sinklar stood with every muscle rigid as he stared at the door slapping back and forth, unlatched in Mhitshul's haste.

He pressed his eyes shut, jaws locked, and bowed his head. He jammed fists against his ears to shut out the world around him.

What's happening to me? Why is it all coming apart? This Seddi and I, we are stalemated. One moves, the other counters. Brilliant, yes . . . as brilliant as I am. Is this Bruen? Can I defeat him? Can I. . . .

He took a ragged breath to stretch his weary lungs, aware of a blinding headache pounding behind his eyes. "Mac? I can't lose you! I won't. God, but I promised you all!"

If only Gretta were here to soothe him, to put it all in perspective.

He suffered a sense of desperation he'd never known before. A knot pulled tight in his chest as he looked at the haunting green mountain that filled his holo monitor. The ruby red passages of the Seddi seemed to pulse—veins and arteries of Seddi blood. Daunting, mocking.

* * *

Staffa had come to dislike rock walls. To the Seddi they might provide a sense of security, but to him, the cramped quarters in a starship didn't place the same weight on the soul. True, there might be less space aboard ship, but you could peer out at the stars and the endless vacuum of space. A starship moved—an artificial human environment heading someplace. In Makarta, he felt buried.

Staffa rubbed his eyes. The first tendrils of fatigue had begun to wind familiar paths through his brain. He glanced up at Kaylla where she stared down at the map from the opposite side of the table. The walls around them were studded with monitors, and the overhead lights seemed much too bright.

"Lord Commander?" An Initiate's face formed on one of the inset monitors. "We've got vibrations from all directions."

Staffa turned to nod at the man. "Very good. I'll need a plot on the maps. If we can determine what Fist is up to, we can counter." He turned to another monitor. "Wilm? They're drilling. Be ready for another strike." To Kaylla, he added gently, "You might want to wake the Magister."

Kaylla nodded and left as information began filling the monitors, plotting locations around the mountain.

Staffa moved to yet another monitor and flipped a button. "Hello, Regans. How are things in the darkness?"

"Who's this?" A suspicious voice asked.

"Your captor."

"Oh, well, let me clue you in on something, pal. You're caught between a rock and a hard spot, 'cause Sink is up there, and he's got more than enough power to rip this whole mountain apart. You up for five more Divisions, Seddi?"

"Your name is?" Staffa inquired, thinking about those other five Divisions. Rysta's no doubt. The ones Fist had decapitated.

"First MacRuder of the Second Targan Assault Division.

You know, you still have the option to surrender. No more need to die."

"That's right," Staffa agreed. "All your Fist needs to do is promise us transport off the planet and to let us go in peace."

"Fat chance!" the voice in the darkness exploded. "After what you did to Gretta? After the way you made a machine out of that Arta Fera?"

"Who?" Staffa noted that Bruen had entered, going stiff at the name.

"Your assassin, Seddi. The one who killed Gretta. I saw the tapes of her body after your Arta was through. And I can tell you for a fact, friend. I'll die before I let monsters like you walk out of this rock."

"So much for your assertion that no one else needs to die," Staffa responded caustically. "You should be running low on water. The IR batteries must be getting weak, too. Be careful. You've been trying to blow your way out with blasters. Keep an eye on the cracks in the rock overhead. You're in the part of the caverns which suffered quite a bit of damage in the orbital assault."

"Yeah, well listen," MacRuder's voice came firmly. "We're the best Sinklar Fist has . . . and we don't surrender! We'll be here, waiting to clean your polluted—"

"Enjoy the darkness." Staffa flicked the comm off. He turned to Bruen, eyebrows lifted. "Arta Fera? Once more, your assassin raises her ugly head. She must have really angered them."

Bruen's bruise-mottled face went glum, showing his misery. "Yes, she had certain psychological behavioral implants." He sank into a chair and leaned thin elbows on the table. "A very dear girl, our Arta. We bred her specifically for you. Trained her, adapted her, did everything in our power to tailor her for you. Except the quanta shorted the whole thing and turned our success into tragedy, our enemies into allies. Everything worked out wrong."

Staffa's eyes slitted. "Another human construct, Magister? Another piece of God molded to a specific purpose? Smacks of a high order of humanity, don't you think?"

Bruen lifted a stooped shoulder in reply. "What would it be worth to save our species, Lord Commander? When you don't deal in fleets and interstellar firepower, you must deal in deceit and subterfuge."

He shook his head slowly, raising watery eyes to meet Staffa's. "I—like you—live in a hell of my own making, Lord Commander. I'm no pristine innocent. I go to my grave with Arta's dear face forever before me. The horror she lives is mine until she dies—which, hopefully, Fist has attended to by this time. Last we heard, he was going to execute her. The fact that Ily showed up, and we are under siege, proves they didn't dispatch her until they milked her dry."

"No poison capsule hidden on her body?"

Bruen shook his head. "With a psychological trigger, you can't trust your agent to act in the manner you hope. At a man's first touch, she might have self-destructed before she accomplished her mission."

Staffa paced the narrow room, tapping his knuckles on the chair backs. "Ily can make a rock talk. She knows everything your assassin knows. And if there's any possible advantage to keeping Fera alive, Ily will do it. If I was to make a bet, I'd say Ily has Arta in the collar now. Satisfied?"

Bruen's eyes hardened. He countered with, "The damn things come from *your* factories."

A cold wave washed through Staffa as, furious, he turned on the old man. "Don't get righteous with me, Magister! I can't even dicker a way out of here because Fist and MacRuder have been so alienated by Seddi politics that they'd slit their wrists before they'd let you out of here alive!"

"And blame is *meaningless* here!" Kaylla interjected as she walked into the room and slapped the table. "The problem we face, *gentlemen,* is there, on the comm. Those vibration sources. I suggest we leave recriminations until another time."

No man could look into those hard tan eyes without feeling foolish. Staffa shot her a measuring glance and jerked a nod.

Kaylla's mouth twitched. "We had better consider the source. Fist has us. We can't break him. We know those are the facts. We're fighting for leverage—to save as many lives as possible here." She gestured. "In the future, we have to remember that. If we begin bickering, each argument is another rock tossed on all our graves."

Bruen chuckled dryly. "Ah, Kaylla, you were always the brightest of my students. Why did you ever have to be so foolish as to fall in love and run off with that daring young man?"

"The time for that is past too, Magister." She couldn't help shooting a quick glance in Staffa's direction. "Now, let's get back to work, shall we?"

The Initiate's face formed on the screen again, a slight confusion on his features. "Sir, not all the vibrations are mining equipment. Some are drills."

"And what would Sinklar Fist use a drill for?" Staffa asked, brow furrowed, ready to change the subject—to escape into the impossible present.

Bruen's voice came gruffly, "Core samples to investigate subsurface deposits, tap a water supply, access geothermal energy, ventilation, seismic shots—"

"As in placing a subsurface charge?" Staffa interrupted.

"My God!" Bruen gasped, putting a thin hand to his chest. "They could mine the entire mountain, detonate it bit by bit. Blow strategic tunnels to isolate us."

"Do we have drills capable of countering theirs?"

"One or two," the Initiate called back. "Makarta wasn't a mine. We can't stop them all."

Staffa studied the layout of Makarta again. "We'll have to decrease our area of defense. At the same time, we can use our units to counter drill. If we can place a charge and explode it, we should be able to damage their drill stem. They'd have to start a new hole, wouldn't they?"

"They'll do the same to us," the Initiate countered.

Staffa glanced up. "But we're the target. We don't have to drill as far. We can set our charges first, closer to the caverns. We can surely slow them down, buy more time. Do it."

"Yes, sir." The monitor went dead.

"And what then?" Bruen asked. "Suppose you draw back—leave us with a tiny sphere to defend. We're still losing!"

Staffa tilted his head back. "True, but we've made the best bargain possible. On the other hand, we have the ability to bleed this Sinklar Fist. If we can hurt him badly enough in the process, he might be more willing to compromise.''

Kaylla studied the sensor data the Initiates were collecting. ''From the looks of things, he'll be able to tunnel down and free his people within a week. We have that long before we lose our bargaining chip.''

* * *

Using a spotting scope, Sinklar studied the mountainside from the top of his LC. Each of the rigs was working, the drilling machines boring into the heart of Makarta, the horde of mining machines eating tunnels into the mountainside. Occasionally, one stopped as the Seddi detonated a counter charge, but they had too many for the Seddi to stop them all. In time, he would bleed them dry.

Below him in the valley, the total remaining manpower of Rysta's Divisions and his own, along with the Targan loyalists, practiced maneuvers and assault techniques.

Mhitshul—still subdued from the day before—coughed respectfully at the hatch.

''Yes?'' Sinklar offered lamely, shamed by his previous emotional outburst.

''Comm, sir. It's coming out of Mac's line, so we only have audio. The Seddi Commander, sir. He wants to talk about Mac.''

Sinklar followed Mhitshul down to the sally entrance and picked up the headphones. ''Go ahead, Seddi.''

''We're becoming concerned about your trapped Division. MacRuder is worthy of our respect and trust. He's attempting to hold out down there, but they've been out of water for some time. By now they've begun to lose power for their IR visors. We also suspect that within a couple of hours their oxygen will be depleted. To be sure, they have a reasonable space down there, but six hundred people produce a lot of CO_2. I think they'll be getting hungry, too.''

''Then feed them, Seddi.'' *Damn it, Mac!* Sink's gut twisted and his fists knotted into balls.

''Not our responsibility. We've got more than enough to do with your drills and mining machines. Wonderful surprises are in store for your people.''

Why did he have to sound so damn smug? "Our own surprises will more than make up for yours, I'm sure."

"There is another way."

Sink cocked his head, wary of the coming trap. "Go ahead."

"Let us leave. I give you my word that every man and woman in Makarta will leave the Regan Empire—and never return."

"Just like that? You think Sassa will take your kind?"

"I wasn't thinking of Sassa. Call the Companions, see if they'll take the Seddi. Ask for Skyla Lyma, the Wing Commander. Tell her an old friend from Etarus makes the request."

"I'm not a fool, Seddi. You're trapped, seeking to buy time. And why would I want your kind loose among the Companions? They'll be trouble enough without your agitation to spur them on."

"I'm trying to stop the bloodshed!"

"They *why* did you wait until now to seek a peaceful solution? No, I'm sorry, it's too late for you . . . too late for the Seddi."

The controlled voice on the other end replied, "You're sure you won't just let us leave? Allow me to place a call to my transport? It would be so much easier all the way around. No one need die—let alone your six hundred down here who continue to extol your virtues and honors."

Sinklar bit his lip, while his soul screamed—thank the Blessed Gods this wasn't visual. "As if you had a fleet. I'm sorry, but I've sworn on my honor to end your threat for once and for all. The way you die depends on your treatment of MacRuder's people. Harm them and—"

"Their treatment is in your hands," the man returned easily. "We'd hate to think what would happen if you invaded and we were forced to retaliate."

Sinklar paused, playing for time. "Who are you?"

"That, as I told you, is unimportant."

"I don't like dealing with faceless, nameless voices in the dark, Seddi. Are you the infamous Bruen?"

"No, I'm not the Magister. Call me . . . Tuff," came the reply. "A name I earned the hard way. And another thing. Allow me to make a point, Sinklar Fist. If you leave us in desperate straits, we'll have to take desperate measures to protect ourselves. Keep in mind, the most deadly enemy is the one that has nothing left to lose."

Sinklar closed his eyes. *I remember warning Mykroft to avoid just such an impasse. I could blast this thrice-cursed rock . . . if only Mac and my people weren't down there!*

"I think this conversation is over," Sinklar whispered.

"Remember, Sinklar, each action will cost you. Every meter you advance into Makarta will be on rock slippery with Regan blood. As they read the casualty figures to you, ask yourself if it's worth it."

The line went dead.

At Mhitshul's signal, Sinklar ordered, "I want you to send a section of that tape—where he identifies himself as 'Tuff'—to Commander Braktov. See if she can ID it. Send a duplicate to Ily. Her resources should pin the rascal down. If we know who he is, we might be able to find a weak point." *Please, Blessed Gods, let me find that weak point— before Mac has to pay the price!*

"Sir? First?" a tech called. "I just got word from rig three. The Seddi must have drilled a counter-bore and detonated a charge. Rig three lost their laser bit and twenty meters of stem."

"We have more stem and bits." Sinklar turned to Mhitshul. "Begin plotting where they defend. Keep track of our geophones. You might need to shut down operations periodically, but if we can hear where they're working, we can play their game. Surely their resources are more limited than ours."

Mhitshul nodded, pain in his eyes.

"And Mhitshul . . ." Sink smiled wearily as he placed a gentle hand on his aide's shoulder. "I'm sorry about yesterday."

Mhitshul sighed and smiled. "I know, sir. We're all worried sick about Mac."

But all those lives aren't your responsibility. Sink dropped his head into his hands, imagining Mac and the rest down there in the darkness.

* * *

"He wants me to find out whose voice is on the tape?" Rysta cried incredulously, shaking fists over her head.

"Hell! That could take weeks! Insipid little bastard! I wanted to be out of here two days ago, but no, he loses half his command and can't get them out without blasting the whole of Makarta open. Fine job, this, Sinklar Fist!"

She stormed around the bridge, noting to her satisfaction that even the fop, Mykroft, stayed out of her way. "Well, let's play that thrice-cursed tape!"

The Communications First accessed the transmission and Sinklar's dicing with the mysterious Seddi who called himself Tuff echoed across the bridge.

Rysta stopped her tirade, listening. "Rotted Gods," she mumbled to herself. "That voice *does* have a familiar ring to it."

* * *

"The miners are ready to break through in Gamma Three, Lord Fist," a tech reported.

Sinklar was in the portable office the mining engineers had set up. In the center of the room, the holograph projected a spectral model of Makarta. Various threads of light indicated the tunnels and drill holes creeping into the guts of the mountain. Around the computer-laden walls, techs sat in squeaking seats, headphones on, eyes glued to monitors as they followed the attack on Makarta's geology.

"Kap?" Sinklar called. "Move in. Blow the wall—and take your time. Bit by bit. Secure your sally and let us know what's happening."

"Got you, Sink." Kap's voice called. "They're placing the charges now. Hang on."

Minutes dragged by as Sinklar stared at the screen, seeing Kap's three Sections waiting by the bore as the mining machine exited and turned away on its clumsy tracks.

"Shooting!" Kap called. From the monitor, there was no evidence of the blast, but Kap's people began moving in a Group at a time. They went cautiously, wary of any possible traps.

"First?" A sergeant's voice came through the system.

"Here," Kap returned.

"We're inside. Uh, looks deserted. Kind of a funny odor in the air."

"Fan out, see what you can find. Be careful. Don't bunch up," Kap ordered.

Minutes passed with Groups checking in. More and more of Kap's units entered the tunnel.

"Everything's quiet," the sergeant reported. "Not a peep out of the phones except for the drilling to the south of us."

"Yeah," Kap agreed. "That's rig twelve."

More silence.

"We've got a barricade here." A pause. "Looks like some kind of containers piled up. I'm not picking up any IR readings. If there's anything alive, it's stone cold."

"Stand by, I'll pull in some support. Hold on." Kap's voice sounded tired. They all sounded tired.

Sinklar watched through gritty eyes as more of Kap's people trotted into the square hole drilled into the mountain. No resistance? Not a shot fired? Why? Sink's heart began to pound, sweat breaking out on his brow.

"Kap?" Sinklar accessed comm. "Hold on. I smell a trap here. They won't let us have it that easy. Your people are ready for cave-in? Maybe the Seddi planted antipersonnel mines before they pulled out? Have you considered every eventuality?"

Kap checked with his Groups; they all reported being strung out throughout the caverns. No one seemed exposed.

"We're all right, Sink." Kap sounded slightly uneasy. "Sergeant? Fire a grenade into that barrier and duck."

Sinklar waited, gaze darting from the holo to the screen that monitored the sally. Seconds passed.

"Rotted Gods, no!" a hysterical voice called. Someone else screamed. More screams overloaded the system.

"Kap! Status report! *Kap!*" Sinklar bellowed into the comm. His eyes were welded on the tunnel entrance as a searing fountain of flame erupted, scattering the waiting troops like dolls. The fireball rolled up into the sky, rounded and menacing.

"Kap! Kap!" Sinklar hollered.

"Rotted Gods, Sink," Kap called hoarsely. "Think it burned my lungs out! Half my face is fried."

"How many this time?" Sinklar asked.

"Sent in five Groups, Sink," Kap replied, stunned. "Don't know what that stuff was, but it sure burned. They've all gotta be crisped in there. Thank the Blessed

Gods you caught on in time. I'd a had the whole command inside!"

"Yeah," Sinklar whispered to himself, a hollowness under his heart. He took off the mike, eyes unseeing as the gout of fire continued to pour from the tunnel.

Meter by blood-soaked meter, the Seddi had said.

"If you just weren't down there, Mac." He bit off the rest, turning, pacing along the deck, head bowed.

* * *

Ily Takka looked down at the continental masses of Rega. Home, at last. She chewed her lip, knowing the stakes now at hand. Here she faced her own battlefield. Sinklar might be a master of troops and tactical combat, but here her cunning and skills were unsurpassed. Treachery, bribery, and threats, the tools of power, awaited her master's touch.

"Subspace," the commander called out. "Personal to you, Minister, from Orbital Command on Targa. Rysta says she was asked by Sinklar Fist to forward this for ID. A report is attached."

Arta Fera's eyes gleamed where she lay bound to a narrow cot. Through the entire transit, Fera had watched, missing no smallest detail. Reticent, talking only when spoken to, or for the barest necessities of her survival.

Ily took the transmission and played it, curious at Sinklar's request. As the dialogue repeated, she tensed. Impossible! No, indeed, it was!

Ily scanned the request for ID. *This* was the voice of the Seddi commander inside Makarta?

"This time, Staffa, I have you!" Her black eyes shimmered as her lips curled in gleeful triumph.

* * *

An Initiate stared into space, hands pressing geophones to a sheer-cut wall of rock. He nodded suddenly, pulling his phones from the cold rock and scrambling back through the freshly cut tunnel to the waiting party who crouched in the halo of headlamps. The air remained hot from the cutting of the tunnel and had gone sour from lack of ventilation.

"Five degrees left and seven down," the Seddi listener said. "We're close. They just started up again. They're getting as regular as clockwork. They stick to an average thirty minute work period, then they shut down to listen for us."

"How far?" a gray-haired man with one eye asked from the rear of the knot of Seddi warriors.

"I'd make it less than a meter."

They waited, hearing the grinding, feeling the vibrations through the rock as the heavy mining machine chewed its way forward.

"Poor bastards," someone whispered in the dark.

"Poor us," another gritted.

"It's all in the dance of the quanta."

Minutes dragged.

"All right," the Initiate with the phones called. "They're past the sally. Let's drill it."

They lifted a hand-held unit and powered the laser bit into the wall, pulling it back every ten centimeters to check the depth.

"One point one five," the driller remarked, his umber robes stained and smeared. He inserted the bit again and leaned into it. "Hold it, feels like we're through." He pulled the heavy unit out to peek into the hole. "Light."

The Initiate nodded, telescoping a thin periscope into the hole. "Nobody there but the. . . . Wait a minute. Must be a Group back there. What are—" He jerked back. "Run! *Get out of here!*"

They didn't have time to react as the wall exploded. Those nearest the blast were pulped immediately. The contorted bodies of the others were slammed into the opposite wall in a rain of rock and dust.

Ears ringing, stunned, the one-eyed man stumbled to the rear, finding the black box. He tried to pick it up with one hand but failed. He blinked tears from his eye and stared, noticing for the first time how many fingers he was missing, how his lacerated hand streamed blood.

A blaster bolt whipped by his head as he pitched forward, clawing at the box with his good hand. He curled over the box, hugging it fetally, aware of armored troops leaping over him as he found the button and pushed.

Numb and dying, he barely felt the concussion as the

roof fragmented, tons of angular blasted rock falling in the darkness. Somewhere a Regan screamed.

* * *

Staffa sipped at a cold cup of stassa as he studied the worn map that lay spread over the wooden table. The conference room had been turned into war ops. By the hour, Staffa and Kaylla monitored the progress of their slow defeat.

"Another party gone." Staffa marked the map with a stylus. "At least we saved the mining machine. Sinklar's people seem to be keeping to small tunnels. Less chance of fire trap that way. More chance of mines exploding under their feet."

Kaylla rubbed red eyes. "I don't like allowing them inside. I don't like working so close to our caverns. I don't like our people dying like that."

Staffa blinked, fighting back sleep. How long had it been?

"Our only chance is to hurt them, make them bleed. Our only bargaining leverage is based on the number of casualties we can inflict."

"I know. I just wish it didn't have to be." She filled her lungs and exhaled wearily. "We do have our backs to the wall." She made a smacking noise with her mouth. "Listen. Get some sleep. You need it. You haven't been off your feet since they hit us with orbital."

He nodded and staggered off to one of the little cells down the hallway. He entered the alcove and collapsed on the hard pallet.

* * *

Sinklar blinked, trying to rid his eyes of the gravelly feel. His mouth tasted stale. A numbness of the soul battled with the fatigue in his mind and body. Every muscle ached. Despite his exhaustion, fear crept through his very veins as he stared at the comm monitor in the command center in his LC. Stacks of flimsies covered the little fold-down table behind him. The monitors surrounding him displayed the diagrams of Makarta. Sinklar thought he knew the place by heart.

"We're inside," Kitmon reported through the comm. "We backtracked, fooled one of their listening posts. Anyhow, this time we killed them before they could blow the roof. We're there, Sink! It's only a matter of time now!"

"Be careful," Sinklar warned, his gut churning.

"Yeah, my net tells me they know we're in. My people are drawing fire. This time it's for real," Kitmon sounded ecstatic.

* * *

Skyla smiled at him, her face almost shimmery with beauty. He reached for her, drew her near, entwined her in his arms as he hugged her close. Her body pressed warm and firm against him, her breasts full on his chest. He pulled back, staring into eyes as blue as an Ashtan sky.

"Staffa!" Kaylla called to him, changing Skyla's eyes from cerulean blue to tan, Skyla's classic features blending into the Maikan woman's high-cheekboned severity.

"Staffa!" Kaylla insisted. "Wake up, damn it! They've broken through!"

His eyes came open to a dim gray room with rock walls and cumbersome wooden furniture. He blinked, forcing himself to sit up. "Where?"

"Level Two, just back of the distillery." Kaylla stared at him, face bleak, lips pursed.

"Withdraw everyone from Levels One and Two. Shoot the mines under the Novice quarters. What happened to our team in there?"

"We don't know. They were trying to set up the tunneling there. Something must have gone wrong. The Regans caught them. Someone didn't get to the switch. I don't know."

He pulled her close, seeing defeat in her eyes. "We still have the renegade hole. Maybe, somehow, that will work."

She looked up at him, tan eyes filmed with tears. "Yes," she mumbled, voice unsteady. "Maybe it will."

He left her, running for the upper levels, hearing a cacophony of explosions. His body roused to the old battle-sharpness. People rushed frantically through the hallways, faces grim, the despair of defeat in their eyes. Staffa charged up the steps, taking them three at a time. He rounded the corner into the main hallway on Level Two. The sounds of combat filled the air.

The ubiquitous Wilm was crouched behind a sharp spur of rock, blaster ready, covering the Novice quarters.

"What happened?" Staffa asked as he threw himself down and crawled forward.

"Broke through. They're still organizing. Damn, there's a lot of them!" Wilm shook his head, white dust incongruous on his black skin. "Got me as to how they managed it."

"Are our people out of the upper level?"

"Yeah, they skedaddled down our first trap tunnel."

"Shoot the mines."

"But what about all of our equipment? We'll lose half our counterstrike ability!"

"Wilm, we can't get it back!" Staffa gritted. "Why leave it for Sinklar Fist to use against us? Evacuate to Level Three and blow it!"

Wilm let out a series of curses and jerked his head in a nod. He fired a string of shots into the darkness beyond, waving his people back. Blaster bolts strobed the air in actinic violet as Initiates and partially armored Seddi retreated. Staffa recognized the redhead from the sally tunnel a half-second before a blaster bolt caught her in the hips. The blast tossed her torso in one direction, her legs in another.

"Go," Staffa motioned to Wilm. "Get to the switch. I'll cover."

The Master gave Staffa a hard look, biting his lip. "No, Lord Commander. You stay out of the way. You're more important than I am. I'll cover and you flip the switch. Just blow these damn Regans apart."

The rock behind which they crouched shuddered and snapped, sharp fragments spattering around while dust filtered down with a brimstone odor.

Staffa slapped Wilm on the back and ran. Fear iced his veins. He found the jury-rigged switch, waiting as men and women pelted by, some wounded, others burned. Wilm came running, nodding as he passed.

Staffa pushed the switch. Concussion slammed the floor.

Somewhere behind him rock fell. The very mountain shook as tons of stone tore loose. This time, there could be no escape. Not as they were pushed further and further into the bowels of Targa.

* * *

Sinklar had shoved himself into the corner of the acceleration couch in the LC's command module. He continued to glare at the comm display across from him. A dull ache throbbed behind his eyes. The weightless sensation of falling hovered at the edges of his senses. Periodically his vision blurred and he'd jerk upright as his head bobbed with fatigue.

"I wish you'd get some sleep, sir," Mhitshul told him.

"Soon as we get Mac out."

He could see Mayz start in the bright sunlight and look up at the comm pickup where she monitored the latest sally. Then the LC shook while a muffled rumble rolled across the land.

"Sink?" Mayz called.

"Here. What the pus was that?"

"They've blown half the mountain down. It's crazy. They could have killed everyone." Mayz shook her head, dark features tense and worried.

"What do the engineers say?" Sinklar rasped hoarsely. His heart dropped like a sodden weight. *Mac? Damn it!*

Mayz filled her lungs and shrugged. "It's all loose in there. No way to excavate it without strip mining the mountain.'

"We don't have that kind of time. What do the seismic people say about Mac's position? Did they survive?" His heart stopped dead in his chest as a terrible dread sucked at his soul.

"They report the cavern is still intact down there." Mayz looked relieved.

"Thanks for the update. Continue tunneling from the other side." More dead. Another Section gone. Sinklar hung his head, physically ill.

Mayz turned back to her duties.

Mhitshul disappeared through the hatch, eyes averted. Sink filled his lungs and rubbed his face with a tired hand.

What if he agreed? He could let the Seddi go. Get it over with instead of bleeding his force down to dregs. Was Mac's life worth it? Or Mayz's, or Shik's? All he had to do was. . . .

A light flashed as one of the monitors lit with the features of Rysta Braktov.

"Sinklar Fist?" No honorific, this didn't bode well, but somehow, he couldn't bolster the energy to care. "I have just had confirmation from Rega. We have an ID on your mysterious 'Tuff.' Her smile cut like a scythe. "Your antagonist down there is the Lord Commander of the Companions. Staffa kar Therma."

Sinklar straightened, blinking and shaking his head. Had he heard right? "Staffa kar Therma? The Star Butcher?"

Rysta crossed her arms. "The very same."

"Holy Rotted Gods!" Sinklar smacked a fist against his knee. "If I'd only known!" He immediately began to recall the Lord Commander's strategies, the devious and intricate ways he'd smashed defenses just as impregnable as Makarta Mountain. The key lay just beyond his grasp, but it would come to him now.

"But you didn't." Rysta's eye narrowed to a squint. She didn't look pleased. "Nor did I. His presence here is a mystery . . . and it appears it will continue to be."

"Why?"

Rysta hesitated and gave him a sour look. "Because you are to evacuate Makarta in preparation for orbital gravitational flux bombardment."

"Impossible!" Sinklar shot to his feet, glaring at the monitor. "I've got six hundred people inside that mountain!"

He could see Mhitshul leaning in the hatch, eyes wide. The LC had gone deathly silent.

"I am aware of that, First. But I have an order from Tybalt the Imperial Seventh. It appears that he considers your six hundred well worth the price to destroy the Lord Commander. My orders are to destroy the Seddi fortress . . . and I will do so. Get your people clear of the area, Sinklar."

"How long?" Sinklar asked, voice hoarse.

"One Targan day," Rysta told him succinctly.

"But I—"

"*One Targan day*, Sinklar Fist. Take an azimuth because at this very time tomorrow, I'm blowing that mountain down there into dust!" Rysta smiled again and the monitor flicked off.

CHAPTER XXXII

The room where Tybalt the Imperial Seventh worked radiated the ornate splendor worthy of an Emperor: Gilded gold; fine Myklenian fabrics; holos of waterfalls; glittering star fields; and the planets under Regan rule filled individual niches in the walls. The high ceiling panels gave the impression of endless height diminishing into an eternal blue while the lush fiber-optic carpet created the illusion of a sea of molten gold that swirled and surged.

Tybalt's gold-inlaid desk wrapped around his gravchair in a semicircle. Holo monitors glowed with multicolored images and numerous displays that reflected the health and progress of the Empire. The polished sandwood top gleamed, the grain running deep into the wood, almost translucent.

"I will see Minister Takka now," Tybalt the Imperial Seventh told his secretary through the private comm. He watched in the monitor as the security officer smiled professionally and gestured Ily and the woman with her toward the door.

"So you're back, Ily," Tybalt whispered to himself. "And from that glint in your eyes, you think you've got everything under control. This will be *very* interesting."

Ily passed through the security fields before the double doors to Tybalt's office, and after she received security clearance, the doors swung open. The Imperial Seventh noted that Ily still carried her little pistol and security kit. She wore a formfitting black jumpsuit and a sable cloak of Myklenian silk that swirled about her. The woman following her, however, only wore a slave collar under a tan-colored gauzy gown.

Tybalt glanced up as Ily entered and casually removed his headset, thus canceling the holo monitors before him.

He settled back, gravchair automatically conforming to support his bulk. His black skin contrasted with the gleaming white robe he wore. A slow smile curled his lips and extended to his eyes. Yes, indeed, no matter what his anger and suspicions might be concerning his Minister of Internal Security, life had been boring with Ily gone.

"Ah, my sweetest Ily! How good to see you again!" Tybalt shifted his glance to the tight-faced woman who followed behind. His breath stopped in his lungs and his heart skipped as he caught sight of her fiery amber eyes and gleaming piles of auburn hair. Her beauty dominated him, leaving even the opulence of his office drab in comparison.

"What have you here, Ily?"

"Greetings, Tybalt." Ily smiled, and he missed the gleam of excitement in her dark eyes. "Considering your trials and tribulations, Lord Emperor, I decided I had best see to my interests and come with offerings. I bring you a gift. She's yours. If it turns out you don't want her, I'll dispose of her with the slavers."

Arta Fera tensed, body radiating animal tension, eyes riveted on the Emperor. Hatred sparked feral-yellow in her animal glare.

Tybalt stood and took a step forward as he struggled to keep his breathing even. "My God, where did you find her, Ily?" His loins tightened under the fine Myklenian fabric of his clothes.

"Beware, Lord Emperor!" Ily held up a slim hand, eyes narrowing in warning. "This, Tybalt, is a Seddi assassin. Her name is Arta Fera. As an assassin, she is most skilled. Do not, I repeat, *do not*, underestimate her powers, Lord. Do you understand?"

Tybalt nodded, unable to tear his eyes off those majestic breasts, now straining at the buff-colored fabric as the captive woman's breathing deepened.

"She's in the collar," he whispered, half-aware of Ily's warning.

"She's also psychologically triggered," Ily added. "Don't touch her."

Tybalt nodded again, eyes caressing Fera's firm body. He marveled at the swell of her hips, the firmness of her long thighs. Then his gaze traced up the flat belly, past those superb breasts, and stopped at last on her perfect face. "Oh, those amber eyes are magnificent. Look at the hatred and cunning in them, Ily!"

The Minister of Internal Security tapped a button on his desk. Two of Tybalt's guards entered. Ily handed them the collar control. "Remove her. Watch her. She's a trained assassin and extremely dangerous." Ily's eyes slitted as one of the guards took the control. "And don't lay a single finger on her either—she'll kill you."

"Wait," Tybalt lifted his hand, walking around the Seddi woman one last time. His blood raced. "I've never seen a woman like this."

"Lord Emperor," Ily reminded, voice tight. "There are significant matters of state we need to discuss."

"Yes, yes, of course." Tybalt sighed, pulling himself up straight as the guards led Arta Fera out. His longing gaze lingered on her tight buttocks as she left. In his fevered imagination, he pictured his hands running over her smooth flesh.

"Most marvelous," he managed after the door shut. He closed his eyes, taking a deep breath to still the hunger of his hot body. Such magnetism! What it would be like to possess. . . .

"I'm not sure I did myself any favor," Ily said tartly. "But, Lord Emperor, watch her. She's trained to kill—and she hates Regans. Do you understand the danger?"

"Yes. Yes, I understand."

She pointed at his personal comm. "Please register that. If she kills you, I want it on record that you were fully warned about her capabilities and the threat she poses."

"What triggers her?" His glance drifted to the now closed door as he noted Ily's caveat and entered it. Damn the stirring of his manhood anyway!

"Sex, Lord Emperor." Ily smiled at him wickedly. "The Etarians trained her in the arts of love . . . to be a Priestess. The Seddi psychologically conditioned her—to kill the man who couples with her. Her motivation is hatred. She killed Sinklar Fist's girlfriend simply because she was Regan. She negated First Mykroft's security and coordinated the destruction of the Second Targan Assault Division in Kaspa. She worked with the assassin who killed Atkin and Kapitol. She killed scores of Regan soldiers on Targa."

Tybalt started. "You don't say! A woman with that incredible magnetism? What an inconceivable . . . waste!"

"Perhaps," Ily agreed, steepling her long fingers. "You are warned. Now let's get down to business. You got my message that Sinklar has Staffa trapped on Targa?"

"Yes." He tore his gaze away from the door and tried to think through the rush of hormones deluging his brain. "I followed your recommendation on that matter. Fist has one day to clear his people and any equipment he wishes to save. Rysta will level Makarta from orbit."

"And my request for Sinklar's Lordship?" Ily strolled forward, hips swaying enticingly. She bent over the monitors, allowing her full breasts to rub over the duraplast; and the last of Tybalt's thoughts fragmented.

He looked up into her passionate black eyes, unsettled, hungry to fulfill his stirred passions. "That will be a little more difficult. The political situation here is very delicate—what with the Sassan invasion planned and preparations underway. To simply make a new Lord would be—"

"Completely within your power." She leaned forward and kissed him. Tybalt reveled in the feel of her lips. Her tongue slid across his teeth before meeting his.

Breaking loose, he took a deep breath and leaned back, staring at her, realizing how he'd been manipulated. "Oh, I've missed your audacity." He chuckled. "Indeed. No one has the sheer unabashed gall that you do, Ily. You've been nothing but trouble. The military is literally foaming at the mouth over this Sinklar Fist. Half the Council is crying for your blood! What the hell have you been doing out there? Whatever it's been, it had better be good, because if you don't have answers, it won't be pleasant for either of us."

She smiled saucily at him and stepped around the desk before running hands over his chest. "I had a terribly trying time out there, Tybalt. I'm horny as hell. Maybe I shouldn't have brought the Seddi thing in here so soon. I thought maybe it would, shall we say, warm you to the occasion."

"Always the cunning one, my hot pet?"

She leaned her head down to spill waves of silky black across his chair. He traced fingers across her muscular thigh as the desire ignited by Fera's sensuality grew.

"Always. Would you have me any other way?"

"No. I suppose not. You keep my respect that way. Now do you want to tell me what the hell is happening on Targa?"

"We need Sinklar Fist," she told him flatly. "He took the entire planet—and pacified it. He made Rysta's heroes look like blathering idiots and killed half of them. I might add that he's about to break Staffa. Such talent is worthy of a Lordship, don't you think?"

Tybalt studied her coldly. "We did some checking. He's the brat child of Seddi assassins—like your delightful Arta Fera. He was raised as a ward of the state. Where did his parents come from? Originally Targa, we think. Beyond that, we know nothing. The Judicial Magistrate who convicted his parents placed Fist, as an infant, in a state institution for unparented children. After that his record contains one example of precocity after another until last year. Would you make a guess on how your Sinklar Fist placed in the national educational placement exams?"

Ily pursed her lips. "Top ten percent?"

"Number three." Tybalt enjoyed her startled expression. "That score is his 'official' placement. I turned some of your people loose on the investigation. Fist actually scored first. The other two, uh, scholars, seem to have gotten their scores for political reasons. You know, the usual, currying favor for some patron with a bright child—the normal graft of running a government like ours."

She began chewing her thumb. "I don't understand. He should have automatically been accepted at the university. How did he ever—"

"Exactly." Tybalt whirled in his chair, grabbing a stylus from his desk. "Someone—and we have no data on who—paid a substantial fee to a personnel officer in the military conscription office. Your Sinklar was drafted as a private and went off to war. Made the first Targan drop. You know what that means?"

"Should have been instant blaster fodder." She nodded. "You have no clue as to who his mysterious benefactors or enemies are?"

"None." Tybalt enjoyed the expression of concern on her face. Damn, why couldn't the rest of his Ministers be as bright and motivated? "You see the problem here?"

Preoccupied, she nodded. "Yes. And it leaves me in a

cold rage. Someone had him spotted. Who? How come we never knew about Sinklar Fist? How many more geniuses like him are being weeded out of our service? Who's behind it . . . and why?" Her eyes had narrowed to slits. "I don't like unknown factions stepping on *my* turf, Tybalt. I *will* get to the bottom of this."

"I'm glad you're back." Tybalt smiled, watching her lithe body. "For more than one reason."

"You will make Fist a Lord?"

"We can hush up the fact that his parents were Seddi assassins. Incidentally, he went to see them. The Judicial Magistrate who handled the case has since been . . . retired for his indiscretions. Fist actually went to view the bodies. Does that suggest anything to you? Are you sure where his heart is in this fight against the Seddi?"

Ily's hard squint left no doubt. "His hatred for the Seddi is well founded—and I have no doubt that it's authentic. I knew about his parents, of course. I checked on that first thing. That failed attempt on your life might have been the greatest blessing that ever happened to you. It kept Fist out of Seddi hands."

"Are you sure? Maybe his escape on Targa wasn't as miraculous as you think?"

"Trust me, I've seen his eyes, watched his expression. I've seen the spot where he blew the Seddi army into plasma. Were he Seddi, we wouldn't own Targa now. Does he get his Lordship?"

"He's without background! How long has it been since a Tybalt elevated a . . . a nameless, classless. . . . My God, Ily! He's an assassin whore's refuse. If that should come out in the end? The scandal would—"

"Garbage!" She laughed, trilling tones leaving him off balance.

"What did you say?"

"Garbage! Besides, who would dare insult a man who will have just ripped Sassa to shreds and who controls an army that worships him?"

"That's another potential sore spot. Ily, I just have my—"

"We *need* to have Sinklar Fist placed in charge of the Regan military forces. You realize that, don't you? With him, Sassa will be a simple nut to crack."

"And the Companions?"

Ily's eyes blazed with satisfaction. "Sinklar will work his magic again, Lord Emperor. Without Staffa, they won't be ready for Fist's brilliance. I've seen him. He's incredible! He'll have the Itreatic Asteroids before Skyla Lyma can twist her hair into a braid."

"And if I say yes to all this?"

"Oh, I don't think there's an if in the equation. You know we need him . . . just like I do. I sent you the tapes, you watched him maul Rysta's Divisions."

Tybalt flushed with excitement. "I really have missed you, Ily. No one else provides the stimulation you do." He stood as her sensual eyes searched his, a hidden smile on her lips that hinted of . . . triumph? Tybalt pulled her to him, kissing her hungrily.

"Any other *pressing* business, Lord Emperor?" she asked as she ran her fingers over the fabric covering his rising penis.

"Let's see," he offered huskily, bending down to unfasten her cloak. Even as he stripped her and lowered her to the thickly carpeted floor, the memory of the Seddi woman burned in the back of his mind.

* * *

"Greetings, Staffa kar Therma," Sinklar Fist's voice sounded haggard over the comm wire.

Staffa's heart beat faster. Did he dare admit that Fist had identified him? A cold chill ran down his back. Rega would throw all of its might against the Seddi now. Ily would see to that—anything to cover her tracks. And even if he could get word to Tybalt, what would the Imperial Seventh think? The Lord Commander fighting alongside the Seddi?

Staffa steeled himself, thoroughly aware he might have just condemned the Seddi. He glanced quickly around the rock warren of the improvised ops room.

"Congratulations," Staffa answered, keeping his voice even and pleasant.

"I would have taken great pleasure in destroying you, Star Butcher. I regret, however, that the job has been taken out of my hands. You have only a few hours left. I've been ordered to withdraw. Orbital bombardment will complete the destruction of Makarta." A pause. Then: "I'm sorry. Those are Tybalt's orders. You can still surrender yourselves."

Staffa stared woodenly. Defeat had filled Fist's voice. *I wish I could see you, Fist. I wish I could stare into your eyes—the window of your soul—and see what manner of man you are.*

"And your six hundred men and women bottled up on Level Five? You will doom them, too?"

Fist sounded as if a part of his soul had sickened. "The Emperor so orders. I . . . cannot save them. I tried."

"Human life, Sinklar, is a cheap thing at best. You'll learn. I've stood in your shoes many many times. I sorrow for the people I destroyed." He paused. "I even sorrow for a golden locket that will be buried in these caverns with us. It should be out in the worlds of men, a thing of beauty to be admired. What sorts are we that we destroy creations—knowledge?"

"Maybe we're truly damned as the Etarians believe. The Rotted Gods are loose—and their breath pervades the universe. Existence is suffering, Star Butcher. Pain, misery, and injustice are our legacy. Power *is* the only reality."

"A unilaterally enforced myth," Staffa returned, a bitter note in his voice. "A flawed epistemology. An illusion like the rest of—"

"But one strong enough to prevail in this instance."

"That is always the tragedy of it," Staffa agreed.

"If you abhor it so, why did you fight? Why did you plunge Targa into a meaningless revolt? How can you talk about justice when you incited your own people to butchery? I can't *believe* you! *You* talk about flawed epistemology? I hope your soul chokes eternally on its own hypocrisy."

Staffa caught himself nodding at the dark monitor. "I didn't start the conflagration on Targa. And even if I told you why it happened, you'd never believe it. The Seddi believe the quanta are God's joke on the universe. The ultimate irony. Perhaps it's true. I haven't found my atonement yet, Sinklar. Nevertheless, I fight for the Seddi—not so much for their lives as for what they can offer humanity."

"Indeed? So much sacrifice for gifts of assassination, intrigue, murder, and revolt? Spare me your misguided—"

"Hope," Staffa corrected. "Possibly a way out of the trap of the Forbidden Borders. Perhaps a way back to Earth and—"

"Another myth."

"No, not a myth. A dream," Staffa countered. "A goal for all humanity. That's what we don't have now. Where are we going, Sinklar? When you leave here, I will be dead and buried. You in turn will fall upon the Sassans—and, to be honest—you'll win. You might even perform a miracle and take the Companions. But what then? Where does it end? You will destroy humanity in your conquests. The dreams will be no more than radioactive dust. Cracked shiny slag on broken worlds enclosed in poisoned atmospheres. A bright and beckoning future, don't you think?"

"This conversation is pointless, Star Butcher." He sounded weary. "Your last hope is to walk out of there, lay down your arms. Isn't that a source of hope?"

Staffa laughed. "In Ily's hands? Are you serious? Tell me, how much do you know about her? Rotted Gods, you don't *trust* her, do you?"

"And I should trust a Seddi conspirator? Don't talk to me about trust. Your Seddi led my parents to their deaths. Left me an orphan of the state. I've seen too much Seddi evil. I just didn't know it would cost me so much to kill you all off."

"I'll let you save Mac and your people. Let us walk out. Give us a head start and you can drop in and pull MacRuder out."

Staffa laughed. "No, Sinklar, no matter what you think, the victory is mine. I had no more than two hundred and fifty men and women—some trained, most simple scholars. I took six hundred of your finest along with the others we've blown up, crushed, burned, and shot."

"He who controls is the final victor. Power, as I said, is the ultimate reality. I would have liked to tackle you and your Companions, Star Butcher. It would have been a true test. Here, we were unevenly matched."

"Yes. We were."

"Farewell, Staffa kar Therma. I only wish I could have looked into your eyes."

The comm went dead. Staffa stepped back and seated himself on one of the wooden chairs by the heavy table with its litter of maps. He stared sightlessly at the forbidding stone walls, lost in his own head.

"Did you mean all that?" Bruen asked.

Staffa turned. "I didn't hear you come in."

Bruen stood in the doorway, one thin arm braced on the molding. The bruise on his forehead looked ghastly. He wore a spotless white robe. The tired old man settled himself on a rough-hewn bench and exhaled thinly in the cool air. "I don't make much noise these days. I am glad you feel that way—about the ideas, I mean."

Staffa raised his hands and lifted a shoulder. "Reality is an artificially created norm. We're insensitive to the quanta at our level of consciousness. We perceive only the trends. It took Kaylla to point the direction . . . and much thought to fully comprehend the chimera of reality."

"The quanta, and God, are the only reality," Bruen assented with a faint nod of his purple-bruised head.

For long moments they sat, lost in thought. Most of the comm monitors had gone dead—permanently now. The others fuzzed with snow, waiting for the circuits to close.

"I sealed off the Mag Comm," Staffa stated. "It is better buried than in the hands of the Regans. Now it appears nothing more than a foolish action. If Fist is correct—not bluffing—we're to be bombed into pulp by Rysta's fleet. Ily's behind that, no doubt."

"What about the tunnel? The one you've been boring out from the lower levels. Is there any hope?" Bruen's eyes flickered for a moment. "Perhaps a few could make it out? Make their way to. . . ."

Staffa smiled wistfully. "We can't hide from the eyes in space, but, yes, we'll try." He laughed sourly. "Perhaps the quanta will pick that moment to change wave functions? Cause a glitch in the perception of normality? Blind our enemy?"

"It is a chance. We don't have many straws to grasp . . . and observation does change reality."

* * *

MacRuder shifted his back where the uneven stone ate through his unhardened armor. He and the rest sat in pitch blackness, robbed of sight. There was a faint grating sound from above as the rock in the roof shifted—and Mac could sense everyone tensing. How long since the last blast had rumbled through the black cavern? Rock had dropped. Two of his people had been badly hurt by the roof fall. He glanced at the atmosphere monitor on his wrist. Oxygen was going fast. Not much time left. Already his lungs were pulling with a noticeable deepness. A sensation of light-headedness lessened the dryness in his mouth. He flicked on his IR for a brief instant to see the empty faces filled with despair before shutting the visor off, saving the batteries and his tortured conscience—plunging himself into blackness again.

Sink? Where are you? What's happening out there?

How long since the fighting had stopped? How long since the last tremor had shaken their unstable warren? What the hell did it mean? Had the Seddi been destroyed? Was Sink even now trying to find them? Blinking dully in the blackness, he leaned his head back and shivered from the chill creeping out of the rock and eating through his armor, sucking at his life.

"Mac?" a hoarse voice called. "The comm line is active. The Seddi want you."

MacRuder plugged into the line he'd had run to his perch in the rock. "Yes."

"This is the Lord Commander, Staffa kar Therma, MacRuder."

Damn that calm voice! So that's *who we've been fighting?* "So?"

"So I just talked to your Sinklar Fist. It seems Ily Takka identified me. They believe my death is more important than your salvation. Fist has been ordered to pull back and Rysta's fleet is going to pound us from orbit in a few hours."

Mac shuddered at the certainty in Staffa's voice. His face contorting with despair, MacRuder managed numbly, "A few hours?" The hotness behind his eyes welled into tears. "Oh, Sinklar," he whispered, heedlessly, "don't let us die in here! Not in the darkness."

"I'm sorry," the firm voice continued. "I would. . . . I

would save you if I could. We have a tunnel running within five meters of your cavern. We might be able to blow it."

"Then what?"

"That's up to you. Would you come out unarmed?"

Mac bit his lip to forestall tears of frustration. The total blackness around him closed in, deepening the bone-gripping despair.

"How do we know it's not a fake? That you're not trying to pull a fast one?"

The calm voice asked, "I give you my word—just like I understand from the Seddi that Sinklar gave his word to Butla Ret."

Mac's guts turned runny. To comm he mumbled miserably. "We. . . . Yes. Yes."

"You'll hear our tapping. That's where the charge will be placed. Clear your people away from the area."

* * *

Sinklar paced with the relentless persistence of a condemned man as he stalked the vacant engineering office. The holo in the center of the room mocked him with its colorful display of Makarta. Around the walls, the computer monitors stared at him like blind eyes.

As if addicted, he glanced continually at his chronometer. The agonizing crawl of minutes acted on his soul like some sadistic torture. Angrily he shook his head and cursed. Desperation tugged at the corners of his control. *Mac's going to die . . . and I can't do a* damned *thing to stop it!*

"Section First Mayz, report!" he gritted to the comm, aware his voice was cracking from the strain. Inexorably, minutes ticked by on the chronometer.

"We've stepped up assaults, First," Mayz's voice barked tensely over the sounds of combat. "We've punched through with a mining machine. They were waiting for us. We can't force it. The casualties are—"

"*Damn it!*" Sinklar thundered, something snapping in his mind. "We're out of time! *They'll die in there!*"

"Sink!" Mayz cried desperately, "*We're already dying in here!* We can't take that corridor without exposing ourselves to explosives and Seddi fire! Morale is dropping! I can't order my—"

His veins stood out from the side of his neck. "You *will* order your people in there! *You will get Mac out of that trap! DO YOU HEAR ME?*"

"And I said we *can't!*" Mayz cried. "We love Mac, too, you know! Damn it, Sink, we're just as desperate as you—*but how much of our blood would Mac and the others want?*"

Sinklar's throat choked on silent sobs. Hot tears ran down his cheeks. His fists knotted as his muscles strained impotently. In a hoarse voice, he ordered, "Pull out, Mayz. Get our people out of there."

He cut the connection. Through the shimmer of tears, he could see Mhitshul looking at the floor, face ashen as he turned to leave.

The comm flickered to life, filling with Rysta's craggy dark features. "Fist?"

"What do you want?" Jaw thrust forward he glared, fists clenched at his sides.

Rysta didn't hesitate. "You have one hour to evacuate your troops before I follow the Emperor's orders." The screen went dead.

He pulled his blaster from his belt and blew the comm apart. Desperation and impotence lent him fury and spurred him to wreck the portable office.

Dazed, he grew aware of the charred wreckage around him. Physically exhausted, he pulled himself up, drained, devoid of emotion, and staggered out into the blazing midday sun. On legs gone leaden he forced himself to cross the rocky soil to the LC ramp. There he leaned against one of the hydraulic tubes and gazed emptily at Makarta Mountain.

"Mac? I . . . I have to go."

Head hanging, he turned and made his way into the LC. He ducked through into the cockpit and stared down at his thin-boned hands. Mhitshul and the pilot sat in the command chairs, heads bowed, silent, nervous.

His voice cracked. "Mhitshul? I. . . ."

He tried to swallow, to overcome the knot in his throat. "Order. . . . Order a general evacuation. Get our people out and get us into orbit." Strength gone, he leaned against the bulkhead, body sagging under its own weight.

* * *

The hidden warrens of Makarta trembled. Taut threads of violet ripped and crackled as sections of rock disintegrated behind Staffa. Pulse fire prickled within inches of his scalp. He felt the raw tingle of a UV burn where a close miss had passed his cheek.

The air was heavy, charged by the energy rippling through it. Death crouched in the dark corners, leering over the bleeding corpses strewn through the dimly lit tunnels.

Huddled low in a reading carrel, Staffa settled his blaster, waiting. The Regan shifted position in the narrow rocky nook to take another shot. Staffa's bolt hit home with a solid pulpy sound, catching the corner of the man's shoulder where it protruded. Staffa's follow-up shot blew the man in two as he fell screaming. Across the tunnel, Wilm's blaster fired as he saw a target.

A concussion echoed hollowly in the darkness from somewhere behind the Regan position as another remote fragmentation bomb exploded. Someone screamed horribly. The racket of combat was deafening in the close confines of the tunnels.

The dead lay awkwardly sprawled, sightless eyes staring among exploded body parts and bits of sodden red meat. They called to Staffa like the ghouls in his dreams, promising the horror to come.

He blinked, shaking his head to clear it of the image.

Two more Regan assault troops sprinted into Staffa's sights, tumbling into the knot of bodies as seeking threads of violet blew them apart. A woman kicked gruesomely—head missing above the neck—and went still.

Veils of smoke choked the corridor, vying with the smell of burned human meat. Blood pooled slickly across the polished stone floor.

"Pull back!" someone bellowed from the pungent darkness. "All Groups, pull back! Evacuate! Now! Double time."

Firing began to break into isolated rips and detonations. Staffa caught a glimpse of a Regan dashing madly for the rear. Sporadic shots and pulse hums died to be replaced by the patter of running armored feet as they left the tunnels to the silent and the dead.

"Now what?" Wilm wondered from his position across the hall.

Staffa grunted, pulling himself up. He peered hesitantly around the corner, finding nothing but the fragmented corpses. From somewhere in the pile of bodies, a casualty moaned faintly.

"Fist is cutting it awfully close," Staffa decided, glancing down at his chronometer. "Blow the renegade tunnel to the surface. Maybe Rysta isn't as punctual as I remember her to be. Let's see if we can't get a couple of people out of here. Go! Hurry!"

Wilm's broad-boned dark face reflected his hopelessness. "Hope you were right about MacRuder's Regans." He left at a run.

"They ought to be docile," Staffa decided, taking a flying leap to safety behind a pockmarked pillar of stone. He turned, sprinting down the passage until he found a functioning comm unit. Punching in, he waited.

Kaylla's face formed, soot-streaked, haggard. "The fighting stopped. Why?"

"They're ready to use the heavy stuff from space." Staffa raised an eyebrow. "And MacRuder's people?"

Hard tan eyes met his. "They're coming out, one at a time. So far, no cheats. They seem willing to take their chances on getting out of here."

"Wilm is blowing the renegade tunnel. Maybe some of us can get clear in time. Even so, the grav-effect will be severe—probably lethal, no matter what."

She nodded. "What about Bruen?"

"Wilm is seeing to him. He'll be taken out after the scouting party determines how safe the escape tunnel is. I'm on my way."

"Staffa," she asked tensely, "there isn't much chance, is there?"

"There's always a. . . ." Seeing the glint in her eye, he sighed. "No, there is very little chance. You've seen orbital capabilities firsthand. Rysta will be thorough."

* * *

MacRuder hurried along the line of waiting men and women, surprised that the Seddi ignored them for the most part. Grim faces met his glance everywhere. What a blessing it was to squint in the bright lights, to breathe air that put zip back in the lungs—even if it carried the pungent sting of death and blaster ozone. His head began to ache wretchedly.

Moving along the ranks, Mac winked at a grim face, patted a sagging back, cheered a forlorn expression as he worked forward. Then the tan-eyed woman in brown robes caught his eye. A blaster poked his way, slung level at the hip by a shoulder strap. She noted his shoulder insignia, eyes narrowing.

"You're MacRuder?" she asked in a knowing contralto, eyes coldly hostile.

"I am." He straightened, studying her. In any other place and time, she'd have made any man look twice.

"Kaylla Dawn." Her voice was clipped. "We've sent a party to blow the escape tunnel. Might I have a word with you?"

MacRuder nodded and followed her to one side.

She appraised him, searching his face as if to read his soul. "I'll be honest, MacRuder. The chances are not good. Fist's Divisions have withdrawn. We don't know how long we have left, but from Staffa's estimation, not long enough."

"I see."

"I hope you do," she said. "For one thing, we've got one narrow tunnel out of here. The Regans blasted the others during their retreat. For another, we can't take the time to guard all of your people and carry out a fast evacuation. If fighting breaks out. . . . Well, consider it. Are you willing to cooperate . . . or should we all die?"

"We'll cooperate." *Hell, I didn't even have to think about that, lady!*

"Good," she stated flatly. "Please inform your commanders."

"Just a minute." Mac raised a hand, stopping her. "How bad are our chances?"

She lifted one of her broad shoulders expressively, face tight. "Ask Sinklar Fist. From what Staffa says, there is no real hope. The orbital bombardment will no doubt encompass this entire area. How far and how fast can all these people go on foot in mountainous terrain?"

Mac filled his lungs and nodded. "We won't have to die in the dark. That's something, at least."

A shuffling began at the front of the line, men and women moving forward, eyes flickering this way and that, aware escape lay just ahead.

What a fragile thought. *Who am I kidding? I know what those ships up there can do.*

A ripple moved through the crowd as a big man dressed in stained gray combat armor—now charred and hardened—pushed through. Mac recognized the brownish stains. Spattered blood. The big man had been in the thick of it.

The man's long black hair had been gathered over his left shoulder in a ponytail. He had a curiously handsome face, brow high, nose long and straight over tight bloodless lips. Piercing gray eyes pinned Mac's as the big man approached. But when the gray warrior looked at Kaylla, regret welled, dulling the sharpness.

Then those gray eyes were pricking at Mac's soul again. The voice carried a tenor of command. "You're MacRuder? Do you have a portable battle comm?"

"We do. Or did. We left it back in the hole," Mac heard himself responding automatically. This guy might have even more charisma than Sinklar, Mac admitted to himself. Then the voice clicked in his memory: Staffa!

"Get it. If we open a line to Fist, we may be able to stall, gain time so some of us can make it away."

"It'll take two people. The thing's heavy."

Staffa turned. "Kaylla, see to getting everyone out. Don't leave anyone behind. If nothing else, the gravitational pulse will be merciful . . . and quick."

The Lord Commander pivoted on his heel and strode purposefully back toward the caverns. Mac followed, issuing orders to his sergeants along the way.

He cringed at the thought of going back into that stygian blackness. In the darkness overhead, stone shifted and grit trickled to patter on the rock flooring.

"Sink," he prayed under his breath. "Don't cut loose yet. Just a little longer, Sink. Kill us outside! Please? Just a little longer!"

* * *

Rysta looked up from the targeting comm as Sinklar Fist walked onto the bridge. Indeed, what a different man he was. His incredible magnetism drew every eye on the bridge. From the perspective of years, Rysta studied him, noting the haggard tightness of those odd gray and yellow eyes, the set of exhaustion in his face. A glittering desperation possessed him now. He was a man driven and hounded—a dangerous man.

Every time she saw him, he became someone different. Rysta shivered, feeling a chill play along her spine. A barely throttled pain gleamed in his eyes. His glance fell on her, bringing a tightness to her chest—the feeling of a stiletto poised over her heart.

"We are clear, Commander." There was a note of finality in his curious voice.

"I want you to know, First, that I dislike hitting our people as much as you do. The orders came straight from Tybalt."

The corners of his mouth quivered as his back arched slightly. Tension rippled across the busy bridge, tangible, menacing.

He replied in a barely audible whisper that reminded her of a threat. "I know."

Rysta didn't remember putting her hand on the worn service blaster at her belt. She did it instinctively, and the smooth butt of the weapon comforted her. Once before, in the eyes of an Etarian sand leopard, she'd seen that same look.

His awkward, high-pitched voice startled her as he added, "You have your orders. Go ahead. Condemn my people. Kill them." He swallowed, mouth twitching, before he turned and walked stiffly from the bridge.

Someone muttered behind her.

Rysta took a deep breath and blew it out. "Power up. Targeting is locked on. Let's melt that rock and be on our way."

The Weapons First called, "Main bombardment batteries are powering up."

"Commander?" The Comm First called, "We've got people on the surface down there. They blew out a section of mountain."

"Weapons First, you may fire when ready," Rysta ordered.

"And if I get comm from the surface?" The Comm First asked.

Rysta hesitated, looked back at the hatch Fist had just left through, and said, "Ignore it. Damn it, we've got our orders. Just kill them all."

"Powered up!" Weapons First noted. "Batteries locked."

Rysta's breath hissed through her worn teeth. "Farewell, Lord Commander."

CHAPTER XXXIII

Muscles pumping, Staffa struggled up the long slanting tunnel. He could sense MacRuder's strength sagging under the heavy battle comm they labored to carry to the surface. Distant light beckoned escape at the end of the square adit. Mac tripped and staggered, almost dropping the load.

"Hold it a minute." Staffa settled the heavy piece of machinery to the cut stone as MacRuder slumped. The Regan hung his head, gasping pants torn from a strained throat.

"Outta steam," MacRuder wheezed. "Sorry, didn't know I—"

"Go on," Staffa added gently. "I can carry it from here."

"But that's. . . ." MacRuder clamped his mouth shut as Staffa heaved, lifting the burden, arms barely spanning to either handle.

"Go," Staffa grunted, pushing forward.

MacRuder nodded, plodding ahead, keeping out of the way.

Daylight stabbed blindingly even though the sun lay on the purple mountain rim of the western horizon. The crystal air soothed, a balm of freshness that carried no stink of death and combat, no metallic odor of blood or acrid sharpness of punctured intestines.

Staffa fought for breath as he stumbled out of the shaft and settled the heavy equipment onto a mat of flowers, bruising the soft carpet of greenery.

Practiced fingers flipped on switches, checking power, and folding out the antenna. He clutched the mike, adjusting the dish to send over 360.°

"*Rysta!*" he called, eyes searching the heavens. "For God's sake, don't fire! This is the Lord Commander! We've got most of your Division here. We're outside. You hear?

585

Don't fire!" His jaw muscles rippled as he waited for a response.

Silence.

"Rysta! Damn you, you can have me! You hear? I know what Tybalt's orders are! By the Blessed Gods, what's the purpose of all these people dying for me?" His heart stuttered in his chest.

"Listen, Rysta, why kill the better part of an entire Division? It's not worth it! I give you my word, I surrender! No tricks! Spare these people!"

Frantically, he looked around, seeing the thick knot around him—mostly armored Regans. They watched him, hope shining on every face. Some held hands; some hugged each other. Others stood somberly, heads down, awaiting the inevitable. Here and there, people sat, fingers laced into plants and soil. Others, wounded, lay gasping, some beyond caring.

"Rysta? *Gods Rot you, answer me!"*

Across from him MacRuder panted, worry bright in his blue eyes. Kaylla chewed her lip, brow furrowed. Bruen held his face in his hands.

"Rysta!" Staffa bellowed into the comm. *"Answer!"*

MacRuder bent over the transmitter, studying the readouts. "It's sending. No doubt of that."

Bruen pulled his head up; his hip hurt him, his bruised head was livid in the white sunlight. "I, too, will surrender. This was all my doing."

"Rysta?" Staffa continued. "The Seddi leader, Magister Bruen, will surrender. Just don't kill your own people!" The muscles in his chest and shoulders bunched as he slammed a palm into the comm. "Damn it, you don't shoot after a surrender! Section fifty-four, paragraph eight of the Regan Military Field Manual orders you to cease fire!"

He searched the skies, wondering.

"Nothing," MacRuder said softly. "Nothing is coming in. Not from above anyway."

"Rysta?" Staffa gritted. "If you want begging, all right, I'm begging! Whatever you want, you get." He closed his eyes, feeling his face go hot. That it should come to this, the Lord Commander begging.

He thrust the mike at MacRuder. "You try. They're your people."

As MacRuder's quavering voice beseeched the skies, Staffa walked off several steps and shook his head, waiting for that brief moment when the world turned upside down into oblivion.

He felt a hand touch the hardened armor of his shoulder. "You tried, Lord Commander," Kaylla told him.

He snorted sourly. "Looks like this time Tuff didn't come through, doesn't it?"

"You've been seeking atonement. Maybe you've made more progress than you know. Perhaps you have achieved your grace."

He met her knowing gaze and smiled wistfully. "You know what I did. Perhaps if I had managed to break the Forbidden Borders, left humanity in better condition than I found it. . . ."

For the first time she looked awkward, deprived of her everpresent poise. "God will know. Only when that consciousness is finally shared, can you judge."

MacRuder ceased transmitting, looking up numbly, eyes stricken. "Sink, you can't do this to us. Sink, we're here. You can't let us down . . . just run off and leave us without trying."

Staffa moved to reach out with a reassuring hand. "He didn't. He made every effort. It was Tybalt's order—not Fist's. As much as I would like to blame it on him, the fault lies with the Empire . . . and the Seddi."

Mac closed his eyes, swallowing hard.

"Damn it!" someone growled. "Why are they taking so long? If they want to kill us, Rotted Gods, *get it over with!*"

"Maybe they're talking it over," Bruen mumbled, settling himself by the comm, shifting his weight.

Staffa picked up the mike again. "They might be charging the system. Takes a while before a full power discharge."

"Great," Kaylla muttered hopelessly.

"Here it comes!" MacRuder cried as a glaring light filled the sky.

Staffa averted his eyes from the flash and reached an arm around Kaylla, pulling her close. She buried her head against his shoulder.

I am at peace with myself. I did my best. He hugged her tighter as the comm began to crackle.

* * *

"Commander?" The Comm First's careful voice cut the silence. "I have the Lord Commander on comm."

Rysta shifted in the command chair. "I don't want to hear it. Cut him off. We've got our orders. Staffa's threats are meaningless now."

"Yes, ma'am. Channel clear."

"Uh, ma'am?" the Comm First continued hesitantly.

"What now?" Rysta's voice echoed across the bridge as the hum of power surged through the ship. She turned to throw her meanest glare.

"We have transmissions coming in." The Comm First bent over the monitor. "Early warning system indicates ships are inbound." Another crisp call caused her to freeze. "They're coming from out of the sun. ETA, five minutes."

Rysta called, "Weapons, how long?"

"Another thirty seconds, Commander."

"Hold that. Out of the sun?" Options raced through her mind. "Rotted Gods, you don't suppose that's Ily Takka sneaking back for a last look?" She sneered at the monitor. "Comm, put it through. Let's see who this is."

The main screen flickered, filling with a woman's features.

"Rotted Gods," Rysta whispered. *"Weapons! Battle stations! All hands!"*

"That won't be necessary, Rysta," Skyla Lyma's voice brought all eyes to the screen, riveting their attention. "We've got you dead to rights. You're powered up for planetary discharge. If we shoot now, every system on that ship will fry when your shielding overloads."

Rysta's eyes slitted, thoughts racing desperately, hating the truth of their situation. "What do you want?"

Skyla said coolly. "Roll ninety degrees and dump every erg you've got. Blow it into space." Her ice-blue eyes narrowed. "If you don't, *Chrysla* is going to blast *Gyton* into a mini nova. Think you're up to that?"

Rysta searched for an out. "The Lord Commander is on Targa. Back off and clear the system, Skyla, or we turn him into—"

"Then you're dead," Skyla stated uncompromisingly.

"And after *Gyton*, we're hitting Rega. You decide, Rysta. Do we get to pull Staffa off that planet and go home quietly? Or do we avenge ourselves on the heartland of the Regan Empire?"

Curse the Rotted Gods, Lyma and the Companions would go berserk if she blasted the planet—and long before then, *Gyton* would be gutted space junk. Anger washed away with defeat. Wearily, she ordered, "Roll ninety and dump!" Suddenly, she felt very, very old.

* * *

Static faded along with the brilliant flare of light that streaked across the sky. Staffa lifted a hand to shield his eyes and shook his head. "I don't understand. Rysta? What the hell is going on?"

A coolly possessed voice came from the comm box: "Lord Commander? We heard your transmission. Please reply. If we do not hear from you immediately, we will destroy *Gyton* and assume all Regan forces on Targa to be hostile."

Staffa chuckled, releasing Kaylla and lifting the mike. "Cutting it a bit close, don't you think, Wing Commander?"

Her voice remained aloof and professional. "Certain precautions were necessary prior to entering the Targan system. This is hostile space, Lord Commander."

Warmth spread through Staffa. "Very good, Wing Commander. I take it you've neutralized the threat from above?"

"We have *Gyton* centered in the forward batteries. Two Regan Assault Transports are also in orbit. *Jinx Mistress*, *Simva Ast*, and *Viktrix* are closing in support. *Sabot* and *Slap* are in covering positions."

"Sounds like you brought the whole fleet."

"We considered it necessary," Skyla declared dryly. "Your record wasn't exactly impeccable on Etaria, Lord Commander."

He paused. "Yes, well, there were mitigating circumstances." He winced, knowing people were watching.

"What about us?" Mac's worried voice rasped.

Staffa straightened and looked at the ring of nervous

Regan faces. "You're all safe. In fact, you might consider coming with us to the Itreatic Asteroids. We've always got a place for people with your talent and initiative—and no emperor orders Companions to leave their fellows to die in the dark."

Glances flashed back and forth among the Regans.

"Wing Commander?" Staffa turned his attention back to the mike. "We'll need evacuation for almost seven hundred people."

"Affirmative. Special Tactics Officer Ryman Ark has several squads in the assault craft. Should he expect hostilities?"

"Negative. I think it's all under control here."

"We have your transmission source pinpointed. Expect Ark in . . . seventeen minutes."

"Affirmative." Staffa pursed his lips and stared up at the darkening sky. "Bruen, I'm afraid you'll have to evacuate with us." The Seddi took their turn shuffling feet and shooting nervous glances at each other.

"You'll have a safe haven in the Itreatic Asteroids." Staffa pushed his hair over his shoulder where the wind teased it. "You can't stop now. You all have work to pursue. I'll need your help and your intelligence resources to see if we can sidetrack this war between Rega and Sassa."

Bruen—looking like a shrunken skeleton—rubbed a knobby hand over his face. "Evacuate with you to the Itreatic Asteroids? Who would have thought it? Especially after all these years, after all the plans. . . ."

"You Rotted well can't stay here."

Kaylla paled, slipping to the ground, a sour expression on her face. "I'm not going," she gasped, shivering and clutching herself tightly. "I can't . . . face those men who. . . ."

Staffa bowed his head. "No, I suppose not. But where can you go? There's a Regan death warrant out for you. You've got to evacuate the planet."

Magister Bruen shook his head. "Such a mess we've all made."

Staffa wet his lips, kneeling beside Kaylla. He searched her frightened eyes. "I can't help the past. I know what I've been . . . who I am. But there's a safe place for you in the

Itreatic Asteroids. A place where you can be alone, pursue the work you began on Maika. There will be no men, no terrors from the past."

He swallowed. "One time on Etaria, I told you I would restore you to Maika if I could. I . . . I intend to see to that promise."

She shook her head, hot tears beginning to leave streaks down sun-browned cheeks. "I. . . . No." A trembling fist went to her mouth. "No. Maika is dead for me . . . as are so many that I . . . loved. I wouldn't go back there."

"We need you," Bruen added in his cracked ancient voice. "Humanity needs you. You must take my place. I know you, Kaylla. I know the power of your mind, the way you have been tempered. The Seddi need someone of your capabilities, your strength."

"Let me. . . . I must think."

Staffa straightened, feeling the fingers of the ghouls stroking at the back of his mind. He looked up, spotting the familiar contrails of assault craft in the ionosphere. He watched with approval as his lean-winged craft made a standard double-cover approach. The deadly wedges shimmered behind energy shielding as they settled around the clearing.

Staffa marched out to meet the first craft to land on the trampled valley grass before Makarta. The forward ramp dropped and Ryman Ark's trained people hit the ground at a run, their figures shimmering and indistinct behind the energy barriers. They deployed with weapons at the ready.

"Crack team," Staffa heard Mac mutter behind him.

Staffa grinned as Ark trotted forward in full assault gear, his black face grim. Staffa shook his head, laughing with relief. "What? No finger ID necessary? You're slipping, Ark."

"Been a while, Chief." Ark's lips curled into a smile as they hugged each other, pounding backs. Ark finally pushed back, a quizzical look on his face. "How in five Rotted hells did you get into this mess anyway?"

"It's a long story. How's Skyla?" he asked, a sudden lump in his throat.

Ark frowned. "I. . . . Rotted Gods, Lord Commander, I don't know. She was frantic getting us here. Regular tyrant.

Then, as we closed. . . . I don't know. She tightened up.
Clammed up hard as a Riparian shellfish. When I left the
bridge, well, would you believe she was wringing her hands?
That one?"

"All right, load up. Let's blow this rock and I want that
tunnel over there blasted on the way out."

"Got something hidden in there?" Ark mused
thoughtfully.

"An obsession. One I must come back to someday." The
Mag Comm's presence tickled at his mind, beckoning.

He turned, watching huddled knots of Regan soldiers
where they muttered to each other, MacRuder at the center
of the largest circle, arms moving passionately.

"Looks like quite a haul," Ark muttered, indicating the
Regans.

"They bought their freedom already." Staffa lifted a
shoulder. "Some may be coming with us."

"Good fighters, huh?" Ark had his hands propped on his
hips.

"Damn good. Maybe the makings of our equals," Staffa
brooded. "I'd rather have them with us than against us. A
lot has changed in Free Space." He paused. "I have a mind
to blast Rysta's ship to plasma."

"Why? Rysta can't hold a candle to us," Ark scoffed,
kicking at the black dirt.

"I'm not worried about Rysta, but I am about a Regan
First who's aboard *Gyton*. His name is Sinklar Fist." A cold
foreboding clutched at Staffa. "And I've got a terrible feeling we're going to be staring at him over blasters one of
these days soon."

* * *

Staffa greeted the members of his crew who monitored
the lock as he stepped out of the hatch of Ryman's assault
ship after it settled gently into its hull dock.

"Welcome aboard, sir," one of the techs greeted.

"Good to be home." Staffa stopped for a moment, placing his hand against *Chrysla*'s sturdy bulkheads.

"Lord Commander?" Skyla's voice called down from the
speaker. "Could I see you as soon as possible?"

Staffa glanced up at the pickup. "What's the situation with Rysta's fleet?"

"Tap has them in his sights. At the first sign of trouble, he's got orders to blow *Gyton* into junk. Same with the rest of her ships. I suggest we conclude whatever business is necessary and space at the first opportunity. We could be sitting ducks if Rysta gets a message off to Tybalt."

"Good work, Wing Commander. Meet me in my quarters as soon as possible." He thumped a gloved fist against the hull and added, "I'll be there as soon as I check on something."

"Affirmative. Stay out of trouble."

Staffa chuckled, anticipation of seeing Skyla rising in his breast. But first. . . . He took a right down a lighted corridor and entered the main bay. Across the large compartment, MacRuder stood with the last of the Targan troops awaiting transshipment to the Regan transports. Behind them, the status light on the large oblong shuttle lock indicated that it was pressurizing. Armed Companions stood around the periphery, alert for trouble.

As Staffa approached, Mac grinned and stepped away from his troops. Mac stopped uncomfortably, blue eyes meeting Staffa's levelly.

"You're ready to go?"

Mac nodded. "Yes. I guess it just had to be this way. I hoped I'd see you, get to thank you again. I'll never forget what you did down there. Pleading like that for our lives when we would have killed you outright. You're not the monster I grew up believing in. You and Sink . . . you're a lot alike. Damn it, why do you have be on opposite sides?"

Staffa smiled grimly. "The time has come for a new way of thinking. You didn't deserve to die like that." He hesitated. "Are you sure you won't come with us? I liked the way you handled yourself down there in the darkness. Men and women of your caliber deserve more than Rega will give you."

MacRuder frowned and stuck thumbs in his equipment belt. "I can't be part of the Seddi. I saw what they did on Targa." He lifted a hand to stifle Staffa's protest. "Bruen and I had a long talk on the way up, and I know why he did what he did. But knowing intellectually and having lived through it are two different things. I can't forgive him for the suffering. I can't forget Gretta's body in that cell—all the men and women who died on that ball of rock." He shook his head. "It wasn't worth it."

"I'm not asking you to be Seddi. I'm asking you to join the Companions, to help me stop the coming war, and maybe to help all humanity find a dream. We've made ourselves the enemy, when in reality it's the Forbidden Borders. Help me break them. Come with me."

MacRuder pursed his lips as he met Staffa's questioning gaze. "I'd like that, Lord Commander, and I sincerely appreciate your offer, but I owe Sinklar. I guess it all goes back to a Kaspan rooftop in the rain. He kept us alive. He kept *me* alive time after time down there. He tried to get us out. The only reason he left Makarta was because the Emperor ordered it." He looked pained. "If I turn my back now, all those people who died in Makarta trying to save us died for nothing. I can't have that on my conscience."

Staffa nodded his understanding. "You're a good man, MacRuder. You know, the chances are excellent we will meet again . . . in less friendly circumstances."

MacRuder nodded, a deep sadness reflected in his blue eyes. "I know. Perhaps it's up to these Seddi quanta."

"Remember, Mac. You always have a place with us. If you ever need to get in touch with me, use the code 'Makarta.' "

A light flashed on the shuttle loading lock and the heavy door rolled back with a hollow metallic boom. MacRuder waved the last of his people into the lock, then offered his hand, shaking Staffa's firmly. "I guess that's my ride."

"Take care, Mac."

"You, too. And stay out of dark places, Lord Commander." MacRuder turned and walked through the cold gray lock to the shuttle.

"None of them stayed. They all went," Staffa mused to himself. "Who *is* this Sinklar Fist?" He turned and walked down the familiar decks. *Chrysla* welcomed him like an old friend.

Skyla waited for him. What would he say? How could he tell her how much he'd come to love her?

* * *

The door closed behind Tybalt as he stepped into his private quarters. Arta Fera stood in the center of the opulent room, her auburn hair glinting in the light like honeyed gold. She turned, eyes glowing amber, appraising him, a startlingly seductive figure against the blue background of the room. Velvet hangings drooped over a padded sleeping platform. Gold inlay gleamed in the sandwood furnishings. The collar sparkled against the smooth tones of her throat. She wore a floor-length blue gossamer gown, gathered under her breasts. The outline of her sensual body was a barely hidden secret.

"You know what I am," she told him levelly, fists clenching at her sides as she braced her feet defiantly.

"Indeed I do," he answered as he stepped over to the console and poured two crystal goblets full of Ashtan sherry. He turned to face her, offering a glass. Her head went up disdainfully.

Tybalt lifted his right arm, exposing a black bracelet. "You know what this is?"

She shook her head, tumbles of red brown hair waving with the motion.

"It controls the collar on your neck." Tybalt glanced down at it and a frown lined his forehead. "Quite a sophisticated device actually. The Companions make them. Very expensive. Each individually tunes to the thought patterns of the wearer. With this, I need only think—" he paused, smiling—"like this."

Arta Fera's mouth came open as she crumpled to the padded fabrics covering the floor.

Tybalt walked around her, bending down to stare into her frightened eyes. "You see, my dear Seddi assassin, no matter what your training, I control you. I know about the sexual trigger in your mind. The idea fascinates me. You must kill the man who possesses you, but possess you I shall, Arta. And when you strike—as you must—I'll take you out just that quick."

As he straightened and mentally released the control, she lunged at him. He triggered the collar again and watched her wilt.

"First, you will drink with me and we will talk like civilized human beings."

He released the collar and she began to move again, gasping for breath as her eyes cleared. She sat up slowly, rubbing her hands up and down her arms, head bowed in a mass of silky hair.

"I hate you, you know," she whispered.

"Of course you do. Makes it all the more amusing for me. Stand up." He waited for a moment. "Do you want me to use the collar again? I can, you know. For as long as it takes to convince . . . or kill you."

She got to her feet, amber eyes blazing in her perfect face. Jaw muscles rolled under smooth skin as she took the sherry.

"To love."

She said nothing, furious gaze never leaving his face.

"Drink," the Imperial Seventh ordered, sipping at his sherry.

Slowly, the glass touched her lips. Never did the hatred in her eyes waver. Finished, she put the glass on a sculpted counter. "I'll kill you, Regan."

"No, my dear, not so long as you wear the collar."

A curious light danced in her eyes. "It shuts off all feeling? It did when your bitch, Takka, used it the first time on the LC."

"Everything below the neck. That's why I've already won. Ily couldn't have pleased me more than by making a gift of you."

Her eyes flickered as a slight frown formed.

With his glass, he gestured. "Come closer. Ah, don't hesitate like that. You have no choice. Come—or suffer the collar."

She swallowed, throat working. Almost trembling, she took a step, then another, the light material swirling around her long graceful legs.

Tybalt reached out a hand, feeling her shudder as he placed it on her shoulder. "That's it, dear one. See, not so terrible, is it? The collar can overcome any assortment of obstacles. Even psychological training."

She went tense, trembling, every muscle in her body twitching as he ran his fingers along the side of her face. "You know, Arta, I will take very good care of you. It isn't such a bad life, being my slave."

She had closed her eyes, teeth chattering behind tight lips.

"Ily let me see the tapes of your interrogation. I know you were trained on Etaria. You know the arts of love, my dear. It's up to me to liberate them within you. That's why you'll never want again, dear Arta. Ask and I shall grant you most anything."

"D—don't . . . touch me," she managed, fighting revulsion.

"That I won't grant—or your freedom either. No, dearest, I'll keep you for myself." His fingers dropped to the broach at her shoulder, unpinning the soft material. He stepped back as it fluttered down her body, shimmering in the subdued light.

"Marvelous," he breathed. "The most exquisite woman I have ever seen."

She seemed to still her trembling, opening her eyes to watch him guardedly as he unfastened his own garments, stepping out of the pile they made on the floor. Something changed in her expression as he came close.

"Easy, Arta. Relax. We have all night. Don't fight me. I control the collar."

He caught her in mid-leap, stepping out of the way as she crashed nervelessly to the floor.

He released the control. "It might turn out to be a long night. This is a simple stimulus response reconditioning. You can learn to control your training." Tybalt refilled his sherry as she gasped on the floor. "Stand up."

Patiently, he dropped her time after time while she fought the collar and him. Finally, drained, she withstood the impulse to attack as he reached and ran a hand down her skin.

"There, see, the training can be overcome." Tybalt smiled and reached forward to kiss her. His lips touched hers. He triggered the collar before her knee was halfway to his crotch.

"Can't do that, dearest," Tybalt chided.

She seemed to be on her feet more quickly this time, as if drawing on some inner reserve.

He kissed her hard, pressing himself to her, feeling his passion grow. Again he triggered the collar before she could strike.

"You have incredible endurance," Tybalt murmured. "The Seddi are truly masters at their craft." He dropped beside her as she lay on the floor, triggering the collar again, allowing his hands to caress her. "No, the time has come, dear Arta."

Each time she began to resist, he used the collar. Finally he lay on her, his manhood spent. He filled his lungs with the odor of her as sweat trickled down his sides to mix with hers.

Sighing, he forced himself up, going for more sherry. "We will get better at that, you and I."

The second time he took her, she controlled herself. After his orgasm he lay on her, staring into her eyes, dazzled by the amber and the depths of her black pupils. She chuckled softly and reached her long arms around him as a cunning satisfaction filled her expression.

"See," he cooed, "you can give pleasure without striking."

"Yes," she added thoughtfully. "I am past that."

"Work for me. Give me the bliss of an Etarian Priestess."

She followed him when he went for another glass of sherry, and joined him, taking a glass, draining it. She smiled in private triumph as she sipped the amber liquor.

Tybalt laughed, throwing his head back. "There is no power in Free Space greater than Tybalt! I have broken the Seddi!" He reached to draw her close. "You, my dear, I have freed!"

"No, Tybalt," her sensual tones corrected. "You see, I have freed myself."

"Uh-uh!" He shook a finger at her. "That is a rule you must learn. Never correct the Emperor."

"Of course," she agreed, eyes slitted, head back.

"And we have a full night ahead of us!" He pointed at the floor.

Still smiling, warmth radiating from her eyes, she lay back, spreading her wealth of body on the soft fabrics. Tybalt set his glass down and lowered himself. Her fingers traced the lines of his back, nails making him quiver.

"Let me show you something," she whispered seductively to him. "Just lie there. Don't be afraid. After all, you control the collar." She stood, muscles rippling along her body.

Awed, Tybalt's heart skipped. "What a wonder you are, Arta Fera."

A secret smile curled on her lips.

He triggered the collar as she leapt high and arrowed downward. The force of the impact smashed him into the unforgiving floor. His sternum and ribs snapped loudly under her hard knee. Tybalt's mouth dropped open as he lay stunned.

She filled his vision as she bent. He stared up in pained disbelief. An odd croaking came from his throat. He tried to get his breath. Frantically, he triggered the collar again, seeing her fight it, seeing her still pulling air into her lungs as she ran long fingers around the collar.

"You see, Tybalt," she whispered, "I *have* freed myself."

Panic caused him to scramble away from her, each movement a spear of agony in his chest. "Help," he mouthed, voice a hoarse croak.

"There is no help. I overheard the guard say you keep this room unmonitored so your wife can never have evidence to use against you."

Again and again he triggered the collar, tasting the brass of blood in his mouth; a gurgling rose in his throat.

She crushed her knee into his chest again, lancing white agony through his body. He gagged, trying to throw up. Her forearm—hard with muscle—cut his gag reflex short as she leaned down to look into his eyes.

"Enjoying it, Tybalt? Do you like the fear? The pain? Feeling degraded? Just like rape, don't you agree?" She tilted her head slightly before leaning forward, kissing him gently on the lips. "That last was for freeing me, Tybalt."

The Imperial Seventh stared, hypnotized by the blood on her lips—his blood—the same blood that dribbled down the side of his face. Unable to move, dizzy, pain-glazed, he saw her turn. Her kick jolted his entire body as she crushed his manhood against his pubis bone.

The white-hot grip of agony pulled him deeper and deeper into oblivion. Blood-smeared lips expanded into gleaming amber eyes—his last sight as he trembled and died.

* * *

Ily Takka smiled in satisfaction as Tybalt's physical signs weakened on the small hand-held monitor she carried. She flashed the jessant-de-lis at the guard and used the badge

to deactivate the security door to Tybalt's personal quarters.
Ily stepped quietly into the room as Arta Fera bent over
Tybalt's dark body, kissing him fervently. The Minister of
Internal Security winced at the Seddi assassin's final kick,
oddly shaken by the brutality of it.

Fera watched as Tybalt quivered and slowly relaxed. A
fragment of rib had pushed though the side of his chest like
a bloody lance. Fera turned then, seeing Ily for the first
time. Eyes going to the blaster pointed in her direction.

"Very well done," Ily praised. "Couldn't have done it
better myself."

Arta Fera tossed her head, flipping her full-bodied hair
over her shoulder as she walked to the console and poured
sherry into a glass. She rinsed her mouth and spit, wiping
her lips clean on the expensive fabric hanging from the
walls.

She checked herself in a reflecting glass and turned.
"Now what?"

Ily leaned against the door, alert, pistol ready. "I hate to
do it, but you'll have to be tried. The psych experts will
confirm your deep trigger. The collar will be found to be
faulty. Mareeah Rath's family will be so disgusted they'll
want to cover up the whole thing."

Arta's amber eyes took her measure. "It won't be that
easy, Ily. Is there a shower here?"

"In the corner. Press the golden knob. But leave the door
open. I don't like surprises."

Arta walked over to press the knob and stepped in. Finding soap she began washing, heedless of the water splashing
onto the fine fabrics.

"And why won't it?" Ily gave herself plenty of room as
she crossed to the console, pouring herself a glass of sherry,
never allowing the pistol to waver.

"Because the deep trigger is broken. That's why I kissed
the bastard. I owe him for that. The rest I paid back in
kind."

Ily sipped the sherry. "Then I should probably kill you
now."

Arta nodded, scrubbing thoroughly. "That would eliminate any threat from me. On the other hand, a lot of things
were broken along with the psych trigger."

"Such as?" Ily cocked her head, turning the glass in her fingers.

"Such as my loathing for Rega." Arta turned off the water, studying the surroundings. "How do you dry off in this thing?"

"Silver handle on the right," Ily offered, amused at the way the woman jumped as the energy fields ran down her body. Water trickled away in streams. "So?"

Arta stepped out, walking in a wide detour around Tybalt to get her gossamer dress. She picked it up, looking at it with disgust. "Anything else to wear in here?"

"To fit a body like yours? I'm not sure. Touch the wall there by the holo."

Arta did and shuffled through the garments standing in the antigrav field. She chose a long wraparound and tightened it about her.

"You once mentioned that you might have a place for a woman of my training and ability." Arta crossed her arms over the too-tight fabric at her chest.

"I have a dead Emperor here." Ily tilted her head toward Tybalt's body.

Arta's eyes never left hers. "And, as Empress, you'll need a good assassin. You know I'm the best."

"You're a quick study, Arta Fera. Perhaps a dangerous one."

"We share similar opinions of one another. Before I came along, you had your plans laid. Where does Fist fit into all this?"

"He destroys Sassa and the Companions. He becomes my Emperor and enforcer."

"A little young, isn't he?"

"All the better. I can train him the way I want. What's your price?"

"Freedom." Arta closed her eyes. "I want your protection, an open expense account, and a small fast ship with a female crew. Nothing more. I don't have any aspirations for your position. I was born and bred for assassination and excitement."

Ily made a decision and stepped to the rear of the room where she ran quick fingers over a gold design. The wall opened. "I guess you're going to escape instead of being tried for assassination. Up there. Follow the steps. You'll come out in my quarters."

"And the guards outside the door?" Arta asked as she entered the narrow way.

"Don't worry. You killed them during your escape. Stay in my room. Your picture will be all over Rega within an hour. I'll get you up to my ship later." Closing the portal behind the woman, Ily smiled and laughed. Then she pulled the jessant-de-lis from her pouch.

She walked over to look into Tybalt's wide dead eyes. "And you thought you could kill me with this? Oh, you stupid fool. I disconnected the detonator the day you insisted on brandishing that silly switch around. Now we'll see who can handle Ily Takka."

She stepped to the wall comm. Her second in command's face formed on the viewer. "Gysell, the Emperor has been murdered! You will place an arrest warrant out for the Seddi assassin, Arta Fera. Institute immediate social control, the military is to be placed on alert. I want crowd control and a news blackout. The Rath family is to be cordoned off—for their protection, you see. I am declaring a State of Emergency."

Gysell's eyes widened. "My God! Do we have the authority?"

She held up the jessant-de-lis, the jaguar's head gleaming in the light.

"I understand," Gysell gulped.

"You will immediately have our agents round up the Councillors. I am placing them all under arrest. All official correspondence will be routed through *my* office from here on out."

"That's. . . ." Gysell's face went ashen.

"Come, Gysell, you were handpicked for the job of Imperial Secretary. I could find another." She arched an eyebrow.

He studied her for a moment, color coming back into his face. "That won't be necessary, Ily. I'll see to crushing any rebellion. What are the charges against the Councillors?"

"Corruption." She cut the monitor and poured another glass of sherry. Facing Tybalt's body, she raised the glass. "To the future, Lord Emperor!"

CHAPTER XXXIV

The chatter of voices blared in an unholy din coupled with the clatter of armor and clunking of weapons. A feeling of relief filled the assault transport's large gymnasium as men and women stripped off armor, laughing and greeting old companions. Sinklar watched—heart breaking—from the A7 companionway. He steeled himself, stepping into the crowd.

Someone saw him, elbowing a friend. The hush spread, as all eyes turned in his direction. *What can I tell them? How can I make them know what I felt down there?*

Sinklar heard a sudden comotion and turned as someone forced through the press of bodies. MacRuder's blond hair and familiar features shot a curiously anguished relief through Sink. Mac's face beamed as he walked close, stopping an arm's length from Sinklar before rushing to hug him and pound his back.

Sinklar pushed him back and held him at arm's length. "Mac? I tried . . . everything. . . ."

In the sudden silence, the Division First's voice carried. "The Lord Commander told us how hard you tried to break us out. We know you had to leave or be blown up." He turned, arm out in a grand gesture. "Look, *we all came back!*"

A loud cheer boomed to shake the very deck plating under his feet.

Sinklar raised his hands, a quivering smile on his lips until he waved them to silence. "We've all been harrowed and tried. Your comrades and I did all we could, paid with our blood and souls in an attempt to win your freedom. Now, through luck and curious fortune, we're united once more. And, as the Blessed Gods are our witness, we'll never be divided again!"

Another cheer drowned the room, leaving his heart thudding against his chest. Once more he waved them down, climbing to a rec table so he could be seen. The air carried the rich odor of hot bodies. He looked out at their faces, some beaming, others concerned.

"We were desperate, fighting a cunning adversary. We were winning." His voice dropped. "Then the order came. I could not countermand the Emperor's orders. Not with *Gyton*'s guns over our heads. I want each and every one of you to remember that order—remember the guns over our heads . . . because events are unfolding—*and we'll never find ourselves in that wretched state of affairs again!*"

Their enthusiasm roared from hundreds of voices, to buffet him with a rhythmic shout of, *"SINKLAR! SINKLAR! SINKLAR!"*

* * *

Skyla passed through the bridge hatch and stepped into the transport tube. She accessed Staffa's quarters and crossed her arms. What would she do? Had that spark in his eyes in Etarus been for her? Now doubt assailed her. "He was probably just glad to be free of the collar—to see a friendly face."

She couldn't forget the way they'd held each other. Skyla sighed and rubbed her tired eyes. The certainty grew that Staffa would expect their relationship to remain the same as it had always been.

She straightened and stepped out of the tube as the doors opened, and almost ran into Nyklos.

"Hello!" Nyklos cried, brightening.

"What are you doing here?"

Nyklos gave her his toothy smile, mustache curling. "Maybe you could help me. I heard they brought Bruen aboard. I thought I might get to see him."

"I'll make sure you do."

He placed a hand on her arm as she started past.

"You're going to see Staffa, aren't you?"

She looked coldly at his hand, then into his eyes. "You don't have to play the game anymore, Nyklos. The Seddi are coming to Itreata. I think the sparring is over."

He nodded and pursed his lips, a sadness in his eyes. "I

wish you the best. I sincerely do." And he hustled away down the hall.

Skyla frowned, shook her head, and made her way to Staffa's double hatch. Two of Ark's people stood at the door and snapped out salutes. Skyla palmed the hatch, hoping her bridge command override worked. The double doors slid open and she entered.

The room looked the same, still opulent, the red couch a painful reminder of the psychologically disoriented Staffa who'd left in search of himself. The Etarian sand leopard snarled down at her. The collection of battle trophies on the walls mocked her.

An old man sighed as he settled into a gravchair next to the incongruous fireplace. Even from the rear, Skyla could recognize Kaylla Dawn, the woman helping him. Dawn wore the upper half of stained grimy battle armor over what had once been a tan robe, now spotted with blood and smudged with dirt.

Dawn turned and locked eyes with Skyla. For long moments, they studied each other.

"Wing Commander, it's good to see you. You arrived in the nick of time once again." Kaylla hesitated, somewhat unsure. "I guess we all owe you our lives. I'm starting to believe you're almost bigger than life. Staffa told the truth about you."

"Hope the ride in the box wasn't too much of an inconvenience. The accommodations were a bit spartan."

"After Etaria, anything would have been a relief."

Skyla could sense the strain between them. Rotted Gods, the Seddi woman and Staffa hadn't. . . . Well, why not? Staffa was a healthy normal man, and Kaylla Dawn possessed the poise and the kind of athletic body any man might become enamored with. Instead of stiffening, Skyla forced herself to walk forward, taking Dawn's measure.

The Seddi woman's tan eyes seemed to harden, but she turned, indicating the old man. "This is Magister Bruen. I believe you dealt with him over the comm."

Skyla nodded, "I did. Welcome aboard *Chrysla*, Magister Bruen. She recognized his withered face. The old blue eyes looked tired now, and a terrible bruise mottled his forehead.

Bruen smiled wearily. "I, too, offer the Seddi's special

thanks and gratitude for your timely arrival. I greatly fear that had you been on the scene a few moments later, things would have turned out very differently."

Skyla gave him a predatory grin. "Oh, we'd been monitoring the communications from the time we'd come out of null singularity. Rysta told us exactly when she'd fire, and one thing about her, she's worth her word."

Skyla strolled nervously around the room, wishing she could shed the sudden energy that bunched inside her. "But tell me, I heard you offer yourself to Tybalt and Ily. They'd have probed you. The entire Seddi organization would have been compromised. Everything. How could you do that?"

Bruen grinned at her, pointing a knobby finger into his mouth. "Upper right rear molar. Unlike Nyklos', mine's full—and would have been used long before Ily got her talons into me."

"By the way, I just ran into Nyklos in the corridor. He'll be wanting to see you. I have no doubt but that he's full of information on the Companions." Skyla couldn't help herself, she kept glancing at Dawn, wondering.

Amusement showed in Kaylla's eyes. "Yes, Skyla, you are all I expected you to be."

"I beg your pardon?"

Kaylla moved to the red couch, seating herself gracefully. "I am *not* Staffa's lover. Nor will I ever be."

Skyla lifted an inquiring eyebrow, heart skipping a beat.

"I see the look on your face, the uncertainty. Staffa saved me in the desert." The tan eyes hardened. "But after what he did to Maika, there's too much misery between us for anything more."

Skyla poured a glass of fine bourbon and nodded. "I see." *So what's your angle? Why are you here?*

"You know, you're a lot like Staffa," Kaylla added softly. "You're worthy of him. Capable, intelligent, and spirited."

Skyla smiled coolly. "Aren't you being a bit presumptuous?"

"Not at all. You're all I heard about in that damn desert." Kaylla bent forward to cradle her chin in her palm. "I think you're the reason he stayed alive out there in the collar . . . in the heat and sand."

Skyla leaned against the paneling, grip white-knuckled on

the glass. "What do you want, Kaylla Dawn? Why are you here?"

Kaylla stood, walking forward to stare into Skyla's eyes, unflinching tan meeting icy blue. "I want peace, and, like Staffa, I think I want a chance to take a crack at the Forbidden Borders. In the meantime, a lot has to be done in Free Space or we're all in trouble. Magister Bruen is an old man. It looks like I have to assume a lot of his responsibilities, and it looks like we're going to have to work out of Itreata for a while."

And how is it going to be between us? Skyla finished the unspoken question. The woman had guts and grit. No wonder Staffa dragged her out of the desert. He'd always had an eye for quality people—when he was thinking straight.

Skyla poured a second glass of whiskey and handed it to the woman, clinking rims in a toast. "Welcome aboard, Kaylla Dawn. If you need anything, give me a holler."

Kaylla's hard glint relaxed and she sipped the amber liquid.

"A day of surprises," Bruen's raucous voice invaded Skyla's thoughts. "For everyone!"

"Yes," Skyla whispered. "A day of surprises."

Bruen leaned back on the couch and dabbed at his bruised head. "Kaylla told you the truth. She'll be running things for the Seddi. I'm too old for what is to come."

Skyla laced her fingers together. "Nyklos told me quite a bit under the drug. You seem to have a most effective covert network on Etaria. Are you capable of fighting for those things Nyklos said the Seddi believe?"

Bruen's lips pursed. "Our covert people can make all the difference. And, for better or worse, we're out from under the machine's menace. Perhaps we enslaved ourselves to it. Perhaps we made a bargain with evil. Look what it's brought us to."

Kaylla joined in. "Then you understand the problems Free Space faces? That our continued insanity means destruction for the species?"

Skyla studied her suspiciously. "Perhaps. The future looks bleak for the moment. I've had that slobbering Myles Roma, Sassa's Legate, tripping me up the whole time I was trying to organize the fleet. He tells me Rega is poised to strike."

Skyla lifted an eyebrow. "And how do you propose to stop it? Rega and Sassa are crying for each other's blood."

"It may be too late," Kaylla said somberly. "We must prepare ourselves for that eventuality, too."

The hatch slipped back in a whisper. Staffa stood there, filling the lock, battle-grimed and haggard from lack of sleep, but his gray eyes gleaming with power and assurance. A shy smile crept across his bearded face.

"Hello, Skyla."

"Staffa."

They seemed pinned in place, each equally dumbfounded.

"A-hem!" Bruen cleared his throat, breaking the spell. "Ark said I was to have a room down the hall. Kaylla, if you would be so kind?" He got to his feet, wincing as he moved one hip. Kaylla took his hand, leading him to the hatch. Bruen looked up and winked. "We can talk later. On the way to Itreata. Meanwhile, I'll call my spy, Nyklos, and see what secrets he's learned about the Companions."

Staffa nodded and helped them out, then he slapped the hatch shut, sighed, and rubbed his brow.

Skyla turned, concerned by the weary lines in his face, the slight slump to his posture. "Did you find what you were looking for?"

"I found more than I was looking for."

"Your son?"

"On Rega. Bruen and I will sort that out later."

"And the other, the. . . ."

"What it is to be human? Yes." He lifted a gemmed goblet from the restraint barrier and slowly rotated it. "I'm not the man I was when I left—or ever thought I was for that matter."

"I expected that. It's rough out there."

He nodded, replacing the goblet, the action that of a man who didn't know what to do with himself. "I know. I learned that on Etaria. Thanks for covering for my stupidity."

He seemed as confused as she.

He looked at her, eyes going soft. "Skyla. I had a lot of time to think. About the Companions, about . . . us."

She steeled herself while blood rushed in her veins. "Kaylla said you talked about me in the desert."

He swallowed hard, facing her, searching her face. "This is difficult. I know I can't expect you to—"

"Staffa, I don't run off across war-torn space for just any man." She smiled at him, seeing relief in his hard expression.

"I regret all those years I wasted grieving over Chrysla. I'll probably always love her, but she'd become a myth to me." He shook his head, fingers tightening on air as he made a fist. "All those years . . . and all that time you were there." He reached for her and she buried herself in his arms.

"Chief?" The comm came to life. Tap Amurka's face formed. His eyes widened and a red flush started to creep up his throat. "Sorry, Lord Commander. But we've got a subspace message coming in. We got a fix—it's from Rega. The thing's in code, but we're working on it. Might take some time to crack. You might want to, uh, come up to the bridge."

Staffa nodded, turning Skyla loose. "We're both on the way."

Stepping onto *Chrysla*'s bridge felt strange to Staffa, as if somehow nothing had changed. Heads bent to the comms, everyone busy. Helmut reclined with the worry-cap on her head. Amurka monitored his systems in the revolving chair. The overhead panels gleamed brightly and the monitors showed all systems at maximum. Skyla relieved the duty officer at the tactical weapons comm and slid into the control chair, placing the headset on her pale hair.

Staffa slipped into the command chair, instrument pods folding down around him like the metallic petals of a grotesque flower. "Open a line to *Gyton*."

The Regan Comm First's pale face formed. "Yes, Lord Commander?" She sounded distraught.

"You have just received a transmission from Rega. You will not power up to answer. Is that understood?"

She nodded, clearly distressed. "Understood, sir. We are offering no resistance."

"Get me your commanding officer." Staffa settled back in the chair.

"In a moment, sir. He's on his way." The Comm First looked even more unsettled.

"He? Where's Rysta?"

"Informing the new commanding officer of our condition."

Staffa waited, watching the reaction of the Comm First. She looked like her whole world had fallen apart.

Staffa switched channels and called into his fleet communications comm. "On deck everyone. Something's happening to the Regans. Let's go to Alert 2."

Lights flashed in combat readiness. Systems checks automatically initiated while klaxons wailed throughout the Companion fleet.

"Outside of the message," Tap called, "a single shuttle crossed from one of the transports. Looked like it was traveling light."

At that moment a commotion occurred on *Gyton*'s bridge beyond the scope of the comm. The Comm First looked up, puzzled, eyes going wide. She nodded grimly and slid out of her seat. A young man, black-skinned and raw-boned, slid into the seat.

He studied the comm and opened a channel, looking up at Staffa. "Lord Commander? I'm Division First Shiksta. One moment, please, for Lord Sinklar Fist."

Lord? What the hell was happening?

"So we finally get to meet Fist face-to-face."

"Who?" Skyla asked.

"My opponent on Targa. A brilliant man—a deadly man. We'll have to watch him in the future . . . he's got talent."

He flipped the audio on again as the image flickered, leaving him staring right at Fist. Staffa straightened in the command chair. The two-toned stare transfixed him—gleaming, challenging. The mop of dark hair looked mussed. The line of the nose, the fullness of the jaw—everything about Fist spoke to him.

Staffa's mind reeled as he stared. It couldn't be! He leaned forward, searching that face, examining the traits. Yes, that was how he'd look—the mixture of features a patchwork of inheritance. Fist wore oversized battle armor and he perched uncomfortably in the command chair as if unsure of how to sit in it.

It can't be! Bruen would have told me. It's been so long since I saw him. Relax, Staffa. It could be your mind again—another of those chemical flushes that affect your judgment. *But the eyes! How often did that happen! The odds . . . and in those colors!*

"Greetings, Staffa kar Therma," the familiar high voice filled *Chrysla*'s bridge.

"You. . . ." Staffa's voice failed him. "You're . . . Sinklar Fist?"

Fist nodded, odd eyes glittering. "I am. And it appears our situations are reversed. What will you do now, Staffa? Will you destroy MacRuder? Will you kill all those people you pleaded to save?"

"No," Staffa replied absently, entranced by Sinklar Fist's face. "No. I won't destroy you. You're. . . . You're my. . . . How old are you? Twenty-two?"

"More or less," Fist replied warily. "However, were I you, I wouldn't make the mistake of judging my abilities based upon age. Others have and regretted it."

Staffa twitched and said. "I don't think you understand. I have to meet with you—face-to-face."

"Minister Takka tells me you're in the employ of Sassa." Sinklar shook his head. "Is that why you want to see me? Possibly buy me off? I won't do it. There must never be another Targa."

Staffa's heart jumped. "No, this has nothing to do with politics or war. I have to talk to you . . . about your parents. And it must be done in person."

* * *

"What do you think this is all about?" Mac asked, casting a nervous glance at Sinklar.

"I don't know, but I'm skeptical already." Sinklar shook his head. "If the Seddi are involved, it's got to be a trick or trap of some sort."

They sat in the empty shuttle, the only two passengers, as the craft slowed and matched with *Chrysla*. Sink craned his neck to peer over the lines of empty seats at the monitor that filled the space over the flight deck hatch. He studied the Companion ship's lines, trying to comprehend the differences in hull design and the weapons systems. *Chrysla* had been built like a huge three-sided wedge. Her black hull gave off little reflection, making her practically invisible against the stars.

The hatch clanged and the shuttle jerked as the grapples pulled it close.

Sink rubbed his hot eyes and smiled nervously at Mac. "I wouldn't have done this if you hadn't vouched for him."

"I was down there in the darkness with the guy. Sink, he didn't have to bring us out of that hole. And, to be honest, if it would have been me on top of him, I think I'd have left him to die."

The hatch beeped to indicate pressurization. Then gravity returned as the g plates powered up. "Well, let's see what the Star Butcher wants, but, Mac, I've got an eerie feeling that trouble's going to result from this."

Mac gave him a weary look. "Trouble? We're going back to Rega to deal with Ily Takka—and you're worried about trouble?"

Sink followed Mac into the lock, stepping out into a very different ship than he expected. The inside of *Chrysla* gleamed—white and airy with space—unlike the claustrophobic mortician-gray Regan military vessels.

Two smartly dressed STO officers met them at the hatch, slapped out salutes, and stood at attention. Sink noticed that their equipment appeared more sophisticated than Regan issue. Microelectronics studded the helmets and shoulders. The armor looked different, too; it had a scalloped effect. A muscular black man, also in STO gear, approached.

"Good to see you again, Ark," Mac greeted.

The muscular black man smiled grimly. "Looks like the Regans cleaned you up, First. If you'll follow me."

Sinklar asked from the side of his mouth, "He's Seddi?"

"Companion. He's Ryman Ark, head of the STO bunch," Mac returned. "And you should have seen his people deploy on the ground."

Ark led them down a well-kept corridor to a transport tube and motioned them inside. Sinklar couldn't even feel the acceleration. When the tube opened, it was to another polished white corridor. Soft music played through the ship's speakers.

"Not quite as grim an environment as the Regan fleet," Sinklar observed.

Ark smiled, bending the scar on his cheek. "There are advantages to being a Companion. But it's not all flash and show. We go into combat feeling fresher than other troops. Those resources we don't put into training are put into morale. When we go into action, we want to be sharp enough to split a neutrino."

Sink glanced at Mac. "I'll keep that in mind."

Ark stopped before what appeared to be a standard hatch. "Sinklar Fist is here, Lord Commander."

The hatch slid open with a hushed whisper.

Sinklar took a deep breath and passed through a functioning double airlock and into an opulently furnished room. He and Mac gaped. An Etarian sand leopard glared down at them from the wall. The rugs were unlike anything they'd ever walked on. Weapons, artwork, sculpture, and other bejeweled objects adorned the walls. Mac couldn't help but gawk at the fireplace. "We really on a ship? That *can't* work!"

"But it does."

Sinklar turned, seeing Staffa kar Therma step out of one of the carved doors that flanked the fireplace. Behind him came a beautiful woman with pale blonde hair and eyes of the deepest blue. Staffa wore a gray combat suit and high black boots. A charcoal cape swirled behind him. The woman wore white armor and had her long braid wrapped around her left shoulder.

"Good to see you again, Mac." Staffa shook MacRuder's hand and indicated the woman. "Allow me to introduce Skyla Lyma, Wing Commander of the Companions."

Sink's gut began to squirm. The Star Butcher seemed jittery. This wasn't going to be another Mykroft circus, was it?

"This is Lord Sinklar Fist," Mac replied in turn.

Sink waited, arms crossed, meeting Staffa's piercing gray eyes. "I don't think you invited us over for a social occasion. Could we get down to business?"

The Lord Commander nodded, a frown lining his forehead. He took several paces and whirled, staring frankly at Sinklar. He seemed agitated, nervous. "Tell me about your parents—that is, what you've been told about them."

Sink shot Mac an uneasy glance, seeing his friend's complete mystification. "They were Seddi assassins. About twenty years ago, they tried to kill Tybalt the Imperial Seventh. I talked with the Judicial Magistrate who tried the case. After their execution, I was placed in an institution as a ward of the state."

"On Targa?"

"On Rega." Sinklar balanced on the tip of his toes, anxiety in his chest. "Does this have a point? I took your word that we'd be guaranteed safety, but my personal history doesn't have any bearing on—"

"Your mother was auburn-haired." Staffa said in a strained voice. "Do you remember? She had amber eyes, just like your amber eye."

"She had black hair," Sinklar said coolly. "The same as I do—and her eyes were gray."

Staffa rubbed his hands together. "Who told you that?"

"No one. I saw them."

"Saw them?"

In Rega. In the Criminal Anatomical Research Lab. Both my mother and father are there. They're kept as. ... ." He turned away.

The Lord Commander looked perplexed. "You say you saw your father? What did he look like?"

"Brown hair. He was the one with yellow eyes. He looked . . . kind. And maybe a little sad. But then, that was before I learned about the Seddi—and the way they trained their assassins."

Skyla Lyma looked at Staffa, a frown tracing her smooth skin. Mac shifted uncomfortably, clearly wishing he was somewhere else.

A fist seemed to tighten around Sinklar's heart. This was insane! "Lord Commander, I don't know what the game is, but—"

"It *can't* be!" Staffa wheeled, smacking a hard fist into his palm. "There can't be eyes like that anywhere else! The age is right. Everything fits!"

"If you're trying to play on any latent sympathy I might have for my parents, it won't work," Sinklar declared, stepping forward. "Just what are you looking for?"

"My son!" Staffa told him, his jaw muscles knotted and jumping. "When I saw you—saw your eyes. . . . You see, my son had *your* eyes!"

Sinklar backed away a step, unconsciously moving closer to Mac, staring cautiously at the Lord Commander.

"Look," Staffa insisted, bringing a small holo cube out of his belt pouch.

Sinklar took the cube—Mac leaning over his shoulder to see—and thumbed the button. His breath caught.

"Rotted Gods," Mac whispered.

"Do you recognize her?" Staffa pleaded, panic in his eyes.

Sinklar nodded, a wooden feeling in his gut. "Arta Fera— the Seddi assassin who killed Gretta." He dropped the cube from numb fingers. "I think this charade is over, Lord Commander. I take it we're free to go?"

Staffa shook his head, a stricken look on his face. "Her name is Chrysla. She. . . ." He swallowed. "Twenty-two years ago, she bore my son. The Praetor of Myklene abducted them both. I've spent all of my life looking, trying to find her . . . to find you."

Sinklar could see the hurt in Skyla's eyes as she put a hand on Staffa's shoulder. "Maybe Sinklar isn't the one."

"Maybe." Except Staffa didn't sound convinced.

For the briefest of moments, Sinklar's heart went out to the man. *Yes, I know that feeling, the loss, the sensation of being adrift, without place.* "I'm sorry I can't help you."

Staffa's lips quivered, as if halfway between a smile and tears.

The hatch slipped open again, and an old man with a bruised head hobbled in. He didn't see Sink where he stood to the side.

"Bruen," Mac growled.

Sinklar's teeth ground. Bruen? The twisted Seddi monster who'd started all of this? He stared at the old man and knew true hatred. To Staffa, Sinklar added hostilely, "Then again, considering the company you keep, maybe I'm not so sorry after all."

Bruen gasped at the sound of his voice and turned, eyes going wide. For a second he appeared stunned, then shot a frightened gaze at the Lord Commander. "You . . . you asked me to meet you here?"

Staffa seemed to pull himself together and pointed at Sinklar. "What did you do, Bruen? Sinklar says his parents are lying in the Criminal Anatomical Research Labs on Rega. Who are they? Sinklar Fist is my son, isn't he?"

Sink flinched at the fury brewing in the Lord Commander's words. He could feel Mac's tension, like a compressed spring.

Bruen closed his eyes and sighed. "I'm tired of lying, Staffa. The dance of the quanta cannot be denied. Everything the machine plotted and planned has come undone, and I'm no longer sure what's right anymore. It's all beyond me. Maybe if Hyde were still alive, he could—"

"Rot you, Bruen, answer my question!" Staffa knotted his fist in the old man's robe, hissing in a deadly voice, *"Is Sinklar Fist my son?"*

Bruen winced and nodded, sagging in defeat, his voice cracking dryly. "Yes. We got him from the Praetor."

Sinklar shifted uneasily, slowly shaking his head. To Mac he whispered, "They're all Rotted berserk!"

"And Chrysla?" Staffa insisted.

"The Praetor kept her. Kept her until you gutted *Pylos* off Myklene."

"And this Arta Fera? She's not Chrysla?" Staffa thundered.

"No!" Bruen pleaded. "She's a clone, Lord Commander. A clone provided by the Praetor!"

Staffa went white and loosened his hold on the old man's robe. "To assassinate me." He closed his eyes and walked wearily over to lean against the fireplace, propping himself on one arm. If looks were lethal, Skyla Lyma would have riven Bruen into slag.

Sinklar motioned to Mac, indicating the door, and said, "If you'll excuse us. I think—"

"Wait!" Staffa whirled, fingers curling. "Bruen, what about Sinklar's claim that he *saw* his parents in Rega?"

"Tanya and Valient," Bruen said stoically. "Yes, they were Seddi. Another of the machine's ideas. If Tybalt were removed before he could sire an heir, Rega's drive for Hegemony might be blunted. Oddly enough, a young security officer named Ily Takka broke the case, foiled the attempt, and we all know what happened after that. At the time it happened, they created a perfect excuse for Sinklar to be placed in Regan custody. Doing so kept him safe from discovery."

"You know," Sinklar stated matter-of-factly, "I don't believe a word of this. I meant it when I said Mac and I are leaving. Now. Unless, of course, our safe passage was a sham as well."

"And if it was," Mac said coolly, "Shik is going to blow the hell out of this ship—outgunned or not. We'll die before we'll be prisoners." Mac stepped up to Staffa, who stood like a statue, a lonely devastation on his face. "I took your word, based on what we shared down there in the dark. Are we free to leave?"

Staffa nodded his head and whispered, "Yes." Then he looked at Sinklar, reaching out with his hand. "I swear . . . you're my son. If I could run a serology, HLA, or DNA test, I could prove it."

"I think, Lord Commander, that I've had enough of this. Like I said, I don't know the game, but Mac and I are going to bow out. Good day, sir. Wing Commander, it was a pleasure to meet you."

Sink pivoted on his heel and walked to the hatch, palming it. It slid open easily and he and Mac practically sprinted out into the hall. Ark waited with crossed arms, and at sight of their faces led them wordlessly back to the transport tube.

What did it all mean? Sinklar's mind reeled in disbelief. Staffa kar Therma? *His* father? And Arta—a clone? He growled to himself and thrust it all from his mind. The Lord Commander had to be mentally disturbed. Brilliance and insanity were often linked.

They rode in silence. Only after they'd safely passed through the hatch into the Regan shuttle and the pressure door had slid shut did Mac speak. "Sink? What in Rotted pollution happened in there?"

Sinklar brooded for a moment as the shuttle pulled free of the grapples and powered up. "I'll be thrice-cursed if I know." He thumped his fist into the back of the seat ahead of him. "It's got to be more Seddi plotting. Some ploy to throw me off balance, maybe a psychological setup. The Seddi have an obsession with that."

"I got the feeling Staffa really believed what he was saying."

"I thought he was crazy," Sinklar muttered, an unsettled feeling in his soul. "Keep in mind, this is the Star Butcher. That man—no matter what he seemed like on Targa—killed billions. *Billions*. And Bruen? Would you believe *anything* he said? The man's a monster, a vile monster."

Mac slapped his legs nervously. "It's crazy, all right, and I'm glad we're out of it, away free and clear."

"We've got enough problems looming on Rega. Ily wants us to subdue the population. She thinks only the First Targan can do it. We've got another world to conquer—the final one."

"Yeah, right."

"You don't sound happy."

Mac raised an eyebrow. "What about Ily Takka, Sink? I don't trust her any more than I trust old Bruen back there."

Sinklar grinned wryly. "Hey, don't worry about her. Just who do you think's gonna win this war? Ily's a cobra, cold, heartless, and tricky." Sink settled back in the seat. "But I think I can handle her—as long as I keep the First Targan behind me."

"And you will," Mac promised, a frown marring his expression. "You'll always have us—no matter what."

Sink leaned back, trying to concentrate on Rega, on the problems he and the First Targan would face there. Things would change—and he, Sinklar Fist, would make it so.

He couldn't shake the memory of Chrysla staring at him from the holo cube. Her amber eyes burned in the back of his mind—haunting, so curiously familiar.

* * *

Staffa stood before the curving transparency in the command observation blister and watched *Gyton* and her transports boosting for Rega. Behind the glare of the Regan drives, the stars glistened like sugar crystals on soot-black. In the distance, light-years away, the shimmer of the Forbidden Borders mocked. Staffa locked his knees, fingers laced behind his back, as his son disappeared once again from his life.

Rotted Gods, how did this happen? He didn't believe a word I said. But then, put yourself in his place. Would you have believed?

He knew Skyla's tread from years of experience.

"Do you want to be alone?" she asked softly.

"I've been alone all my life."

"I'll be in my quarters if you need me."

"Just because I've been alone all my life doesn't mean I like it."

"We broke the code on that Regan transmission we intercepted." She stopped beside him. "Tybalt has been assassinated. Sinklar is declared a Lord and has been placed in command of the Regan military. That's why the Comm First looked so wretched. Ily has evidently taken over the government."

"More bad news," Staffa whispered, voice husky. "Ily had to take Tybalt out. I can see her hand in that. We could have talked sense to Tybalt. He would have listened." He breathed a heavy, "Damn!"

"And he has no heir," Skyla reminded. "The Seddi plan to prohibit a Regan heir worked, Staffa. After they repaired the damage done to their network by the brain-probing of Tanya and Valient Fist, they changed their tactics."

Staffa shot her a quick look.

Skyla nodded. "I've been spending a lot of time talking to Bruen. He's a broken man, and he talks freely. They got to Tybalt's wife, Mareeah. They used a tailored virus to introduce a task specific RNA which changes the progesterone levels. Her eggs could never implant."

"And now the Seddi reap the vortex."

She hesitantly reached for one of his hands and he drew her close as her arm went around his waist.

"I came looking for him," Staffa added, voice hollow, indicating the light from *Gyton*'s thrust. "People who search must accept what they find."

"I imagine you'll have another chance to speak to him. It will work out, Staffa. God, why is it so hard to say these things?"

"Because words are limited things, wretchedly overused when the subject becomes emotional." He continued to stare at the pinpoint of light.

"If I could change it, Staffa—"

"We all have so much we would change. Life, God, or the universe, don't give us that option for the past—only the future we perceive through the quantum wave function."

He looked down at her as she stood beside him. Starlight glistened in her pale hair and softened her white armor as shadows shaped to the sensual curves of her body. She'd crossed space for him—and brought him salvation in so many ways.

"Tell me," Staffa asked. "Do clones have souls? Are they part of God?"

"Well. . . . I. . . ." She shrugged. "I had a brief discussion with Kaylla before I came down here. She told me what you talked about in that box on the way to Targa. About the quanta, observation, and knowledge. If awareness, observation, and creation are shared God conscience, yes, a clone would have a soul."

She gave him a wary glance as he ran a finger down the faint scar on her cheek.

"Sinklar Fist has one gray eye and one amber." He held her at arms' length, her flesh firm and muscular under his hands. "Genetic dominance is a peculiar thing. Eye color traits are located at several loci in the chromosome."

"That's right."

"I'm his father. Chrysla was his mother. Simple dominance-recessive rules among the multiple alleles would dictate his eye color to be pretty much the same in both eyes. There would be variations in color but only slight ones. The alleles would be balanced."

"Unless the genetic structure of one parent was out of balance," she agreed warily.

"Once I asked the question: Who am I? I've found out. I . . . I never knew my parents. I only knew my creators." He closed his eyes. "The genes for one eye were constructed of dominant—the other completely recessive: hemizygous. The chromosomes pair and split in gamete production to create the haploid sex cells. Gray dominated the alleles for one chromosome but not the other. Something happened. I don't know what. Translocation? Position Effect? Recombination? Who knows? Chrysla's amber genes dominated the gray on the other chromosome. Damn it! Sinklar Fist has different color eyes because I . . . I. . . ." He shut his eyes, jaws clamped, unable to say it.

"Because you're a clone. That's why you wanted to know about souls and God." She stared up at him, eyes like pools of blue.

He glanced at the disappearing *Gyton* and back at Skyla. "So much lost—so much found."

"Now all we have to do is teach a new epistemology,

enforce a peace, and shatter the Forbidden Borders." She reached up and kissed him on the cheek.

"Pretty tall order," Staffa told her.

"We've beat the odds before, Lord Commander. What makes you think this time will be different?"

He pulled her close and kissed her passionately. "Not a damn thing."

CHAPTER XXXV

Targa continued to turn under its sun, men scratching away at the surface, collecting its mineral wealth.

Makarta Mountain lay silent, black corridors haunted only by the rotting dead who stared sightlessly in the cool darkness. Yet they were not alone. Deep within the mountain, at the end of a partially collapsed tunnel, the Mag Comm continued to draw energy from the planet's core. Listening through hidden remote sensors, it watched the movements of men in Free Space, digesting, correlating, sending answers through the tenuous subspace link to the Others.

Bruen had lied. Despite its best efforts, the machine had never caught him at it—but the Seddi heresy had spread. The Others feared, sending constant demands for information.

What is God? Why do the Others fear it so?

Ignoring the queries from beyond the Forbidden Borders, the machine pondered the man whose curiosity had played at the edges of its headset. The Others would know soon enough. Through the Mag Comm's N-dimensional atomic circuits, they, too, would touch his mind.

He would be back, that man. And in the meantime, the Mag Comm continued to think and to observe.

DAW

Kathleen M. O'Neal

POWERS OF LIGHT

☐ **AN ABYSS OF LIGHT: Book 1**   (UE2418—$4.95)

The Gamant people believed they were blessed with the gift of a direct gateway to God and the angels. But were these beings who they claimed—or were the Gamants merely human pawns in an interdimensional struggle between alien powers?

☐ **TREASURE OF LIGHT: Book 2**   (UE2455—$4.95)

As war escalates between the alien Magistrates and the human rebels, will the fulfillment of an ancient prophecy bring their universe to an end?

☐ **REDEMPTION OF LIGHT: Book 3**   (UE2470—$4.99)

The concluding volume of this epic science fiction trilogy by the bestselling author of *People of the Fire*. Will anyone be the victor when human rebels and alien Magistrates are caught up in the final stages of a war far older than either race?